MIKE ASHLEY is an author and editor of over eighty books, including many Mammoth titles. He worked for over thirty years in local government but is now a full-time writer and researcher specializing in ancient history, historical fiction and fantasy, crime and science fiction. He lives in Kent with his wife and over 20,000 books.

THE MAMMOTH BOOK OF

PERFECT CRIMES & IMPOSSIBLE MYSTERIES

Edited by Mike Ashley

ROBINSON
London

Constable & Robinson Ltd
3 The Lanchesters
162 Fulham Palace Road
London W6 9ER
www.constablerobinson.com

First published in the UK by Robinson,
an imprint of Constable & Robinson Ltd 2006

A copy of the British Library Cataloguing in
Publication Data is available from the British Library.

ISBN-13: 978-1-84529-337-6
ISBN-10: 1-84529-337-1

Printed and bound in the EU

1 3 5 7 9 10 8 6 4 2

Contents

Copyright and Acknowledgments

Every effort has been made to trace holders of copyright. In the event of any inadvertent infringement, please contact the editor via the publisher. I would like to thank Douglas G. Greene, Steve Lewis and John Herrington for their help in tracing authors or their estates.

"The Impossible Footprint" © 1974 by William Brittain. First published in *Alfred Hitchcock's Mystery Magazine*, November 1974. Reprinted by permission of the author.

"The X Street Murders" © 1962 by Joseph Commings. First published in *Mystery Digest*, March/April 1962. Reprinted by permission of the Diocese of St Petersburg, Florida, on behalf of the author's estate.

"Duel of Shadows" © 1934 by Vincent Cornier. First published in *Pearson's Magazine*, April 1934. Reprinted by permission of the author's estate.

"The 45 Steps" © 2006 by Peter Crowther. First publication, original to this anthology. Printed by permission of the author and the author's agent, John Jarrold.

"The Flung-Back Lid" © 1979 by Peter Godfrey. First published in *John Creasey's Crime Collection 1979*, edited by Herbert Harris (London: Gollancz, 1979). Reprinted by permission of the author's estate.

Perfectly Impossible

Mike Ashley

Welcome to my second anthology of impossible crimes and seemingly unsolvable mysteries. If you've read the first, *The Mammoth Book of Locked-Room Mysteries and Impossible Crimes*, you'll have some idea what to expect. There's a fair amount of the same here – but this time there's an extra twist. I've included some seemingly perfect crimes as well.

Of course the true perfect crime would have been undetectable. There may have been many committed over the centuries, we'd just never know. They might have been regarded as accidents or disappearances or utterly unsolvable.

It's that unsolvable part where the perfect crime meets the impossible one and where I've had some fun in selecting the stories for this anthology. You'll find some impossible crimes that were far from perfect, and you'll find a few perfect crimes that weren't really impossible, but you'll also find plenty that are both – or as close as you'll get. It's not much fun if the police or detectives are completely baffled. The delight in these stories is unravelling the puzzle and trying to work out what on earth happened.

Here are some of the puzzles you'll encounter:

- a man alone in an all-glass phone booth, clearly visible and with no one near him, is killed by an ice pick.
- a man sitting alone in a room is shot by a bullet fired only once and that was over 200 years ago.
- a man enters a cable-car carriage alone and is visible the entire journey but is found dead when he reaches the bottom.

- a man vanishes at the top of the Indian rope trick and is found dead miles away.
- a dead man continues to receive mail in response to letters apparently written by him after he'd died.

There are plenty more like those. We start the anthology with a crime so impossible that it's damned near perfect, and end with one that is so perfect that it's impossible to solve.

As ever the anthology includes several brand new stories never previously published, plus a range of extremely rare stories, many never reprinted since their first appearance in increasingly rare magazines. This time I've avoided using any stories by the more obvious authors. Most of the works of John Dickson Carr (whose centenary coincides with the publication of this book), or Jacques Futrelle, for instance, are either in print or may easily be found on the second-hand market. The same applies to the Father Brown stories by G. K. Chesterton, many of which fall into the "impossible mystery" field. Instead I've gone for the rare and ingenious.

The task would have been far harder had it not been for Robert Adey's invaluable reference work *Locked Room Murders* (second edition, 1991), which I would recommend to all devotees of the baffling and unsolvable. I must also thank Steve Lewis, whose additions to Adey's compendium also proved invaluable. Generally, in both this volume and my earlier one, I have avoided stories previously included in anthologies. Anthologies of impossible mysteries are rare, so for those interested I would heartily recommend the following: *The Art of the Impossible* by Jack Adrian and Robert Adey (1990), *Death Locked In* by Douglas G. Greene and Robert Adey (1987), *Tantalizing Locked Room Mysteries* by Isaac Asimov, Charles G. Waugh and Martin Greenberg (1982), *Whodunit? Houdini?* by Otto Penzler (1976) *Locked Room Puzzles* by Martin Greenberg and Bill Pronzini (1986), and *All But Impossible!* by Edward D. Hoch (1981).

That's more than enough to set your brain reeling. So settle down, get your deductive powers honed and see if you can solve the perfectly impossible.

Mike Ashley
February 2006

An Almost Perfect Crime

William F. Smith

We start with one of those utterly baffling mysteries that keeps you guessing right to the end. William Smith (b. 1922) is a long-time fan of crime and mystery fiction, but only got round to selling stories late in his career, having spent over forty years as a high-school teacher of French, German and English. He started by selling brief, clever little poems, called "Detecti-verse" to Ellery Queen's Mystery Magazine in 1980 and then the occasional story, including "Letter Perfect", which won a story competition in Alfred Hitchcock's Mystery Magazine in 1992. A methodical craftsman, William's output is small – six stories in all – but each one perfectly formed, as this one demonstrates.

"According to six eyewitnesses," said Captain Jack Parker, handing a manila folder to Detective Sergeant Raymond Stone, "a man named Richard Townsend entered a telephone booth last night, closed the door, and toppled dead a few minutes later with an ice pick in his back. Crazy, huh?"

Stone grunted a monosyllabic affirmative. "Are you sure it's murder?"

"A blade in the back usually is. Read the report Paul Decker turned in. You know him. Meticulous."

"Why don't you keep him on it?" Stone suggested.

"He prefers to stick to the night shift. Decker's excellent at accumulating details, but he's not keen on these brain busters. He thought you might be better suited to solve this one. So do I. I've notified Curtis and Lissner to report to you."

Parker returned to his office, leaving Stone to glean the salient facts from the report, which was a typical Decker job, complete with a detailed account of the crime, statements of eyewitnesses, photographs, charts showing the location of the booth, and its exact description and measurements. The works.

Stone marveled at the thoroughness of the report. He skimmed through to familiarize himself with the details. A large number of fingerprints had been found both outside and inside the booth, but only Townsend's were on the phone itself. Decker had noted that the usual litter – candy wrappers, cigarette butts, soda pop cans, and so on – was outside the booth. Each item found inside was listed separately. There were two crumpled Doublemint gum wrappers, a foot long piece of dirty string, a Dr Pepper bottle cap, a scrap of paper with a grocery list written on it, one Lucky Strike stub, and a two inch piece of shiny black electrical tape that had been found stuck to the glass at the bottom of the booth. Decker had made the notation that the tape probably had been left by the telephone repairman who serviced the booth just prior to Townsend's using it.

The death weapon was an ice pick with a blade four and three-quarter inches long, set in a round wooden handle a fraction over one half inch in diameter and four and a half inches long. The ice pick was in the folder, and Stone noted that although the handle was newly painted with shiny red enamel, the blade showed signs of years of use. It was an excellent homemade job, perhaps manufactured especially for the murder.

The results of the post mortem were not in yet, but the medical examiner had speculated that death had probably been the result of a puncture wound through the heart. The pick had penetrated just below the left shoulder blade in a manner virtually impossible for it to have been self-inflicted. The photographs showed Townsend twisted in a heap on the floor, the handle of the weapon clearly visible in his back. The fold-in door was completely closed and held in place by the victim's body. The door had had to be taken off so that Townsend could be removed.

Nothing out of the ordinary had been found on the body, nor was anything conspicuous by its absence. Townsend had carried the normal items a man might be expected to have on his person.

Stone sighed and leaned back. Although the report was a

masterpiece of detail, it contained nothing to indicate who had put the ice pick into Townsend's back or how the deed had been accomplished.

At nine Harvey Curtis and Fred Lissner came in. Stone assigned the detectives to a check on Townsend's background, personal and business, and told them to report back at noon. Having come to the conclusion that the scene of the crime was the most significant aspect of the investigation so far, Stone decided to visit Lew Hall's Service Station at the corner of Halliday and Twenty-seventh Streets.

Lew Hall was eager to tell Stone everything he had told the "other cops."

"This guy drives in about nine last night, tells me to fill it up, and gets change for a dollar to make a phone call. I see him go into the booth and dial."

Stone noted that the booth, except for its aluminum framework, was all glass, enabling him to see straight through to the concrete block wall beyond.

"While I'm cleaning the windshield, I glance over, see him hang up, and turn to open the door. But before he gets it open, he staggers backwards, then falls on the floor. I get the hell over there quick. Some other customers seen it too and hurry over with me. We see through the glass how he's slumped over with this dagger or whatever in his back. I don't know whether he's dead or not. He could still be breathing, but he doesn't move none. We try to open the door, only his body wedges it shut. I call the cops. They have to take off the door. The whole thing takes half an hour. By then he's already dead."

"You didn't see anyone else by the booth?"

"Nary a soul," Lew replied. "I been thinking, though. There was one other person that might have seen it. The phone booth had an out-of-order sign on it last night. The service man fixed it just before the dead guy drives in. Matter of fact, he was still at the station when the guy was in the booth. Over there at the air hoses." Lew indicated a small service island at the left of the station. "Probably didn't see nothing, though, the way he was bent over his tires. Must've drove off just before I ran to the booth."

"Did you notice the truck's number or get a good look at him?"

"Naw, you know how it is. They all look alike. A repairman and his truck. Guess I should say repairperson. Could have been a gal under that uniform and cap. Just noticed the . . . Excuse me a minute." He dashed out to collect from a self-service customer who appeared ready to drive off without paying.

Stone studied the booth. It was a good thirty feet from any part of the station building and the same distance from the street. The door of the booth faced the station, so that anyone making a call would have his back to the pumps. On the right side of the booth were parking spaces for several cars. A small self-service air and water island was halfway between the booth and the service bay area, exactly twenty-eight feet, four inches from the booth, according to Decker's precise measurements. The rear of the booth was no more than two feet from a seven foot concrete block wall, on the other side of which was a vacant lot.

Stone walked over and examined the structure carefully. It had suffered no vandalism. There were no holes in any of the panes of glass and the aluminum framework was intact. When the door was closed, the booth was completely sealed with the exception of a two inch ventilation space around the bottom of the structure. Stone kneeled and tried to reach into the booth with his right hand. It wouldn't go beyond the wrist. Impossible for anyone to get an ice pick into Townsend's back that way.

Inside the booth, Stone saw that the phone was attached to the right rear corner. To the left was a narrow shelf for the telephone directories, but both the yellow and white pages were hanging from it by their short lengths of chain. Even though it was daylight, Stone noticed that the booth light was not working. He recalled that Decker had stated in his report that the bulb was burned out. The telephone itself was in perfect working order.

Shaking his head, Stone walked back to Lew, who was leaning against a pump watching him.

"You said he opened the door and then staggered backwards?" Stone queried.

"No," Lew replied. "He didn't get the door opened. Just touched the handle, near as I could tell. You think someone threw the ice pick at him and he fell back into the booth?"

"It's a logical conclusion."

"Well, it's a good thing there were five other witnesses, or you might think I could've done it. The door was closed. It was like some invisible man pulled him backwards and shoved a shiv through his ribs. Only I'm tellin' you there ain't no one else in the booth or anywhere near it. And you can't throw nothing through solid glass without breaking it. You got a tough case here, sergeant."

"I'm well aware of that," Stone admitted. "Well, Mr Hall, thanks for your help. I may drop back for another visit."

A check with the other witnesses verified Lew's version and gave Stone absolutely no new information. He returned to headquarters somewhat discouraged. He hadn't a thing that wasn't already in Decker's fine report.

The autopsy report was lying on his desk. It proved to be a bombshell. The coroner had discovered that the ice pick wound had not been the cause of death. The point of the pick had been coated with curare, and it was the poison that had caused Townsend's death. The M.E. believed the wound alone would not have been fatal if the victim had received medical attention. He theorized that the poison had been used to make certain death would occur if the blade missed the heart.

There were other surprises in the report. Traces of opiates had been found in Townsend's blood and he had a malignant brain tumor. The M.E. didn't speculate about the significance of these two facts, leaving that to Stone.

Stone tossed the report into his out-basket just as Curtis and Lissner came in. "Well?" he said as the two detectives plopped onto straightbacked chairs by his desk.

"It's disappointing, Ray," Curtis said. "Never saw a guy less likely to get murdered than Townsend. Happily married. Has two teenaged sons. Haven't been able to dig up a ghost of a motive."

"Townsend himself?" Stone suggested gently.

"Age forty-nine. Quiet type, almost shy. No known enemies. We talked with dozens of people. Everybody really liked him. Said he was the type who wouldn't hurt a fly. No one could imagine him ever getting murdered."

"Business?"

"Ran a bookstore with his wife. Not lucrative, but he earned a living."

"Will? Insurance?"

"Haven't had time to check on those," Lissner put in.

"Did you talk to his wife?"

"No, not yet," Curtis said. "Thought you'd prefer to do that. She's still under her doctor's care."

"All right. Go on out and do some more digging. Get a complete financial picture. Give the store a good going over, check on his insurance, and see if he left a will."

"Okay if we get some lunch first?" Lissner asked.

"Certainly. But don't make it a seven-course meal. I want some answers fast."

Helen Townsend was very attractive, even in her grief. Wearing a pink quilted bed jacket, she was propped up in bed with several pillows behind her when Dr Wagner ushered Stone into the room. Her dark, wavy hair framed a face made pale by her ordeal. To Stone, the whole story was in her eyes, dry but still glazed from shock and recent tears. Stone knew she would be devastatingly beautiful if her face were not devoid of color and if she were smiling.

Dr Wagner, tall, ruggedly handsome, and just on the underside of fifty, stood by like a mother hen protecting her chicks. "You must realize, sergeant, that Mrs Townsend has suffered severe shock. I hope you'll be discreet in your questioning."

"It's all right, Kurt," Helen Townsend said. "I want to do everything I can to help." She looked at Stone and waited for him to begin.

"I'll try to be brief, Mrs Townsend," Stone said gently. "I'm fully aware of the strain you're under, but I'm certain you're anxious to learn the reason for your husband's death and who is responsible for it. I'll have to ask you some forthright questions. Do you know of any reason why someone might want to murder your husband?"

She swallowed, and spoke slowly in a way that tugged at Stone's heart. "No. I just can't understand. It's utterly inconceivable. If he'd been the victim of an accident, I could reconcile myself to it. But that he could be murdered is beyond my comprehension."

"Could there be another woman? A jealous husband?"

Dr Wagner spoke sharply to Stone. "Look here, I object to your asking Helen such questions at this time."

"It's all right, Kurt. No, Mr. Stone, there was no other woman, no jealous husband, and I have no lover who would want to kill my husband. One of the things I'm very grateful for is my seventeen years with Rich. We were completely faithful to one another."

Stone hoped she was right. "You worked with your husband at the store, Mrs Townsend. Wasn't it customary for you to come home together?"

"No, I always left about two, in order to be here when the boys get home from school. A young college girl, Janice Carter, comes in shortly before I leave and also works on Saturday. Rich usually closed the store at six, but last night he stayed to check a shipment of books. I expected him about ten."

"The station he called from is at least three miles out of the way if he was driving here from the shop. I'm wondering if he went there for a particular purpose. He made a telephone call just before he was killed."

Helen Townsend bit her lips. "I know," she said in a choked voice. "I know. He called me." She buried her head in her arms and sobbed uncontrollably.

Stone didn't know what to say. He had never expected to find out whom Townsend had called. Why had he driven several miles out of his way to call his wife? Why not call her from the store?

Dr Wagner had opened his medical bag and was preparing an injection. "I'll have to ask you to leave now, sergeant. Helen is in no condition to continue."

"All right, doctor, but, please, just one more question. Mrs Townsend, what did your husband say to you?"

Dr Wagner injected the sedative.

"He said he was on his way home. Then he said goodbye in a strange way. It was," she fought for control, "almost as if he knew he wouldn't be seeing me or the boys again." She closed her eyes and lay back quietly. Stone couldn't tell whether she was asleep or not.

Closing the bedroom door behind him, Dr Wagner escorted Stone to the living room.

"I'm sorry if I disturbed her," he apologized. "Please let me know when I can talk to her again."

"Not for a day or two at least," the doctor said. "Now I think you'd better go."

"Of course. But may I ask you one or two questions?"

"What do you want to know?"

"The autopsy showed traces of drugs in Townsend's blood. I'd like that explained. Was he an addict or had you given him medication?"

Wagner considered for a moment. "Rich Townsend was no drug addict. As a matter of fact he took the prescription only with reluctance. About four months ago, he came in for a checkup. He mentioned he'd been having headaches which aspirin didn't help. I gave him a thorough exam and found he had a brain tumor. Inoperable. I told him he had six months to a year at the most. He took it better than I expected and asked me not to tell Helen or the boys. I probably will now that he's gone. It might help."

"I see. Tell me, was he in much pain?"

"He said no, but he could have been lying. A tumor like that can be relatively painless at first, but as the pressure increases, so does the pain. I gave him a prescription, and I suppose he had it filled. He wasn't a great talker, you know. Preferred to suffer in silence."

"Would the end have come quickly, or would it have been a long, lingering one?"

"Hard to say exactly," Wagner said. "He might have had several months in severe agony, or he could have gone just like that." He snapped his fingers. "The odds are for the longer period, but we'll never know for certain now. I can't see that it has anything to do with his murder. Or are you thinking it was suicide?"

"We're looking into all possibilities," Stone said. "I need all the information I can get. Have you been his doctor long?"

"For over sixteen years," Wagner admitted. "I've been his friend even longer."

"Do you know if he took out an insurance policy recently?"

"I don't think so. I happen to give all the physicals for the agency that insures him. I couldn't have signed a favorable exam report, which is required before a policy is issued. I suppose he could have gone to another company, but I don't think he could have fooled the doctors. You might check with his agent, Hal Harris. I'm sure he'll know more about it."

"I'll do that," Stone replied, moving toward the front door. He turned to face the physician. "By the way, doctor, do you happen to know anything about curare?" He noticed his question brought a slight smile from Dr Wagner.

"I don't wish to seem immodest, but I happen to be an expert in that field. Why do you ask?"

"The coroner has attributed Mr. Townsend's death to curare on the point of the ice pick." Stone paused slightly to allow Wagner to make a comment, but the doctor betrayed no reaction to the news. "Now I'm wondering how easy it would be for a person to get his hands on some of that poison."

"Not too easy for a non-medical person unless he has friends along the Amazon," Wagner replied. "Curare does have medicinal uses. Someone working for a pharmaceutical firm might be able to obtain it. Say, here's a coincidence. Some crude curare I had in my office was stolen just a few weeks ago."

Stone's eyebrows shot upward. "Oh?"

"You can get complete details from your burglary department,"

Wagner said. "When I reported the theft, I assumed the burglar was a drug addict, since my entire supply of drugs was taken. But it could have been the curare he was after, and he took the rest as a cover-up."

"Possibly. May I ask why you had such a bizarre poison in your office?"

"It's not so bizarre, sergeant," Wagner explained. "It's quite a natural hunting tool for South American Indians, and refined forms of it are often used in the medical field as a muscle relaxant. For the past several years I've been doing research to find additional uses for it. As an avocation I've made many canoe trips on the Amazon River, and I became interested there in curare. I was able to obtain a considerable quantity of it for research purposes."

"Is it always fatal?"

"If the dose is large enough. In its crude form, curare is a deadly poison when injected into the victim's bloodstream. Death occurs because, to put it simply, the respiratory muscles are paralyzed, and the victim dies because he is unable to breathe. If it's injected into a vein, a man could die almost instantaneously. With a smaller dose, a person would live longer, depending on his size, and might even recover. There are antidotes which, if administered soon enough, can reverse the effect and save the victim's life. If taken orally, the poison is ineffective. This is why the natives are able to eat the meat of poisoned animals."

"Who knew you had the poison in your office?"

"Only several thousand local TV viewers, in addition to my office staff and a few patients."

Stone paused to let this startling news sink in. "Would you mind explaining?"

"Not at all. It's really very simple. I've taken movies of all my Amazon journeys and show them on TV. Channel 12 has a program called *Adventurous Voyage*, which I appeared on a few weeks ago. During the interview portion of the show, the host asked me questions about the poison the Indians in the film had used to kill game animals. I explained everything, even mentioning that I was doing research with the poison in my office lab. I didn't know someone was going to steal it in order to kill Rich Townsend."

"We don't know where the curare came from, but it's a good bet it could have been yours. You don't suppose Mr Townsend could have taken some from your office?"

The doctor reflected a moment. "He had the opportunity. But for what purpose?"

"Perhaps to bring a swift end to his painful headaches," Stone suggested.

"Not Rich. He wasn't one to take his own life. Yet if the pain were unbearable . . ."

Stone extended his hand. "Thank you, Dr Wagner. You've given me some very useful information. I'll try not to disturb Mrs Townsend again unless it is absolutely necessary." The front door was closed behind him, and Stone returned to headquarters.

Curtis's second report was in Stone's in-basket. Lissner had yet to return from the bookstore. Curtis had been able to ascertain that all of Townsend's property was held jointly with his wife. The big surprise was that Townsend had taken out life insurance for half a million dollars just three months previously. Stone whistled and gave Hal Harris a call.

Harris was on edge. Stone could hear the worry in his voice as he explained the situation. "Mr Townsend had all of his business and personal insurance with my agency. Until about three months ago he had only twenty-five thousand in term on his life. Then he came in and wanted a policy for half a million. That's not so uncommon nowadays. You know, when a man reaches his late forties he begins to be a little more concerned about what might happen to his family if he should suddenly die. He wants a lot more protection. I was only too happy to service his insurance needs. I sent him to Dr Kurt Wagner, who does all our insurance physicals. Townsend came back with a report stating he was in excellent health and fully insurable. However, he did seem somewhat concerned about making the monthly premiums."

"Did you try to talk him out of it?"

"Of course not. My business is trying to talk people into buying insurance. He paid the first month's premium right away, of course, but he was considerably late with the second, and missed the third completely. The policy is still in force because there's a thirty-day grace period. Sergeant, the company that underwrote the policy is not going to like paying. Any chance it was suicide?"

"You're the second person to ask about that today," Stone replied. "All I can say is that we are exploring all possibilities. Does his policy have a suicide clause?"

"You bet. Standard two-year," Harris said. "By the way,

sergeant. I've got a very special policy for police officers. If you're interested, I'll send you a brochure."

"Well, thank you very much, Mr Harris. I'll get in touch with you if I need any more information."

Stone hung up and mulled over the conversation. Dr Wagner had stated he could not have signed a favorable physical exam report for Townsend, yet Harris had just told him that Townsend had a clean bill of health from Dr Wagner. Why would Harris lie? Stone could think of no reason. Why would Wagner lie? Townsend was his friend, and he might do it for a friend, especially if he were in love with the friend's wife. The doctor could have wanted to be certain the window would be well provided for after her husband's death. Stone decided it would be interesting to see a copy of that report.

Lissner's rushing in caused Stone's train of thought to run off the tracks. The young detective had a smile a mile wide across his face.

"I see you've had some luck," Stone remarked.

Lissner could hardly contain himself, but he wanted to milk the suspense. "You call it luck. I call it hard digging."

"Well, let's have it."

The burly detective took a crumpled slip of paper from his pocket and spread it out on the desk. "Found this in the waste-basket in Townsend's office at the bookstore."

Stone read the note. *Call from Lew's station* – 9 P.M.

"Know who wrote it?"

"Townsend himself," Lissner replied. "The bookstore was closed today, of course, but Townsend's salesclerk, Janice Carter, showed up while I was there and helped me search. She identified the handwriting. The paper's from a pad by the telephone. Someone set him up for the kill."

"Could be," Stone said. "On the other hand, he could have simply written himself a reminder. But it does show he knew where Lew's is located. Didn't even have to write down the address. Did you come up with anything else?" He noticed that Lissner was still grinning.

"Not much. Everything was in good shape, especially Janice. Now there's one bright chick. When I mentioned insurance, she dug these out of the files. I can't see they have anything to do with the case."

He handed Stone two letters. The first one was from some

insurance company's main office, informing Townsend that the enclosed check for $3,482.87 was in full payment for his accident claim, policy number 987 756 32. The second letter was from Hal Harris, thanking Townsend for returning the insurance company's check for $3,482.87, which had been sent to him inadvertently by the head office of one of the firms Harris represented. The letter went on to explain that such checks were normally sent to the local representative, who then presented them to the claimant. Through a computer error, the check had been erroneously sent directly to Townsend; moreover, it actually was intended for another Richard Townsend, a man who had been involved in an automobile accident. Harris thanked Townsend and commended him for his honesty in returning a check he could easily have cashed.

"More evidence that Townsend was a real nice guy," Lissner commented.

Stone just hummed, not mentioning the matter of the spurious physical report. Or was it spurious? Dr Wagner might have lied about telling Townsend about his tumor. He had volunteered much confidential medical information. He could have given Townsend a favorable report for personal reasons. A beautiful widow with half a million could be sweet temptation.

After Curtis returned, without much useful information, Stone sent him and Lissner out with instructions to check very carefully on Dr Wagner, Hal Harris, Lew Hall, Janice Carter, and any other close friends or business associates of Townsend. He specifically instructed them to be alert for any connections one might have with another.

For a few minutes Stone sat thinking. The threads of evidence he had were now beginning to form a pattern in his mind. Then he called the telephone company. As he had expected, he was told that the phone booth at Lew's station had not been out of order and that no service truck had been dispatched to repair it. Mr Larking, the manager, added that the truck seen at Lew's was probably one that had been stolen and was later found abandoned a mile or so from the station. Larking was of the opinion the truck had been taken by a gang of coin box burglars. Numerous other trucks had been "borrowed" for a few hours during the past several days. It was the gang's M.O. to place an out-of-order sign on a booth, then send a "service" man, who calmly emptied the coin box as he "repaired" the phone. The company had lost several thousands of dollars in the past few days.

Although Larking said officers from Burglary had already checked the stolen truck, Stone insisted that it be kept out of service until he personally released it. He thanked Larking for his cooperation, hung up, and dialed Burglary. Sergeant Kendrick answered.

"Kenny," Stone asked, "what can you give me on the phone truck stolen last night?"

"Not much. Wiped clean. Not a single usable print. We think it was used by the coin box looters. It's their M.O. all the way, and they're known to be working this area."

"How much was taken from the booth at Lew's station?"

"Funny you should ask," Kendrick replied. "Nothing."

"How do you explain that?"

"On that kind of job they use a key or pick the lock and put everything back in order. Ordinarily we don't know a booth's been hit until a company collector opens the box and finds only a few coins. We wouldn't have checked the box at Lew's station if Townsend hadn't been killed there, but when we did, we found it nearly full. I figure Townsend's coming scared the guy off. He was probably waiting around the water and air hoses until the coast was clear so he could have another try. When he sees all the commotion, he beats it."

"But the phony repairman was there almost ten minutes before Townsend arrived. Wouldn't that have given him time to clean out the box?"

"Normally more than enough. But he could have run into difficulties. The phone company's been installing tougher locks recently."

"Sounds logical," Stone conceded. "Okay, Kenny, thanks. Ring me if anything you find ties in with Townsend's death."

Kendrick's explanation fit Lew Hall's story all the way, but Stone had an uneasy feeling that something wasn't as logical as Kendrick's version made it seem. The sudden arrival of Curtis and Lissner interrupted his thoughts.

The subordinates dragged up chairs and plopped into them. It had been a tedious shift and Stone could tell from their demeanor that they were anxious to call it quits for the day and go home. Stone felt the same.

"Okay, boys, let's hear it."

"Hell, Ray," Curtis complained, "we're up a blind alley. We can't find a motive for anyone to kill Townsend."

"Just tell me what you've learned."

"Wagner's been a friend of Townsend for nearly twenty years. He's been a widower for six. No children. Admittedly he's fond of Helen Townsend, but we couldn't come up with any evidence of hanky-panky. Wagner knew Townsend had only months to live. All he had to do was sit around and wait if he wanted the wife. He's got a good practice. Makes great money. Several years ago he helped out Townsend financially." Curtis unwrapped a stick of chewing gum and slid it into his mouth. He caught Stone looking at him. "You don't mind, do you?"

"Not if you keep it noiseless. Continue."

Curtis shifted the wad to the side of his mouth. "Hal Harris moves in an entirely different social circle than Townsend did. He's the country club type. Young, dynamic. Hell, he's only twenty-nine, but he has an extremely lucrative business. He has a gorgeous wife, no kids. His only connection with Townsend is that he happens to be his insurance agent."

"What about any others? Lew Hall, the bookstore girl?"

Lissner stirred uneasily. "Nothing there, Ray. Janice Carter is just a college student who works part time at the bookstore. No romantic involvement with Townsend. She's got a steady boyfriend. Townsend bought his gas regularly at a station downtown. Probably had never been to Lew's before, but he could have driven past it many times because it's near Dr Wagner's office."

"It would be great to find a motive," Curtis added. "A motive would lead to a suspect. Now we don't have either."

"So where does that leave us?" Lissner answered his own question: "With an unsolvable murder. Cripes, let's face it, this one's impossible. No one could've killed Townsend from either inside or outside the booth."

Curtis was quick to agree. "Right. And even though Townsend had a motive for suicide, he couldn't have stabbed himself in the back. Not even a well-trained contortionist could have done that. And even if he could have, he would have left prints on the ice pick handle. And there were no prints."

All three sat silent, thinking. After a few moments, Stone said, "Look, either it's murder or suicide. There's no way we can call it an accident. Now, Townsend did have a compelling motive for suicide. He had a brain tumor and could have been suffering unbearable pain. But why would he want his suicide to look like murder?"

Curtis's eyes widened with sudden understanding. "The insurance! His wife couldn't collect if he took his own life."

"Right. But why such a bizarre death?" Stone wanted to know. "He could have 'accidentally' stepped in front of a vehicle moving at high speed or driven his car into a telephone pole, and there would have been no question of suicide or murder."

Lissner was right on it. "Townsend was a really nice, thoughtful guy. He never wanted to do anything to hurt anyone. He probably felt a car accident might involve others or that he might be horribly injured but not killed. I think he figured if he set up an impossible murder, no one could be charged with the crime, and his family would be certain to collect his insurance. He'd taken one of those pain-killing pills and put curare on the ice pick to make death quick and certain."

Curtis put a damper on this theory. "Yeah, but how?"

Stone didn't answer the question. "That's what I want you two to think about. Go on home, get a good night's rest, and we'll talk it over in the morning."

After Curtis and Lissner had left, Stone sat meditating. He let his mind replay the conversation with Sergeant Kendrick and suddenly it was clear to him why Kendrick's logical explanation was not so logical. Stone decided it would be very wise to visit the scene of the crime once more.

Lew waved to him as he pulled into the station. It was nine p.m. – about the same time that Richard Townsend had died on the previous night.

"Hi, sergeant! What can I do for you?"

Stone nodded a greeting. "Mind keeping an eye on me the way you did on Townsend?" He walked over to the booth, stepped inside, closed the door, and performed a brief experiment. Then he went back to the pumps.

"Well, Mr Hall?"

Lew pushed back his cap and scratched his forehead. "Looked like you were reenacting the crime. You went through all the same motions the dead guy did, 'cept you didn't fall down dead. How come?"

"It helps me immensely in solving crimes if I don't fall down dead," Stone retorted with a suggestion of a smile. "Now pretend I'm the telephone repairman. Tell me if what I do is about what you saw last night."

Stone drove over to the booth. He got out of his car, entered the booth, closed the door, took the receiver off the hook, put it back, bent down, straightened up, then stepped outside to the back of the booth. He knelt for a moment, then moved slowly over to the air and water service island, returned to the booth, and drove his car to the island, where he checked the tires. He walked back to where Lew was standing.

"Pretty good show, sergeant," Lew laughed. "Like I said this morning, I didn't see him all the time, but I'd say he did pretty much what you just went through."

"Thanks for your help, Mr Hall." Stone extended his hand and got a firm return shake from the station operator.

"Don't mention it. Think it'll help you find the killer?"

"It wouldn't surprise me at all," Stone flung over his shoulder and he got into his car and drove off.

Harvey Curtis was already in the squad room when Stone arrived at eight the following morning. Lissner came swinging in moments later with that mile-wide grin across his face.

"Looks as if you have something to tell us," Stone said.

"Would you believe I've solved this one? I knew my TV watching would pay off."

"Well, don't keep us in suspense," Curtis said.

"You know how we were talking about Townsend being the only one with a motive but we couldn't figure out how he could have got that ice pick in his back? Well, I can tell you, thanks to a movie I saw last night. It's called *Rage in Heaven*. Stars Ingrid Bergman and Robert Montgomery. Both dead now, but they live on in the movies. Maybe you saw it?"

"Can't say that I have," Stone replied. "Well, get on with your story."

"The picture's about this nutty millionaire who kills himself so it looks like murder, so the guy he thinks is his wife's lover will get executed. The guy wedges a knife in the door jamb, then walks backwards into it. He falls on the floor and it looks like somebody has stabbed him in the back. That's how Townsend did it. He wipes the handle of the ice pick clean, and holding it by the tip, puts it into the return coin slot, which held it at the right height and angle to penetrate his heart. Then all he had to do was to be sure someone was around to witness his murder and fall backward onto the blade. Sort of *hara-kiri* in reverse."

Curtis slapped his thigh. "Hot damn, Fred, that's it! Suicide made to look like murder. That's the only solution. Well, Ray, it looks like we can toss this one in the closed file."

"I don't think so," Stone said. "Townsend didn't kill himself; he was murdered. A very clever murder, which was supposed to be termed suicide. Just as you two did."

"Come again," Lissner blurted.

"I don't get it," Curtis admitted.

Stone sighed. The two detectives were good investigative officers, but without much imagination. "The murder of Townsend was well planned and executed. Incidentally, Fred, I thought of the ice-pick-in-the-coin-slot ploy yesterday and nearly came to the same conclusion you did. I let you go through the suicide theory to see if you would agree it was the only solution, and you did. That's the conclusion the killer wanted. He knew we'd sooner or later figure out how Townsend could have put the ice pick into his own back. Once we thought of that, we'd call it suicide and close the case. I'll admit I was almost ready to do it. But a few things didn't fit."

"Such as?" queried Lissner.

"First, the telephone booth was supposedly out of order and had been fixed just before Townsend used it. Logically the repairman's fingerprints should have been all over the phone, yet only Townsend's were found. That told me that the repairman must have wiped the phone clean. No legitimate repairman would have done that. He might have cleaned the phone, but his prints should have been on it. Also a genuine company employee would have replaced the burnt-out light bulb and swept out the booth before putting it back into service. This one didn't. That tells me he was a phony."

"But," Lissner interrupted, "the phone company told us he was a fake attempting to rifle the coin box. We know that."

"We know nothing of the kind," Stone said gently. "Sure, he could have been one of the gang. Stranger coincidences have happened. But a couple of things told me he wasn't. If he had been attempting to break into the coin box, he wouldn't have taken down the out-of-order sign before successfully looting it and putting everything back in order. If he hadn't opened the box in a few minutes, he would have run. He certainly wouldn't have waited around for a second chance."

Both Curtis and Lissner were more than a little dubious. Lissner had come up with a perfectly good explanation of Townsend's death, and they were reluctant to abandon it. However, they could see some logic to Stone's reasoning. "What else?" Lissner asked.

"That piece of electrical tape found in the booth. We assumed that the phone company's serviceman left it there. But remember the phone company hadn't sent out anyone to fix the phone, so that little piece of tape set me thinking. It convinced me that the fake repairman murdered Townsend and then drove off in the stolen truck while Lew and the other witnesses were discovering the body."

The two detectives looked at each other and shook their heads. Curtis spoke for both of them. "I can see how Townsend could have killed himself, Ray, but what you say is impossible. The booth was completely closed. How could anyone get the ice pick into the booth without breaking the glass?"

"Very simply," Stone explained. "He put it into the booth before Townsend entered."

Curtis seemed puzzled. "Okay, say the ice pick was in the booth when Townsend entered. Why didn't he see it? How'd the fake repairman get it into his back when he was at least thirty feet away?"

Stone hesitated. In his mind he had already worked out the solution to how the crime was committed and he was positive he was correct. "The ice pick wasn't in the coin return slot. The killer used compressed air to project the ice pick into Townsend."

"Compressed air?" The puzzled look remained on Curtis's face.

"You know that Lew's station has water and air hoses situated at a distance from the gas pumps, so drivers using those facilities don't hold up the gas lines. It's the only place in town with a setup like that. That's why the murder occurred there. That's why Townsend was lured to that telephone booth. It had been converted into a death chamber. The mechanics of the thing are simple. Dr Wagner's mentioning South American Indians hunting with the poison started me thinking. The hunters use poison darts and blowguns. The killer used the ice pick as his dart and had his own version of a blowgun."

"Sounds complicated to me," Lissner remarked.

"Not really. This is the way I think it happened. The murderer, posing as a telephone repairman, arrives in the stolen truck ostensibly to fix the phone. Earlier he had put an out-of-order sign on the booth to keep it free for his use. He then attaches his blowgun – a light-weight cylinder of some kind, probably cardboard or plastic, and about five inches long – to the underside of the telephone book shelf with some electrical tape, so that it hangs just slightly below the shelf and points to a predetermined spot which he is sure will coincide with the victim's heart. The shelf is just slightly lower than the shoulder blade of a man of Townsend's height. The killer inserts the ice pick into the tube, which is just a fraction wider than the diameter of the handle. Hanging phone books effectively conceal the device from anyone entering or standing in the booth."

Stone paused to see if Curtis or Lissner wanted to make a comment. Neither did.

"Attached to the closed end of the cylinder is a length of transparent flexible tubing – probably plastic – which the killer runs through the rear ventilation opening at the bottom of the booth. He uses a couple of short pieces of electrical tape to hold the thin hose against the framework, where it is virtually invisible. Then he goes over to the air and water island, connects his tubing to an air hose, and pretends to be checking his tires. A few seconds later Townsend enters the death chamber. The killer uses the free compressed air supplied by Lew to blow his 'dart' into Townsend's back. He gives a hard tug on the tubing; the cylinder comes loose from the shelf and drops to the floor. The killer pulls it and the tubing over to his truck and drives off just as Lew and the other witnesses are rushing to the booth. Unfortunately for the murderer, one small piece of his tape remains in the booth. Any questions?"

Lissner was dubious and blunt. "Well, it's a helluva lot more complicated than my suicide theory, but I'll have to admit, it does account for all those bothersome little details."

Curtis went further. "Okay, suppose we agree that the phony repairman is the killer. How do we find out who he is? He wasn't recognized and left no fingerprints."

The reaction of the two officers to his splendid deductions was not as enthusiastic as Stone would have liked. To give them time to appreciate his mental efforts, he got up and walked to the window. The view wasn't good – the police parking lot with a couple of billboards thrown in for good measure. He turned to face his subordinates.

"I know," he teased. "Don't you?"

Both shook their heads.

"I take it we agree that Townsend was murdered. Okay, then we have to accept as fact that the murder was conceived to lead the police to label it suicide, just as you did, Fred. The murderer has to be someone who knew Townsend might have a reason to kill himself and make it appear to be murder."

Jumping to conclusions was one of Curtis's weaknesses. "Dr Wagner! He was the only one who knew Townsend had a tumor. And he had possession of the poison. He could easily have faked that robbery. He could get his hands on the insurance money by marrying the widow."

"Wagner knew Townsend was going to die," Stone said, "but I don't believe he knew about the insurance, since he was aware Townsend was not insurable. And even if he did know about it, he had no motive to kill Townsend, since the man was going to die in a few months. Now, we know that Townsend didn't tell his family about his illness, and Wagner says he told no one. I believe him. But Townsend himself may have told another person, and I'm certain he did."

Curtis and Lissner sat there with open mouths.

"Fred, get a warrant and search for rubber or plastic tubing, red paint, and electrical tape. Also check the area where the telephone truck was abandoned. The blowgun device may have been discarded near there. I'd sure like to get a look at that thing. Harve, you bring in the suspect for questioning."

"Who?" both detectives asked.

"Hall Harris."

By five in the afternoon proof that Stone's deductions were amazingly accurate started coming in. A search of Harris's garage yielded some plastic tubing, a can of paint that matched that on the ice pick handle, and a roll of tape like the piece found in the booth. Detective Lissner even managed to come up with the death device Harris had put together. It was found by neighborhood youngsters in a trash dumpster a few blocks from where the phone truck had been abandoned. Lissner had enlisted the kids in the search and it had paid off for both the detective and the children. It had cost him twenty dollars in rewards, but it was well worth the money, for Harris's fingerprints were all over the gimmick. The device looked almost exactly as Stone had envisioned it – a five-inch piece of PVC sprinkler pipe on one end of a forty foot length of quarter-inch plastic tubing and a connecting tire valve on the other. The files at Harris's office contained a copy of the medical report supposedly signed by Dr Wagner. It was an obvious forgery.

The result of all this evidence was that Hal Harris, after having been questioned for more than two hours in the presence of his attorney, calmly dictated and signed a full confession. It was probably his best move, for by doing so he was certain to avoid the death penalty.

At six in the evening Sergeant Ray Stone sat in an upholstered chair in front of Captain Jack Parker's desk. Parker wanted some personal explanations. "I still don't see how you knew it was Harris."

"It had to be Harris or Wagner. Those were the only two who knew of Townsend's impending death. Wagner had no reason to murder Townsend. Harris was the only one with a motive. Townsend was blackmailing him."

Parker leaned forward eagerly. "How'd you figure that out?"

"Townsend managed to get a whopping big insurance policy when he had only a short time to live. Dr Wagner said he didn't give Townsend an insurance physical, yet Harris told me Townsend came in with a clean bill of health from Wagner. He was lying. No doctor lets the patient carry the exam report back to the company. He sends it. Harris had to have forged the examination report that was sent in with the policy application. It wasn't worth the risk to do that unless someone forced him. That someone could only have been Townsend."

This explanation did not completely satisfy Parker. "What did Townsend know that enabled him to blackmail Harris?"

"It's not so much what he knew, but what he guessed," Stone replied. "Those two letters we found in Townsend's files put me onto it. Harris was filing false claims and pocketing the proceeds. Townsend threatened to tell Harris's parent companies to examine his claims for fraud unless Harris got the policy approved. Townsend, normally a very nice and honest guy, was not concerned for himself when he learned of his terminal illness. He wanted his family to be without financial worries after he was gone. That's why he felt forced to blackmail Harris."

Stone leaned back, lacing his fingers behind his head. "Any more questions, Jack, or have I completely satisfied your curiosity?"

"Not quite," Parker said. "How did Harris get Townsend to go to the telephone booth? After all, he was the blackmailer. You'd think he'd set up the meeting."

"We got the answer from Harris himself. Townsend wasn't able to come up with the third month's premium, so he asked Harris to give him a receipt stating the premium had been paid. Now Harris began to sweat. If Townsend didn't die soon – and many who are given months hang on for years – he was afraid he would be paying all the future premiums for Townsend. He had to come up with a way to get rid of Townsend and have the policy canceled without an extensive investigation. 'Suicide' was the answer. It would appear as if Townsend were trying to bilk the insurance company by faking his own murder."

Stone's pausing briefly caused Parker to blurt out, "So what did Harris do?"

"He telephoned Townsend and suggested that for formality's sake the premium should be sent to the main office. He persuaded Townsend to go to Lew's station at nine o'clock that night and make a phone call from the booth there. Harris told Townsend that when he got back to his car he would find the necessary cash in an envelope on the front seat. Then all Townsend would have to do was to deposit the money in his account and send in a check for the premium."

"You know, Ray, Harris's plan was ingenious," Parker remarked. "It would have succeeded, too, if it hadn't been for your keen observations."

"Could be," Stone said. "It was an almost perfect crime."

The X Street Murders

Joseph Commings

Joseph Commings (1913–92) was one of the masters of the impossible crime story. He started his career in the old pulp magazines in the 1940s. He stockpiled stories written during the Second World War and some of these, possibly rewritten, did not appear in magazines until well into the 1950s. Most feature the larger-than-life and frequently over-bombastic character of Senator Brooks U. Banner. Banner has an uncanny knack of stumbling across baffling crimes of which the following is generally regarded as his masterpiece. Amazingly, although he later sold a number of erotic novels, Commings never published a collection of his stories. Fortunately for impossible-crime enthusiasts, Robert Adey assembled a collection called Banner Deadlines, *published in 2004, which contains plenty more like the following.*

Carroll Lockyear came out of the attaché's private office at the New Zealand Legation on X Street, Washington, D.C. He was tall and skinny. The sallow skin of his gaunt face was drawn tight over his doorknob cheekbones like that of an Egyptian mummy. The resemblance to a mummy did not end with the tightness of his skin. Sticking out from his sharp chin, like a dejected paintbrush, was a russet-colored King Tut beard. He looked like a well-dressed beatnik. In his left hand he carried a brown cowhide briefcase, his long fingers curled under the bottom of it.

The secretary in the reception room, Miss Gertrude Wagner, looked up at him. He approached her desk and laid his briefcase carefully down on it, then towered over it toward her.

"Yes, Mr Lockyear?" she said.

"I have another appointment with Mr Gosling on next Tuesday, Miss Wagner."

Gertrude penciled a line in an appointment pad.

"Good day," said Lockyear. He picked up his briefcase and walked out.

Gertrude smiled thinly at the Army officer waiting on the lounge. He was reading a copy of the *Ordnance Sergeant*, but it wasn't holding his attention as much as it should. He wore a green tunic with sharpshooter medals on the breast, and his legs, in pink slacks, were crossed. Gertrude stopped her professional smile and picked up the earpiece of the interphone and pressed a button.

"Mr Gosling," she said, "Captain Cozzens is waiting to see you." She held the earpiece to her head for a moment, then lowered it. "Captain," she said. Cozzens looked up with bright expectancy from his magazine. "Mr Gosling wants to know if you'd mind waiting a minute."

"Not at all," said Cozzens, eager to agree with such a good-looking girl. No doubt, visions of dinners for two were dancing in his head.

Gertrude stood up suddenly and tugged her skirt straight. She had black hair cut in a Dutch bob and dark blue eyes. The austere lines of her blotter-green suit could not entirely disguise her big-boned femininity. She gathered up a steno pad and a mechanical pencil and started to walk toward the closed door of Mr Gosling's private office. Glancing at the slim bagette watch on her wrist, she stopped short. It was as if she had almost forgotten something. She went back to her desk. On it lay a sealed large bulky manila mailing envelope. A slip of paper had been pasted on its side. Typed in red on the paper was the Legation address and:

Deliver to Mr Kermit Gosling at 11:30 a.m. sharp.

Gertrude grasped the envelope by the top and proceeded into Gosling's office, leaving the door open. This private office, it was carefully noted later, was on the third floor of the building. It had two windows and both these windows were protected by old-fashioned iron bars. It was a room in which an attaché might consider himself safe.

Captain Cozzens had been following Gertrude's flowing progress with admiring eyes. Those narrow skirts did a lot for a girl if she had the right kind of legs and hips. And Gertrude definitely had the right kind.

Another man sitting near Cozzens was watching her too. He was red-haired and young, with a square face and a pug nose. The jacket of his black suit was tight across his shoulders. He was Alvin Odell and it was his job to watch what went on in the office. He was an agent from the Federal Bureau of Investigation. But he too was watching Gertrude with more interest than his job called for.

From where Cozzens and Odell sat they could see the edge of Gosling's desk. They saw the closely observed Gertrude stand before it, facing across it, and she held the bulky envelope up waist-high.

There was a slight pause.

Then three shots spat harshly.

Cozzens and Odell, shocked at the sudden ripping apart of their daydreams by gunfire, saw Gertrude flinch before the desk. Then the two men sprang up together and rushed in to her side.

Gosling, a heavy-featured man with limp blond hair, was tilted sideways in his desk chair. Blood stained his white shirt front. Odell stared at the three bullet holes under the left lapel of the grey business suit.

Captain Cozzens' voice was hoarse. "Those three shots – where did they come from?"

Gertrude's blue eyes, dazed, searched Cozzens' face as if she had never seen him before. Dumbly she lifted up the heavy envelope.

Before Cozzens could move, the FBI man was faster. Odell snatched the envelope out of her hand.

It was still tightly sealed. There were no holes or tears in it. Odell started to rip it along the top. A wisp of bluish smoke curled up in the still air.

Odell tore the envelope wide open and out of it onto the desktop spilled a freshly fired automatic pistol.

Heavy blunt-tipped fingers on speckled hands turned over the brown State Department envelope. It was addressed to *Honorable Brooks U. Banner, M. C., The Idle Hour Club, President Jefferson Avenue, Washington, D.C.*

The addressee was a big fat man with a mane of grizzled hair and a ruddy jowled face and the physique of a performing bear. He wore a moth-eaten frock coat with deep pockets bulging with junk

and a greasy string tie and baggy-kneed grey britches. Under the
open frock coat was a candy-striped shirt. On his feet were old
house slippers whose frayed toes looked as if a pair of hungry field
mice were trying to nibble their way out from inside. He was an
overgrown Huck Finn. Physically he was more than one man – he
was a gang. Socially and politically he didn't have to answer to
anybody, so he acted and spoke any way he damned pleased.

He was sipping his eighth cup of black coffee as he read the
letter.

It was from the Assistant Secretary of State. In painful mechanical detail, it reported the murder on X Street with as much passion
as there is in a recipe for an upside-down cake. Toward the end of
the letter, the Assistant Secretary became a little less like an
automaton and a little more human. He confessed to Banner that
both the State Department and the FBI were snagged. They
couldn't find an answer. And considering the other harrowing
murder cases that Banner had solved, perhaps he could be of some
help in this extremity.

Banner crumpled the letter up into a ball and stuck it into his
deep pocket. Thoughtfully his little frosty blue eyes rested on the
white ceiling. He had read about the case in the newspapers, but
the account had not been as full as the State Department's.

He pulled the napkin from under his chin, swabbed his lips, and
started to surge up to his feet. He looked like a surfacing whale.

A waiter hurried up with a tray. On it were three more cups of
black coffee, "Aren't you going to drink the rest of your coffee,
sir?" asked the waiter in an injured tone.

"Huh?" said Banner absently. Already his mind was soaring out
into space, grappling with the murder problem. "I never touch the
stuff," he said and went lumbering out.

Jack McKitrick, who looked like a jockey trainer, was an FBI
department chief. He stood near Captain Cozzens in the New
Zealand Legation office. When Banner came trotting in the door
McKitrick said sideways to Cozzens: "That's Senator Banner.
They don't come much bigger."

Cozzens shook his head as he eyed the impressive hulk that
rumbled forward.

"Morning, Senator," said McKitrick to Banner.

Banner grunted an answer, mumbling words around a long
Pittsburgh stogie clamped in his teeth.

"Senator," continued McKitrick, "this is Captain Cozzens of the Ordnance Division, U.S. Army." The two men clasped hands. "Cozzens is a small firearms expert."

"Mighty fine," said Banner.

"You were an Army officer yourself, weren't you, Senator?" said Cozzens.

Banner truculently chewed on the stogie. "Yass. I never got above the rank of shavetail. We were the dogfaces who gave 'em hell at Chateau Thierry. But I'll tell you all about my war experiences later, Cap'n. We'll all work together on this. Not nice seeing our New Zealand friends getting bumped off. Not nice at all."

"No, certainly not," said Cozzens.

Banner struck an attitude of belligerent ease. "Waal, I'm listening, Cap'n. You were one of the witnesses to this murder. What were you doing at the Legation?"

Cozzens frowned. "I was here by appointment, Senator. Mr Gosling wanted me to suggest a good handgun for his personal use and to give him instructions in how to handle it."

"Why?"

"I think," said Cozzens slowly, "he wanted to use it to protect himself."

"Against what?"

"He never had a chance to tell me. But I think *this* might supply part of the answer." He held up a wicked-looking pistol. "This is what did the trick, Senator. It's all right to handle it. No fingerprints were found on it."

Scowling, Banner took it from him. "So that's the Russian pop-pop."

"Right," said Cozzens. "A Tokarev, a standard Russian automatic. It's a 7.62-mm. with a Browning-Colt breech-locking system and it uses Nagant gas-check cartridges."

"This was the gun in the sealed envelope," said Banner. "Are you sure it wasn't some other gun you heard being fired?"

Cozzens slowly shook his head. "I've spent a lifetime with guns, Senator. I've got to know their 'voices' just the way you know people's. When you hear an accent, you know what part of the world the speaker comes from. That's the way I am with pistols and revolvers. So I'll stake my reputation that the shots we heard had a Russian accent, meaning they were fired from a Tokarev automatic, slightly muffled. Besides that, ballistics bears me out.

The bullets found in Gosling's body were indisputably from that gun."

Banner grunted. "And all the while the gun was sealed up tight in an envelope and you could see the secretary holding the envelope while the shots were fired?"

"That's right," answered Cozzens.

"How d'you explain it, Cap'n? What's your theory?"

"Theory? I haven't any. I can't explain it. If I hadn't seen it with my own eyes, I wouldn't believe it."

"Anything else you have to offer?" asked Banner.

"Nothing. That's all."

The stogie in Banner's mouth was burning fiercely. He looked around the office where the murder had been committed. It was a completely equipped modern office. Nothing had been disturbed. He mumbled: "*Gosling knew his life was in danger!*"

Banner turned to McKitrick. "I'll see Odell."

Cozzens left while Banner was being introduced to the FBI agent, Odell.

"You heard Cozzens' story about the shooting, Odell," said Banner. "Have you anything to add to it?"

Odell shook his red-haired head. "No, it happened just that way, Senator." His frank boyish face was grave.

"Why were you stationed here?"

"At a request from Mr Gosling. He asked for our security."

"How long've you been hanging out here?"

"About a week, Senator."

McKitrick interrupted to say: "Odell asked for this assignment."

Banner studied the young man with the rusty hair. "What's the reason, Red?"

Odell hesitated, growing crimson around the ears. "Well, Senator – a – Miss Wagner – Well, you'll have to see her to appreciate her—"

Banner suddenly chuckled. He was thinking of his own misspent youth chasing the dolls.

Odell sobered. "She's a hard girl to make friends with," he admitted ruefully.

"It's tough, Red," grinned Banner. "Fetch in the li'l chickie and we'll see if I can't make better time with her than you did."

Odell went out of the office and returned with Gertrude. She looked scared at Banner. Big men in authority seemed to have given her a sudden fright. Her shoulders were hunched up as if she were cold. Odell held her solicitously by the elbow.

"Hello, Gertie," boomed Banner as familiarly as if he had helped to christen her. "Siddown."

She dropped gratefully on the leather lounge as if relieved to get the strain off her shaky knees.

"Gertie, there's no reason why you should think I'm gonna panic you. I'm your big Dutch uncle, remember?"

She smiled at him.

"Now, Gertie," he resumed, "you live with your people, don't you?"

"No," she said hoarsely, then she cleared her throat. "No, Senator. I have no relatives in America. They're all living in Germany."

"Germany?" Banner made a quick pounce. "What part of Germany?"

"On a farm outside of Zerbst."

Banner's little frosty blue eyes looked shrewd. "That's in East Germany, ain't it, Gertie?"

"Yes."

"Tell me about 'em. And how you got out?"

It wasn't too complicated a story. Gertrude had been born just after the end of World War Two. She grew up in a Communist dominated land, where everybody was schooled in the Russian language. She learned to speak English too – from an ex-Berlitz professor who ran a black market in verboten linguistics. Farm life had been stern, as she grew big enough to help her father and crippled mother with the chores, but Gertrude had become sturdy on plenty of fresh milk and vegetables, and she used to walk back from the haying fields with her rakehandle across her back and shoulders and her arms draped over it. It made her walk straight and developed strong chest muscles.

"Yass," muttered Banner at this point. "Like those Balinese gals carrying loads on their heads." He dwelt silently on Bali for a moment, then he said: "Go on. How'd you get outta East Germany?"

She had, she explained, visited East Berlin several times, helping to bring farm products to market. Each time she came an urge grew stronger in her to see all the things she had heard rumors about, the free and wealthy people of the West, the shops and cinemas along the Kurfurstendamm, and the opportunities for a better life. One day, at the Brandenburg Gate, the urge overcame her. She made a wild, reckless dash, eluding Soviet soldier guards, and made it, panting, falling into the arms of sympathetic West Berliners in the American Sector. She had thought that she would surely find somebody who could help to get her crippled mother and her father free too, but so far there was nobody who could perform that miracle.

Her good looks and quick learning ability eventually got her sponsored for a trip to the United States. Mr Gosling, of the New Zealand Legation, had proved kind to her and had got her the job.

She stopped talking, her brunette head with the Dutch bob bent low.

"Haaak!" Banner cleared his throat, making a sound like a sea lion. "Who're you living with now?"

"Nobody. I have a small apartment to myself. I have become an American citizen."

Banner sourly eyed the chewed wet end of the stogie in his hand. "Now about this envelope with the gun in it. When did it come to your desk?"

"Sometime near 11:00 o'clock in the morning, Senator."

"Who brought it?"

"A man from the special messenger service."

"Would you know him if you saw him again?"

"I think I would."

"Was your boss, Mr Gosling, engaged at 11:00?"

"Yes, Mr Lockyear was in there."

"What time did Cap'n Cozzens come into the reception room?"

"Around 11:15."

"Did anyone tamper with that envelope once it reached your desk, Gertie?"

"No, sir. No one."

"What time did Lockyear come outta the private office?"

"It was nearly 11:30."

"When he came out," said Banner carefully, "did he go straight out?"

"Yes – he stopped only to make an appointment for next Tuesday. I jotted it in my pad."

"Then what'd you do?"

"I spoke to Mr Gosling on the interphone," she said in a low hushed voice. "I told him that Captain Cozzens was waiting to see him next. He told me to withhold him for a minute and for me to come in with my notebook. I started to go in, then remembered the envelope. The sticker on it had said: *Deliver to Mr Kermit Gosling at 11:30 a.m. sharp.* I went back to my desk for it."

"It was now just about 11:30, eh? When you went into the private office, what was Gosling doing?"

"He was sitting at his desk."

"He was perfectly all right?"

"Yes, Senator."

"Did he say anything to you?"

She opened her mouth. She paused. "No, he didn't actually say anything. He just smiled and motioned me toward the chair I usually take dictation in. I held up the envelope. I was just about to tell him about it when the gun went off."

"And you saw Gosling being hit with the bullets?"

She nodded wretchedly. "He jerked back, then started to sag over. Then Captain Cozzens and Mr Odell rushed in."

"Is that all?" rasped Banner.

She bowed her head again.

McKitrick, the FBI departmental head, stirred uneasily by the wall. "Now," he said, "you see what's got the wits of two organizations stymied!"

Banner was looking down at his stogie. It had gone out, but he wasn't even thinking about it. He said: "I'll tell you what I think about it."

McKitrick looked at him hopefully. "What?"

"It couldn't've happened! *It's too damned impossible!*"

Ramshaw must have been about forty-five. A cigarette dangled limply out of his slack lips as he sat on the bench at the special messenger service. He wore a weather-faded blue uniform with shrunken breeches and dusty leather leggings.

Banner loomed over him, his enveloping black wraprascal increasing his already Gargantuan size. "You remember the envelope you delivered to the New Zealand Legation yesterday?"

"That's easy, mister. I never handled one like that before. A 10-year-old kid came into our agency about 10:00 in the morning and said somebody told him to leave the envelope with us to be delivered immediately. We didn't ask too many questions, seeing as the kid had more than ample money to pay for the delivery."

"Did he say whether the *someone* was a man or a woman?"

"Nope."

"Did anyone tamper with the envelope while it was here?"

"Nope. I was assigned to do the job, mister. I kept the envelope right in front of me till I delivered it to the Legation at 11:00. It had written on it, *Deliver to Mr Kermit Gosling at 11:30a.m. sharp*, so I wanted to be sure it got there in plenty of time."

Banner glowered. "Didja know there was a gun in it?"

Ramshaw squirmed as if his shrunken breeches chafed him. "I – I thought there was. That's what it felt like through the heavy paper."

"Nobody stopped you on the way to the Legation? Tell me if someone even bumped into you."

"Nope, nope. Clear sailing all the way, mister."

Banner looked down at a pocket watch that must have been manufactured by the Baldwin Locomotive Works. He muttered: "I can still ketch Lockyear before lunch."

He went out of the agency, leaving behind him a grinning messenger. "Say, mister! Thanks for the tip!"

Lockyear, in his office on Pittsylvania Avenue, played with his King Tut beard as Banner made himself known to him.

"It's the strangest thing I ever heard of, Senator," said Lockyear. "But I'm afraid I can be of very little help. Gosling was far from dead when I left him."

"While you were in the office," said Banner, "did you notice anything threatening?"

"Threatening? No, not a thing, Senator."

"Perhaps you'd tell me what you were seeing Gosling about."

"Of course I have no objection, Senator. I'm an exporter-importer. I've been seeing Gosling about clearing some shipments that have been going in and out of New Zealand. Governments are touchy these days about cargoes."

"That's all?"

"That's all, Senator."

In a few minutes Banner was on his way back to the Idle Hour Club. As he entered the convivial surroundings and lumbered into the dining room, he found McKitrick waiting for him.

"The only thing about this case that's plain," said McKitrick abruptly, "is the motive. We know why Gosling was killed."

"Do you?" Banner squeezed in behind a table and told a waiter he wanted some straight whiskey.

McKitrick said in a lower voice: "Gosling was collecting information on a spy who's been selling all our secrets to the Russian Government. Gosling didn't know exactly who it was, but he was getting dangerously close to that truth. Unfortunately the spy got to Gosling first. The Russian pistol is evidence of that."

McKitrick stopped talking long enough to allow the waiter to place Banner's whiskey before him.

"Yass?" Banner fired up another big stogie.

McKitrick continued: "I've been thinking about Gertrude Wagner. She admits she's from East Germany. Her sympathies might easily lie with the Commies. We have only her word that she'd broken with them. What's more to the point, Banner, she was in the room with Gosling when he was killed. The *only* person in the room with him. And she was holding the gun that killed him!"

"So?" muttered Banner. "Mebbe you can explain away the sealed envelope." When McKitrick didn't answer, Banner shrugged. "How was she able to shoot the gun through the envelope without making any holes in it?"

McKitrick sighed. "Times are getting brutal for us investigators when all a murderer has to do is send his victim a gun by mail and it does the killing for him."

The wind coming across the Potomac River that afternoon had the icy sting of early winter on its breath.

Gertrude Wagner, wrapped up in a cloth coat, walking on the park path, stopped suddenly. She stared nervously around her. A man in an oystercolored balmacaan, who had been following her, veered around a turn in the path. When he saw her looking straight at him he hesitated for a fraction of a second, then he kept on coming, his pace more deliberate. Under the slant brim of his hat Gertrude could see the bright red hair. The wide shoulders were familiar.

She stood there until Odell came up to her. He grinned sheepishly. "Hello, Gertie. Mind if I walk the rest of the way with you?"

She drew back a pace as if she was afraid he might contaminate her. Her face looked pale and scared. "You've been following me," she accused him.

Odell was sober. "To tell the truth, Gertie—"

"Why do you have to hound me? Can't you leave me alone?"

"I'm not hounding you," he said, disheartening to know that she had interpreted his actions that way.

"You are, Mr Odell. I haven't been able to make a move since you came to the Legation without having your eyes on me. You people are watching me all the time, waiting to pounce on me for the least slip I make. I thought America was a free country, but the police watch you here as much as they do over there . . . You think I killed Mr Gosling!"

"Did it ever occur to you," he said through clenched teeth, "that I might have other reasons for wanting to be near you?"

"What?" she said, hardly believing her ears. "What did you say?"

"You're not hard to take, Gertie," he said.

"Take?" she said in confusion. "Oh but—"

"You never gave me much encouragement. You always seemed to have so much on your mind, Gertie."

"If that's really true, Mr Odell, I'm sorry I – if I offended you just now."

"*If* it's really true! You don't think I'm telling you the truth?"

"I can't be sure of anything any more."

"I was in that office to protect Mr Gosling – and you." He looked at her steadily. "You believe me, Gertie."

She looked back at him for a long moment, and he thought her eyes were watering.

She lowered her gaze. "Yes, Mr Odell, I do. I do believe you."

"Well, then," smiled Odell, "I hope you're not doing anything tonight, as I want—"

"Oh," she said, "I'm sorry. Not tonight. I have an appointment I can't break. Shall we make it some other time?"

"Sure, Gertie. I'll see you tomorrow."

"Tomorrow." She smiled. "So long then." She had her right hand in her coat pocket. She took it out and held it toward him. He grasped her palm. And then he felt that she had something in her hand – a slip of paper. When she drew her hand away she left it in his palm. He felt, with a rush of intuition, that everything was wrong. He pretended not to notice what she'd left in his hand. As she turned on her high heels to walk swiftly away from him, he thrust his own hand into his pocket.

He watched her go out of sight along the path, then he walked out of the park in the opposite direction. He was curious about what she was trying to convey to him. He went into the first street corner phone booth he came to and took the slip of paper out of his pocket and unfolded it.

The wrinkles of perplexity increased on his forehead.

The paper was blank except for two circles, a small one inside a much larger one, drawn on it in pencil.

Gertrude, the cold night wind whipping the coat about her knees, went up the legation steps. All the windows were dark. X Street was dark. Fumbling in her handbag, she took out a key, unlocked the front door, and slipped into the vestibule. It was all cold marble, like a mausoleum. She left the front door unlocked behind her as she went in, as if she was expecting someone else to follow her.

She flicked on a cigarette lighter to light her way up the plush carpeted stairway to the third floor. This was the floor on which the murder had been committed. She went into the office, tiptoeing past her desk in the reception room, going into the private office.

She looked at Gosling's empty chair behind the desk. Gosling's bloodied ghost still seemed to occupy it. And she shuddered.

She remembered a line from one of the newspapers . . . *A nameless horror has stalked through the Legation* . . .

The watch on her wrist ticked away loudly. She was painfully conscious of time. Everything had depended on time.

She did not know anyone was in the room with her until she heard the door between the offices click softly closed.

She turned around with a violent start. The cigarette lighter flicked out when she released her thumb. A shadow moved against the closed door.

"Is that *you*?" she gasped.

A powerful flashlight blinded her.

"Yes," answered a voice. "Have you done all that was expected of you?"

She nodded miserably.

"Fine." She heard a heartless chuckle.

And that was all she heard, for it is doubtful if she heard the two quick coughs before the lead slugs tore into her breast.

She was dead before she hit the floor.

McKitrick was saying: "The patrolman on the X Street beat saw the door of the Legation swinging open in the wind. He thought something was up, so he took a prowl through the building. He was the one who found her."

Someberly Banner looked down at all that was left of Gertrude. "It's a crying shame," he muttered.

Odell sat gloomily on the edge of the desk. He roused himself up enough to say: "Well, this isn't as puzzling as the first shooting. I talked to Gertie in the park this afternoon, Senator. She said she was going to meet someone tonight. Whoever it was just followed her in here and shot her. If I had any inkling this would happen, I never would have left her alone."

Banner nodded. "It's not your fault, Red." He glared around. "What kinda gun this time? D'you know?"

McKitrick answered: "The medical examiner thinks it's a .38."

Banner snorted. "An American gun! This's striking closer to home."

Odell said: "There's something else I've got to tell you, Senator. It might help you. I confess it doesn't mean a thing to me. In the park today Gertie slipped this into my hand. She acted mighty secretive about it." He gave Banner the paper with the circles drawn on it.

"Whatzit mean?" snapped Banner.

"Circles within circles. Wheels within wheels. You tell me, Senator."

Banner looked at it front and back and held it up to the light to see if there were any pinpricks in it. Then, without saying anything, he crumpled it up and shoved it into his marsupial pocket. Plainly he could not make head or tail of it, but he wasn't going to say so.

Though they stayed there till dawn they found no other clue to point to Gertrude's murderer.

McKitrick woke up to find his phone ringing insistently and Banner on the other end of the wire.

"You never sleep, do you?" snorted McKitrick.

"Hardly ever, Mac. We ain't got time for that now. It's after breakfast. Come to the Legation and bring that small arms expert with you."

"Captain Cozzens?"

"Yaas. Him. I've figgered out what everything means."

"What put you on it?"

"Those circles."

"Suppose you quit being so damned mysterious, Banner, and—"

"Get cracking to the Legation," interrupted Banner. He hung up.

Banner was sitting in a leather chair, comfortably waiting for them to arrive. He bobbed his big grizzled head at McKitrick and Cozzens. His grizzled mane looked like a fright wig this morning, as if he had been trying to comb it with an eggbeater.

"Gennelmen," he said, "this won't take too much of your precious time. Lemme get on with it. First off, you will swear that there ain't any Tokarev pistols hidden in that private office."

"Of course not," responded McKitrick a little testily. His face bore the results of a very hasty shave. There was a nick on his chin. "There isn't as much as a needle hidden in there that we don't know of."

"And you can search me and find out I'm not packing a Russian pop-gun."

"We'll take your word for it, Senator," said McKitrick shortly.

"We get on together," chuckled Banner. He got up with a heave and a vast grunt. "You two sit here on the lounge, the way you were the other day with Odell, Cap'n." He watched them sharply as they followed his suggestion. "I'm going in there." He entered the private office, where Gosling and Gertrude had been killed, leaving the intervening door open. He was out of sight from the two watchers for about five minutes, then he reappeared and stood in the doorway, filling the frame with his bulk, his hands deep in the bulging frockcoat pockets. "Nothing up my sleeve, mates," he announced.

They both stared at him, not knowing what to expect. Then both of them leaped to their feet.

Three loud shots had crashed out in the empty office behind Banner's back!

Banner did not even take his hands out of his pockets. "And there you have it," he said.

"But, great Godfrey!" yipped McKitrick, pushing past Banner to see who else was hidden in the private office. "Who fired that pistol?"

"It was a Tokarev automatic!" said Cozzens. "I'll swear to that!"

"But there isn't anyone here but you!" McKitrick glared helplessly around the room.

"Neverthless—" began Banner. "But let it keep awhile. There're more important things like searches and seizures to be made."

"Confound you, Banner!" said McKitrick, but he was in good humor about it.

"You can begin by arresting—"

The search was fruitless until Banner suggested that what they were after might be on microfilm and if they could not find microfilm in all the obvious places, it might be hidden in the electric light sockets.

That was where they found it.

They had all the proof they needed to arrest their man for espionage and murder.

And Carroll Lockyear, the export-import man, almost pulled his King Tut beard out by the roots when they confronted him.

McKitrick and the Assistant Secretary of State made impressive members of Banner's small audience. Banner was prancing back and forth, gnawing a long stogie, as if he were holding a press conference. But he had not let the reporters in yet. They were all ganged up outside in the hall, waiting.

The Assistant Secretary of State fingered his chin reflectively. "The riddle of the sealed envelope—"

"Yaas, yaas!" Banner chuckled. "It's simple when you know the sorta thimble-rigging that went on behind the scenes. I said in the beginning that I thought the murder was too damned impossible cuz one person alone couldn't've accomplished it. Lockyear is the murderer and spy, all right, but he had forced poor Gertie to help him. Y'see, he was a Commie agent and Gertie told us that her crippled mother and her father are still stranded in East Germany. You can now see how easy it was for him to get her to agree to his scheme. He could tell her he'd get 'em outta East Germany if she played ball. If she still didn't agree, he could easily threaten to turn the old folks over to the untender mercies of the MVD agents."

He paused a moment before going on. "Gosling was getting onto Lockyear's trail. Some time before the murder, Lockyear used a standard tape recorder. Lockyear let the tape run silently for three minutes, then he fired his Tokarev pistol three times near the recorder. He now had a tape recording of three minutes of dead silence, followed by three quickly fired shots. He handed that roll of tape over to Gertie for her to put in Gosling's private office where he could get his hands on it later on. When he went into Gosling's office to commit the murder that morning he had in his briefcase the Tokarev pistol with silencer on it, and also in the briefcase was a large manila mailing envelope that was a duplicate of the one to be delivered to Gertie's desk by the messenger service. The gun that was delivered to Gertie by the special messenger route was probably a toy pistol, so that if the envelope were opened prematurely the whole thing could be laughed off as a practical joke.

"It was all timed to the split second. Lockyear stalled with Gosling till almost 11:30, talking business, then swiftly he pulled the silenced automatic outta the briefcase and shot Gosling in the chest three times with it before his victim could blink or cry out. Naturally the shots were not heard outside the room with the door closed. He whipped out the prepared envelope, snatched the silencer off the pistol-barrel, and shoved the pistol, still smoking, into the envelope, sealing it immediately. Next he set the prepared reel of tape on the recorder alongside Gosling's desk – there's one in every office and you've noticed that Gosling's office had all the modern equipment – and then picked up the envelope and brief-case. It was now, according to his watch, 11:27. He flipped the tape recorder switch to on. Three minutes of dead silence, remember, then three shots. He put his arm around both the envelope and the briefcase so that the briefcase would entirely conceal the envelope to anyone waiting in the lounge. He came out of the private office and walked to Gertie's desk on which the second envelope with the toy gun in it was lying, waiting to be delivered at 11:30 sharp. He put his briefcase down on her desk, so that it covered both envelopes. After getting Gertie to jot down his phony appointment for next Tuesday, Lockyear picked up his briefcase again – *together with the envelope that had been lying on Gertie's desk!* In its place he left the one with the real murder weapon in it. He carried the other envelope out with him, still concealed behind his briefcase, and nobody was aware of the switch. So the gun that had just been used to commit the murder was now waiting for Gertie to carry it back in. She had been forced into it. She knew Gosling was already dead. She had to play out her part. She pretended to talk to Gosling on the interphone to give the illusion that Gosling was still alive after Lockyear left. Then she started to go into the private office, looked at her watch, knew the three minutes were almost up, then carried the sealed envelope in."

He stopped and glowered around the room. "The three shots that were heard by the two witnesses were the ones already on the tape recorder! Cozzens even remarked that they were somewhat *muffled!* ... The tape recorder ran itself out silently again, till Gertie, in the excitement that followed the discovery of Gosling's dead body, managed to flip the switch off."

"Good God!" muttered somebody in the room,

Banner cleared his throat with a big sea lion noise. "Haaak! Although Gertie had been terrorized into helping Lockyear remove a threat to his existence as a spy, she wanted desperately for one of us to know the truth. She knew she was being watched by everybody, their side as well as ours, so she couldn't come right out and tell us about it. She drew two circles, one inside the other, on a piece of paper. She didn't dare hint further. She was trying to call our attention to the reel of the tape recorder – circular. Yunnerstand? And she was trying to help us, boys. If she had completely obeyed the instructions of the murderer, I never would've found the tape still on the recorder in that office – she would've destroyed it. Last night the murderer killed her as a safety measure, thinking that his trail on tape had been completely wiped out."

Locked in Death

Mary Reed & Eric Mayer

Those of you who have seen my anthologies of historical who-dunits will know that Mary Reed and Eric Mayer are the authors of the stories featuring John the Eunuch, set in 6th-century Constantinople. One or two of those stories have been locked-room mysteries. John the Eunuch also features in a series of novels that began with One for Sorrow *(1999). Besides John, they also have another continuing character, Inspector Dorj of the Mongolian Police, who first appeared in "Death on the Trans-Mongolian Railway" in* Ellery Queen's Mystery Magazine *(March 2000). The following is a brand new Inspector Dorj story involving a travelling circus and a puzzling corpse.*

During his years with the Mongolian police Inspector Dorj had witnessed crimes in sufficient variety to inspire several Shakespearean tragedies, but until the crowbar-wielding midget sent the locked door of the circus caravan flying open the inspector had never seen a man murdered by a corpse.

Hercules the lion-tamer was, it is true, an exceptionally large and powerful corpse, but a corpse nevertheless. He lay wedged between the bed on which Dorj had last seen him and the blood-smeared door of the ancient caravan's lavatory cubicle. His enormous hands were still reaching for his victim. Nikolai Zubov, sprawled partly under the table near the door, was now beyond Hercules' reach, but the ugly welt ringing the circus owner's neck made it clear what must have happened. Dorj said so.

"Clear?" muttered Dima, the midget, peering around Dorj into the disordered caravan. Dima's bone white clown makeup ran with sweat from his efforts with the crowbar, turning his face almost as ghastly as Zubov's. "How can you say it is clear when it seems Zubov was strangled by a dead man?"

"Of course the lion-tamer was dead," said Batu, Dorj's assistant. "The lion went berserk and practically disembowelled him. No one could have survived a gaping wound like that. You're lucky you got bored and left the performance before the lion-taming act started."

Dorj now regretted dragging the young man to the circus, which had turned out to be a sorry affair even before the accident. "You kept an eye on the caravan while I returned to town to make arrangements?"

"I would have seen anyone approaching."

"So only Zubov and Hercules were inside?"

A cloud-like frown passed over Batu's round, flat moon of a face, a typical Mongolian face in contrast to Dorj's sharper-angled features. "The names of those deceased should not be spoken so soon after death. Souls linger. So many people, saying their names – they may call the dead back from the lower world."

Dorj had long since abandoned trying to talk Batu out of his native beliefs and instead had taken to occasionally exposing the young man to some culture – unfortunately, as it turned out, in the case of the circus. So now he simply instructed his assistant to begin the tedious collection of evidence and then, to be alone to consider the conundrum, walked away from the caravan and the abandoned Russian airplane hangar the circus had borrowed for its performances.

A rutted track led into the desert where a cold September wind rolled small bits of gravel against his carefully polished shoes. Unlike Batu, who had grown up in a *ger*, the traditional movable tent of the Mongolian nomads, Dorj was city bred. Until the great earthquake that some called freedom had driven him to a posting in the Gobi, he had rarely strayed far from the relatively cosmopolitan world of Ulaanbaatar.

He was not comfortable in his own country. He hated the Gobi, a featureless immensity beside which men and the culture Dorj valued so highly seemed small and insignificant. Out here Batu's half-civilized ideas about returning souls seemed almost plausible.

Or at least as good as any explanation the inspector had for a murderous corpse.

Staring out to the far off horizon where mountains sat like clouds, Dorj tried to recall what he had witnessed earlier. It was possible those events might have something to tell him about Zubov's mysterious death. But since the lion-tamer's death had been a grisly accident, Dorj had not examined the scene as carefully as he would have if a crime had been committed, and he regretted it now.

The inspector had arrived at the hangar door just as the lion-tamer's corpse was being laid beside it, beneath a line of carelessly slapped on posters advertising that those who visited the circus would, among other delights, view a recreation of:

"The First Labour of Hercules. See The Mighty Hercules Slay the Nemean Lion."

Dorj had been struck by the irony of Hercules's death because, while some survived the vagaries and misfortunes of life by seeing dark humour in it all, he survived by noting the irony.

And thinking back now, what else had he noticed, aside from distressed circus-goers edging past the corpse?

Zubov was standing outside the hangar, still wearing his ring-master's top hat, speaking to a muscular young man decked out in spangled tights.

"Perhaps if I go back and perform my act, it will distract the crowd," the young man suggested.

"Conceited fool!" the older man snapped back. "Go help direct them out the exits and make sure they don't panic. Do you think anyone wants to see you preening and swinging like a monkey, with a man lying dead right outside?"

Zubov was soft featured, chubby around the middle, but his voice was harsh. His magic tricks involving a red ball and three boxes with obviously false bottoms had driven Dorj outside.

Dorj also remembered a woman standing beside the door, head bent. She was a tall, striking blonde, perhaps nearing middle age but it was difficult to be certain, given her heavy make-up. She was dressed in layers of diaphanous sequined material that billowed in the bitter wind, but she stood motionless, a great glittering icicle.

Because he was a government official at the scene, Dorj introduced himself to Zubov. There were arrangements to be made.

"We'll put the fat man in my caravan where I can keep on eye on him for now," the circus owner said brusquely. "Dima! Get the wheelbarrow!" He looked around for the clown.

"Where's that idiot runt?" Turning back to Dorj, he continued, "You can't rely on anybody these days. But you must know how it is, Inspector. I suppose you deal with enough underlings yourself – and all of them slackers and idiots."

Dorj followed as the dead man was taken to the ringmaster's caravan and laid on the bed. A few moments later, the blonde woman appeared at the caravan door. She resembled a ghost, icily composed, arms folded around herself as if she were trying to hold in a terrible storm of emotions. At last she was overwhelmed.

"Ah, Cheslav! My poor husband, I am so sorry! So sorry!" Weeping, she threw herself onto the corpse.

"Stop it, Ivana," barked Zubov. "It's too late to be sorry."

But Ivana continued to sob hysterically, embracing her dead husband, smoothing his hair and rearranging his blood-soaked clothing as if to somehow repair the damage the lion had inflicted.

Dorj had hesitated, uncertain whether to intervene. He preferred the theatre where tumultuous emotions could be safely observed, caged upon the stage. He had been thankful when some of the other performers finally escorted Ivana away. The chilly wind no longer billowed out her robes; they had been soaked with her husband's blood.

And those few impressions seemed to tell Dorj nothing at all about how the dead man had committed a murder. Perhaps there was something in Batu's theory of returning souls after all.

"Watch out!"

As he approached the back of the caravan, returning from his solitary walk, Dorj felt a hand on his shoulder and paused in midstep. There was a loud metallic snap. Glancing down, he saw a trap, rusty jaws now locked shut, sitting on the gravel a centimetre or two from his foot. Turning around, he saw he had been warned by a woman. It was difficult to tell her age because of her beard.

"We catch marmots to feed to the animals," she explained in Russian. Seeing Dorj understood, she added, "You're lucky you didn't step in one of these traps before. I saw you wandering around out here during the show, didn't I? I'm sorry our performance drove you out into the cold."

Dorj tried to think of something polite to say while at the same time trying not to stare too obviously at the woman's somewhat sparse but unmistakable dark beard.

He had a soft spot for circuses. They had a certain magic, an otherworldly air, reminding him of Prospero's island. Lights, sequins and distance transformed even the plainest of performers into fabulous creatures. But in truth, the Circus Chinggis had immediately struck him as the sort of seedy undertaking where the owners would be more likely than not to toss the main tent into the back of a 25-year-old Russian military lorry, herd the trained fleas onto a dusty lion and slip out of town under cover of darkness. Except, in a nation where thousands of people actually lived in tent-like *gers*, this forlorn circus apparently had no tents to call its own.

"You sold a programme to my colleague earlier, didn't you?" was all Dorj could think to say.

"I suppose you're one of those who never forgets a face! My name is Larisa Sergeyevna."

Her voice was soft, her skin fair. To his chagrin Dorj found his gaze, leaving her beard, caught by her eyes, as blue as the sky over the Gobi.

Embarrassed, the inspector introduced himself. "I regret I will have to ask you some questions. For instance, I gather you haven't been the Circus Chinggis for long." He indicated the fresh and badly painted lettering on the side of the caravan.

Larisa glanced quickly at the caravan and then looked away, perhaps mindful of the two dead men inside. "You're right. A few weeks ago Zubov decided he would have a better chance of meeting expenses by charging tugriks rather than rubles, not that any of us have actually seen either since we crossed the Mongolian border.

"But," she continued, "Since you asked, let's see, we were the Comrades' Circus at one time, not to mention the Paris Troika. I even recall a time when we were just plain Buturlin's. But I expect we'll have to remain Mongolian for a while since we're nearly out of paint, as well as running low on food. Perhaps you'll give us another chance, and not want your admission money back?"

"I'm sure you put on a fine show. Perhaps it is just that I am out of humour. Or more in the mood for Shakespeare. Not that a circus doesn't have more than a touch of Shakespeare."

"You have a silver tongue, Inspector Dorj! I've never heard a circus compared to Shakespeare before. He wrote mostly about boring old kings killing each other, didn't he?"

"But even his historical plays have a lot of magic in them, really. All manner of ghosts and portents, witchcraft and unnatural creatures . . ." Realizing his gaffe, his voice trailed off, but the bearded lady just smiled quietly at him. Then, to his distress, her blue eyes pooled with tears.

"Poor Cheslav," she said. "He was always so afraid of the lion."

Dorj gave her a questioning look.

"Cheslav – Hercules – was no lion-tamer. He was our strong man," she explained. "Alexi, our real lion-tamer, he left us in Erdenet a few weeks ago. He thought he could find work in the copper mines. So Zubov ordered Cheslav to take over. Just like Zubov, that was!"

She turned away and pitched forward suddenly. Dorj caught her arm to keep her from falling. In the instant her warm weight was on him, his breath caught in his chest.

"My weak ankle," she said. There was anger in her voice. "I used to be an acrobat. Imagine that. Then I got injured, but Zubov insisted I keep performing. He even forced me to keep training on the trapeze. My back is bad now, too. So I'm reduced to hawking programmes." A tear ran down Larisa's pale cheek and into her beard. "He was a hateful man. I could almost believe a corpse would rise up to kill one like him!"

When Larisa had gone Dorj remained aware, uncomfortably so, of the pleasurable sensation of her warmth near to him. It occurred to him that she was not so much ugly as she was . . . exotic . . . magical.

He checked around the caravan again. The murder had occurred, it seemed, just before Dorj returned from Dalandzadgad, where he had gone to arrange for an ambulance to take the dead man away. It would have been much easier to have been able to call one with the aid of a portable telephone, but nothing of the sort had been made available to him out here in the desert. Batu, whom he had left at the circus as an official guard, had heard strange noises from the caravan. When there was no reply to the young policeman's shouted inquiry, he had finally tried the door. It had been securely locked from the inside.

The small caravan was of vintage nineteen fifties design; no doubt it was towed behind one of the circus's old lorries as the troupe moved from place to place. But now it stood alone, surrounded by flat, empty ground, some distance from both the hangar and the other circus vehicles. Dorj's footsteps crunched on the gravel as he circled it. Batu would probably have heard, and surely seen, anyone trying to approach by stealth.

The caravan was as decrepit as the rest of the circus, Dorj thought as he noted a couple of badly patched holes in its rusted walls, half hidden by the freshly applied paint. There was a tiny window in each side wall and a vent in the curved roof. Dorj paced back a short distance, to get a better look at the vent. The opening was far too small for anyone to squeeze through. Dorj, thin as he was, wouldn't have got more than an arm through it. For a moment he wondered about Dima, the small clown, but decided that even Dima could never have managed to squeeze through the vent. As for the windows, he noticed on closer inspection that they were sealed shut by carelessly applied and obviously undisturbed paint.

Glancing through the window, he saw the two dead men, Zubov now on the bed and his apparent murderer on the floor near him, were decently covered by a couple of pieces of canvas, perhaps the remains of the Circus Chinggis's missing Big Top.

"Ah, Cheslav, I wish you could speak," muttered Dorj. Then he recalled what Batu had said about calling back the souls of the dead, and hurried away from the caravan.

"Everyone hated Zubov," Dima stated, confirming what Larisa had told Dorj. The midget, wiping dry, cracked make-up from his chin, was seated on a crate near the hangar door.

The inspector inquired why Zubov had been so hated.

"You saw the way he treated me! Do you doubt it?"

"He treated everyone the same, then?"

"Of course he did. Isn't that always the way with people like him?" Dima climbed off the crate. He barely came up to Dorj's waist. "He used to constantly criticize me for not being short enough," he continued. "Can you imagine that? He'd laugh and shout at me that I couldn't even manage to be small enough to be a proper midget."

"He kept you on, though," the inspector reminded him.

"He had no choice."

Dorj asked him what he thought would happen to the little circus once the investigation was closed.

"I won't be running it, that's for certain!" Dima replied. "But as to that, Zubov didn't confide in anyone. Who knows what his arrangements were?"

As patches of Dima's make-up were removed, wrinkles were revealed at the corners of his mouth. Dorj realized that the man was middle-aged. It was difficult not to think of him as a child.

"Why was it that the others hated him?"

"You mentioned Larisa's story, how the beast turned her into a cripple, but all the women had reason to hate him, the old lecher."

"What about Ivana, Cheslav's wife?"

Dima nodded. "They all did, as I said. And then there's Fabayan Viktorovich, our aerial artist. He was angry that Zubov refused to take the circus to Moscow to perform. And he – Fabayan, that is – thought he should be the headline act. Zubov did not agree. Now, if you don't mind, there's work to be done, whatever our future might be. If I were you, Inspector, I would look no further. A corpse can't be punished and Zubov's murderer deserves no punishment. So perhaps there's justice for the downtrodden, after all."

"I'm glad you found me, Inspector," Ivana said as she opened the door to let Dorj into the trailer. "For I have a confession to make. I'm afraid I am a murderer."

Dorj had had opportunity to keep his Russian polished, but still he was not certain he had understood her words correctly.

"Yes, that's right, Inspector. I'm a murderer," she repeated calmly. She had changed from her bloodied clothing into a tight pink leotard. It did not conceal her body as had the diaphanous robes; it was hardly mourning apparel, Dorj thought.

Dima had told Dorj that he would find the others in what he called "the back yard", the area where the rest of the circus lorries, animal trailers and caravans were parked. Their age and condition caused the back yard to resemble a junk yard.

Dorj had noticed a light on in a long trailer, and knocked on its door. Ivana had answered his summons.

Illuminated by a single bare bulb, the trailer was a dim confusion of shadows. It had an exotic smell, a mixture of animal dung and something worse. Evidently it was used to haul circus animals around from place to place.

"Take care you don't step in that pile of marmots," Ivana warned him after her astonishing confession. "They've been dead for quite some time." Then she began to sob.

Dorj had never cared much for Russian literature of the more melodramatic kind, and was beginning to think that it perhaps reflected national characteristics more accurately than he had hitherto imagined.

Amid the stark shadows striping the trailer, he could distinguish a few empty cages and pens. The faded paintings on the trailer's outside walls depicted lions and tigers, trained poodles, alligators and snakes and a trumpeting elephant. A quick look around the interior showed a ragged cockatoo perched sleepily in a bird cage. One of several aquariums held an iguana. A rumble from the darkness at the back of the trailer reminded him that there was, at least, a lion.

"You're understandably upset," Dorj assured the woman softly.

Under normal circumstances he would have dismissed Ivana as a suspect, simply because a normal woman could not have inflicted with her bare hands the damage he'd seen on Zubov's neck. But, he had to keep reminding himself, circus people could not necessarily be judged by what some might call normal standards. After all, so far he had spoken to a man the size of a child and a woman with a beard. Nevertheless, it still seemed impossible that anyone except Cheslav and Zubov could had been locked inside the caravan.

Ivana, who appeared to be unusually normal by circus standards, retreated toward the back of the trailer and Dorj followed her. In the deeper shadows at the far end, the lion's holding cage was bolted securely to the floor. The lion, which looked scrawny and mangy when viewed at close hand, was asleep. Dorj hoped it would not have to be euthanized.

"We don't suspect you of anything. You surely could not have strangled Zubov," Dorj reassured Ivana.

"I'm not speaking of Zubov. It was my husband I murdered." She quickly shoved something small between the bars of the lion's cage – a marmot – and wiped her hands on her pink leotards before rummaging in a small cabinet near the cage. "Look here."

Dorj glanced over her shoulder and saw several glass bottles and a frighteningly large hypodermic on the shelf above them. He began to point out that in fact a dreadful injury had caused her husband's death. Then another thought occurred to him.

"Are you saying you drugged your husband before he went in the ring with his lion taming act?"

"Not Cheslav. No, I drugged Raisa – the lion. Cheslav could never be a real lion-tamer. A timid man, he was. Raisa is not that fierce, but we always drugged her, for safety reasons, you know? We even drugged her for Alexi, to make her more manageable, or rather Alexi did that himself.

"Since he left, I've taken over looking after the animals. Not that I can do much for them. We're beginning to run out of tranquilizer, as well as their food. It is so sad. Perhaps hunger is what made Raisa so fierce."

She slammed the cabinet door shut and Raisa, disturbed by the noise, rumbled in her sleep. Dorj felt the raw power of the deep sound vibrating in his chest and through the thin soles of his shoes.

"So Zubov ordered me to cut down on the dosage to make what we had last longer," the woman continued. "I should have known better. But I was afraid of him, so I did what he said. And now my poor husband is dead. So you see, as I said, I'm guilty."

"If what you say is true, it was not murder, it was a terrible accident. But in any event, it is Zubov's murderer I'm interested in finding." He did not add that the more he found out about the man the less interested he was in the task. Yet, one did one's duty.

Ivana's eyes glinted as they reflected the light of the bare bulb. "But the evidence is clear. Surely it shows that my husband got up off his death bed to take his revenge on the man who turned me into a murderer?"

As he walked away from the trailer Dorj found himself looking for Larisa. There were things he had forgotten to ask her about, he told himself. Instead he ran into the young man in spangled tights whom he had seen earlier talking to Zubov.

"I'm Fabayan Viktorovich, the aerialist," the young man said, after Dorj had introduced himself. "In fact, I'm the Fabulous Flying Fabayan, as the posters say. Or would have said, if Zubov had ever got them printed."

Dorj, shivering in his thin coat as the wind picked up, suggested they talk somewhere more sheltered. Fabayan led the way back to the hangar, where the fluttering circus posters Zubov had hand-printed in bold red letters, and that long ago from the crumpled looks of them, still promised a brave show with jugglers and clowns, fortune-tellers and snake-charmers, acrobats and contortionists, and of course, the mighty lion-taming Hercules.

"I just want to check on my rigging, though I doubt we'll be putting on another performance tonight. Accidents happen in threes, we always say. I'm sure you will have many questions."

As they entered the ill-lit, empty hangar, Dorj asked the muscular young man about the lion tamer.

"Cheslav was a roustabout, not a performer," replied Fabayan, contempt evident in his tone. "He was an out-of-work stone-mason. Zubov spotted him leaving after a show in Chelyabinsk. We needed some muscle to set things up, to help move cages, to haul up the rigging." He indicated the complicated arrangement of ropes, nets and trapezes half hidden above them. "I couldn't trust him with the knots or getting the nets in the right places, or any of that. Eventually Zubov gave him the lion-taming act."

Nothing at the circus was what it seemed, thought Dorj. Its amazing and glittering wonders were nothing more than tawdry deceits. Yet what about a murderous corpse? What sort of deceit was that? Or was that real?

Dim light outlined the web of ropes high up in the cavernous hangar. Certainly the distance between Fabayan's trapeze, up near the ceiling, and the hard concrete floor far below was real enough.

"It takes true skill to perform up there," boasted Fabayan, following Dorj's gaze. "Buturlin recognized talent. He was born to the circus. He was the one who engaged me. If he were still alive, it would be different."

"Buturlin was the former owner?"

"Yes, and then Zubov and he became partners. Buturlin died a year or two ago. But Zubov, he was originally just the accountant; he knows nothing about talent or the circus."

"Zubov did perform some magic," Dorj pointed out.

"Anyone can buy a trick box. The only thing Zubov made disappear was our pay cheques. If he had headlined my aerial act rather than a fat, unemployed labourer and a drugged big cat, we would be the toast of Moscow by now."

Fabayan's voice echoed around the empty hangar as he walked about, testing several thick ropes dangling from above. Dorj followed a few steps behind.

"Why did Zubov imagine you would do better business in Mongolia?" he finally asked.

"Because we would have no competition, or so he said. But, more importantly, as it turned out, he did not realize that you Mongolians don't have enough tugriks to keep the traffic lights working, let alone pay for art."

Not put diplomatically, but true enough, reflected Dorj. It struck him that the deaths of both the owner and his favoured lion tamer had at once removed two impediments to Fabayan's career. He wondered who else might have been angered by Zubov's refusal to headline aerialists. "Do you perform alone?"

"At the moment, yes. However, I have been training Ivana. Naturally, the audience wants thrills and artistry such as I provide, but I also needed a vision of beauty on the wires, to complement my performance."

The young man stared up into the shadows, a bird with its wings clipped.

"Isn't it dangerous, trying to learn something like that at her age?" Dorj ventured delicately.

The other dismissed the suggestion. "Ivana is closer to my age than Cheslav's," he said, somewhat heatedly it seemed to Dorj. "Besides, she is an accomplished acrobat. She took over for Larisa when she could no longer continue her act. Her acrobatic act, at least. We no longer have a contortionist. Larisa was the only one of us with that talent."

Larisa had mentioned only her acrobatic skill. For a moment Dorj said nothing. He was thinking about her remarkable blue eyes. It was hard to imagine those blue eyes belonged to a woman who was, or had been, a contortionist, as well as . . . Dorj forced his thoughts back to more important matters.

"Is it true that the women had reason to hate Zubov?" he asked, recalling Dima's comment.

"You mean because he was constantly propositioning them? Actually, the way he was always looking at Ivana, I am surprised poor Cheslav waited until he was dead to kill the old lecher. If I had been her husband, I would have strangled him long ago!"

Dorj immediately recognized the possessive jealousy in Fabayan's voice. How often had he encountered that fierce tone while investigating a crime? Perhaps that was why he so distrusted his own emotions. So often strong emotions led to disaster.

He might have felt compelled to ask whether the young man had been having an affair with Cheslav's wife, but the aerialist grabbed one of the hanging ropes and hauled himself up into the shadows. A few seconds later, Dorj heard the creak of the swinging trapeze.

Dorj climbed into Zubov's caravan. Having spoken to the last two or three members of the small troupe, he had discovered that, predictably, they all claimed that everyone else but themselves had good reason to hate the circus owner.

It was hard to remember he had driven out here hoping that for a few hours the circus's dazzling lights, nimble performers and sideshows would free him from the dreariness of the vast grey desert and cramped grey offices of his official life. In Ulaanbaatar he had had the consolation of the State Theatre. Out here in Dalandzadgad culture was a traveling circus.

Dorj removed his wire-framed eyeglasses and carefully wiped their round lenses with his handkerchief. But when he put the spectacles back on, the scene remained unchanged and just as murky.

He examined the interior of the caravan. It held no revelations. Its few cupboards contained only household necessaries, and in any event they were too small for purposes of concealment. Nor had anyone been hiding in the lavatory cubicle, waiting to escape in the general excitement. He would surely have been noticed.

The blood smears on the floor and the imprint of a bloody hand on the lavatory door mutely reproached his lack of understanding.

Dorj positioned himself beneath the closed roof vent and reached up to touch it. When he had noticed it earlier, while examining the outside of the caravan, he'd guessed it was too small to serve as an entrance. Now he was certain. His shoulders were much wider than the opening and Dima, although short, was at least as broad. Not a proper midget, as Zubov had said. In addition, the vent gave no evidence of having been opened recently. Indeed, a ropy bit of cobweb hung down from it.

The cobweb made him think about Fabayan's rigging. Didn't aerialists fly through the air, in a manner of speaking? He would have had a motive, certainly, unless Dorj were mistaken about the aerialist's relationship with Ivana. For that matter, Ivana was an acrobat. Dorj tried to imagine some way aerial or acrobatic skills might breach a locked caravan.

After a moment's thought, Dorj replaced Zubov's wooden chair to the spot he had seen it while assisting Dima to lay Hercules' body on the bed. He sat down where Zubov had sat. Why had the circus owner locked the door until the ambulance came? As a precaution, no doubt. People who were hated had reason to lock their doors.

He glanced around again. By the disordered bed an empty vodka bottle had rolled into a corner.

So, he reasoned, perhaps Zubov had felt the need for a drink, sitting in his cold caravan with the corpse of his headline act. It was not surprising. Dorj tried to imagine how it would have been, sitting there with the dead man, drinking, perhaps eventually dozing.

And suddenly the dead man is rising from the bed. Impossible. It must be the vodka, or the tail end of a nightmare. Half awake, he is confused. He jumps to his feet. The chair topples over as the dead man advances. Convulsed with panic, the ringmaster backs away, but there is no escape. The corpse staggers against the lavatory door, steadies itself with a bloody hand. Then those huge hands fasten on Zubov's throat. Trying to push the nightmare away, the ringmaster finds only a barrel chest gashed by a hideous wound.

Dorj shuddered. Trying to imagine the scene he had felt himself being drawn into it, almost like the shaman he had once seen performing for some tourists. Certainly the masked man, beating a drum and dancing about, had known as well as his spectators that he was not descending into the lower world. But as his gyrations became wilder it seemed to Dorj that the man was convincing himself that he was actually taking the impossible journey and in so doing was also persuading the spectators – most of them, at least – of the fact.

But what Dorj had imagined – a murderous corpse – was simply not possible.

And yet, the lion-tamer had been dead. The wound had been so terrible, he must have gone into shock instantly and died within minutes.

Dorj's thoughtful gaze was drawn again to the bloody handprint on the door. Nor could he forget the welt around the strangled man's neck.

Again he tried to picture the performers, and how their skills might have contributed to Zubov's death. All the exercise did was remind him of a snippet of his limited knowledge of native Mongolian culture. Along with masks, shamans – religious magicians, scoffers called them – wore mirrors on their clothing. Weren't the sequins sewn into circus performers' outfits tiny mirrors? Perhaps it was just as Batu said, the soul being called back, simple magic. Was it so dreadful to believe there might be magic in the world?

Dorj finally found Larisa standing outside the cookhouse among the vehicles in the back yard.

"Do you have a few spare moments?" he asked.

The bearded lady shrugged. "We won't be leaving until tomorrow."

"You'll continue to tour?"

"What else can we do? Eventually some legal person will let us know who owns the circus. Meanwhile we have to make a living."

Dorj paused, gauging the light. It would be more than an hour before it was completely dark. "I need to ask you a few more questions. And there's something you might like to see. A local landmark."

"How mysterious. It's been a long time since I've been asked out walking by a gentleman! I'd be pleased to accept."

"Well, it isn't exactly, that is to say – there are questions . . ."

"What? You aren't shy about being seen with a girl who looks like me, are you?"

As they followed faint tyre ruts up a small hill that rose almost imperceptibly several minutes' walk from the abandoned hangar, Dorj had to admit to himself that although he might indeed be shy about being seen with a bearded woman, it was nevertheless a marked, almost welcome, change from his grey official life.

"Here's something you might want to know," Larisa said, when they were well away from the back yard. "Dima is Buturlin's son. Illegitimate. I understand when Buturlin made Zubov a partner, their agreement required the circus to keep Dima on, even in the event sole ownership passed to Zubov. The agreement apparently didn't specify that Zubov had to treat him like a human being."

Dorj nodded, wondering why Larisa was offering the information. Perhaps it was just to be helpful. People did not always need ulterior motives, he reminded himself. "Perhaps Zubov hoped to force him to leave?"

"It would be his way," agreed Larisa.

"Does Dima have any interest in the circus, now that his father's partner is gone?"

"I don't know. You don't suspect Dima, do you? Perhaps I shouldn't have said anything."

The wind was still cold, but walking made Dorj feel warmer. Perhaps it was his slight build that made him mind the chill. It was not a good trait for a Mongolian, even a city dweller as he had been, since in Ulaanbaatar in the winter it was not unknown for the temperature to reach 40 below.

He asked his companion about Ivana and Fabayan. Larisa confirmed his suspicion. "She married Cheslav in a fit of pique shortly after Zubov hired him, because she'd just had a big quarrel with Fabayan. Ivana is impetuous and emotional, always has been.

She and Fabayan quickly made it up. Poor Cheslav. I often wondered how he could not have known."

They had reached the windswept brow of the hill. From this vantage point, they could see the black bulk of the hangar. Beyond it lay a litter of abandoned Russian military equipment, left there to rust into oblivion in the Gobi's vast emptiness.

Here at the top of the hill was the much older landmark Dorj had wanted to show Larisa. It was a pile of rocks standing higher than his head, a sacred *obo*, built stone by stone by passing travellers over the span of hundreds of years. Up here, looking at such a thing, it was easy to believe the impossible.

"So Cheslav avenged himself on the wrong man," mused Dorj.

"You don't really believe a dead man got up and strangled someone, do you? You're thinking like Shakespeare, with all those ghosts stamping about calling for bloody vengeance!"

"You know Shakespeare?"

"Circus people know everything."

"I really can't make anything of it," Dorj admitted. He related his conversation with the dead man's wife.

Larisa pondered for a few moments. "What if she somehow gave the tranquilizer to Cheslav?" she finally suggested. "Not to kill him outright. Just to make him slow, perhaps affect his reactions. Give the lion its chance, you know? He was frightened of the lion, and I think they can sense it. Well, she was too, especially having to feed it. Though she disliked the reptiles even more."

Dorj nodded. It almost seemed a reasonable theory, given the character of the widow. A tawdry triangle and a more than melodramatic way to get rid of an unwanted husband.

Larisa continued. "But here is another idea. About that terrible wound Cheslav had – perhaps it didn't kill him immediately because of the tranquilizer in him? And he came to in the caravan? He probably thought that Zubov had plotted with Ivana, and that would be enough. He would want revenge before he died." She sighed and continued, "But it is all too fantastic, even for a circus, don't you think?"

Dorj shrugged without comment. Her theories made as much, or as little, sense as anything he had been able to think of up to that point.

Sunset was a purpling bruise on the horizon. In its soft light, they stood looking at the pile of stones that formed the obo. It was not the sort of thing to which Dorj was usually drawn. But it was the only magic he could think to offer this strange woman.

"This is an ancient place of power," he explained.

"A good spot to solve your mystery, then."

Dorj listened to the wind sighing around the *obo*. He thought of the unknown number of ancient hands, belonging to forgotten people all now turned to dust, this single action of their lost lives, the placing of a stone, now all that was left of them.

"It is a good place to make one believe the dead might return," he said, quietly. "We should go back before it gets dark."

He picked up a pebble and added it to the *obo*. As Larisa bent to do the same, she stumbled and, as he had earlier, Dorj caught her arm. This time he was not so quick to let go.

"You would never guess I was an acrobat once," she said.

"And, so I am told, a contortionist. You didn't mention that."

Larisa's blue eyes widened slightly. "You don't suspect me, do you? Do you suppose I managed to wriggle into the caravan somehow?" She looked away from him. "I'm sorry, Inspector. But in fact, I have indeed misled you about something else. You didn't think this was real?"

She grabbed the edge of her beard and pulled. Dorj stared for a second at the suddenly smooth face. "Now there is a magical transformation which the Bard himself would have been proud to preserve in his work," he finally said.

To his distress he saw that the unveiled face was set in a frown.

"I have never suspected you, Larisa," he quickly assured her. "In fact, right now I need your assistance." He grabbed her hand – he could hardly believe he had done so – and hurried her back down the hill.

"There may be another trap around here," Larisa worried. "Be careful. Dima might have put some more out. I wish you'd tell me what you're looking for."

So far she and the inspector, searching around the back of the hangar with the aid of a fading torch, had located perhaps a dozen traps, finding only one sprung, and that holding an unfortunate rat. Dorj merely insisted they continue looking. She swung the feeble yellow light across the ground until it lit upon a metal stake. The flickering beam slid down the stake's attached chain to reveal another trap, and beside it a semi-comatose snake.

"It belongs to the circus, doesn't it?" said Dorj.

"Yes. It's Nikita. How do you know?"

"I grew up in the city, but I don't think boa constrictors are native to the Gobi. Not even ones as small as this."

"He's just a baby," Larisa pointed out. "Zubov traded our big python for it. He eats less. Ivana didn't say anything about him being missing."

"There were pictures of snakes on the animal trailer, but I didn't notice any inside. At least one aquarium was empty, though. When you wondered whether I suspected you'd managed to wriggle into the trailer caravan, it reminded me."

Sluggish from ingesting whatever it had found in the trap, the snake was quickly popped into the empty feed sack Dorj had brought with him. "We'll need this for evidence," he commented.

"You're saying the snake killed Zubov?"

Dorj hefted the sack, hoping the snake would not emerge too quickly from its post-prandial lethargy.

"I should have realized that manual strangulation would leave finger marks on Zubov's neck, not a continuous welt all around it," he explained. "If nothing else, the bloody handprint in the caravan should have reminded me.

"It got there during the struggle. What I surmise happened is that Zubov, having drunk heavily, fell asleep." Dorj continued quickly, wanting to finish without distressing the woman too much. "The snake, having escaped, got into the caravan. Snakes are attracted to warmth and the only warm thing in the cold caravan was the slumbering Zubov."

"The first and last time anything was attracted by Zubov's warmth," the woman said wryly.

"Then he was suddenly woken up by the boa tightening around his neck. He couldn't call for aid. Trying to get it off him, he crashed around, and in doing so knocked the corpse off the bed."

He paused momentarily. "That would explain the blood on the floor and the lavatory door."

Larisa shuddered. "It must be true. Boas that feel threatened instinctively tighten their coils, so I hear."

"Once Zubov was dead," Dorj continued, "he was too big to ingest. Or perhaps the snake was scared away by Batu's pounding on the door. It crawled off through one of those badly patched holes in the caravan wall, in search of other prey. It was probably hungry. In fact, I don't doubt hunger also contributed to the lion attacking Cheslav."

"You don't think it's what Ivana said – not enough tranquilizer?"

They had arrived at the unlocked animal trailer. Dorj looked around for the empty aquarium. The bag he was holding shifted alarmingly.

"I'm not certain about the lion. Perhaps it was just as Ivana said, an accident with the tranquilizer. Or possibly she saw her chance."

"So both deaths were nothing more than accidents. How very strange."

"Yes. Strange indeed. Too strange. Unless . . ." Dorj frowned. He stared into the dimness. "What if Nikita didn't escape? In the confusion, after her husband was killed, Ivana could have returned to this trailer and tranquilized the boa. It isn't a large boa and easily concealed under that billowy outfit she was wearing. Under the circumstances we would never have noticed. And when she threw herself so dramatically onto the corpse – well, he was a big man and there was plenty of room inside that wound for a smallish boa. It would have awakened in a cooling corpse, in a cold caravan, and gone for Zubov."

Larisa blanched.

The sack Dorj had all but forgotten jerked suddenly open. The head of the snake whipped into view. Another convulsive twist of its body and it had knocked the sack from Dorj's hands. The freed boa slithered across the floor. But in the wrong direction. A leonine paw flashed out from between cage bars, and then Raisa was rumbling contentedly as she ate the unfortunate killer.

So accidents did come in threes, as Fabayan had said, Dorj thought.

Larisa and Dorj left the trailer and stood gazing up at the impossibly enormous moon sitting on the edge of the horizon. Its bright light, flooding down from the dark sky, painted the world silver. Ebony shadows pooled here and there. Inside the trailer the lion was devouring the only credible evidence for Dorj's unlikely story.

The strange bearded creature he had met only hours earlier, now transformed into a beautiful woman, leaned nearer to brush a magical kiss onto his cheek. Dorj felt certain he must have fallen into some Shakespearean enchantment.

"I am sorry," whispered Larisa. "But in a way I am not. We circus people stick together. And only Ivana knows what really happened. There is no proof of anything, really."

Dorj wondered what his superiors would say about the report he would be submitting in due course. His reputation would certainly suffer, and he suspected that over the next few months he would be finding rubber snakes hidden in his office desk with monotonous regularity.

But at least he could state the murderer's identity with certainty. How the boa had got into the caravan would be difficult to ascertain, and indeed he was beginning to doubt the fantastic tale he had spun. Perhaps the snake had arrived in the caravan by its own efforts, without anyone's assistance. That part he would leave to his superior's imagination.

"Larisa," he said softly, "Did you know Shakespeare mentions a snake around someone's neck? A beautiful gold and green snake. And there's a lioness in the same scene. In fact, now I think about it, the original Hercules strangled the Nemean lion. What happened here almost makes some sort of sense."

The woman smiled. "Though it is the wrong season, do you mean it almost makes sense in a dream-like midsummer night's sort of way, Inspector Dorj?"

Wingless Pegasus

Gillian Linscott

Gillian Linscott (b. 1944), a former reporter and Parliamentary journalist, is the author of the Nell Bray series of suffragette mysteries that began with Sister Beneath the Sheet *(1991) and includes the award-winning* Absent Friends *(1999). Gillian has a fascination for intricate mysteries. She began a series set in the 19th century featuring journalist Thomas Ludlow and the less-than-reputable horse-dealer Harry Leather, but only completed two stories. I reprinted one of them, "Poisoned with Politeness" in* The Mammoth Book of Historical Whodunnits *(Third New Collection). Here's the other one.*

There was a terrace behind the house with swags of cream and apricot roses, steps leading down to a broad lawn with a cedar tree. The lawn sloped away to a deep ditch, separating the garden from a meadow where cattle grazed. At the boundary of lawn and meadowland was a small lake a couple of acres in extent. The island was not quite in the centre of the lake, nearer the shore on the meadow side, about the size of a large drawing room, with a marble statue of Venus, half-draped, rising from a tangle of rushes and meadowsweet. Nothing else to see at all except, early on that June morning, a horse. A white horse, standing up to the hocks in meadowsweet and early morning mist from the lake, looking itself like a statue, except when you got closer you'd have seen that it was shivering and its nostrils flaring, not being the sort of horse used to spending its nights in the open, even in an English summer. No ordinary horse either. If half-draped Venus had grown tired of English country life and summoned the gods' horse Pegasus to carry her back up to Olympus, this was what might have arrived in answer. Only Venus couldn't fly away after all because the instant his Olympian hooves touched the damp soil of Berkshire, Pegasus had lost his wings and became, like her, marooned in 1866 on a small island on the moderate-sized estate of a man who had made his fortune from railways.

That, at any rate, is how it might have looked to a fanciful observer with a rudimentary knowledge of classical mythology who happened to be looking out from the terrace early that morning. In fact it was a housemaid glancing from her window in the attic who first saw it and she – knowing nothing of Pegasus or Venus – went downstairs and informed the undercook that one of the carriage horses must have got let out of its stable and there'd be the devil to pay when the head groom found out about it. From there the news went out to the stables where a hasty check of heads found that all six equine members of Sir Percy Whitton's establishment were present and correct in their boxes. A delegation of stable staff, along with some of the gardeners picked up on the way, hurried across the lawn to the edge of the lake, and realised at once that this was no ordinary horse. Where it came from and how it had arrived overnight, saddled and bridled, on Sir Percy's little island, was a cause of universal puzzlement overtaken by the necessity of getting it to more solid land. This presented problems because the small rowing boat that was usually kept on the lawn side of the lake for the amusement of Sir Percy's guests had been reduced to splinters in an accident with a garden roller the week before and its replacement had not yet arrived. After some discussion several grooms and gardeners took off their boots, waistcoats, and jackets and waded into the lake. At its deepest it came up to chest height but they went on firmly, encouraged by shouts from their friends on the bank and, possibly, the prospect of some substantial sign of gratitude from whoever turned out to be the owner of the animal which was watching them apprehensively, showing every sign of wanting to bolt but, of course, with nowhere but the lake to go. I would guess that at this point, in spite of the difficulties, the rescuers were lighthearted. It was a diversion from the work of the morning and there was no reason to think that they were engaged in anything more sinister than the recovery of a fine animal.

A groom was the first to step ashore. I suspect that the ardour of the gardeners decreased as they came closer to the dancing, snorting object of their quest. He put hand on the rein, made calming noises. Then he gave a shout and the horse reared up, almost dragging the rein from his hand.

"There's a man here, a man hurt. I think it's Sir Percy."

But long before the swaddled form was carried on a hurdle up the lawn and under the cedar with silent gardeners and grooms around it, the whole household knew that the groom had been only half right. The man on the island was indeed their employer, Sir Percy, but he wasn't hurt – he was dead.

The bare outline of Sir Percy's death reached me on a June evening in London. I read it on a damp galley proof in my place of work, a subeditors' room in inky Fleet Street.

We have received reports from Berkshire that the director of the South Western Shires Railway Company, Sir Percy Whitton, has been killed in a riding accident on his estate near Maybridge. An inquest is to take place tomorrow. Funeral arrangements will be notified.

I hardly knew the man personally, having been in the same room as him on a couple of public occasions, and my first thought was what a sad loss this would be for the lawyers. Sir Percy and his neighbour Charles Clawson of the Wiltshire and Berkshire Railway were at daggers drawn. The Wiltshire and Berkshire had got an Act of Parliament to drive their new branch line along the hill opposite Sir Percy's house. He said it was an abomination, and if a gentleman couldn't live in his own home without steam engines scaring his cattle and blowing smuts all over his guests, it was all up with the rights and liberties of old England. This in spite of the fact that his own money came from railways. The resulting court case, due to open in a week's time, had been anticipated as one of the great events of the legal season. Sir Percy was expected to win, if only because his purse was longer than Clawson's and he'd take it all the way to the House of Lords if necessary. There was extra spice in the fact that the combatants were related by marriage. Clawson had given the hand of his only daughter, Emily, to Sir Percy at a time several years earlier when the two men were business partners, before they fell out.

It's an unfortunate fact of working for a newspaper that all the most interesting things you get to know are those that law or society won't allow you to print. I collect such stories as other men collect ferns or butterflies. I sniffed one here and, by grace of those same railways that began the battle, I was in the little market town of Maybridge before lunchtime next morning. I already had a direct line into the gossip of the area through my old and disreputable friend, Harry Leather. Harry is a groom, jockey, livery keeper, dealer, in fact, in anything you please as long as it has a lot to do with horses and as little as possible to do with the law. He's as small and agile as a street urchin but I suppose is a man in middle years, although from the wrinkles on his weatherbeaten face he looks old enough to have traded horses with the Pharaohs – probably to their disadvantage. At that time he was managing a livery stables at Maybridge, so when I got there I made straight for his establishment on one side of the market square, knowing that nothing that moved on four legs and precious little on two escaped his network. I found him in the saddle room, cleaning tack, and after an exchange of civilities asked him the time of the inquest.

"You've missed it, Mr Ludlow. They opened it at nine o'clock and it was all over by eleven."

"What was the verdict?"

"Misadventure."

"Much interest in it locally?"

He hooked up a stirrup leather and ran a cloth slowly down it. The meaty smell of neat's-foot oil hung in the warm air, along with whiffs of horse from the loose boxes.

"What do you think?"

"Was he well-liked?"

"Well enough by those as liked him."

With Harry, this kind of game could go on all day. But I knew he was hugging information of some kind as closely as a child hugs a puppy. I watched while he oiled a few more leathers then asked him what he knew about the riding accident. It was then that I got most of the details about the island, the shivering white horse, and the man lying dead, with Harry going on with his work all the while, watching me sidelong to see what I was making of it.

"Do you want to see him?"

The sudden question jolted me. I thought at first that he was talking about Sir Percy's corpse, surely now in the hands of the undertaker.

"See who?"

"The horse."

He got up unhurriedly and led the way across the yard. We went past the lines of worthy hacks and dependable carriage horses, round the corner to the few isolated boxes that he keeps for invalids or mares close to foaling. As we turned the corner a high whinnying came from one of the boxes. A head as white as new milk came over the half door, large wild eyes, wide pink nostrils.

"An Arabian. A fine one, too."

We stood looking over the half door while the horse rolled his eyes and snorted at us. He wasn't large, under sixteen hands, but every line of him, from his long back to his clean cannon bones, sang out speed and breeding.

Harry ran a calming hand down the arched neck.

"We have to keep him here because he's entire. Cover every mare in the yard if he had his way."

A stallion, not gelded, therefore as wild as the wind and as unpredictable.

"No wonder Sir Percy got thrown. I suppose he was out for a hack, got bolted with into the lake and onto the island, then the horse reared up and threw him."

Harry snorted, making a noise much like the horse.

"And I'm the Queen of Fairyland."

I suppressed the picture of Harry in rosy wreaths and diaphanous draperies.

"You don't think it happened that way?"

"No, I don't, and if you think about it, neither do you."

"Oh, and why don't I?"

"For one thing, you know horses a touch better than that. Have you ever met an Arab in your life that was any use over water? Can't stand it, coming from deserts like they do."

"If he was bolting . . ."

"If he was bolting, he'd bolt away from water, not across it."

"But he was on the island. I gather nobody disputes that?"

"Nobody's likely to, given the trouble they had to get him off it."

"So how did he get there?" Harry turned towards me with the glint in his eye that usually means the other man is about to get the worse of a bargain.

"That, Mr Ludlow, is the second most peculiar thing about this whole business."

"Oh? So, what's the first, Harry?" He paused, enjoying his moment.

"The most peculiar of the lot is what Sir Percy was doing with him in the first place."

"Hacking out on him, surely."

He gestured towards the horse, calmer now and watching us with interest, although still as ready to fly as a bird from a cage.

"You look at that animal and tell me if he'd let a fat counting-house man like Sir Percy Whitton throw a leg over him. A racing lord might ride him, a tinker boy as wild as he is might ride him, but he wouldn't let any ordinary hacking man as much as put a toe in his stirrup iron."

I looked at the horse and had to admit that I knew what he meant. Harry, seeing my face, nodded.

"Sir Percy couldn't have ridden a hair of his tail."

"But they were on the island together, and Sir Percy was dead."

"That's it."

"So there must have been somebody else there?"

"Not when they got there. The chief groom's a friend of mine. I had it all from him direct."

"He can't have dropped from the clouds. Was there any sign anybody else had been there?"

"By the time they'd got Sir Percy off the island, then the horse, the whole lot was as trampled as if they'd fought a battle over it."

I thought of Charles Clawson and my mind went racing.

"Supposing, for the sake of argument, that somebody had wanted to harm Sir Percy. If he managed to get him alone on a little island with a horse that might be dangerous . . ."

"Be a damned sight easier to wait for him behind a bush with a brace of pistols, begging your pardon. Anyhow, you've still got to get the horse to the island."

And Charles Clawson, as I remembered, was a hacking sort of counting-house man too – no rider for the white horse.

"It would be a complicated way to murder anybody."

At the word murder, Harry turned away. He said, under his breath: "Suppose a man's got to have an interest in life, but yours seems a damned odd one to me."

We'd had this out before, but he'd keep worrying at it.

"Why so? Doesn't it interest you, thinking that a person may be killed by another person and nobody ever know how it happened, or why? You could write whole books about it."

"Funny sort of books they'd be. Who'd want to read them?"

"Just about everybody who's curious about his fellow men and women."

He shook his head. "What that doesn't take into account is that there are what you might call public murders and there are private murders, and it doesn't do to confuse the two of them."

"What do you mean?"

We began walking slowly back across the yard. A dog dozed in the sun and a boy swept the already immaculate brick paving.

"What I call a public murder, let's say a poacher shoots a keeper, everybody knows who's done it, he's tried at the assizes, people go to see him hanged, and that's an end of it. A private murder – somebody kills somebody for a good or a bad reason and doesn't want the whys and wherefores of it known, and mostly you wouldn't do any good to anybody making them known, only stir up more trouble. What you're doing is intruding on private murder."

"You think it was murder then?"

He didn't answer. I asked him how the Arab had come to be in his yard.

"Had to go somewhere until they find out who owns him, and he couldn't have stopped at Sir Percy's place, could he?"

"Why not?"

"The young widow. As soon as she hears about the white horse she faints clean away – thinking, I suppose, of her poor husband being trampled and so on. The doctor says he won't be answerable if she sets eyes on the animal, so they call me in and I ride him over here."

"Ah yes, the widow. Charles Clawson's daughter. She must have been a lot younger than her husband."

"About a quarter of a century younger. Down here they reckon her father gave her to Sir Percy in return for a parcel of railway shares." Harry said it as matter-of-factly as you'd talk of trading one horse for another.

"She'll be a rich widow now, Mr Ludlow, and a nice-looking young lady at that. Good chance for somebody." He laughed and looked at me sidelong.

"I'm not bidding. Was she at the inquest?"

"Yes. Had to answer questions from the coroner about when she'd last seen her husband."

"When had she?"

"Dinner the night before. She went up to bed early, having a headache from the heat. First she knew about it was when her maid woke her up in the morning."

"Had he said anything to her about going out?"

"Not a word, but then he wouldn't, would he?"

There was something odd about the way Harry said that, but I left that for later.

"It must have been a sad ordeal for her."

"Very composed she was, while she was telling it. Afterwards, while she was walking out, she nearly collapsed on her brother's arm. He'd come back from Oxford especially when he heard about it."

"Did they say at the inquest whether Sir Percy was trampled? Were there marks of horseshoes on him?"

"Not one, just the back of his head caved in. The head groom said it looked as though he'd fallen and hit it on the base of the statue, the Venus."

He stopped in front of another loose box in the middle of the long row. There was a dark bay mare inside, cobby sort, sixteen hands, facing away from us and munching hay. She looked quiet and steady, as unlike the Arab as anything on four legs.

"She's Sir Percy's."

"What's she doing here in a livery yard? Did his wife send her away too?"

He shook his head.

"I got up early in the morning and there she was tied to the hitching ring outside the gates. She was covered in mud and tired fit to drop, but whoever left her there had knotted up the reins and run up the stirrups properly."

"When was this?"

"The morning they found Sir Percy's body."

"How far away from here is Sir Percy's place?"

"Four miles."

I could hardly take in what he was telling me, and I must have spluttered my questions. How did he know the mare was Sir Percy's? Could the man have ridden her four miles in the night and walked back in time to be dead on his own island by sunrise, and if so, why? Had Harry told the coroner's officer? The answer to that last question was no, as I should have guessed knowing his dislike for the law. As for how he'd known, it turned out that the mare was a frequent guest at his livery stables when Sir Percy rode into town.

"But you told me that the head groom checked the stables that morning and all Sir Percy's horses were there."

"So they were, all as were meant to be there. This mare was never in his stables. He kept her in his estate manager's stable half a mile from the house and his wife never knew she existed."

There could only be one reason for that.

"You're telling me that Sir Percy kept a *petite amie* in the town here and used the mare to visit her?"

No need, with Harry, to pretend to be shocked. He lives by the morals of the reign before Her Majesty's, if he can be credited with any at all.

"Tuesday and Thursday nights," was all he said. Sir Percy's body had been found early on Wednesday morning.

"Didn't any of this come out at the inquest?"

"Wouldn't have been decent, would it, with his body lying cold and his poor wife sitting there hearing it. I reckon half the jury knew about it and probably the coroner as well for that matter, but nobody was going to say so."

"But it was relevant, wasn't it? Sir Percy has dinner with his wife. Some time after that he walks to his estate manager's house, collects the mare, and starts riding into town. Either on the way there or on the way back he is diverted, for no good reason, onto an island in his lake along with an Arab stallion from God knows where that doesn't like crossing water. His mare, meanwhile, somehow finds her way back to your livery stables and ties herself neatly to a hitching ring. Isn't that a sequence a coroner should know about?"

"Put that way, I'm not saying you're wrong, Mr Ludlow, but I still don't see what good it would do."

"This woman he visited – do you know her?"

"Name of Lucy Dester. House with the green door, opposite the baker's."

I stood making up my mind, staring at the back view of the cobby mare. Aware of eyes on her, she twitched her tail, shifted her hind legs.

"Looks a touch short-tempered."

"Not her. Quiet as a cushion, only she's in season at the moment. Anyway, if you're set on finding out what happened, you've seen both of them that matter now."

He meant both horses in the case – horses being more important to Harry than people. He said just one thing more before we parted at the gate.

"Now don't you go making her miserable. She's a decent enough party in her own way."

There was a man in bloodstained clothes hammering at Lucy Dester's green front door. He looked as if he'd been there for some time, and a small crowd had gathered. I asked a loitering boy who the bloodstained man was and gathered he was the local butcher. I loitered with the rest of the crowd and when, after a few more minutes of beating, the door opened a crack I was able to get a glimpse of the person inside. At risk of being ungallant, she struck me as being ten years too old and a couple of stone too heavy to qualify as any sort of nymph. Her voice, when she told the butcher to go about his business, was not refined. He thrust a solidly booted foot into the door crack and pulled a paper from his pocket.

"Two pounds, three shillings, and fourpence halfpenny."

That was the burden of his song, several times repeated. Mrs Dester owed him two pounds, three shillings, and fourpence halfpenny, and he wouldn't budge from her doorstep until he got it. I fumbled in my pocket, approached the door.

"This is most uncivil behaviour to a lady. Now take your money and be off with you."

He stared open-mouthed at me, then at the coins in his hand, and withdrew muttering. The crack in the doorway opened a little wider and I stepped inside. There were broken expressions of gratitude, explanations about money orders not arriving. I found myself sitting opposite her in a neat parlour, sipping a glass of Madeira.

"I kept it for him," she said. "He always enjoyed his Madeira."

There was no need to ask to whom she was referring. She'd taken me for a friend of his who knew about the relations between them and had come to offer sympathy. She was not an unpleasing woman in either person or conversation, with quantities of lustrous black hair, pink rounded cheeks, and a warmth of manner that compensated for her lack of refinement. She had been, by her account, employed as an actress in London until Sir Percy set her up in a small establishment in town. When he decided to spend more time on his estate, he moved her to the present lodgings.

"And last Tuesday night . . . ?"

She sighed deeply. "There was a nice cold collation laid out for him, ham and fowl, and his claret decanted all ready. He never came."

"Did you think something had happened to him?"

"Not that, oh no. Unexpected guests, I thought, or business that had kept him at home. Nothing like what happened."

"When did you know?"

"It was all round the town. I went out to buy some ribbons for my bonnet and that b— I mean a customer at the haberdashers said she supposed I'd heard about the accident." Two plump tears trembled on her cheeks, ran down.

"I haven't put a foot outside since, and it's been nothing but people at the door with bills, bills, bills. When he was alive, you see, they all knew he'd meet them, but now he's gone they don't have any pity and there's not so much money in the house as a third-class fare back to London."

She bent her head and wept in earnest. I tried to comfort her, although there was very little I could do or say. She looked up at last, eyes brimming with tears.

"I was fond of him, you know. I really was fond of him."

Before I left I asked if she knew anybody who owned a white Arab stallion. No more than the man in the moon, she said.

I borrowed a hack from Harry and spent the rest of the afternoon riding out to Sir Percy's estate to look at the island, to no effect whatsoever. When I got back to the livery stables we had supper, chops and eggs cooked on the old stove in Harry's den next to the saddle room. It seemed that my rescue of Lucy Dester from the butcher was the talk of the town and he made a few heavy-hooved jokes on the theme.

"You're right, though, she seems a decent enough woman in her way, and she has nothing to gain from his death – quite the reverse."

We'd already agreed that I should stay the night in the hayloft, and we were sorting out horse rugs when there was a knocking at the yard gate. Harry's head came up.

"Who the devil is it at this hour?"

It was past ten o'clock, deep dusk, with no sound but the horses munching hay in their boxes. The big double gates to the yard were bolted, but there was a smaller door cut into them. Harry unlatched it and we both looked out. At first there was nothing to see, then a figure stepped out of the shadows and in at the door as quickly as a bat flying. It came in a swish of silk, black garments fluttering.

"I want to buy a horse."

It was a woman's voice, a young woman's. There was a desperate determination in the way she spoke and moved. She had a black bonnet covering her hair, framing a small face as pale as a frost-struck white rose. Her sudden arrival and the unlikeliness of her words left me speechless, although she'd addressed them to me. But Harry, by nature and calling, couldn't help responding to an opening like that, whether it came from man, woman, or hobgoblin.

"What kind of a horse, ma'am?"

"The white Arab."

I was on the point of explaining that he wasn't ours to sell when Harry nudged my arm and drew me to one side. He whispered in my ear, "The widow." Then, back to her: "He's not a lady's horse, ma'am."

"I don't care about that. What's your price?"

If you listened very hard you could hear the tremor in her voice, like a high note on a violin, but to look at her she was snow and steel.

"Fifty guineas, ma'am."

A black-gloved hand came out of her draperies, holding a small pouch.

"Count them out."

Harry counted them on the edge of the mounting block, the coins gleaming in the last of the light, and gave the diminished pouch back to her.

"Where shall I send him, ma'am?"

"Don't send him anywhere. Shoot him."

I'd never have thought to see Harry thunderstruck, but if the heavens had landed on him he couldn't have been more amazed.

"Sh . . . shoot him?"

"Shoot him tonight and bury him."

"But . . ."

Her black glove came up, signing him to be quiet.

"He's my horse now. I've bought him and paid for him, and I can have done as I like with him."

Then, as suddenly as she'd come, she stepped out through the little door and was gone. In the stunned silence I could hear her feet tapping away round the corner. Harry looked sick.

"Well here's a fine thing," I said. "You've accepted money for another man's horse and now you're obliged to shoot him."

"I'd shoot my brother first. The sheer malice of it, to want a good horse shot just because she thinks it killed her husband."

Now she'd taken that frost-rose face away, my mind was moving again, faster than poor Harry's.

"I don't think that's the game."

"Then what is it? For pity's sake, what is she at?"

"I think I know. I really think I see it. Harry, you should see it too."

"I've got no time for guessing games. The thing is now, I've got to get that horse away before . . ."

"Leave it where it is."

"I can't do that. If she comes back in the morning and . . ."

"She won't do that. Now listen, you know this town. Is there a public house where all the grooms drink?"

"'Course there is, The Three Tuns, but . . ."

"Will it still be open this time of night?" He nodded. "Then get over there as quick as you can and tell everybody who'll listen what's just happened, only don't let them know her name. Tell them you're going to shoot the horse first thing in the morning, then come back here."

He looked at me, snatched up his hat from the tack room, and went at a run.

There was an empty box next to the Arab. We spread rugs on the straw by the light of a candle lantern and lay down. Aware of our presence, the white horse snorted and fidgeted on the other side of the partition. Harry had got back from The Three Tuns at about midnight, with beer on his breath and a gleam in his eye.

"Every household from here to Swindon will know about it by morning."

"Did anybody ask questions?"

"Plenty, but I only answered what I wanted to." He pressed something metallic against my hand. "Pistols, in case we need them. Is this person you're expecting dangerous?"

"I should say not to us. I don't know."

Through the short night, between sleeping and waking, he was trying to make me tell him a name. Wait and see, I said, or guess. He knew all that I knew. By half-past three in the morning a pale light was coming in through the half door of the box. The horses in the main yard began to shuffle their straw and whinny. From the box beside us the Arab responded with gentle whickering sounds. I felt Harry's pistol by my side and thought of that pale face.

Then: "It's the door latch."

I hadn't heard it above the horse sounds, but Harry's hearing is acute as an animal's. He signed to me to be quiet and listen and I heard steps coming across the yard. To the horses at that time of the morning a human being signaled the first feed, and the whinnying became a fanfare. The steps hesitated at the onslaught then came on faster, almost running round the corner towards us. We were both on our feet and Harry was bounding for the door of the box, pistol in hand. I grabbed his arm and mouthed, "Wait." The steps came past us and stopped at the box next-door. The white Arab had been whinnying along with the rest of the chorus but now his tone changed to a squeal of relief and recognition. Then there was a bolt being drawn, a man's voice making wordless, soothing sounds, and the click of a buckle tongue on a head collar.

"Now," I said, and Harry and I burst out just as the white Arab was being led from his box. The man on the end of the leading rope looked at first as if he intended to make a run for it, taking the horse with him, but then he looked at our pistols and stood stock still. His face was as white as hers had been, emphasizing the likeness.

"I think," I said, "Your sister has bought the horse."

"You had no right to sell him. Talisman is mine."

He recovered his nerve and stood very upright at the stallion's head. He was a good-looking young man, though a shade too fine and highly strung, like the horse itself. It struck me that he looked like a young knight from the works of the poet laureate, Mr Alfred Tennyson, and that he was possibly conscious of that fact.

"He's a horse that killed a man," Harry said. I don't know if he believed it or was trying to put young Clawson at a disadvantage. The young man practically came to attention.

"Talisman isn't guilty of killing him. I am."

"Suppose," I said, "you come inside and tell us about it."

With Talisman back in his box and the three of us sitting in Harry's cramped little den, it was hard for the young fellow to go on being noble. He told his story straightforwardly enough once he realised that I'd guessed it anyway. The point I had to help him over was the centre of it all – those twice-weekly visits by Sir Percy to my lady of the butcher's bill. Young Clawson was ashamed of a

father who'd married off his sister for money and that shame
turned to raging disgust when news got to him that the brute
couldn't even be faithful to her. He was in his final term at Oxford
when he heard (well provided with money and horses by that same
mercenary father, but that's by the by). He'd taken Talisman from
his stable and ridden two days from Oxford to Maybridge to give
his sister's lecherous husband a piece of his virtuous young mind.

"I knew he'd be going to that woman on the Tuesday evening.
Talisman and I waited on the edge of his grounds, near the lake.
All I meant to do was reason with him, make him turn back and beg
Emily on his knees for forgiveness."

Harry made a noise that might have been a suppressed sneeze
from the hay dust.

"He came riding along in the dusk on that mare of his. I went
through the gate and rode towards him. He must have panicked.
He tried to gallop away from us, but there's no speed in that mare
and he rode like a sack of coals. When he heard us gaining on him
he turned her into the lake, or perhaps she bolted that way, and up
onto the island. We followed. The mare shied away from us. He fell
and cracked his head against a statue. I took his mare and rode
away. I thought Talisman would follow, but he didn't."

He was panting a little, even from telling it. Then he took a long
breath and looked at me.

"So now you have it. I am guilty of the death of Sir Percy
Whitton and you can't shoot the horse for it. Now, sir, if you would
be kind enough to give me the loan of your pistol for a few
minutes . . ."

I almost wished I had Excalibur to give him. Instead, I put on a
very steely air.

"That's all very well, Mr Clawson, but you haven't told us the
truth. The point you've left out of your story is that you yourself
were overcome by brute, animal lust."

Another explosive sneeze from Harry and a "Sir!" from Clawson, equally explosive. He glared, and I think he'd have challenged
me if duelling weren't out of fashion, but he had to listen.

"I've no doubt you're a fine horseman, but even a fine horseman
couldn't have induced that Arab to swim into a lake. Only one
power on earth could make him do that, and she's standing in a
loose box in this yard."

"By God," said Harry, "Sir Percy's mare. A mare in season."

"A case of man proposes but horse deposes. Oh, I believe you about the first part of your story, Mr Clawson. But both your horses had interests that were nothing to do with your concerns. The female fled, the male followed and had his way with her. In the grip of that force of nature there was nothing whatsoever that either of you could do about it. In short, you were bolted with too."

In confessing to murder, young Clawson had been a picture of dignity and control. Now he went as red as a schoolboy and hung his head. I went on more gently.

"While your Talisman was having his way, Sir Percy fell off the mare and cracked his head on the plinth." (Paying, with ghastly appropriateness, a final tribute to Venus, though I didn't add that at the time.) "When you found he was dead, you panicked. Your own horse – once his appetite was sated – wouldn't cross the water back again in cold blood even for you. You took the mare and swam her to land, hoping he'd follow, just as you said. I'm right, aren't I?"

He murmured yes without looking up. I put a hand on his shoulder.

"You mustn't blame your sister for wanting the horse killed. The moment they told her about him she knew he was yours. She was only trying to protect you. Now, I suggest you start on your way back to Oxford before people are up and about. You can write to her from there."

Harry led out Talisman and held the stirrup while young Clawson mounted. I said, standing close to the horse's shoulder:

"Forget it all now. You meant no harm, and nobody will know about it from me."

We opened the gates for him and stood watching while they rode away across the deserted market square, the rider motionless, the horse looking like something going back into a legend. When they were out of sight Harry went back across the yard and stood looking over the half door at Sir Percy's cushion-quiet mare.

"Wonder if she took. Could be a good foal with that Arab blood." I suggested he might make an offer for her to the young widow when he took her fifty guineas back, but knowing Harry, thought it unlikely that the lady would ever see her money again or her husband's mare at all.

Duel of Shadows

Vincent Cornier

*One of the great treasures of the world of baffling mysteries is the
work of Vincent Cornier (1898–1976). A journalist, war reporter, and a much-travelled man, Cornier created some of the
most bizarre and unusual crime and mystery stories to appear in
the magazines from the late 1920s through to the 1960s. In all
that time he never once sought to have them collected in book
form and, although a few have been anthologized, most are now
extremely rare and difficult to find. Cornier created a couple of
continuing characters, of which the most popular proved to be
Barnabas Hildreth, whose stories ran in* Pearson's Magazine *in
the mid-1930s. Cornier would announce in advance to the editor
what the next story would be about and in each case the editor
could not believe the author could pull it off. The following is
generally regarded as the most ingenious of them all – the bullet
that took over 200 years to find its target.*

I n the calculation an allowance has to be made for the *Gregorian
Correction* of the calendar in 1752. Then it becomes apparent
that the time elapsed between the firing of that bullet and its
plunge into Westmacott's body was exactly two hundred and
twenty-two years, two months, one week, five days, twelve hours
and forty-seven minutes . . .

The duelling pistol from which it was shot was fired by Ensign
the Honourable Nigel Koffard. He was a young officer in one of
Marlborough's crack squadrons and had but recently homed to

England after the decisive bloodiness of Malplaquet. The man whom his shot wounded two hundred odd years after was Mr Henry Leonard Westmacott, a branch-cashier of the London and Southern Counties Bank, Limited.

Nigel Koffard pressed the trigger of that pistol, in the park of Ravenshaw Hall, Derbyshire, at precisely eight o'clock on the radiant morning of August the second, 1710.

Henry Westmacott was sitting by his own hearthside in the drawing-room of The Nook, Bettington Avenue, Thornton Heath, Surrey, when Koffard's bullet struck him and shattered his right shoulder. He had just settled down – on the dismal and rainy night of October the twenty-third, last year – intending to listen to a concert broadcast from the Queen's Hall. The ball hit him as the B.B.C. announcer was concluding an apology for the programme being late by saying: "It is now eight forty-seven, and we are taking you straight over—"

Thus was the second time most accurately determined.

All the day long, young Mrs Westmacott had been anxious about their little boy, Brian. He was running a slight temperature.

Hence she no sooner had dinner ended when she needs must go up to the nursery. In the swift way of tummy-troubled baby boys, Brian had contrived to lose his pains. He was sleeping serenely. Except for a slight flush and a dampness in his hair, he was normal.

Pamela Westmacott smiled ruefully as she smoothed his rucked sleeping suit and re-arranged his cot clothes . . .

The shot, the groan and the stumbling fall among the fireirons all sounded on that instant. With mechanical acumen Mrs Westmacott also noted that some china crashed to ruin in the kitchen, and that the opening chords of the Symphony Orchestra's performance were lost to a thud and a sudden silence.

She rushed down the stairs to collide with her maid-servant, who had burst with almost equal speed from her domain.

"Oh, ma'am! Wh-what in the name o' glory's happened?"

"Hush, Biddy, and stay there! I–I'll go in myself and see what's the matter."

Westmacott had raised himself to his knees and was delicately pawing at his right shoulder.

"Henry! Henry – darling!" Pamela Westmacott was down beside him. "What's gone wrong?" Then she saw the sodden red horror of his shoulder. "Oh, my poor old boy! . . . *Biddy* – phone

Doctor Smithers and the police. Tell them to hurry. Say it's serious: Mr Westmacott has been shot!"

When doctor and police arrived Westmacott had been got to bed. He was fully conscious and calm, despite his excruciating pain. His wife had managed him in a way that won Doctor Smithers' admiration. Her first-aid had stanched most of the bleeding.

Smithers turned to her with a smile as he unscrewed the nozzle of the syringe with which he had administered an opiate.

"Sensible woman, Mrs Westmacott! You made everything very easy . . . What's that? . . . *Dangerous?* Oh no, not at all! Direct compound fracture of the *scapula* socket and a flake chipped off the head of the *humerus*. Abominably painful, but that's about all."

Old Smithers patted her hands and definitely pressed her to the door. "Now run along and leave hubby to me. Go down and satisfy the curiosity of those exceedingly impatient policemen. Above all, don't – you – worry."

Pamela Westmacott went in to see Brian before returning to the drawing-room. He had slept through all the hubbub.

The police were certainly impatient. Their cross-examination had foundered poor Biddy. After their dismissal of her she had gone back to the kitchen to blubber among the neglected crockery.

In Mrs Westmacott was discovered harder and less hysterical material. She told them all she knew. Essentially because it tallied so exactly with Biddy's account, the officers became more and more confounded . . .

"But are you absolutely *sure*, Mrs Westmacott, no one came out of this room as you rushed down the stairs? Or slipped out by the front door without your seeing 'em?"

"Oh dear, how many more times must I tell you? *No!*" Wearily she smoothed her forehead. "Who could have done so?"

"Whoever fired that shot," grunted Inspector Ormesby, "there's no weapon to be found. The windows are all properly secured. There isn't any glass broken. Your husband wasn't potted at by someone lurking in the garden, that's self-evident. And he couldn't possibly have shot himself." The Inspector nodded toward the wireless cabinet which the bullet had struck. "The position of his wound and the subsequent flight of the missile settles *that* . . . Somebody shot him! Then who was it?"

A plain-clothes officer turned from his inspection of the

damaged cabinet. He had been pencilling notes referring to the tarnished ball of lead which showed itself, half embedded, in the seven-ply veneered woodwork. It had struck a spot directly in front of a valve, and the impact had been sufficient to shatter filaments, so stopping reception.

This man's talking was far less truculent than that of Inspector Ormesby. But it was deadlier.

"You've told us that the front door was locked for the night. Have I got that right – *hey*?"

"Yes; you have."

"I noticed that a little brass bolt is on the inner side of the door. Then there's the main lock and a Yale latch. All of 'em secured?"

"No. The key of the big lock wasn't turned, but the bolt was pushed home. Naturally the latch held as well."

"Had you to open those to let us in?"

"I had."

"Wasn't it natural for your maid to open that door? Why yourself?"

"Why not? Especially in – in such a crisis! As a matter of fact, Biddy was hopeless – helpless."

The plain-clothes man watched her through half-closed eyes.

"Now, you remember, you also told us that you came helter-skeltering down the stairs at such a rate that you bumped into this Bridget O'Hara woman at the bottom. And she'd just flown out of the kitchen – *hey*?"

"Perfectly correct. When the shot was fired, Biddy dropped a plate or something. Then she rushed here. We – we converged on the room like two mad things."

"No one went out of the door." It seemed that the plain-clothes man was musing aloud. "No one, so you say, went up the stairs past you. No one could have doubled out by way of the kitchen, and no one could have doubled out of here back into the dining-room or into the cupboard under the stairs, without you or your servant seeing 'em . . . *Um-m-m*!" He paused, and ignored Mrs Westmacott completely, to smile past her at Inspector Ormesby. "*And no weapon found*," he slowly murmured. "You carry on here, Inspector. Strikes me I'll have to have another heart-to-heart talk with our faithful Bridget – our exceptionally clever and faithful Bridget. Perfect treasure of a maid, I'll bet!"

Pamela Westmacott flinched as though a viper had reared itself before her eyes as she watched the inimical C.I.D. man saunter from the room. Mad as it seemed; horrible, fantastic and unreal as it was, nevertheless she realised she was the suspect here.

Now let interpolation be made of the somewhat astounding experience of an official police photographer, called Coghill.

A genial little fellow, Egbert Coghill; a craftsman of infinite patience and capability. He was the man who went to The Nook the next day and, acting on police instructions, set about securing photographs of the drawing-room and, more especially, the bullet-splintered radio-set.

Mr Coghill was highly gratified by all he saw. Plenty of light, artificial and otherwise; plenty of space, and most admirable contrasts of dark furnishings against pale matt walls.

Cheerily, with an incessant whispering whistle, he moved about and made himself quite at home. He dumped his big camera on a table. The black leather case, which contained his plates in their mahogany slides, he placed in front of the wireless cabinet. Still softly whistling, he pottered around, making his notes and selecting his objects and angles.

Thereafter he erected his camera and screened its peerless lens with a precisely-chosen colour-filter, designed to obtain for him the correct qualities and the infinitude of detail that the satisfaction of his craftsmanship demanded.

He made various long exposures. He took photographs of the door, the windows, the blood-stained rug, the untidy hearth, and the arm-chair in which Westmacott was sitting when he was wounded. After these, Coghill concentrated on his most important work. He removed his plate carrier from its place in front of the wireless set and focused on the half-embedded bullet and the starry matrix wherein it lay. He expended his remaining four plates on this.

When he came to the development of his material, Coghill was astonished and alarmed. Without exception, each dripping negative held – superimposed on its actual detail – a wee portrait of something that appeared to be an astronomical portrait view of the planet Saturn. These were ring-impounded orbs which had a quality of eerie brilliancy that had struck the plates with something amounting almost to halation. Yet they were mottled by shadows of an intensity and a delicacy Mr Egbert Coghill had never previously developed out of any sensitive emulsion.

*   *   *

More than this phenomena, the four exposures of the wireless cabinet were useless. These, which should have been Coghill's acme, not only bore the eerie imprint of the tiny incandescent "planet", but a great maelstrom of fog about the place where the bullet should have been. The cabinet was clear enough. Only that area which should have been occupied by a representation of the leaden slug was at fault.

Mr Coghill equipped himself with another camera and a new assortment of plates. Back he went to the drawing-room of The Nook. He duplicated his previous exposures and again developed them.

None of this second group of negatives showed the Saturn-like globe. Equally, none of the seven plates he had, secondarily, exposed on the cabinet front was in any better state than the former four. Except for the non-appearance of the queer orb, there were the identical coils of fogginess about the splintered woodwork – *and no sign of the bullet*.

Mr Egbert Coghill made a number of prints from all these negatives. Together with his notes and the plates themselves, he gave these into police keeping. This done, he fared forth and drank deeply.

Without much loss of time those photographs went, by way of Scotland Yard, to a Home Office department in Whitehall: to Barnabas Hildreth. He studied them and puzzled over them, as he afterwards told me, until he was sick to death of the very sight of them. Disgruntled and bewildered, Barnabas then went out to Thornton Heath and interviewed the Westmacotts.

The unfortunate Henry had nothing of much value to relate. He had been reading, he said, and had just put aside his evening paper to listen to the broadcast. As he leaned back in his chair, taking off his *pince-nez* and rubbing his closed eyes, he heard a curiously violent hissing as of air escaping from a pin-punctured tyre. Then there was a detonation and a fierily enormous blow at his shoulder. The next thing he realised was that he was wambling about the floor, suffering pain.

He scouted the idea that anyone could have been in the room with him without his knowledge. And on the subject of the police theory – that his wife had shot him and, in collusion with Bridget O'Hara, had thereafter established incontestable *alibi* – he was sardonically and sulphurously vehement. When he discovered

Hildreth so far agreed with him under that head as to veto further official brow-beating, Westmacott became a different man. He was so relieved, so pathetically relieved, that Hildreth was touched – actually was humanised sufficiently to accept an invitation to stay for tea!

So it came about that the grim Intelligence Service officer and Master Brian Westmacott became friends. Hildreth chuckled over this.

"There was no resisting the little beggar, Ingram. He's a sturdy kid and as sensible as the deuce. No sooner had I finished examining the drawing-room than he lugged me off to build what he called a 'weal twue king's palace' – from bits of wood; wood such as I've never seen a child playing with before. He had a big box full of sawn-up chair legs and rails; 'pillars' for his palace. And he'd scores of miniature arches and so forth – all shaped out of carved walnut and mahogany and oak and elm – little blocks, battens and angle-pieces that had originally been parts of furniture. One glance at 'em showed they were scores of years old and had come from the workshops of masters like Hepplewhite and Chippendale."

I sensed something of extraordinary import here.

"*Oh*, and where'd he got 'em from?"

"Out of the family woodshed. Or, at least, his father had." Hildreth grinned. "I looked it over – lots of the same stuff there. Y'see, Westmacott has a brother in the antique furniture trade: does restorations and repairs and so forth. Westmacott gets all the waste from his brother's workshops. The likely bits he cuts up to add to Brian's collection of blocks and pillars. The remainder is burnt.

"While I was in the drawing-room, old man" – he deliberately went off at a tangent – "I poked that bullet out of the wireless set and took a pair of callipers to it. It's a pistol ball right enough. But where in the name of glory did it come from? And, who cast it – *when*?"

" 'Who cast it?' " I echoed. "What, isn't it an ordinary revolver slug?"

"Mass-produced?" Barnabas rubbed his hands together in glee. "Not on your life! It's as big as a marble and perfectly spherical. And it has marks on it that only the closure of a beautifully accurate bullet-mould could have made. More than that. It's of an unusual calibre – one so unusual that it opens up a tremendous field of conjecture, yet, at the same time, defines the narrowest of tracks. A track, indeed, that a fool could follow."

Silently I watched the peculiar fellow twiddle about with his smoking cigarette. He was looking through its writhing spirals at me with a glitter of satanical humour in his dark eyes.

"Calibres of firearms," he softly stated, "are not little matters left to individual discretion, Ingram. They're registered and pedigreed better than bloodstock – at least, in this country. Ever since 1683 any armourer or gunsmith drilling a new size of bore has had to deposit a specimen barrel and exact measurements with the Tower authorities before he could fit it to a stock or sell or exploit it in any way.

"Remembering that, I asked for records to be searched. The answer is, that ball was cast to be shot out of only two particular types of weapons. It's of a size that's quite obsolete to-day. Either it could have been shot from a long gun, registered in London by Adolph Levoisier, of Strasbourg, in 1826, or out of a duelling pistol fashioned by Gregory Gannion, a gunsmith who had an establishment in Pall Mall between the years 1702 and 1754.

"The exact date of Gannion's application for a licence to put on the market a weapon of a new type and calibre which he called '*an excellently powerful small-arm, for the practise of the duel, or in other uses, for delicacy and swiftness of discharge in defence or offence*' . . . was February the ninth, 1709. And, according to all accounts, the bloodthirsty young bucks of that day went daffy about it. Y'see, it was the first 'hair-trigger' pistol on the market: ugly, but useful.

"I'm working up from that. I've a shrewd idea that good English lead wouldn't come out of a continental long-gun. *No*, a Gannion duelling pistol seems indicated."

I am getting ever more used to Barnabas Hildreth's tortuous tricks. The queerly precise ordination of those words, "good English lead", made me curious.

"How does one determine the nationality of – er – lead?" I suavely asked.

"All as easily as one differentiates between a Chinaman and a Zulu," he sourly grinned. "All as simply as one distinguishes Cleveland iron-ore from Castillian hæmatite; Poldruinn copper from Norwegian; Aberdeen granite from that of Messina – by looking at it first of all, ass, and studying it afterwards.

"According to the assay-notes, furnished me this morning, the lead from which that ball was cast came from one particular area of Derbyshire, *and nowhere else!* What's more, it's almost pure native stuff" – his face shone with some inner ecstatic light – "and, as it chances, so absolutely unique . . . that it's worth its weight, and more, in gold. In fact, if the fervours and excitements of the metallurgical chemists are anything to go by – and they're simply frazzling over it – it's the clue to a pretty fat fortune for someone!"

He got up then, and growling something about my hospitality and his thirst, calmly stalked across to my tantalus and mixed whisky and sodas. Then he challenged me across the brim of his glass.

"Well, old man, all the best! And here's to the speedy solution of one of the neatest mysteries I've struck for months."

So far as I recollect, it was two days later that Hildreth descended on me. He wanted me to go to Thornton Heath with him, and I went. We visited the premises occupied by Westmacott's brother Ralph – Westmacott and Company, Ltd.: "Antique Furniture Restored, Renovated, Repaired and Reproduced" – reproduced mainly, if my layman's eye had any common sense behind it.

Admittedly, Ralph Westmacott had certain specimen pieces in his workshops. These were the magnificent possessions of connoisseurs, to whom the factor of financial worth hardly counted. They were all undergoing tiny but incredibly painstaking forms of restoration, and guarded jealously for the treasures they were.

However, as Hildreth said, these were not our meat. Westmacott took us to the larger, general workshop. Here we saw really valuable, but ordinary, examples of olden furniture in the processes of repair and "faking".

"We pride ourselves," Westmacott told us, "on our ability to replace a faulty participle with a sound one, so meticulously reproduced and fitted – grafted on, one might say – that no one outside first-flight experts can detect the addition."

"That, of course, necessitates," smoothly came Hildreth's question, "your carrying an amazing stock of old cabinet-making woods, I presume?"

Westmacott looked curiously at my friend.

"*Aye*, amazing is the word," he laughed. "Come and have a look in here!"

He preceded us to a vast loft that was filled by racks and shelving – and all of them packed with broken parts of old-fashioned furniture.

"Here you are," he exulted, "from Tudor to Early Victorian;

from linenfold panelling to pollard-oak sideboard doors . . . gathered together from the auction rooms of half the globe. We couldn't carry on a day without 'em. Unless similar old stuff is used on replacement jobs—"

"Stuff like this, for instance," Hildreth interrupted to point at a great stack of dirty wood, looking to me like huge half-cylinders of amber-flecked bog oak: split tree trunks. "This lot seems to be pretty ancient."

Ralph Westmacott moved delicately to Hildreth's side.

"*Aye*," he concurred, "it's old enough! That wood's been buried in the earth for a century and more."

Brightly, blandly, almost with the alert cockiness of a schoolboy, Barnabas Hildreth replied:

"I don't doubt that for a moment, Mr Westmacott! They're elm-wood water conduits, aren't they? And, judging from their boggish appearance, they've come out of moorland or country where there's plenty of peat about."

Ralph Westmacott scratched his grizzled hair.

"Yes, they *are* conduits, and they certainly came out of peaty loam – from Derbyshire, as a matter of fact. We've men on the job up there now. They came from Ravensham Park, near a place called Battersby Brow . . . we bought the whole line of wooden water-pipes that used to serve the hall and the village. Finest tackle in the world for reproduction purposes."

Grimly enough Hildreth chuckled.

"What a game it is!" he drily stated. "Now, 'Battersby Brow,' in Derbyshire" – he was jotting down these particulars in a notebook – "and 'Ravensham Park,' you say?"

"Yes, that's all correct." Westmacott seemed puzzled.

"And this hall you mentioned? What d'you call it?"

"Ravensham Hall, the residence of General Sir Arthur Koffard, you know."

Hildreth put away his book and began to fumble among the blackened elm-wood. He pointed to one or two big fragments which lay about.

"Might I have a chunk to take away with me?" he inquired. "I want it for certain experiments that have to be made." Westmacott nodded. "And will you ratify this? Certain lumps of this wood that you knew would be useless for your work you gave to your brother Henry, didn't you?"

"I – I did! What's the—"

"That's right! I thought I recognised the stuff again. I saw some in his wood-shed." Hildreth smiled. "*Thanks!*"

With that we went away and back to London.

From the "Black Bull," at Battersby Brow in Derbyshire, a letter came to me on the twenty-ninth of October:

> My dear Ingram,
>
> If you can leave your mouldy rag to look after itself for the week-end, come over here and be interested. Of all the intricate bits of work I've ever struck, this is the trickiest! Don't let me down, old chap. I promise you a really noble *dénouement* for the mystery of the Westmacott bullet: an ending that, I suppose, you'll stick on one of your scandalous chronicles of my cases and complacently claim as your own.
>
> Sincerely,
> B. H.

So I set out for Battersby Brow and the "Black Bull" as soon as I put my paper to bed in the early hours of Friday, the thirty-first. At nine o'clock the next morning I was in a beautiful and brilliant country of whistling airs and mighty hills.

Over breakfast, Barnabas crowed mightily.

"Done a lot of work since I saw you, old man! Only one tiny coping-stone to be put on, and the job's complete.

"It *was* a Gannion duelling pistol that fired that ball. I've seen it. There's a pair of 'em, and they've been laid away in a case since seventeen hundred and ten . . . One was discharged. The other was loaded, but I got permission to draw the charge. I drew it right enough!" He chuckled. "D'you know, it was a curious experience. There I had in hand another ball, similar to the one that wounded Westmacott. And there were tiny tattered fragments of a news-paper that had been used for a wad between bullet and powder – an issue of the *Northern Intelligencer* for August the first, seventeen-ten.

"The Koffards of Ravensham Hall have been awfully decent about everything. At first they were inclined to be stand-offish, but when I told old General Koffard the story you know, he tucked into things like a good 'un."

"Sorry to butt in, Barnabas – but, tell me, what story *do* I know? It occurs to me that I've only a few strikingly dissimilar and baffling incidents in mind, all hazily mixed up with lead that's 'worth its weight in gold' and old elm logs which you proved had come from this district."

Hildreth finished eating and lit a cigarette.

"Listen, old man, and follow me carefully . . . Go back in thought to the night of the twenty-third. You have Westmacott sitting in his chair. A bullet, apparently fired out of the void, strikes his shoulder and is deflected into the wireless set. Point the first to be made: direction of bullet's flight proved it was shot from somewhere in the region of Westmacott's feet. Got that?" I surveyed the scene in mind . . . I had to agree. "Now for point the second. Had a ball of that size possessed a high velocity, it'd have made the dickens of a mess of the *humerus*. It'd have caused a comminuted fracture, and, without much doubt, it would have glanced across and gone through his throat.

"But no, it was a missile of low velocity – only a direct compound fracture of the *scapula* socket and a lazy glide off, to smack the front of the wireless set.

"No one can say where the ball came from. The ineffable Egbert Coghill goes to photograph it . . . He puts his platecarrier dead in front of the set, incidentally in front of the bullet. For fully a quarter of an hour he footles about, then, when he comes to take his photographs, he carries on each plate he afterwards exposes a portrait of the ball, transmitted by its own power through the leather case, through the whole clutter of his mahogany slides and, in fact, through everything within eighteen inches of the radio cabinet!"

I jumped at that.

"D'you mean those Saturn-like globes were—"

"Photographs of that ball! *Precisely!* It emitted a short, hard ray of far more intensity than the usual X-ray apparatus employs!"

"But how on earth could that come about?"

"*Pitch-blende*," said Barnabas Hildreth, "that's why! Apart from certain areas in Cornwall, only the Peak district of Derbyshire and some isolated caverns round about Ingleborough in Yorkshire have *pitch-blende* deposits. Usually, it's in association with lead that has a high silver content . . . The assay of that ball not only showed lead and silver, but definite traces of *pitch-blende* striations, all melted together.

"To clinch that part of the business, however" – Hildreth

glanced at the time – "remember that the second batch of Coghill's prints did *not* show the eerie little 'planet'. That was because he did not bung his plate-carrier in front of the set on his second venture. The active emissions were powerless outside a small range.

"But neither set of plates would betray anything except a fogginess where the bullet should have been. What could you reasonably expect?" Hildreth shrugged. "A long exposure, with powerful lens concentrating radium rays on a speedy photographic emulsion – nothing but fog *could* result!"

In the end I realised that Hildreth was right. Radio-active properties in that leaden slug would explain everything. Incidentally I caught the drift of what he meant when he spoke about the value of the bullet and its potentiality as the clue to a fortune.

"Do you mind" – Hildreth was on his feet and again looking at his watch – "if we hustle? We've a walk of a few miles if we're to get that coping-stone set, y'know. And I want it done to-day."

That long tramp across the sage-green acres of the Derbyshire countryside terminated in the park of Ravensham Hall. A group of navvies, excavating a snakish trench, paused in their work and watched us curiously. And, from out of a near-by hut, a podgy and bespectacled man clad in a white coat, and an old iron-haired fellow with a face of claret, came to greet us. One was a chemist called Sowerby and the elder man was Major-General Sir Arthur Koffard, the owner of the estate.

"Well, Sowerby," Hildreth briskly questioned when introductions were completed, "had any luck? Tried my little experiment – *eh*?"

Sowerby smiled unctuously and beckoned us back to the hut. In there, he pointed to a fire-clay retort that glowed above a fierce petrol-air lamp. Around the squat nozzle of the retort a big plume of intensely blue and brilliant flame was glowing. It made the popping sound of the burst of gorse-pods to August sun: an infinitesimal tattoo of whispering explosions.

"Yes, Mr Hildreth, your surmise was right enough. It's *methyl hydride*, without a doubt." He pointed to the halcyon fire. "Almost pure, to burn like that."

"Most 'strordinary – most 'strordinary thing," this was the crisp clacking of Koffard, "tha' one can live a lifetime, 'mong things like these, an' never know – never know. 'Course, this land's been full o' will-o'-th'-wisp lights for years, but one never stops to give 'em much thought – what?''

Barnabas abstractedly nodded and walked out. We followed him to the side of the trench. For a long while he studied the enormous hollow trunks that the navvies had dug out of the black and oozy earth.

"Magnificent trees," he muttered. "Veritable giants! Took some labour, I should say, to gouge their innards out!"

Then he turned to Koffard and asked him something about a map.

"Aye, I've got it here." The rattlevoiced old officer produced a tin cylinder and drew out of it a scroll inscribed by rusted lines of ink. "The avenue stood across there. Nigel Koffard fought his duel" – he pointed to a level sward forty yards away – "just on that patch. At the beginning of the avenue, exactly."

When we went to this place we could plainly see a series of little hummocks stretching, in parallel, for almost half a mile. It was explained to me that here had been a hundred and more elms making a great avenue that was felled in 1803 – under each knoll was a mighty stump. The trunks, hollowed out, had gone into the formation of that pipe-line (for conveying drinking water from a hillside spring) the navvies were excavating.

Hildreth stopped exactly on the spot on which one Nigel Koffard had taken his stance to fight a duel on the morning of August the second, 1710.

"Now Sir Arthur," Hildreth murmured, "let's work things out. Your ancestor challenged his cousin to a duel, primarily over the intentions of that cousin toward your ancestor's sister. When the affair came to its head, Nigel Koffard was fully determined to put a ball through his cousin. But that doughty lad, conscious of honour and innocence, did not so much as lift his own pistol. Refused, point-blank, to defend himself."

"Tha's right; quite right!" Koffard applauded. "He must ha' had guts, y'know – simply stood there. Completely broke Nigel's nerve."

"And the said Nigel," Hildreth grinned, "thereupon did a bit of quick thinking. It dawned on him that he had misjudged his man. So, to show his regret and to extend an olive branch, he turned and fired his bullet straight into the nearest elm. Whereupon the youngsters shook hands. The cousin got permission to marry

Nigel's fair sister, and the Gannion duelling pistols – one discharged and the other loaded – were put back in their case and guarded thereafter, for the sake of the episode, as family heirlooms. And everyone lived happily ever afterwards."

"Precisely, sir!" said General Koffard. "Admirably put, sir! B'gad quite neat, I say – *neat!*"

"Then, if that's so" – Hildreth was already on the move – "we'll trouble that invaluable plan of yours once again. Now we want to see this place called Skelter's Pot, where lead was mined in those days."

. . . We tramped a full mile up a mountainous slope and were eventually rewarded by the view of a bite into a pinkish face of spar, which the old map told us was "Skelter's Pot."

"Out of here," Sir Arthur Koffard told us, "came all the lead used hereabouts. The hall is roofed by it. That pistol-ball was certainly cast from it. But it doesn't pay to work it now."

Hildreth took a geologist's hammer from his pocket and knocked away at a piece of semi-translucent quartz in which dull grey patches showed and on which strangely green filaments were netted.

"I would like," he softly returned as he put this specimen away, "to own your roof! At a modest estimate, it'll be worth more than the hall and this estate put together."

"Now, you see, old chap" – Hildreth tapped the rough pencil sketch he had made – "this was the way of it." I leaned across the table, and under the steady oil-lamp light of the old Black Bull, I looked at the drawing. "Here we've all we need."

I smoked my pipe and wondered.

"When Nigel Koffard shot that ball, at closest range, into the living elm-tree it made a deep cavity, a tunnel, in which it stopped. In a few more years a 'rind-gall' was formed. The elm closed over the wound in its structure by a growth of annular rings. The cylindrical little tunnel remained and the ball remained, precisely as they were.

"Then our elm showed signs of what is called 'doatiness' – incipient decay. It, together with all the others in the avenue, was felled, hollowed out, and used for an aqueduct. Y'see, old man, elm is the *one* wood which never changes if kept constantly wet. They've actually dug Roman elm-wood conduits out of the middle of Piccadilly, as sound as the day on which they were laid. . . .

"This is a queer countryside, Ingram. And the elm is a queer tree. Get those facts in mind.

"That chamber which held the bullet also held the gases of the elm's former disruption, and to these were added those similar gases which lurk in peaty land. 'Similar,' did I say? *Identical* would be a better word. . . . You heard old Koffard talk about marsh-gas; natural gas, that is. . . . Well, that's what we're considering. You saw that chemist fellow, Sowerby, with a retort full of elm-wood burning such gas at the mouth of the apparatus.

"*Methyl-hydride; methane; carburetted-hydrogen* – call it what you will, and still you're right – is marsh-gas. Also it's the dreaded and terribly explosive thing which miners call *fire-damp* . . . when mixed with air.

"You see it burning away in every fireside in the land. It's the illuminating property of coal. And it *always* results when bodies of a peaty, woody or coaly constituent are subjected to great heat."

I began to have an inkling of what Hildreth was getting at.

"However, to the mechanics of the situation." He laughed and drank some beer. "Ralph Westmacott, the furniture man, buys some old weathered elm-wood from Derbyshire in order to fake his manufactures. What he has to spare – useless – he gives, as usual, to his brother, Henry Leonard. Our good Henry Leonard diligently saws it up into chunks and fills the family woodshed.

"Now comes a rainy and dismal October night. Henry puts a log on the open-hearth fire, extends his slippered feet and prepares to enjoy the evening.

"But the wild mystery of the ever-burgeoning earth comes into the simple household of The Nook and claims him. . . . He hears a violent hiss. That was air rushing into the vascular tissue of that hot elm-log, combining with the incredible chemistry of Nature with the terrible potential of that hydro-carbon, *methane, in the hollow where the bullet lay concealed.*

"Nigel Koffard's powder had not half the fulminating property, in the steel barrel of his pistol, that *fire-damp* had in the smooth wound of the elm-log . . . Pressure increased, since the hollow was filling every second with more and more gas, and air was in combination with it. At last, the hungry fire, eating away the inner face of the log, reached the terribly explosive mixture. Then *bang*, up and outwards shot the ball into Henry's shoulder.

"So we're back at our beginning – the very first point I made: that the ball was fired from somewhere about Westmacott's feet.

I recalled flying fragments of coal and co-related things . . . allowing, always, for the unusual.

"But, instead of coal and cinders, the well of the grate was filled with half-burned fragments of wood – like fragments of furniture, surmounted by a big tricorne hunk of charred elm-wood. I wondered, vastly, about those fragments. Then, when I saw the little boy, Brian, playing with his home-made building blocks, I was definitely set on the second line which led me to solution."

He picked up his tankard and smiled.

"That green network you saw on the surface of that spar *was* pitch-blende! I'm told it's more than usually rich in radium and uranium salts.

"The land on which Skelter's Pot is situated belongs to the Commissioners. It's an open common land. Anyone procuring the necessary faculty, and entering into serious negotiations, can mine it . . . So, with the joyous approval of Mr Henry Leonard Westmacott, I have entered my innocent ally Master Brian's name on our list—"

" 'Our list'?" I was puzzled by his most deliberate pause. "What list?"

"Oh, the little company I'm forming: myself, yourself, Koffard, Westmacott and young Brian, to exploit the pitch-blende deposits of our property in Skelter's Pot, Derbyshire." He laughed and stretched his long arms. "It ought to provide for us in our old age, if nothing else!"

. . . Judging by my latest returns from that adroitly-contrived concern, I am inclined, stoutly, to agree.

THE 45 STEPS

Peter Crowther

Here's another brand new story. It was written for the last locked-room anthology I compiled but arrived too late for me to squeeze in. I was thus delighted to find that the story was still available as it includes one of the most audacious methods of murder I have yet encountered – and in the smallest locked room of them all. Peter Crowther (b. 1949) is a highly respected author, editor and publisher primarily of science fiction and fantasy, but of all things unusual. He runs PS Publishing which has won many awards, and which includes books by Brian Aldiss, Ray Bradbury, Michael Swanwick and Ramsey Campbell. Amongst Peter's own books are Escardy Gap *(1996) with James Lovegrove and* Songs of Leaving *(2004) with Edward Miller, as well as the fascinating anthology sequence that began with* Narrow Houses *(1992). Several of Peter's stories have common settings and amongst those is the northern town of Luddersedge, which will one day coalesce into another book. In the meantime, we can peer into part of the town's strange life in the following disquieting tale.*

To say that hotels in Luddersedge were thin on the ground was an understatement of gargantuan proportions. Although there were countless guest houses, particularly along Honeydew Lane beside the notorious Bentley's Tannery – whose ever-present noxious fumes seemed to be unnoticed by the guests – the Regal was the only full-blown hotel, and the only building other than the old town hall to stretch above the slate roofs of Luddersedge and scratch a sky oblivious to, and entirely disinterested in, its existence.

The corridors of the Regal were lined with threadbare carpets, hemmed in by walls bearing a testimonial trinity of mildew, graffiti and spilled alcohol, and topped by ceilings whose anaglypta was peeling at the corners and whose streaky paint-covering had been dimmed long ago by cigarette smoke. The rooms themselves boasted little in the way of the creature comforts offered by the Regal's big-town contemporaries in Halifax and Burnley.

For most of the year, the Regal's register – if such a thing were ever filled in, which it rarely was – boasted only couples by the name of Smith or Jones, and the catering staff had little to prepare other than the fabled Full English Breakfast – truly the most obscenely mountainous start-of-the-day plate of food outside of Dublin. Indeed, questions were frequently asked in bread-shop or bus-stop queues and around the beer-slopped pub tables at the Working Men's Club, as to exactly how the Regal kept going.

But there were far too many other things to occupy the attention and interest of Luddersedge's townsfolk and, anyway, most of them recognized the important social part played by the Regal in the lives of their not-so-distant cousins living in the towns a few miles down the road in either direction. Not that awkward questions were not asked about other situations in which the Regal played a key role, one of which came to pass on a Saturday night in early December on the occasion of the Conservative Club's Christmas Party, and which involved the one hotel feature that was truly magnificent – the Gentlemen's toilet situated in the basement beneath the ballroom.

To call such a sprawling display of elegance and creative indulgence a loo or a bog – or even a john or a head, to use the slang vernacular popular with the occasional Americans who visited the Calder Valley in the 1950s, the heyday of Luddersedge's long-forgotten twinning with the mid-west town of Forest Plains – was tantamount to heresy.

A row of shoulder-height marble urinals – complete with side panels that effectively rendered invisible anyone of modest height who happened to be availing themselves of their facility – was completed by a series of carefully angled glass panel splashguards set in aluminium side grips and a standing area inlaid with a mosaic of tiny slate and Yorkshire stone squares and rectangles of a multitude of colours. It was an area worn smooth by generations of men temporarily intent on emptying bladders filled with an excess of John Smith's, Old Peculiar and Black Sheep bitter ales served in the bars above.

Two wide steps down from the urinals was a row of generously sized washbasins, set back and mounted on ornate embellishments of curlicued brass fashioned to resemble a confusion of vines interlinked with snakes. They nested beneath individual facing panels split one-half mirror and the other reinforced glass, the glass halves looking through onto an identical set of basins on the other side of the partition, behind which stood the WCs.

It was these wood-panelled floor-to-ceiling enclosed retreats – with their individual light switches, oak toilet seats and covers, matching tissue dispensers, and stained glass backings behind the pipe leading from the overhead cistern – that were, perhaps, the room's crowning glory. They were even more impressive than the worn leather sofas and wing-backed chairs situated on their own dais at the far end of the toilet, book-ended by towering aspidistras and serviced by standing silver ashtrays and glass-topped tables bearing the latest issues of popular men's magazines.

But while these extravagant rooms – albeit small rooms, designed for but one purpose – had rightly gained some considerable fame (particularly as the town was not noted for anything even approaching artistic or historical significance) they had also achieved a certain notoriety that was not always welcome.

Such notoriety came not merely from the time, in the late 1940s, when an exceptionally inebriated Jack Walker pitched forward rather unexpectedly – after failing to register the aforementioned double step leading to the urinals – and smashed his head into one of the glass-panelled splashguards. Nor did it come from that legendary night when Pete Dickinson was ceremoniously divested of all of his clothes on his stag night and reduced to escaping the Regal, staggering drunkenly through Luddersedge's cold spring streets, wearing only one of the toilet's continuous hand towels (those being the days before automatic hand dryers, of course), a 50-foot ribbon of linen that gave the quickly sobering Dickinson the appearance of a cross between Julius Caesar and Boris Karloff's mummy.

Rather, the toilet's somewhat dubious reputation stemmed solely from the fact that, over the years, its lavish cubicles had seen a stream of Luddersedge's finest and most virile young men venturing into their narrow enclosures with their latest female conquests for a little session of hi-jinks where, their minds (and, all too often, their prowess and sexual longevity) clouded by the effects of ale, a surfeit of testosterone and the threat of being discovered, they would perform loveless couplings to the muted strains of whatever music drifted down from the floor above.

The practice was known, in the less salubrious circles of Calder Valley drinking establishments, as "The Forty Five Steps Club". The name referred, in a version of the similar "honorary" appellation afforded those who carried out the same act on an in-flight aeroplane ("The Mile High Club"), to the toilet's distance below ground – three perilously steep banks of fifteen steps leading down from the ballroom's west entrance.

And so it was that, at precisely 10 o'clock on the fateful night of the Conservative Club's Christmas Party, it was to this bastion of opulence and renown that Arthur Clark retired midway through a plate of turkey, new potatoes, broccoli and carrots (having already seen off several pints of John Smith's, an entire bowl of dry roasted peanuts and the Regal's obligatory prawn cocktail first course) to evacuate both bladder and bowel. It was a clockwork thing with Arthur and, no matter where he was or whom he was with, he would leave whatever was going on to void himself – on this occasion, all the better to concentrate his full attention and gastric juices on the promised (though some might say "threatened") Christmas Pudding and rum sauce plus a couple of coffees and a few glasses of Bells whisky. Arthur's slightly weaving departure from the ballroom, its back end filled with a series of long dining tables leaving the area immediately in front of the stage free for the inevitable dancing that would follow coffee and liqueurs, was to be the last time that his fellow guests saw him alive.

"Edna. *Edna!*" Betty Thorndike was leaning across the table trying to get Edna Clark's attention, while one of the Merkinson twins – Betty thought it was Hilda but she couldn't be sure, they both looked so alike – returned to her seat and dropped her handbag onto the floor beside her. Hilda – if it was Hilda – had been to the toilet more than fifteen minutes ago, while everyone else was still eating, her having bolted her food down in record time, and had spent the time since her return talking to Agnes Olroyd, as though she didn't want to come back and join them: they were a funny pair, the Merkinsons.

When Edna turned around, from listening – disinterestedly – to John and Mary Tullen's conversation about conservatories with Barbara Ashley and her husband, she was frowning.

"What?"

"He's been a long time, hasn't he," Betty said across the table, nodding to the watch on her wrist. "Your Arthur."

"He's had a lot," Edna said with a shrug. The disc jockey on the stage put on Glen Campbell's *Wichita Lineman*.

"Oh, I love this, me," Mary Tullen announced to the table, droopy-eyed, and promptly began trying to join in with the words, cigarette smoke drifting out of her partially open mouth.

"You've been a long time, Hilda," said her sister Harriet, pushing her plate forward. Hilda noted that the food had been shuffled around on the plate but not much had been eaten.

"Been talking to Agnes Olroyd."

"So I saw."

"She was asking me about the robbery," Hilda said.

"Robbery? I thought you said nothing had been taken."

Hilda shrugged. "Robbery, break-in – it's all the same thing."

Hilda worked at the animal testing facility out on Aldershot Road where, two days earlier, she had come into work to discover someone had broken in during the night – animal rights protesters, her boss Ian Arbutt had told the police – and trashed the place.

Not wanting to talk about the break-in again – it having been a source of conversation everywhere in the town the past 36 hours, particularly in the Merkinson twins' small two-up, two-down in Belmont Drive – Hilda's sister said, "How's her Eric?"

Hilda made a face. "His prostate's not so good," she said.

"Oh." Harriet's attention seemed more concentrated on Edna Clark.

As Mary elbowed her husband in the stomach, prising his attention away from a young woman returning to a nearby table with breasts that looked like they had been inflated, Betty Thorndike said to Edna, "D'you think he's all right?"

Edna said, "He's fine. He always goes at this time. Regular as clockwork. Doesn't matter where he is." This last revelation was accompanied by a slight shake of her head that seemed to convey both amazement and despair.

"I know," Mary Tullen agreed. "It's common knowledge, your Arthur's regularity."

"But he's been a long time." Betty nodded to Arthur's unfinished meal. "And he hasn't even finished his dinner."

"He'll finish it when he gets back," Edna said with assurance.

Behind her, somebody said, "There's no bloody paper down there."

Hilda Merkinson knocked her glass over and a thin veil of lager spilled across the table and onto her sister's lap. "Hilda! For goodness sake."

"Damn it," Hilda said.

Edna threw a spare serviette across the table and turned around. Billy Roberts was sliding into his seat on the next table.

Sitting across from Billy, Jack Hanlon burst into a loud laugh. "You didn't use your hands again, did you, Billy? You'll never sell any meat on Monday – smell'll be there for days."

Billy smiled broadly and held his hand out beneath his friend's nose. Jack pulled back so quickly he nearly upturned his chair. He took a drink of Old Peculiar, swallowed and shook a B&H out of a pack lying on the table. "If you must know," Billy said, lighting the cigarette and blowing a thick cloud up towards the ceiling, "I used my hanky." He made a play of reaching into his pocket. "But I washed it out, see—" And he pretended to throw something across the table to his friend. This time, gravity took its toll and Jack went over backwards into the aisle.

As Jack got to his feet and righted his chair, Billy said, "I flushed it, didn't I, daft bugger. But I was worried for a few minutes when I saw there wasn't any paper – course, by that time, I'd done the deed. They need to check the bloody things more regular." He blew out more smoke.

"Aren't you going to tell somebody, Billy?" Helen Simpson asked, her eyes sparkling as they took in Billy Roberts's quiffed hair.

"Can't be arsed," Billy said. "There's some poor sod down there now – probably still down there: he'll have something to say about it when he gets out," he added as he did a quick glance at the entrance to see if he could see anybody returning who looked either a little sheepish or blazing with annoyance.

"That'll be Arthur." Edna looked over her shoulder at Betty. "I bet that's my Arthur," she said. She tapped Billy on the shoulder. "That'll be my Arthur," she said again.

"What's that, Mrs Clark?" Billy said, turning. "What's your Arthur gone and done now?"

"He went to the toilet ages ago. Billy says there might not be any paper. There'll be hell to pay if there isn't."

Harriet Merkinson shuffled around in her handbag, produced a thick bundle of Kleenex and she held them out. "Here, why don't you take him these?"

Edna nodded. "Thanks, er—"

"Harriet," said Harriet.

"Thanks, Harry – good idea." She passed the tissues back to Billy and gave a big smile. "Here, be an angel, Billy and go back down and push these under the door for me."

"You haven't been down to the gents, have you, Mrs Clark?" There was a snigger at the last part from Jack Hanlon. "You can't get sod all under them doors."

"Well, can't you knock on his door or something?" She nodded to the table behind her. "He hasn't even finished his meal."

Hilda looked across at Arthur's plate and noted that it didn't look much different to her sister's – the only difference was that one meal was finished with and the other wasn't.

When he got back to the toilet, Billy saw one of the young waiters about to go into each cubicle to fasten a new roll of tissue into the dispenser. "Somebody tell you, did they? Was it Arthur Clark?"

The boy shook his head, his cheeks colouring. "It was some bloke, don't know what he's called," the waiter said, shifting his weight from one foot to the other. "Said he'd come down and a lot of the—" The boy paused, searching for the word.

"Traps?" Billy ventured.

The boy smiled. "Said a lot of the traps didn't have no paper."

"When was that?" Billy asked.

"Well, when he was down here, I suppose," he said, frowning and holding up an armful of toilet rolls. "I just said—"

"No, when was it this other bloke mentioned about there been no paper."

"Oh," the boy gasped. "I see." He frowned and chewed his lip. "A while back. I had to get the key to the stock cupboard first and I was still collecting dishes."

Outside the entrance to the toilet there was a sudden burst of high-pitched giggling. "There's a bloody waiter in there!" a girl's voice said. Billy chuckled. Presumably only the waiter's presence was preventing the girl from coming into the gents with her partner and not the fact that the toilet area was filled with men, young and old, either standing at the urinals or washing at the basins. Alcohol was a wonderful thing and no denying.

The chuckling continued and was complemented by the sound

of feet hurriedly ascending the 45 steps back to the ballroom. A man Billy didn't know wafted through the doors, unzipping his flies and grinning like a Cheshire cat.

Billy exchanged nods with the man and turned his attention back to the waiter. He was still smiling – until he saw that the door to the cubicle which had been occupied while he was down here was still firmly closed.

"Has somebody just gone in there? I mean, while you've been down here."

The boy glanced at the closed door and shook his head. "Not while I've been down here."

Billy looked down at the Kleenex in his hand and felt the waiter look down at them at the same time. He jammed them into his jacket pocket, walked across and tapped gently on the door. "Hello?"

There was no response.

"He'll be sleeping it off, lad, whoever he is," a stocky bald man confided to Billy as he held his hands under the automatic drier. "You'll need to knock louder than that."

Billy nodded slowly. He rapped the door three times and said, "Mister Clark – are you in there? We've got toilet paper out here if you've run out."

No answer.

The bald man finished his hands off on the back of his trousers and moved across so that he was standing alongside Billy. Although he was short, a good six inches shorter than Billy and three or four beneath the lofty height of the young waiter, the bald man had a commanding air about him. The waiter shuffled to one side to give the man more room.

The bald man hit the door several times with a closed fist and shouted, "Come on, mate, time to get up. You'll be needing a hammer and chisel if you stay in there much longer, never mind bloody toilet paper."

Still no answer.

"He must be a bloody heavy sleeper," Billy said. "Either that or he's pissed as a newt."

The bald man turned to the waiter. "Is there any way into these things? I mean, some way of getting in when they're locked."

"I don't know," the waiter said.

"Well, can you find somebody who does know? And can you do it bloody sharpish?"

The waiter turned around and ran to the door and disappeared, his clumping feet echoing up the steps to the ballroom.

The man lifted his hands and felt around the door. "Do you know this bloke, whoever he is?"

Billy shook his head. "No. Well, I do; I know his name and that, but I don't really know him. His wife asked me to come down."

The man nodded. "Why was that, then?" he said, turning around.

"Well, there's no paper in any of the toilets."

"How did his wife know that?"

"She heard me telling them on my table. I'd just got back from, you know—"

"Having a crap, I know, get on with it lad."

Billy straightened his shoulders. He would usually square up to anyone who spoke to him like that – after all, he wasn't a lad: he was almost 25 – but there was something about the bald man that made him shrink back from confrontation. "That trap was closed when I came down here and it was still closed when I went back up."

The bald man reached into his inside pocket and removed a packet of Marlboro. While lighting a cigarette he said to Billy, "Did you hear anything while you were down here?"

Billy shrugged. "Like what?"

The man blew smoke out. "Groans, plops, farts, throwing up – the usual."

"No; no, I didn't."

The man nodded. He hammered on the door again, louder this time. "What did you say his name was?"

"Arthur Clark."

"Not the bloke who wrote *2001*, I suppose? I loved that picture."

"I don't think so," Billy said with a chuckle.

"No, me neither." He hammered again. "Mister Clark, if you can hear me, open the door. It's the police."

Billy was watching the door but when he heard that he turned to the man. "Are you really the police? I mean, are you a, a copper?"

Before the man could answer, the waiter came back into the toilet. He was trailing behind a tall man with bushy eyebrows that met over his nose. His face, which was scowling, was a mask of excess, folds of skin lined with broken blood vessels. He said, "What's going on?"

"Who are you?" the bald man asked.

"Sidney Poke. I'm the manager of the Regal."

The bald man nodded. "Any way into these things when they're locked on the inside?"

Sidney Poke said, "Who are you?"

The bald man jammed his cigarette in the corner of his mouth, pulled a credit-card holder from his inside pocket and shuffled through the little plastic flaps. He found what he was looking for and held it out for inspection. "Detective Inspector Malcolm Broadhurst, Halifax CID," he said.

"What's the problem, Inspector?" Sidney Poke said, his manner suddenly less aggressive.

"Somebody's in there and we can't get them to open the door. Been there a while, this lad says," Malcolm Broadhurst said nodding at Billy Roberts.

"Who is it? Who's in there?" Sidney Poke asked Billy.

"Never mind who he is," the policeman said. "How do we bloody well get in to him?"

Sidney Poke shrugged. "I suppose we have to knock the door down."

Malcolm Broadhurst nodded. "Why did I know you were going to say that? Right—" He threw his cigarette on the floor and ground it with his foot. "One of you go upstairs and call for an ambulance – just to be on the safe side."

A blond-haired man said, "I'll do it," and disappeared at a run out of the toilet.

The policeman took hold of Billy's left arm and squeezed the biceps. "What do you do for a living, lad?"

"I'm a butcher."

"Just the job," he said, and he stepped back out of the way. "Right, break that bloody door down – and, daft as it sounds, try not to go mad: he could be on the floor at the other side."

As he squared up to the door, Billy said, "How the hell do I do that? Knock the door down but go steady, I mean."

"Just do your best. Now, you others stand back and give him room."

The door jamb splintered on the sixth try. It came away on the eighth, still fastened but only loosely.

"Brilliant job, lad," Broadhurst said taking Billy's arm. He pulled him back and stepped close to the door, squinting through the small gap that had appeared. "It's still fastened, but only just."

He stepped back and frowned. "No time to bugger about looking for something to prise it open. If the fella couldn't hear all that din then he's in a bad way." He stepped back and nodded to Billy. "Break it down, lad."

Billy pulled himself back onto his left foot and hit the door with all his strength. The lock snapped and they heard something – a screw, maybe, or part of the actual lock – clatter inside the cubicle. The door stopped against something on the floor.

Malcolm Broadhurst pushed Billy out of the way and, holding the door, squeezed his way into the cubicle. When he was inside, the policeman closed the door again.

They heard shuffling.

"Is he all right?" Sidney Poke asked. Billy thought it was a pretty stupid question.

For a few seconds there was no answer and then the policeman said, "He's dead." Then, after a few seconds more of shuffling sounds and sounds of exertion, he said, "Bloody hell fire."

Billy said, "What is it?"

When the door opened again the policeman was rubbing his face, looking down at the floor.

Billy and Sidney Poke and the young waiter – whose name was Chris and for whom this was his first night working at the Regal – followed Malcolm Broadhurst's stare.

Arthur Clark was now sitting up against the side wall of the cubicle, the toilet paper dispenser – containing almost a full roll of paper – just above and to the side of his left ear. He was fully clothed but his shirt had been ripped apart at the stomach. Worse than that, the man's flesh looked to have been flayed, with thick red welts and deep gashes covering the skin, and the top of his light grey trousers seemed to have been dyed black around the waistband: but they knew the original colour had been a deep red.

Chris the waiter gagged and turned away, his hand clamped over his mouth as he made for the washbasins. He made it just in time. When he was through, he leaned his head on his hand to one side of the basin and, in a surprised voice, said, "Hey, that's where they were."

The boy crouched down and reached his hands to the deep metal basket on the floor between his basin and the one next to it. When he stood up he was holding an armful of toilet rolls, some full and still thick and some partly used.

"Bloody idiots," said Sidney Poke. "Do anything for a laugh but they wouldn't think it was so damned fun—"

"Get everyone out, Mister Poke," the policeman said. His voice sounded tired. "Get everyone back upstairs. But not you, butcher boy," he said, turning to Billy. "You can give me a hand getting him out of here."

The toilet was completely empty when they finally struggled out with Arthur Clark and laid him on the floor beside the washbasins.

"He looks like he's been got at by a wild animal," Billy said. "And scared to death, by the look on his face."

The policeman shook two Marlboros from his pack and handed one to Billy. "Give it up tomorrow," he said as he held his lighter under Billy's cigarette.

Billy drew in the smoke and watched the bald man crouch down by the body. He turned over Arthur Clark's hands one by one and said, "He was the wild animal. He did it to himself. See—" He held one of the hands up for Billy to see. The nails were caked with blood and skin – they looked like the hands of a butcher.

"Why? What did he think he was doing, do you think?"

"Looks to me like he was trying to get into his own stomach."

"Arthur?" a woman's voice shouted from outside the toilet door.

Then a man's voice said, "You can't go in there, madam."

"Arthur!" the woman's voice screamed.

There was a crash outside the door that sounded unquestionably like someone falling over.

"Shit," said Detective Inspector Malcolm Broadhurst.

The ambulance arrived with siren wailing but it left silently.

Malcolm Broadhurst sat with Edna Clark for a long time, initially with Betty Thorndike, Joan Cardew and Miriam Barrett by her side, offering consolation in the undoubtedly heartfelt but seemingly sycophantic way that people have when they feel *there but for the grace of God*. To the policeman from Halifax CID, the trio was doing more harm than good and he sent them packing. "Like the bloody witches from *Hamlet*," he said to Billy Roberts over at the bar, ordering a couple of stiff Jamesons from Sidney Poke, who had assumed bar duties for the duration.

The rest of the guests and all the staff had given their names to a couple of uniformed officers from Halifax and had gone home.

"*Macbeth*," Sidney Poke said quietly.

Billy looked up from his Irish frowning. He would have been happier with a pint but the policeman had ordered. "What?"

"The three witches. It was *Macbeth*, not *Hamlet*."

"Oh."

"And what about Bill and Ben? That was a turn-up for the books."

"Who's Bill and Ben?"

"Oh, the Merkinsons. The two old women."

"Oh, the one who collapsed."

Billy nodded. "And her sister."

"Which one of them was it who collapsed?"

Billy shrugged. "You can never tell. They both always look the same – dress the same, talk the same; it's really weird."

The two "old" women, as Billy Roberts had called them, were 53 years old. Malcolm Broadhurst wouldn't have been far out with his own estimate of 50–51. The same age, give or take a year – he always forgot his own age but he knew he'd had his fiftieth because of the stripper they'd bought for him down at the station – and he didn't consider himself as old. But then again, maybe he was. "Twins, are they?" he said.

Billy nodded.

Broadhurst had noticed them, standing by while he was talking to Edna Clark, because they were identically dressed, right down to the two-string necklace of fake pearls hanging over the first half-inch of their maroon dresses. One of them was looking after the other, the one who had collapsed, feeding her sips of brandy brought over by Sidney Poke.

"Like a couple of weirdos," Billy Roberts said, remembering the scene in vivid detail. "Funny though, her keeling over like that."

Now it was the policeman's turn to nod. "She the Hilda Merkinson who works at the animal rights centre? The one that was done in this week?"

Billy frowned. "Don't know. But she's the only Hilda Merkinson in Luddersedge."

"Cheers!" said Malcolm Broadhurst. He lifted his glass and drained it, then set it back on the bar top. "How much do I owe you?" he said to the Regal's manager.

Poke shook his head. "On the house. Think I'll have one myself."

It was one o'clock.

"What was it, d'you think?" Billy asked. He lit a B&H from the packet he'd retrieved from the table and offered it to the other two. Poke waved a hand and the policeman simply produced his Marlboros and took one out.

"We'll know when the autopsy boys know," Broadhurst said

around a cloud of smoke. "His missus says he didn't have a bad heart or anything, but it's either that or something he ate."

"I thought that," Billy offered, and then wished he hadn't when he caught the glare from the Regal's manager.

"Or drunk," Broadhurst said. "I've had his meal wrapped up for tests, along with the pint he was working his way through."

"Fancy," Billy said, more to himself than to the others, "getting up for a crap halfway through your meal."

"His missus says he does it regular as clockwork," Broadhurst said.

"That's right," Billy said. "Doesn't matter where he is or who he's with. Come ten o'clock he has to disappear to do the deed. It's legendary around town – everybody knows."

"Another?" Poke said, holding the bottle of Jamesons over the policeman's glass.

Broadhurst frowned over the answer to that and other questions that were already forming in his mind.

It was almost two o'clock when Broadhurst made his way from the ballroom and along the corridor towards reception. At the steps leading down to the Gentlemen's toilet he paused. The steps were well lit but only in stages, the main house lights of the hotel having been dimmed an hour earlier. Now only single bulbs, secured behind half shells equally spaced down the flights, lit the steps leaving a well of darkness at the bottom.

The darkness seemed inviting and off-putting, both at the same time.

The policeman shook a cigarette from his packet, lit it and breathed smoke around him. It felt good . . . felt normal somehow. For there was a lot about what had happened that was not normal.

Before he even realized he was moving, Broadhurst had reached the landing at the foot of the first flight, his hand on the rail and his eyes squinting into the gloom. He took the next two flights two steps at a time but when he reached the bottom, with the ornate doors leading into the toilet right in front of him, he stopped and listened.

What was he listening for, he wondered. Was he listening for the sounds of Arthur Clark, screaming in agony? For didn't some folks say that no sound ever died but only grew faint, waiting to be heard once more by those with the most finely tuned sense of hearing? No, it was something more than that; something more than the late-night campfire thoughts of ghoulies and ghosties and things that went *phrrp!* in the night.

He threw his cigarette stub to the floor and stepped on it hard, pushing open the doors and stepping inside.

The toilet was silent. There was no sound save for the distant chuckle of water moving through ancient pipes, turning over in radiators and cisterns, and *dlup dlupping* down drain holes.

He looked around.

Someone else had been in here, someone who knew more about Arthur's tragic death than he did. A lot more. Broadhurst felt it – felt it in his water, he thought, cringing at the unintentional pun. The death was neither natural nor unintentional. But he couldn't understand how it could be anything else.

He walked along the row of cubicles, their doors either fully open or ajar, and felt a sense of threat, as though someone was going to step out of them, perhaps someone recently dead come to exact his revenge, or someone who knew more about the death, come to prevent being caught. Broadhurst stepped away from the line of cubicles and stopped, staring at the open doors.

What was he thinking of? How could the death be anything other than natural? The cubicle walls went from floor to ceiling, the door the same . . . save for barely an inch of space top and bottom – certainly far less than would be required to get into the cubicle if the door were locked from the inside. And, of course, the same went for getting out again when the deed was done.

"What deed?" Broadhurst said softly. There was no answer, just a giggle of water over by the sofa at the far end of the room.

He leaned on one of the basins and continued to look around. He moved from the basin, reluctantly turning his back on the cubicles until he was reassured by their reflection in the mirror over the basin in front of him, and looked some more. *What are you looking for, Kojak?* a small voice whispered in the back of his head, using the name granted to him long ago by his colleagues in Halifax CID. *It's an open and shit case, seems to me*, it added with what might have been a wry chuckle.

"Funny!" Broadhurst snapped, and he looked along the basin-tops, down to the floor and then along beneath them. There was a basket beside each one.

Hey, that's where they were.

The young waiter's voice sounded clear as a bell in his head. Broadhurst could half see him, stooping down to lift an armful of toilet rolls.

Then Sidney Poke's voice chimed in. *Bloody idiots . . . Do anything for a laugh.*

Broadhurst frowned.

The ghost of Billy's voice said, *That's right, doesn't matter where he is or who he's with. Come ten o'clock he has to disappear to do the deed. It's legendary around town – everybody knows.*

Broadhurst turned around to face the cubicles—

everybody knows

– and walked slowly towards them, his back straightening as they came nearer. He started at one end and walked slowly, pushing open each door and staring at the empty tissue holder—

Hey, that's where they were

– attached to the wall of each cubicle, right next to where an arm would be resting on a straining knee, where so many arms had rested on so many straining knees—

It's legendary around town

– until he reached—

everybody knows

– a cubicle with toilet paper. *The* cubicle.

He stared down at the now empty floor and closed his eyes. He saw Arthur Clark writhing in agony, crying out for help; so much pain that he could not simply unlock the cubicle door and crawl for help.

Broadhurst removed his handkerchief from his pocket and, stepping into the cubicle, wrapped it around the toilet roll.

Seconds later he was going up the steps away from the Regal's Gentlemen's toilet, two steps at a time; and wishing he could move faster.

Sundays in Luddersedge are traditionally quiet affairs but the events of the previous evening at the Conservative Club's Christmas Party had permeated the town the same way smoke from an overcooked meal fills a kitchen.

In the tiny houses that lined the old cobbled streets of the town, over cereals and toast and bacon butties, and around tables festooned with open newspapers – primarily copies of the *News of the World*, the *Sunday Mirror* and the *Sunday Sport* – voices were discussing Arthur Clark's unexpected demise in hushed almost reverent tones.

Conversations such as this one:

"I'll bet it was his heart," Miriam Barrett said from her position at the gas stove in the small kitchen in 14 Montgomery Street.

Her husband, Leonard grunted over the *Mirror*'s sports pages. "Edna said not," he mumbled. "Said he hadn't had no heart problems."

Miriam was unconvinced as she fried her bacon and sausages, and a few pieces of tomato that looked like sizzling blood-clots. "All that business with his – *toilet*," she said, imbuing the word with a strange Calder Valley mysticism that might be more at home whispered in the *gris gris* atmosphere of a New Orleans speakeasy. "Can't have been right."

Leonard said, "He was just regular, that's all."

"Yes, well, there's regular and there's *regular*," Miriam pointed out sagely. "But having to go in the middle of your meal like that, just 'cos it's ten o'clock, well, that's not regular."

Leonard frowned. He wondered just what it was if it wasn't regular, but decided against pursuing the point.

But not everyone in Luddersedge was talking.

In his bedroom over his father's butcher's shop at the corner of Lemon Road and Coronation Drive, Billy Roberts opened his eyes and stared at the watery sun glowing behind his closed curtains. His mouth was a mixture of kettle fur and sandpaper and using it to speak was the very last thing on his mind. It was all he could do to groan, and even then the sound of it sounded strange to him, like it wasn't coming from him at all but maybe drifting from beneath the bed where something crouched, something big and unpleasant, waiting to see his foot appear in front of it.

Billy turned to his side and breathed deeply into his cupped hand. Then he stuck his nose into the opening in his hand and sniffed. The smell was sour and vaguely alcoholic, almost perfumed. He slumped back onto the pillows. It was those bloody whiskies that did it. He should have stuck to the beer, the way he usually did. It didn't do to go mixing drinks.

Billy had had a bad night, even after all the booze. He supposed there was nothing like messing around with a dead body – particularly one that had smelt the way Arthur Clark's had done, Arthur having so recently dumped into his trousers – to sober a person up. It had taken Billy more than an hour to drop off after getting in – despite the fact that it was three in the morning – and even then his dreams had been peppered with Arthur's face . . . and the man's ravaged stomach.

*   *   *

Work had been underway in the ballroom of the less than palatial Regal Hotel for several hours when Billy Roberts was beginning to contemplate getting out of bed.

The wreckage was far worse than usual somehow, even though the festivities had been cut short by the tragic events in the gentlemen's toilet. But at least most of the explosive streamers were still intact and there were fewer stains than usual on the cloths and the chairs. The most surprising thing was the number of personal possessions that had been left in the cloakroom, particularly considering the very careful population of the town. But then the unceremonious way the guests had been dispatched for home after been questioned made a lot of things understandable.

Chris Hackett had arrived after the clear-up had begun, clocking into the ancient machine mounted on the green tiled wall leading to the Regal's back door at 7.13. He didn't think anyone would object to the fact that he was almost quarter of an hour late, not after last night. He set to straight away, throwing his yellow and blue bubble jacket onto one of the chest freezers in the kitchen and emerging through the swing doors into the ballroom. It was a hive of activity.

Elsewhere, various men and women were dismantling trestle tables, creating a mound of jumbled tablecloths, loading glasses and bottles and plates and cutlery onto rickety wooden trolleys, the sound of their labours dwarfed by the sound of similar items being loaded into the huge dishwashers in the kitchens.

Wondering where he should start, Chris Hackett saw a table that had been untouched, over by the far wall. He went across to it, moving around to the wall side to begin stacking the plates. Halfway along the wall he caught his foot on something and went sprawling onto the floor, knocking over two chairs on the way.

Somebody laughed and their was a faint burst of applause as Chris got to his feet and looked around for the culprit of his embarrassment.

It was a lady's handbag.

Malcolm Broadhurst sat smoking a cigarette. He had been up since before dawn, having snatched a couple of hours' fitful nap lying fully clothed on the eiderdown; unable to settle to anything, his mind full of the previous evening.

The call came through at a little after ten o'clock.

A man's voice said, "You up?"

"Yeah."

"Been to bed?"

Broadhurst grunted. "Didn't sleep though."

"Well, you were right not to," the voice said. "We've been on this all night – well, all morning would be more accurate."

"And?"

"We've not finished yet but we've got a pretty good idea."

The voice with the "pretty good idea" belonged to Jim Garnett, the doctor in charge of forensic science at Halifax Infirmary and who doubled as the medical guru for Halifax CID. He chuckled. "It's a goodie. You were right to be suspicious."

The policeman shook another cigarette from his packet and settled himself against the bed headboard. "Go on."

"Okay. Two hours ago, I'd've been calling you to tell you he'd had a heart attack."

"And he didn't."

"Well, that's not exactly true: he did have a cardiac arrest, but it wasn't brought on by natural causes." Garnett paused and Broadhurst could hear the doctor shifting papers around. "What made me a little more cautious than usual – apart from your telephone call last night – was the list of symptoms, all classical."

Broadhurst didn't speak but it was as though the doctor had read the question in his mind.

"There were too many. Profuse salivation—"

"Profuse – is that like, there was a lot of it?"

"You could say that," came the reply. "The poor chap's shirt was soaked and he'd bitten through the back left side of his tongue; he'd vomited, messed his pants – diarrhoea: most unpleasant – and there were numerous contusions to the head, arms and legs."

"Suggesting what?"

"The contusions?" Garnett smacked his lips. "Dizziness, auditory and visual disturbances, blurred vision, that kind of thing – and not what you'd want to experience when you're stuck in a WC. It's my bet he shambled about in there like a ping-pong ball, bouncing off every wall. And, of course, the pain would have been nothing to what he was having from his stomach – that's why he'd clawed at himself so much. By then, he'd be having seizures – hence the tongue – and he'd be faint."

"Why didn't he just come out, shout for help?"

"Disorientation would be my guess. And panic. He'd be in a terrible state at this point, Mal."

Broadhurst waited. "And?"

"And then he died. I've seen cases before – cardiac arrests – with two or three of the same symptoms, but never so many together . . . and never so intense. This chap suffered hell in his final minutes."

Garnett sighed before continuing. "So, we checked him out for all the usual bacteria – saliva, urine, stool samples; and there were plenty of those, right down to his ankles – and—"

"So he hadn't even been to the toilet?"

"No, he *had* been. His large bowel was empty. This stuff came as the result of a sudden stimulation to the gut and that would release contents further up the bowel passage. Anyway, like I said, we checked everything but it was no go. Then I checked the meal – bland but harmless – and the beer . . . nothing there either."

Garnett moved away from the phone to cough. "God, and now I think I'm coming down with a cold."

"Take the rest of the day off."

"Thanks!" He cleared his throat and went on. "So, in absolute desperation, we started checking him for needle marks: thought he might be using something and that was why he always went to the toilet so regularly. But there was nothing, skin completely unbroken. And then . . ."

"Ah, is this the good bit?"

"Yes, indeedy – and this is the good bit."

Broadhurst could sense the doctor leaning further into the phone, preparing to deliver the *coup de grâce*.

"Then we turned him over and we found the rash."

"The *rash*? All that and a rash too?"

"On his backside, across his cheeks and up into the anus. A nasty little bastard, blotches turning to pustules even five hours after he died. At first I thought maybe it was thrush but it was too extreme for that. So we took a swab and tested it."

The pause was theatrical in its duration. "*And* . . . go on, Jim, for God's sake," Broadhurst snapped around a cloud of smoke.

"Nicotine poisoning."

The policeman's heart sank. For this he had allowed himself to get excited? "*Nicotine* poisoning?" he said in exasperation. "Nicotine, as in *cigarettes*?" He glanced down at the chaos of crumpled brown stubs in the ashtray next to him on the bed.

Garnett grunted proudly. "Nicotine as in around eight million cigarettes smoked in the space of one drag."

"What?"

"That was what killed him – not the heart attack, though that delivered the final blow – nicotine: one of the most lethal poisons known to man."

"And how did he get it, if it wasn't in the drink or in the meal, and it wasn't injected? And assuming he didn't smoke eight million cigarettes while he was sitting contemplating."

Garnett cleared his throat. "He got it in the arse, Mal, though God only knows how."

Broadhurst glanced across at the solitary toilet roll sitting on his chest of drawers. "I know, too," he said. "But the 'why', that's the puzzler."

"And the 'who'?"

"Yeah, that too."

Edna Clark sat at her kitchen table, her hands wrapped around a mug of steaming tea. Sitting across from her was Betty Thorndike.

When the knock came on the front door, Betty said, "You stay put, love – I'll get it."

Hilda Merkinson had been in every room in the house but her sister was nowhere to be found.

Worse still, she couldn't find her handbag.

"Harry?" She had already shouted her sister's name a dozen times but, in the absence of a more useful course of action, she shouted it again. The silence seemed to mock her.

Hilda knew why Harriet had gone out. She had gone out to clear her head, maybe to have a weep by herself. No problem. She would get over it. It might take a bit of time, but she would get over it – of that, Hilda was convinced.

They had lived together, Hilda and Harriet Merkinson, in the same house for all of their 53 years; just the two of them since their mother had died in 1992.

They had a routine, a routine that Hilda did not want to see altered in any way. It was a safe routine, a routine of eating together, cleaning together, watching the TV together, and occasionally slipping along to The Three Pennies public house for a couple of life-affirming medicinal glasses of Guinness stout. It was a routine of going to bed and kissing each other goodnight on the upstairs landing and of waking each morning and kissing each other hello, again in the same spot; a routine broken only by Harriet's job in Jack Wilson's General store, and Hilda's work at the animal testing facility on Aldershot Road, where she'd been for almost seven years. The same length of time that Harriet had worked.

During that time, the routine had persevered.

It had been all and its disappearance was unthinkable.

Not that there hadn't been times when things looked a little shaky, namely the times when Ian Arbutt had cornered Hilda in the small back room against the photocopier and sworn his affection – despite Ian's wife, Judith, and his two children. But basically, Ian's affection had been for Hilda's body and Hilda had recognized this pretty quickly into the relationship – if you could call the clumsy gropes and speedy ejaculations performed by her boss on the back room carpet a relationship.

Hilda had had to think of how to put an end to it – thus maintaining her and Harriet's beloved routine – while not having it affect her position at the testing centre.

The solution had been simple, if a little Machiavellian. She had sent an anonymous letter to Judith Arbutt saying she should keep a tighter rein on her husband. "I'm not mentioning any names," the carefully worded (and written) letter had continued, "but there are some folks around town who think your Ian's affections might be being misplaced." Hilda had liked that last bit.

A very anxious and contrite Ian had suggested to Hilda, on the next occasion that they were both alone in the centre, that he felt he wasn't being fair to her. "Trifling with her affections" is what Hilda imagined he was wanting to say but Ian's pharmacological expertise did not extend to the poetic. "I hope you're not leading up to suggesting I look for other work," Hilda had said, feigning annoyance, brow furrowed, "because that would mean something along the lines of sexual harassment, wouldn't it?"

The answer had been emphatic and positive. "A job for life", is how he worded it. "You're here for as long as you want to be here, Hilda," he said. And he had been true to his word, at least Hilda could give him that.

No, Hilda would have nothing come between her and her sister. They were all either of them had and their separation was something she could not contemplate. She had thought that Harriet felt the same way.

And then came the fateful day, almost a week ago – was it really only a week? it seemed so much longer – that had threatened to change all that.

Every Thursday, without fail, Harriet always walked along to the fish-and-chip shop on the green – Thursday being Jack Wilson's early closing day – and had the tea all ready for Hilda when she got in. But on this particular Thursday, following four days of solid rain, when Hilda – a little earlier than usual because Ian also had flooding and wanted to get off – had gone past the General Store, she had seen Harriet helping Jack with moving boxes around due to the leakage through the front windows. He had asked her to stay back and give him a hand, and Harriet couldn't refuse, despite her other "commitments".

"We'll just have some sandwiches," Harriet had shouted through the locked door of Jack's shop, looking terribly flustered. "You just put your feet up and I'll make them when I get in," she added.

Hilda had nodded. Then she had gone home, put the kettle on and, at the usual time Harriet always left the house en route for the fish and chips, Hilda had embarked into the darkness on the very same journey. Imagine her surprise when, from behind the big oak tree on the green, a shadowy figure leapt out, grabbed her by the shoulders and planted a big kiss on her mouth.

It was Arthur Clark.

"Thought you weren't coming," Arthur had announced to a bewildered Hilda. "Been here bloody ages," he had added. "Edna'll be getting ideas – mind you," Arthur had confided, "it won't matter soon. Must dash." Then he had given her another kiss and had scurried across the green bound for home, calling over his shoulder, "See you on Saturday anyway, at the Christmas do."

Hilda had stood and watched the figure disappear into the darkness, and she was so flabbergasted that she almost forgot all about the fish and chips and went home empty-handed. But already she was thinking that that would not do. That would not do at all.

The "meeting" had given her advance knowledge of a potential threat to the beloved routine. And by the time she was leaving the fat-smelling warmth of the shop, Hilda had hatched a plan.

She knew all about poisons from Ian's explanations, long-drawn-out monologues that, despite their monotony, had registered in Hilda's mind. Which was fortunate. She knew about nicotine, and about the way it was lethal and produced symptoms not unlike heart failure.

Getting a small supply would not be a problem. There were constant threats against the centre – notably from animal rights groups based out in the wilderness of Hebden Bridge and Todmorden – so a small break-in, during which most of the contents of the centre could be strewn around and trashed, was an easy thing to arrange . . . particularly after administering a small dose of sleeping tablets to her sister, who obligingly nodded off in front of the TV.

Hilda scooted along Luddersedge's late night streets, let herself in with her own key – thanking God that he had seen fit to make Ian make her a joint key-holder with him – did what she considered to be an appropriate amount of damage, and removed a small amount of nicotine from the glass jar in Ian's office cabinet, to which, again, she had a key. She left the cabinet untouched by "the vandals" who had destroyed the office. Then, after resetting the alarm, she had smashed in the windows with a large stick and returned home.

It wasn't until she was almost back at the house that she heard the siren. She had smiled then – it had been long enough for whoever had broken in to do all the damage and escape without challenge. The night air had smelled good then, good and alive with . . . not so much possibilities but with continuance. Back in the warmth, she had settled herself down in front of the TV and, after about half an hour, had dropped off herself. The icing on the cake had been the fact that it was Hilda's sister who woke *Hilda* up. A wonderful alibi, even though none would be needed.

Two days later, on the night of the Conservative Club's Christmas Party, Hilda had bolted her meal and – though she knew she was risking things – had gone to the toilet at ten minutes to ten (Arthur Clark's toilet habits being legendary). Once out of the ballroom, she had run down to the Gentlemen's toilet, removed the tissue rolls from all but one WC, and had treated the first few sheets of the remaining roll with the special bottle in her handbag. It was four minutes to ten when she had finished.

She had arrived back in the ballroom at 9:58 just in time to see Arthur get up from the table and set off for his date with his maker. She had not been able to go straight back and was grateful for Agnes Olroyd catching her to talk about the break-in and about her Eric's prostate. By the time they had finished talking, Hilda's composure was fully restored and she was able to rejoin the table.

And now Harriet was nowhere to be seen. But that could wait.

The main thing as far as Hilda was concerned was to find her bag.

And she had a good idea as to where it was.

* * *

Harriet's revelations had hit Edna Clark harder even than her husband's death less than twelve hours earlier.

In Edna's kitchen, with the sun washing through the window that looked out onto the back garden and with steam gently wafting from the freshly boiled kettle, Edna sat at the table feeling she had suddenly lost far more than her life partner: now she had lost her life itself. Everything she had believed in had been quickly and surely trounced by the blubbering Harriet Merkinson when she burst through the front door, ran along the hall – pursued by a confused Betty Thorndike – and emerged in the kitchen, tears streaming down her face. And now Edna's 27 years with Arthur lay before her in tatters; every conversation, every endearment whispered to her in the private darkness of the their bedroom, every meal she had prepared and every holiday snapshot they had taken.

While Harriet continued sniffling and Betty simply stood leaning against the kitchen cabinets (installed by Arthur, Edna recalled, one laughter-filled weekend in the early 1980s), her eyes seemingly permanently raised in a mask of disbelief, Edna looked around at the once-familiar ephemera and bric-a-brac of a life that now seemed completely alien. These were things from another life – another *person's* life – and nothing to do with Edna Clark, newly bereaved widow of one Arthur Clark, late of this parish.

The story had been a familiar one. Even as Harriet Merkinson had been burbling it out – the clandestine meetings, the whispered affections, the promise of a new life once Arthur had built up the nerve to leave his wife – Edna felt that she had heard it all before . . . or read it in a book someplace, maybe even watched it on television. The Arthur revealed by Harriet was not the Arthur she remembered, save for one thing: his toilet habits. At least something was constant in her husband's two lives.

And now, while Edna's mind raced and backtracked and questioned and attempted – in the strange and endearing way of minds – to rationalize and make palatable the revelations, the "other" woman continued to burble a litany of regret and sorrow and pleas for absolution and forgiveness.

"I can't forgive you," Edna said at last, her words cutting through the thick atmosphere like a knife through cheese. "Never," she added with grim finality. "I can understand, because I know these things do happen, but I can never forgive you. You haven't taken only my husband's memory, you've completely removed my entire life."

It was the most articulate statement Edna had ever made, and the most articulate she would ever make in what remained of her life. Of course, she would come to terms with what had happened, but she would never get over it.

"Edna, Edna, Edna, Ed—"

"Now get out," Edna said, cutting Harriet's ramble off mid-word. Her voice was quieter now, more composed, gentle even. There was no animosity, no aggression, no threats of retribution: just a tiredness and, the still silent Betty was amazed to see, a new-found strength that was almost majesterial. "I never want to speak with you again."

Minutes later, Betty and Edna heard the distant click of the front door latch closing. It sounded for all the world like the closing of a tomb door or the first scattering of soil on a recently lowered coffin. Edna leaned forward and placed her face in her hands, and she began to sob, quietly and uncontrollably.

While Malcolm Broadhurst was greeting the two uniformed policemen on the steps of the Regal's ornate front door, two things were happening, both of them personally involving the Merkinson twins.

For Harriet, the routine so cherished by her sister had been a chore. More than that, it had been the bane of her life.

Harriet had long wanted to get out of the repetitive drudgery of the existence she shared with Hilda, and Arthur Clark – dear, sweet Arthur, with his strange toilet habits – had been her ticket to salvation. Love was a new experience to Harriet: for that matter, she did not know – not truly, down in those regions of the heart and the soul where such things reside – whether she really loved Arthur, for she had never experienced such feelings, even as a teenager and a young woman. But she did see in him the means whereby she could attain a new life, a life of relative importance. "Harriet and Arthur", "Arthur and Harriet" – she couldn't decide which she preferred, but she preferred either to "The Merkinson twins" or "Hilda and Harriet".

As she fished out the old clothesline from the kitchen cupboard, taking care to replace the various bottles and cartons of disinfectant and packets of soap powder, she felt a calmness come over her. Arthur's death had effectively removed her last chance for salvation, and she had been destitute. But now, thanks to the clothesline, she saw a solution. It wasn't the one she would have preferred but it was now the only one available. The only game in town. She could neither face life with Hilda nor life without the constant frisson of excitement she got prior to meeting Arthur, and she certainly could not face the comments and whispers around town when she walked down the high street or around the green. No, this way was best for all concerned. It was best for Edna – who might at least derive a little satisfaction when she heard – and it was best for Hilda, who would have to put up with her own share of her sister's shame.

She climbed the stairs wearily and attached one end of the clothesline to the upstairs banister rail. Then, after ensuring that the line's drop was sufficiently short to do the job, she fashioned a noose of sorts and slipped it over her head. With one final look around the landing she climbed over the rail and sat on the banister, staring down at the floor far below. As she jumped, in that fleeting but seemingly endless second or two before the line pulled taut without her feet ever touching the hall floor, she wondered where Hilda was . . . and what she would say when she came home.

"You've got something for forensics?"

Broadhurst nodded. "It's inside. I didn't want to be seen with it outside."

They started to walk.

"I came up last Wednesday," Malcolm Broadhurst explained to the two uniforms. "To check into the break-in down at the animal testing centre."

"Oh, yeah?" one of the policemen observed. His name was James Proctor and he had perfected that same aggressive and questioning response to even the most innocent facts or snippets of information, seeming to require confirmation or substantiation to anything said to him.

"Yeah," Broadhurst confirmed. They were now walking up the Regal's steps and approaching the wide, oak-panelled revolving door. "Your Inspector Mishkin asked me up because there were a few things he wasn't too happy about. I take it you two aren't working on that case?"

"We didn't know it was a case," the second policeman said as they emerged from the revolving door into the hotel's reception area. He said the word "case" with a heavy-handed touch of sarcasm. "Thought it was just a simple break-in."

"Yes, well," Broadhurst continued. "That's the way it looked, and Inspector Mishkin and I decided to keep it that way until things made a little more sense."

"And have they now?" the second policeman asked.

Broadhurst hit the bell on the reception desk.

"Look at it this way," the policeman said, turning from the desk and looking the two uniforms in the eye. "Whoever broke in through the window managed to trash the place and then place all the broken glass on top of the wrecked office." He nodded, smiling. "That's a pretty good trick, don't you think?"

"So—"

"So," Broadhurst continued, watching the main staircase as a young man appeared and started down, "the 'vandal' clearly had access to the centre and wanted to cover up the fact that they had been there. Now that reason could be simply a matter of their wanting to fight the animal testing, kind of like a fifth columnist, or it could be another reason. I think we now have that reason – although the reason itself must have a reason – and that's what I now bloody well intend to find out."

"Yes, sir?" the young man said as he reached the bottom of the stairs and approached the three men at the desk. "Sorry to keep you waiting."

"Is Mister Poke around?" Broadhurst asked. "I gave him something to look after for me."

The man nodded and moved around the desk. "I'll give him a call, sir," he said.

As Harriet Merkinson was swinging gently from side to side in the hallway of the house she shared with her sister, Hilda Merkinson slipped quietly into the back door of the Regal.

"Hello, Miss Merkinson," Sidney Poke said. His tone was quite reverential, a tone he would use when speaking with anyone who had been at the previous evening's party, and particularly those who had been closely involved with the tragic death of Arthur Clark.

Hilda nodded. "I wondered," she said, "if you had found anything this morning. When you were cleaning up, I mean."

Sidney frowned attentively. "Have you—" The ring of his mobile phone interrupted him. "Excuse me just a minute," he said, pulling his phone from his side pocket. He pressed a button and said, "Yes?"

Hilda looked around as Poke listened on the phone.

"Right," he said. "I'll get it and bring it through." He waited another few seconds and then said, "Very well, I'll meet them on the way."

"Now," Poke said as he returned the phone to his pocket. "Where we were? Ah yes, have you lost something?"

They started walking slowly through the ballroom, which was now cleared. Tables were folded and leaning against the far wall; chairs were stacked in towering piles in front of the stage; and an army of young men and woman were busy with vacuum cleaners, criss-crossing the floor, their attention fixed on the carpet.

"My handbag," Hilda shouted above the drone of the cleaners. "I think I must have left it last night." Poke nodded and looked around absently. "In all the excitement," Hilda added, suddenly wondering if "excitement" were the correct word to use under the circumstances.

"Ah!" Sidney Poke motioned Hilda towards a small occasional table set up by the door leading out to the toilets. The table contained a few jackets plus an assortment of bags.

"All those were left last night?" Hilda said in astonishment.

Poke gave an approximation of a laugh sounding more like a snort. "No, these belong to the cleaners," he said, "but your bag – if you did leave it, and if it has been found – is most likely here as anywhere."

As they reached the table, Hilda saw her bag. Her heart rose – or surfaced . . . or whatever it was that hearts did that was the opposite to sinking – and she reached out for it, careful not to appear too anxious. "That's it," she said triumphantly.

She picked up the bag and unfastened the sneck. She removed her purse, noting with grim satisfaction that the small bottle was still there, nestled in the bottom amongst Kleenex tissues, lipstick, comb and all the other rudiments of a woman's handbag, and flipped it open. "There," she announced, proudly displaying her library card, "just to show it's mine."

Hilda replaced the card and dropped the purse back into the depths of the handbag. Fastening the sneck, she said, "Well, I'll get off then."

Sidney Poke nodded. He took her arm and gently led her towards the main door that went on to the toilets and out to the reception area.

"How are you today? I mean, how are you feeling?"

Hilda made a face. "Oh," she said, "you mean after—"

Poke nodded with the quietly attentive air of an undertaker.

"It was my sister. It was Harriet who collapsed. Not me."

"Ah." He pushed open the door and ushered her through ahead of him. "Well, I'll leave you here, if that's okay, Miss Merkinson." Poke stopped at a desk in a small recess and shuffled in his pocket. He produced a set of keys and set about opening the desk's deep drawer. "We're running a little behind, what with – you know."

Hilda nodded, watching Poke reach around into the drawer.

Somewhere far off, but coming closer, she could hear footsteps.

"Ah, here it is," Poke grunted. "Must have pushed it further back than I thought." His back to Hilda, Poke pulled out a small bundle and closed the drawer.

The footsteps were getting closer. Hilda tried to ignore the yawning staircase on her right, the fabled 45 steps that led down to the Gentlemen's toilets. Deep in her mind, the footsteps belonged to Arthur Clark as he descended less than 12 hours earlier to empty his bowel and meet his end . . . except they seemed to be coming towards her rather than away from her. She shook her head and turned back to see the Hotel manager holding a toilet roll enclosed in a polythene bag.

"Right then," Poke was saying, though his words sounded like rushing water in Hilda's ears. Rushing water and footsteps, now getting very close – echoing – as though there were more than just Arthur coming back.

Poke moved the bag from one hand to the other as he returned the keys to his pocket. Hilda frowned at the bag, looked at Poke, smiled awkwardly, and turned around to face the toilet steps, half expecting to see Arthur climbing up to see her, to ask her why she had done what she had done, and bringing other people with him, friends of his, friends who – *wanted toilet paper* . . .

– wanted to talk to her and smooth her troubled brow with grave-cold hands. She turned sharply, took a couple of steps in the direction of the reception area and then stopped. There were figures approaching, figures making footstep-sounds. Her initial relief at discovering that the footsteps didn't belong to her sister's fancy man quickly evaporated when Malcolm Broadhurst called out to her.

"Ah, one of the Misses Merkinson." Broadhurst's tone was cheery. There were two policemen with him. "Now which one are you?"

Hilda started to speak and then, clutching her bag tightly, she spun around. Behind her, Sidney Poke was still standing by the doors leading into the ballroom, the toilet roll in his hand.

"Miss Merkinson?"

Hilda looked all around, clutching the bag even tighter, willing it to disappear . . . willing it to be a week earlier, willing there to have been no rain so that Jack Wilson's General Store had not been flooded and Harriet had not had to stay and so Hilda had not gone for the fish and chips and so met Arthur who believed that she was her own sister . . . willing herself, back seven years ago, not to take the job at the animal testing centre . . . so many things. So many opportunities for her to have avoided this single instant.

But it was too late.

The footsteps were growing louder and slightly faster, moving towards her along the polished floor.

"Miss Merkinson?"

Then it all became clear.

She could escape through the toilets somehow. Escape and find Harriet and they could run off together, start a new routine . . . just the two of them.

She turned and almost leapt forward.

The piece of slanted ceiling that descended with the steps stayed straight for a second or two and then tilted.

Just as she was wondering why that was, Hilda hit her head on the side railing. She felt something warm on her cheek, spun around, and smashed her shin on one of the steps. For a second, amidst the confusion and the pain, she thought she could see a figure standing at the foot of the 45 steps, a figure patiently waiting for her to come down. She heard a crack.

Hilda slipped backwards and to the side somehow, hitting the back of her head on another step before turning over fully and ramming her face into one of the rail supports. More warmth . . .

And then blackness.

Another step broke her nose and her pelvis, another her third and fourth ribs – sending a splinter of bone into her left lung and scraping a sliver of tissue away from the second and third ventricles of her heart.

Two more steps fractured her skull, broke her left collarbone and smashed the base of her spine. The final step on the first flight sent another piece of rib through her heart.

She rolled onto the first landing and then proceeded down the second flight. And then onto the third.

*   *   *

It was Betty Thorndike who found Harriet.

She had called around on her way back from Edna Clark's house, just to see if Harriet was all right. Of course, she wasn't.

By Monday afternoon, it was all over bar the shouting. And as far as Malcolm Broadhurst was concerned, there would be little of that. He had been to see Edna Clark on the Sunday afternoon, with both of the Merkinson sisters lying on metal trays in the cold and strangely-smelling basement of Halifax General.

In the silent loneliness of Edna's kitchen, the widow had told him everything that Harriet had told her. Broadhurst put the rest of it together himself.

He had spoken with his boss at Halifax CID and they had agreed between the two of them that there was little to be achieved by releasing all of the gory details. They decided that Hilda had been a keen promoter of animal rights, using her position at the centre to obtain vital information of the testing Ian Arbutt was carrying out – hence the break-in.

Harriet, meanwhile, had been unable to come to terms with her sister's death and had hanged herself. Only a slight discrepancy in timing suggested that such might not be the case and nobody would hear about that discrepancy. Now the two of them were united again . . . in whatever routine they could arrange.

Edna Clark cried when the policeman explained what he had organized. It meant that her life had been partially restored. To all intents and purposes, she was still the grieving widow of a fine and upstanding member of the Luddersedge community. Betty Thorndike, who had not said anything to anyone about Harriet Merkinson's revelations – and had had no intention of doing so – consoled Edna and assured her that everything was all right.

"He was a good man," Edna whispered into her friend's shoulder. "Deep down," she added.

"I know he was, love," Betty agreed. "They all are – deep down."

Driving back to Halifax late afternoon on Monday, there was just one thing that niggled Malcolm Broadhurst. He could not understand why Ian Arbutt had seemed somehow relieved – albeit momentarily – when he was told of Hilda's unfortunate accident.

But the policeman did not believe Arbutt was in any way involved in either the break-in or Arthur Clark's murder. There was another story there, somewhere, as, of course, there always is.

Contrary to the Evidence

Douglas Newton

Douglas Newton (1885–1951) was a prolific writer of books, articles and stories for well over forty years. He achieved a certain fame when his novel War *(1914), which pretty much predicted and depicted the First World War, appeared a few months before the real War broke out. He did it all again with* The North Afire *(1914), which looked at the future conflict in Northern Ireland. A journalist by profession, Newton was selected to accompany the future Edward VIII on his tour of Canada just after the War and wrote about it in* Westward with the Prince of Wales *(1920). Newton was immensely prolific, so much so that despite having some fifty books published, that represents scarcely a tenth of his total output for magazines during the 1920s and 1930s. One such series that never made it into book-form featured Paul Toft, an investigator who served as an unofficial consultant for the police, but who acted on intuition and instinct rather than hard facts and deduction. The series ran in* Pearson's Magazine *during the mid-1930s and includes the following ingenious and near perfect crime.*

We sat in the room where old Stanley Park had died so suddenly that morning. As the witnesses unfolded the story, even Paul Toft seemed to grow a mere huddle of sharp knees and elbows in his arm-chair, while Inspector Grimes became a bouncing mass of irritation as he realised that he had been dragged out to Friars' Vale on the mere reasonless suspicions of a headstrong young woman. The local police sergeant and I sympathised with him.

This was no crime, but a sheer waste of time.

Gerald Park was perfectly frank about the part he had played in the tragedy of his uncle's death.

He had come out from Stripe to old Stanley Park to borrow money. He hadn't had much hope of getting it, he admitted, because there was bad blood between him and his uncle – who had kicked him out of this very house for stealing, less than a month ago. He was so desperately hard up, however, he had had to make the try.

He had come out by train to Friars' Vale Halt and had taken a taxi from there. He had timed himself to arrive about 10.30, because that was the time his uncle always read his papers in this sitting-room. He let himself in with the door-key he had kept when his uncle had turned him out. He did that because he knew that if he rang, Mrs Ferris, his uncle's housekeeper and only servant, would not let him in. It would have been more than her place was worth, seeing how his uncle had come to hate him.

Anyhow, his idea was to slip in quietly, getting into his uncle's presence before anything could intervene. But "springing" himself on the old man like that had proved to be a horrible mistake. His uncle saw him even before he could get into the room, and rose from his arm-chair by the fire with such a snarl of rage that Gerald stopped dead in the very doorway.

The old man made furious gestures at him to get out. Gerald spoke, attempting to placate him, but that only made matters worse. At the sound of his nephew's voice, old Stanley Park took a step forward as though he meant to throw the weedy young man out with his own hands – and then, quite suddenly, he crumpled up and fell to the floor.

Gerald, terrified, sure that the old man had had a stroke at the sight of him, called over his shoulder to Grass, the taxi-man – for the thing had happened so swiftly that he had never even moved inside the sitting-room door. Grass ran in and together they went to the old man. Or, rather, Gerald left that to Grass, who was more competent, while he himself ran back into the hall and called out to Mrs Ferris in the kitchen, before hurrying across the hall into the dining-room to get brandy from the cellarette.

Mrs Ferris was coming up the hall as he came out with the

brandy, and they went into the sitting-room together. By then Grass was sure that there was very little hope for old Stanley, though on Gerald's instructions he drove at once for a doctor, there being no telephone in the house. Mrs Ferris had, meanwhile, taken charge of the old man, Gerald standing by doing anything she ordered. But it was plain there was nothing to be done, and indeed old Stanley was dead before the doctor arrived, about ten minutes later.

Gerald Park, a weedy, rather slick fellow in the early twenties, was clad in smart clothes now gone to seed, rather shamefacedly "supposed" that the sight of him *had* given his uncle the shock that killed him. He admitted his uncle had good cause for anger against him – he'd behaved like a heartless young fool. Although his uncle had taken him into his home when his father died a few years ago, and had been as kind as his strict nature allowed, he, Gerald, had played fast and loose, got himself into bad company and ways and ended – well, by robbing his uncle on the sly.

He hadn't any excuse. Of course, he'd hoped to pay the money back sometime, and he probably would have if someone hadn't sneaked to his uncle and so caused the final explosion. After that he hadn't a chance. His uncle was terribly down on that sort of thing. He'd been absolutely beside himself with fury and had turned Gerald out of his house then and there. That was his way. Drove his own nephew right out of his life from that moment, warning him never on any account to show his face in Friars' Vale again.

Perhaps he oughtn't to have risked coming back, seeing how bitterly the old man felt, but, as he'd said, he was absolutely on the rocks and had to get money somehow – and then, how was he to know that the sight of him would have such a fatal effect?

A straightforward story. Grass, the taxi-driver, not only confirmed it, but strengthened it by several items Gerald Park had left unsaid.

For instance, he had kept his taxi waiting beside the door because Gerald had given him the wink . . . Well, wink was a manner of speaking. Gerald had asked him to wait in a sheepish sort of way, and Grass, knowing how things were between old Stanley and that young blackg— this nephew of his, as all the village did, anticipated a quick return fare with Gerald being booted out.

While Grass waited he watched Gerald. That was easy. Gerald left the front door wide open – for a quick run out, of course, should his uncle turn nasty. As the sitting-room door was just to the left of the hall, Grass naturally saw Gerald open that. Saw him all the time, in fact, for he never really went over the threshold of the sitting-room – never had the chance from the look of it.

Yes, Gerald stopped dead in the doorway. He seemed scared to go in. Grass heard him call out loud something like, "But, Uncle, give me a chance . . ." After that there was a crash inside the room, and Gerald turned a frightened face over his shoulder, yelling that his uncle had had a fit or something.

Gerald was so paralysed with surprise that Grass had to push him out of the sitting-room doorway to get at the old man. He found Stanley Park in a heap beside his arm-chair – yes, right across the room, by the fire – and, from the look of him, there wasn't much chance. Oh, he was still alive, but it was plain his heart had burst or something, at the sight of Gerald, and it was all u.p.

No, Gerald hadn't gone near him. He stood hovering away off by the door like a frightened puppy, until, suddenly, he thought of the brandy and Mrs Ferris. Grass had heard him yelling for Mrs Ferris. She came in ahead of Gerald, who handed her the brandy and glass; he was still that scared and helpless. In fact, the only thing the feller did try to do was to take off his coat and hand it to him to put under his uncle's head. Even then Mrs Ferris had stopped him and made him fetch a cushion instead.

Mrs Ferris, a rabbit-mouthed, but plump and motherly sort of woman, bore all this out. She had been at the scullery sink washing the breakfast things when she heard Master Gerald call. She had come at once, after drying her hands. Master Gerald was coming from the dining-room with the brandy and glass in his hands as she reached the sitting-room door. He shouted that his uncle had been taken ill, and she ran into the sitting-room. She didn't like the look of the old gentleman at all, and sent Grass for the doctor.

No, it was she who gave that order; maybe Master Gerald repeated it to Grass, but the poor boy was so terribly upset he did not know what he was doing. Yes, he stood about helpless the other side of the room, so flummoxed at what had happened that he seemed terrified of coming near his uncle. Yes, he did take off his coat for his uncle's head, which only showed how struck all-of-a-heap the poor boy was, seeing he could have reached for any of three cushions from the settee.

Mrs Ferris's manner made it plain that she had a warm corner in her heart for Gerald. She agreed that he'd been wild and reckless, and that his uncle had been terribly set against him because of his theft. But she held he'd been led away by his kind heart. Also, though she didn't want to cast no aspersions, there was those who had worked against him, too. Yes, Miss Barbara Tabard, if they *must* have it. All she would say was that if Miss Barbara had only let well alone, poor old Mr Stanley would be alive and happy now.

Miss Barbara Tabard was the reason why we were in the case. She was the daughter of Stanley Park's sister, and she and Gerald were the only living relatives of the dead man. She lived in Stripe, where she taught in an elementary school, for she was an independent, pretty, and vehement girl in the middle twenties.

For these reasons she had an enmity for Gerald, whom she considered a slimy, unscrupulous little sponger who had wormed his way into their uncle's good graces solely to feather his own nest. She had already told us quite frankly that it was she who had discovered his thefts and so caused the break between him and his uncle.

Barbara had made the twenty minutes' journey from Stripe immediately on receiving the wire about her uncle's death. Finding Gerald on the scene, she had become suspicious at once. Also she found Stanley Park's doctor puzzled. He could not understand how the old man had come to die from heart failure – as it seemed. Only a few months before, he had given Stanley Park a thorough overhaul, and his heart had then been as sound as a bell. Of course, a shock might have made a difference, but he was perplexed.

Barbara had seized on that ("She would," Grimes had snarled). She at once became sure there had been foul play. She declared that Gerald would stop at nothing when it was a question of money. And there was a question of money. Stanley Park had been a rich man. He had meant the bulk of his fortune to go to Gerald, as his natural heir, with a smaller sum for her, Barbara. But after Gerald's exposure and disgrace he had decided to make a fresh will, cutting Gerald out entirely and leaving everything to her.

Gerald, Barbara insisted, must have learnt that he was altering his will and so taken a desperate step to prevent his own disinheritance. The doctor and even the local sergeant thought her suspicions too wild in the face of the evidence, but the impetuous girl promptly tackled the indulgent Mrs Ferris and forced from her an admission that, not only had she been in correspondence with Gerald, but that she had told him that his uncle had actually made an appointment with his lawyer for the next week in order do put the alteration of his will finally in hand.

On learning that, Miss Barbara went off the deep end, as the local sergeant put it, telling him that if he did not move she herself would go to headquarters at Stripe and force the police to take action. As she was plainly the sort to keep her word – with interest – the harassed sergeant decided that the best way out would be to let Stripe hold the baby, so to speak; so he had 'phoned head-quarters. That was why Inspector Grimes and Paul Toft had picked me up at my consulting-room on the way to Friars' Vale. As Medical Officer I might find something that Stanley Park's doctor had missed. But they hadn't much hope. As Grimes said when we'd finished with the witnesses.

"Sheer waste of time an' tissue. On the face of it, this Gerald Park never had a chance o' doing anything to his uncle, even if he wanted to. There never was a case in it . . ."

"I don't know . . . I feel . . ." Paul Toft muttered, and at that ominous "Ifill," we swung on him – and gaped. He had not uncoiled his lank limbs, but his left hand was churning away at a soft piece of india-rubber, that unmistakable sign that his queer mind had sensed crime.

"But – but you *can't* feel," Grimes protested. "Everything's against foul play. There's no hint of wound or bruise on the body, for instance, an' there couldn't be. Gerald never went within fifteen feet of his uncle. An' that taxi-driver, who was watching him all the time, saw nothing suspicious."

"Yes, that taxi – odd," Paul Toft's great domed forehead frowned. "Less than ten minutes' walk from the station – yet this youngster, though he's financially on the rocks, took a taxi . . . Queer extravagance, eh?"

"No! Just the sort o' fool thing his sort does," Grimes was curtly brushing the suggestion away, when I found myself blurting with that strange impulse that is so often helpful to Toft's curious gift:

"That driver made a very useful witness, though. Only one who could, with those trees screening the carriage-way. That might be a reason for taking a taxi . . . And doesn't he seem to have made the most of it? I mean leaving the front door open and so forth."

"That's been explained," Grimes began, but Toft flashed at me the smile that always tells I have given him a lead, and nodded.

"Ah, Doctor, you always touch the point . . . You're right. There's a certain overemphasis . . . His strange keeping away from his uncle, for instance . . . He let the taxi-driver and Mrs Ferris do everything while he stood afar off. Seems a bit over-done – pointed . . ."

"Yes," I agreed, "as though he was definitely trying to create the impression that he could not possibly have had anything to do with his uncle's death."

"What – you mean you think he *had*?" Grimes cried.

"I feel – yes, I feel that murder was done here," Paul Toft said with his most dreamy conviction.

We stared at him. When Paul Toft talked like that we no longer scoffed, he'd proved those extraordinary "feelings" of his too often. But even I could not feel quite convinced. If ever there was a case when the whole mass of the evidence made murder seem quite impossible, this was it. In fact, Grimes all but bellowed:

"How in the name o' Job *did* he do it then? Look, the old man was in this chair, by the fireplace. Gerald stood in the door there, fifteen feet away. He was under observation all the time. He simply couldn't ha' done a thing, or raised a hand without the taxi-man knowing all about it. How then? Did he mesmerise the old chap to death – or what?"

Even Toft had no answer to that. On the face of it, it was quite impossible for Gerald Park to have struck his uncle down. Unless, as I said: "He shot him from the doorway."

Directly I spoke I knew I'd said a foolish thing. Though Toft looked at me sharply, Grimes let go a savage bark. "Funny how we've all overlooked the loud report of a pistol. A darn loud report, get me, seeing it was fired inside the house. I wonder why the taxi-driver forgot to mention hearing a little thing like that . . . aye, an' seeing Gerald using his pistol."

I wanted to kick myself for blurting without thinking. Not only would it have been impossible for the taxi-man to miss such pistol play, Mrs Ferris must have heard the report too. Crestfallen, then, I was surprised when Toft unlimbered his reedy limbs, and, ignoring Grimes' "What the devil –?" crossed to the door to call the taxi-man into the room again.

But even the suggestion of hope that brought proved vain. The taxi-man was as contemptuous of the pistol idea as Grimes.

"A pistol? *Not* a chance," he said emphatically. "I tell you I had my eyes on Gerald all the time . . . Expecting fireworks when his uncle saw him, you see. He couldn't ha' used a pistol without my seeing – let alone me hearing."

"That's sure – you heard nothing?" Grimes insisted.

"Not a thing – an' I know what pistols sound like, too."

"He might have been using one with a silencer," I put in. "You say he called out loudly to his uncle . . ."

"He did, sir. But that made no manner o' difference. I mean, I'm ready to swear there wasn't even the ghost of another noise."

"Your engine was still running though," Toft put in.

"Maybe," the man shrugged. "But that wouldn't make any difference. We get so used to it we hear other sounds agin it – and I'd have heard even a silencer. . . . An' then, as I say, I was watching him close. He didn't make the motions like shooting. Just stood still an' stiff all the time."

"How can you be so sure?" I objected. "Can you remember exactly how he stood?"

"Well, I can then," the man snapped. "He stood practically half out o' that sitting-room door all the time. His hand was holding it open by the knob all the time . . . the nearest hand that'd be, the left. His right hand was in his pocket. His arm never lifted or moved or anything – no, not even up to when I shoved him aside to go in to his uncle."

"But that means his right hand was hidden from you by his body," I fill muttered. "I've heard of people shooting from their pockets . . ."

Grimes cut in: "You say Gerald took off his coat to put under his uncle's head – were you able to see if there was a pistol in its pocket, or anywhere on him?"

"There wasn't, sir," the taxi-man declared. "I'm certain of that. I'll tell you why: I noticed how ragged the lining of that coat was, thinking what a come-down it was for a chap like him. It was so ragged that I couldn't ha' missed seeing a pistol poking out or bulging. Another thing. It was me he handed the coat to before Mrs Ferris told him to get a cushion – an' from the weight o' that coat, there couldn't have been a pistol in it."

That seemed conclusive enough, yet Paul Toft muttered: "Odd bit of by-play, that coat business . . . as though it were part of a thought-up alibi . . ."

We did not pay much attention to him. The pistol theory was destroyed, especially as the taxi-man went on:

"An' it's all stuff, anyhow. As if I didn't know what bullets do to people . . . I saw plenty enough in the War. An' there was no sign o' wound on poor old Mr Stanley."

That clinched the matter, as it were, but it also reminded me that it was about time I took a look at the dead man. The body had been taken into the sitting-room behind the one we were in, and as I examined it the thought of foul play receded farther and farther from my mind. There was simply no sign of wound or violence. I pointed this out to Paul Toft, who stood brooding over me as I worked.

"Eh? Nothing there, Doctor?" he muttered, coming out of his medium's trance . . . "Nothing that would show, no . . . I feel that's it . . . Something that was sure *not* to show . . . How?" He examined the body. "Hair, maybe . . . Hair still thick and black . . ."

"It couldn't hide a bullet wound," I said.

"No . . . no, not a bullet wound, but . . . How would he have stood as Gerald came into the door? Left front to Gerald, eh . . . ? Shave the head on the left side, please, Doctor . . ."

I did this, not with much hope, but rather because I was always peculiarly under the spell of this strange, lank man's strange powers. The more of the surface of the skull I uncovered, the more pessimistic I became – until Toft's bony finger prodded forward and he muttered:

"What do you make of that, Doctor?"

It was a tiny puncture in the skin well above the left ear, a little red speck so small that it might have been anything from a flea-bite to the prick of a needle-point. I said as much.

"Needle-point!" he breathed. "Ah, we're getting warmer."

"How?" barked Grimes, who had joined us after a routine search of the house. "You suggesting that Gerald jabbed a poisoned needle into the old fellow? Just when did he manage that – never having been near him?"

"A dart might have done it"; I had taken fire at Toft's suggestion. "A poisoned dart."

"Fine!" Inspector Grimes jeered. "An' Gerald being a rackety one was no doubt a first-class darter from practice in pubs. Only you're forgetting the taxi-man swears he never took his hand from his pocket. Also. . . ."

"An air-pistol fires darts," I said excitedly. "And, by Jove, an air-pistol makes next to no noise, not enough to be heard above the sound of a taxi-engine, I'll bet."

"Fine, Doctor," Toft smiled at me, but the Inspector went on grimly:

"As I was about to finish – *also* even air-pistol darts aren't invisible to the naked eye. They're quite solid bits of metal, with a point and a lead butt an' tufts o' silk to steady 'em. How is it the taxi-man missed such a dart sticking in the old man's head? Remember Gerald never went near enough to pull it out."

"I feel . . . it fell out," Toft said, but I could not support him there. From the nature of the wound it would have remained sticking into the head.

"The doctor doesn't think so," Grimes said, reading my face. "Also, say it did fall out, it would have dropped close to the body. It's a plain dark brown carpet in that room. Would the taxi-man, Mrs Ferris, and the other doctor have missed seeing it as they worked on the body? It's a thousand to one against. There was no sign of it in the room then – no sign of it now. I've been over that room with a hand-brush. I'll show you."

He called out, and the local sergeant brought in a dust-pan with the sweepings of the sitting-room. There was little more than a litter of fluff and scraps, tiny bits of coal, fragments of paper, a couple of wireless screws, a thin, capped pencil, also the little red cylinder of indiarubber that belonged to it though it had been trodden out, one or two buttons, the half of what looked like the elastic button strap of a pair of braces . . . stuff like that, but no sign of anything like a dart.

"You're going to say Gerald might have picked his dart up," Grimes said. "Well, I don't think he could have, not before it was seen. What's more, I don't think he'd risk his neck on anything so conspicuous . . . And then, there's the pistol? What became of that? There's no sign of it anywhere about or on Gerald . . . No, it won't wash. You're only making a case out o' moonbeams, Toft."

It seemed so. I stood dejected. Paul Toft said in his dreamy calm:

"There's no getting over that." He touched the tiny puncture on the skull. "That's how he died . . . I feel that. And he was deliberately wounded under the hair so that we'd miss it."

"Oh, heck!" wailed Grimes; "an' I've just been telling you that all the facts say NO!"

"Of course they would. The whole thing was carefully, brilliantly schemed to make facts say no," the reedy man mused on. "From the careful employment of that taxi-driver as a witness, to the firing of an all but silent air-pistol from the pocket . . . a helpfully ragged pocket, remember . . . And you'll probably find that Gerald Park is a first-rate marksman."

"I probably will," the Inspector said bitterly. "That won't be so hard as to find how he managed to make a dart and a pistol vanish into thin air under the noses of witnesses. Just crank up a really good *feeling* to explain that, my lad."

Toft only blinked and looked at me, and in trying to think of a way out I did remember something.

"Just precisely *when* did Gerald offer his empty coat to his uncle?" I asked.

"Didn't you hear Mrs Ferris say it was after she came into the sitting-room," Grimes said sourly.

"After he'd fetched the brandy," Toft put in swiftly. "Yes, that's the loophole, Doctor. He was out of sight of witnesses, at least while he was in the dining-room getting the brandy."

"An' a fat lot that's going to help," Grimes said as we went into the dining-room. It was, indeed, sparsely furnished; just a gate-table, six stiff chairs, and a side-board with two cupboards, one of which was the cellarette.

"I've even searched behind the pictures; there's nothing here," Grimes began, and added as Toft walked straight towards a French window in the rear, that opened on to the garden. "An' that's no good, either. It's been locked all winter, an' the key's not in it."

"That's what makes it queer," Paul Toft said. "The key's usually left in this sort of window from year's end to year's end. Did someone want to create the impression that nobody could have got out through this window to-day?" He stood still, staring at the lock with his queer other-worldly gaze. Then he muttered:

"Hum! Someone locking this window, snatching out the key, moving on the run to the room across the hall . . . where would he hide the key?" His eyes twinkled at me. "How's this for real pukka police deduction, Doctor? There's a hall stand full of umbrellas on the way. . . . Wouldn't he toss the key into them in passing?"

I went to the hall stand. The third bulgy umbrella I upended and shook, shot a key to the hall floor. It fitted the French window.

We stepped through it on to a small redtiled veranda overlooking the garden. This was without railing, but it had an inclined glass roof supported by pillars to keep off the rain. We stood and looked at half an acre of neat garden.

"You think he might have nipped out here and chucked his pistol into one of them bushes, or hidden it in one of the flower-beds?" Grimes asked in a voice not so assured as it had been. "A mug's trick. He'd ha' known bushes and flower-beds are the first things *we* think of."

"And being a smart fellow he would think of a cleverer place," Toft said. "Cleverer but handy . . . easy to use in a hurry, handy to get at when suspicious people like ourselves had gone."

He stepped out into the garden and looked up at the roof of the veranda. A gutter ran along the edge of it, terminating in large, old-fashioned rain-water heads and down pipes at each end. With his left hand churning away at its indiarubber, Toft walked to the nearest down pipe, stretched his reedy arm up into the rain-water head, and, after a sharp tug, brought his hand away – with an air-pistol.

It was a short, but obviously powerful weapon with a rather full bore, and looked of foreign make. Toft broke it, charging its air chamber, and fired. It made very little sound, and was plainly in perfect working order.

"Job!" Grimes said in grudging admiration. "Your feelings do *get* you there, I fill. . . . He's a smart one, that Gerald, just fancy his thinking of locking the window after hiding this and then hiding the key to keep us from looking here . . . All the same, there's the dart. He's got everything so neatly alibi-ed that you'll have to prove that dart before you can be sure of pinning it on him."

That was a fact. Paul Toft stood, his great head brooding as he churned away at his indiarubber. Grimes and I examined the pistol, talking quietly not to disturb him. It was an interesting pistol, and I pointed out some oddnesses about it to Grimes – the size of the bore, for instance.

"Too big to carry any air-gun pellet I know," I said. "Why, you could shoot a pencil from that."

"Pencil!" Toft's voice came suddenly, alight with eagerness. "That's it, Doctor. . . . I wonder why I felt? . . . But I remember reading about it now."

"What?" both Grimes and I demanded in one voice, but his lank limbs were carrying him headlong into the house, and he was calling to the sergeant for the pan of sitting-room sweepings.

He was in the sitting-room when they were brought. Toft picked from the mess the little cylinder of rubber that had dropped out of the cap of the pencil.

"Clever," he muttered. "Devilish clever. . . . Dropping that pencil, too . . ."

"What's the pencil got to do with it?" Grimes frowned.

"*Nothing*," Toft grinned, "but you'd never suspect that, would you? This bit of rubber looks as if it belonged to that pencil, doesn't it? Just an ordinary eraser off the top of a pencil. But look—" Toft broke the pistol, exposing the breech hole, and into that he shoved the rubber cylinder. "It fits the pistol as perfectly as any lead slug, you see. Doctor, will you put that big book on top of that arm-chair. Good, now put a sheet of clean notepaper against it . . . and stand clear. I'm not such a good shot as Gerald Park."

But he was good enough. He walked to the door, just where Gerald had stood, though instead of shooting from his pocket he took aim in the orthodox way, and fired.

Again the pistol made only a slight sound; a much sharper rap came from the paper where the rubber pellet struck. It struck with such force, in fact, that it bounded right across the room, and only Toft's sharp eyes followed it to a corner under the book-case some twelve feet away.

"Your eyes show you the first advantage of such a bullet," Paul Toft said. "Being rubber – having, in fact, a pneumatic tip – it bounces away with great violence from whatever it strikes. Bounces, you might say, right out of range of the victim, so that there is little chance of its being connected with him . . . and being innocent rubber, anyhow, it is likely to be over-looked. Only it's not innocent rubber . . ."

He walked across the room and lifted up the sheet of notepaper the bullet had struck. On that paper we saw a faint ring impression made by the head of the rubber, and in the centre of it a tiny puncture – just such a puncture as had pierced the skin of Stanley Park's head. It was then that we realised that there must be a needle bedded in that rubber cylinder. Paul Toft proved it to us.

Rescuing the bullet from under the book-case, he held it delicately by one end, and, taking a pair of tweezers from his pocket, pressed the outer edges of the circular top down. As he did that, a tiny needle-point emerged from an almost imperceptible hole in the nose, a needle-point no more than an eighth of an inch long, but, if that point was poisoned – deadly.

"I read about this some time ago . . . but forgot it until Doctor Jaynes stirred my memory," the dreamy fellow smiled. "They've been using this deadly weapon in several countries of Europe for safe and secret murder. You can see how horribly efficient it is. An assassin can shoot at his man anywhere, in the street, in a crowd, in a theatre. Nobody hears the report of the air-pistol, so nobody can trace the shooter. The victim falls dead, but nobody knows how he dies. There is only that tiny poison hole, hidden by the hair, no doubt, as in Stanley Park's case. The bullet – that has already bounced off into the litter of the street . . . it automatically vanishes when it has done its work. Even if fired in a room it can be covered up, as Gerald Park so nearly covered it up, by dropping a pencil from which the rubber eraser is missing . . . so you would think the bullet merely part of that . . ."

"Almost fool proof," Grimes nodded. "When the murdered man tumbled down without wound, without any hint of anybody attacking him, it'd naturally be taken for heart failure or a stroke, as we thought Stanley Park's death was; and all the murderer has to do is to walk away . . . Just as Gerald Park nearly did – *but won't*."

But I am afraid Gerald Park did. When Grimes arrested him he was startled, but took it quietly. He simply couldn't believe we had caught him until he heard the charge read over to him, and saw the pistol. Even then he went quietly to his cell – and committed suicide. He'd been searched, of course, very carefully, but the police had overlooked a further quality of that deadly little indiarubber bullet. It could be too easily hidden. He'd hidden another bullet in the turn-up of his trousers, we thought. But we could never be sure. He was found next morning with the rubber cylinder gripped tight in his fist. The point driven into his palm, so that the hydrocyanic compound on it had done its deadly work. Thus we never knew how he had come to plan his murder – even though Paul Toft had brought it home to him.

The Impossible Footprint

William Brittain

William Brittain (b. 1930), a retired high-school teacher, is one of those authors who has consistently produced clever crime stories for the magazines for the last forty years and yet has had none collected in book form. That in itself is a mystery. He has written a long-running series featuring Leonard Strang, also a high-school teacher, who unravels unusual problems and whose adventures are long overdue for book publication. I reprinted one of the Strang stories in my earlier volume of locked-room mysteries. The following story does not feature Mr Strang, but is another baffling mystery. Just how can someone who has lost his foot leave a footprint?

Matt Kehoe leaned his hunting rifle against one of the small pine trees that encircled his hiding place in the still woods and beat his mittened hands together to get some circulation stirring in his fingers. Even through the two sweaters and the thick parka he was wearing the icy cold crept up his spine and made him shiver uncontrollably. His snowshoes creaked loudly as he shifted his weight from one foot to the other.

"Mister Kehoe, will ye hold still, if ye please? Oi'm a guide, sor, not a worker of miracles. If ye expect a deer to pass this way so's ye kin get a shot at it, ye've got to stop soundin' like a boiler factory at full production."

The whispered voice with its rich Irish brogue conjured up visions of the morning sun rising over the green fields of County

Cork and the smoke of peat fires issuing from the chimneys of sod huts in Galway. Kehoe looked at his companion and shook his head in amazement.

For the man who had spoken, crouched down on his snowshoes in a position Kehoe would have sworn it was impossible to achieve, had the swarthy skin, high cheekbones and thin, hawklike nose of a full-blooded Indian. His blue denim jacket could provide little in the way of warmth, while his wide-brimmed hat was perforated with several bullet holes as well as a few larger openings which looked suspiciously as if they had been made by human teeth. Yet the cold didn't seem to affect him at all. The look of repose on his face might have been graven from stone.

"Joshua, I'm going to freeze to death if we don't start moving around," Kehoe said through chattering teeth. "Wouldn't it be better to go looking for deer instead of just waiting for them to come to us?"

Joshua Red Wing shook his head slowly and looked up at Kehoe with reproachful eyes. "Yesterday when I agreed to guide ye in yer huntin'," he said, "I understood ye wuz one o' them detective chaps like oi've read about in the penny-dreadful magazines. Oi thought ye'd be used to a bit uv hardship, what with runnin' down alleys an' climbin' fire escapes like I see on the tellyvision. It's a sad disappointment to discover yer as soft as the rest uv the hunters from the city. Next oi'll be findin' out ye can't shoot worth a damn, neither."

Joshua reached into a pocket and drew out a dented tin flask. "Here," he said, passing it to Kehoe, "this'll warm yer blood a bit."

Kehoe grasped the flask, removed the top and took a single long swallow, then suddenly jerked the flask from his lips. Strange gasping sounds came from his throat, and his face turned bright red as the liquid, which felt as if it had been produced from sulfuric acid liberally laced with ground glass and old razor blades, streaked down his gullet.

"Luscious, ain't it?" asked Joshua, retrieving the flask. "It's from an old family recipe me sainted mother gave to me at the time of—"

"Joshua," Kehoe said, tears streaming from his eyes, "I'd pull you in right now for attempted poisoning if I hadn't seen you drink that stuff yourself. Is it that brew that makes you sound like an Irish Geronimo?"

"No," replied Joshua with a twinkle in his eye. "Fact is, oi spoke nothin' but Injun up to the age uv four. At that point oi began workin' at a church in the village in exchange fer an eddication. Me English wuz learned from a Father McGrath and a cook named Bridget O'Toole. They wuz both first-generation Irish, which accounts fer me way uv speakin'. If it offends ye, why oi kin do 'ugh' and 'how' ez good ez any Injun ye'll see in the movies."

Before Kehoe could reply, Joshua stood up, gripping his rifle in one hand and motioning for silence with the other. "Oi heard somethin' off in the woods," he whispered to Kehoe. "Comin' this way, it wuz. Now ye sees the wisdom uv me ways. Let the other hunters drive the game ahead uv 'em. We'll be here to greet it when it arrives."

Kehoe nodded, pumping a cartridge into the chamber of his own gun.

"Wait fer a good shot, an' try to drop the animal in its tracks," Joshua breathed. "Old Karl Spearing's land begins about two hundred yards over to the left. If a wounded deer makes it that far, no sense chasin' it. Spearing's a mean one an' won't have anybody comin' on his land to hunt. The few who tried hev wound up with a rump full uv buckshot."

"I think I see something off there in the woods," Kehoe said, pointing. "I'll just—"

"Don't be too hasty," Joshua warned. "It could be anything. Mebbe a black bear that got up too early from its winter nap."

A loud shout established the inaccuracy of the bear theory. "Help! Is anybody around? Help!"

Through the trees Kehoe caught sight of a man headed toward them at a dead run. He envied the man's ability to handle snowshoes without tripping over them.

"It's Tip Spearing, Karl's lad," Joshua said. "Over this way, young fella."

Joshua stepped out of the grove of pines. As the running man approached he tripped and would have fallen if the Indian hadn't caught him in his arms.

"Take it easy, lad," Joshua said to the gasping man. "Now then, Tip, what's the trouble?"

"Josh, I–I—" Tip Spearing was in his mid-twenties, at the peak of his manhood, but judging from the ghastly expression on his face, he had looked into the deepest pit of hell itself.

"It's terrible," Tip went on. "I can't believe—"

"Calm down," whispered Joshua soothingly. "What is it now?"

"It's Dad. He didn't come back home last night. I've been out looking for him and—" He gulped convulsively. "I'll take you to where he is."

Beckoning to them, Tip turned, and retraced his tracks. Joshua followed at an easy trot, while Kehoe stumblingly brought up the rear. They passed through a large clearing where the ground had been blown free of snow, and Kehoe almost tripped as twigs and leaves caught at the webbing of his snowshoes.

Reentering the forest, the men finally reached a vertical mass of shale that jutted upward like some monstrous grave marker. Tip signaled for Joshua and Kehoe to stop. "Over . . . over there."

Leaning their rifles against a tree, the two men left Tip and moved off in the direction that he had indicated. The white snow on the ground caught the sunlight that filtered through the branches and threw it back into their eyes so they squinted from the glare. They burst out onto what appeared to be a game trail amid the trees – and suddenly the snow wasn't white anymore.

It was red. The bloody, frozen circle was almost six feet in diameter.

Kehoe had seen dead men before, but he clamped his teeth together and swallowed loudly as he beheld the body of Karl Spearing spread-eagled in the snow, its lower part across the bloody stain. The body's left foot was shod in a calked boot with the letter "S" worked into the sole – but all that was left of its right leg was a stump, ending in a raw, open wound.

"Cut clean through the leg bones, just below the knee," Kehoe said to Joshua. "Knife's missing from the sheath at his hip, too. What do you suppose happened?"

"Oi've got a fair idea," replied the Indian. "Not too pretty, either. Oi've heard about such things often enough in this country, but this is the first time oi've seen it. Would ye mind followin' me? An' hev a care where ye step, if ye please, so's not to destroy tracks. Eventually we'll hev to call in the local law. No sense ruinin' all such things fer 'em."

They moved off down the trail, keeping well clear of the wide swath in the snow where Karl Spearing had evidently dragged his tortured body in a desperate attempt to seek help. The trail led past a thick stand of willow shoots. Joshua pulled aside the leafless branches.

"Yonder's the trap, Mr Kehoe. Hev a look."

Kehoe gaped at the shiny-toothed jaws of the bear trap in the midst of the white snow of the willows. They were clamped inexorably together on a bloody booted leg.

His eyes riveted on the leg, Kehoe spoke to Joshua. "You said you knew what happened here. What was it?"

Quickly the Indian sketched in the story. A lone man in mid-winter, the chance misstep, and the heavy jaws of the trap, chained to a thick tree, leaping up out of the snow to grip the leg. In such a fix there was only one desperate chance, to be taken before cold seeped too deeply into the bones and blood.

A tight tourniquet was applied, after which the imprisoned limb was packed with snow to numb it as much as possible. Then, in a grinding hell of shock and pain, the pinioned man performed an amputation – on himself. Finally, if cold and loss of blood did not take their toll, it might be possible to make one's way to where help was available. A slim chance at best, but Karl Spearing knew what must be done. He had tried – and he had lost.

"Spearing's house is but a short ways beyond the trees there," Joshua said, pointing. "Great big stone buildin' it is, with a telephone line down to the village. If he'd been able to get to it, he might be alive now."

"Rotten business," added Kehoe. He pointed to a bone-handled hunting knife lying on the flattened snow. "Must be what he did the operation with. The poor devil hardly had a chance, did he? Well, what now?"

"We'd best get back to Tip and take him to the house. Oi'll call Vern Lefner from there."

"Lefner? Who's that?"

"He's our sheriff. When he's done makin' out his reports on this – that'll take several hours, ez Vern loves to scribble on official papers – the two of ye kin talk about police work fer the rest uv the day. What with all our shoutin' and hollerin', oi doubt there's a deer left in the whole county."

"Do you think it'll be okay to leave the body unguarded? I mean, couldn't it be mutilated by wild animals?"

"Oi'd doubt it. There's some bears ez travels this game trail during the summer, but they're all hibernatin' now. Besides, they're not too partial to human flesh. And the body's too cold and stiff to attract wolves."

The two men flanked the wide trail in the snow that led back to Karl Spearing's body. Kehoe gave the corpse a wide berth, but

Joshua seemed intent on examining it at close range. Suddenly he paused, peering quizzically at a spot on the ground.

"There's a queer thing," he breathed softly.

"What's the matter?" called Kehoe, who had moved a few paces ahead.

"Oi've found a bit uv an oddity here. Yer the detective. Come and tell me what you make uv it."

Kehoe padded closer on his snowshoes.

"Hev a care," Joshua said. "Ye'd not want to destroy evidence, would ye?"

"Evidence? What evidence?"

Joshua pointed to a spot near the toe of the left snowshoe. "What hev ye to say about that?"

"Karl Spearing's footprint, that's all. There's no mistaking that 'S' from the bottom of his boot. He probably tried to stand before he became too weak to do so, and—"

"Mister Kehoe, would ye take note uv the fact that the print wuz made by the right foot? An' the leg to which that foot's attached is now caught fifty yards back down the trail in a bear trap."

"Why yes, that's true, but—"

"Then tell me, sor, how did the print get up here next to the body?"

"Well, it . . . that is . . . Oh, there's got to be some simple answer."

"Then would ye care to offer an explanation? Is it yer contention that the severed leg, takin' on a life uv its own, somehow got out uv the trap an' then hippety-hopped down here to the body like a Pogo stick? An' then later returned and put itself back into the trap?"

"No, of course not. But . . . well, maybe Karl Spearing left the print several days earlier. If there was no new snow since then . . ."

"He just happened to be in the area, I suppose? An' how would you suggest he arrived here that first time? There's no second set of footprints. Just the ones that lead to the thicket where the trap is."

"Oh. Then perhaps Spearing walked ahead on the trail a little way and came to this spot. He went back for some reason, and that's when he got himself caught. Dragging his body along, he'd have covered up the other tracks he made."

"Oi see." Joshua's voice dripped sarcasm. "He walks up to here. 'Oh my!' he sez, 'oi've forgotten somethin'.' So he turns about, walks back down the trail and thrusts his foot into a trap he'd set hisself. After cuttin' off his own leg he crawls back, destroyin' all tracks except this one by the body, which he leaves to confound us. No, Mr Kehoe. There's more to Karl Spearing's death than meets the eye."

"Josh, according to what you told me yourself, this whole thing is open and shut. Karl Spearing cut off his leg and then bled – or froze – to death. Stop trying to make such a big deal out of it. Why, if you hadn't seen that footprint—"

"Ah, but I did see it, Mr Kehoe. An' so did you."

"Yes, and I'll bet when this Lefner fellow gets here, he'll have a dozen logical explanations for how it got there. Better leave detective work to the police, Josh."

"Very well. But oi'll hev no part uv any explanation uv Karl Spearing's death that doesn't take that footprint – that damned impossible footprint – into account."

The two men returned to where the weeping Tip Spearing was waiting and half-led, half-carried him through the woods to his house. While Kehoe looked for the telephone to put in a call to the village, Joshua laid logs in the huge fireplace and soon had a roaring blaze going. From the liquor cabinet he took a bottle and administered a healthy tot of whiskey to Tip as well as taking a mammoth swig for himself. Then he laid Tip on the couch and repeated the dosage. Within half an hour the bottle was nearly empty, Tip was asleep, and Joshua was honoring Kehoe with a nasal rendition of "The Rose of Tralee".

It was almost noon when Sheriff Vernon Lefner's jeep stopped at the edge of the dirt road that ran past the house. Matt Kehoe met him at the door.

"Glad to know you," Lefner said when Kehoe had introduced himself. "Always good to meet another cop. How's the hunting been going?"

"Got me a new guide this time," Kehoe said. "His name's Joshua Red Wing. He looks Indian but talks like he was mayor of Dublin. Do you know him?"

"Know him?" was the reply. "I've run him in for hunting and fishing out of season more times than I can remember. He's a good guide though, at least when he's sober. By the way, what's that sound? Is somebody using a chain saw out back?"

In reply Kehoe opened the door to the livingroom. In front of the embers of a dying fire Joshua was sprawled out in a leather easy chair. His eyes were closed, but his open mouth resembled the entrance to a mine shaft. The gargantuan snores coming from his throat reverberated from the room's beamed ceiling.

Lefner, considering the empty bottle on the floor near the Indian's right hand, said, "He'll be out for quite a while, but it's just as well. It'll give the two of us a chance to examine Karl Spearing's body."

"Fine." Kehoe hauled his parka from the closet. "By the way, Josh found a footprint down there. A little strange, its being where it is, I guess. But he's trying to make a big thing of it."

"Between his police magazines and what he sees on TV, Josh considers himself another Sherlock Holmes," Lefner commented. "C'mon. Maybe we can get back before he wakes up and decides he's being attacked by a herd of pink elephants."

It was almost sundown when Joshua woke. He got up from his chair, holding his head as if it were about to burst, and gingerly walked to the kitchen.

"Cold lamb," he groaned, looking from the two men at the table to the platter in front of them through bloodshot eyes. Within the Indian's head a gang of tiny miners seemed to be excavating his brain with pickaxes and dynamite.

"We found it in Karl's refrigerator," Lefner said. "I had some men come up and take the body to Dr Fanchion's in town for a medical examination, but I wanted to be here to ask Tip a couple of questions when he wakes up. I thought we might as well eat while we're waiting. Slice some off, Josh, and dig in."

"No sense me even tryin' to eat," moaned Joshua softly. "With a bit o' luck, oi'll be dead within the hour anyway."

He shuffled to the door, threw it open, and took several deep breaths of the cold, clear air. Slowly his eyes focused, and the mining operations within his head closed down. "An' what, Vernon, is yer conclusion ez to Karl Spearing's death?"

"An accident, no question about it, Josh. Spearing did everything he could to save himself. If he hadn't cut off his leg he'd have frozen to death right there in the trap. As it was, well, at least he went a lot more quickly his way."

"An' the footprint? Ye did see it, didn't ye?"

Lefner nodded. "I saw it, Josh. It's gone now, of course. When the men came for the body they scuffed up the area pretty badly."

"So it's gone, eh? An' with it, any embarrassin' explanations ye'd hev to make about it."

Lefner gestured toward Kehoe. "We both saw it, Josh. We admit it was there. It's just that we don't think it's that important."

"Oh." Joshua slumped into a chair. "Oi see. Then how d'ye explain its presence by the body?"

"I don't know, Josh, but . . ." Lefner shook his head in annoyance. "Kehoe, talk to this knothead, will you? Tell him what police work is really like."

Joshua turned to Kehoe, a look of intense interest on his face. "Do that, Mr Kehoe," he said. "Talk to me about how the police ignore clues that's right in front of their noses."

Kehoe cut himself another slice of lamb, the knife grating on the bone of the roast. "What Lefner is trying to say," he began, "is that real police cases aren't like the shows on TV. On the crime shows everything's neatly wrapped up at the finish. But in real-life criminal cases there are a lot of loose ends—"

"Ez the police," interrupted Joshua, "oi merely want yez to explain how that one footprint got up by the body, when the foot that made it wuz fifty yards away, caught tight in a bear trap. Is that too much fer a tax-payin', law-abidin' citizen to ask?"

Lefner was taken with a sudden fit of coughing. "Josh, we've got to be getting back to town," he said finally, getting control of himself. "Now we're going to have to wake Tip, and when we do, I don't want to hear anything more about that footprint. The boy's been through enough for one day."

"Then ye wouldn't be interested in me theory."

Kehoe and Lefner looked at one another and then both stared at Joshua. "What theory?" asked Kehoe.

"About the footprint, uv course. But if you two detective gintlemen are too busy, why . . ."

Lefner, red-faced, began rising from his chair. Kehoe restrained him. "Just a minute, Vern. How long will this take, Josh?"

"P'rhaps thirty minutes. Oi'm sure Tip'll sleep that much longer. He drank almost ez much ez oi did from that bottle, an' he ain't had near the practice."

"Okay!" Lefner pounded the table. "Okay, Josh. We'll hear you out. But it had better make sense. And after this, no more talk about that blasted footprint. Agreed?"

"Yer charmin' manner puts me completely in yer power," Joshua said. "Agreed."

The Indian stood up and dug a hand deep into a trousers pocket. Then he held the hand over the table and allowed three scraps of grimy paper to fall lightly in front of Lefner. "Oi'd ask yez to look at these," he said. "Meanwhile oi'll be outside, lookin' about a bit."

As Joshua left the room, Lefner took one of the bits of paper and passed another to Kehoe. "Looks like an IOU," Lefner said. "From Tip Spearing to Joshua. Seven dollars and eighteen cents."

"Mine's the same," Kehoe said. "But the amount's different. A dollar and a quarter."

"Less than a week old, both of them. The third's for five dollars even. Josh probably got 'em in one of those poker games they hold at the hotel. Everybody in town knows Tip gives IOU's. But he always makes good on them."

"But what's this got to do with the footprint?" Kehoe asked. "I still don't see—"

He was interrupted by the thump of something being deposited on the back porch. Then the outside door burst open, and amid a blast of frigid air, Joshua entered, smiling broadly at the two.

"We saw the IOU's, Josh," Lefner said. "What's the matter, don't you think Tip will make good, now that his father's dead?"

"Oi'll disregard yer remark ez unworthy uv ye," Joshua said, grinning expansively. "Fer while yez two were sittin' here stuffin' yerselves, oi've been solvin' the murder of Karl Spearing."

"Murder!" Lefner's face turned a beet-red. "Josh, I've heard enough already. Nothing's been said at all about Karl Spearing's being murdered."

"Yes there has. Oi just said it meself. Now if ye'll calm down a bit, oi'll elucidate fer ye."

Lefner turned to Kehoe, shaking his head.

"Ye see, Vernon," Joshua began, "there wuz somethin' about Karl Spearing lyin' there in the snow that disturbed me from the first. In addition to the footprint, oi mean. A couple of things, in fact. In the first place, while the snow around the body itself wuz drenched with blood, there wuz none to speak uv back at the trap. What oi mean to say is, the leg wuz covered with it, but none at all on the snow. Even if Karl had wrapped his tourniquet to the tightest, seems ez if there'd be a drop or two, don't it?"

Kehoe was seeing the Indian through new eyes. "You know, you're right," he said. "But that's still not conclusive, Josh."

"P'rhaps not. But try this. Karl Spearing had a sheath knife to do his cuttin' with. The blade wuz mebbe six inches long. Oh, t'was sharp enough, and he could hev performed the amputation with it. But only if he'd cut off his leg at the knee where the joints come together. But no. The bones wuz sheared through cleanly, a few inches below the joint. An' ye just can't cut a bone like that with a knife without doin' a good bit o' hagglin' at it. Ye kin experiment on the lamb roast right now, if ye'd like.''

Both Kehoe and Lefner let their confusion show in their faces. Their preconceived notions were trickling out of their minds like sand through an hourglass.

"Karl Spearing's leg,'' Joshua went on, "wuz cut off with the one weapon an outdoorsman might carry that could slice through bone with a single cut – a finely-honed ax.''

"Wait a minute,'' protested Lefner. "Karl Spearing didn't have an ax with him.''

"Ah.'' Joshua held up a finger triumphantly. "So finally yer comin' around to me way o' thinkin', eh? Ye'll admit, then, the presence uv a second party?''

"Well . . . yeah, I suppose so,'' Lefner said. "But I still don't see how the other person got there. I mean, there were no tracks around except Karl's.''

"But there wuz other tracks, don't ye see? Don't forget the trail Tip Spearing, Mr Kehoe an' me made when we went to view the body.''

"Why, sure we did,'' Kehoe said. "But neither of us killed—'' He stopped abruptly.

"Yer beginnin' to see what oi'm drivin' at, ain't ye?'' Joshua said, smiling.

Kehoe jerked a thumb in the direction of the livingroom. "Are you saying you think Tip killed his own father and then retraced his trail back to where we were?''

"Somethin' like that. O' course the killin' wuz probably done a day or so ago. But ez long ez Tip walked in the tracks he'd first made, there'd be just the single trail. When Tip located us in the woods an' took us to the body, we figured the tracks had been made when he discovered his father. But they could just ez easy uv been put there a day or two before, when the killin' wuz done.''

"Josh,'' Lefner said, "I don't care when the trail to the body was made. I still can't see that Tip's guilty of murder. I mean, what motive did he have?''

"Karl Spearing owns this house and a good deal uv the land around here. A man uv considerable means. An' yet Tip, his own son, wasn't allowed to have enough pocket money even to play a few hands uv penny-ante poker. He had to use IOU's an' then account to his father for every cent he lost. A most degradin' situation fer Tip. Might it be that he went searchin' fer his father to ask fer money to pay his debts? Tempers flared, an' there wuz a fight, with Karl comin' out the loser. Oi tried to point out this possible motive by presentin' yez with them IOU's uv mine, but I suspect ye wuz hard put to divine their true meanin'."

"So you think Tip killed his father, eh?" asked Lefner. "Well what about the foot in the trap? And that footprint by the body?"

"All right, let's sum up the whole operation. At some time yesterday – or p'rhaps the day before, I dunno, what with the body bein' froze the way it wuz – Tip is out in the woods, carryin' an ax. He sees his father on the game trail an' decides to ask fer money. There's an argument, ez I said, an' a brief struggle. Tip loses his temper an' swings the ax, takin' off Karl's leg. Karl falls to the ground, fast bleedin' to death, right at the spot where we seen his body. Out there in the woods, who wuz to hear his cries of pain?

"But Tip's mind is on other things. He knows if the body is found in its present condition, he'll be the number-one suspect.

"Then, an inspiration. Tip's heard stories, ez oi hev, about men bein' caught in a trap an' what they had to do to save themselves. He knows the bear trap's nearby. So he picks up the bloody leg, and off he goes down the trail. Once in the willow thicket, he jabs around with that grisly member 'til he hits the pan uv the bear trap under the snow. The jaws crunch together on the leg. Then Tip drops Karl's sheath knife by the trap to complete his alibi and muckles up the trail between the trap an' the body so it'll look like a man's dragged himself along it. All the footprints are destroyed, or so Tip thinks. But there's still one uv Karl's near the body that he overlooked an' oi found."

Joshua leaned back in his chair and spread his hands expansively. "An' that's the way it wuz, ez they say on the tellyvision. This mornin' Tip went lookin' fer someone to be witness to Karl bein' dead with one leg cut off an' caught in the trap. He found Mr Kehoe an' me. If we didn't immediately assume what Tip wanted us to, oi'm sure he stood ready to point out what he wished us to believe. Ye must, uv course, give Tip credit fer his actin' ability. He'd uv succeeded, too, if me sharp Injun eyes hadn't spotted that footprint in the snow by the body."

"He could beat the rap yet," Kehoe said. "You've got an interesting theory there, Josh, but no real proof."

"Would the murder weapon do?" Joshua asked. "Oi found an ax out in the shed. Somebody did a hurry-up job uv tryin' to wipe it clean, but there's still some reddish stains on the handle an' blade. Oi dropped it off on the steps on me way in from outside. Could yer police chemists make somethin' uv them stains, Vern?"

"Yeah." Lefner got up and peered into the livingroom to check on Tip Spearing. "If the stains are human blood, we'll have a pretty tight case."

"Well," Joshua said, "at least ye'll hev it easy apprehendin' yer suspect. Oh my, the hangover he'll have when he wakes. Oi hope, Vern, that ye won't be too severe with him."

"Hell, Josh, he killed a man – his own father."

"True. But what kind uv a man wuz the father? Seems to me the milk uv human kindness might uv turned to gall in the man's veins."

"Look, just because he didn't give Tip any money—"

"No, oi wuz thinkin' about how that bear trap wuz placed. It's winter. No need fer a trap with the bears all hibernatin'. Besides, no bear's about to hide in a thicket. That'd be the place where the hunters would lurk, waitin' fer game to pass by on the trail. Like we wuz doin' this mornin', Mr Kehoe."

Kehoe stared wide-eyed at Joshua. "You mean . . ."

Joshua nodded. "Karl Spearing couldn't stand to hev people huntin' his land. He'd do anythin' to keep 'em away, even shoot at 'em. So I don't believe he wuz after bear when he set that trap.

"It wuz put there to catch a man."

Three Blind Rats

Laird Long

*Laird Long (b. 1964) is a prolific Canadian writer whose stories
have appeared in a wide range of print or on-line magazines,
including* Blue Murder, Handheldcrime, Futures Mysterious,
Hardboiled, *and* Albedo One. *His story "Sioux City Express"
from* Handheldcrime *was included amongst the top 50 mystery
stories of 2002 by Otto Penzler in the anthology* The Best American Mystery Stories – 2003. *In this brand new story, he demonstrates how criminals can use the latest technology to commit the
perfect crime – if only an impossible crime hadn't got in the way!*

Pinero said, "Marciano or Lewis – who'd you take in that one?"
He lowered his *Ring Magazine* and looked at McGrath,
watched the little man down his fourth cup of coffee of the
morning, rub his grey face.

McGrath played around some more with his Blackberry, his
right eyelid twitching as he stared at the glowing screen. "I told
you, I don't follow boxing. It's too violent." Thumbs flying like a
twelve-year-old video-gamer chalking up kills on *God of War*, he
added, "You should see all the great features on this thing."

Pinero raised his magazine again, recrossed his feet on top of his
desk. "You're gonna get radiation poisoning from all those gadgets
of yours," he warned, taking some satisfaction in his partner's
stricken expression.

Pinero was young, liked to wear his clothes flashy, gel his jet-
black hair into a subtle Mohawk. But despite all that, he considered

himself old-school, less concerned with the geeky forensic fantasies of criminal investigation, than the pavement-pounding, door-dusting street solving of it. And he was good at it, like his father had taught him.

"Pretty soon we'll be able to break cases without ever even leaving the office," McGrath stated. "Like fighting a war by remote control." He tilted his empty mug against his lips, almost choked on the plastic stir straw.

McGrath was well past the age when most cops were puttering around their Victoria condos, bald as a bagel and just as rubbery. But he'd carved out a niche for himself in the Department by becoming a tech-savvy guru, an indispensable computerized tool in the 21st-century assault on crime.

The men's mutual loathing went back to the first day they'd been paired together in Homicide. Pinero despised McGrath's foul coffee breath and chronic health whining, his holier-than-Intel attitude. While McGrath didn't envy Pinero his smooth good looks and muscular physique; he detested him for them, in fact. And the young detective's apparent indifference to all things chip-driven earned him a special place of contempt in McGrath's ebook.

Pinero was two weeks away from transfer – bait for trolling John's with the Vice Unit – and both men were counting the days, one on his Dukes of Hazzard wall calendar, the other on his Outlook software.

Sergeant Bugler walked into the Squad Room, barked, "McGrath, Pinero!" They looked up. "Got a job for you two." They waited. "Lenny 'The Rat' Laymon's been found dead."

It was a skid row bungalow bordered by a boozecan on one side and a crack house on the other; smack-dab in the middle of the sour armpit of Vancouver – the downtown eastside. Inside: the nude body of Lenny Laymon, curled up in a fetal ball on the bottom of his bathtub, like a rat in its hole.

Pinero stared at the hunk of limburger on the toilet lid, gestured. "That a joke?"

McGrath slurped java out of a paper cup. "Air freshener, more likely."

Constable Mullings laughed. "The Rat did like his cheese."

The two detectives and the uniformed cop looked down at Lenny's sunken body. The water had still been running from the showerhead when the girl had discovered him, both he and the water ice-cold by then. Even with the long soak, Lenny still looked dirty, the yellow skin on his hairless body going blue, backbone spined like a Stegosaurus. His eyes and mouth were wide-open, back of his blonde-fringed head a bloody mess.

"When'd the girl find him?" Pinero asked Mullings.

"'Bout an hour ago," the Constable replied, wiping a big, red nose with a big, red hand. "She couldn't reach him on the phone all of yesterday, so she decided to pay him a visit this morning."

"How old is she, anyway?"

"Fourteen."

"How'd she get in?"

"Had her own key."

Pinero mauled a hunk of bubblegum. They could hear the girl, Kristal, crying away in the next room, lamenting a life gone down the drain: a con artist, fraud artist, sneak thief, pickpocket and stool pigeon.

"Look what I found when I made her empty her pockets," Mullings added, pulling something out of his jacket. He held it up. It sparkled in the light of the bare bathroom bulb.

"A diamond ring," McGrath said, taking it from the Constable and examining it.

"Rock's gotta be at least one-carat," Mullings guessed. "She claimed Lenny gave it to her – like anyone'd believe The Rat was gonna pop the question, eh – then finally admitted she'd found it on Lenny's dresser and palmed it, after she found the guy soaking in the tub."

"It's got ZJ stamped on the inside of the band," McGrath stated.

"Zammy Jewelers," Pinero responded. "They've got a store in the Centre Mall – make their own rings. And right now I'm betting they're at least one bauble short of a glitter palace."

He pulled a couple of Kleenex's, a pair of latex gloves out of his pocket. He set the Kleenex carefully down on the grimy tile floor and knelt beside the tub, dressed his hands in the throwaway gloves. He ran a finger along the bottom of the tub, up to and around Lenny's body. He poked the corpse.

McGrath turned his head and spoke to the two guys from the Fire and Rescue Service who were lounging in the doorway, "Looks like an accident, huh?"

They nodded.

"If it was anyone but The Rat, we wouldn't even be here," he grumbled, fingering what he suspected was a cellphone tumor growing behind his right ear. "Hey, I heard you guys get Workers' Comp now, if you develop lung cancer, or have a heart attack twenty-four hours after a fire. That right?"

The guy with the Stalinesque mustache nodded, smiled a self-satisfied smile. "You're darn right it is. The Union got the legislation passed a couple of months ago, eh."

"I just started smoking again myself," the other firefighter joked.

"Cops should have something like that," McGrath groused. "I'm sure I'm getting cancer from using my computer and cell-phone all day, in the line of duty. My doctor even said—" He halted his grievance when he saw his partner tilt Lenny's stiffened body face-up, so he could check out The Rat's other profile.

Pinero dug around in Lenny's right ear. "Gimme a pair of tweezers, someone."

He was handed a pair, and everyone watched as he pulled something out of Lenny's oversized ear. He held the small, brown object up for inspection. "How many guys take a shower with their hearing aid still in?" he asked.

McGrath was working his wireless keyboard like the Chicago Stadium organist when Pinero reemerged from Robbery. "There was a heist at the Zammy Jewelers store in the Centre Mall last night alright," he informed his partner. "Estimated loss: four hundred grand."

McGrath whistled. "Lenny pulled a couple of jewel snatches back in the day, didn't he?"

"Yeah, with a little help from some friends – turned enemies." Pinero glanced at the piece of paper in his hand. "The last one that we know of was the Big Rock Diamond Mountain store on Granville – five years ago. The Rat weaseled out of heavy jail time by squealing on all his partners, including the inside guy, the fence, a couple of US Customs slobs, and half the local Hell's Angels starting line-up."

The phone on Pinero's desk rang. He scooped it up, growled, "Yeah?"

"Detective Pinero, Dr Rampersand, Coroners Office."

"Yeah, Doc?"

"Yes, you wanted us to phone as soon as we had some pre-liminary results from our examination of Leonard Laymon."

"The Rat. Yeah, go, Doc." Pinero snagged a pad and pencil.

"Yes, well, cause of death appears to be a single blow to the back of the head – blunt force trauma – as you no doubt observed for yourself. Time of death was approximately two to four a.m., the morning of 16 November."

Pinero glanced at his watch, the comely picture of Daisy Duke: 2:10 p.m., Wednesday the 17th. "What else?"

The doctor cleared his throat. "Well, not much, I'm afraid. There appear to be no other untoward signs of trauma on the body, other than the usual assortment of bruises, burns, cuts, scabs, pimples, and warts that come from a bad diet and a life lived close to the streets. We found soap scum, lime scale, and tile grains in the wound, consistent with someone knocking their head on the edge of a bathtub after losing their footing."

"Thanks, Doc." Pinero hung up, thought for a moment, then reconnected. "Hey, Doc, forgot to ask – what about the hearing aid?"

"It's a completely-in-the-canal type of hearing aid, very small. It's not waterproof, of course, but someone could well forget about it when taking a shower."

"Thanks, Doc." Maybe The Rat had actually gone out the same way he'd come in – accidentally, Pinero thought. He relayed the information to his partner.

McGrath's cellphone chimed the alien greeting from *Close Encounters of the Third Kind*. He plucked it off his belt. "Okay, we'll be right down." He stood up and reholstered his cell, swallowed dregs and said to Pinero, "The Lab's got something for us to see."

The two men trotted on down to the basement.

"The Zammy Jewelers' cameras, all the mall cameras, went blank as a blacked-out Canucks game at midnight – for ten minutes," Cordweider explained.

"Covered up?" Pinero asked the lab technician.

"Naw. Off-line," Cordweider snorted, "along with the alarm system. Everything came back up like the new programming day at 12:10 a.m. But by the time the security company got there, the jewelry store was a whole lot less sparkly."

"Did the cameras see anything interesting before they blinked off?" McGrath asked, fondling the bag under his left eye and staring at the bank of monitors.

"Indeed," Cordweider teased. "We've been running the mug-shot file against the surveillance camera facial shots, looking for matches, and you wouldn't believe who turned up."

"Who?" Pinero gritted impatiently. He and Cordweider had gone a few rounds during a late-night stakeout once, when bad food and conversation had turned decidedly personal.

Cordweider grinned. "Take a look at this, hot-shot." He pointed to a blank monitor, pressed a button. People started walking in and out of quadruple doors. "That's the entrance to the mall on West Georgia. Note the date and time."

Pinero and McGrath noted: 16 Nov 2005, 2103:44 and counting.

Cordweider pressed another button and the picture froze. A guy in a bulky jacket was coming through the door. Cordweider fingered a roller ball, locked on the guy's face, clicked. The face jumped up and filled the screen, unmistakable.

"Lenny 'The Rat' Laymon," McGrath exhaled.

Back in the Squad Room, the detectives went to work. What had been a simple slip-up in the tub – one more bad guy washed away – was now something strangely different. If the Coroner was right – and he had a lucrative book deal and speaking calendar to attest to his brilliance – then the unanswered question was: how could a Rat lying dead in a bathtub early Tuesday morning slink into a shopping mall late Tuesday night, with the intent, it seemed, of knocking over a jewelry store?

It didn't make sense. And when something doesn't make sense, you work some sense into it. Pinero hooked up with Forensics, while McGrath mined Lenny's computer for pertinent information.

"Tolmeyer speaking?"

"Pinero. What'd the boys in Forensics get off the crime scene?"

Tolmeyer laughed. She had a soft spot for Pinero – right between the legs whenever he wanted it. "We 'boys' are still on scene. But so far, everything looks pretty clean – from a crime perspective, that is, not a housekeeping one. No signs of forced entry, lots of fingerprints – Lenny's and the girl's – nothing else unusual, so far."

"No Athabaska Terrier hairs? Albino herb roots native only to Cape Breton Island? Poisoned tea bags? Furry creature suits with DNA-identifiable sweat?"

Tolmeyer laughed again. "You've been watching too many TV shows, Detective."

"What about the tub? Any evidence someone dusted it with a Zamboni – made it extra slippery for the bathing beauty?"

"In my professional opinion, that bathtub hasn't been cleaned since it was installed. And nobody greased the soles of Laymon's feet, either, before you ask."

Pinero grunted, shelved the phone as Tolmeyer was enquiring about his dinner plans for the evening.

He was chewing things and a wad of gum over when McGrath pointed at his computer screen. "Take a look at this," he said.

Pinero strolled over, looked at the listing up on the LCD flat screen.

"This is Lenny's email history," McGrath explained, his hand stroking his optical mouse with caffeine jitters. He highlighted the first message listed after a backlog of porn and penis enlargement spam. It was dated Monday, 15 November, from meatman@yahoo.com, subject: "Ready to go to work?"

McGrath looked at Pinero. Pinero looked back. They both knew The Rat didn't work – honestly, anyway. McGrath clicked on the message. It read: "Job's a go. Come prepared."

"Did The Rat respond?" Pinero asked.

"Not by email, no."

"Who's Meatman? J.M. Schneider?"

"Don't know." McGrath admitted. "The account information's as phony as a three-dollar coin. But I ran a trace on all Internet activity associated with the account, and found something fairly interesting."

"Give."

"Meatman is a 'member' of an adult dating site – kinkyluvers.com. The profile is of a thirtysomething guy with a peccadillo for morning toe jam, I kid you not. No picture, though. And the membership contact info is limited to the email address."

"Don't you need a credit card or something to sign up to those sites?"

"Not this one. It's run free of charge by The Friends of Fetish – a government-subsidized think-tank operating right here in the downtown. Anyway, I already sent Meatman a message – with an attachment." McGrath clicked, and Pinero ogled a busty brunette with black-stockinged, red-ribboned legs long enough to span Burrard Inlet, her silky feet close-up displayed in open-toed, patent-leather red pumps. Her hair covered up her face, if she had one.

"Just call me Clarissa," McGrath chuckled, coughed. He took his hand off the mouse long enough to pour himself a mouthful of mocha.

The two detectives kept at it, logging frustration and overtime at time-and-a-half. Pinero ran a check on Lenny's known associates; McGrath and the lab techs continued to pour over Lenny's hard-drive and the mall surveillance video.

Lenny's "associates" were the scum de la scum of the Vancouver crime scene. "Rainy Day" Izzo: part-time drug dealer, full-time drug user; ratted out by Lenny on a heroin deal that went bust; parole records stated that he was currently weaving hemp into saleable product in Nelson, four hundred miles due east. Sylvia Wojawoski, aka "Skye Flowers", so named because she was always on her back, looking up at the sky: Stanley Park prostitute and bit-player MILF in locally-lensed porn; cohabitated with Lenny for five years; currently suing the deceased rodent for child support – three kids that he denied were his despite their enormous overbites; busted on a low-track sweep Sunday night, now cooling her high heels in lock-up. John Jorossismo, aka "Jarhead", aka "Jason" (of *Friday the 13th* movie fame): US Marines deserter and Hell's Angels patch prospect, weapons smuggler, loansharker, goalie in an industrial beer league, and recent Vancouver Port Authority employee of the month; stiffed out of a grand and stooled on by Lenny – the Big Rock Diamond Mountain job; current whereabouts a gated subdivision in White Rock. And . . .

"Matthew Kolvin," Pinero and McGrath spoke as one.

They looked at each other. "Why'd you say—" they both said.

McGrath pointed a shaky digit at his computer screen. Pinero trucked on over, stared at a picture of a bare-chested Matthew Kolvin, shaved head gleaming, blue eyes glinting hard as diamonds, thick lips curled into a smirk, torso tanned and rugged as Desert Storm khaki.

"Clarissa received a response to her email," McGrath said, grinning triumphantly.

Pinero recited the file he'd just been looking at: "Matthew Kolvin: strong-arm specialist, extortionist, cigarette, alcohol, and Lotto ticket smuggler – and sometime jewel thief; handed a ten-year sentence for his role in the Big Rock Diamond Mountain job; served half, release date: 10 November – one week ago today."

"Maybe you, me, and Clarissa should pay Matthew Kolvin a visit," McGrath added unnecessarily.

The detectives rousted Kolvin and an underage hooker out of bed at the fleabag rooming house address he'd given his parole officer. He was spitting mad. Pinero calmed him down only slightly with a shot to the groin.

"I never robbed no goddamn jewelry store!" he gasped. "Don't know nuthin' about any dead Rat, neither!"

"Listen, Meatman," McGrath countered, knocking back a caffe latte and eyeballing a laptop, scanner, camcorder, and printer huddled together on a ratty couch, along with the hooker. "We've got an email that you sent Lenny talking about a 'job' – a day before Lenny did a back flip in his bathtub and a day-and-a-half before the Zammy Jewelers store was hit."

Kolvin glared at the men.

"You hated Lenny's guts, didn't you – for ratting you out on the Big Rock Diamond Mountain job?" Pinero stated. "But not bad enough to turn your nose up at another good heist, team up with the guy again?"

Kolvin's incisors glinted silver. "I ain't talked to that bum in five long years."

"How do you explain the email then?" McGrath asked.

"I don't," Kolvin growled.

Silence.

"What's your brother up to these days – Bertrand?" Pinero asked, changing tactics. "You talk to him since his release?"

"I talk to that bum like I talk to Lenny and you bums!"

The detectives exited the flophouse with the exact same thing they'd entered it with – one flimsy cyber link between Lenny Laymon and Matthew Kolvin that would vaporize in the ether of a court of law, without plenty more supporting evidence.

"Maybe we should brace Bertrand?" Pinero suggested, as the two men sat in their unmarked and stared at the constant drizzle. "He knew and hated Lenny, was in on the BRDM job, too."

"Maybe . . ." McGrath mused.

Matthew and Bertrand Kolvin were, in fact, identical twins, but that's where the similarities ended. Matthew was a muscle boy, Bertrand a finesse man – an accountant gone bad, writing a ticket to the easy life through cheque kiting, money order doctoring, credit card fraud, and embezzlement. He wore his blond hair long, usually in a ponytail, build: slender.

The two brothers hated each other with a passion reserved for only the overly intimate, since their teen years. They'd nonetheless worked together on a number of jobs since graduating from young offenders status, business being business – the last one the BRDM job. They'd demanded separate trials, then jails, and been granted both by the accommodating Canadian judicial system.

"But how *do* we explain Lenny walking into a mall – presumably robbing a jewelry store, presumably with Matthew Kolvin's help – eighteen hours after he's supposed to be dead?" McGrath continued.

"Reincarnation?" Pinero suggested. "He picked right up in the new life where he'd left off in the old? Or maybe it was a guy in a Lenny Halloween mask, like bank robbers wear Nixon masks and cheating husbands wear Clinton's?" Pinero laughed.

McGrath didn't. "A mask . . ." he pondered, sucking the last drops of life out of his latte. "Did you happen to notice all that computer equipment in Kolvin's apartment?"

"I noticed. What about it?"

"The mall surveillance system is digital – computer-controlled. I wonder . . ."

"Wish upon a star while you're at it," Pinero growled. "I'm gonna grab me some gym time then sack out."

"Good idea," McGrath said, eyeing a street-corner Sally Ann that served all-night joe. "I think I'll log some sleep myself. Then first thing tomorrow morning, I think I'll consult with a high-placed friend of mine. A friend who sees all, knows a thing or two about subterfuge." He winked a pouchy eye at his partner.

Pinero snorted.

Early next morning, Pinero dropped McGrath off at the Defence Department Building downtown, then proceeded to Lenny's bungalow for another look-see. He lifted the yellow tape, ducked inside the squalid digs.

Everything was just as crummy as before, the dust settled back to where it had lain for the fifty years before Forensics had disturbed things. Pinero went into the bedroom, looked at the dirty clothes strewn on the floor, the unmade, sheet-soiled bed, the battered nightstand with the "barely legal" skin mags on top, the splintered garage sale card table where Lenny's powerful stolen computer had sat.

He walked over to the doorless closet, fingered through the tie-dyed and BC Bud T-shirts, the Manitoba Moose jerseys, getting nothing more out of it than a probable skin rash. Kristal had told the detectives that lover-boy Lenny was nutso over the Moose, a minor league hockey team playing in the frozen tundra of Winnipeg, Manitoba – Lenny's birthplace.

And as Pinero stared at the jerseys, something suddenly tumbled inside his skull. He retraced his steps, to the front door of the rathole, where a Manitoba Moose jacket hung on a hook. He examined the bulky jacket, fingered the sewn-on crest – a smug-looking cartoon moose holding a hockey stick, a frozen pond in the background. He plucked the jacket off the hook and took it with him.

When Pinero entered the Squad Room he found Sergeant Bugler hanging over one of McGrath's bony shoulders, their eyes glued to something on the computer screen. Pinero admired Bugler's tight, round bottom for a moment, then said, "Found another good Jimmy Neutron site?" He flung his leather jacket over the back of his chair.

Bugler glanced up, annoyed. McGrath's pavement-hued face tinged slightly red.

Pinero took up position behind an unoccupied shoulder.

"The lab technicians have finished stripping Lenny's computer equipment," McGrath told his partner. "They found enough child porn to put the Thailand Bureau of Tourism out of business, but look what they found in his webcam history." The detective took a long, suspenseful slurp of fresh-brewed coffee.

"Why would a rat like Lenny even have a webcam?" Pinero asked no one in particular. "To see him is to hate him."

McGrath finally swallowed. "Lenny was technologically armed, like all professional criminals are getting these days." He looked up at Sergeant Bugler meaningfully. "Like all law enforcement officials need to be to keep up with them."

Bugler nodded vaguely, squeezed his shoulder.

McGrath stroked the keyboard, and Lenny's ugly mug popped up on-screen, wispy whiskers framing a buck-toothed mouth. McGrath dragged the bar at the bottom, and Lenny went all fast and jerky. Then his jaundiced face suddenly turned mouse-white, his beady eyes registering panic. McGrath lifted his finger, returning the action to normal speed.

Lenny leaped out of his chair and skittered to the bedroom door. Someone was yelling at him from the hallway: "You put me away and I'm going to put you away, Rat!"

Lenny backed away, paws up and out in supplication, and a face briefly appeared in the shadowy doorway. McGrath froze the picture, cleared away some of the shadow, locked onto and enhanced the face: Bertrand Kolvin, delicate features twisted with rage, ponytail in a knot.

"Hmmm," Pinero commented. "So Bertrand Kolvin threatened Lenny's life. Who hasn't? I heard the Doukhobors even put out a contract on the guy once."

McGrath's brown-toothed grin was a thing of triumph for everyone but the BC Dental Association. He restored the full picture, pointed to the timeline at the bottom of the screen. It read: 14 Nov 2005, 21:45:24. He said, "We know Bertrand Kolvin threatened Lenny Laymon on Sunday at 9:45 p.m. Now, let's just see if he followed up on that threat. There's nothing more of interest on the webcam, but remember that high-placed friend I was telling you about? Well, he CSIS's all. Take a gander at this video, and note the time and date again."

Pinero cracked his knuckles. Bugler sighed. McGrath clicked. The computer revealed a black world inhabited by white images, a timeline reading: 16 Nov 2005, 01:47:38 PTZ. The view was from on-high, way high, the white figure emerging out of a parked car a thermal image. The figure crossed a street with the jerky movement of time lapse photography, paused at the door of a house, and then went inside.

"Location?" Pinero asked.

"Two hundred block of Alexander Street," McGrath crowed. "That bungalow," he pointed, "is Lenny's place – right around the time of his death."

"Lenny coming home after a hard day's night of working the back pockets of the bar crowd?" Pinero suggested.

McGrath shook his head, replayed the sequence. "See how the figure dips to the right when he walks? Do you know what that is?"

"A limp," Bugler breathed.

McGrath beamed. "A limp is right. A noticeable limp. Lenny didn't limp. But—"

"Bertrand Kolvin limps," Pinero admitted.

The three police officers watched some more, watched a figure come skulking down the sidewalk, pick something up out of the gutter along the way, slip into Lenny's house at 02:15:52 PTZ – Lenny returning home? Watched the limper exit Lenny's house at 02:30:21 PTZ, get in a car and drive away.

"Like I said before, we should brace Bertrand Kolvin," Pinero stated. Then added, "Too bad none of this is admissible in court, privacy laws and Charters of Rights and Freedoms being what they are."

"It's all strictly on the qt," McGrath agreed. "I have to delete everything in an hour. But . . . the show's not over yet." He pointed and clicked and dragged some more, seemed to replay the scene of the limper exiting a car and entering Lenny's house. Only now the timeline read: 17 Nov 2005, 02:02:13 PTZ. A full day later.

"What!? Why would Kolvin risk returning to the scene the next night?" Bugler asked.

"Good question," McGrath replied, as they watched the limper leave Lenny's death trap at 02:06:37 PTZ.

Bugler straightened up, her back cracking, head shaking. "But if Lenny was actually bumped off by Bertrand Kolvin early Tuesday morning, then how in heck did he participate in a jewelry store robbery Tuesday night?"

"Another good question," McGrath responded, browning his nose still further. He looked at his partner. "Did anyone think to bring in Lenny's jacket, by any chance?"

"Yeah," Pinero replied, blowing a bubble. "I did – just now. It's in the Lab, undergoing intense comparison with some surveillance video."

McGrath nodded, grinned, tried to wash back the rising tide of his excitement with a shot of coffee. "My friends at the Canadian Security Intelligence Service also provided me with some useful information about making faces – false faces."

Bugler glanced at Pinero as McGrath cackled, choked and coughed up some coffee. Pinero just shrugged.

Search warrants were issued, served, and executed on Bertrand Kolvin's swank Port Coquitlam condominium, Matthew Kolvin's downtown dump, that afternoon. McGrath and Pinero happily split up so they could cover both searches, and two hours and ten phone calls later, they felt they had enough evidence to bring the Kolvins in for questioning.

The twins were placed in Interrogation Room 104. It was the first time they'd met since they'd been busted five years earlier, and much like that time, it didn't go well. They attacked one another on sight.

"Sit down and behave yourself!" Pinero commanded, shoving Matthew into a wooden chair, sending him and it skidding into the wall.

The brothers glared at each other, twin faces of hate.

Pinero kicked off the proceedings, talking about Lenny "The Rat" Laymon's fateful tumble in the tub. "It looks like an accident, it smells like an accident – a guy taking a shower makes a wrong step and one-and-one-half-gainer later, he's cold as a Coho. Happens all the time, right? No signs of forced entry, violence, lube on the porcelain, nothing incriminating like rat poison lying around." He paused. "But does it sound like an accident? You didn't know Lenny had a hearing aid installed two years ago, did you, Bertrand? Because you were doing five for a crime Lenny stooled you on."

Bertrand folded thin arms across a bony chest, tilted his fine, blonde head up in a haughty manner that would've done the CEO of a Crown Corporation proud. "I didn't know, and I don't care. I'm glad the little rat's dead, but I had nothing to do with it."

"Then how come your face shows up on Lenny's webcam – your voice threatening to do him bodily harm – only a couple of days before the guy's soft head met hard surface in a love embrace?"

"What!? That's preposterous!" Bertrand wailed.

"What!? That's preposterous!" Matthew mimicked, an octave or two higher.

Bertrand lunged at him. Pinero, McGrath, and Bugler wrestled the two siblings apart, planted them firmly back in their chairs again.

McGrath struggled to catch his breath, mop up and strain into a cup his spilled coffee. Then he said, "We have surveillance pictures of a man entering Lenny's house – easily picking his lock – Lenny coming home, the man exiting, right around the time of Lenny's death. A man limping rather badly. That puck to the knee back in junior hockey put a permanent crimp in your stride, didn't it, Bertrand?"

"Thanks to my brother, yes," the man sniffed.

"I was aiming for his balls," Matthew gritted. "But they were too small a target."

Bertrand ignored him, said to McGrath, "I was home in bed when Lenny died, nowhere near his rat hole."

"And what about the mystery of a man caught on a surveillance camera, entering a mall, eighteen hours after he's supposed to be dead?" Pinero intoned. "How's that possible?"

The Kolvins went stone-faced.

Pinero leaned into Matthew. "You emailed Lenny about a 'job' – Meatman. Was it the Zammy Jewelers job at the Centre Mall? A diamond ring was found at Lenny's place – a down payment maybe, before the loot was fenced?"

Matthew snorted. "I told you dickheads already I had nuthin' to do with that job."

"Funny thing about that surveillance video, though," McGrath interjected, tonguing the rim of his coffee cup. "Detective Pinero noticed something strange about the jacket 'Lenny' was wearing in the video. It's got a Manitoba Moose logo on it – the new logo, that is: a stylized angry moose baring its teeth, set against a background of trees."

Pinero held up Lenny's jacket, fingers covering the logo.

"But Lenny hadn't bought the new one yet," McGrath went on. "It only came out in September, just before the start of the season. The jacket we found at his house still has the old logo on it . . ."

Pinero moved his fingers aside.

". . . a smug-looking cartoon moose holding a hockey stick, a frozen pond in the background."

Matthew glanced at Bertrand; Bertrand glanced at Matthew.

"It's like the man in the video knew Lenny wore a Moose jacket, but when he recently purchased one, he unknowingly got a slightly different moose than the one Lenny sported," McGrath said. "It's tough to keep track of all these marketing gimmicks, isn't it?"

"And while I was taking note of Mick E. Moose's facial expression," Pinero clocked in, "Detective McGrath was taking note of the zipper on the jacket – the zipper tongue, specifically. It looked wider, shinier than the narrow black one on Lenny's jacket. Reason?" He plucked it out of McGrath's shirt pocket, held it up.

Everyone looked at the glinting tongue, waiting for it to speak.

McGrath interpreted. "We ran it through the Lab. It can be used to mesh metal teeth together alright, but it's also a device used for what's called 'facial provocation'. A device developed by a certain spy agency which shall remain nameless, that can be purchased on the black market or rigged up at home by a real tech expert. A device that when triggered throws up a prepro-grammed, made-to-specs image – almost like a hologram, except more realistic. In this case, a preprogrammed image of Lenny Laymon's face, masking the face of the real man who entered that mall and hid in it until after closing, then shut down the Zammy Jewelers security system and the mall security cameras just long enough to rob the store and make his escape."

Gum chewing. Foul, ragged breathing. Twin sets of teeth grinding.

"Someone wanted to pin the robbery on Lenny; someone with technological expertise. Someone who didn't know The Rat was already dead when he was supposedly knocking over a jewelry store."

Pinero said, "I talked to the warden at Stony Mountain, Matthew, asked how you spent your five years. He said you were a royal pain in the ass the first three, until you discovered the computer lab your last two. They had to almost drag you out of there when your sentence was up. Boning up for crime in the new millennium, eh, Matthew?"

A single finger – the middle one – in the upright and locked position, was the Kolvin response.

Pinero slapped it aside. "And guess who was doing exactly the same thing fourteen hundred miles away in the William Head pen? Your twin brother Bertrand. You guys might hate each other, but you still think alike, like identical twins will."

"You're the one tried to frame me and Lenny for the jewel heist," Matthew snarled at Bertrand, "hacking into his computer and planting that phony email, his ugly mug on your stinking face, that ring at his place!"

"You're the one tried to pin a murder rap on me," Bertrand snarled back, "hacking into Lenny's computer and planting my face in his webcam, your voice – our voice – threatening him, limping around like you were me!"

They launched themselves at one another. Mutually assured destruction.

Sergeant Bugler walked into the Squad Room. Detectives McGrath and Pinero were at their desks eating, yammering, the crumbs and insults flying. "Well, Bertrand Kolvin just signed his confession to the jewelry robbery," she informed the pair, "admitting to trying to frame his brother and Lenny Laymon for the job. Apparently, he doesn't want to face a possible murder charge."

Pinero stuck a pencil behind his ear, chewed corned beef and said, "Lucky we found that zipper tongue in his condo, along with enough computer equipment to stock a Radio Shack. He tossed the Moose jacket, but I guess the tongue was just too valuable – for other jobs and other frames."

"You think Matthew will confess to murdering Lenny?" Bugler asked, hands on her hips.

"Maybe, once we break his alibi. We know where he was the morning Lenny was killed – faking a limp in front of Lenny's house to implicate his brother, just to be on the safe side in case there were any witnesses around. Like ones in the sky that he may or may not know about."

"How do you think he killed Lenny?"

McGrath fielded that one in a spray of coffee cake. "We're guessing he just caught Lenny in the bathroom and overpowered him, slammed his head against the tub, killing him instantly. He worked it out to look like an accident, but he set his brother up to be the fall guy just in case it was ruled foul play. There's no such thing as a perfect crime, after all, Sergeant."

Bugler nodded. "But it *was* actually Bertrand going into Lenny's house the night after the murder, right? He says so, anyway."

"Right," McGrath confirmed, picking his teeth. "He was planting that diamond ring to really tie Lenny into the jewelry heist. He never even saw the body – just heard the water running and assumed Lenny was taking a shower. That two man limping oddity, along with the 'dead' Lenny going shopping mystery, of course, is what made us realize there was a frame going on – in this case, a double frame."

Bugler gave her head a shake. "Instead of working together, like good twins should, they were working at cross-purposes – and didn't even know it."

Pinero nodded, belched. He interlaced his fingers behind his head and propped his feet up on his desk, almost toppled over backwards. "Yup. They were going to fix The Rat for what he did to them – each in their own way – so why not kill two jailbirds with one stone by framing each other for their crimes at the same time?"

Bugler let out a sigh. "Well, thank goodness that unlike the Kolvins, you two work so well together."

McGrath spluttered java. Pinero untangled hands and feet and shot upright. "Huh!?" they gaped.

"So well, in fact," Bugler continued, smiling, "that I've canceled your transfer out of Homicide, Detective Pinero. This is one pairing that's just too valuable to split up."

Death and the Rope Trick

John Basye Price

The legendary Indian Rope Trick is such an obvious choice for an impossible mystery that I'm surprised it hasn't been used scores of times. In fact, I'm only aware of this one story which in itself has been tucked away in the pages of the London Mystery Magazine *for over fifty years and never reprinted.*

I have been unable to trace much information about John Basye Price, who was born in 1906. He followed in his father's footsteps in his interest in zoology and was for many years a biologist and science teacher at Leland Stanford University. He published several learned papers on his chosen subject, but just once or twice dabbled with mystery fiction, of which this is a particularly cunning example.

On the plane *en route* to Central America my uncle and I paused for a moment, then lowering our voices we resumed our conversation.

"But, Uncle Edward," I asked, "what can this Dr Marlin hope to gain from all this? He must know he *can't* do what he claims."

"He sounds like a monomaniac with delusions of grandeur, who may become violent when his demonstration fails," my uncle replied. "That's one reason I asked you to come with me."

"One reason?"

"Yes, Jimmy, the other is I need someone I can trust – absolutely."

*   *   *

Filled with curiosity at the summons from my uncle, Mr Edward Dobbs, Chairman of Western University's Board of Trustees, I had joined him at the airport, but we had no time for conversation until we were in the plane and on our way.

Then at last I asked my uncle what it was all about. In reply he handed me a newspaper clipping, and I read:

"CAN DO INDIAN ROPE TRICK," SAYS SAVANT LAYS CLAIM TO $500,000 REWARD

San Francisco, July 6 – It was announced at Western University to-day that an attempt to claim the $500,000 reward offered by the late Richard Welton to anyone who can perform the Indian Rope Trick will be made in the Republic of Del Rio. The claimant is a Dr Clive Marlin, self-styled student of the occult, who has resided in Central America for a number of years.

Richard Welton, who died three years ago, provided in his will that the reward could be claimed outside the United States in some country which had no income tax.

Mr Welton, a life-long student of spiritualism, considered that a successful performance of the Indian Rope Trick under test conditions would be an absolute proof of the genuineness of psychic phenomena, as even Houdini – exposer of many fraudulent mediums – never attempted it.

As often described, but never by an eye witness, the "Indian Rope Trick" is supposed to be a demonstration of mind over matter. The yogi causes a rope to rise in the air by supra-normal means; then a boy climbs to the top of the rope and vanishes, to be rematerialized a mile or more away.

Harry Price, the English expert, once offered a similar reward for anyone who could perform the trick, but no one ever tried to claim it. But Mr Welton thought that a much larger reward might be more effective.

I put the clipping down. "Welton must have been crazy," I said.

"The courts said not, Jimmy. . . . He *was* eccentric – no doubt of that – but still legally sane."

"But how does this concern us?"

"Directly, Jimmy. Mr Welton left two million dollars to Western University, but on the condition that we administer this

$500,000 fund. I, myself, as Chairman of the Board of Trustees, have the sole discretion to grant or withold the reward to any claimant."

"So that's why we're going to Del Rio?" I said.

"Yes. It's all nonsense, of course, but under the terms of the trust I have to make this trip. Crazy or not, Dr Marlin has the right to attempt his demonstration."

A thought came to me. "This Dr Marlin may be sane but crooked," I said. "Not knowing you, he may try to bribe you with part of the reward to give a false report on the test."

"No, Jimmy, if he had that in mind, he would have tried it before he put up the thousand-dollar forfeit. The will requires one to keep the University from being bothered by cranks."

I smiled to myself at the idea of anyone trying to offer my uncle a bribe. A slight man in early middle-age, partly bald with a fringe of dark curly hair, he had keen blue eyes that usually managed to see everything going on. By profession he was a geologist, who might have made a fortune in mining but who preferred to retire on a moderate income to devote himself to scientific studies and to his duties at Western University as Chairman of the Board of Trustees.

"No doubt you're right," I said; "but why has Dr Marlin stipulated that only two persons watch his demonstration?"

"He says that more might set up too many conflicting thought waves and make his success more difficult."

"I wonder," I said. "He may be an expert magician who thinks he can deceive two persons easier than a crowd."

"I doubt it, Jimmy, If even Houdini couldn't work the rope trick, I don't think this Dr Marlin can."

The next morning my uncle and I left the American Consulate in Del Rio City, and in a hired car drove for half an hour along a desolate coast to Dr Marlin's coffee *finca* (plantation). The house was on a slight rise near a secluded bay with a small island about two miles off-shore. At hand was a wharf with a motor-boat moored to it. Dr Marlin's house, to my surprise, was a white two-storied mansion suggesting the Southern United States rather than Central America.

As our car pulled up, we saw three figures awaiting us on the veranda. One, slightly in the lead, a European wearing a white linen suit, stepped forward and introduced himself as the claimant,

Dr Clive Marlin. I looked at him with interest mixed with apprehension, but his manner was perfectly normal. He was a tall, distinguished-looking man of about fifty with thick iron-grey hair and a clipped moustache. A monocle was in his right eye, and his speech was apparently that of a cultured Englishman. But I thought I noticed just a trace of some foreign accent.

After a few words to us, Dr Marlin beckoned the other two forward and presented them as his assistants, Mustapha and his son Ali. My uncle and I spoke to them in Spanish, but the two only bowed and Dr Marlin explained that they only understood Hindustani.

Except that the two both seemed Hindus, I found it hard to believe that they were father and son. Mustapha was a big man, as tall as Dr Marlin but thicker. He wore a white Oriental costume with a turban, and most of his brown face was covered by a dark beard. His son Ali (seemingly about twenty) was shorter and very thin. I could see the ribs under his dark skin, for, unlike his father, he wore only a loin-cloth. He had no hair on his face, wore no turban, and his entire head was shaved so that his scalp glistened like rubber in the sun.

"I suppose," my uncle said, "Ali is the lad who will climb the rope?"

"That is correct," said Dr Marlin. "But not today. First you must witness the pouring of the concrete."

"Concrete?"

"Yes, Mr Dobbs, we don't want to leave any room for doubt. Today I am laying a concrete pavement over the testing-ground so that no one can claim later that Ali vanished into a trap-door under the rope."

We had been following Dr Marlin as he spoke, and a short distance from the house we came to a level field of about an acre, surrounded, except for two gaps, by a thick, six-foot hedge.

In the centre were four iron poles, six feet high, set in the ground so as to form a twenty-foot square. The poles were connected at the tops by four wires designed to hold curtains.

About a dozen native workmen surrounded a bin filled with a freshly mixed concrete. At Dr Marlin's command they poured it on the ground, and smoothed it until the entire square between the poles was covered to a depth of two or three inches.

"Now," said Dr Marlin, "just as a check, will you gentlemen write your names in the concrete? It is very rapid setting, and will be hard to-morrow."

We did so. Before we left, my uncle managed to get a few words in private with Juan, the overseer; but Juan declared that he and all the rest of the workmen had only been there two weeks, and they knew nothing of Dr Marlin. We had already heard from the American Consul that Dr Marlin had bought his *finca* three years ago; he seemed to be an Englishman with plenty of money; but, aside from that, nothing was known of him.

My uncle and I were up early the next morning, and drove to Dr Marlin's after breakfast. I took my pistol and had a small but excellent camera hidden in my pocket. My uncle had accepted the offer of a loan of another camera from Dr Marlin the day before. But this was only misdirection. Secretly *I* was to take the pictures.

We found everything ready for us. Dr Marlin escorted us to the field, after offering us cigarettes. We each took one, but when his back was turned we exchanged them for two of our own brand.

The concrete was hard and we verified our signatures. At the sides of the poles were curtains ready to enclose the pavement. Now, however, they were open. On the pavement was Ali, clad only in a white loin-cloth.

"Where's the rope?" I asked.

"Mustapha will bring it shortly," Dr Marlin replied. "Here he comes now."

Through the gap in the hedge appeared a motor-tricycle. On it was Mustapha clad in his white robe and turban. He drove up on the pavement, dismounted, and from an open wire basket on the handlebars (the machine did not have a rear compartment of any kind) produced a coiled rope about twenty feet long, with a large knot on one end and a snaphook on the other. He uncoiled it and fastened the hook to an iron ring set in the centre of the concrete.

"All ready?" asked Dr Marlin. "Oh, I forgot one thing. After the demonstration is over this morning, you may think that perhaps Ali had a twin brother who tricks you in some manner. So, Mr Dobbs, will you please take Ali's finger-prints? As you know, even with identical twins the finger-prints are different."

My uncle agreed and Dr Marlin beckoned Ali forward and reached in his pocket. An expression of annoyance crossed his face. "I'm sorry," he said, "but I forgot to bring an inkpad. But never mind, I have one in my laboratory over this way. It will take only a few minutes."

We three, accompanied by Ali, started off towards the other gap in the hedge, away from the house. Mustapha, seated cross-legged on the pavement, started to arise to follow, but Dr Marlin motioned him to stay where he was.

The laboratory turned out to be a hut filled with chemical apparatus. It took some time for Dr Marlin to find an ink-pad among the odds and ends that cluttered up the place, but finally one was located. My uncle inked Ali's fingers; secured his prints on a sheet of paper, made a private mark below them; and, after drying, folded the paper and put it in an inside pocket.

We four then returned to the field, where Dr Marlin and Ali rejoined Mustapha on the pavement. Suddenly, in spite of myself, I gave a tremendous sneeze. At the sound Dr Marlin barely started, and Mustapha, like a true yogi, never moved; but Ali jumped as if he had been stung. "He seems to be under a genuine nervous strain," I thought. My uncle and I compared watches, both showed exactly 10.10 a.m.

As directed, my uncle and I took separate stations. I was about twenty feet from the post at the eastern corner of the square, while my uncle had a similar position at the western corner. Dr Marlin then closed the curtains on all four sides, leaving the three demonstrators inside but shut off from view. My uncle and I could each see two sides of the square, and thus covered all four sides between us.

Dr Marlin seemed so confident that in spite of myself I could not help a wondering excitement. But there was to be another interruption. A petrol motor started up behind the curtains, and Mustapha emerged and drove away on the cycle towards the house. I noticed that the rope was back on the handlebars. Dr Marlin called out from behind the curtains that the rope had proved defective and that Mustapha would soon be back with another one. But it was quite a while before Mustapha reappeared, on foot this time, with a coil of rope over his shoulder. Parting the curtains just enough to squeeze through, he rejoined Dr Marlin and Ali inside. All was ready.

Mustapha's voice was heard, shrill and eerie, in a loud chant or wailing. From behind the curtain came the sound of a blank cartridge. I gave a gasp of incredulity and my uncle shouted with amazement. As if by magic, the rope shot high into the air twenty feet or more above the curtains. I forgot to breathe, but still the rope was up there like a snake twisting and writhing in the air above us. It was like a trick on a movie screen, but there was no screen there – only the rope and the blue sky. A fantastic thought of mirrors came over me. I picked up a stone and threw it at the rope, and it went right past it and fell to the ground on the other side. My scalp contracted, my spine tingled as I kicked myself to make sure I was awake.

Another shot from behind the curtains. Simultaneously all four curtains burst into flame, giving off a thick, black smoke. Through the smoke I could dimly see something ascending the rope. The fire died down an instant later and soon the air cleared. The curtains were gone. Dr Marlin and Mustapha were seen alone, at the base of the rope, staring up at Ali. With his white loin-cloth, shaved head, and brown skin clearly visible in the air, Ali was clinging to the top of the rope twenty feet above us.

Raising my camera, I took picture after picture.

Then – Dr Marlin raised his pistol and fired again. Instantly Ali vanished like a soap-bubble. All that was left was his white loin-cloth, which dropped to the pavement below. The rope still twisted and writhed above our heads for a few seconds more. Then it suddenly collapsed and fell to the concrete. Mustapha picked up the loin-cloth, turned and gave it to Dr Marlin, who handed it to my uncle. It was empty, and nowhere in the enclosed field was there any sign of the vanished Ali!

My mind was in a turmoil; I wondered if I could be crazy. I turned to my uncle for reassurance, but did not get it. He was as flabbergasted as I.

Dr Marlin suggested that we return to the house, and led the way, while my uncle and I followed with Mustapha. With an effort my uncle seemed to rouse himself as from a trance.

"I wouldn't have believed it," he said, "but we both must have been hypnotized. Thank God, you had your own camera. If your film shows nothing up in the air, we'll know it was only an hallucination."

"But suppose the film does show Ali at the top of the rope?"

"Then," my uncle said grimly, "under the terms of my trust. I'm afraid I will have no choice. I will have to give Dr Marlin a draft on the University for $500,000."

"It may have been a trick of some kind." I suggested.

"How could it be? There couldn't have been any mirrors used, and, anyway, you and I were on opposite sides of the pavement. It's appalling!"

"Well, it isn't your money," I said.

"It's worse than that, Jimmy. Everyone will believe what you mentioned before – that I gave Dr Marlin a false certificate that he made the demonstration."

"But he did make it." I said.

"Yes, but no one will believe it. Everybody will think that Dr Marlin bribed me with part of the reward. And why shouldn't they think I was bribed? I'm not a rich man. They'll say that Dr Marlin and I conspired together to 'fake the film and split the cash.' I'll be expelled from my scientific societies, and will have to resign from the Board of Trustees. . . . Still, no doubt, when we develop your film we'll see that the whole thing was only an hallucination – but, my God, what an hallucination!"

Dr Marlin led us past the house and down a steep path to the wharf. He picked up a robe and tossed it into a motor-boat. "Ali will be needing that," he remarked. "As you noticed, I could transport Ali, but he had to leave his loin-cloth behind. The subject has to co-operate to be dematerialized. The power doesn't extend to inanimate objects such as clothes."

"Where is Ali now?" my uncle asked.

Dr Marlin pointed to the island about two miles away. "He has rematerialized over there. I thought it would make the demonstration more dramatic to transport him over water. As you see, the only boat is on this side. Shall we start?"

Mustapha took the wheel and we four set out for the Island. About half-way there, Mustapha gave a cry and pointed. Ahead was a dark figure struggling feebly in the water. As we almost reached it, it sank below the waves. Jerking off my coat and shoes I plunged in. Again and again I dived, but without success. I was almost exhausted when finally by luck. I reached the motionless figure. Grabbing an arm, I brought the body to the surface.

"My God, it's Ali," exclaimed my uncle as he and Mustapha lifted the nude figure into the boat. My uncle tried artificial respiration as Dr Marlin took the wheel and we headed back to the wharf. On shore, my uncle continued his efforts, but it was useless. Ali was dead.

Mustapha seemed stunned at the death of his son. Dr Marlin himself seemed shaken. "Poor Ali!" he said. "He must have made some error in concentration. He rematerialized too soon, before he reached the island, and fell in the water. I blame myself! But we never had any trouble before. If only he could have kept afloat a little longer . . ."

Then, with an abrupt return to his old manner, Dr Marlin said, "But, Mr Dobbs, this tragic accident doesn't affect the result of my demonstration. Here is an ink-pad and some paper. I suggest that you take the finger-prints of the corpse and compare them with those in your pocket."

My uncle seemed taken aback for a moment, but he complied, while Dr Marlin took me to the house for some dry clothes. On my return my uncle was putting his magnifying-glass back in his pocket. "There isn't any doubt," he said. "The two sets of prints are identical."

"Yes," said Dr Marlin, "Now, I suggest that you two gentlemen retire to the dark-room in the house to develop your pictures, while I telephone the police about the accident. When you have examined the films, come out on the verandah. We will all have a drink together, and then, Mr Dobbs, I shall be most happy to receive your cheque for $500,000!"

It would have been more decent, I thought to wait at least until Ali's dead body had been taken away, but my uncle disagreed and we retired to the dark-room. My hands were shaking as I put my film in the developer.

As the image appeared, I gave a shudder. In the dim red light we saw the rope extending twenty feet in the air with Ali clinging to the top. We printed enlargements, and when they were fixed my uncle turned on the light and examined them with his glass. "It's Ali, all right," he said. "What we saw, Jimmy, wasn't any hallucination."

We went out to the veranda. I gave a loud cry and my stomach turned over. There at the top of the cliff in a pool of blood lay Dr Clive Marlin, stabbed to death and with a knife in his heart.

I was nearly overcome with the succession of shocks. For an instant so was my uncle, but he drew himself together. Glancing at his watch, he took out a notebook. "One ten p.m." he said. "I'd better write it down."

I looked at my own watch. "It's 1.15," I said; "your watch must have stopped."

"No, it's still going. Didn't the water affect your watch, Jimmy?"

"No, it's waterproof, and, anyway, water wouldn't make a watch run *faster*."

Just then a police car, followed by the hearse for Ali, drove up.

Two police got out, stiffened as they saw the body of Dr Marlin, then turned to stare at us.

An hour later, after the police had been reinforced by their superior officers, my uncle and I were summoned to a room in the house, where a police inspector and his sergeant were questioning Mustapha and Juan, the overseer. As we entered I gasped, for Mustapha, who supposedly spoke only Hindustani, was, in fluent Spanish, pouring out a flood of accusations against my uncle and me.

According to him we were desperate criminals who had not hesitated to murder Dr Marlin when he demanded the reward for demonstrating the Indian rope trick. "They want the five hundred thousand dollars for themselves!" he shouted. "They didn't know I understand English. I heard them talking about it on the way to the wharf!"

With horror I remembered my uncle's conversation. The police looked ominous, and I remembered stories of accused persons in Latin America who had not been held for trial, but who had been shot out-of-hand "while attempting to escape".

But my uncle remained cool, and said in Spanish. "Inspector, before we do anything else, let us find out the correct time." The police, puzzled but courteous, compared watches, and we found that my uncle's and mine were both fast – his by seven minutes and mine my twelve. "I thought so," he said to me.

Turning to the police he said, "My nephew and I were developing pictures when Dr Marlin was killed. Unless one of the workmen did it, the only person who could have killed him was this man – Mustapha!"

Juan broke in, "But, Señor, I and all my men were working together, by Dr Marlin's orders, at the far side of the house. We saw this man – Mustapha – the entire time seated in his upstairs room. We could see him through the window."

"I don't doubt it," my uncle said, "but Mustapha could have been in two places at the same time."

"Surely you don't think he left his astral body upstairs for an alibi while he went down to the cliff to kill Dr Marlin?" I asked.

"Something of the sort, Jimmy . . . Inspector, I suggest that we search this man's room at once."

Mustapha objected vehemently, but was overruled. In the room my uncle's eyes fell on a closed door. It was locked, and Mustapha insisted that he had lost the key; but the police soon forced the door open. I gasped, for seated on the floor of a small closet was Mustapha.

My uncle gave a tug, and the figure collapsed like an over-sized doll. "A very fine dummy," my uncle said as he parted the clothes at the back. "See, the figure is entirely hollow. Clever but not quite original. Walter Gibson reports that Houdini designed a similar hollow dummy for one of his illusions shortly before he died."

Turning to the dejected Mustapha, my uncle said with authority, "Your only chance is to tell the truth! Isn't this what happened? You killed Dr Marlin in self-defence when he tried to kill you because you knew that he had murdered Ali!"

Mustapha started and nodded vigorously, "As God is my witness, that is the truth! . . . But how did you know?"

"I missed it at the time, but Dr Marlin made a slip when we were taking the finger-prints. He said, 'You may think that Ali *had* a twin brother?' Already, before the demonstration, Dr Marlin was thinking of Ali in the past tense."

"But, Señor Dobbs," the police inspector objected, "how could Dr Marlin have murdered this Ali? Do *you* believe in magic?"

"There was no magic at all, Inspector. The whole rope trick was only a 'stage illusion,' but quite an elaborate one. But Dr Marlin made one mistake. He forgot about the watches. When I learned that Jimmy's watch and mine had suddenly become erratic, I guessed part of the truth."

"How so, Señor Dobbs?"

"I'll start at the beginning and describe what I think happened," my uncle replied. "Mustapha can correct me if I go wrong on details. But let's go and sit on the veranda, as this will take some time."

On the veranda my uncle resumed, "There are really two parts to the Indian Rope Trick – both universally considered impossible. The first is to make a rope rise miraculously in the air. The second is to make the boy suddenly disappear from the top and have him reappear at a distant spot.

"There can be no doubt that this morning something like a rope really did rise in the air – the photographs prove it. Now, there is no way to make a *rope* do that, but this 'rope' must have had as a core either a wire or chain of magnetic metal. Isn't that so Mustapha?"

Receiving a nod, my uncle continued, "The fact that both

Jimmy's watch and mine behaved erratically could mean only one thing – that they had been exposed to a strong magnetic field and had become magnetized. This gave me the clue. As you know, while opposite poles of a magnet attract each other, similar poles repel each other with equal force. I remember at the exposition in San Francisco in 1939 seeing an exhibit where a metal bowl was made to float in the air by a powerful electro-magnetic field underneath. Later I read that mediums used this method to make metal tables rise from the floor during fake seances. Perhaps Dr Marlin first got his idea there."

Mustapha nodded again, as my uncle continued, "Dr Marlin made his 'rope' a chain or wire of highly magnetized metal covered with a thin layer of hemp. Under the ground in the field he had built a very large system of electro-magnets designed to project a cone of force. When the current was turned on magnetic repulsion raised the 'rope' above the ground as if by magic."

"But, Uncle Edward," I objected, "if it's as easy as that, why hasn't someone done it before?"

"It's far from easy, Jimmy. As the 'rope' rises above the ground, the magnetic force diminishes very rapidly. To raise a 'rope' twenty feet takes something like a baby cyclotron. Making one would take years of work and cost a small fortune."

"Three years and fifty thousand dollars," Mustapha broke in. "At least so Dr Marlin told me. But the reward was enormous."

"But what happened to Ali; how did he vanish from the top of the rope?" I asked.

"Let's take things in order," my uncle said. "When we arrived yesterday, Dr Marlin took us to the field to watch the pouring of the concrete. The real reason for the pavement was to keep us from digging later and finding the electro-magnets. Dr Marlin also introduced us to his two assistants, supposedly from India. Where do you really come from, Mustapha?"

"From Mexico City, Señor. Ali and I have had a Hindu act for some time."

"You might have chosen better names," said my uncle. " 'Mustapha' and 'Ali' sound more like Mohammedans than Hindus . . . To come to this morning. At the start of the demonstration Mustapha, Ali, and Dr Marlin were all present on the pavement. But that was the last time the three were really together until we found Ali in the water.

"Dr Marlin 'forgot' his ink-pad, and we three, with Ali, went to the laboratory to take the finger-prints. As soon as we had left, Mustapha produced the hollow dummy of himself from some hiding-place nearby (perhaps in the hedge) and arranged it in a sitting position on the pavement. Leaving it there, he, himself, ran up to the house.

"When we came back from the laboratory we never doubted that the dummy was Mustapha. (But remember, Jimmy, 'Mustapha never moved' when you gave that loud sneeze.) Dr Marlin and Ali rejoined 'him' on the pavement and closed all four curtains.

"Then Dr Marlin 'discovered' that the rope was 'defective' and sent 'Mustapha' for another one. What really happened was that the hollow dummy was placed on the cycle, and Ali crept inside it, came through the curtains and rode rapidly up to the house in the semblance of Mustapha. He had no trouble balancing on the tricycle; all he had to do was to sit still and steer. We never doubted that Ali was still behind the curtains, but, really, at that time Dr Marlin was there alone.

"When Ali reached the house, out of our sight, he emerged from the dummy, took it upstairs and hid it; while the real Mustapha walked back to the field, to give Ali more time, and 'returned' to us with another rope."

"But," I objected, "we saw Ali at the top of the rope."

"No, Jimmy, we only thought we did. After the real Mustapha rejoined Dr Marlin behind the curtains, he started a chanting wail while Dr Marlin pressed a concealed switch – probably in one of the iron rods. This turned on the electro-magnets underneath and, as if by magic, the 'rope' rose in the air.

"Then either Dr Marlin or Mustapha brought from his pocket a collapsed rubber dummy which, when inflated, was an exact life-sized replica of Ali. Incidentally, that was why Ali had to shave his head. Hair would be hard to imitate, but the rubber looked just like dark skin.

"Instead of using air, Dr Marlin inflated the rubber dummy with helium. I don't know just how; did you have a small cylinder of it under your robe, Mustapha?"

"No, Señor, the helium was under pressure in a tank beneath the concrete. One of the iron rods was really a pipe with a concealed nozzle. It took only an instant to inflate the dummy, which looked exactly like Ali. Dr Marlin paid three thousand dollars to have it made by an expert in magical supplies in Mexico City."

"Next," continued my uncle, "Dr Marlin placed a loin-cloth on the figure to weigh it down in position, and attached the dummy with dark threads to the bottom of the 'rope'. Then he fired a blank cartridge, set fire to the curtains, and under cover of the dense smoke the released dummy, filled with helium and exactly weighted with a light ballast, rose to the top of the 'rope,' where the large knot prevented it from going higher. You must have used a very light loin-cloth, Mustapha?"

"Made of paper, Señor."

"I see. That instant must have been the trickiest part of the whole illusion. We might notice that 'Ali' was rising, not climbing. But the dense smoke and the thrashing about of the 'rope' – caused by slight magnetic variations – entirely deceived us. Then, too, our critical faculties had just been almost paralysed by the miraculous rising of the 'rope.' After that we were in a state to see and believe almost anything. I don't say we would have been fooled a second time, but Dr Marlin only had to make the demonstration once."

"It certainly fooled me," I said.

"No more than me, Jimmy. Next the smoke cleared, and in the air above us we saw 'Ali' at the top of the rope – not for long, but long enough to take photographs. Then Dr Marlin raised his pistol; but this time, instead of a blank he fired a real bullet, which pierced the dummy. The dummy instantly collapsed, and the shrunken rubber was drawn back inside the loin-cloth where we couldn't see it as it fell to the ground. Ali had vanished before our eyes! What happened to the paper loin-cloth, Mustapha?"

"I picked it up, Señor, and by sleight-of-hand exchanged it for a real one I had under my robe. I gave the real one to Dr Marlin, who handed it to you."

The police inspector broke in, "All this is most interesting, Señor Dobbs, but what about the murder?"

"We will come to that in a minute. The plan was that after the demonstration we should find Ali on the island – rematerialized there by magic – or rather by supra-normal powers. Apparently the only boat was still on this side, but there must have been another one hidden. Did it have a silent engine, Mustapha?"

"Yes, Señor, it was a small aluminium canoe with a battery and electric motor. Dr Marlin had it hidden, hung above the water, under the floor of the wharf. Ali was supposed to discard his loin-cloth, launch the canoe, cross to the island, and then sink the boat to complete the illusion."

"Now we come to the first death," my uncle said. "Just what

happened, I don't know. My guess would be that before the demonstration Ali demanded more money than Dr Marlin wished to pay him. Mustapha, do you know about it?''

A look of misery crossed the bearded face. "I didn't, but I do now. The boy was too ambitious. Dr Marlin told me just before he himself died that Ali demanded half of the entire reward, instead of the ten thousand dollars apiece that we had been promised. He threatened to give the whole thing away to you if Dr Marlin didn't agree.''

"So that was it," my uncle said. "No doubt he promised Ali everything, and then killed him before he could try to collect. Dr Marlin must have tampered with the boat.''

"He boasted of it to me!" Mustapha cried angrily. "He opened a seam in the bottom and filled it with a plastic that would dissolve soon after Ali launched the canoe. It must have sunk about half-way across. But Ali was a better swimmer than Dr Marlin thought. He nearly managed to keep up until we came.''

"Surely you suspected something afterwards?" my uncle asked.

"I did, Señor, but I wasn't sure. So I put the dummy of myself at the window while you two were in the dark-room, and went outside to have it out with Dr Marlin. He was ready for me though, and pulled a gun with a silencer out of his pocket. He told me how Ali had died, and then forced me to the edge of the cliff and tried to push me off – apparently a grief-stricken suicide. But he didn't know that I had a knife in my sleeve. I threw it and it pierced his heart. Then I lost my head, tossed his gun into the water, and ran back to my room to hide the dummy in the closet. I deeply regret, Señor, that I accused you, but I didn't think anyone would believe me.''

"Don't worry, Mustapha," my uncle said. "The police, no doubt, will recover Dr Marlin's pistol and raise the canoe from the bay. That evidence will prove your story of self-defence. But it's fortunate for me that I happened to notice the magnetized watches. I suppose that Dr Marlin never thought of them giving the show away.''

"Yes, he did, Señor; he thought of that as a remote possibility just before he sent the wire to you. We considered hiring someone to steal your watches in California, and having him bribe a jeweller to sell you non-magnetic ones. But Dr Marlin decided that it would take too much time. He was always afraid that someone else would claim the reward.''

"Why," asked my uncle in surprise, "did he think some rival knew his secret?"

"No, Señor, and, besides, very few mediums would have enough money. But it's a strange thing – all his life Dr Marlin had been a charlatan and a fraud, but always he believed that some of the other mediums were genuine. All the time he was getting things ready, he was afraid that some yogi from India, with genuine psychic powers, would appear and claim the reward by *really* demonstrating the Indian Rope Trick."

The Problem of
The Black Cloister

Edward D. Hoch

Let us bow to the Master. No, not John Dickson Carr. Carr may have set the rules for the impossible crime story and created most of the templates, but Edward Hoch (b. 1930) has now written considerably more stories than Carr and created far more variations on old ideas as well as plenty of new ones. I never cease to be amazed at Hoch's output. He has now been selling short fiction for over fifty years and has had at least one story, sometimes more, in every issue of Ellery Queen's Mystery Magazine *since May 1973. He's steadily creeping towards having written and published one thousand stories, and precious few living writers can say that. Of the eighteen or so new stories that Ed produces each year, three or four of them are impossible crime stories – so he's probably written around 200 of them by now. Many of his stories fall into one of a number of series, and almost all of his series characters have had to face an impossible crime now and then. One of them, Dr Sam Hawthorne, who narrates his stories to his anonymous guest about cases from his early years in practice, encounters nothing but impossible crimes. So far there have been two collections of Hawthorne's cases,* Diagnosis: Impossible *(1996) and* More Things Impossible *(2006).*

I could clearly have filled this book solely with Ed's baffling mysteries, and certainly felt that only one selection did not do justice to the Imp of the Impossible, especially as Ed has also written the occasional perfect-crime story. So here are two by the Master. The first is a Sam Hawthorne story, followed immediately by a non-series story containing one of Ed's most creative crimes.

L ess than a week after the 1942 election that insured a seventh and final term for Sheriff Lens, the Allied invasion of French North Africa began. It was a joyous time for everyone, a sign that we had launched a major ground offensive at last. (Dr Sam Hawthorne paused to refill the glass of his listener.) It was also a time for war-bond rallies in the cities, when celebrities sometimes came to help raise money for the war effort.

Towns like Northmont ordinarily would not have attracted a war-bond rally on any large scale, but as it turned out we had a local celebrity hardly anyone knew about. The November election brought us a new mayor, Cyril Bensmith, a slender, vigorous man of forty, a bit younger than me. I'd hardly known him before he ran for office, and I didn't know him much better now. His family had a small farm over near the town line, almost into the adjoining township of Shinn Corners, which probably explains why I hadn't heard about him or his boyhood chum Rusty Wagner.

Rusty'd been George Snider at the time. He didn't become Rusty till he moved to New York and landed the villain's role in a mildly successful Broadway play. From there he went off to Hollywood and became Paramount's answer to Humphrey Bogart. He was never as big a star as Bogart, but by April of 1943, with the Allies advancing in Tunisia and many of the younger male stars in the service, Rusty Wagner was doing his part by touring the country selling war bonds. Health problems and his age, just turning forty, had kept him out of the army. When Mayor Bensmith heard he'd be at a rally in Boston he invited his old friend to make a side trip to his hometown.

"Did you hear the news?" my nurse April asked that morning. "Rusty Wagner is coming here for the war-bond drive."

"We don't go to many movies," I admitted, though the town boasted a pretty good theater. "I guess I've seen him once or twice."

"I'm going to help out on the drive," she said. April's husband André was away in the service and I could understand her urge to get involved.

"That's good. I'll come and buy a bond from you," I promised.

That night at home I mentioned it to my wife Annabel, who showed a bit more excitement than I had. "That's great news, Sam! Something's finally happening in this town."

I smiled at her remark. "A lot of people think too much happens here already. Our murder rate—"

"I wish you wouldn't blame yourself whenever somebody gets killed in Northmont. I'm sure there were murders here before you ever came to town. I'll have to ask Sheriff Lens when he and his wife come to dinner."

The sheriff had been elected to his first term in 1918, just days before the armistice that ended the war. I hadn't moved to town and set up my practice until a few years later, in January of '22, and for some reason we'd never really talked much about Northmont's past crimes.

We dined with Sheriff Lens and his wife Vera every couple of months, and it was their turn to come to our house two nights later. While Vera helped Annabel with dinner in the kitchen I engaged the sheriff in conversation. "Annabel and I were talking the other night about Northmont's crime rate. How was it before I came here in 'twenty-two? Did you have just as many murders?"

Sheriff Lens chuckled, resting his hand on the glass of sherry my wife had provided. "Can't say that I remember any at all before you came to town, Doc. Guess you brought 'em with you." He took a sip from the glass and added, "There was the fire over at the Black Cloister, of course, but no one ever suggested that was murder."

I'd driven past the burnt-out building several times during the past twenty years, wondering why the county didn't just tear it down and sell the land at auction. "Exactly what happened there?" I asked.

"Well, it was in the late summer of 'twenty-one. The place had been built late last century as a sort of farming commune for disenchanted monks and other religious men who'd left their various orders but weren't ready to return to the secular world. Occasionally they took in one or two juvenile offenders if the courts asked them to, on the theory that a hard day's work might set them straight. Nobody paid much attention to them out there, except about once a month when a couple of them came into town for supplies. They called it the Black Cloister, named for the Augustinian monastery in Germany where Martin Luther lived.

After the Reformation the monks moved out but Luther continued to live there, offering shelter to former monks and travelers. Upon his marriage in fifteen twenty-five the building was given to him as a wedding gift."

"You know a good deal about it, Sheriff."

"Well, Vera's a Lutheran even though we were married by a Baptist minister. We got talking about the Black Cloister one night and she filled me in on all that history."

"I heard my name mentioned," Vera Lens said as she came in to join us. "Dinner will be ready in three minutes."

"Doc was just wondering about the Black Cloister," the sheriff explained.

"Funny you should mention that, Sam. We're putting together an antique auction for the war-bond rally and someone donated the ornate oak front door from the Black Cloister. You can see it along with the other antiques down at the town hall."

"Maybe I'll take a look. When is this all going to happen?"

"Next Tuesday, the twentieth. That's the day after the Boston rally. They're tying it in with Patriots' Day and the Boston Marathon." Easter Sunday that year was not until April twenty-fifth, the latest it could be.

We took our seats at the table as Annabel came in with our salads. "I was just talking to Vera about the rally," she told me. "I told her I wanted to help out, too."

"A lot of people are. April at my office said she'd help. There's nothing like a movie star to brighten things up."

"Rusty Wagner isn't exactly a heartthrob," Vera remarked, plunging her fork into the salad. "Sometimes his face looks like it went through a meat grinder."

"He makes a perfect villain, though," Annabel said. "I saw a couple of his films before we were married." Turning to me, she said, "Sam, we have to start going to the movies more."

Somehow the conversation never did get back to the fire at the Black Cloister. It wasn't until Sunday afternoon, two days before the scheduled rally, when I accompanied Annabel to the town hall and stood before the fire-scorched door, that I remembered the burned building. The thick oak door was indeed a thing of beauty, leaning against the wall. Its front showed a bas-relief of a hooded monk kneeling in prayer, and this is what would have greeted visitors to the Cloister.

"You can see the door was badly scorched in the fire," Vera said as she came up to join us. We were in the ornate lobby of the town hall, where a score of items of all shapes and sizes had been assembled for the auction.

I ran my fingers over the bas-relief, admiring the carving. "Looks as if there are a few little wormholes in it, though," Annabel remarked.

There were indeed, toward the sides and top of the door. I pulled it away from the wall, but the back was smooth and unmarked, without a trace of scorching. "What was the story about this fire?" I asked Vera. "It was before I moved here."

"I was pretty young then myself, but I remember the Cloister as some sort of religious community. There was a fire and one young man died. After that the rest of the community just scattered."

"Who owns the property?"

"I have no idea. Felix Pond at the hardware store donated the door. He said it had been in the family for years, but I don't know that they ever owned the place."

"How does this charity auction sell war bonds?" Annabel asked.

Vera Lens explained. "People bid by purchasing the bonds, so it's not really costing them anything. They get their money back when the bonds are redeemed. The items are all donated and I don't imagine they have any great value. But something like this door could be cleaned up and painted and put to good use. Some church might even like it."

I ran my fingers over the wood once more, again impressed by the workmanship. "I wonder who carved this. Was it someone locally, or perhaps one of the residents at the Black Cloister?"

"It's possible Mayor Bensmith might know."

"I think I'll ask him."

Cyril Bensmith had a dairy farm on the North Road. His tall, gaunt frame reminded some of Abraham Lincoln, though he'd never thought of entering politics until his wife died a few years earlier. They had no children, and perhaps in search of a new beginning he'd run for mayor and been elected handily. He still worked his farm every day. Being mayor of Northmont was not a time-consuming occupation.

He had just arrived at the town hall and was greeting people with a handshake when I went up to him. "How are you, Sam? Good to see you here. I think the rally on Tuesday's going to be a big success."

"It should be," I agreed, "especially with Rusty Wagner's appearance."

"Rusty's an old friend. I haven't seen him in years, but we've stayed in touch."

"I was admiring that door from the old Cloister," I explained, gesturing toward it. "Know anything about it?"

"No more than you. Felix Pond at the hardware store donated it."

"I was wondering if the carving was by a local person."

"I couldn't tell you that. If there's an opportunity you might ask Rusty when he's here Tuesday."

"Rusty?"

"He was living at the Black Cloister at the time of the fire."

"How old would he have been at that time?"

"Eighteen, I think. Same age as me. He and another boy, Fritz, were caught stealing a car in Hartford. The judge suggested they could avoid jail by spending the summer doing farm work at the Cloister and they agreed quickly enough. That's how I got to know Rusty. His name was George then, but he never liked it. We saw a lot of each other that one summer, before the fire."

He moved on to greet others, and I was left with unanswered questions.

On Monday Sheriff Lens stopped by my office in a wing of Pilgrim Memorial Hospital. He was chatting with April as I finished seeing the morning's last patient and I invited him into my examining room. "Everything set for the bond rally tomorrow, Sheriff?"

"I guess so. Vera's had me run ragged, picking up donations for the auction."

"I was talking to our mayor yesterday and he tells me Rusty Wagner was a resident of the Black Cloister. You never did finish about the fire."

"It was so long ago I can barely remember it now. Like I said, it was the summer of 'twenty-one. The Cloister was home to about a dozen men, some from a Trappist monastery that had closed, and others from various Protestant denominations. They were men with problems or at loose ends. There were also those two kids doing farm work to avoid prison. I guess Rusty Wagner was one of them. The other fellow was killed in the fire."

"Tell me about it."

Sheriff Lens sighed. "Don't you have enough mysteries in the present to satisfy you, Doc? This was no impossible crime or anything. No crime at all, far as I know. The fire started in the kitchen somehow and spread to the rest of the house. It was in the afternoon and the other residents were out in the fields working. Wagner and this other young fellow, whose name I don't recall—"

"The mayor said it was Fritz."

"That's right, Fritz Heck. Anyway, they were preparing the evening meal when it happened. Wagner managed to get out with a few bad burns, but the other boy didn't make it. I suppose that little scarring on Wagner's face didn't hurt when he started playing villain roles."

That was pretty much all he remembered, but I was still interested in tracking down the origin of that door. I drove over to Felix Pond's hardware store on my lunch hour and waited while he took care of a couple of customers. Pond was a bristling, bearded man who seemed strong as an ox, constantly carrying lumber and supplies out to waiting wagons. I was not one of his regular customers, but he knew me by sight. "Dr Hawthorne! What brings you here? Got a need for a hammer or screwdriver?"

"Curiosity brings me," I told him. "I was admiring that door from the old Cloister and they told me you'd donated it. I wondered how you came by it."

"That's easy," he said with a grin. "I stole it, years ago. The place seemed to be just rotting away after the fire. The residents had all scattered and no one was even sure who owned the property. It was a sin to see that fancy door just sit there and decay like that so I took it home with me. Stored it in my supply shed out back and forgot all about it till somebody asked me about it last year."

"It might be worth some money," I speculated.

"Sure might! It's fine workmanship, made by one of the original residents of the Cloister. But I figured I couldn't really sell it since it wasn't mine to begin with. When someone suggested I donate it for the bond auction it seemed like a good idea."

"I'm sure people will bid on it. I might even do so myself." But then something clicked in my mind. "Tell me, Felix. Did you decide to donate this to the bond auction after you heard Rusty Wagner was going to be here?"

He frowned at my question. "Why would I do that?"

"Someone told me he was living in the Cloister at the time of the fire."

"Really?" He thought about it. "I guess maybe it was after we heard he was coming. Can't remember who suggested it, though."

I left the hardware store, wondering more than ever what was bringing Rusty Wagner back to Northmont.

Tuesday was sunny and mild, a perfect spring day to greet the crowd that had turned out for the war-bond rally. It was nothing compared to the Boston crowd, of course, but I recognized several people from Shinn Corners and other towns who'd driven over for the event. We'd set up a stage in the town square, with a billowing flag bunting as a backdrop. The auction items were all on view, including the Cloister door standing upright against one of the backdrop supports.

Just before the rally began, Mayor Bensmith made a point of introducing me to the star attraction, Rusty Wagner. He was shorter than I'd expected, and his features were a bit sharper. Close up I could see the scarring on the right side of his face. It appeared that the skin had been burnt, apparently during the Cloister fire. The damaged area was not large and could have been easily covered by make up if he wished. Accompanying him was his manager, a fellow named Jack Mitchell, looking uncomfortable in a suit already rumpled from their train trip.

"I understand you lived here for a time," I said, shaking Wagner's hand.

He smiled pleasantly. "A long time ago, one summer before I moved to New York City. The town has changed a lot since then."

The mayor rested a hand on his old friend's shoulder. "We're going to start in a few minutes. You'd better get in position on the stage." He turned to me with a wink. "We want to open with a bang, like in Rusty's movies."

For a moment I didn't know what he meant. Then, as Wagner took the stage amidst an outburst of applause, a man in a German officer's uniform suddenly appeared from behind the flag bunting and stood before the Cloister door, taking aim at him with a Luger pistol. There were screams from the spectators as a shot rang out and Rusty Wagner clutched his chest, falling to the floor.

Immediately Mayor Bensmith sprang to the microphone, holding up his arms to calm the audience. "That, folks, is what could happen right here if not enough of us support our government with war bonds! Happily, the German officer is really our own Milt

Stern, and Rusty Wagner is alive to fight another day." He motioned to the downed star. "Time to greet your public, Rusty!"

But Wagner remained sprawled on the floor of the stage without moving. I went quickly to his side. There was no blood, no sign of a wound, but I knew at once that he was dead.

When a well-known movie star dies before hundreds of people at a bond rally, it makes news all over the country. Mayor Bensmith and Sheriff Lens both knew Northmont would be on the front pages the following day and they turned to me for help. I urged them to calm down, reminding them that we didn't yet know the cause of Wagner's death. "One thing we know for sure, whatever killed him, it wasn't a bullet from Milt Stern's gun."

Nevertheless, while the mayor tried to calm the crowd and get on with the war-bond auction, Milt was the first person the sheriff and I questioned. He was a ten-year resident of Northmont, in his mid thirties, married with two children. For the past several years he'd worked at the local feed store. "Is Wagner dead?" he asked us at once. "They took him away in the ambulance and somebody said he was breathing."

"He's dead, son," Sheriff Lens told him. "We just didn't want to announce it right away and put a damper on things. After the bond rally's over there'll be an announcement."

Stern passed over the German Luger for our examination. "All I had was one blank cartridge in it." I slid out the clip and confirmed that it was empty. "The mayor got the gun and uniform from a theatrical costume place in Boston."

"It was the mayor's idea?" I asked.

"Well, he was talking about something like that to start things with a bang. I volunteered to play a Nazi and fire a blank at him."

The facts were clear-cut and I would have been awfully surprised if the autopsy showed Rusty Wagner had been poisoned or choked to death. It didn't. By the following morning we knew that he'd died of a heart attack. There was no wound anywhere on his body.

Still, I stopped by the mayor's office to have a talk with him. "Apparently the man had a weak heart," I said. "Maybe that's what kept him out of the army, that and his age."

"It's just a tragedy it had to happen here," Mayor Bensmith said. "He could have dropped dead in Boston just as well."

"Tell me something. Did you explain to Wagner exactly what

you had planned, with the Nazi officer and all? Did he know someone would fire a blank cartridge at him?"

"Certainly. I went over every bit of it with him as soon as he arrived. My secretary, Rita, was with us at the time." He called her into the office. "Rita, what did I tell Rusty Wagner when we met him at the station?"

Rita Innes was a prim middle-aged woman who'd worked in Bensmith's office at the farm before his election as mayor. He'd taken her with him to the elective office and she'd settled in well. Now she answered, "You explained about the man dressed as a Nazi who'd fire a blank at him. He'd fall to the stage and you'd tell the audience to buy bonds. He wasn't surprised. He said he'd acted out scenes for audiences in other cities, too."

"The heart attack was just a coincidence, happening when it did," Bensmith decided.

I had to agree with him. From both a medical and a legal viewpoint, there'd been no crime.

Wagner's death had completely overshadowed the war-bond auction, and it was a couple of days later before I saw Vera Lens and remembered to ask her about it. "We did well," she reported, "considering everything."

"Who bought that door from the Black Cloister?"

"Funny you should ask. It went to a man named Jack Mitchell. He was Rusty Wagner's manager and was making the tour with him. The door's still here. We're supposed to ship it to him in California."

On the following Monday, the day after Easter, I was driving past the ruins of the old Cloister and decided to stop. Walking through the high grass to the gaping front entrance, I found a roof partly burned through, and weathered walls still showing scars from the fire. There was evidence of children playing there, and ground into the dirt out back I found a used shotgun shell. Every farm family kept a weapon close at hand. There were always varmints on the prowl.

After lunch I stopped in to see Sheriff Lens at his office. "I drove by the Black Cloister this morning and took a look. Can you tell me any more about the fire and your investigation?"

The sheriff gave one of his familiar sighs. "Doc, there's no crime for you to solve, neither here nor back in nineteen twenty-one. That Rusty Wagner could be killed by a shot from a blank cartridge isn't an impossible crime, it's no crime at all!"

"Let's get back to the Cloister fire for the moment. Tell me about the young man who died there."

He went over to the file and opened the bottom drawer. "I haven't looked at that folder myself in years. Probably should have discarded it after all this time." Opening the slender file, he took out some papers and a few photographs. "The victim's name was Fritz Heck. He was eighteen, same age as Wagner. Nice-looking fellow. That's him on the right in this photo."

"Is this Wagner with him?"

"No, it's Heck's younger brother."

I nodded. "I should have guessed that from the resemblance."

"We got the photo from the family in Hartford, for identification purposes. There was no doubt it was him, though. Heck's finger-prints were on file with the Hartford police. Him and Wagner stole a car but didn't know much about driving it."

"How did the fire start?"

"Wagner told me they were preparing dinner, chatting about a girl they'd met in town, when Heck got careless and some hot grease caught fire. They tossed water on it but that just spread it around. The flames went up along the ceiling and into the living room." He referred to his notes and Wagner's statement. "Heck ran into the living room and tried to beat it out, but it was too late. He was trapped by the fire and smoke, and died inside the front door, trying to get it open."

"Why is the house still standing after all these years?"

Sheriff Lens shrugged. "I heard tell Heck's family bought it, wanted it as a memorial to their son. But they never did anything except pay the taxes."

"Did you ever meet any of them?"

He shook his head. "If they came here I didn't see them. Of course the body was shipped back to Hartford for burial."

"What about Rusty Wagner? What happened to him after the fire?"

"They took him back to Hartford, too, for treatment of his burns. We heard later that he moved to New York and was in a play. Mayor Bensmith was a friend of his and stayed in touch over the years." He squinted at me over the tops of his glasses. "You're tryin' to make something out of all this, aren't you?"

"I'm trying," I agreed with a smile. I picked up the snapshot of Fritz Heck and studied it. "Do you have an autopsy report there?"

"Well, not really. Back in 1921, Northmont's coroner was just a local sawbones eager to make a few extra bucks. He just had to look at the body to know the fire killed Heck. The Hartford police furnished us with medical records on the two boys, though."

He passed them over to me and I glanced quickly through them. There were the usual childhood illnesses, plus a serious bout of influenza for Heck during the nineteen epidemic. Wagner had suffered from rheumatic fever twice as a child, but had escaped the flu. "What else do you have there?"

"Just Wagner's statement on the fire, which I've told you about. His face was burnt trying to save his friend."

I thought about that. "Do you have a phone number for this manager of his, Jack Mitchell?"

"I think it's here somewhere. Why do you want it?"

"Vera says he was high bidder on that Cloister door. It seems an odd thing to bother about when your client has just died."

I phoned Mitchell's West Coast office and after some delay was put through to him. "Mr Mitchell, this is Dr Hawthorne, back in Northmont. We're still investigating Rusty Wagner's unfortunate death."

"Yes," he replied. "I just got in the office. I've been making arrangements for the memorial service. What can I do for you?"

"I'm told that you were high bidder for the door from the Black Cloister, where Rusty lived for a time."

"That's correct. He wanted me to bid on it for him. It seemed very important to him. When the ambulance took him away I was hoping he was still alive. I entered my bid on the door before following him to the hospital."

"What do you plan to do with the door?"

"Do with it?" his voice rasped over the phone. "Nothing. Now that he's dead you can keep the door, auction it off again."

"Did he have any reason for wanting it so badly?"

"None that I know of. He'd lived at that Cloister for one whole summer. I suppose it brought back memories."

"I'm sure it did," I agreed. "His friend died in the fire, and he was badly burned."

"He never went into detail about it. He just asked me to buy the door at the auction."

I thanked him and hung up. Sheriff Lens asked, "Did you learn anything?"

"He doesn't want the door now that Wagner's dead. He said we should keep it and auction it off again."

"I'll tell Vera."

"Where's the door now?"

"Still over at the town hall. In the mayor's office, I think."

"Let's go have another look at it," I suggested.

We walked across the square to the town hall. Mayor Bensmith hadn't yet returned from lunch, but his secretary Rita showed us the door leaning against his office wall. "We're waiting for shipping instructions," she informed us.

"He doesn't want it," I told her. "We'll auction it again."

I moved over to examine the door more closely and asked Rita, "Do you have a pair of tweezers?"

"I think so." She went back to her desk and returned with them.

"What are you after, Doc?" Sheriff Lens wanted to know.

"I'm not sure, but I know Wagner wanted this door, and his statement to you at the time of the fire wasn't completely accurate."

"How's that?"

"He said Fritz Heck died inside the front door, trying to get it open. But look at this door. The scorching is on the outside, while the inside is unmarked by flames. This door had to be open at the time of the fire, and if that was the case how could Heck have been trapped there by the fire and smoke? He could have simply run outside."

"I never thought of that," the sheriff admitted.

I took a penknife from my pocket. "I wish we'd had a more complete autopsy report."

"In those days—"

"I know." I concentrated on one of the wormholes Annabel had noticed earlier, enlarging it a bit with my knife. Then I went to work with the tweezers. After a moment I extracted what I was seeking.

"What is it, Doc?"

"Buckshot. Annabel thought they were wormholes, but I noticed the other side was unmarked. These were worms that went in but didn't come out. Notice the unusual pattern they formed." I pointed out a half-dozen small holes toward the sides and top of the door.

"A buckshot pattern would be more circular," he argued.

"Not if something or someone had been in its way. Don't you see, Sheriff? Fritz Heck was standing by this open door when someone fired a shotgun at him. I know they probably had one on the premises because I found an old shotgun shell in the dirt there. The missing pellets from the pattern are in Heck's body, and judging by the close grouping of these other pellets that shotgun blast was probably enough to kill him."

"Rusty Wagner was the only one in the house at the time."

"Exactly," I told him. "We'll never know now what happened, but Wagner told you they'd been chatting about a girl they met. Maybe they argued about her, maybe Wagner picked up the shotgun that every farmhouse had in those days and tried to drive Heck from the Cloister. Maybe it went off accidentally by the front door."

"Then he started the fire deliberately?"

I nodded. "To cover the crime. He probably made a special point of burning the body, to cover up the wounds from the shotgun pellets. When he got too close and burned his own face it added verisimilitude to his story."

"Any coroner today would have found those shotgun pellets."

"Probably. He certainly would have spotted the absence of smoke in the lungs, a sure sign that Heck was already dead when the fire started."

Sheriff Lens sighed. "With Wagner dead there's not much point in exhuming the body now."

"None whatsoever."

"I only wish you'd been around here a year earlier, Doc, and I wouldn't have missed all this. It was a perfect crime."

I shook my head. "No, Sheriff. The perfect crime was the murder of Rusty Wagner in front of this building last Tuesday. And there's not a thing we can do about it."

As it happened, Annabel and I were dining at Max's Steakhouse, our favorite restaurant, a few nights later when I spotted Milt Stern drinking at the bar. "Excuse me for a few minutes," I told her. "I'm going to talk to him."

"Sam! You said you wouldn't."

But I got up anyway and went over to him. "Got a few minutes, Milt?"

"Sure. What's up?"

"I just want to chat. Over in that empty booth would be best."

He glanced toward Annabel at our table. "You shouldn't leave her alone."

"This won't take long."

He followed me to the booth and slid in the other side. "So what's this all about?"

"Rusty Wagner."

"God, I feel terrible about that! It's as if I'd murdered him."

"You did."

He moistened his lips and gave a half laugh. "Well, not really. The gun had a blank cartridge in it."

"What was it that made you move here, Milt? Did you know your brother had been murdered that day up at the Cloister?"

"He wasn't—"

"Yes he was, Milt. I saw the snapshot of the two of you and even then I noticed the resemblance. Ten years ago you left Hartford and moved here, changing your name from the German Heck to its English meaning, *stern*. You suspected all along that Wagner had killed your brother. Perhaps he hinted at trouble between them in one of his letters. Once here you settled down and married. Somewhere along the line you saw the Cloister door that Felix Pond had rescued from the place, and recognized those little 'wormholes' for what they were. When you heard that Wagner would be coming here to take part in a war-bond drive, the idea came to you."

"What idea?"

"You would suggest to Pond that he donate that old door for the war-bond auction. Then, when the mayor was discussing a clever way to bring Wagner on stage, you volunteered to dress in a Nazi costume and fire a blank pistol at him. You knew, of course, that he'd had rheumatic fever twice as a child. Perhaps your brother mentioned it or you read it in a movie fan magazine. Such a medical history almost certainly would have left him with a weak heart, probably the reason for his draft deferral."

"He knew in advance I was going to fire a blank pistol at him," Milt Stern said. "That wouldn't have caused a heart attack."

"Perhaps not alone. But when he came onto that stage what he saw was the friend he'd killed twenty-two years ago, aged a bit but still recognizable, standing in front of that same door and pointing a gun at him. In the instant the gun went off, his weak heart failed."

"Do you really expect anyone to believe that?"

"No," I admitted. "Certainly not a jury."

Milt Stern smiled at me. "Then why are you telling me this? Who else have you told?"

"Sheriff Lens knows, and the mayor soon will know. They can't bring any charge against you, but it might be better if you left Northmont, moved back to Hartford."

He studied my face for a long time. "Don't you understand it's something I had to do? Whether he lived or died was out of my hands."

"Whether you stay or go is out of my hands, too," I told him.

"All right," he said at last. "I'll take your advice."

I left the booth and went back to join Annabel. I'd done all that I could.

A Shower of Daggers

Edward D. Hoch

Susan Holt awoke with a start, wondering why her bed felt so hard. Then memory flooded back in a blinding instant of terror and she knew she was in a jail cell, accused of murder. She opened her eyes and saw a woman in the next holding cell staring at her through the bars. "You're awake," the woman said.

"What? Yes. Yes, I'm awake. What time is it, please?"

"Barely daylight. Quarter to seven."

Susan groaned. She'd slept less than three hours and her mouth felt as if it was full of cobwebs. She glanced at the lidless toilet in one corner of the cell. "Do they give you anything to eat here?"

"Pretty soon now. They'll bring something around seven o'clock. What you in for?"

"Murder, I guess. I haven't been charged yet." The other woman gave a low whistle of appreciation and Susan hastened to add, "I didn't do it."

"Have you called a lawyer?"

"Not exactly. I called someone who'll get me a lawyer." She had called Mike Brentnor, her coworker in promotions at Mayfield's, Manhattan's largest department store. He was hardly a friend, but in the middle of the night in a strange city she was feeling desperate. Considering that she'd awakened him from a sound sleep, he'd been both concerned and reassuring, promising to be on the first morning plane out of LaGuardia, a flight that would take less than an hour.

Presently a guard brought her a breakfast tray with some juice, coffee, and a hard roll. "You'll be brought before the judge at ten o'clock," he said, not unkindly. "Have you seen your lawyer yet?"

"No. I think someone's on the way."

Mike Brentnor arrived a few minutes before nine, looking just a bit flustered. He was slim and slyly handsome, around thirty, the sort of man Susan used to see by the dozen in Manhattan singles bars. She met with him now in one of the interrogation rooms. "I phoned Marx from the airport and he gave me the name of a good criminal lawyer up here," he told her.

For an instant she was dismayed that he'd reported to their superior, but of course Saul Marx would have to know about it. She wouldn't be flying back as planned this afternoon. She'd be in a jail cell in upstate New York. "What did he say?"

"That it must be a mistake. Who is this person you're supposed to have killed?"

"Betty Quint. It's a long story. I'd rather just go over it once when the lawyer's here."

"I left word at his office. They were going to try catching him at home so he could come directly here. Mayfield's name carries some weight, I guess."

"I'm glad of that!" The coffee had revived her and she was feeling a little more human.

"I'm pleased you phoned me, Susan. I heard you broke up with Russell and I can't say I'm sorry about that. You know I've always had a fondness for you."

"Fondness? Is that what you call it?" She decided to make things clear from the beginning. A night in a jail cell had intensified the anger she sometimes felt toward Brentnor, though she knew none of what had happened was his fault. "I phoned you because I didn't want to wake Saul in the middle of the night, and yours was the only other Mayfield's home phone number I had with me. I do appreciate your flying up here, but let's not get the wrong idea."

"All right," he agreed, flushing at her harsh words. "Now tell me what—"

A guard came to announce that her lawyer had arrived. He bustled in looking like an upstate version of Mike Brentnor, though with more style. She had a sudden vision of him in a courtroom defending her on the murder charge.

"Hello, Miss Holt," he said, holding out his hand. "I'm Irving Farber from the firm of Freeman and Farber. That's my father in the firm name, not me." A smile flashed across his face, then was gone. He was all business. "What happened here?"

"I've been arrested for murder is what happened," Susan said, her anger rising again.

"Have you made a statement to the police?"

"I told them what happened. They questioned me for hours until I demanded a lawyer."

"That's good." He took a yellow legal pad from his briefcase and started to make notes. "What about the assistant D.A.? Was he in to see you?"

She nodded. "After they photographed and fingerprinted me. I told him I wanted to phone a coworker to get me a lawyer. By that time all I wanted was some sleep."

"All right, Susan. May I call you Susan? Suppose you tell me your story from the beginning."

He glanced questioningly at Mike Brentnor and Susan said, "It's all right if he stays. I have nothing to hide."

"Let's start at the beginning. What brought you to our city?"

Susan took a deep breath, as if she was about to dive into a swimming pool. "I work for Mayfield's, the Manhattan department store. We're opening our first location in western New York at your new shopping mall in Pembroke and I flew up to work out the details of some special promotions. Betty Quint was my contact here."

More notes. "How long had you known Miss Quint?"

"I'd met her once at our New York office about six months ago. She stayed overnight at my apartment. We'd been in constant touch by phone, fax, and E-mail since then. This is my first trip up here because there was no point in coming until the store was almost ready to open."

"When does it open?"

"Next Tuesday. A week from today."

"Go on. Describe everything that happened."

I took the Monday afternoon flight up from LaGuardia (Susan continued), arriving at midafternoon. Betty met me at the airport and drove me to the new store. She was a friendly, uninhibited young woman of about my age, around thirty. Seeing her again confirmed my impression of her from our initial meeting at the New York store. She was a good worker, perfect for this store, but perhaps lacking the cool sophistication needed for the Manhattan retail scene. She liked jokes and didn't mind attracting attention to herself. I wasn't surprised when she mentioned she was active in a local theater group.

We toured the completed Mayfield's store, where clerks were busy unpacking merchandise for the shelves and racks. Betty consulted her notebook frequently as she led the way through the store, pointing out special features of interest. A small cafe was already open for the employees and we took advantage of it for coffee and a snack.

"I'm so excited to be part of the Mayfield's team!" Betty gushed. "Have you been with them long?"

"About nine years. Ever since college."

"I thought Manhattan was very exciting when I was there in the spring."

"It is, but most of my excitement has come from traveling for the store. I've been to Tokyo, Iceland, Switzerland, London, and all over America."

"Do you meet lots of men on the job?"

"Not too many," I said. "I told you about Russell."

"Are you back living with him?"

"No." I felt like saying it was none of her business. Instead, I shifted the conversation back to the new store. "Do you have anyone helping you on promotions?"

"Sadie Shepherd, she's my secretary." Her face brightened. "There she is now! I'll introduce you." She called out to a slender dark-haired woman in her twenties who was already headed in our direction. "Sadie, this is Susan Holt, the promotions coordinator at Mayfield's flagship store in Manhattan."

The young woman had a pleasant smile and seemed eager to please. "So glad to meet you! Betty told me about the great time she had in New York."

"It was fun for me too. Perhaps you can come down and see our store sometime."

"I'd love that," Sadie said, then turned her attention briefly to Betty. "I wanted to catch you before you left. Here are a couple of phone messages."

"Thanks, Sadie." She glanced at them and slipped them into a pocket of her notebook. When we were alone again she turned back to me. "It would be great if you could stay and help me through next Tuesday's opening."

"I'm afraid that's impossible, Betty. I have to fly back tomorrow afternoon. But we can go over lots of things while I'm here. If you're free we can have dinner tonight. My expense account is fairly generous."

"That would be great! We have a wonderful new French restaurant down by the harbor."

"I'll have to check in at my hotel first. I don't want to inconvenience you. I should rent a car."

"Why bother, for just one night? I'll drive you to the hotel and then we can go to my place while I change."

It wasn't quite as simple as it sounded. Just as we pulled up at my hotel Betty received a call on her cell phone. She seemed annoyed at the caller, someone named Roger, and tried to get rid of him. "Look, I'm working right now, Roger. Sadie gave me your messages, but I was too busy to get back to you. Can't we talk about this later?" She listened for a moment and then said, "I'm with someone from the New York office and we'll be going back to my apartment." When he said something else she uttered an obscenity and pushed the Off button on the phone.

I gave a grunt of approval. "Is Roger an old boyfriend?"

"Worse than that," she said, but explained no further.

It took me a few minutes to check in and she accompanied me to my room.

"I just want to slip into a dress and we can be on our way," I told her.

"It's not a fancy place."

"I've gotten a bit rumpled from traveling. I'll only be a minute." She sat down on the bed. "Do you smoke?"

"Tried it. Gave it up."

She'd opened her purse to take out a cigarette but then thought better of it. Meanwhile, I'd unzipped my overnight bag and removed this simple print dress I'd brought with me for early fall wear. I didn't bother retreating to the bathroom for a modest change of clothes. We'd seen pretty much all of each other the night Betty stayed over at my Manhattan apartment. That was also the night she'd startled me by suggesting we stop for after-dinner drinks at the Plaza bar and then paying for them with a hundred-dollar bill.

"Can I use your phone?" she asked as I was freshening my makeup.

"Go ahead." I motioned toward the nightstand.

She got an outside line and punched in a local number. When the party answered she started right in. "Roger phoned me awhile ago." A pause and then, "Well, I don't like it."

I tried to keep busy with my make-up to avoid being too obvious about my eavesdropping. "I'm at the hotel now," she said, "but I'll be back to my apartment shortly. What'll I do if he comes up and wants the money?"

She listened intently after that, finally said, "All right," and hung up with a sigh.

"Is anything wrong?" I asked casually, finishing with my makeup.

"No, no. Just man trouble. You know how it is."

We started out for her apartment but she was openly nervous, keeping an eye on the rearview mirror as if fearful of being followed. I wondered about that but asked no further questions, even when she seemed to double back on her route and take the long way through a number of narrow residential streets. "Less traffic this way," she muttered, sensing my questioning gaze.

Presently we entered a neighborhood of large older homes, many of which had been split into apartments and needed ugly second- and third-floor fire escapes to comply with housing codes for multiple dwellings. Betty Quint parked in front of one of these. "Come on up. I want to take a quick shower and then we'll be on our way."

It was already after six and starting to get dark. Thick gray clouds had rolled in, threatening rain. She led the way to a side door which she quickly unlocked. I noticed there were two mail-boxes, one with her name and the other with Mr & Mrs R. James Liction. "The landlord," she said by way of explanation. "A retired couple. They live downstairs. Come on up." She led the way to her second-floor apartment.

"It's so large!" I marveled.

"I have the entire second floor," she answered with pride. "These old houses are great bargains." She dropped her things on the coffee table and walked to the front window, gazing down at the street. "Damn!"

"What's the matter?"

"He's down there in a car. I think we were followed."

"Roger?"

"I'm going to shower," she said, walking into the bedroom as she shed her outer garments. I hesitated to follow but then she called to me. "Here's something you might like even if you did quit smoking."

I walked into the bedroom and found her holding out a cigarette with crimped ends. "What is it, pot?" I asked.

"Sure! It's good stuff. Helps you unwind after a day's work."

"No thanks. But go ahead if you want one."

She shrugged and tossed the joint on the bedside table. "I don't like to smoke alone."

Wearing only a bra and panties she went into the bathroom and turned on the shower, rummaging in a cabinet for a bath towel. "Come on in, Susan. Talk to me while I shower." She handed me the towel to hold.

I sat on the closed toilet seat, feeling uncomfortable as she shed her underwear and tossed it into a laundry hamper. Then she felt the spray of water with her hand and stepped into the shower, pulling the curtain closed behind her. "Tell me about the Manhattan store," she called out over the rush of water. "Is it true a homeless man lived there for days before he was discovered?"

"I've heard stories like that, but I—"

Betty Quint screamed, just once, chilling my spine. Then there was a thump as her body went down in the tub. "Betty!" I yanked open the shower curtain and stared at her body, drenched in the pounding spray of hot water.

She'd been stabbed once in the back with a slender dagger that still protruded from the bloody wound. A second, identical dagger lay in the tub near her foot. Otherwise the tub was empty.

I was alone in the steamy bathroom with her body.

Irving Farber scratched his nose and stared at Susan. "That story is impossible, you know. It couldn't have happened the way you told it."

"But it did!" she insisted. "I called 911 and the police were there within minutes."

"And they arrested you."

"Not right away. They questioned me for hours, trying to make me change my story. They accused me of all sorts of wild things, especially after they found the pot. I told them neither of us had smoked it but they kept pounding at it. One of the detectives suggested we'd been high on pot and made love to each other, and then I killed her to hush it up. That's when I demanded a lawyer."

Farber's face was grim. "What was the detective's name?"

"Sergeant Razerwell."

He made a note of it. "Tell me, Susan, what's your explanation for Betty Quint's death?"

"I have none. I agree it's impossible."

"Did you touch anything in the apartment after you phoned the police?"

"No. I didn't even turn off the shower. I couldn't go back in there and see her again. I just sat in the bedroom and shivered until I had to open the door for the police."

Farber glanced at Mike Brentnor. "Will the store go bail for her?"

The question startled him. "I – I don't know. Depends on how much it is, I suppose." He wasn't about to admit he had no authority in the matter.

"Who's your boss?"

"Saul Marx."

Irving Farber glanced at his watch. "Is he in the office by now? It's nearly ten."

"He should be."

"Get on the phone and ask him about bail. Meanwhile, I'll talk to the assistant D.A. and find out how much they'll be wanting."

"Is there a chance I'll get out of here?" Susan asked, her hopes soaring at the thought of it.

"Depends on the D.A.'s office. Don't get your hopes up." He put the yellow pad in his attaché case and snapped it shut.

Susan glanced at her watch. "I'm supposed to be in court in ten minutes."

"They'll come for you when they're ready. Sometimes these things are a bit loose. If they don't get you there, it's their fault, not yours."

The attorney and Mike Brentnor departed, leaving Susan to wonder just where she stood. She'd investigated a few murders in the past, during her travels for Mayfield's, but she'd never been accused of committing one herself. The killing of Betty Quint while she was alone in the shower seemed so impossible that, paradoxically, Susan felt the solution must be a simple thing she could easily discover once she was free.

Presently one of the guards came for her. "Am I going before the judge?" she asked.

"Not yet. They want to question you some more."

Susan was immediately on guard. "My attorney—"

"He's been notified."

She was ushered into one of the interrogation rooms, where she sat down at the bare table to wait. Presently the door opened and a stocky red-haired man she'd never seen before entered. He was carrying a briefcase and Irving Farber was right behind him. "Good morning, Miss Holt," the redhead said, flashing a smile that was quickly gone. "I'm Adam Dullea, US Secret Service." He flashed an ID that looked like miniature currency with its finely engraved borders.

Susan panicked, imagining some labyrinthian plot against the president. What had she gotten herself into? "What do you want?"

"I just have a few questions regarding your relationship with Betty Quint." He opened his briefcase and took out a clear plastic envelope with a hundred-dollar bill inside. "Have you ever seen one of these?"

"A hundred dollars? I guess I've seen a few."

"Did Betty Quint ever show you one?"

"No." Then she remembered something. "She came to New York for a meeting about six months ago. We went out for dinner and drinks later and I remember she paid for the drinks with a hundred-dollar bill. I was a bit startled, but some people like to use big bills when they travel."

"This one is counterfeit," he said.

Susan peered at it more closely. It looked fine to her. "What's its connection with Betty?"

"She passed it at a local restaurant. There've been a few other incidents too. We've had her under surveillance."

"Is it true you can do these on a good color copier?" she asked.

"Not of this quality. We think it was printed overseas."

"How—"

"I'm asking the questions, Miss Holt. Did Betty Quint ever show you or give you a hundred-dollar bill?"

"Just that one time when she paid for the drinks. And she gave it to the waiter, not to me."

"I understand from your statement to the police that she received a phone call from someone named Roger while driving you to your hotel."

"That's correct."

"Did she identify him further?"

"Not to me, no."

"And she made a call from your hotel room?"

"Yes. I'm sure you could trace that. Most hotels keep a record of phone charges for billing purposes."

Adam Dullea looked at her sadly. "The call was made to the local Mayfield's store, Miss Holt."

That surprised Susan and she must have shown it. "We'd just left there. Why would she –?"

He took a deep breath. "Look, Miss Holt, we're inclined to accept your story for the moment, and so are the local police. If you had killed her, you would certainly have come up with a better story than you did – a burglar on the fire escape or a prowler under the bed, for example. Also, your coworker Mike Brentnor has informed the police that you've been helpful with other murder cases in the past. You'll be released on your own recognizance, but you're to remain in the city for at least forty-eight hours pending another court apperance on Thursday, when charges may be dismissed. Is that agreeable?"

"I suppose it'll have to be." What were they doing, giving her two days to find the real killer?

The Secret Service agent departed and Farber smiled encouragement. "Come on, Susan. You're on your way out of here."

In the courtroom it went exactly as predicted. The preliminary hearing was adjourned until Thursday morning at ten and she was released on her own recognizance. Mike Brentnor was waiting in the back of the courtroom. "Let's go celebrate!"

"I've nothing to celebrate, Mike. A woman's been murdered and I'm the only one who could have killed her."

That was when Adam Dullea reappeared, his smile a bit more sincere this time. "Now that you're released from custody, I wonder if we could talk."

"About the murder?"

He nodded. "If you'll excuse us, Mr Brentnor—"

Susan was happy to escape from Mike's eager clutches. She allowed herself to be guided out of the courthouse and into Dullea's car. "Where are we going?" she asked.

"Back to the scene of the crime. Isn't that how these things are done?"

She laughed. "I'm no psychic, you know. I don't pick up the killer's thoughts or visions. Sometimes I notice things that others have missed."

"That's what I'm hoping for."

This time as the car pulled up to the house a white-haired man came onto the front porch to greet them. He introduced himself as James Liction. "I own the place. You folks more police?"

Dullea showed his identification. "Secret Service. The victim was part of an ongoing investigation into counterfeit currency. Could I ask you if she paid her rent in cash?"

He shook his head. "Always a check, first of the month. My wife Mona was just saying what a nice tenant she was. Never any trouble. I can't believe she was involved with counterfeiters."

His wife a stocky woman who moved slowly, came out to join them. "Tell 'em about that suspicious-looking guy across the street, James."

"Well, I already told Sergeant Razerwell."

"Tell me too," Dullea requested.

Liction shifted his gaze to Susan. "I happened to see the two of you drive in. After that a fellow parked across the street. He just sat there in his car for a long time. It was too dark to get a good look at him. When he heard the sirens coming he left quick."

Susan remembered that Betty Quint had glanced out the front window and become upset when she saw the car. "We're going to take another look upstairs," Dullea told him.

James Liction shrugged. "Go ahead." He and his wife went back inside.

The apartment was much the same as the day before, except that the door was sealed by yellow police crime-scene tape. Dullea pulled it away and used a key to enter. Inside Susan noticed signs that the drawers and closets had been searched by the police or Dullea's people. "What are you looking for?" she asked. "More counterfeit money?"

He nodded. "A great deal of it. Before she went to work for your store, Quint was employed on the reservations desk of a major airline. Her boyfriend, a copilot on international flights, brought back several small packages of counterfeit money, all hundreds like this one. They're often printed overseas and used as bulk payoffs for drugs." He brought out the bill he'd shown her earlier, in its clear plastic envelope. He pointed to the lower right of the portrait where it read "Series 1996" in small print. "Notice anything wrong with it?"

She shook her head. "There's Ben Franklin, looking the same as ever."

"That's what's wrong. Beginning in 1996 the hundred-dollar bills changed significantly. The portrait is larger and off-center. There's a new watermark and other safety features. Skillful as this job is, the counterfeiters made a fatal mistake in using the old design and dating it 1996. These bills couldn't be passed in bulk overseas, where a suitcase full of drug money would be carefully examined by the seller, so they were smuggled into this country to be passed individually."

"You think Susan's boyfriend hid them here?"

"Yes."

"And then killed her?"

Dullea shook his head. "His name was Lloyd Baker. He was found shot to death last week in the parking lot at Kennedy Airport."

Susan sat down on the couch. "You think the same person killed Betty?"

"No, as a matter of fact, Baker's killer is in custody. We were moving in on Betty Quint and obtaining a search warrant for this apartment. The easy answer is that she feared being caught with the counterfeit money and committed suicide."

"She stabbed herself in the back? And where did she get the knife? She didn't take it with her when she stepped into the shower. I was right there."

"All right, then. If it wasn't suicide, what happened?"

Susan recalled the scene vividly. "I don't know. It was almost as if a shower of daggers hit her, instead of water."

"Daggers? There was only one."

Susan had gotten up and gone into the bathroom. She opened the cabinet that held the towels, then turned her attention to the shower itself. It was made of molded plastic, recessed into the wall. The plastic was solid and there was no clear sight line to the room's only window, which had been closed in any event. The ceiling was smooth and unmarked, with the room's only lights arranged on the wall above the mirror. The showerhead was normal. It had not dispensed daggers. The shower curtain was ordinary white opaque vinyl. "There were two daggers," she called out to Dullea. "One in her back and another in the bottom of the tub."

Susan turned on the water and couldn't hear Dullea's reply. Something caught her eye. She reached down and peeled it away from the bottom of the tub. It was a piece of Scotch tape, several inches long. Stuck fast near the drain, it had been all but invisible. "Look at this," she called to him.

He came into the bathroom. "Tape. Where was it?"

"Stuck to the bottom of the bathtub. They could have overlooked it in their crime scene search."

"What does it tell us?"

"I don't know." She stared around the bathroom. "You mentioned a search warrant. When were you planning to use it?"

"Last evening."

Susan thought about it. "Someone named Roger phoned her in the car, before we arrived at my hotel."

"I read that in your statement."

"Maybe he was going to take the counterfeit money off her hands. With her boyfriend dead she'd need to do something."

"You don't just get a friend to deal in counterfeit."

"Maybe it's the same friend who was selling her pot. He might have been interested."

"Roger?"

"Roger," Susan agreed. "When she made the call from my hotel room she sounded a bit frightened of him. And she'd had other messages from him earlier. Maybe she was afraid he'd kill her for those counterfeit hundreds. Maybe he did kill her, but I'm damned if I know how."

Susan still didn't have a car of her own, and after Dullea left her off at the hotel she asked the room clerk where she could rent one. He directed her to a place just a few blocks away. As she was turning from the desk another thought struck her. "Do you keep a record of guests' outgoing phone calls, with the numbers called?"

"Yes, ma'am, we do."

"Could I see mine, please? I've mislaid a local number that I need."

He brought it up on the computer and jotted it down for her. "This is the only call from your room."

Susan glanced at it, a bit puzzled. "Yes, that's the one. Thank you." Dullea had told her that Betty Quint phoned Mayfield's from her room, but the number at Mayfield's new store ended in 6700. This number ended in 6743. Susan went up to her room and dialed it.

A woman's voice answered with, "Store promotions."

"Whose office is this?" she asked.

"I – it was Betty Quint's office."

"Sadie? Is this Sadie Shepherd?"

"Yes. Betty is—"

"I know. This is Susan Holt."

"Oh! Miss Holt!"

Susan made a snap decision. "I'd like to speak with you after work today. Could we have a drink together?"

"I don't know. I'm busy tonight."

"I have to rent a car. What time do you finish up?"

"Usually five, but until the opening I can pretty much leave any time. Since Miss Quint's death—"

"I'll pick you up at five, Sadie. If you don't want to go anywhere we can talk in the car."

She was outside the store in a new Chevy when the young woman emerged, exactly on the hour. Sadie heard her beep the horn and headed over to join her in the front seat. "It's good to see you again, Miss Holt. That was terrible news about poor Betty."

"How do you think I felt, being right on the scene?" Susan left the motor off since Sadie had indicated she had no time for a drink.

"How did it happen?" the young woman asked.

"I was hoping you could tell me."

Her face froze into a mask of ice. It could have been fright or defiance. "I don't know what you mean."

"How was Betty Quint killed in that shower, Sadie? You know, don't you?"

"Why do you say that?"

"Because I think you were responsible for her death."

Sadie Shepherd exploded into fury. "That's a damned lie! I know nothing about it!"

"Calm down and listen. This is what I know so far. Betty's boyfriend was killed after smuggling a large quantity of counterfeit hundred-dollar bills into this country from overseas. They had a flaw in them that made it necessary to pass them individually rather than in bulk, where they'd be closely examined. After her boyfriend's death, Betty tried to find a buyer for the money and she went to a man named Roger who was supplying her with pot and maybe other drugs. You two became friendly and she confided all of this to you. Somehow Roger frightened her, perhaps by demanding the counterfeit hundreds for less money than she wanted. He phoned her yesterday and made more threats. Back at my hotel, she phoned you at the store to tell you what was happening. She phoned her own direct number, but of course you answered. At the store yesterday you gave her some messages you'd taken in her absence, so I knew you answered her phone. Just as you did when I called that number earlier."

"You think you know everything, don't you? We didn't become

friendly only recently, as you say. We've been friends for two years, since we were in a local theater production together. She got me the job as her assistant at Mayfield's. I liked her. She was lots of fun, always joking and doing crazy things."

"What about her drug problem?"

"She smoked a little pot, sure, but nothing more than that."

"Roger was her supplier?"

She nodded. "I told her not to go to him about the money, but she had all these hundreds and she was afraid to pass them herself. She'd tried a few here and in New York, but it made her too nervous."

"Her boyfriend had hidden the counterfeit money with her?"

"Sure. He thought it was the safest place, but it didn't keep him from getting killed."

"Roger followed us back to her apartment last night. He was parked across the street."

Sadie turned away. "I told her what to do on the phone earlier."

"What was your advice?"

"I said if he was at the apartment she should manage to make her escape somehow. If he went after her, I'd go up there and take the money before he got it. She'd given me a duplicate key."

"She made her escape all right, by getting killed. Did you go there last night?"

"God, no! When I heard about her death on the news I knew there'd be cops all over the place."

"Where was the money hidden?" Susan asked.

"Inside a folded towel in the bathroom cabinet."

"If it was still there, the police certainly found it. They were all over that bathroom."

She touched the door handle. "Look, I've got to go. I've told you everything I know."

"Not quite everything. Where can I find Roger?"

"I don't know. He was just a name to me. Betty never told me anything about him."

She left the car quickly, walking across the paved lot to her own little white Neon. Susan sat where she was until Sadie Shepherd had pulled out and vanished down the highway. She wanted to make certain she wasn't being followed.

Back at her hotel she found the Secret Service waiting for her. Adam Dullea intercepted her on the way to the elevator. "You're a tough one to keep up with. I leave you alone for a few hours and you're off on your own."

"I thought I had to clear myself by Thursday morning. I can't do that sitting in a hotel room."

"Where did you go?"

"You mean you didn't have me followed?"

He laughed. "That was my job."

Susan just stood there in the lobby, wondering how much she could safely tell him. Finally she said, "All right, come on up and I'll tell you what I learned."

In the room she opened the minibar and offered him a drink which he declined. "Maybe a Coke, if you're having something." She joined him in one and he said, "Your friend Brentnor's been worried about you."

"I should be so hard on Mike. He did fly right up here and help rescue me from a jail cell. I just always have the feeling he's waiting for a chance to paw me."

"Has he tried it before?"

"Once or twice. But he backs off when he sees I don't like it." He sipped his drink. "Where were you this afternoon?"

"Out at the store. I still work for a living."

"So do I. Who did you see there?"

"Betty's assistant, a young woman named Sadie Shepherd."

"Does she know anything about the killing?"

"Betty was an old friend. She told Sadie about the counterfeit money. She was afraid this Roger fellow wanted to take it without paying her price."

"That's about what we figured."

"The money was hidden in the bathroom cabinet with her towels."

"It was?" The news seemed to startle Dullea. "Sergeant Razerwell told me he personally searched the entire bathroom, including the toilet tank."

Susan looked up. A sudden thought struck her. "What's Razerwell's first name?"

"Eric. Don't let your imagination run wild."

She brooded about it for a moment, then remembered something else. "While I was in her bathroom earlier, you said something about the dagger that killed her and I told you there were two daggers."

He shook his head. "Only one."

"There was a second dagger at the bottom of the tub."

"No, just the weapon that killed her. It was still in her back."

She held her breath, eyes closed, and asked one more question. "Were you parked across the street at the time of the murder, watching the apartment?"

"Sure. I told you we were going to use the search warrant last night. I had to make sure she didn't remove the money before my men arrived. When the police came I drove away until I could find out what was going on."

Susan opened her eyes and smiled. "Then I know how it was done."

It was back to Betty Quint's apartment once more. Darkness had settled in and a strong breeze was blowing a few dead leaves down the center of the street. White-haired James Liction opened the door in answer to their ring and seemed more resigned than surprised at seeing them. "What is it? You want to examine the apartment again?"

"I don't think that'll be necessary right now," Susan told him. "I just want to ask you one question."

"Well, you might as well come in. You too, Mr Dullea. Now what's the question?"

The answer came before she had a chance to ask it. From the kitchen, his wife called out, "Who is it, Roger?"

"It's just—" Liction began. Then he must have seen the expression on Susan's face and realized what had happened. He tried to twist away as Dullea reached out to grab him.

When the Secret Service man had him under control, Mrs Liction came into the room. "Hey, what's going on?"

"We just have a few questions for your husband, that's all."

She seemed resigned to it. "About the drugs, I suppose."

"That and other things."

Then Susan spoke. "I was going to ask you what the 'R' stood for in R. James Liction, the name on your mailbox. I thought maybe it was Roger. That's what Betty Quint called you, wasn't it?"

"I guess so," he mumbled. "I might have sold her a little pot. Nothing wrong with that."

"Are you growing it in the basement?" Dullea asked. "Some people do."

"Can I call you Roger?" Susan asked, then went on. "Roger, we know Betty offered to sell you a quantity of counterfeit hundred-dollar bills from overseas. She was frightened that you might try to steal them from her."

"I didn't kill her," Liction insisted. He could see where the conversation was leading. "I couldn't have killed her. You were alone with her when it happened."

"How did you know that?" Susan asked. "By looking in the bathroom window from your perch on the fire escape? Yes, I know there's a fire escape outside that window even though I didn't actually look at it. I saw the fire escape to the second floor when I drove up with Betty yesterday, and Mr Dullea here even commented on the unlikely prospect of a burglar coming through the bathroom window from the fire escape."

Liction moistened his lips. "I think I want a lawyer."

"You'll get one," Adam Dullea said, formally stating his rights. "First thing, we're going to get Sergeant Razerwell down here to make the formal arrest. The murder is his job. I'm just interested in the money."

Mrs Liction spoke from the doorway. "If we give you the money, will you forget about the killing?"

"Shut up, Mona!" he nearly screamed.

"You see," Susan continued, "I made a big mistake. Betty had seen someone in a car across the street and that frightened her. I thought it was Roger, but she knew it was Mr Dullea here. She was caught between the two of them, with no way out. Maybe she'd even spotted you on the fire escape, Roger. Anyway, she decided to fake an attack on herself in the shower and escape by being taken to the hospital in an ambulance. She'd done some community theater work and had a fake dagger with one of those collapsible blades, the sort that ejects imitation blood when the blade retracts. It has adhesive to stick to the skin. While she was rummaging for a towel, she took the fake dagger and a real one and attached them to her body with Scotch tape, probably under her arm where I couldn't see it. Her secretary Sadie said she was a great joker. Maybe she'd even pulled this stunt before."

Dullea was shaking his head. "Are you saying she accidentally killed herself?"

"No, no! She meant to tell me she was wounded and to call an ambulance. Then she'd give herself a flesh wound with the real dagger before they arrived, and she'd be rushed to the hospital, escaping both Roger and the Secret Service. But after sticking the collapsing dagger to her back, she let herself fall in the shower and accidentally hit her head, knocking her out for a moment. The real dagger, still taped to her body, came loose and fell in the tub. I saw the daggers and thought she was dead. Roger here had heard her scream, and while I was phoning 911 he came in the window of the bathroom to get the package of money. He must have seen her hide it there earlier. She was beginning to stir in the tub and he stabbed her with the real dagger. He saw that the first one was a fake, so he pulled it off her back and took it with him, along with the money. He went back out the window and closed it behind him."

"How long would that have taken?"

"Not more than thirty seconds, and any sounds would have been covered by the water from the shower, which I hadn't turned off. I stayed out of the bathroom completely after I called the police."

"What would she have told you and the doctors after the hoax was discovered?" Dullea asked.

Susan shrugged. "She'd have had a slight flesh wound to show the doctors, and she'd have thought up some story to explain the knife. She'd have told me it was meant to be a joke and it backfired. At least she'd be safe from both Roger and you. That was the important thing."

Dullea allowed a brief nod of agreement. "How did you know it was Liction? That first initial wasn't much evidence to go on."

"There was something else. When Betty called Sadie from my hotel room, she said she was going back to her apartment and what should she do if Roger came up and demanded the money. She was saying that Roger lived downstairs, if I'd only known how to interpret her words. And once I knew Roger was so close, the method of murder wasn't so hard to work out. One of the daggers had disappeared, and that meant someone had entered the bathroom before the police arrived. No one came through the door and the window was the only other entrance. If I hadn't killed Betty, the person who entered through the window must have done it. Roger was too likely to be ignored."

It was Mona Liction who returned with the package of counterfeit money while they waited for the police. "Here! Take it! I told him not to get involved in this. Take it and leave us alone."

Adam Dullea reached out a hand as a police car pulled up in front. "I'll take it, but I'm afraid we won't be leaving you alone for quite some time."

The Hook

Robert Randisi

Robert Randisi (b. 1951) is a powerhouse of creative energy. Not only does he write scores of crime stories and westerns, some ghost written for others, he also founded the Private Eye Writers of America Association in 1981, inaugurated the Shamus Awards for the best P.I. fiction, and co-founded (with Ed Gorman) the news magazine of the field, Mystery Scene. *Before writing full-time Randisi worked as an admin. assistant for the NYPD, which gave him plenty of material for his series featuring the New York police detective Joe Keough, whose adventures began in* Alone with the Dead *(1995). Amongst his many books is* The Ham Reporter *(1986) in which an ageing Bat Masterson teams up with a young Damon Runyon in 1911. The following story, set a few years earlier, also features the legendary Bat Masterson in a series of inexplicable murders.*

1

Denver, 1899
George's Weekly
Normally, this is a sports column, but something has happened in this city and no one seems to be doing anything. Three women have been killed on the streets of Denver and the police department seems to be unable – or unwilling – to do anything about it. All citizens of Denver – decent and otherwise – have a right to be able to walk the streets in peace and safety. The old west – they keep telling me – is gone. The

twentieth century is upon us, and yet these young women are dead and the killer is still at large. Shame on you, Chief Flaherty, and shame on the Mayor.

The banging on the door woke Bat, who reached out for Emma only to find her gone. This was not unusual. She often rose before he did, as she often retired before him. If she was up, she would answer the door, and would not allow anyone to disturb him unless it was . . .

"Bat?" she said, softly. "It's the police."

When Bat entered Chief Flaherty's office there was one other man there, seated in front of the Chief's desk. Flaherty's normally florid face was redder than ever as he told the police officer who had delivered Bat, "You can go."

"What's this all about, Chief?" Bat asked. "I don't usually get up this early in the—"

"Masterson," Flaherty said, cutting him off, "this is Inspector House. Inspector, Bat Masterson."

House stood up and turned to face Bat. He had a genial grin on his face as he extended his hand and said, "Quite a column in today's paper."

"Oh," Bat said, accepting the younger man's extended hand, "so that's what this is about."

"That's right, Masterson," Flaherty said. "Since you think the Denver police are so inept, I'm gonna accept your offer of help in this case."

"I didn't offer—"

"Or I'm gonna toss your ass in jail for obstructing the investigation."

"I didn't obstruct—"

"One or the other," Flaherty said. "The choice is yours."

Bat could see that the Police Chief was deadly serious. It had been a few years since he'd seen the inside of a cell, and his recent spare of soft living had not left him in shape to handle the food.

George's Weekly was owned and edited by Herbert George, who was so thrilled to have the likes of Bat writing for his paper that he allowed the western legend to cover any subject he wanted. Ostensibly a sports columnist, on this morning Bat was berating the Denver police for their inability to track down and capture the man who had, in recent months, killed three women on the streets of Denver. Two were what polite society called "decent" women, and the third was what that same group referred to as "fallen". To Bat Masterson, whether the women were somebody's wife or a street whore didn't matter.

Actually, it did matter to Bat. The person it didn't matter to was his wife, Emma. She was the one who was particularly upset about the murders, since she and her friends no longer felt safe on the streets.

"It's the job of the police to catch this maniac, isn't it?" she'd asked him yesterday morning while he dressed.

"Yes, dear."

"And they're not doing their job, are they?"

"No, dear."

"Well, then, somebody should light a fire under their asses, shouldn't they?" she demanded.

"Yes, dear." Bat wasn't surprised at his wife's language. When they'd met she had been performing on stage at the Palace Theater, which at the time he'd owned (and had since sold). Stage people, he'd found, often "salted" their language.

"Somebody with the public's ear," she finished, and stared at him.

It suddenly became clear that she was talking about him, so he fixed his tie, turned to her, kissed her cheek and said, "Yes, dear."

He'd written the column, half expecting that Herbert George would not run it.

But he did . . .

Bat sighed. "I guess you got yourself a volunteer, Chief."

"Excellent," Flaherty said. "House has been working on the case so far, so he will catch you up on what's been going on. I think you two should work well together."

"Shall we go?" House asked, standing up.

Bat stood and said, "Lead the way."

"Oh, and one more thing," Flaherty said before they reached the door. "When this thing blows up it ain't gonna be blowin' up in my face. It's gonna be your faces. You two got that?"

"Got it," Bat sad.

"Yessir," House said.

The two men left the office.

2

"I don't get it," House said, out in the hall.

"What is there to get?"

"You're Bat Masterson," House said. "Why would you agree to this just because of some threats from our blowhard police chief?"

"Are you married, son?"

"No, sir."

"Then you wouldn't understand."

Inspector House led Bat to an office and closed the door behind them.

"Have a seat."

The detective walked around and sat behind his desk. On it were three folders. He put his hand on them.

"Want to read them, or do you want me to tell you what we have?" he asked.

But sat across from the man. "Just tell me."

"How much do you know?"

"Only what I read in the newspapers, like everyone else."

House sat back in his chair. "Well, forget everything you read," he said. "It's all false."

"Why?"

"We've kept the truth to ourselves."

"And has that helped?"

"No."

"All right, well," Bat said, settling back in his chair, "tell me what you've got."

"We reported that the three women were robbed and murdered," House said. "We deliberately left out the method that was used to kill them. Because of that, all these 'Jack the Ripper' rumors have started."

Bat had the good grace to experience some chagrin. He had, after all, mentioned Jack the Ripper to Herbert George only yesterday.

"And were they killed the same way Jack the Ripper's victims were?" he asked.

"Not at all," House said.

"So how were they killed?"

"We don't know," House said.

"What does that mean?"

"It means there was no sign of violence on them," House said. "They were just . . . dead."

"Natural causes?" Bat asked. "All three?"

"No," House said. "They had to have been killed. They were dumped where they were found. Somebody killed them, we just don't know how."

"It's impossible to kill somebody and not leave a mark on them," Bat said. "Where were they found?"

"Different parts of the city," House said, "but the odd thing is . . . the family of the third woman."

"What about them?"

"Well . . . she was found down by the docks," the Inspector said. "They claim she never would have gone down there."

"Why not?"

"She wouldn't have reason to," House explained, "and she was afraid."

"So maybe a man took her there?"

"They say no," the inspector said. "She was married. Her husband can't explain what she was doing down there."

"How old was she?"

"Twenty-eight."

"Happily married?"

"By all accounts."

"Where were the other women found, exactly?"

"One was found in a Market Street alley, another at the train station."

"The train station? Where?"

"Behind one of the buildings."

"It sounds like all these girls were . . . discarded."

"Yes."

Bat sat and thought a moment. It was actually a smart move for Flaherty to bring in someone with a fresh perspective. He was just sorry it had been him.

House went on to expalin how he had conducted his investigation, and how he had come up with nothing concrete to point to the killer.

"The women are all in their twenties," he said, "but that's the only similarity. The first was a whore, the second an old maid and the third happily married."

"Old maid? How old?"

"Twenty-nine. Not attractive. No prospects."

"What about the other two and where they were found?" Bat asked.

"Not unusual," House said. "The whore was the one found behind the train station. She could have been doing some business there."

"And the second woman? Was she known to frequent the area where she was found?"

"Not frequent, but friends didn't find anything unusual about it."

"Where did she work?"

"The other end of town," House said, "near where she lived."

"So she was found a long way from either."

"Yes."

"I'm not a detective, but it still sounds like they were dumped, like human refuse. Were they killed where they were found?"

"Hard to tell."

Bat rubbed his face. He hadn't even had a cup of coffee yet.

"What else did the bodies tell you?"

"The bodies?"

"They were examined, weren't they?"

"Well, yes, but . . . I told you, they weren't attacked."

"Was anything done to them after they were dead?"

"What do you mean? Do you mean . . ." House looked horrified.

"People have done things to bodies after they're dead, Inspector. I'm sure you know that."

"Yes, well . . ."

"How about autopsies?" Bat asked. "Were the bodies autopsied?"

"Autopsied?"

"You do know what an autopsy is, don't you?"

"Well, uh, yeah, I guess . . ."

Bat knew that Doctor George E. Goodfellow had conducted autopsies during the time he spent as coroner in Tombstone, Arizona. He also knew until the 1860s autopsies were pretty much confined to execution victims. But this was 1899, the dawn of a new century. Autopsies were being used to find cures for disease, why not use them to find out other things?

"Maybe an autopsy would tell us something we don't know," Bat said. "Where are the bodies?"

"Well . . . the third is at the morgue. She was only killed a few days ago. The others are . . . I assume they've been buried."

"We might have to dig them up."

"What? Oh, no, the families . . . the Chief wouldn't like—"

"The Chief volunteered me for this and I've come up with an idea nobody else had. He'll go along with it."

"But—"

Bat stood up. "Let's go ask him."

3

Chief Flaherty went along with it, but only to a point. He agreed that the third girl should be autopsied, but held off any decision about the other two until after that.

Now they needed to find a doctor who would do it. At that time Denver had no coroner and would not have until 1902.

"Get a doctor the same way you got me," Bat told Flaherty. "Volunteer one."

"I got a better idea," Flaherty said, and that's how it became Bat's job to come up with a doctor. But it was actually Emma Masterson who came up with a suggestion.

After Bat returned home and told Emma what had happened she said, "I have just the woman for you."

"Woman?" Bat asked. "A female doctor?"

She folded her arms across her bosom. "And what's wrong with a female doctor?"

"Emma, we're going to be asking her to cut open these women—"

"Justina is a doctor, Bat," she said. "Cutting into a body is not going to frighten her."

"All right, all right," he said. "How do you know her?"

"I came across her delivering babies in my volunteer work," she said.

"Delivering babies? This is a long way from delivering babies—"

"I told you, she's a doctor." Emma actually stamped her foot in frustration.

"All right," he said, again. "Since it's your fault I'm involved, I'm going to go with your suggestion. Where does this Doctor . . . whatsername live?"

"Doctor Justina Ford," Emma said. "She moved here only a few months ago to practice. She graduated from medical school earlier this year – don't you dare interrupt me again, Bat Masterson!"

*   *   *

The buggy pulled up in front of 1880 Gaylord St and Bat and Inspector House stepped out.

"A lady doctor," House said to him, as they approached the door.

"Yes."

"Women are supposed to be nurses," the Inspector said, "not doctors."

"House, I've already gone through this with my wife," Bat said, the exasperation clear in his voice. "We need a doctor, right?"

"Right."

"I can't keep calling you House. What's your first name? Or do you want me to keep calling you Inspector?"

"My name is Harry."

Bat looked at him.

"Harry House?"

"That's right."

Bat waited a beat, then said, "I'll call you House."

When the black woman answered the door Bat said, "We're here to see Doctor Ford. Would you tell her that we're here, please?"

"I am Doctor Ford," the woman said. "You must be Bat. Emma said you would be coming by to see me. Please, come in."

She turned and went inside, leaving them to follow her or not. Bat and House exchanged a glance. Both men were obviously even more taken aback by the fact that she was black, let alone a woman.

They followed her inside, Bat first. They found her in a modestly furnished living room. She was in her late twenties, her hair pulled back tightly, her skin very dark and smooth.

"My surgery is through there," she said, inclining her head toward a door, "but we can talk in here. Would either of you like refreshments?"

"No, uh, Ma'am," Bat said. "We might as well just get to it. Did Emma tell you what we wanted?"

"No," the woman said, "she just told me that you needed a doctor and she recommended me. What is it you need done, gentlemen?"

"An autopsy," Bat said.

"Just one?"

"At first," he said. "Maybe two more, but those victims are already buried."

She looked at House.

"You're a policeman?"

"Yes, ma'am," he said. "Inspector House."

"Then this is about the three women who have been killed?"

"Yes, ma'am."

"And autopsies have not yet been done?"

"No, Ma'am," House said. "We, uh, didn't even think of it until Bat mentioned it."

"You would be paid by the city," Bat said.

"I'm not worried about that," she said. "If I can help catch this maniac I'm happy to do it. May I perform the autopsy at the St Joseph's Hospital, on Franklin Street?"

"You can have it done anywhere you want, Doctor," Bat said. "We'll have the body brought there . . . when?"

"As soon as possible," she said. "Immediately, in fact. I'll go there now."

"We'll have the body brought right over," Bat said, "and thank you, Doctor."

"Thank you for asking me, Mr Masterson," she said. "I'm happy to help."

Bat and House left. The buggy they'd ridden there was waiting for them outside.

"We'll leave this one here to take her to the hospital. We can find a cab around the corner," Bat said.

"You really think she can do this, Bat?" House asked.

"She's a doctor, House," Bat said. "Let's just go and arrange for the body to be brought to her."

Bat headed for the corner and the Inspector followed him, still dubious.

Bat Masterson and Inspector House were waiting outside the operating room while Doctor Ford performed the autopsy on the third dead woman, Jessica Williams. House kept nervously looking through the window of the closed door.

"Relax," Bat said. "She knows how to cut into a body."

"I hope so."

Bat hoped so, too. He wondered why Emma had not told him that Doctor Ford was black. He was careful not to mention it to Chief Flaherty. It was well known that the Chief hated black people.

House backed away from the door quickly and seconds later Doctor Ford came through, wearing a white surgical gown that was now stained with blood and something else that Bat didn't want to think about.

"What did you find, Doctor?" Bat asked.

"It was a very good idea to have an autopsy performed, Mr Masterson," she told him. "It's not what I found that's interesting – astounding, actually – but what I didn't find."

"And what's that?"

"There are no internal organs," she said.

"What?" House asked.

"This woman's internal organs have been removed."

"But . . . she wasn't cut open," Bat said, "the way the Jack the Ripper victims were."

"Exactly."

"And yet they're . . . missing?" House asked.

"Yes."

"But . . . that's impossible," House said.

"Yes," Doctor Ford said, "it is."

4

Flaherty was irate.

"You allowed a black woman to cut open a white girl?" he demanded.

"We allowed a doctor to cut open a dead girl, yes," Bat said. "If we hadn't, we wouldn't know about the missing organs."

"Does she know what she's doing?" the Chief demanded.

"Yes, Chief, she does," Bat said.

Flaherty rubbed his face with both hands. "The Mayor's gonna be livid."

"Come on, Chief," Bat said. "We need to dig up the other two girls so Doctor Ford can examine them as well, see if the same thing is true."

"The families . . ." Flaherty said. "The Mayor . . . the newspapers . . ."

"I work for a newspaper, Chief, remember?" Bat asked. "I can slant this in a way that will make you look very good."

That seemed to appeal to the Chief.

"All right, Masterson. I'll get an order from a judge to exhume both bodies so this . . . this doctor can examine them. But I'm warning you . . ." The man pointed a finger. ". . . this better result in us catching this maniac." He looked directly at Inspector House. "Understand?"

★   ★   ★

It took two days but eventually Bat and House were standing outside the operating room at St Joseph's Hospital again, waiting.

"If she finds the same thing," House said, "what are we gonna do? We'll have three impossible murders. Yet, how can it be impossible if it's been done?"

"That's a very good question," Bat said. "I guess we'll have to wait for the doctor to answer that one. I'll tell you one thing, I can't wait for this to be over so I can go back to being a sportsman and nothing else."

"I've heard people refer to you that way," House said. "As a sportsman? Is that how you prefer to be known, these days?"

"It's as good a way as any," Bat said. "Especially since I now have my own club."

"I'm sure Mr Floto is not all that thrilled about that."

"Well," Bat said, "that's kind of the point, isn't it?"

At that moment the door opened and Dr Ford came walking out, clad in her white spattered gown.

"Well," she said, "it's the same."

"Damn it," House said. "This is too strange."

"Doctor," Bat said, "did you find anything at all that might explain what's going on?"

"I have found something," she said. "It's on all three women, but I don't know that I can explain it."

"Anything would help," Inspector House said.

"There is an incision, a very small incision, on their left side."

"All three?" Bat asked.

"Yes."

"And that's all?"

"Yes."

"Could the organs have been removed through that?" Bat asked.

"It doesn't seem possible, but . . ."

"But what, Doctor?" Bat asked. "If you've got an idea, don't hold back."

"That's all it is," she said, "an idea. Just something I remember from medical school. If I could have some time—"

"Give us an idea of what you're talking about," Bat suggested, "and then take the time you need."

"Well, I'm thinking about . . . mummification."

"Mummi – what's that?" House asked.

"Mummies?" Bat asked. "You mean like, in ancient Egypt?"

"Yes."

"Egypt?" House asked, still looking confused.

"When they mummified their dead," Dr Ford explained, "part of the ritual was to remove all the internal organs."

"But . . . through a small incision like the one you described?"

"I seem to remember . . . something about a small incision, but I don't recall how it was done. I can do some research at the museum, talk to the Egyptian expert there."

"Can that be done today?" Bat asked.

"I don't see why not?"

"Then I'll take you there, Doctor."

"I don't need to be taken, Mr Masterson—"

"Sorry, Ma'am," Bat responded, "what I meant was, I'll go with you, if you'll allow me to."

"Well . . . why not?"

"Just let me walk the Inspector out and I'll have a cab waiting when you're ready."

"Very well."

Outside the hospital Bat said to House, "You go and tell Flaherty what I'm doing. After the doctor and I go to the museum I'll come and find you."

"What the hell, Bat—" House said. "I can't go back to the Chief with this."

"This could be the only explanation we have for what seems to be impossible," Bat said.

"Ancient Egypt? Mummies? Do you believe all that?"

"Don't you ever do any reading, son," Bat said. "We're talking about history."

"Still," House said, as they headed down the hall, "It's hard to believe."

"Yes, it is."

5

"Who do we ask for?" Bat asked, as they entered the Denver Museum of History, located on Broadway.

"The Egyptology expert," Dr Ford said.

"I'll let you start to do the talking."

"Shouldn't Inspector House be with us?" she asked. "After all, he's the policeman."

"Inspector House had something else to do," Bat said. "Don't worry, we have official standing."

They walked down a long hall until they encountered a man standing at a desk.

"Can I help you?"

"My name is Doctor Ford," she said, "and this is Bat Masterson, the, um, columnist. We are hoping to speak to whoever is your expert on Egyptology?"

"Bat Masterson?" the man asked. He was a small man roughly Bat's age, but he stared at the frontier legend with a little boy's enthusiasm. "Really?"

"Yes," Bat said, "I'm afraid so. Do you have an expert in, um, Egyptology?"

"Ooh, yes, we do," the man said. "You want Mr Vartan. I'll get him for you."

"Thank you," Doctor Ford said.

"Doctor, how many of these experts could there be in Denver?" Bat asked while they waited.

"I would think only one."

"And would he know how to do this, how to . . . what? Mummify?"

"I know what you mean, and I don't know," she said. "I suppose we'll have to ask him."

They waited in silence, and after a few minutes had past the doctor looked at Bat curiously. "Did you mean that you . . . suspect this man, even though you haven't met him yet?"

"No," he said, "of course not. I just thought if he's the only expert that maybe the killer had come to see him, just like we have."

"Oh, I see."

But now that she mentioned it, why couldn't the one man in Denver who had the know how be a suspect in the crime? Bat decided he would give this jasper a real close going over and watch him carefully.

They heard footsteps coking towards them and saw the small man returning with a very tall, dark-skinned man wearing a suit and tie.

"This is Mr Vartan," the small man said.

"I am Michael Vartan. I understand you were looking for me?" Vartan asked. "Sam said one of you is a doctor?"

"I am Dr Ford," Justina Ford said.

Vartan looked at her in complete surprise.

"I did not know we had any black doctors in Denver, let alone a woman. How fascinating."

"Mr Vartan?" Bat said. "My name is Bat Masterson. We would like to ask you some questions about—"

"The famous killer?" Vartan asked.

Bat closed his mouth and glared at the man.

"I am a columnist for the newspaper *George's Weekly*."

"Ah, but surely you are the famous Bat Masterson," Vartan said. "There could not be two men with such a name."

"I am perhaps famous," Bat said, "but not as a killer."

"I am so sorry," Vartan said. "I have offended you."

"Mr Masterson has been many things, Mr Vartan," Dr Ford said, "among them a lawman."

"And now a writer," Vartan said. "How commendable. I apologize again. You have some questions concerning what?"

"The process of mummification," Dr Ford said.

Vartan stared at them for a few moments, then said, "I have an office. Would you follow me, please?"

He led them through hallways of the museum, so that they never saw any displays except through doorways as they passed. Eventually they came to a room with a desk and a few chairs. He invited them in to sit, and closed the door before circling his desk and seating himself.

"Please, tell me your problem."

Dr Ford looked to Bat, who took up the tale. He told Vartan about the three women who had been killed and what had been found by Dr Ford during the autopsy.

"What we need to know is," Dr Ford said, "could the organs have been removed through this small incision?"

"Interesting," Vartan said. He paused to consider and while he did he picked up an instrument from the desk. It was a long copper needle with a small hook on the end. "Do you see this? It was used by the Egyptians to remove the brain through the nasal passage."

Bat remembered Dr Ford mentioning that earlier.

"Could it be used for the organs, too?" Bat asked.

Vartan didn't reply to Bat's direct question, but went on in his train of thought. Bat thought Vartan warmed to his gruesome subject too much.

"No one knows how the brain was removed, but it must have been in pieces," the man went on. "It could not have been removed this way as a whole."

"The organs couldn't have been removed as a whole either," Dr Ford said. "At least, not through that incision."

"The incision you refer to was indeed used to remove the organs," Vartan said, "and then they were put into a jar and buried along with the body."

Bat didn't like the way Vartan's eyes shone during the telling.

"But no one knows for sure how it was done," Vartan continued, "just as we don't quite know how the brain was removed." He set the bronze tool down. "But we know that they were."

"So no one," Bat said, "not even you, who is an expert, would be able to do such a thing now?"

"I?" Vartan asked, looking shocked. "I would never – no, no, too bloody. I would be too . . . squeamish, I think."

Bat doubted that Vartan was squeamish about much of anything. The man seemed to be enjoying the spotlight and also – to Bat's trained eye from years of not only gambling but sizing up men who may or may not try to kill him – he thought the man seemed amused.

"Mr Vartan," Dr Ford said, apparently unaware of these things, "has anyone else come to see you about these things in, say the past six months or so?"

"Unfortunately, no," Vartan said, making a steeple of his hands and fingers and regarding them above it. "I rarely get to speak of these things in this way."

Another thing Bat noticed about Vartan was that the man's gaze never wavered from his own. Even when he speaking to the doctor, he was looking at Bat. Many men had looked at Bat that way over the years, as if they had or were getting his measure. They had all been disappointed.

Oddly, the room seemed bare. There were no Egyptian objects of any kind on the walls, and the only one on his desk was that bronze tool sitting on the edge of his desk.

"I am so sorry these women were killed – how were they killed?"

"That's still something of a mystery," Dr Ford said, "but their organs were removed after death."

"Shocking . . . in this day and age, I mean."

"Yes," Dr Ford said, "quite."

"They were peaceful in death, Mr Vartan," Bat said. "What would make them die so peacefully?"

"Well, certain poisons would have that effect," Vartan said. "There are poisons which cause horrible, painful deaths, but there are several which could cause a person to simply . . . fall asleep . . . forever. Some of these were used in ancient Egypt."

Poison was not a common form of killing in the West – at least, not in what people were now calling the "old" West.

"And you would know what kind of poisons those were, wouldn't you?" Bat asked.

Vartan looked embarrassed and said, "Well, I am an expert on things Egyptian."

"Yes, you are," Bat said.

"That's fascinating," Dr Ford said.

"Well," Bat said, "I think we're done here, Doctor. Obviously, Mr Vartan won't help us with anything more."

Bat got to his feet, stumbled and almost fell, righting himself by catching the edge of Vartan's desk. He knew the man must have been thinking, "What an old fool."

"Can't," Vartan said.

"Excuse me?" Bat asked, back on solid footing.

"You said I won't help you with anything more," Vartan said. "You meant 'can't'."

Bat looked the man in the eyes and said, "Did I?"

Outside the museum Dr Ford said, "What a rude man. He never looked at me the entire time."

"That's because he was lookin' at me," Bat said. "He's the one."

"I beg your pardon?"

"He did it. He killed those women and removed their organs."

"How can you—"

"He looked me in the eyes the whole time, challenging me. Believe me, Doctor, I know what that look means. He did it."

"Is that what you will tell the Chief? Would they arrest him on your word?"

"No," Bat said, "they wouldn't, but I don't think they'll have to."

"Why not?"

Bat put his hand in his pocket and came out with the bronze hook from Vartan's desk. Carefully, he wrapped it in a handkerchief and handed it to the doctor.

"How did you – you took that when you stumbled."

"Yes. Check it. I'm sure there's some flecks of blood on it. He's so arrogant that he still keeps it on his desk. And I'm sure there'll be some rare poison in that museum somewhere – unless he's destroyed it all now."

Dr Ford looked down at the hook in her hands. "You think he used this?"

"I'd bet on it. But even if he didn't, he knows I know," Bat said. "He knows if he stays in Denver, I'll have him."

"But . . . if he leaves, and goes somewhere else . . . is that good enough?"

"It'll have to be, Doctor," Bat said. "It'll have to be."

But it wasn't, not for Bat Masterson. That evening, as Vartan came out of his apartment carrying a suitcase Bat was waiting, leaning against the building. He hadn't been wearing his gun that afternoon in museum, but he was wearing it now. He chose one with a pearl handle, so that it gleamed in the moonlight.

Vartan saw him and stopped. There was no slump to the man's shoulder, no diminishment of his arrogance.

"You stumbled on purpose," he said. "I realized it afterward."

"I was going to let you go," Bat said, "let you run, but I decided I had to know why. Why would you do that to those poor women?"

"I am afraid my explanation will not give you much satisfaction."

"Try me."

The man shrugged.

"To see if I could. I have studied the Egyptians for so long. I believe they were a master race. I wanted to see if I could do what they did. And after I did it once, I knew that if I kept trying, I would succeed."

"Did you do more than those three?"

"No," Vartan said, "Just those – so far."

"Just those, period, Mr Vartan."

"Now that you know the why, perhaps you would . . . ?"

"Put the suitcase down, Mr Vartan," Bat said, pushing away from the wall so Vartan could see the pearl handle, "you won't need it where you're going."

The Mystery of
the Sevenoaks Tunnel

Max Rittenberg

Time for a couple of really old classics. In my earlier volume I looked at the dawn of the impossible crime story and the flurry of interest following the success of The Big Bow Mystery *by Israel Zangwill in 1892. Over the next couple of decades the locked-room mystery blossomed. Conan Doyle used it for at least one Sherlock Holmes story, and the American writer Jacques Futrelle, who alas went down with the* Titanic, *created the first great impossible-crime expert with the Thinking Machine, Professor S.F.X. van Dusen. His story "The Problem of Cell 13", first published in 1905, remains one of the classics of the impossible.*

The years before the First World War saw many writers turning their hand to creating baffling crimes, but not all of these stories became as well known, and many are forgotten in old magazines. One of the most original writers of the years around the First World War was Australian-born (though of German descent) Max Rittenberg (1880–1965). He wrote a couple of popular series for the monthly magazines. One featured the strange cases of psychologist, Dr Xavier Wycherley, which were collected in book-form as The Mind Reader *(1913). But the other series, which featured an early forensic scientist known as Magnum, and which ran in* The London Magazine *during 1913, never made it into book-form. Magnum is the prototype irascible scientist, far more interested in his research than in any social graces, but once presented with an unsolvable problem, nothing will deter him from seeking the truth.*

After the First World War Rittenberg became an advertising consultant, establishing his own firm, and stopped writing fiction all together.

"What does it matter whether it were accident or suicide?" said Magnum into the telephone with decided irritation, because he was being interrupted in the midst of a highly complex calculation of a formula based on crystallographic angles and axes, requiring quaternions and perfect quiet.

"It matters fifty thousand pounds," replied the legal voice at the other end of the wire. "That's the value of his insurance policy. The company contend it was a case of suicide, and therefore the policy is null and void."

"At the present moment," snapped Magnum, "I don't care if he were insured for the National Debt! Find a detective, and don't bother *me!*"

Leaving the receiver off the hook, so that he could not be rung up further, Magnum plunged again into the world of sin α and cos ß.

The interrupter was the junior partner in East, East, and Stacey, a young man of some pertinacity as well as legal ability. He happened to have a very special interest in the case of the deceased, because the next-of-kin was a particularly charming young lady; at least, particularly charming to himself. So he jumped into a taxi and drove from Clifford's Inn to Upper Thames Street, where the scientific consultant had his office and laboratories.

"The deuce!" was Magnum's welcome for him.

"Awfully sorry to interrupt. How long will you take to finish?" was the soft answer designed to turn away wrath.

"Till midnight!" snapped Magnum, hunching his bushy reddish eyebrows, and thrusting out his straggly reddish beard belligerently.

"I'll wait," decided Stacey. "I'll go and talk scandal with Meredith."

Ivor Meredith was a young Welshman, an analytical genius and Magnum's right-hand man. He was the very essence of shyness and modesty. Stacey went into the laboratories and began to chaff him in order to kill time.

"What's this I hear about you and a certain fascinating widow?" was his opening gambit.

Young Meredith, blushing furiously, protested that he didn't know any fascinating widow. Which was perfectly true, as he was mortally afraid of all the feminine sex.

In an hour's time Magnum appeared from his office. His crystallographic analysis had borne out his personal guess exactly, and the thundercloud temper had vanished from his skies. He found that his young Welsh protégé had scored off Stacey by challenging him to blow a glass bulb, which looks delightfully simple and in reality requires months of practice. Stacey, perspiring over the blow-lamp, was surrounded by a score of horrible bulbous monstrosities.

"Better stick to the law," smiled Magnum. "You can make a successful lawyer even if you have ten thumbs to your hands. Now what's this trouble about the insurance policy?"

Stacey answered him seriously with a résumé of the case. Abel Jonasson, a somewhat eccentric recluse, a man of fifty-four and a bachelor, had insured his life for fifty thousand pounds with the Empire Assurance Company six months previously. On a railway journey through the Sevenoaks tunnel he had been alone in a second-class compartment. In some way he had fallen out of the moving train; had been killed possibly by the fall; and had certainly been run over by a train passing on the other line of metals. A coroner's jury had returned an open verdict. On the advice of their doctors and counsel, the Empire Company, a firm of first-class reputation, had decided to fight the claim up to the House of Lords if necessary.

They contended that, for a man of his limited income, a fifty thousand pound policy was far too heavy, unless he deliberately intended to take his life in order to secure a large sum of money for his relatives. Such cases had cropped up before.

"Then they shouldn't have insured for such a heavy amount," interrupted Magnum.

"Well, they did," answered Stacey. "They took his premium, and now they fight the claim. Miss Gerard, his niece and next-of-kin, has very slender means, and so—"

Something in Stacey's tone gave Magnum the clue to this unusual interest in a client of slender means.

"Another wedding present to buy!" he interjected cynically.

Stacey took the remark on the half-volley, and flicked it neatly over the net:

"Help us, and we'll consider it as the wedding-present."

"I don't see that the case lies in my province. Try Scotland Yard."

"I have. No satisfaction. A scientist is wanted. Scotland Yard can't tell me why the dead man carried in his pocket a phial of atoxyl."

"Specific against sleeping sickness."

"A Central African disease. It's unknown in England. Why should he carry the antidote about with him?"

"Have his serum examined."

"That's been done. No trace of the disease has been found. But the Empire doctor claims that Jonasson must have *thought* he had the disease, and therefore committed suicide. A book on the subject was found at his country cottage. Our side will have to prove some other reason for his carrying that phial of atoxyl. That's one point on which I want your help."

Magnum pulled out a disgracefully malodorous pipe from his baggy, shapeless working-jacket, and proceeded to stuff it with a smoking mixture of his own blending, strong to the point of rankness.

Meredith hastened to their library above the office, and returned with one of the twenty bulky volumes of Watts's Dictionary of Chemistry. His chief took it, and turned thoughtfully to the half-column description of the chemical properties of the drug, one of the arsenic derivatives. Presently he remarked:

"Have you considered the possibility of foul play?"

"That was one of our first thoughts," returned Stacey. "But Jonasson was seen alone in the compartment at Tonbridge Junction, only five miles from the tunnel, and there were no traces on the footboard of anyone clambering along from one compartment to another."

"Windows?"

"All shut."

"A man under the seat?"

"No traces."

"When was the discovery made?"

"As soon as the train came out of the tunnel into Sevenoaks Station. The door of Jonasson's compartment was open, and banging to and fro . . . All the evidence goes to show that he was entirely alone in the compartment; that he opened the door himself – fingerprints on the handle – and fell out. We claim that he must have become suddenly frightened – he was a nervous old man – and that he lost his head, opened the door to call for help, and was thrown out by the rush of wind against the open door."

"Sounds very probable."

"The Empire Company say that if he wanted help he could have pulled the alarm-cord. There was no one else in the compartment – that's certain from the footprints in the dust. He had nothing to be afraid of, they claim."

"Equally plausible."

"Can you tell me why he carried that atoxyl with him?"

Magnum was not a man to confess openly to ignorance. He replied curtly:

"I'm not a theorist. Ask me *practical* questions."

For reply, Stacey produced from his pocket a blank manuscript-size envelope, and from the envelope a much-creased sheet of folded paper – blank.

"I found this in Jonasson's study while hunting for his will. I have a strong feeling that it contains a message written in invisible ink. Miss Gerard tells me that he was the kind of eccentric who would do that. Will you try to get the message out?"

"Suppose," asked Magnum shrewdly, "it were to say that he intended to commit suicide?"

"In that case," laughed the lawyer, "I shouldn't call you as a witness."

"You young scoundrel!"

"But it won't do that," answered Stacey, returning to serious-ness. "Miss Gerard knew him well – he was very fond of her in his queer, angular way – and she is perfectly certain that he had no intention of committing suicide."

"If you prove wrong," warned Magnum, "don't count on me to keep silent in a case of fraud."

He passed the sheet of paper to Meredith, who examined it eagerly, his eyes alight at the thought of pitting his chemical knowledge against the secret of the apparently blank paper.

Meredith's first move was to cut the sheet into four quarters, so as to avoid the risk of spoiling the whole of it in the course of experimenting.

The heat test gave no result, nor did the iodide test, nor the sulphuretted hydrogen test.

Magnum, suspecting that they were in for a long session, looked at his watch, found it marking seven o'clock and sent out for three porterhouse steaks, a Stilton cheese and bread, and lager beer.

"I should prefer oysters, a fried sole, and a bottle of claret," suggested Stacey.

"You'll have what's good for you," retorted Magnum, who had unæsthetic views on food.

It was close on nine o'clock before Meredith at length triumphed. Fitting together three-quarters of the sheet of paper – the other quarter had become spoilt in the course of testing – the following wording stood out in roughly written capital letters:

```
TO | A. J.
FROM THE EARTH
FROM THE WATER


     E SKY!
```

Magnum turned to Stacey.

"There's your wedding present," said he grimly.

All Stacey's pose of flippancy had dropped from him. Staring at the paper, he asked, in a hushed voice:

"What does it mean?"

"A warning," returned Magnum. "A warning that must have put Jonasson's nerves on edge. In that railway compartment, alone, passing through the long Sevenoaks tunnel, something happened to terrify him into trying to escape."

"If we could prove it! But what exactly happened?"

"The last words of the warning were, judging on the first two lines, 'FROM THE SKY!'"

"Yes, yes!" cried Stacey eagerly.

"That railway-carriage – of course it's been sealed and shunted into a siding?"

"Naturally."

"Tomorrow morning we'll go and examine it."

"Yes, but what's your theory?"

Magnum's temperament included a strong dash of human vanity. He liked to have his achievements bulk large. He liked to display his results against an effective background. Having arrived at a simple explanation of a puzzling mystery, he preferred to keep silent about it until the morning should bring the glowing moment for the revelation.

Stacey had to be content to wait.

The railway-carriage – possible evidence in a fifty thousand pound law-case – had been shunted into a goods yard of the Chatham and South-Eastern, and housed in a shed under lock and key at the instigation of the insurance company.

A legal representative of the company, as well as a district goods manager of the Chatham and South-Eastern, accompanied Stacey and Magnum to the fresh inspection of it. The insurance lawyer – dry, thin-lipped, pince-nezed, cynically critical, abundantly sure of himself – allowed a ghost of an acidulated smile to flicker around his eyes as he viewed Magnum's air of expectant triumph. The goods manager preserved an attitude of strict neutrality. Stacey was on a hair-trigger of expectation, masked under a pose of legal dignity and self-restraint.

The railway official broke the seals on the door of the compartment, and threw it open for Magnum's inspection. The latter's shrewd eyes darted about the interior, taking in every detail.

To all appearance, it was an entirely ordinary, humdrum, commonplace, second-class compartment, carrying no hint of tragedy. The dead man's ulster, umbrella, and travelling-bag, replaced on the rack in the position where they had first been found, merely suggested that some traveller had left them there while he went out to buy a journal at a book-stall. A small volume of Lamb's Essays, lying on a corner seat, might have been put there to secure his place.

Then Magnum asked to see the two adjoining compartments – one a smoker, one a general compartment. They were bare of extraneous objects and entirely unsuggestive.

"Well?" challenged the opposing lawyer, with his thin and acid smile. "Have you discovered some point we all have been dense enough to miss?"

"There are always two sides to every question," returned Magnum.

"Your side and my side?"

"The inside and the outside," amended Magnum, with a cutting edge to his words.

"And the application of that very sound maxim?"

"The application is that to view the outside one needs a ladder."

"And why a ladder, may I ask?"

"I am not a 'Child's Guide to Knowledge,' but if you are seriously anxious for an answer to your question, it is in order to climb." Having delivered this snub, Magnum turned, and addressed himself to the goods manager: "Please send for a short ladder, so that I can examine the roof."

When it arrived, Magnum mounted briskly to the roof of the carriage, and looked for the footprints or traces of a man having crawled over the roof, which he confidently expected to find. A grievous disappointment awaited him. The roof was streaked with raindrops trickling over soot, now dried into the semblance of a map of some fantastic mountain range. There were no footprints.

"Did it rain on the day of the accident?" he asked sharply.

Stacey, after a moment's thought, replied in the affirmative.

"Unfortunate," commented Magnum. "Rain would have obliterated footprints. Come up here."

At last Stacey understood what Magnum was driving at. "*From the sky!*" had been the concluding words of the warning to the dead man. Someone had crawled on the roof, pulled up the lamp over the compartment in which Jonasson was travelling, and then – In a flash he pictured the old man alone in the compartment, through the long tunnel, where a cry for help would be drowned in the roar of the rushing train, looking upwards to see a menacing face staring at him from the aperture of the lamp, a revolver at cock, and ready to shoot him down in any corner of the compartment. Trapped, helpless, terrified, Jonasson had tried to escape by the door, and had been thrown on to the line.

Magnum, moving forward over the roof, in plain view of the others, went to pull up the lamp and demonstrate his point.

But a sentence from the railway official checked him in mid-action.

"You are thinking of the old type of lamp, sir. These ones are not removable. They're fixtures."

Magnum, incredulous, went on; found the lamp screwed in tight, and the screws rusted in firmly.

The insurance lawyer permitted himself a dry laugh of cynical amusement.

"Facts," said he, "have an unfortunate habit of contradicting the most ingenious and elegant theories."

Magnum was now thoroughly roused by the mocking mystery of the railway compartment. He had, in plain words, made a fool of himself in front of the insurance lawyer. That was unbearable. The only way to get back his self-respect was to wrest out the secret, and flourish it in the lawyer's face.

Before, Magnum had been only halfheartedly interested in a problem which was somewhat outside his professional line; now, he was resolutely determined to work at it with a red-hot concentration of energies.

Hurrying to New Cross Station with Stacey, he took ticket to Paddock Wood, beyond Tonbridge, where Jonasson had lived his recluse life in a country cottage a couple of miles away from the railway line, alone save for a housekeeper-servant. On the way, Magnum plied Stacey with question after question regarding the life-history, the habits and eccentricities of the dead man. Stacey's information was limited; the housekeeper could tell much more.

On their arrival, they found the cottage bolted and barred. A hedger and ditcher, working in a neighbouring lane, expressed the thoughtful opinion that the housekeeper must have locked up and gone away. Where? demanded Magnum, assisting his cerebrations with a couple of half-crowns. He didn't rightly know. Could he find out by asking neighbours? That struck the hedger as an idea of great brilliance, and, dropping his tools, he set off to make inquiries.

Meanwhile, Magnum, impatient of obstacles, broke a window in the cottage, and secured unconventional entrance. With Stacey's guidance, he went through the dead man's books and papers and personal possessions in search of a fresh light on the mystery.

Both were now firmly convinced that Jonasson had come to his death by foul play, or, more exactly, that he had been terrified out of the closed railway compartment by some human agency. Both were equally of the opinion that it was a matter of long-standing revenge, reaching back into the obscurities of Jonasson's past life.

But mere opinions would be poor weapons for a big law-case. They must have *facts*. They must find out whom, why, how. They must be prepared to prove in court how a man, indisputably alone in a railway-compartment, with closed doors, closed windows, and no aperture for human entrance, could be so terrified as to be driven out. In case of danger the first thought of any man would be to pull the alarm-chain running through from compartment to compartment. Why had Jonasson not done so?

A long search through books, papers, and clothes proved annoyingly inconclusive. Jonasson's tastes were evidently cultured and leisured. Whatever he might have been in his youth, in the immediate past he had been a trifler with books, garden, and fishing. That gave them no help.

In the bedroom of the dead man, Magnum on a sudden impulse threw up the window. Outside it, he was surprised to find a screen of fine-meshed wire netting.

"Why this?" he asked to Stacey.

"To keep out summer insects, I should imagine."

Magnum suddenly became very thoughtful, hunching his bushy eyebrows and twisting at his straggly beard.

The hedger and ditcher, beaming with pride at the success of his detective work, came to announce that the housekeeper had gone to visit a married daughter living at Tonbridge.

"We'll go there at once," said Magnum; "and the first question to ask her is why Jonasson put up that wire netting."

Stacey looked at him questioningly.

"The loaded revolver he kept in his bedroom," pursued Magnum, "is nothing out of the ordinary for a nervous man living in a lonely country cottage. But the wire screen is highly unusual. The unusual is worth analysis."

An hour later, they were at Tonbridge. Mrs Pritchett was readily found in the parlour above her daughter's confectionery shop in the High Street – a time-worn, grey-haired, grey-minded woman, resigned to the arrows of misfortune, dull of speech, with that love for irrelevant, side-track detail which goes so often with one of limited interests and narrow outlook. Magnum, with his impatience of slowness, found his temper distinctly tried during his endeavours to get relevant answers to his pointed questions. In essence, her information amounted to this:

Mr Jonasson had had the wire screen fixed up six months previously. He was a very reserved man, liking to give orders without giving reasons. It was in wintertime, so that there was no reason to guard against wasps, gnats, or mosquitoes. No; she had no idea why he wanted it, but he was very concerned about having it put up at once.

"At once?" questioned Magnum, seizing on the suggestiveness of the phrase.

It was directly after he received a visit from the dark gentleman with the gold-rimmed spectacles. High words had passed between them. No; she had no idea who he was. Mr Jonasson was very reserved, keeping his affairs entirely to himself. The dark gentleman was a foreigner – he looked like a half-caste. He was seen in the neighbourhood of Paddock Wood three months later. She believed that this man must have tried to murder Mr Jonasson in the train. She was convinced that he was hiding under the seat of the compartment.

"That has been proved impossible," put in Stacey.

Mrs Pritchett was of the opinion that nothing was impossible to a foreigner.

Regarding the past life of the dead man, her information was mostly conjecture, embroidered fantastically after the fashion of country gossip. The only definite fact was that he had gone to Africa as a young man. The name "Uganda" persisted in her memory. At one time he had kept souvenirs of Africa in his study, but some years back he had made a clean sweep of them, burning them in a bonfire at the end of the garden.

Letters? When Mr Jonasson received letters, he usually burnt them. No, indeed, she never pried into his private papers! She hoped she knew her place! No; she didn't listen to the conversation between Mr Jonasson and the foreigner. She couldn't help hearing that they were angry with one another, but to suggest that she would stoop to listen at a keyhole—

"If you had," retorted Magnum impatiently, "Mr Jonasson might be alive today."

Mrs Pritchett relapsed into the easy tears of old age, and it took all Stacey's efforts to comfort her.

"You'll be saying next as it was me as murdered him!" she cried accusingly at Magnum.

He offered a sovereign as consolation for wounded feelings, and the interview proceeded. But no further information of importance resulted.

Magnum and Stacey returned to town. The scientist chose an empty second-class compartment of the same type as the mystery carriage, and asked Stacey to leave him there alone during the journey.

At Cannon Street, when Stacey went to rejoin his friend, he found Magnum glowing with excitement.

"I think we've got it!" he cried, slapping Stacey on the shoulder with a lusty thump. "First set your detectives on the hunt for that half-caste with the gold-rimmed spectacles."

"Yes, I'd settled to do that," returned the young lawyer; "but even if we find him, it doesn't help much for our side of the case.

Assume that he threatened to murder Jonasson – assume that Jonasson was in deadly terror of him – assume that he travelled in the next compartment to Jonasson. Even then the Empire Company would claim that the deceased threw himself out of the train – suicide while temporarily insane, but still *suicide*. The fifty thousand pound policy money will never come to Miss Gerard unless we can show the court *how* Jonasson was terrified out of an empty compartment."

"I believe I can do it," returned Magnum emphatically. "The phial of atoxyl he carried in his pocket, the book on sleeping sickness, the wire screen to his bedroom window, Uganda the home of the tsetse fly – they fit together like the pieces of a jig-saw puzzle. One more piece in place, and the whole pattern would stand out. To-morrow we'll search that sealed compartment once again."

"In the presence of the Empire's lawyer?"

"Naturally. Arrange it for the afternoon. And if I can show him that Magnum is not quite the fool he imagines—"

As mentioned before, Magnum was not without a dash of very human vanity.

On the following afternoon, the same four were back in the shed where the mystery carriage stood mutely waiting to deliver up its secret. The insurance lawyer's acidulated smile was now fattened out to a mellow tolerance. He was no longer afraid of any of Magnum's theories. The goods manager, while still outwardly neutral, had transferred his sympathies to the side of the Empire Company.

Although it was summer, Magnum wore a pair of thick gloves. In his side-pocket a packet bulged out noticeably.

"I want every inch of the compartment swept out," he said to the railway official. "Will you do it yourself, so as to avoid any suspicion that might arise if I were to do so?"

Tolerantly, the goods manager called for a carriage-cleaner's broom, and proceeded to the task, sweeping around the cornices, behind the cushions, and underneath the seats, and gathering the sweepings into a small pile, while the other three watched intently from outside.

"Stop!" called Magnum suddenly, his eyes alight with unsuppressed triumph. From the sweepings he picked up a large insect, dead, and displayed it emphatically in his gloved hand in front of the insurance lawyer.

"A tsetse fly!" he stated.

"Well; and what if it is?"

"The carrier of the sleeping sickness. Deadly. One sting from it, and a man would stand a poor chance."

"I don't follow your argument," objected the lawyer, with chilly impassiveness.

"That's what drove Jonasson to his death. That one, and perhaps a dozen others. The rest probably flew out of the open door in the Sevenoaks tunnel. This one was killed by him."

"Still, I don't follow you. How could your dozen tsetse flies enter a closed compartment?"

"Get inside, and I'll demonstrate!" snapped Magnum.

The lawyer, with a gesture of disbelief, entered the compartment, and the door was closed on him. Magnum immediately proceeded to the smoking compartment alongside, lit himself a cigar, and then produced from his pocket the box which was causing the bulge. It contained a dozen live wasps, angry at their long imprisonment. Magnum, standing on a seat, took out one of the buzzing insects with his heavily gloved fingers, and placed it in the tube of the alarm-chain passing from compartment to compartment. A few puffs from his cigar drove the insect to find escape through the further end of the tube. The other wasps quickly followed.

What then took place in the insurance lawyer's compartment would have been highly comic had it not been in demonstration of a tragedy.

Fighting with the furious insects, ruffled, dishevelled, and wiped clear of cynical smiles, the lawyer made a hurried and undignified escape to the outside.

"And that," clinched Magnum, "was how Jonasson was sent to his death."

The murderer was never captured, and so the inner history of the tragic feud never came to light. But it became abundantly clear that the dead man had been fearing an attack by the tsetse fly; it was for that reason that he screened his bedroom window and carried in his pocket the drug which might counteract the terrible effects of the sting. No doubt the unknown murderer had threatened him with that particular form of revenge. Jonasson had insured his life heavily, either in the superstitious hope that it might avert death, or in order to leave his niece well provided for, or for both reasons.

The fact of importance which Magnum had demonstrated was the *method* by which Jonasson had been driven out of the railway-carriage. On that, the Empire Company compromised out of court for forty thousand pounds.

Magnum, who did not believe in hiding his light under a bushel, sent to Stacey's wedding-present table a neatly framed sheet of writing-paper with the wording: "To Mr and Mrs Stacey, forty thousand pounds, from Magnum."

The Red Ring

William Le Queux

William Le Queux (1864–1927) was considerably more prolific than Max Rittenberg and far better known. He is regarded as one of the progenitors of the spy novel, producing works of international intrigue just before John Buchan and E. P. Oppenheim. His early works, which rapidly established his reputation, include A Secret Service *(1896),* England's Peril *(1899) and the bestselling* The Invasion of 1910 *(1905). Le Queux was a dab hand at self-publicity, perhaps using some author's licence to add to the mystery. But he was clearly a fascinating character, deeply involved with the secret service, and often acting on his own initiative – all manner of secrets are revealed in* Things I Know *(1923). The following story – first published in 1910 and which so far as I know escaped inclusion in any of his many collections – is presented in the first-person, giving an added verisimilitude to the mystery. Who knows but that something very like this might just have happened in Le Queux's world.*

The Usborne affair, though very remarkable and presenting a number of curious features, was never made public, for reasons which will quickly become apparent.

It occurred in this way.

Just before eight o'clock one misty morning last autumn, Captain Richard Usborne, of the Royal Engineers, and myself were strolling together up and down the platform at Liverpool Street

Station, awaiting the arrival of the Hook of Holland boat-train. We had our eyes well about us, for a man was coming to London in secret, and we, members of the Secret Service, were there to meet him, to examine his credentials, and to pass him on to the proper quarter to be questioned, and to receive payment – substantial payment – for his confidential information.

I had arranged the visit of the stranger through one of our secret agents who lived in Berlin, but as I had never before met the man about to arrive, we had settled that I should hold a pale green envelope half concealed in my handkerchief raised to my nose, and that he should do the same.

"By Jove, Jerningham," Dick Usborne was saying, "this will be a splendid *coup* – the revelation of all the details of the new Boravian gun. The Department ought to make you a special grant for such a service. I hope, however," he added, glancing about him with some suspicion – "I hope none of our foreign friends have wind of this visit. If so, it will fare badly with him when he gets back."

I had kept my eyes well about me and was satisfied that no other secret agent was present.

A moment later the train drew into the station, and amid the crowd I quickly distinguished a short, stout, middle-aged man of essentially Teutonic appearance, with a handkerchief to his face, and in it an envelope exactly similar to my own.

Our greeting was hasty. Swiftly we put him into the taxi we had in readiness, and as we drove along he produced certain credentials, including a letter of introduction from my friend in Berlin.

Herr Günther – which was the name by which we knew him – appeared extremely nervous lest his presence in London should be known. True, he was to receive for his information and for certain documents which he carried in his breast-pocket two thousand pounds of Secret Service money; but he seemed well aware of the ruin which would befall him if his Argus-eyed Government became aware of his association with us.

We had both witnessed such misgivings on the part of informants before. Therefore we repeated our assurances in German – for the stranger did not speak English – and at St Clement Dane's Church, in the Strand, I stopped the taxi and alighted, for Dick Usborne was to conduct our friend to the house of our chief, General Kennedy, in Curzon Street, it not being considered judicious for Günther to be taken to the War Office.

The German was to return by the Hook of Holland route at nine o'clock that same night, therefore he had brought no baggage. Secret visits of this character are always made swiftly. The British public are in blissful ignorance of how many foreigners come to our shores and tell us what we most desire to know – for a substantial consideration.

The Secret Service never advertises itself. Yet it never sleeps, night or day. While pessimists declare that our authorities know nothing of what is progressing in other countries, a gallant little band of men – and women too – are ever watchful and ever travelling across the face of Europe, gathering information which is conveyed to London in secret and carefully docketed in a certain room of a certain Government Department that must, of necessity, be nameless.

We, its agents, often live through exciting times, crises of which the public never dream.

It is one of these which I am permitted to here relate.

On the day in question I played golf at Sunningdale, for I had been some months abroad – living in a back street in Brest, as a matter of fact – and was now on leave at home. I dined at the golf-club, and about ten o'clock that night entered my rooms in Shaftesbury Avenue, where I found a telegram lying upon the table.

It had been despatched from the Brighton station at Victoria at six-thirty, and read.

Am at Webster's. Come to me at once. Cannot come to you. – DICK.

By this message I was greatly puzzled. Webster's was a small private hotel in which I knew Usborne had sometimes hiden himself under the name of Mr Clarke, for we are often compelled to assume fictitious names, and also to keep queer company.

Why had he so suddenly gone into hiding? What had occurred?

At once I took a cab along Victoria Street and alighted before the house, which was to all intents and purposes a private one, save for the lamp outside which stated it to be an hotel.

The black-bearded little manager, whom I had once met before, told me that my friend had arrived there at noon and taken a room, but at two o'clock he had gone out and had not returned.

"And he left no message for me?" I asked.

"None, sir."

"Did he bring any luggage?"

"Mr Clarke seldom brings any luggage," was the man's reply. "He generally just sleeps here, and leaves his baggage in a railway cloakroom."

I was puzzled. If Dick wished to see me so urgently he would surely have remained at the hotel. He was aware I was going out to golf, although I had not told him where I intended playing.

While we were speaking I saw a chambermaid pass, and then it occurred to me to suggest that my friend might have returned unobserved. He might even be awaiting me in his room. He had said that he was unable to come to me, which appeared that he feared to go forth lest he should be recognised.

I knew that Dick Usborne, whose ingenuity and daring were unequalled by any in our service, was a marked man.

Both the manager and the chambermaid expressed themselves confident that Mr Clarke had not returned, but at last I induced the girl to ascend to his room and ascertain.

From where I stood in the hall I heard her knock and then try the door.

She rattled it and called to him. By that I knew it was locked – on the inside.

Instantly I ran up the stairs and, banging at the door called my comrade by name. But there was no response.

The key was still in the lock on the other side, so a few minutes later we burst open the door by force and rushed into the dark room.

The manager lit the gas-jet, and by its dim light a startling sight was presented. Lying near the fireplace, in a half-crouching position, face downwards, was Dick Usborne. Quickly I turned him over and touched his face. The contact thrilled me. He was stone dead!

His eyes, still open, were glazed and stared horribly, his strong hands were clenched, his jaw had dropped, and it was plain, by the coutortion of the body, that he had expired in agony.

Quickly suspicious of foul play, I made a rapid examination of the body. But I could find no wound or anything to account for death. A doctor, hastily summoned, was equally without any clue to the cause of death.

"Suicide, I should think!" he exclaimed when he had finished his examination. "By poison, most probably; but there is no trace of it about the mouth."

Then, turning to the police-inspector who had just entered, he added:

"The door was locked on the inside. It must, therefore, have been suicide."

"The gentleman was a friend of yours, I believe, sir?" asked the inspector, addressing me.

I replied in the affirmative, but declared that he was certainly not the man to commit suicide.

"There's been foul play – of that I'm positive!" I declared emphatically.

"But he locked himself in," the hotel manager argued. "He must have re-entered unobserved."

"He was waiting here for me. He wished to speak to me," I replied.

The theory held by all present, however, was that it was suicide; therefore the inspector expressed his intention of having the body conveyed to the Pimlico mortuary to await the usual post-mortem.

I then took him aside downstairs, and telling him in confidence who I was, and what office my dead friend held, I said:

"I must ask you, inspector, to lock up the room and leave everything undisturbed until I have made a few inquiries myself. The public must be allowed to believe it a case of suicide; but before we take any action I must consult my Chief. You, on your part, will please inform Superintendent Hutchinson, of the C.I. Department at Scotland Yard, that I am making investigations. That will be sufficient. He will understand."

"Very well, sir," replied the inspector; and a few moments later I left the house in a taxi. Each member of the Secret Service is a detective by instinct, and I suppose I was no exception.

Half an hour later I was seated with General Kennedy in his cosy little library in Curzon Street explaining briefly my startling discovery.

"That's most remarkable!" he cried, greatly upset at hearing of our poor colleagues's death. "Captain Usborne brought the man Günther here just after nine, and we had breakfast together. Then he left, promising to return at three to again take charge of the stranger. He arrived about a quarter past three, and both he and the German left in a four-wheeler. That is the last I saw of either of them."

"Günther was to leave to-night. Has he gone?" I asked.

"Who knows?" exclaimed the shrewd, grey-headed little man,

who, besides being a distinguished General, was Director of the British Secret Service.

"We must find him," I said. Then after a moment's reflection I added: "I must go to Liverpool Street Station at once."

"I cannot see what you can discover," replied the General. "If Günther has left he would not be noticed in a crowded train. If he left London he's already on the North Sea by this time," he added, glancing up at the clock.

"Usborne has been assassinated, sir," I declared with emphasis. "He was my best friend. We have often been in tight corners on the Continent together. May I be permitted to pursue the investigation myself?"

"By all means, if you really believe it was not a case of suicide."

"It was not – of that I'm quite certain."

I was suspicious of Günther. The German might have been an impostor after all. Yet at Webster's Dick had not been seen with any companion. He had simply gone there alone in order to wait for me.

For what reason? Ay, that was the question.

With all haste I drove down to Liverpool Street. On my way I took from my pocket a slip of paper – the receipt from a tourist-agency for the first-class return ticket between London and Berlin which I had sent to Günther. It bore the number of the German's ticket. At the inspector's office I was shown all the tickets collected of departing passengers by the boat-train, and among them found the German's voucher for the journey from Liverpool Street to Parkeston Quay.

I had at least cleared up one point. Herr Günther had left London.

On returning to the dark little hotel just after midnight I found a man I knew awaiting me – Detective-Inspector Barker, who had been sent to me by Superintendent Hutchinson, the uniformed police having now been withdrawn from the house.

Alone, in the small sitting-room, we took counsel. Barker I knew to be a very clever investigator of crime, his speciality being the tracing and arrest of alien criminals who seek asylum in London, and for whose extradition their own countries apply.

"I've seen the body of the unfortunate gentleman," he said. "But I can detect no suspicious circumstances. Indeed, for aught I can see, he might have locked himself in and died of natural causes. Have you any theory – of enemies, for example?"

"Enemies!" I cried. "Why, Dick Usborne was the most daring agent in our service. It was he who discovered and exposed that clever German agent Schultz, who tried to secure the plan of the new *Dreadnought*. Only six months ago he cleared out a nest of foreign spies down at Beccles, and it was he who scented and discovered the secret store of rifles and ammunition near Burnham-on-Crouch in Essex. But probably you know nothing of that. We've kept its discovery carefully to ourselves for fear of creating a panic. Dick, however, had a narrow escape. The night he broke into the cellars of the country inn where the depôt had been established he was discovered by the landlord, a Belgian. The latter attempted to secure him, but Dick succeeded in snatching up the Belgian's revolver, firing a shot which broke the blackguard's arm, and so escaped. Such a man is bound to have enemies – and vengeful ones too," I added.

The mystery was full of puzzling features. The facts known were these. At noon Dick had arrived at that place and, under the name of Mr Clarke, had taken a room. Just after three o'clock he had been at Curzon Street, but after that hour nothing more had been seen of him until we had found him dead.

The chief points were, first, the reason he had so suddenly gone into hiding; and, secondly, why he feared to come round to my rooms, although he desired to consult me.

Sending Barker across to despatch a telegram, I ascended alone to the dead man's room, and, turning up the gas, made a minute investigation. Some torn paper was in the fireplace – a telegraph form. This I pieced together, and, in surprise, found it to be a draft in pencil of the telegram I had received – but it was not in Dick's handwriting.

I searched my dead friend's pockets, but there was nothing in them of any use as clue. Men of my profession are usually very careful never to carry anything which may reveal their identity. Travelling so much abroad as we do, we never know when we may find ourselves in an awkward situation, and compelled to give a fictitious account of ourselves to a foreign ponce bureau.

That small, rather comfortless room was of the usual type to be found in any third-rate private hotel in London – the iron bedstead, the threadbare carpet, the wooden washstand, and lace curtains limp and yellow with smoke.

While Barker was absent I carefully examined everything, even the body of Dick himself. But I confess that I could form no theory whatever as to how he had been done to death, or by what means the assassin had entered or left the room.

While bending over my dead friend I thought I detected a sweet perfume, and taking out his handkerchief placed it to my nostrils. The scent was a subtle and delightful one that I never remembered having smelt before – like the fragrant odour of a cottage garden on a summer's night. But Dick was something of a dandy; therefore it was not surprising that he should use the latest fashionable perfume.

As I gazed again upon the poor white face I noticed, for the first time, that upon the cheek, just below the left eye, was a slight but curious mark upon the flesh, a faint but complete red circle, perhaps a little larger than a finger-ring, while outside it, at equal distances, showed four tiny spots. All was so very faint and indistinct that I had hitherto overlooked it. But now, as I struck a vesta and held it close to the dead white countenance, I realised the existence of something which considerably increased the mystery.

When Barker returned I pointed it out, but he could form no theory as to why it showed there. So I took a piece of paper from my pocket and, carefully measuring the diameter of the curious mark, drew a diagram of it, together with the four spots.

Barker and I remained there together the greater part of the night, but without gaining anything to assist towards a solution of the mystery. The servants could tell us absolutely nothing. Therefore we decided to wait until the postmortem had been made.

This was done on the following day, and when we interviewed the two medical men who made it and Professor Sharpe, the analyst to the Home Office, who had been present, the latter said:

"Well, gentlemen, the cause of death is still a complete mystery. Certain features induce us to suspect some vegetable poison, but whether self-administered we cannot tell. The greater number of vegetable poisons, when diffused through the body, are beyond the reach of chemical analysis. If an extract, or inspissated juice, be administered, or if the poison were in the form of infusion, tincture, or decoction, a chemical analysis would be of no avail. I am about to make an analysis, however, and will inform you of its result."

I made inquiry regarding the curious ring-like mark upon the cheek, but one of the doctors, in reply, answered:

"It was not present today. It has disappeared."

So the enigma remained as complete as ever.

Next day I travelled over to Berlin, and there met Herr Günther by appointment. From his manner I knew at once that he was innocent of any connection with the strange affair.

When I told him of the strange occurrence in London he stood dumb-founded.

"The Captain called for me at Curzon Street," he said in German "and we drove in a cab to his club – in Pall Mall I think he said it was. We had a smoke there, and then, just at dusk, he said he had a call to make, so we took a taxi-cab and drove a long way, across a bridge – over the Thames, I suppose. Presently we pulled up at the corner of a narrow street in a poor quarter, and he alighted, telling me that he would be absent only ten minutes or so. I waited, but though one hour passed he did not return. For two whole hours I waited, then, as he did not come back, and I feared I should lose my train, I told the driver to go to Liverpool Street. He understood me, but he charged me eighteen marks for the fare."

"And you did not see the Captain again?"

"No. I had something to eat at the buffet, and left for Germany."

"Nothing happened while you were with the Captain?" I asked. "I mean nothing which, in the light of what has occurred, might be considered suspicious?"

"Nothing whatever," was the German's reply. "He met nobody while with me. The only curious fact was the appointment he kept and his non-return."

In vain I tried to learn into what suburb of London he had been taken; therefore that same night I again left for London, viâ Brussels and Ostend.

Next day I called upon Professor Sharpe in Wimpole Street to ascertain the result of his analysis.

"I'm sorry to say that I've been unable to detect anything: If the Captain really died of poison it may have been one of those alkaloids, some of which our chemical processes cannot discover in the body. It is a common fallacy that all poisons can be traced. Some of them admit of no known means of detection. A few slices of the root of the Œnanthe crocata, for instance, will destroy life in an hour, yet no poison of any kind has been separated from this plant. The same may be said of the African ordeal bean, and of the decoction and infusion of the bark of laburnum."

"Then you are without theory – eh?"

"Entirely, Mr Jerningham. As regards poisoning, I may have been misled by appearances; yet my colleagues at the post-mortem could find nothing to cause death from natural causes. It is as extraordinary, in fact, as all the other circumstances."

I left the Professor's house in despair. All Barker's efforts to assist me had been without avail, and now that a week had passed, and my dead friend had been interred at Woking, I felt all further effort to be useless.

Perhaps, after all, I had jumped to the conclusion of foul play too quickly. I knew that this theory I alone held. Our Chief was strongly of opinion that it was a case of suicide in a fit of depression, to which all of us who live at great pressure are frequently liable.

Yet when I recollected the strong character of poor Dick Usborne, and the many threats he had received during his adventurous career, I doggedly adhered to my first opinion.

Day after day, and with infinite care, I considered each secret agent of Germany likely to revenge himself upon the man who, more than anyone else, had been instrumental in combating the efforts of spies upon our eastern coast, There were several men I suspected, but against neither of them was there any shadow of evidence.

That circular mark upon the cheek was, to say the least, a very peculiar feature. Besides, who had drafted that telegram?

Of the manager at Webster's I learned that Mr Clarke had for some months past been in the habit of meeting there a young Frenchman named Dupont, engaged in a merchant's office in the City. At our headquarters I searched the file of names and addresses of our "friends", but his was not amongst them. I therefore contrived, after several weeks of patient watching, to make the acquaintance of the young man – who lived in lodgings in Brook Green Road, Hammersmith – but after considerable observation my suspicions were dispelled. The reason of his meeting with Dick was, no doubt, to give information, but of what nature I could not surmise. From Dupont's employers I learned that he was in Brussels on business for the firm on the day of the crime.

There had apparently been some motive in trying to entice me to that hotel earlier in the evening of the tragedy. Personally I did not now believe that Dick had sent me that telegram. Its despatch had been part of the conspiracy which had terminated so fatally.

Nearly nine months went by.

On more than one occasion the Chief had referred to poor Dick's mysterious end, expressing a strong belief that my suspicions were unfounded. Yet my opinion remained unchanged. Usborne had, I felt certain, been done to death by one who was a veritable artist in crime.

The mystery would no doubt have remained a mystery until this day had it not been for an incident which occurred about three months ago.

I had been sent to Paris to meet, on a certain evening, in the *café* of the Grand Hotel, a person who offered to sell us information which we were very anxious to obtain regarding military operations along the Franco-German frontier.

The person in question turned out to be a *chic* and smartly-dressed Parisienne, the dark-haired wife of a French lieutenant of artillery stationed at Adun, close to the frontier. As we sat together at one of the little tables, she bent to me and, in confidence, whispered in French that at her apartment in the Rue de Nantes she had a number of important documents relating to German military operations which her husband had secured and was anxious to dispose of. If I cared to accompany her I might inspect them.

Offers of such a character reach us sometimes, for the British Government are known to be excellent paymasters when occasion demands. Therefore, nothing loth, I accompanied her in an auto-cab out towards the Bois.

The lady's apartment, on the third floor of a large house, proved to be quite a luxurious little place, furnished with great taste, and when she had ushered me into her little *salon* she left me for a few moments. We were alone, she said, for it would not be wise for anyone to know that she had sold information of such vital importance to England. Her husband would get into serious trouble for not placing it at the disposal of the Ministry of War.

A few moments later she returned, having taken off her hat and coat, bearing a small black portfolio such as is used by business men in France. Seating me at a table, and standing at my side, she placed the papers before me, and I began a careful perusal.

I suppose I must have been thus occupied for some ten minutes, when slowly, very slowly, I felt her arm steal around my neck.

In an instant I sprang to my feet. The truth that I had all along suspected was now plain. Facing her, I cried:

"Woman, I know you! These documents are pure fabrications –

prepared in order to entrap me here! I believed that I recognised you at first – now I am convinced."

"Why, monsieur!" she exclaimed in a voice of reproach. "What do you mean?"

"I mean, mademoiselle, that it was you – *you*, Julie Bellanger – who killed my friend Dick Usborne, because he exposed you as a spy!" I cried.

"Killed your friend!" she gasped, trying to laugh. "You are mad, m'sieur!"

"Yes, you killed him! And shall I explain to you how you accomplished it?" I said, looking straight into her dark eyes. "Usborne had become friendly with you in Beccles, and you never suspected him in connection with the Secret Service. Among other things, he gave you a bottle of a new and extremely rare perfume which he had brought from Bucharest – that perfume which is now upon you. As soon as we met tonight I recognised its fragrance. Well, Usborne, having convinced himself that you were engaged with others in gathering information in Suffolk for the General Staff in Berlin, informed the police, and you were ordered away. You came to London and, determined upon a terrible revenge, took a room at the hotel where you knew he sometimes stayed. Then you sent him a telegram purporting to come from his friend Dupont, asking him to go to Webster's and meet him there. In response to this poor Usborne went, but almost instantly on his arrival you paid your bill and left the hotel. You then watched my friend out again and, re-entering the hotel unseen, crept up to his room, the number of which you had already ascertained prior to leaving. There you concealed yourself until just before six. When he returned you emerged, and on pretence that you were ready to dispose of these self-same papers, you induced him to sit down and examine them, just as I have done. Suddenly you placed your arm about his neck, while with your right hand you stuck the needle of the little hypodermic syringe – the one you now hold in your hand there – into the nape of his neck where you knew that the puncture would be concealed by the hair. It contained a deadly vegetable poison – as it does now!"

"It's a lie!" she cried in French. "You can't prove it!"

"I can, for as you held him you pressed his left cheek against the breast of your blouse, against that little circular brooch you are now wearing – the ring with four diamonds set at equal distances around it. The mark was left there – upon his face!"

She stood staring fixedly at me, unable to utter a word.

"After you had emptied that syringe you held him until he lay dead. Then you removed all traces of your presence and, stealing from the room, turned the key from the outside by means of that tiny hand-vice which I notice lies in the small bowl upon the mantelshelf yonder. Afterwards you crept downstairs and sent me a telegram, as though from the man who had already died by your hand. And, mademoiselle," I added severely, "I, too, should have shared the same fate had I not recollected the smell of the Roumanian perfume and seen upon your blouse the round brooch which produced the red ring upon my friend's countenance."

Then, without further word, I crossed to the telephone and, taking up the receiver, called the police.

The woman, suddenly aroused by my action, dashed towards me frantically to stay my hand, but she was too late. I had given warning.

She turned to the door, but I barred her passage.

For a moment she looked around in wild despair; then ere I could realise her intention or prevent her, she stuck the point of the deadly needle – the needle she intended to use upon me because I had assisted in clearing out those spies from Suffolk – deeply into her white, well-moulded arm.

Five minutes later, when two policemen came up the stairs to arrest her, they found her lying lifeless.

Observable Justice

Will Murray

Will Murray (b. 1953) is not only one of the most prolific and knowledgeable people in the field of pulp fiction – the author of over 50 books including 40 novels in the Destroyer *series and eight* Doc Savage *novels – he is also a professional psychic and instructor in remote viewing, the subject of the following story. Murray's remote-viewing novel,* Nick Fury Agent of Shield: Empyre (2000) *predicted the operational details of the 11 September 2001 terrorist attacks on America more than a year before they occurred.*

Two uniforms met Detective Raymond Murex at the door to Room 314 of Boston's Park Plaza Hotel. "You won't need that," one told him.

Murex pocketed the Vicks Vapo Rub and asked, "He doesn't smell?"

"No, sir. Must have died overnight. Housekeeping found him when she came to make the bed. Looks like natural causes."

Pulling on latex gloves, Murex stepped in. The dead man lay on the still-made bed in his street clothes, as if napping, hands neatly folded over his stomach. A black sleep mask covered his eyes. On the bedside table lay a calfskin wallet and an open binder-style notebook, both black.

Murex took out his own notebook. "What time was he discovered?"

"Maid said she had to come back several times because of the

'Do Not Disturb' sign on the door. When he wouldn't respond, she used her key. That was 1:45."

Murex wrote it down and asked, "Name?"

"Registered as John Doom."

Murex opened the wallet and confirmed that. Next he looked at the notebook. The page on the left was blank. On the right a set of numbers were centered in 30 point type:

5688
7854

Murex leafed through the rest. Every right-hand page displayed a set of similar numbers. He copied down the exposed set. The binder contained no other writing.

Murex called in the hotel manager, who was waiting outside.

"John Doom, when did he check in?"

"Last night. Reservations were made on Friday."

"Who saw him last?"

"Not sure. It appears he checked in and went straight to bed."

"And never woke up," said Murex. "It happens. Thank you. When can I talk to the desk clerk who checked him in?"

"He comes on duty at 5:00. I'll call him in early."

"Appreciate that."

The ME showed up. Acknowledging Murex, he asked, "What can you tell me about this one?"

"Not much. Found this way in the last hour. Possible natural causes."

A crime scene photographer took several shots of the dead man.

"Let's take a look at the color of his eyes." Carefully, the ME removed the sleep mask. "Hello," he said.

Murex leaned in. The man's eyes were wide open, staring. They almost bugged out of his head. Their color was glassy green.

The ME shone a penlight. "Pinpoint hemorrhages, indicating burst capillaries. Normal under certain conditions."

Murex said, "He looks scared."

"The *eyes* look scared. His face is another matter. Thyroid problems can give the eyeballs that protruding effect."

"So can manual strangulation," Murex reminded.

"Strangulation ivariably triggers bowel elimination, and I smell nothing of the kind." The ME was examining Doom's throat. "No ligature marks. No bruises." He felt of the windpipe. "Larynx is unremarkable."

Taking one of the dead man's hands, the ME started to separate them. "Two chipped fingernails. But no defensive – what's this?"

Murex extracted a thin microcassette recorder from between the man's fingers. Rewinding, Murex played it back. A murmuring voice emanated from the tiny speaker: "5688 7854 January 23. 5688 7854." There was a long pause in which measured breathing could be heard.

"Respiration appears regular," the ME remarked.

The voice repeated "5688 7854." Then: "My perceptions of the target are of a winding stone stairwell leading into the bowels of the Earth. It feels cold. Air stagnant. A sickly greenish light is emanating from far below . . ."

Another pause came in which breathy exhalations were the only detectable sounds. After three minutes of disconnected murmurings, Murex paused the recorder. "Sounds like he just fell asleep."

The ME looked at him. "I wonder what he meant by 'target'?"

"Suddenly 'natural causes' doesn't trip off the tongue so easily, does it?"

Murex went to the window. Outside, afternoon traffic flowed by the hotel. This was the heart of Boston's financial district. The blue glass blade of the Hancock Tower stood just a few blocks north, and beyond that the city's second-largest office tower, the Prudential Building. Murex thought of the twin World Trade Center towers, and shivered.

"I'd better check in with my commanding officer," he told the ME. Using his cellphone, Murex spoke briefly, recounting his findings. He listened, then snapped the device shut.

"Captain Hurley would like a priority on this autopsy."

"Okay. I'll put a flag on it."

Minutes later, as the body was being removed out a side door, Detective Murex was talking to the desk clerk.

"Do you remember a John Doom checking in?"

"Sure. Hear he died."

"In his sleep. Anything unusual about him come to mind?"

"No."

"Any distinguishing features?"

"No. He wasn't very tall, about five-four, medium brown hair. Paid by credit card. He reminded me of my cousin."

"Why is that?"

"My cousin's in the Air Force. This guy gave me that feeling, too."

Murex nodded. "Remember him well enough to identify him?"

"I won't have to go down to the morgue, will I?"

"No. Follow me."

EMTs were rolling the body into the back of an ambulance. Murex called out, "Hold up."

Stripping the sheet off the corpse's face, he asked, "This look like him?"

"Yeah. No, wait. That's not him."

Murex said, "No?"

"No. His hair was browner and the eyebrows much thicker."

"Now take a deep breath," Murex said. "People can appear different in death. Look again. Is this the man who checked in last evening under the name of John Doom?"

"I – Yeah, it is."

"You are positive?"

"Absolutely. Can I go now? I feel kinda ill."

"Stay handy."

A forensics team from the CSI Unit had taken control of Room 314. They dusted for prints, collected hair samples off the bedspread and said hardly a word.

Murex was bagging John Doom's personal effects when he noticed the black binder had a logo embossed into it: A human eye in a starburst over the letters TIRV. Uncolored, it was detectable only under direct light.

Grabbing the sleep mask, Murex gave it a second look. Over the right eye, in modest white letters, were the same initials. Outlined on the mask's brow gleamed a tiny white eye in a starburst.

"What have we here?" he muttered.

Reaching into his coat for his cellphone, Murex discovered the tape recorder. It felt warm. He realized he'd left it on pause. Hitting play, Murex sat and listened. The DOA's breathing continued for a time. He seemed asleep, but came out of it. He began speaking:

"I'm standing in a chamber hollowed out of solid stone. Instead of a floor, I see grates. Iron grates . . . it feels hot . . . the air reeks of sulfur . . . Below me it's like a barbeque pit . . . black smoke . . . leaping flames . . . I perceive two burning eyes . . . like very hot coals. And a black face emerging . . . it's—"

Suddenly, the voice rose into a panicky strangled sound. The voice began gasping, struggling for air. It soon choked off. The tape hummed white noise. The absence of breathing noises was unmistakable.

One of the CSI team said, "Sounds exactly like a heart attack."

Murex called his CO. "Looks like natural causes with a funny twist. Scratch that courtesy call to the FBI."

Back at District A-1 headquarters, Murex Googled the initials TIRV. He got one hit: Technical Institute for Remote Viewing of Nashua, New Hampshire. Linking to the site, Murex was confronted by the eye-in-a-starburst motif, white against a black starfield.

EXPLORE THE UNIVERSE!

During the Cold War, the Pentagon and the Kremlin were locked in a desperate race. Not the space race, but a far more secret enterprise: the Psi Race! Dedicated to penetrating the deepest frontiers of human endeavour, the Department of Defence launched Project Stargate, where specially-selected candidates plucked from every service branch were trained to become true "spooks" – shadowy secret agents who could go anywhere, penetrate any nation's security, all without leaving the confines of the ultra-secret Stargate training center at Fort Meade, Maryland!

Now, you too can become a Stargate-level psychic explorer. Captain Trey Grandmaison, one of the Stargate unit's top Remote Viewers, is now teaching qualified civilian candidates in the advanced 21st-century martial art formerly available only to the military elite!

Hearing the knock, Captain Hurley barked, "Come in."

Murex entered. "Turned up something unusual on that hotel fatality, sir."

"What is it?"

Instead of answering, Murex set down the black binder, the eye shade and a color printout of the TIRV site home page.

"What the holy hell?" Hurley growled. "You have a nice flair for the dramatic, laying it out for me like this."

"I figure you can do the math faster than I could explain it."

"Much obliged," Hurley said dryly. He read the TIRV mission statement aloud: " 'Remote Viewing is the acquisition and description, by mental means, of information blocked from ordinary perception by distance, shielding or time. TIRV is dedicated to placing this powerful mind technology in peaceful hands.'" He leaned back. "Is this for real?"

"Your guess is as good as mine. According to this website, Captain Grandmaison is ex-Army Intelligence. He trains people to do this stuff. John Doom was apparently trying to remotely view whatever these numbers represent when he expired."

"Why don't you take a run up to New Hampshire and see this guy, Grandmaison?"

"I'll do that."

As Murex started out, Hurley called after him, "I got a feeling about this one, Ray."

Former Captain Trey Grandmaison lived in a converted farm-house just over the Massachusetts border. It was a sprawling structure painted Colonial white, edged with stark black trim. A big barn lay behind it, as colorless and weathered as a Cape Cod fishing shack. The drive leading back to the barn had been plowed clean of snow.

A vaguely European woman with intensely black hair answered the door. Dark circles under her eyes marred a natural beauty.

Murex flashed his shield. "Detective Ray Murex. Boston Homicide. Could I have a word with Mr Grandmaison?"

"I'm sorry. But he's in the gray room. He can't be disturbed right now."

"Gray room?"

"His private viewing room. He's working a practice target."

"I should have called first, but I need to ask him about one of his students."

The door fell open. "Perhaps I can help you. I run the registra-tion side of TIRV."

"Then I would like to talk with you, Mrs Grandmaison."

"Call me Effie, please."

The living room was decorated in the Mission style. Murex searched for signs of a military past and found none. No medals. Not even an American flag on display.

Murex took a chair. "What can you tell me about a John Doom?"

Effie Grandmaison looked blank. "I don't place that name. Are you sure he was a TIRV student?"

"He was found dead in bed last night wearing one of your sleep masks, a TIRV binder at his bedside. According to a microcassette recorder found on his person, he was actively remote viewing a number in your binder."

"We call them coordinates. Do you know the cause of death?"

"Not as yet."

"What were the coordinates?"

Murex recited the numbers from memory.

Effie frowned. "I don't recognize them, but of course we create new targets all the time. What were his perceptions?"

"Excuse me?"

"Of the target, I mean."

"I'd like to stick with John Doom for the moment," Murex said impatiently. "Do you have a class registry?"

"Why is this important? Do you think he was murdered?"

"Right now, it looks like he died of fright."

Effie Grandmaison abruptly stood up. "I think this is important enough to disturb Trey. Please follow me."

Rising, Murex followed the woman outside to a cellar door.

"The basement can't be accessed from inside the house," she said, throwing up the bulkhead door. She led him down into a work area, past an oil furnace, to the far end. It was very cold. Murex could see his breath. A cobwebby corner was paneled off in pine. The hard-carved sign on the door read:

DO NOT DISTURB! SESSION IN PROGRESS!

Effie Grandmaison pressed a white button. No sound came back.

"Soundproof?" Murex asked, blowing into his hands.

"And lightproof. A bell would freak him out if it went off in the middle of a session. This simply activates a green light. He'll be a minute or so coming out of session."

It was two minutes before Trey Grandmaison emerged, looking upset.

"What the hell, Effie?"

"I'm sorry, Trey. But this is Detective Murex from Boston. He's here about a man who died while working a target from one of our class binders."

Trey Grandmaison didn't look very surprised. If anything he seemed spacey. He was a compact individual with hair so brown it verged on black. His smoke-gray eyes had trouble focusing.

"Let's take this upstairs," he said at last.

* * *

Trey Grandmaison looked up from the computer screen. "There's no record of a John Doom ever taking one of my classes."

They were in the den. It too was Spartan. The only photos showed Grandmaison in civilian clothes.

Murex asked, "How would he have gotten hold of one of your binders then?"

Effie inserted, "They are part of our course package of materials. There's nothing to stop one of our students from loaning or selling one to anyone they want."

Grandmaison added, "We put a copyright notice on all practice target packs, but many of our target feedback photos are things you can find in any encylopedia – Seattle's Space Needle, Mount Rushmore, the *Titanic*—"

Murex interrupted, "Is there anything about doing this work that might induce someone to have a heart attack?"

"No!" Effie said suddenly.

Trey Grandmaison said, "I teach two types of RV, detective. Coordinate Remote Viewing and Extended RV. If he was lying down with an eye shield, he was doing ERV. It's pretty safe. Half the time, my students drift off into a Delta state."

Murex looked up from his notebook. "I don't follow."

"We RV in different brainwave states, detective. Alpha for CRV. Theta for ERV. Theta is the gateway to the Delta sleep state. If you go too deep, you simply click off like a light."

"It's perfectly safe," Effie reiterated.

"I did hear about a candidate viewer who died of fright while working a target," Grandmaison said slowly.

"Is that so?"

"It was back in '87, just after I joined the unit. In between working operational targets, they would run us against practice coordinates to keep us in our viewing zone. The duty monitor came in one day and claimed he had worked up a really challenging target. The viewer who worked that one was never seen again. Rumor was he'd had a heart attack. But there was talk he'd died of fright."

"Fright?"

"Whatever he was viewing scared him so badly his heart gave out."

Effie said, "But, Trey, that was just a rumor."

"Well, we never saw that viewer again. So I suppose it's possible whatever your guy was viewing scared him literally to death."

Murex asked, "Do you recognize this set of coordinates?"

Grandmaison took the offered notebook. "I don't know these. I use a date system of notation. That way, if another RV instructor steals my targets, I can tell just by looking at the coords."

"Is that a problem for you – theft?"

"My students don't pay upwards of two thousand dollars just to remotely experience the summit of Pike's Peak. My specialty is non-validation targets – UFOS, other planets, historical mysteries. Most were first worked back in Project Stargate. I've developed others. Anyone taking my class can teach others using my target packs, so I have to protect my business."

"Is there any way of determining what these numbers mean?" asked Murex.

"They don't mean anything."

Murex looked his question.

"These look like randomly-generated target coordinates," Grandmaison explained. "That's how we worked back in the Stargate era. A computer would spit out a set of these and a tasker would assign them to the target. We RV off the coords so we're not frontloaded as to the nature of the target. Think of the numbers as a metaphysical longitude and latitude."

"Then how do—?"

"How do they work? Monitor's intention. Once I assign the number to a target, my intention drives the session."

Murex tried to keep his face straight.

"Tell you what, detective," Grandmaison offered. "I have a small ERV class coming in shortly. Why don't we run the group against this one?"

"I don't see how that would—"

"Otherwise, I'm afraid I can't help you," he said suddenly.

Murex stood up. "I'll keep your offer in mind."

On the way out, Trey Grandmaison handed Murex a business card.

"In case TIRV can help in any way, all my contact numbers are on this card. Call me anytime."

"Thanks for your cooperation," Murex told him.

The ME's preliminary report had come in by the time Ray Murex had returned to his desk. He skimmed it, then took it in to his CO.

"According to this, John Doom hadn't eaten in four days before he was found. No signs of poison or foul play. Cause of death appears to be heart failure. But the ME thinks the pinpoint eyeball hemorrhages strongly indicate he was lying face down when he died, and for a period of up to six hours afterward."

"But he was found lying face up, right?"

"Right. With a microcassette recorder carefully nestled in his neatly folded hands."

"You mean, placed there," Hurley said. "Looks like we have an attempt at a perfect crime with locked-room overtones. Let's take it from the top, guy checks in about 9 p.m. Monday night. By which time according to the ME, he could have been dead three or four days. Anyone at the hotel ID the body?"

"Desk clerk who checked him in, but he was a little shaky. However, the driver's license photo fits the deceased."

"So if John Doom couldn't have checked in Monday night, who did? And how did Doom's corpse get there?"

"There's another problem," Murex said. "The body showed no outward indications of decomposition."

"So he couldn't have died in the hotel room."

"Not according to the ME. Wherever he was, Doom was on ice over the weekend. But someone had to flip the body over after those post-mortem pinpoint hemorrhages appeared."

"Hmmm. What did you get in New Hampshire?"

"I found Grandmaison and his wife. They seem to take this Remote Viewing stuff dead serious. If they're running a scam, I didn't detect it in their manner. They claim never to have heard of John Doom. Otherwise, they made absolutely no sense to me. According to them, the coordinates the dead man were working when he died were randomly assigned. Common sense says if they're random, they can't possibly do what he claims they can."

"Go at this from the angle of Doom's last four or five days. I'm going to put you with Knuckles on this."

"Why?"

"You'll see. He's already been informed."

Detective First Grade Robert Knuckles had been on the job a dozen years longer than Ray Murex and acted it.

"Another day, another stiff," he sighed.

"This one is complicated. Let me bring you up to speed."

Knuckles listened with head tilted back and his pale blue eyes gazing off into space, his expression bored. When Murex got to the part about Remote Viewing, Knuckles took his feet off his desk and began to look interested.

"This is a new one," he said. "I could get to like it. Let me see Grandmaison's card."

Murex gave it up. Knuckles read it over, then flipped it. "Whoa. What is this?"

Knuckles showed him the obverse side. Two sets of four digits were marked in blue ink: 2006/0075.

"Look like remote coordinates to you?" Knuckles asked.

"Pretty much," Murex admitted. "Unless the first one is the year."

Knuckles frowned deeply. "You say Grandmaison takes this stuff pretty seriously. I wonder . . ."

"Wonder what?"

"Well, maybe he just happened to give you a card on which he scribbled some stray coordinates. But try this on for size: maybe these coordinates are *you*."

"Me?"

"Could be he's tagged you for remote surveillance."

Ray Murex exploded into uncontrolled laughter.

"You ever work with psychics?" Knuckles asked.

"Never!"

"You know the unwritten rule."

"Sure. If you're stuck, you can consult one, you just can't use what they tell you in a court of law."

Bob Knuckles grinned wisely. "I've invoked that rule a time or two. Never mind the details. Take it from someone who's been at this longer than you. Take this stuff seriously, but treat it skeptically."

"Always." Murex pocketed the card and asked, "What's your take on this?"

"Obviously someone sneaked a corpse into the Park Plaza, pretending to be the deceased. I think we had better find out more about dead Mr Doom. I took the liberty of starting that ball rolling. He's single, 44 and lived waaay out of town. Mission Hill."

Murex frowned darkly.

"I know what you're thinking," Knuckles said. "Why would a single guy rent an expensive hotel room less than three miles from home?"

"Maybe he needed a quiet place to do his thing?"

"Let's see how quiet the home front really is."

*　　*　　*

The house was a triple-decker, dark chocolate brown, at the top of
Parker Hill. Murex and Knuckles had to climb nearly 100 cracked
concrete steps to get to the front door. The black woman who
answered was the landlady.

"A few questions about John Doom, ma'am," Murex said,
showing his shield.

"Come on in then."

They were let into the top-floor apartment.

"Lived here five years," the landlady was saying. "Quiet man.
Kept to himself."

"What did he do for a living?" Murex asked.

"Had different jobs. Didn't talk much about it. Traveled a lot. I
wouldn't see him for a week or two at a time, and he was always
saying as how he'd been to Baltimore or San Diego, or somesuch
place. Never said why."

There were two bedrooms. One was a standard setup with a twin
bed, and the usual furniture. The other was something else.

"What the hell he done with this room!" the landlady burst out.

The second bedroom room was all gray – ceiling, walls, even the
inside of the door. The windows were hung with blackout shades.
Gray, too. Even the rug was battleship gray. In the middle of the
rug was a thin futon, gray as mold.

Murex said, "It's a gray room."

"I can see that!" the landlady sputtered. "But what—"

"Could you excuse us, please?"

"Fine. I need to call a painter anyway . . ." She bustled out.

Murex huddled with Knuckles.

"Grandmaison had one in his cellar. I didn't see the inside. They
remote view in gray rooms for some reason."

"Then why did Doom go to a hotel, if he had this setup handy?"

"Good question."

They looked around. A bookcase was crammed with books and
microcassettes in labeled boxes. Murex selected one, loaded it into
a recorder from his pocket.

A male voice began saying: "9746 0458 April 3rd 9746 0458 My
perceptions of the target are . . ."

Murex hit stop. He popped in the other cassette. The same voice
recited different coordinates and a date.

"Doom was really into this stuff," Knuckles muttered. "I
wonder if it's any good for police work . . ."

Murex shot him a dark look. They began looking for address

books and cancelled checks with the deceased's signature on it. It didn't take long.

"This look like the registration signature?" Knuckles asked.

Murex frowned. "No. Not even close."

A commotion came from down below. Exiting, they found the landlady complaining to a UPS man who was hand-trucking a big burlap-covered box up the 100 steps.

Knuckles demanded, "What's this thing?"

The landlady huffed, "A damned steamer trunk. Belonged to John. Fool hotel sent it over. What am I supposed to do with it?"

They examined the trunk. It was empty.

"We'll take this off your hands, ma'am," Murex said.

Back at the Park Plaza, the hotel manager was saying, "Yes, we did ship the trunk back."

Knuckles demanded, "Didn't you understand that it could be evidence?"

"But it was stored outside the room. I was told not to remove anything from the room proper. We have a basement storage facility for large items."

"Did John Doom arrive with this trunk?" asked Murex.

"The desk clerk will know."

The clerk didn't look happy to see Ray Murex.

"Did John Doom check in with a steamer trunk?"

"No, it was delivered later. I don't remember the company. He requested that it be sent up to his room, and then a few hours later, asked that it be placed in storage."

"What do you remember about this trunk?"

"Well, the bellman complained that it was pretty heavy."

"I want to talk with that bellman."

The bell captain had a poor memory. He couldn't describe John Doom, but he recalled one thing clearly: "That trunk was very heavy going up, and a lot lighter coming down."

Murex asked, "What color were Doom's eyes?"

"Grayish."

"Not greenish?"

"No, grayish."

"Thank you."

Murex and Knuckles conferred. Murex growled, "Doom's eyes were green as seawater."

"If it was Doom who checked in," countered Knuckles.

"My money says that it wasn't."

"Your money's no good in court, Ray."

"Here's how I see it. The victim was delivered to the hotel in that steamer trunk. Bellman takes the trunk up to the hotel room, after which the unknown person who checked in under Doom's name removes the victim from the trunk, lays him out on the bed, calls for the trunk to be removed, then exits quietly."

"You think he was dead going in?"

"Exact time of death will establish that. But where was he for four days that he didn't eat, and didn't decompose if he was already dead?"

"And what really killed him, and how?" said Knuckles.

"I don't buy death by remote viewing," Murex muttered.

"Let's talk to the ME then."

The Medical Examiner was busy trisecting a human liver. He didn't even look up from his work. "Heart failure. Your DOA expired of natural causes on or about last Friday, the 21st."

"Are you sure?" Murex pressed.

"I'm never sure. But I am positive. A contributing factor appears to be malnourishment and dehydration."

"Could he have been scared to death?" asked Knuckles.

"There's no known medical test for that. But yes. Could have. It's within the realm of possibility. But heart failure is what I will certify."

"Anything else?"

"Under three fingernails I found gray deposits. Paint chips."

Murex and Knuckles examined these under a microscope.

"Looks like scrapings," decided Murex.

Knuckles nodded. "Yeah. Probably from his gray room."

"Except for one thing. These scrapings are slate gray. Doom's gray room was battleship gray. A lighter shade."

"Good catch."

On the drive up to New Hampshire the next morning, Bob Knuckles was saying, "The guy dies of a heart attack while doing his thing in a gray room. Whoever has charge of the gray room in question needed to cover it up for some reason. So he transports DOA Doom to the Plaza and stages it to look like the death happened there."

Behind the wheel, Murex growled. "It doesn't fit."

"Sure it fits. What do you mean, it doesn't fit?"

"What are you covering up? Heart attacks happen."

"So do lawsuits. Guy doesn't want to be sued for negligence by the fatality's relatives."

"Trade a lawsuit for criminal mischief and felony transport of a body across state lines? I'll take the lawsuit any day. It was staged. The date of the tape was Monday, not last Friday."

"If you're going to stage a death by remote viewing, why use a TIRV folder?" Knuckles countered.

"Because you're not TIRV. You're a rival RV school. Kill two birds with one stone. Dispose of inconvenient body and screw competition."

"Makes more sense to just dispose of the body, and hope for no traceback."

"I don't see it," Murex insisted.

They were silent for a while. Fresh snowflakes were blowing in the backwash of vehicles ahead. Winter was settling in. After a time, Knuckles spoke. "Try this: it's a murder."

"Murder how?"

"Let's say RV works like they say. No, follow me on this. Victim Doom wants to RV a really hot target. Perpetrator has a reason to want him off the planet. Maybe he knows Doom has a weak ticker. Figures one good scare might – just might – flatline him."

"Okay. It's plausible so far as to motivation."

"Good. So he drops him into the scariest place possible."

"Which is?"

"Hell."

"Hell!"

"Hear me out now," Knuckles said. "What did Doom describe on that first tape? Going down into the Earth and finding himself in a giant barbecue pit with blazing eyes looking up at him. What would that be except Hell?"

"I don't believe it."

"Listen to it again." Knuckles replayed the tape.

"5688 7854 January 23. 5688 7854. My perceptions of the target are . . ."

Murex suddenly pulled over. "Wait a minute. Stop! Give me that."

Ray Murex popped out the cassette and inserted one taken from John Doom's apartment. He let it play for two full minutes.

"Sound like the same guy to you?" Murex asked.

"Not even remotely," Knuckles returned.

"Ouch."

They checked other tapes. All the voices matched. Except for the tape found on the body of John Doom.

"Scratch the theory he died doing what he loved best," Knuckles muttered as Murex got the car back into northbound traffic.

"Suddenly I like Trey Grandmaison," said Murex.

"Doesn't fit."

"What do you mean, doesn't fit?"

"Whoever staged Doom's death scene wouldn't use TIRV paraphernalia if he was connected to TIRV."

"I still like him. He bears a general resemblance to the mystery man who checked into room 314. And he has gray eyes. Let's see how he takes our showing up unexpectedly."

"You still carrying his business card?"

"Yeah."

Knuckles grinned. "Then maybe he'll be expecting you."

"I've been expecting you," said Trey Grandmaison at the door.

Murex kept his voice flat. "You have?"

"Well, either you were going to solve it, or return for more information. Either way, I expected another visit."

"I'm Bob Knuckles. We'd like to know more about RV."

"I'm on my way to teach a class. But follow me."

Grandmaison led them to the barn.

"What is the purpose of a gray room?" asked Knuckles.

"That started in the unit – Stargate. We needed a quiet sealed environment in which to do our work. Gray is a neutral color that won't influence the viewer's imagination."

"Uh-huh," said Murex.

Knuckles said, "We think John Doom died in a gray room. Could we see yours?"

"Not much to see. But come on."

The gray room was a flat hue from floor to ceiling. Behind a drop ceiling hung a battery of indirect lights. A gray blanket covered a floor mattress. It was very cold.

Murex asked, "No heat?"

"Ceiling lights will warm it up enough. Most sessions last less than 50 minutes. And I've had survival training. Cold doesn't bother me."

"What would you call this shade of gray?"

"Slate."

"Doom had a room like this. But it was lighter in color."

Grandmaison cocked an eyebrow. "He had a gray room? Then what was he doing RVing in a hotel?"

"That's what we'd like to know. Where were you over the weekend, Mr Grandmaison?"

Grandmaison didn't blink. "I returned from teaching an Advanced Applications class in Richmond, Virginia on Sunday morning."

"How long were you there?"

"All week. Class started that Monday morning."

"Witnesses?"

"Over 60 people took my AARV class. I can give you their contact information."

"We may or may not need it," Murex said glumly.

Knuckles scratched at the inner door. Gray paint flaked off. "Ever lock yourself in by accident?"

"Impossible. There's no exterior lock."

Knuckles looked. "You're right. My mistake."

"Where was Mrs Grandmaison last week?" asked Murex.

A vein in Trey Grandmaison's forehead began throbbing. "With me. She assists me on the road. Is there anything else? I have to begin my ERV class."

Knuckles asked, "Would you mind if we observe? I'm kinda curious about this RV stuff."

"Happy to. Come on."

The barn was insulated inside, and quartz space heaters radiated warmth from all four corners. It was barely enough. About a dozen people ranging in age from twentyish to fiftysomething sat on pine folding chairs facing a long table. Behind that stood a portable blackboard. Most shivered in their coats.

Grandmaison announced, "We have two guests from the Boston police investigating a mysterious death in the RV community."

A woman raised a hand. "Are we going to work it?"

"If we were, you know I wouldn't frontload you first, would I?"

The class laughed.

"Detectives Murex and Knuckles are just here to satisfy their curiosity."

Murex stepped forward, showing a morgue photo. "Does anyone here know this man? John Doom?"

No one stirred.

"Does anyone here have a gray room, or knows someone who does?"

Heads shook all around. Murex stepped back.

Grandmaison said, "We'll begin by debriefing on the overnight target. Who wants to start?"

A man stood and began reciting from a black binder notebook. "My perceptions of the target were of a tall spidery latticelike structure situated in a wide flat area."

"Good. Next?"

"My perceptions of the target suggest an oil derrick on a land platform—"

Grandmaison interrupted, "Stop. How many times do I have to drill this into you guys? Describe, do not identify. Premature target identification will get you into trouble every time."

"Sorry. Target was metallic, vertical, man-made, and I got strong sensory impressions of cross-braces and oil smells."

"Probably associational noise from the derrick concept. Next!"

As the class went around the room, they described structures ranging from a NASA shuttle on its launch pad to high-voltage power line transmission towers.

Murex whispered to Knuckles, "They're all over the map."

When the last student was done, Grandmaison rolled up a portable overhead projector.

"Target 2004/0013 is very challenging because of the tendency of the viewer's conscious mind to force a familiar identification. Hence, a class will bring back similar descriptions, dimensionals and other data, but will often lean toward different interpretations, usually biased by personal knowledge or analytic overlay."

Grandmaison clicked a switch. The Eiffel Tower appeared on the screen – a white sheet nailed to the wall behind him.

A woman gasped, "No one got it!"

"On the contrary. Most of you got it. The Eiffel Tower is structurally similar to an oil derrick or a electrical transmission tower, and because it also functions as a TV and radio broadcasting antenna, those of you who are sensitive to energetics will perceive it that way. Who described a Shuttle on its pad? You decoded the Eiffel Tower and its elevator as a gantry structure and its elevator. Good signal acquisition. Not so good decoding."

The class seemed impressed. Murex was not.

"How do they know he's not throwing up a picture to match what they get?" he whispered to Knuckles.

"Why were they getting basically the same stuff?" Knuckles countered.

"Okay!" Grandmaison announced. "Ten minute comfort break."

The class made for the house.

A woman walked up to Murex and Knuckles, saying, "If you guys need help with your case, I'm a professional spirit communicator."

When Murex hesitated, Knuckles took the card. "We'll keep you in mind, Miss . . . Carter."

"No problem!"

Grandmaison drifted over, grinning. "Not bad for only three days' training."

Murex asked, "Your class didn't seem to react when I flashed Doom's photo."

"The RV community is exploding. I teach people. My former Stargate colleagues teach other people. We don't all keep track of each other."

Bob Knuckles asked, "Where were you the night John Doom checked into the Plaza?"

"Here. Home. We were selecting targets for next week's ERV class in LA."

Knuckles nodded. "You teach all over the country?"

"And local classes in between."

"We've determined that Mr Doom was dead approximately four days before he checked in to the hotel," Ray Murex said suddenly.

Trey Grandmaison didn't skip a beat, although a vein in his forehead suddenly leaped to life. "You have your work cut out for you. And so have I. Excuse me."

The class was filing back in. The break over, Grandmaison wrote a set of coordinates on the chalkboard and said, "Okay, this is your next target. Go to it."

The class gathered up sleeping bags, futons and the like and spread them out at scattered places on the floor.

"Target is to be viewed in present time. You have one hour. View until the data starts to repeat or the signal line runs dark. Don't interpret. And no snoring."

Grandmaison led them out, saying they needed absolute quiet.

"Where's Mrs G?" asked Knuckles.

"Shopping."

"I have a hypothetical question."

"Shoot."

"Would it be possible, in your professional opinion, to remote view Hell? Assuming of course that there is such a place?"

Grandmaison didn't hesitate. "Absolutely."

Murex asked, "Are there any other RV instructors or schools in this area to your knowledge?"

"No. I'm the only one in New England. There were only a dozen or so people in the unit, and those who are teaching civilians are scattered around the country."

"Would you know of any other gray room in the area other than yours or Doom's?"

"I thought mine was the only one. I would suggest you look into other schools. I didn't train this guy, but if he built a gray room, he's a very serious viewer."

"How do I go about that?"

"Google," smiled Trey Grandmaison.

On the ride back to Boston, Murex was very quiet while Knuckles cleaned his fingernails with a nailfile, carefully placing the scrapings in a napkin.

"Guy had survival training," Knuckles said quietly.

"So?"

"So – he was ex-intelligence. Probably knows a lot of ways to kill a guy so that it looks like natural causes."

"It still doesn't fit."

"No, it does not," said Knuckles, looking at the business card that read *Beverly Carter, Spirit Communicator*. "If Grandmaison made that Hell tape, he's a fabulous voice actor. Guy has a voice like a bullfrog."

The next two days were bleak. The weather was bleak. Progress of the case was bleaker. The weatherman kept promising snow, but all the skies mustered up were flurries.

A forensic handwriting analysis of the hotel signature proved that John Doom had not checked himself into the Plaza. No known relatives or friends of John Doom could be found.

Trey Grandmaison's military records revealed that he received a dishonorable discharge for psychological reasons in 1993. The records were sealed. Otherwise he checked out clean. No record anywhere.

On the third day, Bob Knuckles was trolling the net and came across a website advertising an on-line course called Tom Morrow's Practical Remote Viewing. The instructor's photo caused him to say, "What ho!"

Ray Murex took a look and said, "That's John Doom."

"Now we know what he does for a living. Time to give Miss Carter a buzz."

"Why?"

Knuckles smiled broadly. "Why not?" He dialed a number.

"Miss Carter, this is Detective Knuckles. How are you? Good, I'm calling you rather than bother Mr Grandmaison. Do you keep your class assignments? You do? Good. If I read you a set of coordinates, could you identify them for me? Sure, I'll hold." To Murex, he said, "She's getting her class notes. Hand me that TIRV business card, will you?"

Murex scaled it over.

"The numbers are 2006/0027 . . . You did! When? What did you get? Interesting. What did the class get? Really? Could you do me a big favor? Would it be possible to view those coordinates now? And call me back."

Knuckles hung up. "She's calling back in twenty minutes."

"And?"

"Let's see what she comes up with."

Twenty minutes later. Knuckles took the call. He was on less than two minutes. "That's very helpful. Thank you."

Murex looked his question.

"She got a guy sitting at a desk. Dejected."

"So?"

"So. You're sitting at a desk looking pretty forlorn to me."

"Oh, come off it!"

"She said the class worked those numbers Tuesday night. You interviewed Mr G. on Tuesday. They got the same thing then. A guy at a desk concentrating on something serious. Three students got a law-enforcement vibe. Looks like he tagged you. Why? Forget about whether RV really works or not. Just speculate with me: why would he do that?"

"Because he's dirty."

"Or knows more about Doom's demise than he'll let on," Knuckles countered.

Murex sat up in his chair. "Let's go at this from another angle. Trey Grandmaison is out of town all last week. That checked out.

No holes. He comes back and finds a dead guy in his gray room. He's gotta do something."

"Wait a minute. What's Doom doing there?"

"We'll figure that part out later. But maybe Mrs G – Effie – is moonlighting."

"So why does he stage the death with TIRV material?"

"He figures his airtight alibi makes it a perfect crime. What has he got to lose? Also, this gives him a direct pipeline into any investigation."

"No. It points any investigation directly at him."

"Right, also. If things get hot, he sees it coming. He can take steps."

"How was Mrs G. when you talked to her?" asked Knuckles.

"Nervous. Showed signs of being severely short on sleep too. Seemed worried about the impact of bad publicity on the business."

"But Mr G. isn't, is he? Why not? Think motive."

Murex gave it some thought. "Maybe he wants the publicity."

"Why would he want bad publicity?"

"Maybe in his business bad publicity is good publicity. Or any publicity is better than none."

"Student RV's Hell and drops dead," Knuckles shot back. "How is that good?"

Murex made a face. "Maybe to the whackos who take these classes, it'll sound like the ultimate thrill ride."

"Maybe his business is failing and he's teaching Doom privately. Discovers he's an incognito rival. Offs him somehow and sets it all up."

"Possible. But why is he so cooperative?"

"He's ex-Army Intelligence. Versed in psychological operations. Being cooperative and up front could be a way of deflecting suspicion."

"Which he actually wants in a perverted way."

"Sure. It's basic reverse psychology – mind games." Knuckles leaned back in his chair and gazed at the ceiling. "Try this: DOA Doom croaks. His teacher couldn't find a way to get him back into his apartment – all those steps must have been too daunting – but checking him into a hotel was easier. Calls and makes reservations to boot."

"Why not a motel?"

Knuckles shrugged. "Big hotel, easier to penetrate. Lot of

people coming and going. No car directly involved. No license plate on record with the hotel. He fakes the tape because how else are the investigating parties going to know what Doom was supposedly RVing?"

The phone rang. Knuckles took it. "Yes? Yep. Yep. Good." He hung up. "That was the lab. The paint chips found under Doom's fingernails match the ones I scraped off Grandmaison's gray room. Postive match. No question."

Murex blinked, then remembered Knuckles cleaning his nails. "Can we use that in court?"

"Won't need to. We can get admissible paint samples later. The question is, did Doom die naturally, or was he snuffed?"

"And if so, who did it?"

"That's easy. Mrs G."

"Too many unknowns to assume that." Pressing a button on his desk, Murex picked up the telephone. He dialed the number off the TIRV card and said, "Mrs Grandmaison? This is detective Ray Murex down at Boston Homicide. Sorry to wake you. I have a few more questions, if you don't mind. Were you in Richmond during the week your husband taught that class? You were? No reason. Except this: lab tests have proven conclusively that John Doom did not expire in his own gray room. We only know of one other in this area. That one belongs to your husband. Well, until we can rule something out, we have to consider it ruled in. So we'll be in touch." Murex hung up.

Knuckles looked at him. "Why did you do that?"

"Sometimes, you light a fuse. Other times you're just setting fire to a string. Let's see which it is."

The call came from Trey Grandmaison within the hour.

"I'd love to help you guys close out this investigation," he offered. His tone was fluttery.

"Because we can't rule your gray room out of the picture?" said Murex.

"No. Because my wife is becoming upset with your questions. Look, I offered to help before. Why don't I personally RV John Doom's last hours and see what I come up with? Maybe that will give your investigation a fresh direction."

"It couldn't hurt," Murex said dryly.

"I'll assign the coords and get back to you with whatever data I get."

"Appreciate that."

Knuckles looked at Murex. "This could go either way."

Hours later, the promised pages came sliding out of the office fax machine. Knuckles read it first.

"This is interesting. Seems dead Mr Doom liked to frequent bondage and domination rooms. According to this, he died in someone's 'dungeon' and his mistress relocated his inconvenient remains, using his RV hobby as a cover—"

"Forget it!" Murex snapped angrily. He slid the TIRV business card over.

Knuckles took it, compared it to the coordinates recorded on the session report. "I'll be damned! The same coordinates. He didn't even try. No question now that he's dirty."

"We'll see what the lab says," Murex said darkly.

"About what?"

"About the voice analysis of that call I recorded yesterday."

Knuckles cocked a questioning eyebrow. "Mrs G?"

"I have a hunch her voice patterns will match up with the Doom tape."

"You illegally recorded an interstate telephone call. That's not admissible evidence, either."

"We'll worry about that if there's a matchup," muttered Ray Murex.

The aural spectrography report was three days coming through. It arrived one day too late to do any good.

Bob Knuckles was checking with the Richmond hotel that had hosted the TIRV class the week before. He thanked someone and hung up.

"That's the last staffer," he said. "They all confirm that Mrs G. arrived with her husband and departed with him six days later. But no one can verify her whereabouts in between."

"So she could have flown home any time in that six-day period. Or taken a train."

"Very possible. Boston and Richmond are at opposite ends of the Northeast corridor."

"And the fingerprint bureau says that every print taken off that steamer trunk matches up with the people known to have handled it."

"So Mr G's hands are clean, after all."

"Too clean. John Doom's prints are not to be found, either.

That old trunk was almost forensically pristine. All prints are post check-in."

"And so another perfect crime unravels owing to excessive prep."

"We'll see," Murex said.

The first news reports of the Manchester to Los Angeles airliner making an emergency landing due to a passenger emergency made no immediate impression on either Detectives Murex or Knuckles. The followup, reporting that a female passenger had been taken off dead, also passed by unremarked on. The passenger's name was being withheld pending notification of next of kin. But when the morning papers reported that Efthemia Grandmaison had been found dead in seat 23C on the overnight flight to Los Angeles, Bob Knuckles exploded out of his chair.

"He did it! I know he did!"

"Calm down. Let's go at this the right way."

"Son of a bitch killed Doom, and then took out his wife because she knew he did it!"

"Doesn't fit."

"What do you mean, doesn't fit? Of course it fits. It fits perfectly."

"A wife can't be made to testify against her spouse. There's more to it."

Murex reached out to Los Angeles police department and asked for the detective in charge of the case to contact him ASAP. A detective John Burks returned the call. After Murex explained his interest, Burks gave him what he had:

"The deceased and her husband, this Grandmaison, take the red eye and upon their arrival at LAX, the husband attempts to awaken his wife. She was nonresponsive. EMT's are called to the plane. Wife was pronounced dead at the scene. The husband is telling a crazy story."

"How crazy?"

"Claims he was with some secret project during the Cold War that employed mental powers to spy on the Russians. He and the wife teach this Remote Viewing. The wife, he says, was remote viewing something while the husband slept in the adjoining seat. He says this is not the first time someone expired while doing these experiments."

"Is there an audio tape of the session?" Murex explained. "Usually, they record the experience."

"Yeah, we do have a cassette. But we haven't listened to it yet."

"You might want to call me back after you do."

"Why don't I just play it this minute and we'll both listen?"

Moments later, a hushed voice came over the line.

"2004 8547 January 31st. 2004 8547 . . . I am in a dark room. I can see a door, but it is closed. Something is stirring above the door, where the wall joins the ceiling. Ominous. Black. A cloud. I see eyes . . . It's speaking, 'Death is coming for you!' It's moving toward me. Trey! Trey! Wake up! Ahhhh . . ."

"Sounds like she was having a nightmare," Burks suggested.

Murex snapped, "I don't buy it."

"You say you're investigating a death tied to the Grandmaisons," Burks prompted.

"Right." Murex gave him the investigation thusfar.

"Seems to me like these people were poking their noses into places human noses don't belong," Burks opined.

"Can we get a copy of that tape for voiceprint comparison?"

"Consider it done."

"Thanks. What are you going to do with Trey Grandmaison?"

"Depends on what the ME says. But he's being very cooperative."

"We'd like to be informed either way."

LAPD got back to them the next morning.

"ME says natural causes," Burks reported. "Heart failure. Probably as a result of night terrors, also known as sleep paralysis."

"I'm not familiar with that one," Murex admitted.

"It's a documented medical condition. According to the ME, when you dream at night, your body shuts down so you don't act out your dreams by kicking and flailing around. Sometimes nightmares wake people up in the middle of it, and they find that they can't move for a minute or two. It's apparently a frightening experience when it happens."

"So how does the ME know that's what really happened?"

"Because it happened to him once. Says he was having a nightmare just like the one the woman recorded. A black cloud came at him, threatening to kill him. It roosted on his chest and he discovered he couldn't breathe. Shock woke him up. Found he couldn't move a muscle. But the cloud was gone. The experience scared him so much he talked to his doctor about it. The doc told him about sleep paralysis. End of story."

"Are you satisfied with that explanation?" Murex asked.

"Not especially. But the death technically took place over some other state's jurisdiction. ME says she was dead before she reached California airpace. So we're dropping the matter. The ME will release the body to the husband tomorrow."

"I'll let you know what the voiceprint analysis says."

"Don't run up too big a phone bill on our account," Burks said dryly.

The aural-spectrography report was succinct. Murex frowned as he read it.

"Not the same voice, huh?" Knuckles said.

"The contrary. Perfect match. Effie Grandmaison made Doom's tape. But what good does that do us now? She's dead and can't be questioned."

"Okay. Let's think this through. We're not at rope's end. Yet. Effie Grandmaison slips home during the time her hubby is teaching that RV class down in Virgina, probably by Amtrak."

"Right. While she's home, she snuffs Doom. Leaves him in the cellar gray room where he'll keep for a few days, and returns to Richmond. Later, she accompanies Grandmaison home, where he hatches an elaborate hoax to make it look like Doom died elsewhere. All seems well."

"Until we start digging and making Mrs G nervous. Mr G decides the wife is a growing inconvenience, and somehow snuffs her during the flight to LA while crew and passengers are sound asleep."

"This time, he concocts a more plausible version of the original perfect crime. One that will stand up in court, provided an expert in sleep paralysis is called in to testify."

"Obviously, he recorded the tape."

"Let's see what the Effie tape tells us."

The FedEx package from LAPD arrived later that afternoon. Murex and Knuckles rushed it over to the lab, twisting arms until a technician agreed to look at it over his lunch break. He came back with a fast answer: "Not the same voice at all. Guaranteed."

Murex took Knuckles aside and said, "That leaves only one voice possible: Trey Grandmaison. After he takes out the wife, he makes the tape in the toilet of the plane. Plants it and he's home free, thinking no one is going to see through to the truth."

"Thinking wrong. But how do we prove otherwise? He's off the hook and walking free under the perfect alibi: asleep beside her the entire time."

Murex said, "I don't buy this sleep paralysis stuff."

"It's ironclad, according to that ME. It happened to him, didn't it?"

Murex went to an idle PC and and started a search. He found several websites devoted to sleep paralysis. One read: *Sleep paralysis is an REM sleep parasomnia, and a symptom of narcolepsy, although it can affect about 40 per cent of the general population. It's characterized by frighteningly vivid hypnogogic hallucinations and accompanied by acute respiratory distress. First-time sufferers often assume that they are dying.*

Murex snorted, "I don't buy this at all."

"Says it's a legit medical condition," Knuckles pointed out.

"Not that. The black clouds. Almost every account here says the same thing. Subject is sleeping and has the same nightmare. A malignant black cloud comes into the bedroom, starts threatening them, and lands on their chest. Subject can't breathe. Panic sets in. Fear of death wakes them up. They find they're paralyzed until their body goes back to normal. Ridiculous."

"Maybe it's the opposite of the tunnel of light some people report during the near-death experience," Knuckles suggested. "A trick of the brain."

"Show me where in mythology or literature there are legends of evil black clouds and I'll—" Murex froze at the screen.

"You what?"

"I just found the hole in Trey Grandmaison's alibi."

"Big?"

"Big enough for a black cloud to come in through. Let's find out when Mrs Grandmaison is coming home."

They called every Nashua New Hampshire funeral home until they found the one responsible for waking Effie Grandmaison.

Knuckles hung up. "The body is coming in on a 7 p.m. flight. Odds are Mr G is accompanying said body."

"Let's go meet the grieving spouse."

Trey Grandmaison looked appropriately startled to see Detectives Murex and Knuckles patiently waiting for him at his Manchester Airport gate.

"We're very sorry to hear about your wife," said Ray Murex.

"A true tragedy," added Bob Knuckles.

"We'd like to clear up a few things. The airport has allowed us to use one of their offices."

Trey Grandmaison followed them willingly, but pensively.

"Let me start with what we know for certain," Murex told him after they took seats. "We know that John Doom died in your gray room while you were in Richmond, and was left there for several days while you were presumably absent. We also know that your wife did not expire as a result of sleep paralysis."

Trey Grandmaison looked at both men by turns. "Sleep paralysis is a medical condition my wife had for years," he said gravely. "This time, it killed her."

"It did not kill her. Therefore, you did."

"I did not! Look, Effie developed narcolepsy. Probably from too much RVing in altered brainwave states. Her doctor can produce the medical records proving it."

"The reason we know sleep paralysis did not kill your wife is that tape she made."

A vein pulsed in Grandmaison's forehead. "Tape?"

"The one recorded in-flight," Knuckles put in. "You didn't think we knew about that, did you?"

"I discarded that tape in LA." The vein continued pulsing.

"Not surprising. Loving husband that you are. Of course you'd throw out your wife's last recorded words – except she didn't record them. *You* did."

Trey Grandmaison almost cracked a grin. He turned it into a grimace. "I wish now I had saved that tape. We could disprove your theory electronically."

"Yeah," Murex went on. "Too bad. But let me continue. The reason we know your wife did not die of sleep paralysis any more than she or John Doom died while remote viewing something that frightened them to death is that if Mrs Grandmaison had been suffering sleep paralysis at the time, she would not have been able to record her experience. Sleep paralysis doesn't just freeze the major muscles in the body, but the vocal cords as well. A person suffering from SP *can't* speak. If they can't speak, they can't describe menacing black clouds threatening to murder them. *Can* they, Mr Grandmaison?"

Trey Grandmaison said nothing. But that vein pulsed more strongly.

"You didn't think it through very thoroughly, did you?" Knuckles pressed. "You knew you couldn't pull that remote viewing Hell smokescreen twice. So you had to top it. But plausibly. Maybe Mrs G. did suffer from SP. But we all know she didn't die of it."

Gray eyes opaque, Grandmaison said, "No one knows that."

"I know what you're thinking. If a person dies of fright as result of sleep paralysis, only they and God would know the truth."

Trey Grandmaison threw up his hands. "I wish I had saved that tape. It would resolve everything."

"Fortunately for us, but unfortunately for you, LAPD made a dupe. And here it is." Knuckles slid a microcassette recorder across the table. He hit play.

"2004 8547 January 31st. 2004 8547 . . . I am in a dark room. I can see a door, but it is closed. Something is stirring above the door, where the wall joins the ceiling. Ominous. Black. A cloud . . ."

Murex stopped the tape. "Fair job of masking your voice. How hard do you think it will be to match your voiceprint to that recording?"

Trey Grandmaison turned pale and then flushed. He lunged for the recorder, fumbled it open and almost got the minicassette into his mouth before Murex and Knuckles fought it out of his hands.

After they had cuffed him, and his rights were read, Bob Knuckles asked, "Would you say that we've got your number, or your coordinates?"

Ray Murex said, "You can tell us about it, if you'd like."

Grandmaison surprised them. He did exactly that.

"John Doom was a student of mine. One of my earliest students. He kept taking my courses and then he started teaching RV under another name. Using my coordinates. It was getting out of hand. He'd steal my students from my own classes. Charge half what I did. Between him and the sagging economy, I was having a hard time. Something had to be done."

"So you decided to do away with him?" Murex prompted.

"That was Effie's idea. She came home from Richmond on the pretext of giving Doom some private training and while he was in-session, she sat on his chest, holding a pillow over his face until he suffocated. I showed her how to hold his arms down with padded knees so he wouldn't bruise."

"In other words," Knuckles said, "she burked him."

Murex looked blank. "Burked?"

Grandmaison nodded sullenly. "An old assassination technique.

Leaves no marks. Looks just like natural causes. Effie had him fast for four days beforehand, promising that it would improve his session work. That was so his bowels wouldn't empty and create a sanitary problem while the body cooled in my gray room."

"Except the body was flipped over after telltale pinpoint haemorrhages appeared in the whites of the eyeballs," said Murex. "Either his eye capillaries burst while he was smothered, or gravity did it. Either way, the position of the body gave the show away. You can skip the part about how you staged the death scene in the hotel room. We figured that out. Why did you do your wife?"

"She was starting to become unglued. Guilt. Fear. I don't know. But I knew she couldn't hold it in forever. So while everyone was asleep on the plane, I did the same thing to her she did to Doom."

"What goes around, comes around," clucked Knuckles.

The throbbing vein in Trey Grandmaison's forehead became still. "It was easy. I booked seats in the last row. There was no one for six or seven rows around of us. And they were dead to the world."

"You're kind of a control freak, aren't you?" Knuckles pressed. "That's why you staged the death scene using TIRV class materials, isn't it? To baffle us and provide you the opportunity to send us off on wild-goose chases?"

Grandmaison shrugged. "It's elementary psychological warfare. What kind of murderer would leave a trail leading directly to his front door?"

"One who was drummed out of the Army for reasons of mental instability. You were so wound up in your Stargate razzle-dazzle, you didn't think we'd look beyond it. You were dead wrong."

Murex frowned. "So you killed this rival Doom because he was stealing your coordinates."

"They're worth thousands of dollars," he said leadenly. "And they're my livelihood."

"But they're only numbers. You told me so yourself."

Trey Grandmaison's composed face wavered, recovered, then fell completely apart. His voice broke.

"It's all I salvaged from my military career," he sobbed. "My business was everything I had. You don't know remote viewing, so you wouldn't understand."

Ray Murex stood up.

"Maybe not. But I understand observable justice. Let's go."

On the Rocks

J. A. Konrath

J. A. (Joe) Konrath (b. 1970) is the author of Whiskey Sour
*(2004) and its sequels which feature forty-something Chicago
police detective Jacqueline ("Jack") Daniels. She also features
in several short stories including the following. Although he has
only been writing professionally for three years, Konrath has
already been nominated for several awards and won the Der-
ringer Award in 2005 for his short story "The Big Guys".
Konrath has also had stints as a stand-up improv comedian, and
you can see some of that living-on-your-wits in the way Daniels
has to think fast yet stay sane in this, her first locked-room
mystery.*

"S he sure bled a lot."

I ignored Officer Coursey, my attention focused on the
dead woman's arm. The cut had almost severed her left wrist, a
flash of pink bone peeking through. Her right hand was curled
around the handle of a utility knife.

I'd been in Homicide for more than ten years, and still felt an
emotional punch whenever I saw a body. The day I wasn't affected
was the day I hung up my badge.

I wore disposable plastic booties over my flats because the shag
carpet oozed blood like a sponge wherever I stepped. The apartment's air conditioning was set on *freeze*, so the decomposition
wasn't as bad as it might have been after a week – but it was still pretty
bad. I got down on my haunches and swatted away some blowflies.

On her upper arm, six inches above the wound, was a bruise.

"What's so interesting, Lieut? It's just a suicide."

In my blazer pocket I had some latex gloves. I snapped them on.

The victim's name was Janet Hellerman, a real estate lawyer with a private practice. She was brunette, mid thirties, Caucasian. Her satin slip was mottled with drying brown stains, and she wore nothing underneath. I put my hand on her chin, gently turned her head.

There was another bruise on her cheek.

"Johnson's getting a statement from the super."

I stood up, smoothed down my skirt, and nodded at Herb, who had just entered the room. Detective First Class Herb Benedict was my partner. He had a gray mustache, Basset hound jowls, and a Santa Claus belly. Herb kept on the perimeter of the blood puddle; those little plastic booties were too hard for him to get on.

"Johnson's story corroborates?"

Herb nodded. "Why? You see something?"

I did, but wasn't sure how it fit. Herb had questioned both Officer Coursey and Officer Johnson, and their stories were apparently identical.

Forty minutes ago they'd arrived at apartment 3008 at the request of the victim's mother, who lived out of state. She had been unable to get in touch with her daughter for more than a week. The building superintendent unlocked the door for them, but the safety chain was on, and a sofa had been pushed in front of the door to prevent anyone from getting inside. Coursey put his shoulder to it, broke in, and they discovered the body.

Herb squinted at the corpse. "How many marks on the wrist?"

"Just one cut, deep."

I took off the blood-soaked booties, put them in one of the many plastic baggies I keep in my pockets, and went over to the picture window, which covered most of the far wall. The view was expensive, overlooking Lake Shore Drive from forty stories up. Boaters swarmed over the surface of Lake Michigan like little white ants, and the street was a gridlock of toy cars. Summer was a busy time for Chicagoans – criminals included.

I motioned for Coursey, and he heeled like a chastened puppy. Beat cops were getting younger every year; this one barely needed to shave. He had the cop stare, though – hard eyes and a perpetual scowl, always expecting to be lied to.

"I need you to do a door-to-door. Get statements from everyone on this floor. Find out who knew the victim, who might have seen anything."

Coursey frowned. "But she killed herself. The only way in the apartment is the one door, and it was locked from the inside, with the safety chain on. Plus there was a sofa pushed in front of it."

"I'm sure I don't need to remind you that suicides are treated as homicides in this town, Officer."

He rolled his eyes. I could practically read his thoughts. *How did this dumb broad get to be Homicide Lieutenant? She sleep with the PC?*

"Lieut, the weapon is still in her hand. Don't you think . . ."

I sighed. Time to school the rookie.

"How many cuts are on her wrist, Coursey?"

"One."

"Didn't they teach you about hesitation cuts at the Academy? A suicidal person usually has to work up the courage. Where was she found?"

"On the floor."

"Why not her bed? Or the bathtub? Or a comfy chair? If you were ending your life, would you do it standing in the middle of the living room?"

He became visibly flustered, but I wasn't through yet.

"How would you describe the temperature in this room?"

"It's freezing."

"And all she's wearing is a slip. Little cold for that, don't you think? Did you read the suicide note?"

"She didn't leave a note."

"They all leave notes. I've worked these streets for twenty years, and never saw a suicide where the vic didn't leave a note. But for some strange reason, there's no note here. Which is a shame because maybe her note would explain how she got the multiple contusions on her face and arm."

Coursey was cowed, but he managed to mumble, "The door was—"

"Speaking of doors," I interrupted, "why are you still here when you were given an order to start the door-to-door? Move your ass."

Coursey looked at his shoes and then left the apartment. Herb raised an eyebrow.

"Kinda hard on the newbie, Jack."

"He wouldn't have questioned me if I had a penis."

"I think you have one now. You took his."

"If he does a good job, I'll give it back."

Herb turned to look at the body. He rubbed his mustache.

"It could still play as suicide," he said. "If she was hit by a sudden urge to die. Maybe she got some terrible news. She gets out of the shower, puts on a slip, cranks up the air conditioning, gets a phone call, immediately grabs the knife and with one quick slice . . ."

He made a cutting motion over his wrist.

"Do you buy it?" I asked.

Herb made a show of mulling it over.

"No," he consented. "I think someone knocked her out, sliced her wrist, turned up the air so the smell wouldn't get too bad, and then . . ."

"Managed to escape from a locked room."

I sighed, my shoulders sagging.

Herb's eyes scanned the view. "A window washer?"

I checked the window, but as expected it didn't open. Winds this high up weren't friendly.

"There's no other way in?" Herb asked.

"Just the one entryway."

I walked up to it. The safety chain hung on the door at eye level, its wall mounting and three screws dangling from it. The doorframe where it had been attached was splintered and cracked from Coursey's entrance. There were three screw holes in the frame that matched the mounting, and a fourth screw still remained, sticking out of the frame about an inch.

The hinges on the door were dusty and showed no signs of tampering. A black leather sofa was pushed off to the side, near the doorway. I followed the tracks that its feet had made in the carpet. The sofa had been placed in front of the door and then shoved aside.

I opened the door, holding the knob with two fingers. It moved easily, even though it was heavy and solid. I closed it, stumped.

"How did the killer get out?" I said, mostly to myself.

"Maybe he didn't get out. Maybe the killer is still in the apartment." Herb's eyes widened and his hand shot up, pointing over my shoulder. "Jack! Behind you!"

I rolled my eyes.

"Funny, Herb. I already searched the place."

I peeled off the gloves and stuck them back in my pocket.

"Well, then there are only three possibilities." Herb held up his hand, ticking off fingers. "One, Coursey and Johnson and the superintendent are all lying. Two, the killer was skinny enough to slip out of the apartment by going under the door. Or three, it was Houdini."

"Houdini's dead."

"Did you check? Get an alibi?"

"I'll send a team to the cemetery."

While we waited for the ME to arrive, Herb and I busied ourselves with tossing the place. Bank statements told us Janet Hellerman made a comfortable living and paid her bills on time. She was financing a late model Lexus, which we confirmed was parked in the lot below. Her credit card debt was minimal, with a recent charge for plane tickets. A call to Delta confirmed two seats to Montana for next week, one in her name and one in the name of Glenn Hale.

Herb called the precinct, requesting a sheet on Hale.

I checked the answering machine and listened to thirty-eight messages. Twenty were from Janet's distraught mother, wondering where she was. Two were telemarketers. One was from a friend named Sheila who wanted to get together for dinner, and the rest were real estate related.

Nothing from Hale. He wasn't on the caller ID either.

I checked her cell phone next, and listened to forty more messages; ten from mom, and thirty from home buyers. Hale hadn't left any messages, but there was a "Glenn" listed on speed dial. The phone's call log showed that Glenn's number had called over a dozen times, but not once since last week.

"Look at this, Jack."

I glanced over at Herb. He set a pink plastic case on the kitchen counter and opened it up. It was a woman's toolkit, the kind they sold at department stores for fifteen bucks. Each tool had a cute pink handle and a corresponding compartment that it snugged into. This kit contained a hammer, four screwdrivers, a measuring tape, and eight wrenches. There were also two empty slots; one for needle nose pliers, and one for something five inches long and rectangular.

"The utility knife," I said.

Herb nodded. "She owned the weapon. It's looking more and more like suicide, Jack. She has a fight with Hale. He dumps her. She kills herself."

"You find anything else?"

"Nothing really. She liked to mountain climb, apparently. There's about forty miles of rope in her closet, lots of spikes and beaners, and a picture of her clinging to a cliff. She also has an extraordinary amount of teddy bears. There were so many piled on her bed, I don't know how she could sleep on it."

"Diary? Computer?"

"Neither. Some photo albums, a few letters that we'll have to look through."

Someone knocked. We glanced across the breakfast bar and saw the door ease open.

Mortimer Hughes entered. Hughes was a medical examiner. He worked for the city, and his job was to visit crime scenes and declare people dead. You'd never guess his profession if you met him on the street – he had the smiling eyes and infectious enthusiasm of a television chef.

"Hello Jack, Herb, beautiful day out." He nodded at us and set down a large tackle box that housed the many particular tools of his trade. Hughes opened it up and snugged on some plastic gloves and booties. He also brandished knee pads.

Herb and I paused in our search and watched him work. Hughes knelt beside the vic and spent ten minutes poking and prodding, humming tunelessly to himself. When he finally spoke, it was high-pitched and cheerful.

"She's dead," Hughes said.

We waited for more.

"At least four days, probably longer. I'm guessing from hypovolemic shock. Blood loss is more than forty percent. Her right zygomatic bone is shattered, pre-mortem or early post."

"Could she have broken her cheek falling down?" Herb asked.

"On this thick carpet? Possible – yes. Likely – no. Look at the blood pool. No arcs. No trails."

"So she wasn't conscious when her wrist was cut?"

"That would be my assumption, unless she laid down on the floor and stayed perfectly still while bleeding to death."

"Sexually assaulted?"

"Can't tell. I'll do a swab."

I chose not to watch, and Herb and I went back into the kitchen. Herb pursed his lips.

"It could still be suicide. She cuts her wrist, falls over, breaks her cheek bone, dies unconscious."

"You don't sound convinced."

"I'm not. I like the boyfriend. They're fighting, he bashes her one in the face. Maybe he can't wake her up, or he thinks he's killed her. Or he wants to kill her. He finds the toolbox, gets the utility knife, makes it look like a suicide."

"And then magically disappears."

Herb frowned. "That part I don't like."

"Maybe he flushed himself down the toilet, escaped through the plumbing."

"You can send Coursey out to get a plunger."

"Lieutenant?"

Officer Coursey had returned. He stood by the kitchen counter, his face ashen.

"What is it, Officer?"

"I was doing the door-to-door. No one answered at the apartment right across the hall. The superintendent thought that was strange – an old lady named Mrs Flagstone lives there, and she never leaves her home. She even sends out for groceries. So the super opens up her door and . . . you'd better come look."

Mrs Flagstone stared up at me with milky eyes. Her tongue protruded from her lips like a hunk of raw liver. She was naked in the bathtub, her face and upper body submerged in foul water, one chubby leg hanging over the edge. The bloating was extensive. Her white hair floated around her head like a halo.

"Still think it's a suicide?" I asked Herb.

Mortimer Hughes rolled up his sleeve and put his hand into the water. He pressed her chest and bubbles exploded out of her mouth and nose.

"Didn't drown. Her lungs are full of air."

He moved his hand higher, prodding the wrinkled skin on her neck.

"I can feel some damage to the trachea. There also appears to be a lesion around her neck. I want to get a sample of the water before I pull the drain plug."

Hughes dove into his box. Herb, Coursey, and I left him and went into the living room. Herb called in, requesting the forensics team.

"Any hits from the other tenants?" I asked the rookie.

He flipped open his pad. "One door over, at apartment 3010, the occupant, a Mr Stanley Mankowicz, remembers some yelling coming from the victim's place about six days ago."

"Does he remember what time?"

"It was late, he was in bed. Mr Mankowicz shares a wall with the vic, and has called her on several occasions to tell her to turn her television down."

"Did he call that night?"

"He was about to, but the noise stopped."

"Where's the super?"

"Johnson hasn't finished taking his statement."

"Call them both in here."

While waiting for them to arrive, I examined Mrs Flagstone's door. Like Janet's, it had a safety chain and, like Janet's, it had been ripped from the wall and the mounting was hanging from the door. I found four screws and some splinters on the floor. There were no screws in the door frame.

A knock, and I opened the door. Officer Johnson and the super. Johnson was older than his partner, bigger, with the same dead eyes. The superintendent was a Pakistani man named Majid Patel. Mr Patel had dark skin and red eyes and he clearly enjoyed all of this attention.

"I moved to this country ten years ago, and I have never seen a dead body before. Now I have seen two in the same day. I must call and tell my mother. I call my mother when anything exciting happens."

"We'll let you go in a moment, Mr Patel. I'm Lt Jack Daniels, this is Detective Herb Benedict. We just have a few . . ."

"Your name is Jack Daniels? But you are not a man."

"You're very observant," I deadpanned. "Did you know Janet Hellerman?"

Patel winked at me. Was he flirting?

"It must be hard, Lt Jack Daniels, to be a pretty woman with a funny name in a profession so dominated by male chauvinist pigs." Patel offered Herb a look. "No offense."

Herb returned a pleasant smile. "None taken. If you could please answer the Lieutenant's question."

Patel grinned, crooked teeth and spinach remnants.

"She was a real estate lawyer. Young and good looking. Always paid her rent on time. My brother gave her a deal on her apartment, because she had nice legs." Patel had no reservations about openly checking out mine. "Yours are very nice too, Jack Daniels. For an older lady. Are you single?"

"She's single." Herb winked at me, gave me an elbow. I made a mental note to fire him later.

"Your brother?" I asked Patel.

"He's the building owner," Officer Johnson chimed in. "It's the family business."

"Did you know anything about Janet's personal life?"

"She had a shit for a boyfriend, a man named Glenn. He had an affair and she dumped him."

"When was this?"

"About ten days ago. I know because she asked me to change the lock on her door. She had given him a key and he wouldn't return it."

"Did you change the lock?"

"I did not. Ms Hellerman just mentioned it to me in the elevator once. She never filled out the work order request."

"Does the building have a doorman?"

"No. We have security cameras."

"I'll need to see tapes going back two weeks. Can you get them for me?"

"It will not be a problem."

Mortimer Hughes came out of the bathroom. He was holding a closed set of tweezers in one hand, his other hand cupped beneath it.

"I dug a fiber out of the victim's neck. Red, looks synthetic."

"From a rope?" I asked.

Hughes nodded.

"Mr Patel, we'll be down shortly for those tapes. Coursey, Johnson, help Herb and I search the apartment. Let's see if we can find the murder weapon."

We did a thorough toss, but couldn't find any rope. Herb, however, found a pair of needle nose pliers in a closet. Pliers with pink handles.

"They were neighbors," Herb reasoned. "Janet could have lent them to her."

"Could have. But we both doubt it. Call base to see if they found anything on Hale."

Herb dialed, talked for a minute, then hung up.

"Glenn Hale has been arrested three times, all assault charges. Did three months in Joliet."

I wasn't surprised. All evidence pointed to the boyfriend, except for the damned locked room. Maybe Herb was right and the killer just slipped under the door and . . .

Epiphany.

"Call the lab team. I want the whole apartment dusted. Then get an address and a place of work on Hale and send cars. Tell them to wait for the warrant."

Herb raised an eyebrow. "A warrant? Shouldn't we question the guy first?"

"No need," I said. "He did it, and I know how."

Feeling, a bit foolishly, like Sherlock Holmes, I took everyone back into Janet's apartment. They began hurling questions at me, but I held up my hand for order.

"Here's how it went," I began. "Janet finds out Glenn is cheating, dumps him. He comes over, wanting to get her back. She won't let him in. He uses his key, but the safety chain is on. So he busts in and breaks the chain."

"But the chain was on when we came in the first time," Coursey complained.

Herb hushed him, saving me the trouble.

"They argue," I went on. "Glenn grabs her arm, hits her. She falls to the floor, unconscious. Who knows what's going through his mind? Maybe he's afraid she'll call the police, and he'll go to jail – he has a record and this state has zero tolerance for repeat offenders. Maybe he's so mad at her he thinks she deserves to die. Whatever the case, he finds Janet's toolkit and takes out the utility knife. He slits her wrist and puts the knife in her other hand."

Five inquisitive faces hung on my every word. It was a heady experience.

"Glenn has to know he'd be a suspect," I raised my voice, just a touch for dramatic effect. "He's got a history with Janet, and a criminal record. The only way to throw off suspicion is to make it look like no one else could have been in the room – to show the police that it had to be a suicide."

"Jack," Herb admonished. "You're dragging it out."

"If you figured it out, then you'd have the right to drag it out too."

"Are you really single?" Patel asked. He grinned again, showing more spinach.

"If she keeps stalling," Herb told him, "I'll personally give you her number."

I shot Herb with my eyes, then continued.

"Okay, so Glenn goes into Janet's closet and gets a length of climbing rope. He also grabs the needle nose pliers from her toolbox and heads back to the front door. The safety chain has been ripped out of the frame, and the mounting is dangling on the end. He takes a single screw," I pointed at the screw sticking in the door frame, "and puts it back in the doorframe about halfway."

Herb nodded, getting it. "When the mounting ripped out, it had to pull out all four screws. So the only way one could still be in the doorframe is if someone put it there."

"Right. Then he takes the rope and loops it under a sofa leg. He goes out into the hall with the rope, and closes the door, still holding both ends of the rope. He tugs the rope through the crack under the door, and pulls the sofa right up to the door from the other side."

"Clever," Johnson said.

"I must insist you meet my mother," Patel said.

"But the chain . . ." Coursey whined.

I smiled at Coursey. "He opens the door a few inches, and grabs the chain with the needle nose pliers. He swings the loose end over to the door frame, where it catches and rests on the screw he put in halfway."

I watched the light finally go on in Coursey's eyes. "When Mr Patel opened the door, it looked like the chain was on, but it really wasn't. It was just hanging on the screw. The thing that kept the door from opening was the sofa."

"Right. So when you burst into the room, you weren't the one that broke the safety chain. It was already broken."

Coursey nodded rapidly. "The perp just lets go of one end of the rope and pulls in the other end, freeing it from the sofa leg. Then he locks the door with his own key."

"But poor Mrs Flagstone," I continued, "must have seen him in the hallway. She has her safety chain on, maybe asks him what he's doing. So he bursts into her room and strangles her with the climbing rope. The rope was red – right, Herb?"

Herb grinned. "Naturally. How did you know that?"

"I guessed. Then Glenn ditches the pliers in the closet, makes a half-assed attempt to stage Mrs Flagstone's death like a drowning, and leaves with the rope. I bet the security tapes will concur."

"What if he isn't seen carrying the rope?"

No problem. I was on a roll.

"Then he either ditched it in a hall, or wrapped it around his waist under his shirt before leaving."

"I'm gonna go check the tapes," Johnson said, hurrying out.

"I'm going to call my mother," Patel said, hurrying out.

Herb got on the phone to get a warrant, and Mortimer Hughes dropped to his hands and knees and began to search the carpeting, ostensibly for red fibers – even though that wasn't his job.

I was feeling pretty smug, something I rarely associated with my line of work, when I noticed Officer Coursey staring at me. His face was projecting such unabashed admiration that I almost blushed.

"Lieutenant – that was just . . . amazing."

"Simple detective work. You could have figured it out if you thought about it."

"I never would have figured that out." He glanced at his shoes, then back at me, and then he turned and left.

Herb pocketed his cell and offered me a sly grin.

"We can swing by the DA's office, pick up the warrant in an hour. Tell me, Jack. How'd you put it all together?"

"Actually, you gave me the idea. You said the only way the killer could have gotten out of the room was by slipping under the door. In a way, that's what he did."

Herb clapped his hand on my shoulder.

"Nice job, Lieutenant. Don't get a big head. You wanna come over for supper tonight? Bernice is making pot roast. I'll let you invite Mr Patel."

"He'd have to call his mother first. Speaking of mothers . . ."

I glanced at the body of Janet Hellerman, and again felt the emotional punch. The Caller ID in the kitchen gave me the number for Janet's mom. It took some time to tell the whole story, and she cried through most of it. By the end, she was crying so much that she couldn't talk anymore.

I gave her my home number so she could call me later.

The lab team finally arrived, headed by a Detective named Perkins. Soon both apartments were swarming with tech heads – vacuuming fibers, taking samples, spraying chemicals, shining ALS, snapping pictures and shooting video.

I filled in Detective Perkins on what went down, and left him in charge of the scene.

Then Herb and I went off to get the warrant.

Eternally Yours

H. Edward Hunsburger

Harry Edward Hunsburger (b. 1947) has written a variety of westerns and mystery novels, some under pen names, but he is probably best known for Death Signs (1987), about the murder of a deaf man who leaves a clue in sign language as he dies. It was adapted for the TV series Hunter in 1988. I only know of one short mystery story by Mr Hunsburger and fortunately for us it's also a locked-room puzzle with an added impossibility.

My name is Jeff Winsor and I'd like to say straight off and for the record that I don't believe in ghosts. I never have believed in them. I never will. And I can't think of one good reason why I should.

The whole notion of restless, prowling spirits strikes me as a waste of time. Even in the afterlife there must be better things to do than wander around moaning and wailing, frightening poor mortals out of a good night's sleep. Messages from the recently departed are an even sillier idea. Let's face it, most people say far too much in one lifetime to have anything worthwhile left over for broadcasting from The Great Beyond. And as for things that go bump in the night, all I can say is that they never bump into me.

I figure it's over when it's over. You total up a life's credits and debits, rise quietly from the table, and cash in your chips. Maybe there's an after-life. Maybe there isn't. But either way, there are no such things as ghosts.

Now what I *do* believe in is the scarcity of good apartments in New

York City. The kind of elegant, spacious apartments you find in those old but beautifully maintained buildings surrounding Gramercy Park. The kind of apartment I finally got to move into when Admiral Miles Penny tripped on the carpet and fractured his skull.

I'd like to be more sympathetic, but I never met the man. From everything I've heard, he'd led a long, full, if somewhat tempestuous life. Not to mention all the trouble he caused me *after* he died. But up until I moved in, the only connection between us was that I got his apartment. I'm not even going to go into what I had to do to get it or how much the rent is. Let's just say that wretched excess pretty well covers it all.

I moved into the place on October first, a week to the day after they moved Penny out to a less spacious but far more permanent address. I wanted to concentrate on unpacking, but I had an assignment due. I decided the cardboard carton obstacle course would have to wait for a while.

As it turned out, both projects got sidetracked. Because that was the day the first postcard arrived.

It was jammed in the apartment door mail slot along with some catalogues from a shoe company, a bookseller, and one of those Vermont cheese and smoked ham places. It was an old postcard, yellowed at the edges, with a view of a few ragged palms and a seedy looking pink stucco hotel. All that was on one side. The following brief message was on the other.

> *Miles,*
> *You were right about that adaptation of the Krimsky book. It stank. I didn't like the lizard scene either. Knight to C-3.*
> *Fraternally yours,*
> *Charles*

Nothing unsettling there, nothing ghostly. Right? Just a chess-by-mail crony of Penny's who hadn't yet heard of his demise. That's what I thought too. The incongruity of it didn't hit me until later that afternoon when I was hard at work at my easel.

The adaptation that Charles had referred to was *Cold Moon*. It was a blockbuster novel that had recently been made into a TV movie. It was the recently part that bothered me. The film had had its world premiere just five days ago. So how in the world could Miles Penny have an opinion about a movie televised after his death? I felt something like a chill along my spine. Inside my head a tiny voice started humming the theme from *The Twilight Zone*. Was the late admiral carrying on a correspondence from beyond the grave? Was heaven a seedy resort hotel? And was I, Jeff Winsor, nonbeliever in ghosts, being haunted, indirectly, by means of the US mail?

A ringing phone cut short my crazed speculations. For a wild moment I thought it might be Admiral Penny trying to reach me *direct*. But as it turned out it was the earthy, and earthly, voice of Karen Hunter, the lady in my life.

"You sound a little flustered," she said after the usual preliminaries. "Anything wrong?"

I told her about the postcard. I heard a suppressed giggle, but at least she didn't laugh out loud.

"There has to be a rational explanation," Karen insisted. "You should try to contact this Charles guy who sent the card. Is there a return address? What about the postmark?"

I looked at the card again. "There's no return address and the postmark's too blurred to be legible."

"Well," Karen sighed, "that's all I can think of. You've roused my curiosity about Admiral Penny, though. I remember you told me he died of a fall. Is there any possibility of foul play?" Her rich, contralto voice gave the last two words a lot of dramatic emphasis.

"Give me a break," I said. "The authorities pronounced it accidental death. He was going to get his mail when he tripped on the little rug in front of the door, fell, and fractured his skull. The realtor told me Penny was in his eighties. The bones get thin and brittle at that age. Any kind of bad fall can be fatal. There's no way it could be murder. The door was locked and bolted from the inside. They had a locksmith take the whole door off just to get into the apartment."

"He died on the way to get his mail," Karen said thoughtfully. "Doesn't that strike you as a strange coincidence? And now he's sending you messages, messages that come to the exact spot where the crime occurred."

"What crime?" I practically shouted. "Penny's death was accidental. And he isn't sending *me* any messages. He's writing to some guy named Charlie who's sending his replies here. What the hell am I talking about? Penny isn't writing anyone. Penny is dead."

There was a moment of silence on the other end of the line. "Forget about the locked door," Karen said finally. "It doesn't prove anything. People are always getting murdered behind locked doors in mysteries. All of this," she said solemnly, "can only mean one thing."

"What?" I demanded irritably.

"That Admiral Penny was murdered. His restless spirit is calling upon you to bring his killer to justice. The poor man won't be able to rest in peace until you've solved this murder."

"I don't believe in ghosts," I shouted.

"See you tonight at eight," Karen cheerfully ignored me. "You'd better get busy on this. Painting book jacket illustrations for mysteries is one thing. Actually *solving* one might not be so easy."

Before I could get another word in, she hung up on me. I replaced the receiver and swore for a while. Karen's a terrific lady with more than her share of intelligence, beauty, and charm. The only thing she has too much of is imagination. She not only believed that there was a murder and a ghost involved in this. She really did expect me to solve the mystery. And I knew I'd never hear the end of it if I didn't at least go through the motions.

Slightly dazed by my sudden elevation to amateur sleuth, I threaded my way through the cardboard-box jungle and went back to work. I make a comfortable living painting dust jacket illustrations for mystery and suspense books. I did all kinds of commercial art up until a few years ago when the cover I painted for *Death Is My Interior Decorator* won all the big awards in the field. Now I specialize in the crime stuff, which is fine with me because I like to read mysteries, too.

I'd barely gotten back into the painting when the doorbell rang. If this was the late admiral calling in person, I wasn't even going to bother unpacking. The apartment was nice but not *that* nice. As it turned out, it was only Tom Banks, the doorman.

"Getting settled in?" he asked with a friendly smile. A tall, broad-shouldered man in his early sixties, he has one of those open, expressive faces, the kind that seem readymade for smiles and laughter. I figured him for one of those rare people, a man who actually enjoys his work.

"Settled in," I answered. "I'll be lucky if I get everything unpacked before the two year lease is up."

Banks laughed and handed me a stack of mail. More catalogues, from the look of it, and perched on top of them, you guessed it . . . a neat little pile of postcards. "I've been holding them downstairs," he explained. "Drayton, the postman, asked me to. He didn't want the moving or cleaning people tampering with the mail."

Better them than me, I thought.

"Very conscientious," I said aloud. "I've never been in an apartment building before where they deliver the mail right to your door."

"That's Drayton," Banks nodded. "Very dedicated to the job, he is. Never taken a sick day in twenty years. The perfect postman, I call him. He told me just the other day that he was being considered for mail carrier of the year."

"How about that." Just my luck. If he'd been a little less zealous, I might not have ever seen the damned postcard.

"Do the rugs look okay?" Banks asked. "They spent all afternoon on them. I guess they got all the blood out of that one," he added, peering down at the faded two by three Oriental I was standing on. It was the very same rug on which the admiral's sea legs had a fatal loss of footing.

"They look fine to me. When's the relative due?"

"Well now," Banks was suddenly evasive. "A couple of weeks, I guess. Shouldn't be more than a month or so." He spread his hands in a gesture of futility. "There's nothing I can do, Mr Winsor."

"I'm not blaming you," I reassured him. Part of the deal for my getting the apartment was that I kept the admiral's stuff there until his only living relative arrived from some distant port of call. Apparently there was no more storage space in the basement of the building. I'd managed to cram most of his furniture and personal stuff into the spare bedroom. But there was no way I could get all the rugs in there, too. As a compromise the management had agreed to have the rugs cleaned before I moved in.

After wishing me well with the unpacking, Banks returned to his post in the lobby. I should have gone back to work myself, but I looked at the postcards instead. There were four of them in the pile of mail Banks had brought up, each with the same view of the rundown hotel. They were all from his friend Charles, with a chess move at the end of each message. Two of them seemed normal enough, but the other two carried obvious replies and comments to events that had taken place *after* Admiral Penny's death.

What the hell was going on here? Was there chess after death? Was the US Postal Service a *whole* lot more far reaching than I'd ever given it credit for? I hadn't taken the one card all that seriously, but this was something else again. Charles had signed all of the cards "fraternally yours". I wondered how Admiral Penny was signing the cards he sent to Charles? *Eternally* yours?

I was too keyed up by then to go back to the painting. I grabbed my jacket instead and went downstairs. I needed a walk in the park, something to get my mind out of neutral. Maybe I could come up with a couple of notions that would clear the whole thing up. The worst part of it was that I was actually starting to *believe* what Karen had said. That Admiral Penny had been murdered and that it was up to me, if I wanted the "haunting" to stop, to bring his killer to justice.

One of the advantages of living on Gramercy Park is the park itself. It's a small, fenced-in square of immaculately maintained greenery, to the best of my knowledge the only private park in New York City. A neighborhood association handles the upkeep, and the park is strictly reserved for area residents only. Some people might find it a little on the snobbish side, but I wasn't complaining. Since I now lived there, I intended to make the most of it.

My new key fitted perfectly in the park's wrought iron gate. I closed it firmly behind me and began to stroll the graveled paths, enjoying the autumn sunshine while I tried to think detective-like thoughts.

I almost knocked the girl over before I saw her. She spun around and glared at me, a tall, willowy blonde with the face of a Botticelli angel. "I didn't hear you coming," she sputtered angrily. "You really ought to learn to walk louder." Her wide blue eyes narrowed as she focused in on me. "You're Winsor, aren't you? The fellow who just moved into 3C."

"That's right," I smiled. "And you're Tana Devin, the star of *Maneuvers*."

The recognition and the way I'd phrased it brought on a full-wattage smile. She'd obviously mistaken me for a fan of the show. *Maneuvers* was a new and very popular daytime soap, and Tana Devin played the vixen, the one you *love* to hate. She couldn't act worth a damn, but it didn't matter. Nobody else on the show could, either.

"We're neighbors, you know," she informed me. "I live right next door to you in 3B."

"You must have known Admiral Penny then?" If I was going to do some detecting, now was the time to start.

Her smile did a fast fade, and I could almost see the smoke from the smoldering anger that backlit those bright blue eyes. "Penny," she seethed. "Dropping dead was the only thing that man ever did that made me happy. He was the nosiest old crock in creation. Always looking through the peephole in his door to see who was coming in and going out of the other apartments on the floor. I could hear his raspy breathing every time I walked by. It was getting so I hated to invite anyone over. No privacy at all in my own damned building." Her blue eyes narrowed a little more as she studied my face. "I hope you're not going to be manning the peephole like Penny? I won't stand for any more of that crap." Her soft voice was suddenly as cold and merciless as an Arctic winter.

"Not me," I assured her. "I'm far too busy for that kind of nonsense."

"Glad to hear it," she said. "Just keep it that way and we'll get along fine." On that cheerful note, she turned away and strode down the path without a word of goodbye.

Well, I'd certainly learned one thing about the late admiral. Tana Devin hated him. Now, no one likes being spied on, but it's basically a harmless pastime. What I couldn't figure out was why Tana Devin loathed Penny with such *intensity*. There had to be more to it than that.

After a couple more turns around the park, the answer came to me. The lovely Miss Devin's name had been in the papers quite a lot these past few weeks. Not the *real* papers but those supermarket tabloids they sell at the checkout counters. I vaguely remembered the headlines on one of them, some kind of sex scandal that linked Tana Devin with a prominent but very married politician. I remembered somebody's mentioning that the liaison had very nearly cost Tana her part in *Maneuvers*. While the show portrayed this kind of bedhopping all the time, the chairman of the company that sponsored it was an *uncle* of the politician's wife. I guess rating points won out over family ties because Tana did manage to keep her job. But the way I heard it, it had been a *very* close thing.

What I remembered best about the whole business were the pictures that appeared under the headline. Pictures of Miss Devin and the politico that had that slightly off, distorted quality that tends to catch an artist's eye. Exactly the kind of pictures you'd get shooting through an old fashioned peephole . . . just like the one on the door of my new apartment.

I was positive that that's what Penny had been doing. A few candid snaps of the two lovers as they passed by the door might have fetched a good price. They would also make an obviously secret affair as public as the corner library. Was that motive enough for murder? As far as Tana Devin was concerned, I believed it was motive enough and then some.

I told Karen all about it over dinner that night. After all, it's no good being a detective if you don't have a Watson around to bask in your reflected glory.

"It's a nice start," Karen said, patting my arm. Not exactly the complimentary outpouring I'd been expecting. "But what you need is a few more suspects. Not to mention the *how* part of a locked room murder."

"Details," I muttered. "I just need a couple more days to put it all together." Not necessarily true, but it *sounded* good.

"Glad to hear it," Karen smiled. "Remember, I'm counting on you. I imagine Penny's ghost would like to settle down, too. I doubt haunting is all it's cracked up to be."

"I'm working on it," I said testily. "I do have a few other things to do, too," I reminded her.

The next morning I did one of them, putting in three hours at the easel. It was a cool, gray day with a steady syncopation of rain that drummed on my windows. Atmospheric mystery story weather, but not much good for strolling in the park. So when I finally took a break from painting, I stayed indoors and inspected the scene of the crime.

Feeling as though I should be brandishing a magnifying glass, I knelt down in front of the little Oriental rug on which Penny had tripped and died. The cleaners *had* gotten all the blood out. I couldn't find a trace. I did notice something, though. When they yanked the cleaning tag off, they left a little nylon loop still threaded through the fibers. I teased it free and slipped it in my pocket.

I figured out the *how* part of the murder when I shifted my attention to the door. The mail slot was the key. Visualize Penny standing at the door, staring out the peephole, while someone, the murderer, crouched out of sight on the other side of the door. All the murderer would have to do was quietly open the outside mail slot and shove a stick or a cane through, knocking Penny's legs right out from under him. It was as simple as that.

"Brilliant deduction," I murmured to myself. I thought about phoning the police right away but decided to spring my theory on Karen first. Besides, I still had to figure out the *who* part. Tana Devin was a good candidate for the killer, but I hadn't even talked to anyone else yet. Also, I needed that little thing they call *proof*.

Just past noon I heard the postman at the door. I put down my brush and went to check the mail. It had slid through the slot and was lying on the little rug. Two catalogues and, of course, another postcard. It looked exactly like the other ones except for the message, which read:

Miles,
  How did you guess that the prime rate was going to drop two days before it happened? What have you got? A crystal ball? Thanks for the tip. Bishop to C-6.
  Fraternally yours,
  Charles

Now Penny was giving financial advice from the Great Beyond. The prime rate had dropped earlier in the week, and from the cheerful tone of the note it appeared that Charles had taken advantage of Penny's powers of prediction. Was it just a lucky guess, or did Penny have special, inside information from Up There? I don't know what bothered me more, the postcard or the fact that the admiral hadn't taken the time to write *me* about the shift in the prime. It was the least he could have done. After all, I was the one trying to solve his murder. If there actually *was* a murder. In spite of my theory about the mail slot and cane, I still wasn't one hundred percent convinced.

I figured I ought to talk to the postman, though. He might be able to tell me something more about Penny. I swung open the door and caught him just before he reached the elevator.

"Excuse me," I said. "I'm Jeff Winsor, the new tenant in apartment 3C."

"Lew Drayton," he introduced himself. "I'm sorry, Mr Winsor, but there's nothing for you today. It usually takes a week or so for the forwarded stuff to start coming through." He smiled as if to say the delay was a shame but there was nothing he could do about it. He was a short, pudgy, moonfaced man with thick, rain-misted glasses. His postman's slicker glistened with moisture, and his bulging leather mailbag fitted the contours of his body as though it were a part of it.

"I'm not worried about my mail," I told him. "But I was wondering about Admiral Penny's. Are you going to keep on delivering it here? He died, you know."

"Yes, I heard," Drayton sighed. "A real loss to the community. As for his mail, there are a couple of ways to go. You could mark it 'deceased, return to sender.' Or you could readdress it to his next of kin, but Tom Banks told me the admiral's only living relative is out of the country at the moment. If you want my opinion, the easiest thing for you to do is just keep it here until the next of kin arrives to claim it. But that's entirely up to you," he added quickly. "I'll be glad to arrange it any way you want, Mr Winsor. Just say the word."

His eagerness to oblige threw me for a moment. After all, this *was* New York, a city hardly noted for its zealous public servants. I'd forgotten that Banks had called Drayton "the perfect postman".

"Let me think about it," I said finally.

Drayton nodded. "Take all the time you want. Besides, most of Penny's mail is catalogues, like this one from Pitt's up in Maine." He reached out and tapped the catalogue I'd carried out into the hall with me, ignoring the postcard that rested on top of it. "Those Pitt brothers make a sweet rod and reel," he grinned, "but a little too pricey for me. If there's nothing else, Mr Winsor, I'd better get back to work."

"Did you know the admiral well?" I pressed him. "Get along with him okay?"

"I just delivered his mail," Drayton shrugged. "And I get along fine with *everyone* on my route. Got to get moving," he tipped his cap. "Don't like to keep my customers waiting." He waved and stepped into the waiting elevator where his bulky form was quickly concealed by the closing doors.

Feeling a little deflated, I wandered back into the apartment and spent a couple of minutes contemplating the park through my rain-streaked bay window. I guess after Tana Devin, I'd been anticipating something a little more meaty. But then everyone couldn't be a suspect. Drayton was just the postman. Like the fraternal Charles, an unknowing helpmate, a bearer of haunted mail.

I decided that if I really wanted to learn more about Penny, I should talk to Tom Banks. New York legend has it that doormen know everything about their tenants, all the little details ranging from shoe size to sexual preference. I hadn't thought about Banks before, but if there was any truth to the legend, he could be a regular well-spring of information.

On my way down to the lobby I was nearly bowled over by a big, gray-haired man who came catapulting out of the elevator.

"Sorry about that," he said as I regained my balance. "I guess my mind was somewhere else. I only wish the rest of me was, too," he added with sudden bitterness. He had the look of a businessman gone to seed. His tailor-made gray suit was wrinkled and stained. There were dark circles under his eyes, and the hand that gripped his ebonwood walking stick was white-knuckled with tension. He blinked at me and frowned. "I don't remember seeing you before? Are you visiting someone in the building?"

"Just moved in," I told him. "I'm the new tenant in 3C."

"Penny's place," he said in a harsh whisper, as if the name itself was almost too painful to pronounce. "If I could have spared the time and the shoe-leather, I would have danced on the old bastard's grave. If anyone ever deserved to die, he was the one."

"What do you mean?"

"Mind your own damn business," he muttered, pushing past me. He stomped down the hall, cutting at the air with the gleaming ebon stick as though he were slashing away at some imaginary foe. He paused at the door of apartment 3A, unlocked it, and disappeared inside, slamming the door behind him with a thunderous crash that echoed through the hallway.

"Well now," I said to myself. "The suspect shortage is certainly over." Even death hadn't lessened the man's obvious hatred of Penny. And that gleaming ebon-wood walking stick? I could practically see it cannonading through the mail slot to shove the old admiral's legs right out from under him. But who was this guy? I didn't even know his name yet. And why did he loathe the recently departed Penny?

I found Tom Banks at his post in the lobby, staring moodily out at the rainswept street. "Mr Winsor," he turned and smiled at me. "Surely you're not thinking of going out in that downpour without so much as an umbrella?"

I shook my head. "I just came down to pass the time of day. I wanted to ask you about one of my neighbors, a big, gray-haired man in A? What's he got against Penny?"

"That would be Mr Campbell." Banks sighed and shook his head. "He'll be leaving us at the end of the month. Some recent financial setbacks are forcing him to relocate."

"Why do I have the feeling that Penny is somehow involved in that?" I prodded him.

"Mr Campbell isn't too good at hiding his feelings," the doorman nodded. "I guess there isn't any harm in telling you about it now. Mr Campbell and his partner own a computer company. A few weeks back, the two of them were planning to take over another firm, a small company that unknowingly held a patent that would give Campbell and his partner a virtual lock on a big, upcoming defense contract. Campbell sold off all his assets at a loss to raise the necessary capital, but before he could put in a bid, a rival firm bought the company right out from under them."

"How does Penny figure into it?"

"Well," Banks hesitated, "Mr Campbell can't prove anything, but he and his partner were discussing the takeover when they walked by Penny's door. They had a longish wait for the elevator, so they pretty well covered it all. No one else knew about the deal, and with Penny's reputation for spying on his neighbors, he seemed like the only person who could and *would* have alerted the rival company."

"I could see why Campbell would hate him," I sympathized. "What about you, Tom? How did you get along with the admiral?"

"It's my job to get along with all the tenants," Banks replied with quiet dignity. "But now that he's gone, I have to admit that Penny was a hard man, the only one I've ever met who would go out of his way to make someone else's life miserable."

"You sound as though you might be speaking from personal experience," I said. The sad, regretful tone of his voice gave him away more than any words could.

"It happened a few months back," Banks said softly. "Like the admiral, I'm a retired navy man myself. Now, I'm not one to ask for favors, but I have a grandson, a fine boy with all the makings of a naval officer. Ever since he was a lad he's wanted to go to the Academy. He has all the grades, the qualifications. All he needed was a recommendation, a little pull at the top to get him in. I asked Penny if he'd be willing to put in a word for the boy. All it would have taken was one phone call, a few minutes of his time. Well, first he said yes, then no, then yes again. By the time I realized he never intended to do it, it was too late to ask anyone else. It seemed as though he took a kind of perverse pleasure in keeping me dangling like that."

Although I'd never met Penny I was beginning to hate the man myself. "What happened to your grandson?" I asked Banks.

"He went into the navy as an enlisted man," Banks said bitterly. "There's no shame in that," he added, "but he would have done the Academy proud. He never had his chance, thanks to Penny."

There wasn't anything I could say to that. I left Banks staring out at the rain and went back to the apartment. I was beginning to wonder how Admiral Penny had lived as long as he had. If he hadn't been murdered, he certainly should have been. I'd never come across anyone who was a more suitable candidate for homicide. I was also beginning to regret my own attempt at amateur sleuthing. *If* Penny had been murdered, his killer almost deserved to get away with it. I say *almost* because I still intended to solve the crime if I could. Penny had done some pretty horrible things in his life, but none of them as terrible as murder itself.

I spent the rest of the day and all that evening at the easel, finishing up my assignment. While my hand wielded the brush, my mind arranged and rearranged all the bits and pieces I had about Penny and his death. I had started out with no suspects, not even a proper murder. None of this would have come about if it hadn't been for the postcards and Karen's insistence that I investigate.

Now I had three suspects. Tana Devin and Campbell were the more obvious ones, but Tom Banks was also a possibility. He seemed quiet and friendly enough on the surface, but who could really tell what was going on inside? As for the murder part of it, my cane-through-the-mail-slot theory eliminated the whole locked room element. It should have put Campbell at the head of my suspect list, but it didn't. Any one of them could have bought a cane and shoved it through the slot. And after Tana Devin's description of Penny's "raspy" breathing, any one of them could have easily ascertained if he was at his post on the other side of the door.

I had suspects, motives, and method. I had everything I needed except for the most important thing: a solution to the crime.

It was still raining when I turned in at midnight. The rumble of thunder and the crack of lightning punctuated my futile attempt to sleep. When I finally did doze off, I had the craziest dream. I was being chased through Gramercy Park by a giant postcard. And it would have caught me, too, if it hadn't been for the lifesized chessman. He was a white knight who poked a hole through the postcard with his uptilted lance. The postcard fell to the ground, but then the knight started bearing down on me, with his lance aimed straight at my heart.

That's when I woke up. Not only had I escaped the sinister pursuers of my dream but I'd come up with the solution to the mystery. And it was so simple that I should have seen it right away. I still had some checking to do, though, just to make absolutely certain I was right.

The rain tapered off around six, the last of it disappearing with the dawn of a bright, autumn day. After an early breakfast I went downstairs for another talk with our friendly doorman.

"Who plays chess around here?" I asked after we'd exchanged good morning pleasantries.

The question seemed to take him by surprise. "Well now," he hesitated. "I play a little chess. Strictly amateur stuff. Drayton, the postman, and I often have a game on Sundays. Then there's Mr Campbell. He's won a couple of local championships, and I know he spends a lot of his free time over at the Marshal Chess Club."

"What about Tana Devin?"

Banks frowned thoughtfully and nodded. "Now that you mention it, I believe she's a player, too. She once starred in an off-Broadway show called *The Chess Match*. So she must know at least the rudiments of the game, though I don't think she has much time for it. Are you looking for a game?"

"No," I said smiling. "I'm looking to *end* one."

Leaving Banks more confused than ever, I paid a brief visit to a local shop. After that I returned to the apartment where I spent the rest of the morning experimenting at the scene of the crime.

When the postcard slid through the mail slot at a little past twelve, I was ready and waiting. I didn't bother to bend down and pick it up. I swung the door open instead, startling the mailman so much that he stumbled back, nearly losing his balance.

"Mr Winsor," Drayton grinned. "I'm sorry but there's nothing for you today."

"That's okay," I told him. "I was wondering if you could mail this for me," I asked, handing him a postcard.

"No problem," he said eagerly. "I used to mail cards for the admiral all the time."

"I know you did."

He must have sensed something, either in my face or in the tone of my voice. "Now, what do you mean by that?" he asked quietly. He wasn't grinning any more.

"I figured it all out last night. The whole thing started with the postcards, but I got side-tracked for a while, never realizing that the answer was right there under my nose."

Drayton forced a smile. "You're talking in riddles, Mr Winsor. I still can't figure out what you're trying to say."

"You're the perfect postman, right?"

"The best in the business," Drayton agreed.

I shook my head. "When I asked you what I should do with the admiral's mail, you listed several options, all of them dependent on the mail's being delivered *here*. You never once mentioned the routine procedure of having the post office *hold* it or putting in a change of address that would have sent it directly to Penny's next of kin. It would have been easier on both of us, but you never said a word. Because you wouldn't have seen the postcards any more. After all that time on the sidelines, you were finally in the game. You just couldn't bear to give it up, could you?"

"Are you accusing me of tampering with the U.S. mail?" Drayton bristled.

"I'm accusing you of reading some postcards," I said softly. "The ones Penny gave you to mail for him and the ones you delivered from his friend, Charles. You're a chess player yourself. It's only natural that you'd become interested in a game, especially if it were a good one. I didn't suspect you at first. But last night I realized that somebody else must be carrying on the game with Penny's friend Charles. You were the only one besides me with access to all the incoming postcards. And since Penny was an elderly man who spent most of his time eavesdropping from behind the door, it seemed only logical that he'd give the outgoing cards to you to mail for him. It all came down to your being the one, the *only* person who could keep the chess game going after Penny's death. Charles must be a worthy opponent," I suggested. "Are you enjoying the game?"

"All right," Drayton said with a sheepish grin. "You caught me at it. Charles Fairfield is a top-ranked player just like the admiral was. I couldn't resist the challenge. After all these years of trying to second-guess them, I had to see if I could beat Fairfield myself." The heavyset postman shrugged. "All I did was write a few postcards and sign Penny's name to them. No harm in that, right?"

"No harm if the admiral hadn't caught you reading the cards in the first place," I corrected him. "These past few days I've learned just what kind of man he was. What you did was only a minor infraction of the rules. After all, postcards aren't *meant* to be private. But Penny would have complained just the same, ruining your standing as the 'perfect postman,' spoiling your chance to be named mail carrier of the year. But first he would have let you dangle for a while, enjoying the prolonged agony. The sight of you sweating it out, never knowing exactly when your spotless reputation would be shattered beyond repair. He waited too long this time," I said quietly. "Long enough for you to kill him."

"Are you crazy?" Drayton sputtered. "Penny tripped on a rug behind a locked door. No way that could be murder."

I shook my head. "There are a couple of ways, but I didn't figure out the right one until last night." I dug the little loop of nylon cord out of my pocket and held it out for Drayton to see. "I found this knotted through the rug. The rug Penny tripped on when he fractured his skull." Involuntarily both of us glanced down at the faded Oriental. "At first I thought the loop was left over from a cleaners' tag. But then I remembered Tom Banks's comment that the cleaners had spent 'all afternoon' on them. They'd done the work right here. No reason to tag them if the rugs weren't leaving the apartment."

I prodded the nylon loop in my open palm. "I took this over to a sporting goods store this morning. The man in the fishing department identified it as a piece of deep sea fishing line, strong enough to withstand the pull of a fighting marlin. And I know you're a fisherman. You told me as much yourself when you talked about not being able to afford a rod and reel from the Pitt catalogue."

"What does that prove?" Drayton demanded. Behind his thick glasses his eyes had taken on a narrow, almost glowing intensity. Casually he slipped his mailbag off his shoulder and put it down on the floor. "It's real interesting," he said with a slow smile. "But it still doesn't add up to murder."

"Sure it does," I insisted. "I spent a lot of time this morning standing on that little rug with the door closed. Right off I noticed how the rug gets bunched up from shifting your feet around. It gets pushed up against the door and a little edge of it gets shoved *between* the door and the bottom of the frame. Not much," I emphasized. "Just enough to knot a line in it."

"Go on," Drayton prompted me. He was still smiling, but there was no pleasure at all in his voice.

"You must have done that part of it quietly," I continued. "Keeping well below the sightline of the peephole. It would have been easy. Most of the tenants aren't around this time of day. Then you make your normal appearance, dropping the mail through the slot. When you hear Penny picking it up, you hurry away. The other end of the line was secured to something heavy and tough. Your mailbag is my best guess. It's perfect for the job. The sudden pull on the line yanks the rug against the door and Penny with it. It was a pretty sure bet that something like that would fracture an old man's brittle skull. After you hear the crash, you just walk back and cut the line with scissors or a knife."

"You mean a knife like this?" The short but lethal looking blade suddenly appeared in Drayton's hand.

"Just like it," I gulped.

"I thought he was my friend," he continued with quiet intensity. "He used to meet me at the door every day. I'd hand him his mail and he'd give me the cards to post for him. Then one day he caught me reading one of Charles's postcards. I guess he must have been suspecting it for a while. He wouldn't open the door after that. He'd just stand on the other side and taunt me, telling me over and over again that everyone would find out that I really wasn't perfect. I had to kill him. Don't you see? I *am* perfect. The perfect postman!"

He lurched toward me, the blade upraised. As he crossed the doorstep and stepped onto the rug, I gave the line hidden in my hand a tug. His feet went flying out from under him. The knife fell from his hand. He cracked his head against the doorjamb and sagged to the floor, unconscious but still very much alive.

"Well, that's one ghost laid to rest," I said to myself. I reached behind a pile of boxes and switched off the tape recorder. Then I phoned the police.

Karen came over that night, long after they'd taken the raving postman away in a strait-jacket. I felt sorry for him but not *all that* sorry. He'd tried to kill me, too. I'd told her all about it on the phone, rubbing it in just a little when I reminded her about restless ghosts and hauntings by mail.

I wasn't surprised when she showed up with a peace offering. "Housewarming gift?" I asked, accepting the brightly wrapped package.

"Open it up," she smiled.

I did just that. "But I don't need a chess set," I protested. "I don't know how to play and I'm certainly not going to learn now. I don't believe in chess."

"What about ghosts?"

"I don't believe in them, either."

"Then what do you believe in?" Karen demanded.

I looked around me, taking in the endless stacks of cartons and crates, untouched since the movers had left them there except for the addition of a faint coating of dust. "The scarcity of good apartments in New York City," I said firmly. "That's what I believe in . . . I think."

Murder in Monkeyland

Lois Gresh & Robert Weinberg

Robert Weinberg (b. 1946) is a renowned collector and specialist in pulp magazines and pulp art who turned to writing, starting with a series featuring occult detective Alex Warner in The Devil's Auction *(1988). Lois Gresh (b. 1956) is a computer programmer and systems analyst. Their skills came together on the techno-thriller* The Termination Node *(1999). Their other collaborations include* The Science of Superheroes *(2002) and* The Science of Supervillains *(2004). Lois tells me that she once worked in a research establishment very similar to the one described here, but to say any more would spoil the story.*

1

Once upon a time, after returning from the bank where I had the pleasure of making a six-figure deposit of the week's earnings, I casually asked my boss, Penelope Peters, what special talent made her so incredibly successful. After all, Penelope, due to a genetic imperfection in her cells, suffered from extreme agoraphobia. She was unable to leave her home without suffering major panic attacks that left her a total mental and physical wreck. Yet, working from her office deep in the heart of Manhattan, she earned astonishing sums week after week solving problems that stumped the highest and the mightiest throughout the country, and sometime even the world. Having served as her assistant; chief bottle-washer; and eyes, ears, nose, and legs for the past five years, I had witnessed her genius so often I had become inured to her working miracles. I just wondered how.

"Brains and personality," answered Penelope, with the barest twinkle in her green eyes. It was the punch line to one of the oldest and dumbest jokes around, and she loved using it.

"Yeah, right," I countered, "save it for the newspapers. Tell me the truth. I've devoted the past five years of my life running errands, going to used book stores, attending board meetings, and catching crooks for you. It's time I learned the secret hand-shake." Then, to show that I wasn't actually annoyed with her, I added, "Please."

"Oh, well," said Penelope, rising from behind her imposing ebony desk in the center of her office. "You won't believe using the Magic 8-Ball, I assume?"

"Nope," I replied. "Nor the ouija board explanation or the sack of old bones in the closet. I want the real stuff. So I can finally make my own way in the world, starting with a big advertisement on the internet: 'Sean O'Brien, Investigations; formerly employed by the notorious Penelope Peters, World's Premier Problem Solver.'"

Penelope frowned. "You're not really thinking of leaving?" she asked. "It would take me years to train another assistant."

"Decades," I replied, with a grin. "It would take you decades. If not lifetimes."

"Besides," she said, "I haven't sent you scouring used book stores for years now. I buy everything off the internet and have it delivered by Fed Ex."

"There was that time I took the ferry to Hoboken—" I began, but she cut me off with the wave of a hand.

"Enough, enough," she said. Penelope walked to the mahogany floor-to-ceiling bookcases that covered the left wall and laid one hand on the top of a well-read volume. "Everything I know I learned from studying this book. Read it, absorb it, and don't forget it. That's all you need to do to be just like me."

That I doubted. I stand six foot two, weigh two hundred and forty pounds, and made it through college on a football scholar-ship. I have a degree in accounting, a detective's badge, and a black belt in karate. I'm a fast talker, possess a near-photographic memory, and know how to follow instructions. My hair and eyes are black as coal, and nobody mistakes me for a movie star. Any resemblance between me and my boss is purely imaginary.

At five foot seven, 110 pounds, with green eyes and brown hair, Penelope Peters might have made it as a top fashion model if she lost fifteen or twenty pounds and could manage to leave her home on assignments. Since the second option was out of the question, she obviously saw no reason to consider the first. Not that I think she would have bothered. Penelope didn't like taking orders from anyone, which was why she had set up her consulting business years before, when her agoraphobia was just starting to act up. In the time since, she's become the problem solver that other problem solvers come to when they're stumped. Her IQ number is off the charts, and her office is filled with rare trinkets and expensive gifts sent to her from satisfied clients throughout the world. Her brains didn't come from any one book. But, I'm no dummy. I know what my boss is like. Besides, I was curious. I took the book.

"*The Sign of Four* by Sir Arthur Conan Doyle," I read aloud. "Sherlock Holmes? Everything you know, you learned from Sherlock Holmes?"

"Elementary, my dear O'Brien," said Penelope, with a smile.

"He's not a real person. He's a character in a book."

"Real or not, he knew the secret to solving mysteries," said Penelope. "Any sort of mysteries, be they problems with business to problems with murder."

"Which is?" I asked.

Penelope removed *The Sign of Four* from my hands and flipped the book open to what had to be a familiar page. She read aloud, ". . . when you have eliminated the impossible, whatever remains, however improbable, must be the truth."

"That's it?" I said, somewhat doubtful. I must admit I wasn't particularly impressed. Which explains, I suppose, why I'm the assistant and Penelope is the boss. "That's all?"

"Nothing else," said Penelope carefully sliding the book back into its place on the shelf. "A sharp mind, an attention for detail, and that sentence is all you need to solve the most perplexing puzzles ever encountered."

"I find that hard to believe."

"You'll see," said Penelope.

I did, of course, less than a month later, when Penelope solved the murder in Monkeyland.

2

Imagine if you will a four-story building in the shape of a square. Think of it built out of concrete and steel, with huge panoramic windows on each of the four levels, with a round information desk on the first floor and two large elevators in a concrete hub in the center of the square. In case of fire or any other sort of disaster, the elevators immediately lock into place in the shafts and can't be used until the "all clear" alarm sounds.

Located in the corners of the square are four sets of emergency stairs. In case of an emergency, your only escape from an upper floor is down and out to the first floor. And, try as you may, there is no possible method of accessing any of the top three floors from the first.

Attached to each of the four sides of the square is a stubby concrete and steel rectangular wing, about twenty feet wide and thirty feet long. There are no windows or openings of any kind in these rectangles, and the concrete/steel walls are over two feet thick.

Located in each wing is a single laboratory. During the day, entrance to the labs is by a security card obtained at the desk. The cards are produced each morning by a random number generator and are only good for one day. They have to be carried at all times on the upper floors. If anyone without a card is detected by the many sensors located throughout the building, alarms immediately blare and the entire building complex locks down until the violator is caught. Each lab, due to the nature of the dangerous work being conducted within, has its own air supply and is powered by its own generator.

Still, Homeland Security deemed that these precautions were *not enough*. Which explains the huge movable concrete slabs on each side of the lab entrances.

When I first saw the slabs, my jaw dropped and I stood frozen for a minute in absolute awe. They were, without question, the biggest door jambs ever created. Each slab stood sixty feet high by ten feet across and was two feet deep. They were constructed from concrete laid over a metal frame of thin steel rods. Each massive slab rested on a motorized block of titanium steel. When the complex shut down for the night, the two slabs of concrete per laboratory slide together to meet and form an immovable door – one that couldn't be opened by anyone less powerful than Samson or Hercules.

"You expecting an alien invasion?" I wondered aloud.

"Never hurts to be prepared," said Captain Anthony Rackham, my escort for the afternoon. "Better safe than sorry when you're dealing with plague and ebola bacteria."

I shuddered, the full meaning of the complex's nickname, The Slab, hitting home. The less time I spent in this building, the better. Hopefully, Penelope was going to solve this crime quickly.

"According to the briefing I received this morning," I said, "researchers are permitted to remain in the labs overnight when working on a project?"

"Whenever they want," said Rackham. "Just because we're military doesn't mean we don't understand the needs of scientists. Each laboratory is equipped with a refrigerator, a microwave, a cot, and a bathroom complete with shower stall. Some of our top researchers spend weeks here without leaving their labs. They're dedicated to the safety of our country."

What Rackham considered dedication, I defined as obsessive behavior. But I was too polite to say so. Especially since the Captain was a good two inches taller than me and looked like he stepped out of a Conan the Barbarian movie. Not that he wasn't all slick and polished, from his sharply pressed uniform to his shiny black shoes. Rackham had been assigned to me when I first checked into the complex a half-hour before. I still wasn't sure if he was my escort or my guard. Not that it mattered. I was here strictly as a recording device for my boss.

The call had come in the middle of the night. A man was dead under mysterious circumstances. He'd been discovered in a locked and sealed concrete laboratory. No one was positive if it was a crime or not, but if it was, it needed to be solved immediately. The police and FBI were baffled. Contact Penelope Peters. Which meant I was off early the next morning to The Slab, a secret government complex fifty miles outside of Manhattan. Exactly in what direction that fifty miles was can't be stated. Or so I was warned when given directions. And from the tone of the voice of the man on the phone, I knew he wasn't kidding.

"Now that we've gone over the layout of the building," I said, "how about showing me the scene of the crime."

"You're in charge," said Rackham, waving me into one of the elevators. "It's on the top floor."

I noted with my usual efficiency that there were two cameras in the lift. The chances of someone making it upstairs undetected in this building were absolute zero.

"We don't appreciate surprise visitors," said Rackham, as we stepped out onto the fourth floor, in answer to my unspoken question. "The stuff stored in these labs could wipe out half the planet. Think of it as a terrorist supermarket."

"Terrific," I said. "You think Dr Schneider was killed by enemy agents?"

"I'm not a detective," said Rackham, sounding slightly smug, the first emotion evident in his cold tones. "I have no idea who murdered Schneider, if anyone. He might have died from natural causes. Working in his lab would have given me a heart attack in a week."

Rackham steered me across the floor to a lab sealed off with yellow police tape. A pair of marine guards holding rifles stood in front of the door into the wing. They snapped to attention as we approached. The captain pulled open the door to the laboratory and stepped aside.

"After you," he said. The lights in the lab were on. They were always kept on. "The scene of the crime."

I had no idea exactly what to expect, but whatever I might have imagined was immediately wiped away by what I saw upon entering the lab. What I saw and smell and heard.

"Welcome to Monkeyland," said Rackham. The smugness in his voice was much more pronounced.

3

I should have been prepared, knowing that most of the work done in The Slab involved biological and chemical warfare, but I wasn't. The entire back wall of the laboratory was covered from floor to ceiling with monkey cages. There must have been fifty metal pens in total though I never did spend the time to count them. Each cell, which is what they resembled most, held one small monkey – one small *shrieking* monkey, looking miserable in a boxed environment that barely gave it space to move. Each monkey wore a skull cap with electrodes protruding from it. With horror, I realized that researchers had removed the tops of the monkeys' heads, stuck electrodes into their brains, and then topped the hideous surgery with what looked like party hats from hell. It was no wonder the monkeys were shrieking. The combined noise of *dozens* of monkeys was nerve shattering.

Adding to the beasts' misery, the cages were arranged in rows, and since each pen had a solid metal floor to keep waste and food from dropping through the bars, the monkeys on the lower levels lived in a perpetual twilight. Those on the top row had the light, but because the fixtures were never shut off, they lived in perpetual sunshine. It was cruel torture either way.

Needless to say, the smell of half-eaten food, waste and urine didn't improve my opinion of the lab. How anyone could conduct research in such a place was beyond me, but then again, I'm not a scientist. I turned to Rackham.

"Aren't there laws about treating lab animals?" I said. "Are we really allowed to remove their skulls and literally torture them to death like this?"

"Yeah, we're allowed. It's how basic research is done: on animals. And it's worse than what you're seeing here. From what I hear, the scientists don't let the animals eat or drink much, and they give food and water to the monkeys only if the monkeys cooperate during experiments. As for the lighting and cages and all that sort of thing, talk to the contractor who built this place for Homeland Security," said Rackham. "They cut corners but got the job done fast. Friends in high places wanted results and if a few laws were broken, no one complained."

Call me a naïve bumpkin. I should have realized that even during a time of war against terrorism or terror groups or radicals of any one cause or another, no-bid contracts and kickbacks never went out of style. And I should have realized that, just because the public doesn't hear about the torture, doesn't mean the torture isn't going on.

"Look at the walls," said Rackham, making no attempt to hide the anger and contempt in his voice. "There are cracks in the concrete due to water seepage and not enough support in the foundation. We've got mice in the basement and bats make their nests in the roof."

"Bats?"

"Bats," repeated Rackham. "Concrete walls are nice and dry, better than most caves. Drive by this complex at night and you'll think you're in Transylvania."

Bats, plague, ebola germs, monkey brain surgeries, electrodes, and a building called The Slab. I was starting to feel like I had walked into a bad horror movie. I looked down at the floor. The outline of a body had been drawn in front of the monkey cages in blue chalk. It served as the last testament to Dr Carl Schneider.

The professor, his degree being in neurobiology, had been found the morning before when his assistant entered the lab. Schneider was slumped in front of the cages, with one door open and a monkey sitting on the nearby lab table chattering at the cold corpse. The researcher had been working on a hush-hush project involving monkeys and incurable motor function diseases, and he had spent the night in the lab. He had been alone when the slabs locked him in, and there was no record of the concrete blocks moving during the night. In effect, the scientist had been sealed inside a concrete box. Nobody came in, and nobody left.

All the physical evidence pointed to Schneider having just taken the beast out of the cage when a heart attack dropped him down. Both hands occupied with the scrambling monkey, the doctor never had a chance to grab for the phone and call for help. Everything suggested that Schneider had unfortunately suffered from sudden cardiac arrest and died in an instant.

There was no sign of a struggle. No wounds on his body, not even a scratch. The food and drink in the refrigerator had been tested and no poison detected. Gas was similarly ruled out, as polluting the air supply would have killed the monkeys in the lab as well as the doctor. Even the autopsy results pointed to a killer heart attack.

Why then the frantic call to Penelope Peters and my presence in the lab the next day? Because Dr Carl Schneider was thirty-one years old, was in near perfect health and, as far as anyone could tell, didn't have a bad habit in the world. People like that don't usually die from heart attacks.

"Any phone calls?" I asked, knowing the answer.

"Neither incoming or outgoing," said Rackham. "Phone system works fine, in case you're wondering. We checked it immediately after finding the body. He obviously died before he could contact the front desk. Not that it would have mattered. Once this place is sealed, it stays that way till morning."

I walked around the lab, stared at the concrete walls, noted the tiny holes near the top. Big enough for a spider to crawl through, not much more. Attacked by a baby bat, I wondered, then dismissed the idea as beyond belief. A poisonous insect, perhaps? I was reading too many spy novels.

"Any chance the project he was working on caused his death?"

"No," said Rackham. "Anything that would kill a man would kill all the monkeys in the lab. And they're still alive."

Definitely. The beasts screamed continually as I prowled around, trying to look like I knew what I was doing. Bright lights and screaming monkeys, it was enough to drive a man to drink. But murder? I couldn't see how.

"Could he have been scared to death?" I asked, knowing how preposterous the idea sounded. "Was Schneider afraid of bugs? Maybe the janitor drew invisible paintings on the wall that could only be seen when the lights were turned off?"

Rackham snorted. "Dr Schneider was the most rational person I ever met. He had absolutely no imagination. Not the type to be scared by invisible ink. Besides, all of the maintenance crews are Marines with top-secret clearance. Plus the lights in this lab are never shut off."

On the wall over the desk was an award paper in a gold frame. The paper indicated that Schneider had won a prestigious science award and $100,000 prize only last year. A framed photo of a skinny, pale white man with thinning brown hair dressed in a bathing suit standing next to an equally pale blond woman wearing a modest two-piece outfit rested alone on the desk. Some words were scribbled on the bottom of the picture.

"That Schneider?" I asked.

"The one and only," said Rackham. "With Professor Mary Winfree, from the plague lab, down one floor."

"To Carl, with lots of love, Mary." It sounded like the possibility of a motive to me. Love, as the song said, changes everything. "Let's go visit Professor Winfree."

4

If Schneider's lab was Monkeyland, then Winfree's domain was obviously Mouseville. The lady professor's laboratory was one floor down from the murder scene and was arranged in much the same layout as the room above. Cages to the rear, scientific equipment of all sorts to the left, minimal living comforts to the right. When we entered the lab, Winfree was examining a slide under a microscope while in the rear two assistants in white coats were feeding the mice. The professor peered at us with wide blue-gray eyes. "Can I help you gentlemen? This is a restricted area."

"This whole building is a restricted area, Professor," said Rackham. "We all know that. I'm Captain Rackham, and this is Mr O'Brien. We're investigating Dr Schneider's death."

"Oh, yes," said Winfree, a faint blush rising in her cheeks. "Carl's death. So unfortunate. Investigating? I don't understand. I thought he died of natural causes?"

"A heart attack at thirty-one?" I asked. "Rather young for heart disease, don't you think?"

Winfree stood up, her fingers fluttering. She looked like she was ready to fly away. "I – I never considered that. But why question me? Carl and I weren't close. The last time I spoke with him was a week ago."

"There was a photo on his desk," I said. "Signed by you, *with lots of love*?"

The professor giggled, a high-pitched sound that startled the mice in the rear of the lab, which began squeaking. "A brief flirtation at the beach last summer. A few weeks in the sun. Surely not a reason for foul play. Carl and I were still fond of each other. Sometimes we even talked about going on another trip, but it never amounted to much. That's because neither of us was willing to abandon our first love."

"First love?" I asked.

"Our work, of course."

"Right," I replied. "Anyone you suspect other than terrorists or PETA activists who would have wanted to harm Dr Schneider? Angry relatives, old girlfriends?"

"No-o-o," said Winfree, drawing the word out the length of a sentence. "Carl didn't associate with people outside of the complex. None of us do. We're devoted to our work. It's our life."

I nodded. Obsessed. Great for the country, bad for a murder investigation.

"I wasn't even here the other night," continued Winfree. "I was giving a lecture at the university. You should ask Otto if anything strange happened. He's always around."

We left Professor Winfree after a few more questions. If she was guilty of murdering Schneider, then I was a monkey's uncle. Though, I've been wrong before. Plenty of times.

"Who's Otto?" I asked.

"First floor," said Rackham. "Otto Klax, Professor of Neurobiology, the man in charge of our MEMS program." Rackham sighed. "Another genius with underdeveloped social skills. At least he doesn't work with lab animals. Not enough room in his lab for anything other than him and his ego."

MEMS referred to mechanical components on the micrometer size and included 3D lithographic features of various geometries. They were made using planar processing similar to semiconductor processes such as surface micromachining. Devices using them ranged in size from a millionth of a meter to a thousandth of a meter. Too small to even imagine, yet they were the hottest item in military circles. I noted that both Schneider and Klax were neurobiologists, yet while Schneider concentrated on the brain, Klax's focus was on MEMS. "Why would a neurobiologist be working with MEMS?" I asked Rackham.

He shrugged. "More sadistic torture of innocent animals, I suppose. They build tiny electrical and mechanical devices that they implant into animal brains. Klax builds the devices, Schneider uses them. Klax does a lot of the hard work, Schneider gets the glory. Not that I'd call an award for torturing animals to their deaths, *glory*."

I had to agree with Rackham. Even the salary of a Klax or Schneider was nothing more than blood money.

If Otto Klax had even the slightest trace of personality, he could have played a mad scientist in a horror movie. He definitely looked the part, standing six foot six and weighing no more than a hundred and fifty pounds. Thin enough that if he turned sideways he didn't leave a shadow. Jet black hair, a thin moustache, and tiny black eyes that darted around the room, never making direct contact with anyone. He spoke softly and in a rush, making his speech almost incomprehensible.

"What do you want with me?" he asked, seconds after we introduced ourselves. "I'm much too busy for anything you want to talk about anyway. Much, much too busy for idle chit-chat. Not enough time in the day as it is. What do you want, why are you bothering me?"

"Dr Schneider died in his lab the night before last," said Rackham. "Professor Winfree suggested we ask you if anything strange happened in the complex that evening."

"Mary said that?" said Klax. "I don't know why she would think so. I was in my office working, as usual. All night, every night. Locked in here like a rat in a trap, no way out, nothing to do but wait till morning. If anything weird took place, I wouldn't know. Not me, locked behind these concrete slabs.

"Besides," continued Klax, "Schneider worked with monkeys and I hate monkeys. Dirty rotten little beasts. There's nothing for me to gain from Schneider's death. Only one who benefits is Arronds, his assistant. Talk to him, he's the one with a motive. Now, get out. I have machines to build, reports to write. Get out, get out. Stop wasting my time."

Marvin Arronds had waved good night to Schneider when the slabs closed and locked, and had found the professor's body in the center of the lab the next morning. According to the few locked-room mystery stories I've read, that made him the most likely candidate for murdering his boss. Unfortunately, none of those stories offered any explanation about how Arronds could have managed the task with no one the wiser. Nor did they explain the two Marine guards who had also seen Schneider alive when the slabs had locked shut.

"Me? Kill the professor?" said Arronds, a short, rotund man, with a shaved head and a voice that boomed like a megaphone. Necessary to be heard over the monkeys, I guessed. "That's the craziest thing I've ever heard. Sure, I worked in the laboratory, but Dr Schneider was the genius. Besides, the professor was my friend. Sure, he was a nerd, but that was okay. Everybody liked him."

"Dr Klax suggested that—" I began.

"Dr Klax is nuts," said Arronds, sounding furious. He pointed a finger the size of a sausage at my face. "Guy's a paranoid fruitcake. Thinks everyone is out to steal his ideas."

Five minutes of questioning Arronds further convinced me that, if he had invented a unique method of murder, it was the first thing he'd ever discovered in his life. He was strictly a bottle washer with a degree in biology. More to the point, he genuinely seemed to have liked Schneider. I mentally crossed him off my list of suspects, which left me zero for three.

"You want to interview the professors in the east wing next?" asked Rackham when I was finished with Arronds.

"Sure, why not," I replied. I had a feeling this was going to be a long day – a very long day.

5

I arrived home around nine that night. Penelope was sitting in the TV room, watching a rerun of *Law and Order*. She took one look at the sour expression on my face and ordered me to the kitchen. "Julian made shrimp for dinner. There should be some leftovers in the refrigerator. Eat and drink, then report."

It took me nearly two hours to describe my day. During the entire recital, Penelope only interrupted once. "Bats? Did you actually *see* bats?"

"Flying over the rooftop when I left," I assured her. "Little ones, but definitely not birds. Bats."

Penelope nodded then settled back and let me drone away. I did my usual fine job of imitating a video recorder, describing in great detail everything I had seen, heard, and smelled the entire time I had been away. By the time I finished, she was having difficulty covering her yawns.

"I know, it's not very exciting stuff," I said, "but if anyone committed a crime in that place, I've no idea how."

"That's because you've forgotten your Sherlock Holmes," said Penelope, rising from behind the desk. "I'm going to bed. I suggest you do the same. Tomorrow, we'll need to be at our best for the séance."

"Séance? We're having a séance?"

"Of course," said Penelope. "What better way to identify a murderer?"

What Penelope Peters wants, Penelope Peters gets. Especially when she's working for the government and they're anxious for results. Wearing a black tuxedo and feeling pretty much the idiot, I answered the doorbell the next evening at 8 p.m. Standing on the steps were Captain Rackham, Mary Winfree, Otto Klax, and Marvin Arronds. Backing them up were two Marines. Our guests had arrived.

As instructed, I ushered them into the parlor, which Julian and I had earlier arranged per the boss's instructions. A small round table sat in the middle of the room covered by a black cloth. In the center of the table was a crystal ball I had rented earlier in the day from a Manhattan theater props store. Six wood chairs circled the table. I arranged everyone exactly as Penelope wished. First came Mary Winfree, then Rackham, then Otto Klax, then me, then Marvin Arronds. The blank chair was for my boss.

Penelope entered in a swirl of black silk. She looked very much the gypsy fortune-teller with her hair up in a knot and several strings of costume jewelry around her neck. "Thank you for attending tonight's service," she said, nodding to everyone. "Would you please be seated."

"This is nonsense," said Klax, "pure nonsense," but he sat down. No one else said anything, though they all looked puzzled.

"Now, please form a circle by holding hands," commanded Penelope. "That includes you, Dr Klax."

"This is a waste of time," said Klax, pulling his hands out of his coat pockets and linking his cold fingers with Rackham's on one side and mine on the other. "I should be back at my lab, working."

"Working?" said Penelope. "Or planning another murder?"

"What are you babbling about?" said Klax, trying to wrench his hands free. Not that he could. Which had been the point of this entire charade, making sure Klax couldn't use the miniature control unit the Marine guards later found in his left pocket.

"I never touched Schneider," declared Klax. "I was in my lab all night."

"Yes, you were," said Penelope. "Safe and secure in your laboratory while your MEMS robots, programmed by you, climbed up through the cracks in the concrete walls and killed Professor Schneider."

"Say what?" I was so surprised I almost let go of Klax's cold fingers. Almost.

"MEMS robots are so small they can fit into spaces only a few thousandths of an inch wide," said Penelope. "If artificially intelligent, they can be programmed to assemble themselves into bigger machines once they reach a specific destination. For example, they can go through small cracks between a wall and ceiling, then assemble into a larger flying robot. They can be programmed to seek and attack a specific target: in this case, Dr Schneider. Klax's devices carried a payload of hydrogen cyanide with them and loaded it into the stinger of a mechanical mosquito."

"Cyanide gas kills people almost instantly," I said, Penelope's words starting to sink in. "The results mimic a heart attack, and all traces dissolve into the body within hours. But how could a mosquito deliver enough gas to kill Schneider?"

"It was all a matter of waiting for the proper moment," said Penelope. "Klax knew that sometime during the night Schneider would lift one of the monkeys out of its cage. With both his hands occupied, the professor couldn't stop the attack that killed him."

"The mechanical mosquito—"

"– flew into Dr Schneider's nose and squirted the hydrogen

cyanide into his nasal passage," said Penelope, finishing my thought. "A small dose inhaled at such close range would kill in seconds."

"But why?" said Mary Winfree, her questions directed at Klax, not us. "Why on earth would you want to kill Carl?"

Klax rose from the table, and towering six foot six, and having wrenched his hands free, lifted both fists in the air. "How can you even *ask* that question, Mary? I did all the work. He won all the awards. He got the money, the fame, the glory. And because of all that, he got *you*."

"*Me?*" she said. "What do I have to do with this?"

"He lusted after *you*, and *I* couldn't allow it," said Klax, a very strange note creeping into his voice. "*I* wanted you, and you never even looked my way, Mary. My robot spies heard him talking to you on the phone last week. Trying to seduce you. Take you on another trip. That's when I decided he had to die. He couldn't have the awards that were supposed to be mine, the money and honors that were supposed to be mine, and now *you*, too! I just couldn't allow it!"

"You," said Mary Winfree, "are a very sick and misguided man. You're crazy, Klax!"

And so it was jealousy, after all, that killed Dr Schneider. Not a monkey. Not a bat. And to my surprise, something deadly was able to penetrate the fortress called The Slab. Where nothing goes in and nothing comes out, murder took place.

The Marines found a fistful of tiny machines in Klax's right pocket, a miniature control device in the other. Proof positive that he had used such micro-machines for murder and a grim reminder that Penelope's subterfuge had saved anyone else from being killed.

"I had Captain Rackham bring the two of you with Klax tonight so he wouldn't guess we specifically suspected him," explained Penelope to Arronds and Winfree, once the Marines had left with their prisoner. "I also thought, since you were Dr Schneider's friends, you would want to help capture his murderer."

"An amazing deduction," said Arronds. "How did you figure out it was Klax?"

"She asked Sherlock Holmes," I answered.

No Killer Has Wings

Arthur Porges

Arthur Porges (1915–2006) was another of those writers who wrote prodigiously for the magazines but had very few works preserved between hard covers. You will, though, find a slim volume of his Sherlock Holmes parodies, featuring Stately Homes, in Three Porges Parodies and a Pastiche *(1988), whilst* The Mirror and Other Strange Reflections *(2002) is a collection of his weird fiction. Porges wrote scores of ingenious impossible crime stories and a volume of those is long overdue. Here's just one example.*

I was beginning to think that Lieutenant Ader had finally run out of bizarre cases. He hadn't bothered me for almost six months, or since that "Circle in the Dust" affair.

But I should have known better; it was just a breathing spell. His jurisdiction, mainly the city of Arden, isn't likely to be free of skulduggery for long. Not that I minded too much; in fact, I like playing detective. For that matter, who doesn't?

This was something of a switch, however; because instead of asking me to help solve a murder, it was more a matter of un-solving one first, you might say.

I'm used to being called on by Ader. As the only reasonably well qualified expert in forensic medicine in these parts – I'm chief pathologist at Pasteur Hospital, serving the whole county – I do work for a number of communities in the area. You see they don't trust their local coroners, since most of them are political hacks long out of practice. So whenever they need a dependable autopsy, especially the kind their man would just as soon not handle – say somebody buried a month – they send for Dr Joel Hoffman: me.

Last Tuesday I was happily preparing a slide of some muscle section; it had a bunch of the finest roundworm parasites that you'll ever see. Oddly enough, it occurred to me that these organisms, so loathsome to the laymen, were not only gracefully proportioned, and miracles of design, but never killed each other through greed or hate, and would never, never build a hydrogen bomb to destroy the world.

Well, think of the Devil – in this case, murder – and he's sure to appear. Into the lab came Lieutenant Ader with a young girl in tow. Him I've seen before, but never in such company, so being a man first and a pathologist second, I looked at her. A small girl, dark, and just a bit plump. What my racy old man used to call a "plump partridge." She had been crying a lot; it didn't need eight years of medical study to tell that. As for Ader, he was half angry, and half ashamed.

"This is my niece, Dana," he said gruffly. "You've heard me mention her occasionally."

I smiled. She fixed her enormous, smoky grey eyes on me, and said: "You're the only one who can help us. Everything adds up all wrong. Larry couldn't have done it, and yet there's nobody else who went out there."

"Whoa," I said. "Back off a few paragraphs, and start over again."

"Larry's her fiancé," Ader explained. "I'm holding him on a first degree murder charge."

I must have looked surprised, because he reddened slightly, and snapped, "I had to, but she thinks he's innocent. Why, I don't know. I've told her about your work before, and now she expects you to perform a grade A miracle to order. In other words, Dana's picked you to smash my nice open-and-shut case to little pieces."

"Thanks a lot, both of you," I said sardonically. "But I only do wonders on Wednesday and Friday; this is Tuesday, remember."

"That's all right; you can solve the whole case tomorrow," the lieutenant said, giving his niece a rather sickly grin. It was a noble attempt to cheer her up, and of course a complete failure, as such things always are.

"Look," he added, obviously on a hot spot, and not enjoying it, "I've got the boy cold; the evidence is overwhelming. You'll see what I mean in a minute. But Dana here isn't convinced, and to be perfectly honest, I don't see Larry bludgeoning an old man to death for money, myself. He's pretty hot-tempered, but gets over it fast. I don't think he goes in for physical violence, anyhow. Still . . ." He broke off, and I could almost read his mind. When you've met enough murderers, one thing soon becomes as clear as distilled water: there's simply no way to tell a potential killer in advance of the crime.

"Why are you so sure he didn't do it?" I asked Dana.

Her round little chin rose stubbornly; I liked her for that. I hate the passive, blonde, doughy kind of girl.

"I know he couldn't kill anybody," she said, "especially an old man lying on the sand. He might punch another fellow his own age, if they were both on their feet, but that's all. Do you think I could love a murderer, and be ready to marry him?"

I looked at Ader, and both our faces must have become wooden at the same time, because she gave a little cry of pure exasperation.

"Ooh! All you men know is evidence. I know Larry!"

The lieutenant is married, and so knows about women. Even so, this line of reasoning, being so feminine, made him wince. But the answer was about what I expected. So I merely remarked: "Suppose you give me the main facts, and then we'll fight about who's guilty."

"Right." Ader seemed relieved. He was always at his best with evidence rather than theories or emotions. I imagine that Dana, in cahoots with his very warm-hearted wife, Grace, had been needling him for hours. Not that he's unsympathetic. I've known cops who wouldn't mess with a case that was all sewed up to please their wives, children, or grandparents. He was doing it for a mere niece.

"First," Ader said, "the victim is Colonel McCabe, a retired Army Officer, sixty-two years old. Yesterday morning, quite early, he went down to his private beach, as usual, accompanied by his dog. After a brief paddling in the shallows, he dozed on a blanket, and while he was dozing somebody came up to him, carrying a walking stick, and calmly smashed his skull with the heavy knob. It seems beyond a doubt that the killer must have been Larry Channing, the colonel's nephew, a boy of twenty-four, who lives in the same house."

"And the motive?"

"Money. McCabe had a bundle. Larry's one of the minor heirs, but fifty thousand or so isn't hard to take at his age."

"Larry's going to be a doctor," Dana flared. "He wants to save lives. And he didn't need the money. His uncle was going to see him through med school."

"That's true," Ader said. "But a quick fortune might tempt even a potential doctor."

"Not only potential ones," I said a little enviously, thinking of the ocean cruiser I'd like to own some day. "But just how did you tag Larry as the murderer?"

"Because the young hot-head acted like a complete fool. He left enough evidence – you couldn't call them 'clues'; they're much too obvious – to convict an archangel. Let me show you the sketch."

Here Ader reached into his briefcase, and brought out a scale diagram which indicated the position of the body on the beach and the footprints made by the Colonel and those made by the murderer – to the body, and away from it.

"The sand was quite unmarked to begin with," Ader said, "smoothed out by the tide the night before. We found the colonel's prints, leading from the stairs across the sand to the water, and then back to where he lay down on his blanket. Then there are Larry's tracks from the stairs to McCabe, and back. Nobody else's there except the dog's, which go all over, above and beneath the others. The beach is accessible only from the house and the sea; there's no possible approach at the sides for they're sheer rocky cliffs. That perfect privacy is what makes the property worth $200,000. Now, considering all that, what can any sensible person conclude? McCabe's only visitor, as clearly shown by the tracks, was Larry Channing."

"I suppose you checked all the prints."

"Of course. Although it was hardly necessary. Larry admitted walking out to see his uncle about seven-thirty, while the rest of the family still slept. He even told us that they quarreled again. It wasn't the first time. You see, the colonel didn't want him to marry a poor girl like Dana." A tinge of bitterness came into Ader's voice. As an honest cop, he was always one jump ahead of the finance company. "The old man said that nobody but a fool married except for money, that love was a typically modern delusion, confined largely to soft-headed teen-agers and the women who read confession magazines. It's just as easy to fall for a rich girl as a poor one, he maintained. That's how he got his own fortune – by marrying a wealthy widow, no beauty, needless to say. The hell of it is, that gives the boy a better motive than money alone. The colonel was mad enough to cut him off for picking Dana. In that case, no med school."

"Sounds pretty bad. What about the weapon?"

"Well, since McCabe's skull was crushed, we looked for some kind of club. It wasn't near the body, so we figured Larry got rid of it. But blamed if we didn't find it right in the house, at the back of his own closet. It's Larry's pet walking stick, an ebony one with a roughly rounded, heavy knob for a handle. It had been carelessly wiped. There's still some blood and hair on the thing. Now isn't that a stupid way to commit murder?"

At that Dana leaped up, her eyes blazing. "He didn't do it, that's why! Don't you see it's too obvious, too easy?"

Ader grimaced.

"I've thought of that," he said, "and in a way I agree. Unless he hoped to make us think that way – to believe he was framed, and very crudely at that. Larry is a bit hot-tempered, as I've said, but no fool. And only a prize idiot would leave a damning trail like this one. Talk about painting yourself into a corner. This bird put on a dozen coats."

I had been studying the diagram while Ader talked, and now I groaned. "It was sure to happen some day. I might have known."

"What's that?" the lieutenant demanded.

"I'll tell you. If Larry is innocent, you've got a real classic here – a locked room murder, basically. The tracks on the sand show plainly that nobody else came anywhere near the victim. Are you positive he was killed by a blow from that stick?"

"Not yet, although I'd bet on it. But there's been no autopsy yet, and the stick hasn't been tested by a pathologist. All we've done so far is check finger-prints and tracks. They're all Larry's and the colonel's. The rest is up to you. But the man's skull was dented badly, so if anything else killed him, the blow was superfluous, which makes no sense. However, the body's at the morgue; I'll have it brought here. You can have the stick any time, too."

"What about Doc Kurzin? Going to bypass him again?" Kurzin's the coroner, an ancient incubus who missed his forte as a meat-cutter for some supermarket.

"I'll have to, if we're going to get anywhere. Your standing as an expert in this county gives me that right, officially."

"All right," I said, a little reluctantly, because to be honest, it seemed that the boy must be guilty. After all, most murders are not subtle; they are chock full of blunders. When a man is keyed up to the point of killing, he's not likely to be a cool planner. "I'll do the P. M. as soon as you get the body here to the hospital. Then, if you want to bring the stick later, I'll see if the blood and hair are really the victim's. Meanwhile, do the usual and make me one of your fine lists of suspects. You know, descriptions, character analysis – the works. You've a knack for that."

"There are plenty of possibles," Ader said glumly. "Four other heirs in the house, and I don't think the colonel ever won any popularity contests in the army or out of it."

"How many of the other suspects fly? Because, believe me, it'll take wings or teleportation to explain how the old man got killed without the murderer leaving tracks on the sand."

"That's why I can't help thinking Larry did it. I don't want to believe it, but the alternative, as you say, means a parachute jump, or something. And," he added in a bitter voice, "a similar jump in reverse – upwards."

"Larry is innocent," Dana said firmly to me. "If you remember that, you'll find the explanation. You're our only hope, so please try very h-hard."

"I should warn you of one thing," I told them. "I'm not an advocate, remember; I can't take sides. What if the facts of my investigation—" I was going to say, "– put another nail in the boy's coffin?" but had the good sense to hunt a different metaphor – "make the case against Larry even worse? Maybe you should give the job to Kurzin at that. He'll mess it up so that the jury might give the boy all the benefit of the doubt."

"You won't hurt his chances. He didn't do it, and that's what the evidence is bound to show finally," Dana said, her voice still firm.

Ader shrugged in half humorous resignation.

"You heard her," he said. "I'm inclined to agree that there's nothing to lose, really. The worst D.A. in the business couldn't fail to get a conviction right now, with no further investigation." He led his niece gently towards the door. "I'll have the body brought over immediately. And I'll drop by myself with the stick later, unless I get tied up somewhere." He patted the girl's shoulder sympathetically, and they left.

Watching Dana leave, chin up, I thought that if Larry was smart enough to pick her, he wasn't likely to bungle a murder so badly. Then I thought my logic was getting worse than hers, so I went back to my roundworms.

*　　*　　*

The body arrived about ninety minutes later, and things being slack at Pasteur, I was able to get right to work. Beginning, as usual, with the head, I had to agree with Ader that the crushed skull certainly explained the man's death. In addition, it was also true that the old boy was remarkably healthy otherwise, and could have reached a hundred. There were laborious tissue and toxicological tests possible, but I felt them to be counter-indicated. I had no doubt he was killed by a blow on the head. I was just finishing up these gross tests, when Ader came in with the walking stick.

He studiously avoided looking at the remains, even though everything was back in place. In another minute I was through, and covered the body with a sheet. Then Ader came closer.

"Well?" he demanded.

"He was killed by a clout on the head, all right. Let's see that stick."

He gave it to me. There was a plastic bag over the heavy end of the stick; the stem was thin, tough ebony, thirty-eight inches long. There was little doubt that egg-shaped handle could account for the bone injury. Whether it had or not remained to be seen.

The blood test was fast and simple, a matter of typing the blood. The hair didn't take long either, using a good comparison microscope. I shook my head ruefully at the results, and Ader's face was bleak. He had his tail in a crack, so to speak. On the one hand, he had a dream of a case, with none of the usual rat-race of finding reluctant witnesses and other sorts of elusive evidence. On the other there was his niece, Dana, a favorite relation I inferred, about to lose her beloved to the gas chamber, or, if they were lucky, to a prison for thirty years or so. Either way, the lieutenant wasn't going to be happy. Unless, of course, we found a new candidate for the big jump.

"I'm sorry," I said. "This is no help. McCabe was killed by this stick. I'll stake my professional reputation on that – and will have to so testify under oath."

"I wasn't expecting anything else," he said listlessly. "For Dana's sake, I was only hoping. Anyhow, here's that complete run-down on the rest of the household. Read it over tomorrow, and maybe you'll think of something. You've done it before on more hopeless cases."

"This one out-hopelesses all the others," I said. "And frankly, we don't need suspects as much as we need 'how was it done.' One murder; one rather obvious killer – what's the point in additional names?"

"I don't know," he said wearily. "But begin by assuming Larry is innocent, and then figure out how somebody else might have done it."

"Very simple," I replied. "All I need is another month and fifty per cent more brains. But I'll try, Master."

Ader left, looking desperately tired. He probably hadn't slept much since the murder.

It was after eleven, but I didn't feel pooped at all, so I sat down with the family dossier. Ader is very good at this sort of thing, and I could easily visualize the members of Colonel McCabe's household.

There were five in the family itself, exclusive of the dead man. They were Larry, the nephew, a boy of twenty-four; two sons, Harry, aged thirty-two, and Wallace, thirty-nine; the colonel's brother, Wayne, fifty-seven; and a cousin, Gordon Wheeler, twenty-eight. As for servants, an elderly couple kept the place clean and did the gardening. A middle-aged woman did the cooking.

When it came to motive, they all had it, except for the servants, who were provided for whether the colonel lived or died. For the family, it was a matter of money. McCabe was worth well over a million, his late wife having been the childless widow of a rich manufacturer. The colonel's will was no secret. The two sons were down for $200,000 each; the brother, $150,000; Larry, $50,000; and the cousin, $30,000, all tax free. After a few small annuities to the servants, anything Uncle Sam left would go to the local museum, provided they kept McCabe's arms collection, all of it, on permanent display.

For the old man fancied himself a military expert of high order. But instead of refighting the Civil War, and the one in 1914, he preferred to correct the errors of earlier generals. In short, he intended to rewrite Oman's "The Art of War in the Middle Ages".

One room of the house was devoted to a collection of medieval arms and armor. This was the responsibility of the cousin, Gordon, who catalogued the stuff, and kept it so polished and functional that McCabe could have left on a crusade at any moment, perfectly equipped with plate armor, sword, lance, dagger, and crossbow. Only a horse was lacking.

The late colonel was something of a bully at times, but not really a bad sort. There was no evidence that he interfered unduly with the members of his family, or that any of them had serious cause to hate him. It seemed to me, reading between Ader's lines, that the only reasonable motive was money. For McCabe was possibly a bit stingy on handouts, although everybody had an allowance of sorts.

But, actually, motive wasn't the basic problem here. My real job was just as I'd stated it to Ader: If Larry didn't kill the colonel, *how* was it done? The "who" could wait, and would probably come from the method, I felt sure.

I took out the diagram and photos again. There's a process called "brain-storming", very popular on Madison Avenue. It consists of throwing the rational mind out of gear, and letting its motor race. You give your wildest fancies free rein, hoping to find gold among the dross. I tried that, and came up with some weird notions. The craziest was a theory that the murderer wore shoes giving fake pawprints of a dog. The trouble with that was the obvious shallowness of the prints on the photos. The coach dog weighed perhaps sixty pounds, this weight distributed over four paws. A 160 pound man would leave suspiciously deep prints by comparison. Still, I meant to have Ader check on the actual depth of the prints. I was desperate, you see.

But that "solution" didn't even convince its inventor, so I took another tack, and this one gave me a thrill of hope. What if the approach had been from the sea? According to Ader's notes, all members of the family were waterskiers, and the like – why not skin divers, too? If the murderer came out of the water, with or without special equipment, killed the colonel, and returned the same way, would he have left tracks, or would the tide erase them? Here was a very tenable possibility.

I was tempted to ring Ader at once, but it was after twelve, and I remembered his weariness. Wednesday would be soon enough. So I went home to bed, and dreamed of a skin-diving coach dog that terrorized the bathers.

The next morning I phoned the lieutenant, and told him my two theories. The man walking like a dog, as I'd feared, was nonsense. The plaster casts – this surprised even me, but Ader leaves nothing to chance – showed them far too shallow to have been made by a man.

The second solution, about approach from the sea, however, did excite him. The only question was whether such a feat was possible at the private beach. One way to settle that was to check with Sammy Ames, sports editor of the local paper, a buff on water games. Ader gave him a call, while I listened in, conference style.

Ames was very emphatic. Nobody unwilling to commit suicide would swim within five miles of that coast at this time of the year. The undercurrents made it physically impossible to survive there; not even an Olympic gold medalist could manage it.

That was bad enough, but a call to the Yacht Club brought further verification, plus the fact that some footprints would have been left, at least until the evening tide came in.

It was hard enough finding those two theories; now I had to come up with a third, and it had to be a better one. That made a visit to the house mandatory, so I asked the lieutenant to take me there.

The place was quite impressive: a big, roomy, two-story mansion, with stairs in the back leading down some sixty feet of rock to the private beach. That beach was bounded with those minor precipices on three sides, and the sea itself on the fourth.

I won't waste time describing the family, since their physical qualities are not relevant. All the men were healthy, athletic types, strongly masculine. They seemed genuinely sorry for Larry, but certain he was guilty.

The collection of medieval arms would have made the visit worthwhile in less harrowing circumstances. The walls were lined with daggers, battle-axes, bills, pikes, crossbows, and other ancient man-killers. There were several dummies in full suits of armor, beautifully burnished. Wheeler, the curator of this family museum, was obviously proud of the collection, and had become a trained specialist on medieval warfare through his research for the colonel. He enthusiastically demonstrated the correct use of several outlandish weapons, handling them with the assurance of an expert.

But none of this was clearing up the mystery – if there was one, and Larry didn't happen to be our murderer.

Well, I was pretty discouraged at this point. Maybe John Dickson Carr can make up and solve these locked room puzzles on paper, but this was too much for me. I was ready to throw in the sponge, and go back to Larry as the killer.

But then I recalled other recent cases Ader and I had worked on. In those, a fresh appraisal of the evidence broke the impasse. Besides, I liked Dana. And it makes a difference, when you have a personal interest in an investigation.

So back I went to the lab. The first thing I did was re-read my notes on the autopsy. They didn't change a thing. The colonel's

skull had been fractured just above the right ear. I tried to visualize
how the blow might have been struck. If the killer had stood to the
right of, and just behind the old man, lying there with his feet
towards the sea, and made a golf-like swing from right to left, with
the knobby end of the stick down, hands near the ferrule, that
would account for the injury. Nothing unlikely there; no incon-
sistencies to take hold of.

Rather gloomily, I turned to the remaining evidence, the stick
itself. I held it in the way I had pictured it, and tried to re-enact the
fatal swing. Suddenly I felt a surge of hope. The blood and hair
were in the wrong place! If the stick had been swung, like a golf-
club, by a standing man, the side should be stained. In fact, that
would be true no matter how the thing was manipulated as a
bludgeon. But instead, the very top of the handle had the blood and
hair. How was that possible?

Excited, I experimented again. The only way to hit a person with
the top of the knob would be to make a spear-like thrust forward
with it. But that would be awkward and unlikely even if enough
power was possible, something I doubted. Then a whole new
prospect opened before me, one that suggested many significant
modifications of our interpretation of the evidence. That stick
hadn't been used as a club at all. It must have been projected like a
spear, knob first. But how? Certainly nobody could actually throw
the thing, like a lance, with sufficient force and accuracy to kill a
man from – how many feet? I checked the drawing again. The body
was almost forty feet from the foot of the stairs, which is where the
murderer would have had to stand in order to avoid tracking up the
sand. Such a throw was utterly fantastic by sheer muscle power.
The skull has thick bones, not easily fractured.

Then, looking at that long, slender body of the stick, I had an
idea. I grabbed my lens and studied the metal ferrule. Sure
enough, there were two shallow but definite grooves across the
tip. They could have only one explanation; in them a taut string
would not slip off the end of the ferrule. That meant a crossbow – it
seemed obvious, now. What could be simpler than placing the
narrow ebony rod in the slot of a strung crossbow, knob forward,
and then, from a position on the stairs, aiming at the man lying
there on the sand. The stick, propelled with all the force of a
powerful metal leaf spring, would strike a terrific blow on the
victim's head.

I began to pace the floor feverishly. A perfect solution; one that explained everything. So that's why there were no other tracks. The killer didn't need to leave the stairs. What no mere arm could do, the crossbow made easy. Aiming one was no harder than pointing a rifle, and forty feet was a short range. Even so, the murderer must have practiced a bit to make sure. Perhaps he hadn't hoped to convict Larry, but merely to confuse the issue.

All right, he shot the strange arrow, then leaving it by the body — I cursed. Another good theory gone to pot. The stick had not remained by the corpse. How did the marksman recover it without leaving tracks?

I thought of a string, say a nylon fishline, tied to the missile. But another peek at the photos ruined that solution. There was no long, narrow trail in the soft sand to show where the stick was hauled back.

But I knew there must be some explanation; the rest fitted too well. I examined the stick again, starting at the ferrule. In the middle of the polished stem, I found some indentations. They were not deep, but then the wood is very hard. I measured them, and noticed their spacing. There were no others like them; obviously, Larry took good care of his prize possession. It was baffling, especially because I felt that I was getting close.

Then, seeing the photo again, it came to me. The sort of thing I should have spotted immediately. But any theory needs testing, so I called Ader, and asked him to meet me at the beach. He was to get, on the Q. T., one of the non-suspects, say the housekeeper, to bring Gustavus Adolphus, the coach dog. I wanted somebody the animal knew, and would obey. Since she fed him, that was no problem. He knew and obeyed her.

At the beach, I showed Ader the marks on the stick, and explained the crossbow theory.

"Those marks have been made by teeth," I told him. The Dalmatian was racing about, happy to be out on the beach again for a romp along the shore. At our request the housekeeper, a little bewildered but willing, stood on the stairs and flung the ebony stick end over end towards the water. "Fetch, Gustavus!" she shrilled, and barking joyously, the spotted dog raced out, seized it with his mouth, and carried it to the woman.

I grinned at the lieutenant.

"That completes the story. When the old man was dead, and the killer stood where she is now, all he had to do was shout 'Fetch!' and the dog retrieved the murder weapon. A wordless accomplice. Neat. No footprints on the sand."

"He was sure a lot of help to the poor colonel," Ader snapped, giving the clumsy hound an indignant glare. "Instead of chewing up the murderer, he helps the guy get away with it. Or almost."

"Don't blame the dog," I said. "You can't expect these so called lower animals to understand murder. That takes the higher intelligence; the same that invented it. But Wheeler must be our man; as you saw, he's an expert on all those medieval weapons. Now that I think of it, he didn't demonstrate or even discuss the crossbow. That's pretty significant."

"I've no doubt that's the way it happened," Ader said. "Now to prove it to a jury."

"That won't be easy," I said. "Except for the grooves for the bow-string, and the teeth marks on the stick, there isn't any evidence to impress laymen. I can't prove the stick was actually fired. Maybe we haven't helped Larry very much, even now."

"Don't you believe it," was the grim reply. "I know just how to break Wheeler down. The oldest trick in the game. He'll get an anonymous phone call tonight. Somebody will describe the main points of the murder, claiming to be an eye-witness, and demanding a pay-off. If Wheeler's guilty, and I've no doubt about that, he'll want to meet that Mr X very badly, either to bribe or kill him. We'll have him cold, with witnesses. But first, we'll have to see that the housekeeper doesn't spill the beans. Luckily, Gustavus Adolphus can't talk."

"Don't say that. If he could talk, our job would have been a lot easier."

Well, as Ader promised, the trap worked. I can see why. A murderer is full of fears generally, and the worst of them is an eye-witness to the crime.

Dana says that she and Larry will name their first boy after me. I suggested Gustavus Adolphus instead. Although he was an accomplice, he finally testified for the defense, making our case solid.

Benning's School for Boys

Richard A. Lupoff

Although Richard Lupoff (b. 1935) is most closely associated with the field of science fiction, in which he is an acknowledged expert on the works of Edgar Rice Burroughs, his overall output shows that he is a writer who refuses to stay tied down. He has produced a bewildering assortment of fiction from oriental fantasies (Sword of the Demon, *1978*), *to steampunk* (Into the Aether, *1974*), *to horror* (Lovecraft's Book, *1988*) *and, of course, to mystery, with* The Comic Book Killer *(1988) and others. In my previous locked-room anthology, I included Dick's story "The Second Drug", featuring detectives Chase and Delacroix. That story, along with several others featuring the two sleuths, may now be found in his forthcoming collection,* Quintet. *The following includes another of Dick's detectives, Nick Train, and takes as its setting a place very familiar to the author, as it's where he undertook his army training back in 1954.*

Private Nicholas Train was sitting on his bunk polishing his combat boots, wondering if he hadn't made a mistake when he passed up the chance for an exemption. They considered cops essential, the Selective Service Board did, and he could have filed papers and stayed out of the draft, stayed safely at home. Pounding a beat in Brooklyn wasn't exactly cherry duty, but it beat the hell out of getting shot at by the krauts or the nips and maybe coming home with some pieces missing, or maybe in a box.

But, what the hell, he hadn't liked Hitler from the start, and when his Chinese girlfriend asked him to take her to Mott Street for roast duck lo mein and he'd got an earful from her about what was going on in China he decided that the nips were no better than the Nazis.

Pearl Harbor was the last straw. He was ready to sign up the next morning but there would have been nobody to take care of his mother so he kept pounding his beat, mooning around the house when he was off duty, and taking his Chinese girlfriend to Mott Street whenever she asked him to.

Then, almost a year after Pearl Harbor, Mom died. The day after the funeral Train had dressed in civvies, put in his papers at the precinct and signed up for the United States Army.

And here he was halfway through Basic, sitting on his bed polishing his boots. Somebody had brought a portable radio into the barracks and they were playing Christmas music. A couple of guys were writing letters home. There was a lazy poker game going on, the cards smacking down and coins rattling on a foot locker. And Private Aaron Hirsch was sitting on his bunk crying.

"What's the matter with you, Jewboy?" That was Private Joseph Francis Xavier Schulte, former altar boy, former star fullback of St Aloysius's Academy, designated barracks anti-Semite. "You got no right to cry at Christmas carols, you Christ-killer."

Hirsch jumped up. His face turned the same color as his crinkled red hair. "Shut the hell up, Saint. What I do is my business."

"Oh, listen to the little kike. Ain't you tough, Hirsch? You want some of what I gave that Jewboy halfback from Maimonides? I put that bastard in the hospital, in case you don't remember."

"*Cut it out!*"

Ah, the voice of authority. The soldier standing in the doorway wore two chevrons on his winter OD's. His olive drab uniform was neatly pressed. In it he looked like a military fashion plate compared to the trainees in their baggy fatigues. He wore a brassard around one sleeve, designating him as the corporal of the guard.

"Hey, Pops!" He pointed a finger at Train. "Grab your piece and report to the company office. Captain Coughlin wants to see you."

"Me?"

"Yeah, you."

"Captain Coffin?"

"Very funny. Don't let him hear you call him that."

"What's he want me for?" This had to be something serious. If it wasn't, Corporal Bowden would have handled it himself, or at most Sergeant Dillard. The company first sergeant was as close to God as they ever saw, most days. Officers were some kind of exotic creatures who kept to themselves and spoke to the GIs only through sergeants and corporals.

"Christ, Pops, how the hell do I know?" Bowden took a few steps and clicked the portable radio into silence. "Hey, it's Saturday morning. You guys get a few hours off to polish your gear and get your letters written. What's this?"

He picked up the playing cards and the cash that was laid out on a foot locker between two cots. "You guys know there's no gambling allowed in the barracks. And it's payday. How do you have any mazuma left to play for? Now I have to confiscate this evidence." He stuffed the cards in one pocket and the money in another. "I don't know, I don't know, how are we ever going to make soldiers out of you sad sacks?"

Nick Train had shoved his feet into his boots and tucked his fatigue jacket into his trousers. "Coughlin really wants to see me, Bowden?"

"No, I'm just trying to ruin your Saturday. Of course he wants to see you."

"No idea why?"

"Nope."

Train smoothed out the blankets on his bunk, took his Garrand rifle down from the rack near the barracks door and headed out into the wintry Georgia air. For a December morning the day wasn't too cold, certainly no colder than Train was used to in Brooklyn. The sky was clear and sparkling and the sun was a brilliant disk. There were a few patches of snow still on the ground. The last snowfall had been three days ago. Train held his rifle at port arms and quick-timed across the company area toward the office.

The building behind him was new construction, whitewashed wooden walls under a green tar-paper roof. It would probably be hot as blazes in the summer but he wouldn't know that. It was definitely freezing cold in the winter.

First Sergeant Dillard was working at his desk in the company office. He looked up when Train arrived, then back at his paperwork. He didn't say anything, didn't indicate why Train had been summoned.

Train stood at attention facing the First Sergeant's desk.

After a while, Dillard looked up again and grunted. "Go back to the door and knock the snow off your boots. What kind of pigsty do you think this is?"

Train complied. Then he returned to stand in front of Dillard, his Garrand at his side, butt on the linoleum floor beside his polished boot.

"Captain Coughlin wants to see you, Train."

"Corporal Bowden told me. What's it's about, Sarge?"

"Sergeant."

"Sorry. Sergeant."

"I don't know." First Sergeant Martin Dillard shook his head. "I don't know, but it's something big. He's got Lieutenant McWilliams in there with him. And I heard some walloping a while ago." He shook his head again. "Just go knock on the door, Train, and maybe say a prayer while you're at it."

Lieutenant Phillips McWilliams opened the door to the captain's office when Train knocked. McWilliams was gussied up in officer's dark greens, the silver bars shining on his shoulder straps like miniature neon bulbs, the US insignia and crossed rifles of the infantry on his lapels polished to a sheen. He even affected the Sam Browne belt that every other officer Train knew had abandoned.

Train almost expected him to be wearing a parade ground saber with his uniform, but he wasn't. Instead, there was a holster hooked to his uniform belt, the regulation holster issued to officers along with their .45 caliber Colt automatics.

The lieutenant jerked his head toward Captain Samuel Coughlin's desk.

Train crossed the room, halted, thumped his rifle butt on the floor and executed a sharp rifle salute, the way he'd been taught a few weeks ago.

Captain Coughlin bounced his forefinger off his right eyebrow, then folded his hands in front of him on his desk. Even in December he sat in his shirtsleeves, his uniform jacket with the railroad tracks on the shoulders on a nearby hanger. Train had never been in the captain's office before. He kept his posture but even so he was able to see the pictures on the freshly whitewashed wall behind the captain. There was a standard shot of President Roosevelt, one of old General Pershing and one of General Marshall, and a blow-up that must have been made in France during the First War. It showed a very young Samuel Coughlin standing rigidly while an officer who had to be Douglas Mac-Arthur himself pinned a medal on his khaki tunic.

There was a fire axe on Captain Coughlin's desk. Behind him, Train saw another doorway. The door-frame and the door had been damaged, Train guessed, by the fire-axe.

"They call you Pops, don't they?" Captain Coughlin asked.

Train said, "Yes, sir."

"Why is that?"

"They're mostly kids, sir. All of them, in fact. Seventeen, eighteen, nineteen years old. I guess Hirsch is a little older, maybe twenty. They think I'm an old man."

"How old are you, Train?"

"I'm twenty-four, sir."

"Used to be a police officer, did you?"

Captain Coughlin knew damned well that Train used to be a police officer. He knew how old he was, knew everything else that was in Train's 201 file, the personnel folder that every man Jack in the Army had. Still, he answered.

"Yes, sir."

"Twenty-four." The Captain smiled sadly. "Twenty-four and they call you Pops. Well, I guess we did the same thing in '18." The Captain's face was leathery and etched with lines, his hair graying at the temples.

Captain Coughlin jerked his thumb in the direction of the damaged doorway. "Do you know what's in there, Train?"

"No, sir."

"It's the company safe room. We keep classified information locked up in there. What passes for classified information in this kindergarten. We also put the payroll in there the night before payday."

Captain Coughlin pushed himself back from his desk and stood up. He moved toward the damaged doorway. "Take a look, soldier. Go ahead in there."

It was only a few steps. Once inside the safe room Train stopped. The safe door hung open. Train couldn't tell what if anything was inside. A coffee mug stood on top of the safe. Corporal Miller, the company pay clerk, sat beside it in a battered wicker chair. His arms hung over the arms of the chair, almost but not quite dragging on the linoleum. His head was canted to one side. His hair was matted with blood. He wasn't moving, and Train had seen enough bodies in the line of duty as a cop to know that he was dead.

Even so, he flashed an inquiry to the Captain, got a suggestion of a nod in return, then felt the side of Miller's neck, searching for a pulse. There was no pulse. The body was cold. There were no windows in the room. Most of the light came from a shaded fixture hanging by a long cord from the ceiling, casting macabre shadows on Miller's face. A little more light filtered through the open doorway from the Captain's office.

Train turned around. Captain Coughlin was standing with his fists balled and balanced on his hips. "Poor fellow," Coughlin murmured. "He was one of our good boys, you know. Religious as all get-out. Chapel every Sunday. Rosary in his pocket, Missal in his foot-locker. Poor bastard."

Coughlin didn't use strong language very often.

Lieutenant McWilliams stood in the doorway, looking like a photographer's model.

Turning back to Corporal Miller, Train observed that Miller, too, had been issued a forty-five. The holster hung from Miller's belt, the butt of the automatic visible from where Train stood.

"I should probably call the Provost Marshal right now," Captain Coughlin announced. "It's his business eventually, in any case. But they're looking to put me out to pasture. I shouldn't tell you this, Train, I wouldn't tell it to any of the kids in this outfit, but I'm going to rely on your maturity. If I turn up with a dead payroll clerk and an empty safe, they'll decide I can't cut it any more and I'm out of here on a pension. Not for me, Sunny Jim! Not with a big war going on."

He walked around the safe and the wicker chair with its motionless occupant. "No, sir, not for Samuel Coughlin, USA. If we can solve this thing and present a solution to the Provost Marshal instead of a mystery, I just might get out of this kindergarten and got a chance to do some fighting before I'm through."

"I don't know if that's wise, Captain."

Lieutenant McWilliams had a cultured voice. He was the opposite of the Captain.

Train knew – everybody in the unit knew – that Coughlin was a mustang. He'd been an enlisted man in the first World War, earned a commission and spent the Roaring Twenties and the Depression years soldiering at backwoods Army posts. Now he was overage in grade and hanging on by his fingernails.

But McWilliams was the scion of a high society family. Barracks rumors claimed that his mother had wanted him to live out her own thwarted ambitions, to become a great and famous botanist. Either that, or enter the priesthood. Or both, like old Gregor Mendel. Instead, Old Man McWilliams was delighted when Junior opted for the United States Military Academy. All it took was a couple of phone calls and a generous campaign contribution to a United States Senator, and young McWilliams was in. And he'd done his daddy proud. Cadet Captain, top 10 percent in his class, starting quarterback on the Army football team until a knee injury side-lined him for his senior season. And that might have been a blessing in disguise. The team had played badly and wound up the season losing the Army–Navy game for the third year in a row. At least Phillips McWilliams wouldn't be tarred with that loss. And the 1942 football season hadn't been much better, ending with another loss to Navy, a disgraceful fourteen-nothing shellacking.

But now Phillips McWilliams was a First Lieutenant in the United States Army, executive officer of a training company at the Infantry School with a glittering future before him and only a careworn middle-aged Captain to climb over – at least for the moment. As an officer his duties weren't too rigorous. Train knew that. The ordinary GIs knew more about the lives of officers than the other way around. The people on the bottom always knew more about the people on top. That was one of life's constants. The trainees knew that Lieutenant McWilliams drove a shiny new Packard convertible, one of the last to roll off the line before the factory switched to war production, and he used it to cruise down broad Lumpkin Boulevard to Columbus or across the Chattahoochie River into Phenix City, Alabama, for a night of drinking and gambling and whoring pretty much whenever he felt like it.

McWilliams's Packard was just one car that all the trainees recognized. All the officers and NCOs in the permanent party had cars: Captain Coughlin's gray Plymouth, Sergeant Dillard's battered Ford station wagon, Corporal Miller's little green Nash. They all bore Fort Benning tags, blue for the officers, red for the NCOs, all carefully logged in or out every time they passed through the post gatehouse.

Captain Coughlin was talking again. Train snapped back to the moment. To the – he grinned inwardly – crime scene. "The First Sergeant called me this morning," he said. "Told me that he couldn't get a rise out of Miller. Corporal had spent the night in the safe room, same as every month the night before payday."

The Captain paused. The room was silent. A platoon of officer candidates passed by outside. Train could hear their boots crashing on the frozen Georgia soil, hear them singing the unofficial Fort Benning Infantry School song.

> *High above the Chattahoochie*
> *Near the Upatois*
> *Stands our dear old alma mater*
> *Benning's School for Boys.*

They were past the company office now, their voices growing fainter. But Train knew the song, as well.

> *Forward ever, backward never*
> *Follow me and die*
> *To the ports of embarkation*
> *Kiss your ass good-bye!*

"Safe room door is secured with a hasp and padlock inside and out," Captain Coughlin resumed. "Not exactly Fort Knox, is it, but it's the best Uncle gives us to work with. Miller locked his side, I personally locked the outside. Sergeant Dillard, Lieutenant McWilliams and I all have keys to the outside lock, but that wouldn't get us in if Miller didn't open his. You see?"

Train grunted, then remembered himself and replied, "Yes, sir."

"That's why we had to use the fire-axe." Lieutenant McWilliams sounded as if he disapproved of the whole proceeding.

Train knew the type. It was all beneath him. All beneath Mister Phillips Anderson McWilliams of the Newport and Palm Beach McWilliamses.

Captain Coughlin grasped Train's bicep. The touch came as a shock. Officers didn't touch enlisted men. They might become contaminated. Coughlin's grasp was remarkably powerful. His fingertips dug into Train's arm.

"What are you doing in this outfit anyway, Train?" He released Train's arm, stood eye-to-eye with him. Train was taller by four inches easily but he felt no advantage in facing this older man. "Why are you here? Why didn't you apply for a commission? You ought to be in CID."

"Criminal Investigation Division? Me, Captain?"

"I said that, didn't I?"

"Yes, sir. I – I just have to get through Basic first, don't I?"

"Course you do. All right. Look, I'm calling on your skills, soldier. You know how to deal with a crime scene. You know how to conduct an investigation."

"Sir." Lieutenant McWilliams interrupted. "Sir, you're risking big trouble, sir. This is against regulations. Don't you want me to call the Provost Marshal? I really think that would be best, sir."

Captain Coughlin said, "Train, I want you to get to work on this. I'm relieving you of your other duties. You don't need the training anyway, you know everything a soldier needs to know."

After another silence Coughlin asked, "What do you need, Train?"

"I don't suppose you could get me an evidence kit, sir?"

"I'd have to get it from the Provost Marshal. The jig would be up."

Train pursed his lips. He crossed the room, stood near one wall. He touched his fingers gingerly to the thin structure, then examined them. Fresh whitewash. He laid his rifle carefully on the floor, bolt lever upward. He went back to the doorway and examined the splintered wood.

"Who did this?" he asked.

"Sergeant Dillard."

"Did you see him do it?"

"McWilliams and I were both witnesses."

"What time was that?"

"McWilliams and I had breakfast together at the mess hall. Sergeant Dillard came pounding in there to get us." He looked at Lieutenant McWilliams.

The younger officer said, "We ate at 0530 hours, Train. We were finishing our meal at approximately 0555 hours when Sergeant Dillard arrived. He was out of breath, seemed upset."

Captain Coughlin grunted. "Go on, McWilliams."

The Lieutenant looked annoyed. For a moment Train was puzzled as to the reason, then he realized that Captain Coughlin had called him McWilliams, not Lieutenant McWilliams. Train held back a smile.

"We came through the day room, saw the lock was open from the outside. We tried to raise Miller but we couldn't. So the Captain had Sergeant Dillard use the fire axe."

"And this room—?" Train inquired.

"What about this room?"

"Did you touch anything? Move anything? Sir?"

McWilliam said, "Nothing."

Train stationed himself just inside the doorway, studying the damaged wood and the area around it. The walls themselves were made of thin plasterboard. They had been recently whitewashed. Train bent closer to the door-jamb. He studied the wood and the adjacent plasterboard. He didn't say anything.

Behind him, Lieutenant McWilliams said, "Aren't you even going to look at the corpse, Private?"

Train turned back, made what might have been an almost imperceptible bow to McWilliams, then addressed Captain Coughlin. "I'd like to be alone at the crime scene, sir. If that's possible, please. I know, well, normally in police work there are a lot of professionals present. Photographers, fingerprint men, coroner's people, detectives. I'm not a detective myself, sir, but I've been at a lot of crime scenes and I was hoping for a promotion to detective. But we don't have those professionals here, so if I might, sir, I'd like to be alone in this room."

"Not possible!" McWilliams sounded furious. "This – this buck private, this plain GI – just because he used to be a flatfoot pounding a beat, wants to act like a big shot and order us around, Captain? Who does he think he is? He belongs back in his barracks, the Provost Marshal should be in charge."

Captain Coughlin let out a sigh. "Just go and – I tell you what, Lieutenant, scamper over to the mess hall and get us some coffee, will you?"

"I'll have Sergeant Dillard send a man."

"No, McWilliams, you go yourself."

This time Train couldn't restrain his grin. The Lieutenant looked as if Captain Coughlin had asked him to march around the parade ground in his skivvies. The air in the room was so full of tension you could have picked it up on a Zenith radio. But at last the Lieutenant took his leave.

Captain Coughlin said, "Train, I'll be in my office. You call me if you need anything, otherwise just come on out when you finish in here."

Captain Coughlin winked at Private Train. Yes, he did, he actually winked at the buck private. Then he left the safe room. He stopped and drew the damaged door shut behind him, the hole that the fire axe had gouged out admitting light from the outer room.

Train took one more, confirming look at the splintered wood and the adjacent plasterboard. The whitewash was recent enough to show traces of fingers dragging vertically on the door-jamb, then sliding horizontally onto the plasterboard.

Returning to the corpse, Train knelt and examined the two cold hands, first one and then the other. As he'd already noted, the fingertips were white. He lifted them and sniffed. There was whitewash on them.

He studied the wound on the side of Miller's head, feeling through the bloodied hair to try and determine whether the skull was damaged. It didn't seem to be. He scuttled across the linoleum and returned with his rifle. He stood over the body, holding the weapon so that its butt-plate was adjacent to the wound. He walked around the body and tried again, from behind.

It didn't fit. Miller had been hit with something smaller than a rifle butt.

Train studied the safe. He wasn't an expert safe man, he didn't know very much about locks, but there was no evidence that the safe had been forced or blown open. If it had been, there would surely have been some reaction to the blast. Who had the combination of the safe? He'd have to find out.

In any case, Sergeant Dillard had tried to rouse Miller shortly before 0555 hours and failed to do so. He had a key to the outer lock and presumably used it – something else to check on – only to be stymied by the fact that the inner lock was dogged.

Captain Coughlin, Lieutenant McWilliams, and Sergeant Dillard all had keys to the outer lock. Only Miller had a key to the inner lock. Where was it? The lock itself was in Captain Coughlin's office, still attached to its hasp and the splintered wood that the hasp had been screwed to. But where was the key? Train searched Miller's pockets but failed to find it. The room was not brightly lighted, but Train searched anyway, going to his hands and knees and covering every square inch of floor.

The key turned up in the last place he looked – of course – a darkened corner of the room five or six feet away from the door.

Train stood up, squeezing the padlock key as if it could tell him what had happened. It couldn't, but he was convinced that the contents of the room could, if only he asked them the right questions.

Once again he studied the damage to Miller's head. He was convinced that was not the cause of death. Eventually the Provost

Marshal's people or the Quartermaster's people would come and take away the body, and the Medics would perform an autopsy and pronounce cause of death, and Miller's parents would get a telegram from the Secretary of War and they would go out and buy a service flag with a gold star to hang in their window in place of the one with the blue star that Train was sure hung there now.

But he didn't want to wait.

He knelt in front of the corpse and studied its face. He leaned forward and smelled Miller's nostrils and his mouth but detected no odor. The features were relaxed in death. There was no rictus. He stood up and placed himself behind the wicker chair and tried to imagine Miller's last minutes.

Someone had struck Miller high on the skull on his left side. The blow didn't look serious enough to cause unconsciousness no less death. Who had struck Miller? Who could get into the safe room once it was locked from both inside and out? Only Captain Coughlin, Lieutenant McWilliams, or First Sergeant Dillard, and then only if Miller let them in by opening the inside lock.

He heard voices from the outer office and a moment later Captain Coughlin invited him to join him.

Lieutenant McWilliams was standing in front of Captain Coughlin's desk. There was a tray on the desk, with a steaming pot and three cups. First Sergeant Dillard stood nearby looking uncomfortable.

Captain Coughlin addressed Train. "Come in, soldier. Pour yourself a cup of java."

McWilliams, uniform pressed and buttons polished, was red-faced, his jaw clenched. With an obvious effort he said, "Sir, I must protest. This soldier – there are only three cups – it's a violation of protocol—"

Coughlin waved his hand. "We'll make do somehow, Lieutenant."

McWilliams drew himself up, suddenly taller than he'd been. "If the Captain will excuse me, sir, I have to return to my duties."

Coughlin signaled Sergeant Dillard to approach. "What's today's schedule, Sergeant?"

"We've been pushing the trainees pretty hard, sir. They have the morning off, then grenade drill this afternoon."

"Good."

"And, Captain – it's payday, sir. The men expect to be paid today."

"All right." Captain Coughlin swung around in his chair and raised his eyes. It was impossible to tell whose picture he was consulting: President Roosevelt's, General Pershing's, General Marshall's, or Douglas MacArthur's. Or possibly, Nick Train thought, he was communing his own younger self, the bright young soldier who went to France to whip the Kaiser.

Coughlin swung back to face the others. "McWilliams, Dillard, here's what I want. Lieutenant, find yourself a swagger stick."

"I have one, sir."

"I expected as much. All right. And, Sergeant, grab a clipboard. I want the two of you to inspect the trainees' barracks. I want you to find at least a dozen gigs. I don't care how hard you have to poke around to find 'em. If they're not there, make some up."

Lieutenant McWilliams's anger was clearly turning to pleasure. Sergeant Dillard kept a straight face. Nick Train made a supreme effort to become invisible.

Captain Coughlin leaned back in his chair and drew in his breath audibly. "Go slow. Keep those trainees braced. When you finish, you get out of there, McWilliams. Sergeant, you tell those trainees they're confined to barracks except for meals and training exercises. They'll have a GI party tonight. The works. Swamp out the barracks, polish the plumbing, climb up in the rafters and get the dust out. They have a barracks leader, do they?"

Sergeant Dillard said, "Schulte, sir. Saint Schulte, they call him."

"All right. You tell him that he's responsible for supervising the party. When the barracks is ready for reinspection, he's to notify you. You'll bring Lieutenant McWilliams back in and reinspect."

"Yes, sir," Dillard grinned.

"And tell 'em that we're holding onto their pay for them, they'll be paid as soon as they pass reinspection." He made a sound somewhere between a snort and a guffaw. "That's all. Lieutenant, Sergeant."

They saluted and left.

"Well, Private Train, what do you think?" the Captain asked.

"I think I have an idea, sir."

"All right, soldier, what is it?"

"May I take this with me?" He filled one of the cups on the tray Lieutenant McWilliams had brought back, then held it up.

"All right."

Train took the cup with him, back into the safe room. He placed it carefully on top of the safe, beside the cup that had been there when he first entered the room. He studied the cups. They were identical. Of course that didn't prove much. But there was a small Infantry School crest on each of them. That meant that they came from either the Officers Club or the NCO Club, not the mess hall, despite the instructions that Coughlin had given McWilliams.

He sniffed the coffee in the cup he'd brought, then bent over the other cup. Being careful not to touch the cup or its contents, he tried to detect an odor coming from it, but without success. Even so, he thought, even so, he was making progress.

He'd been attempting to recreate Corporal Miller's actions when Lieutenant McWilliams had arrived. Now he resumed that effort. He squatted beside Miller's wicker chair and reached for his coffee cup, the cup that was resting on top of the safe. He lifted the cup, sipped at the coffee, lowered the cup once more and pushed himself erect.

He crossed the room to the door and extracted the padlock key from his pocket.

So far, so good. But Miller had not opened the lock. Instead he had struck the wood and plasterboard repeatedly with his hands, as if he was trying to grasp the lock and insert the key. The key had tumbled from his fingers and clattered across the room.

Why would it do that? Why did that happen?

If Miller was dizzy, losing consciousness, trying to leave the room, he would have done that. He would have opened the lock, trying to get out of the safe room. Of course he would have failed, the outer padlock would have stopped him. But if he was confused, struggling, he might not have thought that through.

With the key lost, lying in a dark corner of the room, his vision and equilibrium failing, Miller would have staggered backwards.

Train duplicated the act.

Two, three, four steps and – Miller would have collapsed into the wicker armchair. Train collapsed, found himself sitting in the lap of a cold cadaver, leaped to his feet.

No, the blow to Miller's head had not caused his death. It was a red herring, designed to direct the investigation of Miller's death – the inevitable investigation of Miller's death – away from what had really happened. He'd have to have Miller's coffee tested, but in all likelihood that was the means by which a lethal dose had been administered.

Train peered into the corpse's face again. If it hadn't been for the blow to Miller's head, any investigation would have found that he'd died of natural causes. Even young men have heart attacks, and the rigors of military life on a man whose former lifestyle had been sedentary could bring on a sudden deadly embolism.

But who had administered the blow to Miller's head, and why, and when?

Nick Train retraced his route from the door to the wicker chair, to the safe, back to the door, back to the chair. Then he stopped, staring down at the remains of Corporal Fred Miller, company pay clerk.

He wasn't an expert on poisons but he'd learned a little bit about them, first in high school and then at the police academy. Miller had apparently realized there was something seriously wrong with him, tried to get help, then staggered backwards and collapsed into his wicker armchair to die. The only mark on his body was the obviously superficial head wound.

What would cause a death like Miller's?

Based on Train's police training, the likely suspect was digitonin, an easily soluble form of digitalis. That would come from a common plant called purple foxglove, also known as bloody fingers or dead men's bells. The victim might well drink it, for instance in a cup of coffee, and not notice anything for as long as several hours. Then his heart action would slow, he would become dizzy and disoriented, lose consciousness and die quietly.

Just as Corporal Fred Miller had died.

Train made his way to Captain Coughlin's office and told the captain his conclusions. He described his reconstruction of Miller's movements from the wicker chair to the padlock, the struggle with the key, and Miller's collapse and death.

"I don't know what an autopsy will show, Captain. I'm not sure what signs that poison would leave in the body. Maybe none. I'm not a trained toxicologist, sir. But I'd bet my month's pay that a chemical test will show digitonin in Miller's coffee."

Captain Coughlin grunted. "Sounds very plausible, Train. And we'll get the right people in to check those things damned soon. I don't think I can hold out on this thing more than another hour or two." He put his face in his hands and rubbed, as if that would stimulate the blood flow and help his brain to work.

"Great job so far," he resumed. "But if that's how Miller was killed, you still haven't told me how the money was removed from the safe. Not to mention – what do you call it in the detective business, Train – *Who Dunnit?*"

"Sir, I'm not a detective. But I have an idea of how the money was removed. I think that Miller was working with his killer. Whoever was his partner double-crossed him."

Coughlin picked up his cup of coffee and raised it to his lips. An odd expression crossed his face. He lowered the cup without taking any coffee.

"What would you call that, Train – an inside job, right?"

"Yes, sir."

Train paused for a few seconds to gather his thoughts. The silence was punctuated by a booming sound. An artillery unit was practicing coordination with an infantry brigade on the other side of the post. The sound was that of a 155-millimeter howitzer.

"Captain, here's the way I think it happened. Miller's partner opened the outer padlock, Miller opened the inner one. The partner brought a cup of coffee with him. Miller thought that was nice. He left it on top of the safe. Miller's partner opened the safe."

He stopped, then asked, "Who knows the combination to the safe, Captain?"

"Same people who have keys to the padlock. Lieutenant McWilliams, Sergeant Dillard, and myself."

"Yes, sir. Well, Miller's partner opened the safe and removed the cash. Then he hit Miller. The wound looked to me as if it could have been inflicted with the butt of a forty-five. Miller was still conscious. His partner left, taking the money with him. Miller relocked the door from the inside and his partner relocked it from the outside. The idea was that Miller would claim he'd been attacked by an unknown assailant, maybe a masked safecracker who managed to open the safe and get away with the payroll. That would send the CID off on the trail of an imaginary crook from outside, someone who had managed to get copies of the keys to both padlocks, while in fact Miller and his partner had the money."

"And what would they do with the payroll?"

Train shrugged. "I don't know, sir. But I have a suggestion."

There was another boom, another howitzer round fired.

"The first thing to do is check Miller's belongings. No telling what we'll find there."

Captain Coughlin summoned the Sergeant of the Guard and had

a corporal and a private stationed outside the company office. They had strict orders not to step inside, not even to look inside, on pain of court martial. Then the captain told Nick Train to come with him.

Train was feeling less like a soldier and more like a cop by the minute.

Permanent party had better housing than transients at Benning. Corporal Miller had lived in a tiny room, partitioned in an NCO barracks. Train used a pair of bolt-cutters to open the padlock on Miller's door and then to remove a second padlock from Miller's foot locker.

The locker contained clean uniforms, underwear, toilet articles, all in inspection-ready order. Boots and shoes lined up beneath Miller's bunk. Civvies on wire hangers on a wall-mounted rod.

The only non-regulation items in Miller's foot locker were his religious paraphernalia. Rosary, Douay Bible, religious pictures, a couple of saint's medals.

Train was kneeling in front of the foot locker, carefully examining its contents. He sensed Captain Coughlin standing behind him and turned to look at him. Captain Coughlin was studying the contents of the locker, as well.

"I don't see anything here," Train said.

"I do." Captain Coughlin frowned.

"Sir?"

"You know Miller was a very religious man, don't you?"

"Yes, sir."

"His most precious belonging was his Missal. He always carried it around with him. But it wasn't in the safe room, was it, Train?"

"No, I'd have seen it."

"Then it should be in his foot locker. Not here, is it?"

Train shook his head.

"Where is it?"

"Don't know, sir."

"How's this, Train? Maybe the old man can play detective, too. It was just a little book, you know. He could have put it in a uniform pocket. Could have had it with him in the safe room. Probably did. It's a long night in there, no companions, no entertainment, another man might ask permission to bring in a radio, or might smuggle in some comic books or magazines. But a man like Miller would bring either a Bible or a Missal and spend his time communing with the Almighty."

Train struggled to his feet. He was pushing a quarter century and his knees weren't as flexible as they'd been ten years ago.

"You think Miller's partner took the Missal?"

"Yep."

"But why, Captain?"

Coughlin shrugged. "Who do you think Miller's partner was, Train?"

"It had to be someone who had the key to the outer lock."

"Yes."

Another distant howitzer boom.

"Who, Train? Don't be afraid. Who was Miller's partner?"

"It had to be Lieutenant McWilliams or Sergeant Dillard, sir."

"Or – who else?"

"You, sir."

"That's right. We have three suspects now, Train. That's progress. That's real progress. It has to be McWilliams or Dillard or Captain Coffin. Oh, I know what they call me. Don't be naïve." He paused. "Three suspects. Don't be afraid to say it."

He walked to the window. At least Miller had had a window in his room. He peered outside for a long moment. Looking past the captain, Train could see the patches of snow covering the red west Georgia clay.

"Where do you think the money is, Train?"

"I don't know. Sir."

"Try. If you were the killer, Train, if you were McWilliams or Dillard or Old Man Coughlin, Captain Coffin, and you had just robbed the company safe, what would you do with the money?"

"I think I'd try and get it off the post, Captain."

"I think so, too. All right, come on back to the company office, soldier."

The two soldiers posted outside the company office rendered smart rifle salutes to Captain Coughlin as he and Private Train returned. The captain motioned Train to sit opposite him, then picked up a telephone and placed a call. He picked up a pencil and scribbled a few notes, then grunted into the receiver and hung it up.

"McWilliams and Dillard both drove off post last night. McWilliams left around 2300 hours. Returned at 0400 this morning. Dillard left at 2346 hours and returned shortly after 0500. There's no record of my leaving the post, and in fact I did not. What do you make of it, Train?"

"I don't know, sir."

Train followed Coughlin's glance to a wall-mounted clock. It was well into the afternoon. He and Captain Coughlin had missed the noon meal. Train's barracks-mates would be on the practice range, throwing dummy hand grenades at cardboard targets.

From outside the building, Train heard a familiar voice. It was Lieutenant McWilliams, dressing down the two soldiers for what Train knew would be some petty offense. A moment later, McWilliams strode into the office and halted before Captain Coughlin's desk. He snapped a sharp salute and all but clicked his heels, Gestapo-fashion.

"Sit down, Lieutenant," Coughlin instructed. "Good. Make yourself comfortable. Don't worry about sitting next to an enlisted man, you won't catch a disease."

McWilliams sent a filthy glare at Train.

"Where were you last night, Lieutenant?"

"I was here, sir. In the company office. Catching up on paper-work, looking over training schedules."

"Right. And then?"

'Then, sir?"

"Then, Lieutenant. You didn't spend the night here, did you?"

"No, sir."

"Well, where did you go?"

"I went to my quarters, sir. I got a good night's sleep, then I went to the mess hall and met you there for breakfast."

"Right."

Coughlin picked a sheet of paper off his desk, fingered it briefly, then dropped it again.

"Gate guards indicate that you left the post at 2300 hours last night and returned at 0400."

"Oh. Yes, sir. That's true."

"That's all right, Lieutenant. You're an officer and a gentleman. You don't have to stand bed check. So long as you're present for all duties, you can come and go as you please. That's per regulations."

"Yes, sir."

"Where were you, though?"

"Am I required to answer that, sir?"

"I am directing you to answer, yes, Lieutenant."

McWilliams had removed his visored cap and was holding it in his lap. "Sir, I met some friends and enjoyed a social visit."

"Right. And where was that?"

"Columbus, sir."

"Broad Street?"

"Yes, sir."

"You get laid, McWilliams?"

"Sir!"

"Jesus Christ, man, you have a pair of gonads, don't you? What did you do, pick up a woman in a bar? Do you have a steady girlfriend? Go to a whorehouse? This isn't a Sunday School class, Lieutenant, we've had a murder and robbery here. Where were you last night?"

"The, ah, that one, Captain."

There was another boom. It was louder than the howitzer booms, but in fact it seemed to be a smaller explosion, sharper, closer to the company area.

"Which one?"

"Ah, the last one, sir."

"Please, McWilliams, let's have it in plain English."

"All right, sir. I was at the Cardinal Hotel."

"Okay. We all know what that place is. I just hope you were careful, Lieutenant."

"I was, sir."

The young officer's face was crimson.

"All right. One more thing. I want to inspect your vehicle."

"Yes, sir."

"Right now, McWilliams." The captain turned to Nick Train. "Did your police training include checking out vehicles for contraband, Private?"

"It did, sir."

Train wound up inspecting Lieutenant McWilliams's 1942 Packard Darrin One-Eighty. The convertible came up spotlessly clean and innocent, inside and out. McWilliams stood by fuming, Captain Coughlin watched noncommittally. Nothing under the hood but a perfectly maintained straight-eight engine. Nothing in the trunk but a jack, a tire-iron, a tool kit, and a spare tire. At the end, Train crawled out from under the car, dusted himself off and presented himself to Coughlin.

"Nothing, sir."

"All right, Train. Lieutenant McWilliams, you hurry out to the grenade range and have a look-see. That was a nasty pop a little while ago. I hope somebody didn't set off a real grenade. Train, you come with me. We're going to have a look at Corporal Miller's vehicle. McWilliams, you don't mind if we borrow your tire iron, do you? Just in case we need it to pry open Miller's car?"

But Miller's little '36 Nash 400 had been left unlocked. The True Believer in All Things Holy had trusted his fellow man to that extent. Or maybe he had nothing worth stealing. There was no trunk lid in the odd little car. Train scrambled over the seat to get into the trunk. The car wasn't as well maintained mechanically as McWilliams's Packard, nor was the interior quite as clean and innocent.

Train emerged with a half-empty bottle of Bourbon in one hand and a stack of ratty publications in the other. "Girly books," he grinned, offering the loot to Captain Coughlin.

The captain grinned and shook his head. "So little Miller had a pair of gonads, too." He brushed his hand across his forehead. "Well, we'll just toss that stuff. No need to upset his family, they've got grief enough coming. No Missal, though?"

"No, sir."

"Okay, soldier. On to Sergeant Dillard's wagon."

But before they got to that vehicle, a soldier in olive fatigues came panting up, perspiring profusely despite the winter chill. Train recognized the ruddy complexion and the curly rust-colored hair sticking out from under the man's fatigue cap. It was Aaron Hirsch. He wasn't crying, just sweating.

He managed to pull himself together and salute the captain.

"Sir, Lieutenant McWilliams sends his respects and a message for the captain."

"Yes, yes." Coughlin returned the salute. "What is it, Hirsch?"

"It's Sergeant Dillard, sir."

"What happened?"

"He was demonstrating grenade technique, sir. He had a practice grenade. It was painted the way they are, to show they're not armed. He pulled the pin and counted down to show us how long it took for the fuse to burn. It went off, sir. It wasn't a practice grenade. It was a live grenade. He – it went off, sir. It blew him to bits, sir."

"Jesus, Jesus, Jesus, Joseph and Mary. Jesus. The poor bastard. He must have known the jig was up. All right, here comes McWilliams now."

And Lieutenant McWilliams arrived, polished shoes covered with red Georgia dust even in winter, uniform spotless and pressed, every brass button glittering in the December sunlight.

Even before McWilliams got off his salute, Captain Coughlin barked at him.

"You've sent for the medics, of course."

"Yes, sir."

"Cancelled the rest of the session and sent the men to barracks."

"Under command of Private Schulte, sir. A fine soldier, I can see that already."

"I'm sure of it. All right, McWilliams. Let's have a look in Sergeant Dillard's vehicle."

They found it concealed inside the spare tire in Dillard's Ford. Miller's missing Missal. The annotations were in a simple code; the Provost Marshal's men and the CID investigators would have no problem cracking it. Poor innocent Miller, the payroll clerk had made notes to himself in the Missal, notes that gave the key to his carefully maintained records. It was obvious that he never thought anyone would see the contents of the Missal except himself and his God.

Everything was there. The identities of the gamblers, the amounts they owed. The monthly payroll would have got a lot of military men out of debt with whoever held their IOU's. A lot of military men including Sergeant Dillard and Corporal Miller. And Lieutenant McWilliams.

"You, Lieutenant? That's hard to believe. You drive that Packard, you wear custom-tailored uniforms, you're from old money, McWilliams. How could you get in so deep? Why didn't you just ask your family to bail you out?"

"You wouldn't understand, Captain. With due respect to your rank, sir, you really wouldn't understand. I couldn't go to my family. I had to work this out myself."

Captain Coughlin moaned, as if he and not Lieutenant McWilliams had been caught. "It was the Army–Navy game that did it, wasn't it? Loyal to the old school, you went double-or-nothing on everything you owed, and Navy whipped Army again, didn't they? You poor sap, McWilliams. You poor, poor sap."

The captain drew in a deep breath. Then he said, "I take it you and Sergeant Dillard and Corporal Miller were all in this together? Who was your bookie, that's not in Miller's book. Was it Jackalee Jennings in Columbus? Or somebody in Phoenix City? Big Mike Norris? Larry Sunday? You know, those fellows don't keep their operations very secret, they're pals with the sheriffs on both sides of the river. Who was it, son?"

McWilliams looked angry for a moment when he heard Captain Coughlin use that last word. Then he shook his head. "I don't think I should say anything, Captain. Under the Uniform Code of Military Justice I have the right to a civilian attorney and I will ask my family to provide one. That much, I will accept from them."

"Did you kill him, McWilliams? Tell me that much. Was it you or was it Dillard? Which one of you killed Miller?"

"I'm not going to answer any questions, sir."

"Dillard is dead now. Very convenient, McWilliams. You can lay it all on his grave. I suppose that's what your lawyer will do, isn't it?" He looked up, looked over McWilliams's cap with its glittering eagle ornament and its polished leather visor. Train wondered what Captain Coughlin saw. He couldn't guess. Coughlin said, "All right, Lieutenant. Report to the Provost Marshal and tell him to place you under arrest pending investigation."

Nick Train watched Lieutenant McWilliams salute, execute a smart about face, and march off like a good little soldier.

"Where did they get the poison?" Captain Coughlin asked. He didn't direct the question to anyone in particular, but Private Train and Private Hirsch were both within earshot.

"Foxglove is common," Train said, "it grows in every ditch in the State of Georgia."

"Lot of it in Spain, too," Hirsch volunteered. "I was there with the Lincolns, you know. Saw plenty of Foxglove."

Captain Coughlin said, "All right, boys, you go back to your barracks and polish your boots."

The Episode of the
Nail and the Requiem

C. Daly King

Ellery Queen, or at least the Frederick Dannay half of that writing team, regarded the collection The Curious Mr Tarrant *(1935) as containing "the most imaginative detective short stories of our time." The book, rather oddly, was published first in Britain, and that first edition is regarded as one of the rarest volumes of 20th century detective fiction. It was not until 1977 that it saw its first American edition, and more recently it has been augmented with later stories in* The Complete Curious Mr Tarrant *(2003). The author, Charles Daly King (1895–1963) was a psychologist who used his understanding of the workings of the mind in creating often quite simple puzzles but which utterly perplex the reader. He completed six novels, all of which were also first published in Britain, featuring police detective Michael Lord and his psychologist assistant Dr Rees Pons. If you like murders on trains, then* Obelists en Route *(1934) is worth tracking down. The following doesn't involve a train but it does include one of those puzzles that seems so simple when explained but is otherwise so completely baffling.*

The episode of the nail and the requiem was one of the most characteristic of all those in which, over a relatively brief period, I was privileged to watch Trevis Tarrant at work. Characteristic, in that it brought out so well the unusual aptitude of the man to see clearly, to welcome *all* the facts, no matter how apparently contradictory, and to think his way through to the only possible solution by sheer logic, while everyone else boggled at impossibilities and sought to forget them. From the gruesome beginning that November morning, when he was confronted by the puzzle of the sealed studio, to the equally gruesome denouement that occurred despite his own grave warning twenty-four hours later, his brain clicked successively and infallibly along the rails of reason to the inevitable, true goal.

Tarrant had been good enough to meet us at the boat when Valerie and I had returned from our wedding trip; and a week later I had been delighted with the opportunity of spending the night at his apartment, telling him of the trip and our plans and hearing of his own activities during the interval. After all, he was largely responsible for my having won Valerie when I did; our friendship had grown to intimacy during those few days when the three of us, and Katoh too, had struggled with the thickening horror in Valerie's modernistic house.

It was that most splendid time of year when the suburban air is tinged with the smoke of leaves, when the country beyond flaunts beauty along the roads, when the high windows of the city look out every evening through violet dusk past myriad twinkling lights at the gorgeous painting of sunset. We had been to a private address at the Metropolitan Museum by a returning Egyptologist; we had come back to the apartment and talked late into the night. Now, at eight-thirty the next morning, we sat at breakfast in Tarrant's lounge while the steam hissed comfortably in the wall radiators and the brisk, bright sky poured light through the big window beside us.

I remember that we had nearly finished eating and that Tarrant was saying: "Cause and effect rule this world; they may be a mirage but they are a consistent mirage, everywhere, except possibly in subatomic physics, there is a cause for each effect, and that cause can be found," when the manager came in. He wore a fashionable morning coat and looked quite handsome; he was introduced to me as Mr Gleeb. Apparently he had merely dropped in, as was his custom, to assure himself that all was satisfactory with a valued tenant, but the greetings were scarcely over when the phone rang and Katoh indicated that he was being called His monosyllabic answers gave no indication of the conversation from the other end he finished with "All right; I'll be up in a minute."

He turned back to us. "I'm sorry," he said, "but there is some trouble at the penthouse. Or else my electrician has lost his mind. He says there is a horrible kind of music being played there and that he can get no response to his ringing at the door. I shall have to go up and see what it is all about."

The statement was a peculiar one and Tarrant's eyes, I thought, held an immediate gleam of curiosity. He got out of his seat in a leisurely fashion, however, and declared: "You know, Gleeb, I'd like a breath of fresh air after breakfast. Mind if we come up with you? There's a terrace, I believe, where we can take a step or so while you're untangling the matter."

"Not at all, Mr Tarrant. Come right along. I hardly imagine it's of any importance, but I can guarantee plenty of air."

There was, in fact a considerable wind blowing across the open terrace that, guarded by a three-foot parapet, surrounded the penthouse on all sides except the north, where its wall was flush with that of the building. The penthouse itself was rather small, containing as I later found, besides the studio which comprised its whole northern end, only a sleeping room with a kitchenette and a lavatory off its east and west sides respectively. The entrance was on the west side of the studio and here stood the electrician who had come to the roof to repair the radio antenna of the apartment house and had been arrested by the strange sounds from within. As we strolled about the terrace, we observed the penthouse itself as well as the wide view below. Its southern portion possessed the usual windows but the studio part had only blank brick walls; a skylight was just visible above it and there was, indeed, a very large window, covering most of the northern wall, but this, of course, was invisible and inaccessible from the terrace.

Presently the manager beckoned us over to the entrance door and, motioning us to be silent, asked: "What do you make of that, Mr Tarrant?"

In the silence the sound of doleful music was more than audible. It appeared to emanate from within the studio; slow, sad and mournful, it was obviously a dirge and its full-throated quality suggested that it was being rendered by a large orchestra. After a few moments' listening Tarrant said: "That is the rendition of a requiem mass and very competently done, too. Unless I'm mistaken, it is the requiem of Palestrina . . . There; there's the end of it . . . Now it's beginning again."

"Sure, it goes on like that all the time," contributed Wicks, the electrician. "There must be someone in there, but I can't get no answer." He banged on the door with his fist, but obviously without hope of response.

"Have you looked in at the windows?"

"Sure."

We, too, stepped to the available windows and peered in, but beyond a bedroom that had not been used, nothing was visible. The door from the bedroom to the studio was closed. The windows were all locked.

"I suggest," said Tarrant, "that we break in."

The manager hesitated. "I don't know. After all, he has a right to play any music he likes, and if he doesn't want to answer the door—"

"Who has the penthouse, anyhow?"

"A man named Michael Salti. An eccentric fellow, like many of these artists. I don't know much about him, to tell the truth; we can't insist on as many references as we used to, nowadays. He paid a year's rent in advance and he hasn't bothered anyone in the building, that's about all I can tell you."

"Well," Tarrant considered, "this performance is a little peculiar. How does he know we may not be trying to deliver an important message? How about his phone?"

"Tried it," Wicks answered. "The operator says there isn't any answer."

"I'm in favour of taking a peek. Look here, Gleeb, if you don't want to take the responsibility of breaking in, let us procure a ladder and have a look through the skylight. Ten to one that will pass unobserved; and if everything seems all right we can simply sneak away."

To this proposal the manager consented, although it seemed to me that he did so most reluctantly. Possibly the eerie sounds that continued to issue through the closed door finally swayed him, for their quality, though difficult to convey, was certainly upsetting. In any event the ladder was brought and Tarrant himself mounted it, once it had been set in place. I saw him looking through the skylight, then leaning closer, peering intently through hands cupped about his eyes. Presently he straightened and came down the ladder in some haste.

His face, when he stood beside us, was strained.

"I think you should call the police," he grated. "At once. And wait till they get here before you go in."

"The police? But – what is it?"

"It's not pleasant," Tarrant said slowly. "I think it's murder."

Nor would he say anything further until the police, in the person of a traffic patrolman from Park Avenue, arrived. Then we all went in together, Gleeb's passkey having failed and the door being broken open.

The studio was a large, square room, and high, and the light, sweeping in through the north wall and the skylight, illuminated it almost garishly. It was sparsely furnished; a couch, a chair, a stool, an easel and a cabinet for paints and supplies stood on a hardwood floor which two rugs scarcely covered. The question of the music was soon settled; in one corner was an electric victrola with an automatic arrangement for turning the record and starting it off again when it had reached its end. The record was of Palestrina's Requiem Mass, played by a well-known orchestra. Someone, I think it was Tarrant, crossed the room and turned it off, while we stood huddled near the door, gazing stupidly at the twisted, bloody figure on the couch.

It was that of a girl, altogether naked; although she was young – not older than twenty-two certainly – her body was precociously voluptuous. One of her legs was contorted into a bent position, her mouth was awry, her right hand held a portion of the couch covering in an agonised clutch. Just beneath her left breast the hilt of a knife protruded shockingly. The bleeding had been copious.

It was Tarrant again who extinguished the four tall candles, set on the floor and burning at the corners of the couch. As he did so he murmured:

"You will remember that the candles were burning at eight forty-seven, officer. I dislike mockery."

Then I was out on the terrace again, leaning heavily against the western parapet. In the far distance the Orange mountains stood against the bright horizon; somewhat nearer, across the river, huddled the building masses that marked Newark; overhead a plane droned south-westward. I gagged and forced my thoughts determinedly toward that plane. It was a transport plane, it was going to Newark Airport; probably it was an early plane from Boston. On it were people; prosaic people, thank God. One of them was perhaps a button salesman; presently he would enter the offices of Messrs. Simon and Morgetz and display his buttons on a card for the benefit of Mr Simon . . . Now my insides were behaving less drastically, I could gasp; and I did gasp, deep intakes of clear, cold air.

When I came back into the studio, a merciful blanket covered the girl's body. And for the first time I noticed the easel. It stood in the south-east corner of the room, diagonally opposite the couch and across the studio from the entrance doorway. It should have faced north-west, to receive the light from the big north window, and in fact the stool to its right indicated that position. But the easel had been partly turned, so that it faced south-west, toward the bedroom door; and one must walk almost to that door to observe its canvas.

This, stretched tightly on its frame, bore a painting in oil of the murdered girl. She was portrayed in a nude, half-crouching pose, her arms extended, and her features held a revoltingly lascivious leer. The portrait was entitled "La Séduction". In the identical place where the knife had pierced her actual body, a large nail had been driven through the web of the canvas. It was half-way through, the head protruding two inches on the obverse side of the picture; and a red gush of blood had been painted down the torso from the point where the nail entered.

Tarrant stood with his hands in his pockets, surveying this work of art. His gaze seemed focused upon the nail, incongruous in its strange position and destined to play so large a part in the tragedy. He was murmuring to himself and his voice was so low that I scarcely caught his words.

"Madman's work . . . But why is the easel turned away from the room . . . Why is that . . . ?"

It was late afternoon in Tarrant's apartment and much activity had gone forward. The Homicide Squad in charge of Lieutenant Mullins had arrived and unceremoniously ejected everyone else from the penthouse, Tarrant included. Thereupon he had called a friend at Headquarters and been assured of a visit from Deputy Inspector Peake, who would be in command of the case, a visit which had not yet eventuated.

I had gone about my business in the city somewhat dazedly. But I had met Valerie for luncheon downtown and her presence was like a fragrant, reviving draft of pure ozone. She had left again for Norrisville, after insisting that I stay with Tarrant another night when she saw how excited I had become over the occurrence of the morning. Back in the apartment Katoh, who, for all that he was a man of our own class in Japan, was certainly an excellent butler in New York, had immediately provided me with a fine bottle of Irish whisky (Bushmills, bottled in 1919). I was sipping my second highball and Tarrant was quietly reading across the room, when Inspector Peake rang the bell.

He advanced into the room with hand outstretched. "Mr Tarrant, I believe? . . . Ah. Glad to know you, Mr Phelan." He was a tall, thin man in multi, with a voice unexpectedly soft. I don't know why, but I was also surprised that a policeman should wear so well-cut a suit of tweeds. As he sank into a chair, he continued, "I understand you were among the first to enter the penthouse, Mr Tarrant. But I'm afraid there isn't much to add now. The case is cut and dried."

"You have the murderer?"

"Not yet. But the drag-net is out. We shall have him, if not today, then tomorrow or the next day."

"The artist, I suppose?"

"Michael Salti, yes. An eccentric man, quite mad . . . By the way, I must thank you for that point about the candles. In conjunction with the medical examiner's evidence it checked the murder definitely at between one and two a.m."

"There is no doubt, then, I take it, about the identity of the criminal."

"No," Peake asserted, "none at all. He was seen alone with his model at 10.50 p.m. by one of the apartment house staff and the elevator operators are certain no one was taken to the penthouse during the evening or night. His fingerprints were all over the knife, the candlesticks, the victrola record. There was a lot more corroboration, too."

"And was he seen to leave the building after the crime?

"No, he wasn't. That's the one missing link. But since he isn't here, he must have left. Perhaps by the fire-stairs; we've checked it and it's possible . . . The girl is Barbara Brebant – a wealthy family." The inspector shook his head. "A wild one, though; typical Prohibition product. She has played around with dubious artistics from the Village and elsewhere for some years; gave most of 'em more than they could take, by all accounts. Young, too; made her debut only about a year ago. Apparently she has made something of a name for herself in the matter of viciousness; three of our men brought in the very same description – a vicious beauty."

"The old Roman type," Tarrant surmised. "Not so anachronistic in this town, at that . . . Living with Salti?"

"No. She lived at home. When she bothered to go home. No one doubts, though, that she was Salti's mistress. And from what I've learned, when she was any man's mistress he was pretty certain to be dragged through the mire. Salti, being mad, finally killed her."

"Yes, that clicks," Tarrant agreed. "The lascivious picture and the nail driven through it. Mad men, of course, act perfectly logically. He was probably a loose liver himself, but she showed him depths he had not suspected. Then remorse. His insanity taking the form of an absence of the usual values, he made her into a symbol of his own vice, through the painting, and then killed her, just as he mutilated the painting with the nail . . . Yes, Salti is your man all right."

Peake ground out a cigarette. "A nasty affair. But not especially mysterious. I wish all our cases were as simple." He was preparing to take his leave.

Tarrant also got up. He said: "Just a moment. There were one or two things—"

"Yes?"

"I wonder if I could impose upon you a little more, Inspector. Just to check some things I noticed this morning. Can I be admitted to the penthouse now?"

Peake shrugged, as if the request were a useless one, but took it with a certain good grace. "Yes, I'll take you up. All our men have left now, except a patrolman who will guard the premises until we make the arrest. I still have an hour to spare."

It was two hours, however, before they returned. The inspector didn't come in but I caught Tarrant's parting words at the entrance. "You will surely assign another man to the duty tonight, won't you?" The policeman's reply sounded like a grunt of acquiescence.

I looked at my friend in amazement when he came into the lounge. His clothes, even his face, were covered with dirt; his nose was a long, black smudge. By the time he had bathed and changed and we sat down to one of Katoh's dinners, it was near to half-past nine.

During dinner Tarrant was unaccustomedly silent. Even after we had finished and Katoh had brought our coffee and liqueurs, he sat at a modernistic tabour, stirring the black liquid reflectively, and in the light of the standing lamp behind him I thought his face wore a slight frown.

Presently he gave that peculiar whistle that summoned his man and the butler's valet appeared almost immediately from the passage to the kitchen. "Sit down, doctor," he spoke without looking up.

Doubtless a small shift in my posture expressed my surprise, for he continued, for my benefit, "I've told you that Katoh is a doctor in his own country, a well-educated man who is over here really on account of this absurd spy custom. Because of that nonsense I am privileged to hire him as a servant, but when I wish his advice as a friend, I call him doctor – a title to which he is fully entitled – and institute a social truce. Usually I do it when I'm worried . . . I'm worried now."

Katoh, meantime, had hoisted himself on to the divan, where he sat smiling and helping himself to one of Tarrant's Dimitrinoes. "Sozhial custom matter of convenience," he acknowledged. "Conference about what?"

"About this penthouse murder," said Tarrant without further ado. "You know the facts related by Inspector Peake. You heard them?

"I listen. Part my job."

"Yes, well that portion is all right. Salti's the man. There's no mystery about that, not even interesting, in fact. But there's something else, something that isn't right. It stares you in the face, but the police don't care. Their business is to arrest the murderer; they know who he is and they're out looking for him. That's enough for them. But there is a mystery up above, a real one. I'm not concerned with chasing crooks, but their own case won't hold unless this curious fact fits in. It is as strange as anything I've ever met."

Katoh's grin had faded; his face was entirely serious. "What this mystery?"

"It's the most perfect sealed room, or rather sealed house, problem ever reported. There was no way out and yet the man isn't there. No possibility of suicide; the fingerprints on the knife are only one element that rules that out. No, he was present all right. But where did he go, and how?

"Listen carefully. I've checked this from my own observation, from the police investigations, and from my later search with Peake.

"When we entered the penthouse this morning, Gleeb's pass-key didn't suffice; we had to break the entrance door in because it was bolted on the inside by a strong bar. The walls of the studio are of brick and they have no windows except on the northern side where there is a sheer drop to the ground. The window there was fastened on the inside and the skylight was similarly fastened. The only other exit from the studio is the door to the bedroom. This was closed and the key turned in the lock; the key was on the studio side of the door.

"Yes, I know," Tarrant went on, apparently forestalling an interruption; "it is sometimes possible to turn a key in a lock from the wrong side, by means of pincers or some similar contrivance. That makes the bedroom, the lavatory and the kitchenette adjoining it, possibilities. There is no exit from any of them except by the windows. They were all secured from the inside and I am satisfied that they cannot be so secured by anyone already out of the penthouse."

He paused and looked over at Katoh, whose head nodded up and down as he made the successive points. "Two persons in penthouse when murder committed. One is victim, other is Salti man. After murder only victim is visible. One door, windows and skylight are only exists and they are all secured on inside. Cannot be secured from outside. Therefore, Salti man still in penthouse when you enter."

"But he wasn't there when we entered. The place was thoroughly searched. I was there then myself."

"Maybe trap-door. Maybe space under floor or entrance to floor below."

"Yes," said Tarrant, "well, now get this. There are no trap-doors in the flooring of the penthouse, there are none in the walls and there are not even any in the roof. I have satisfied myself of that with Peake. Gleeb, the manager, who was on the spot when the penthouse was built, further assures me of it."

"Only place is floor," Katoh insisted. "Salti man could make this himself."

"He couldn't make a trap-door without leaving at least a minute crack," was Tarrant's counter. "At least I don't see how he could. The flooring of the studio is hardwood, the planks closely fitted together, and I have been over every inch of it. Naturally there are cracks between the planks, lengthwise; but there are no transverse cracks anywhere. Gleeb has shown me the specifications of that floor. The planks are grooved together and it is impossible to raise any plank without splintering the grooving. From my own examination I am sure none of the planks has been, or can be, lifted.

"All this was necessary because there is a space of something like two and a half feet between the floor of the penthouse and the roof of the apartment building proper. One has to mount a couple of steps at the entrance of the penthouse. Furthermore, I have been in part of this space. Let me make it perfectly clear how I got there.

"The bedroom adjoins the studio on the south, and the lavatory occupies the north-west corner of the bedroom. It is walled off, of course. Along the northern wall of the lavatory (which is part of the southern wall of the studio) is the bath-tub; and the part of the flooring under the bath-tub has been cut away, leaving an aperture to the space beneath."

I made my first contribution. "But how can that be? Wouldn't the bath-tub fall through?"

"No. The bath-tub is an old-fashioned one, installed by Saltri himself only a few weeks ago. It is not flush with the floor, as they make them now, but stands on four legs. The flooring has only been cut away in the middle of the tub, say two or three planks, and the opening extended only to the outer edge of the tub. Not quite that far, in fact."

"There is Salti man's trap-door," grinned Katoh. "Not even door; just trap."

"So I thought," Tarrant agreed grimly. "But it isn't. Or if it is he didn't use it. As no one could get through the opening without moving the tub – which hadn't been done, by the way – Peake and I pulled up some more of the cut plank by main force and I squeezed myself into the space beneath the lavatory and bedroom. There was nothing there but dirt; I got plenty of that."

"How about space below studio?"

"Nothing doing. The penthouse is built on a foundation, as I said, about two and a half feet high, of concrete building blocks. A line of these blocks runs underneath the penthouse, directly below the wall between the studio and bedroom. As the aperture in the floor is on the southern side of that wall, it is likewise to the south of the transverse line of building blocks in the foundation. The space beneath the studio is to the north of these blcoks, and they form a solid wall that is impassable. I spent a good twenty minutes scrummaging along the entire length of it."

"Most likely place," Katoh confided, "just where hole in lavatory floor."

"Yes, I should think so too. I examined it carefully. I could see the ends of the planks that form the studio floor partway over the beam above the building blocks. But there isn't a trace of a loose block at that point, any more than there is anywhere else . . . To make everything certain, we also examined the other three sides of the foundation of the bedroom portion of the penthouse. They are solid and haven't been touched since it was constructed. So the whole thing is just a cul-de-sac there is no possibility of exit from the penthouse even through the aperture beneath the bath-tub."

"You examine also foundations under studio part?"

"Yes, we did that, too. No result. It didn't mean much, though, for there is no entrance to the space beneath the studio from the studio itself, nor is there such an entrance from the other space beneath the bedroom portion. That opening under the bath-tub must mean something, especially in view of the recent installation of the tub. But what does it mean?"

He looked at Katoh long and searchingly and the other, after a pause, replied slowly: "Can only see this Salti man construct this trap, probably for present use. Then he do not use. Must go some other way."

"But there is no other way."

"Then Salti man still there."

"He isn't there."

"Harumph," said Katoh reflectively. It was evident that he felt the same respect for a syllogism that animated Tarrant, and was stopped, for the time being at any rate. He went off on a new tack. "What else specially strange about setting?"

"There are two other things that strike me as peculiar," Tarrant answered, and his eyes narrowed. "On the floor, about one foot from the northern window, there is a fairly deep indentation in the floor of the studio. It is a small impression and is almost certainly made by a nail partly driven through the planking and then pulled up again."

I thought of the nail through the picture. "Could he have put the picture down on that part of the floor in order to drive the nail through it? But what if he did?"

"I can see no necessity for it, in any case. The nail would go through the canvas easily enough just as it stood on the easel."

Katoh said: "With nail in plank, perhaps plank could be pulled up. You say no?"

"I tried it. Even driving the nail in sideways, instead of vertically, as the original indentation was made, the plank can't be lifted at all."

"O.K. You say some other thing strange, also."

"Yes. The position of the easel that holds the painting of the dead girl. When we broke in this morning, it was turned away from the room, toward the bedroom door, so that the picture was scarcely visible even from the studio entrance, let alone the rest of the room. I don't believe that was the murderer's intention. He had set the rest of the stage too carefully. The requiem; the candles. It doesn't fit; I'm sure he meant the first person who entered to be confronted by the whole scene, and especially by that symbolic portrait. It doesn't accord even with the position of the stool, which agrees with the intended position of the easel. It doesn't fit at all with the mentality of the murderer. It seems a small thing but I'm sure it's important. I'm certain the position of the easel is an important clue."

"To mystery of disappearance?"

"Yes. To the mystery of the murderer's escape from that sealed room."

"Not see how," Katoh declared after some thought. As for me, I couldn't even appreciate the suggestion of any connection.

"Neither do I," grated Tarrant. He had risen and began to pace the floor. "Well, there you have it all. A little hole in the floor near the north window, an easel turned out of position and a sealed room without an occupant who certainly ought to be there . . . There's an answer to this; damn it, there must be an answer."

Suddenly he glanced at an electric clock on the table he was passing and stopped abruptly. "My word," he exclaimed, "it's nearly three o'clock. Didn't mean to keep you up like this, Jerry. You either, doctor. Well, the conference is over. We've got nowhere."

Katoh was on his feet, in an instant once more the butler. "Sorry could not help. You wish night-cap, Misster Tarrant?"

"No. Bring the Scotch, Katoh. And a siphon. And ice. I'm not turning in."

I had been puzzling my wits without intermission ever since dinner over the problem above, and the break found me more tired than I realised. I yawned prodigiously. I made a half-hearted attempt to persuade Tarrant to come to bed, but it was plain that he would have none of it.

I said, "Good-night, Katoh. I'm no good for anything until I get a little sleep . . . Night, Tarrant."

I left him once more pacing the floor; his face, in the last glimpse I had of it, was set in the stern lines of thought.

It seemed no more than ten seconds after I got into bed that I felt my shoulder being shaken and, through the fog of sleep, heard Katoh's hissing accents. " – Mister Tarrant just come from penthouse. He excited. Maybe you wish wake up." As I rolled out and shook myself free from slumber, I noticed that my wrist watch pointed to six-thirty.

When I had thrown on some clothes and come into the living-room, I found Tarrant standing with the telephone instrument to his head, his whole posture one of grimness. Although I did not realise it at once, he had been endeavouring for some time to reach Deputy Inspector Peake. He accomplished this finally a moment or so after I reached the room.

"Hallo, Peake? Inspector Peake? . . . This is Tarrant. How many men did you leave to guard that penthouse last night?" . . . "What, only one? But I said two, man. Damn it all, I don't make suggestions like that for amusement!" . . . "All right, there's nothing to be accomplished arguing about it. You'd better get here, and get here pronto." . . . "That's all I'll say." He slammed down the receiver viciously.

I had never before seen Tarrant upset; my surprise was a measure of his own disturbance, which resembled consternation. He paced the floor, muttering below his breath, his long legs carrying him swiftly up and down the apartment.

"Damned fools . . . everything must fit . . . Or else . . ." For once I had sense enough to keep my questions to myself for the time being.

Fortunately I had not long to wait. Hardly had Katoh had opportunity to brew some coffee, with which he appeared somewhat in the manner of a dog wagging its tail deprecatingly, than Peake's ring sounded at the entrance. He came in hurriedly but his smile, as well as his words, indicated his opinion that he had been roused by a false alarm.

"Well, well, Mr Tarrant, what is this trouble over?"

Tarrant snapped, "Your man's gone. Disappeared. How do you like that?"

"The patrolman on guard?" The policeman's expression was incredulous.

"The *single* patrolman you left on guard."

Peake stepped over to the telephone, called Headquarters. After a few brief words he turned back to us, his incredulity at Tarrant's statement apparently confirmed.

"You must be mistaken, sir," he asserted. "There have been no reports from Officer Weber. He would never leave the premises without reporting such an occasion."

Tarrant's answer was purely practical. "Come and see."

And when we reached the terrace on the building's roof, there was, in fact, no sign of the patrolman who should have been at his station. We entered the penthouse and, the lights having been turned on, Peake himself made a complete search of the premises. While Tarrant watched the proceedings in a grim silence, I walked over to the north window of the studio, grey in the early morning light, and sought for the nail hole he had mentioned as being in the floor. There it was, a small, clean indentation, about an inch or an inch and a half deep, in one of the hardwood planks. This, and everything else about the place, appeared just as Tarrant had described it to us some hours before, previous to my turning in. I was just in time to see Peake emerge from the enlarged opening in the lavatory floor, dusty and sorely puzzled.

"Our man is certainly not here," the inspector acknowledged. "I cannot understand it. This is a serious breach of discipline."

"Hell," said Tarrant sharply, speaking for the first time since we had come to the roof. "This is a serious breach of intelligence, not discipline."

"I shall broadcast an immediate order for the detention of Patrolman Weber." Peake stepped into the bedroom and approached the phone to carry out his intention.

"You needn't broadcast it. I have already spoken to the night operator in the lobby on the ground floor. He told me a policeman left the building in great haste about 3:30 this morning. If you will have the local precinct check up on the all-night lunch-rooms along Lexington Avenue in this vicinity, you will soon pick up the first step of the trail that man left . . . You will probably take my advice, now that it is too late."

Peake did so, putting the call through at once; but his bewilderment was no whit lessened. Nor was mine. As he put down the instrument, he said: "All right. But it doesn't make sense. Why should he leave his post without notifying us? And why should he go to a lunch-room?"

"Because he was hungry."

"But there has been a crazy murderer here already. And now Weber, an ordinary cop, if I ever saw one. Does this place make everybody mad?"

"Not as mad as you're going to be in a minute. But perhaps you weren't using the word in that sense?"

Peake let it pass. "Everything," he commented slowly, "is just as we left it yesterday evening. Except for Weber's disappearance."

"Is that so?" Tarrant led us to the entrance from the roof to the studio and pointed downwards. The light was now bright enough to disclose an unmistakable spattering of blood on one of the steps before the door. "That blood wasn't there when we left last night. I came up here about five-thirty, the moment I got on to this thing," he continued bitterly. "Of course I was too late . . . Damnation, let us make an end to this farce. I'll show you some more things that have altered during the night."

We followed him into the studio again as he strode over to the easel with its lewd picture, opposite the entrance. He pointed to the nail still protruding through the canvas. "I don't know how closely you observed the hole made in this painting by the nail yesterday. But it's a little larger now and the edges are more frayed. In other words the nail has been removed and once more inserted."

I turned about to find that Gleeb, somehow apprised of the excitement, had entered the penthouse and now stood a little behind us. Tarrant acknowledged his presence with a curt nod; and in the air of tension that his tenant was building up the manager ventured no questions.

"Now," Tarrant continued, pointing out the locations as he spoke, "possibly they have dried, but when I first got here this morning there was a trail of moist spots still leading from the entrance door way to the vicinity of the north window. You will find that they were places where a trail of blood had been wiped away with a wet cloth."

He turned to the picture beside him and withdrew the nail, pulling himself up as if for a repugnant job. He walked over to the north window and motioned us to take our places on either side of him. Then he bent down and inserted the nail, point first, into the indentation in the plank, as firmly as he could. He braced himself and apparently strove to pull the nail toward the south, away from the window.

I was struggling with an obvious doubt. I said, "But you told us the planks could not be lifted."

"Can't," Tarrant grunted. "But they can be *slid*."

Under his efforts the plank was, in fact, sliding. Its end appeared from under the footboard at the base of the north wall below the window and continued to move over a space of several feet. When this had been accomplished, he grasped the edges of the planks on both sides of the one already moved and slid them back also. An opening quite large enough to squeeze through was revealed.

But that was not all. The huddled body of a man lay just beneath; the man was clad only in underwear and was obviously dead from the beating in of his head.

As we bent over, gasping at the unexpectedly gory sight, Gleeb suddenly cried, "But that is not Michael Salti! What is this, a murder farm? I don't know this man."

Inspector Peake's voice was ominous with anger. "I do. That is the body of Officer Weber. But how could he—"

Tarrant had straightened up and was regarding us with a look that said plainly he was anxious to get an unpleasant piece of work finished. "It was simple enough," he ground out. "Salti cut out the planks beneath the bath-tub in the lavatory so that *these* planks in the studio could be slid back over the beam along the foundation under the south wall; their farther ends in this position will now be covering the hole in the lavatory floor. The floor here is well fitted and the planks are grooved, thus making the sliding possible. They can be moved back into their original position by someone in the space below here; doubtless we shall find a small block nailed to the under portion of all three planks for that purpose.

"He murdered his model, set the scene and started his phonograph, which will run interminably on the electric current. Then he crawled into his hiding-place. The discovery of the crime could not be put off any later than the chambermaid's visit in the morning, and I have no doubt he took a sadistic pleasure in anticipating her hysterics when she entered. By chance your radio man, Gleeb, caused us to enter first.

"When the place was searched and the murderer not discovered, his pursuit passed elsewhere, while he himself lay concealed here all day. It was even better than doubling back upon his tracks, for he had never left the starting post. Eventually, of course, he had to get out, but by that time the vicinity of this building would be the last place in which he was being searched for.

"Early this morning he pushed back the planks from underneath and came forth. I don't know whether he had expected anyone to be left on guard, but that helped rather than hindered him. Creeping up upon the unsuspecting guard, he knocked him out – doubtless with that mallet I can just see beside the body – and beat him to death. Then he put his second victim in the hiding-place, returning the instrument that closes it from above, the nail, to its position in the painting. He had already stripped off his own clothes, which you will find down in that hole, and in the officer's uniform and coat he found no difficulty in leaving the building. His first action was to hurry to a lunch-room, naturally, since after a day and a night without food under the floor here, he must have been famished. I have no doubt that your men will get a report of him along Lexington Avenue, Peake; but, even so, he now has some hours' start on you."

"We'll get him," Peake assured us. "But if you knew all this, why in heaven's name didn't you have this place opened up last night, before he had any chance to commit a second murder? We should have taken him red-handed."

"Yes, but I didn't know it last night," Tarrant reminded him. "It was not until late yesterday afternoon that I had any proper opportunity to examine the penthouse. What I found was a sealed room and a sealed house. There was no exit that had not been blocked nor, after our search, could I understand how the man could still be in the penthouse. On the other hand, I could not understand how it was possible that he had left. As a precaution, in case he were still here in some manner I had not fathomed, I urged you to leave at least two men on guard, and it was my under-standing that you agreed. I think it is obvious, although I was unable then to justify myself, that the precaution was called for."

Peake said, "It was."

"I have been up all night working this out. What puzzled me completely was the absence of any trap doors. Certainly we looked for them thoroughly. But it was there right in front of us all the time; we even investigated a portion of it, the aperture in the lavatory floor, which we supposed to be a trap-door itself, although actually it was only a part of the real arrangement. As usual the trick was based upon taking advantage of habits of thought, of our habitised notion of a trap-door as something that is lifted or swung back. I have never heard before of a trap-door that slides back. Nevertheless, that was the simple answer, and it took me until five-thirty to reach it."

Katoh, whom for the moment I had forgotten completely, stirred uneasily and spoke up. "I not see, Misster Tarrant, how you reach answer then."

"Four things," was the reply. "First of all, the logical assumption that, since there was no way out, the man was still here. As to the mechanism by which he managed to remain undiscovered, three things. We mentioned them last night. First, the nail hole in the plank; second, the position of the easel; third, the hole in the lavatory floor. I tried many ways to make them fit together, for I felt sure they must *all* fit.

"It was the position of the easel that finally gave me the truth. You remember we agreed that it was wrong, that the murderer had never intended to leave it facing away from the room. But if the murderer had left it as he intended, if no one had entered until we did, and still its position was wrong, what could have moved it in the meantime? Except for the phonograph, which could scarcely be responsible, the room held nothing but motionless objects. *But if the floor under one of its legs had moved, the easel would have been slid around.* That fitted with the other two items, the nail hole in the plank, the opening under the bath-tub.

"The moment it clicked, I got an automatic and ran up here. I was too late. As I said, I've been up all night. I'm tired; and I'm going to bed."

He walked off without another word, scarcely with a parting nod. Tarrant, as know now, did not often fail. He was a man who offered few excuses for himself and he was humiliated.

It was a week or so later when I had an opportunity to ask him if Salti had been captured. I had seen nothing of it in the newspapers, and the case had now passed to the back pages with the usual celerity of sensations.

Tarrant said, "I don't know."

"But haven't you followed it up with that man, Peake?"

"I'm not interested. It's nothing but a straight police chase now. This part of it might make a good film for a Hollywood audience, but there isn't the slightest intellectual interest left."

He stopped and added after an appreciable pause, "Damn it, Jerry, I don't like to think of it even now. I've blamed the stupidity of the police all I can; their throwing me out when I might have made a real investigation in the morning, that delay; their the negligence in overlooking my suggestion for a pair of guards, which I made as emphatic as I could. But it's no use. I should have solved it in time, even so. There could only be that one answer and I took too long to find it.

"The human brain works too slowly, Jerry, even when it works straight . . . it works too slowly."

The Impossible Murder
of Dr Satanus

William Krohn

William Krohn (b. 1945) has the distinction of being the youngest writer represented in this collection. Youngest, that is, at the time he wrote the following story: he was eighteen when he submitted it to Ellery Queen's Mystery Magazine *where it appeared a little over a year later. Krohn had read his first detective novel a couple of years earlier:* John Dickson's Carr's *masterpiece of the impossible* The Three Coffins, *and he was hooked. Needless to say the following story is heavily influenced by Carr, but you might as well learn from the best. Krohn wrote a second similar story which was rejected as too complex, and he moved on to other fields. He has since become a noted film critic and an expert on the work of Alfred Hitchcock, including the study* Hitchcock at Work *(2003). He is also Director of Creative Services for the Commercial Film Division of New Galaxy Enterprises and the editor of the online webzine* RocketsAway. *The following is where it all started.*

The policeman was thinking about magic.

It was a strange thought for a policeman to have, but even his superiors might have forgiven him on an evening like this. It was late August, and a velvet-dark midsummer night had descended on the streets of the city. On this particular street, with its big comfortable homes and airy lawns turning from green to black in the smoky twilight, the darkness seemed to sing with a kind of summer magic that even a policeman can feel.

But Lieutenant-Detective Jerry Doran was thinking of another kind of magic – the kind which involves playing cards and white rabbits, bouquets of flowers that burst from nowhere and beautiful ladies who vanish at the wave of a silver wand. This kind of magic had somehow got loose from the safe confines of the stage and was causing Lieutenant Doran a severe occupational headache; and now he was ringing the doorbell of the one man who might help him – a man who did not believe in magic at all.

"Sometimes I think," said Richard Sheilan as he ushered his guest into the living room, "that it takes a murder to make you come visiting. Your soul is Machiavellian, Jerry. You should have been a politician."

"I should have been an astronaut," Doran said feelingly, "or a short-order cook. Anything but a policeman."

"Tch-tch," said Sheilan. He stepped over to the liquor cabinet and extracted a bottle and two glasses. "Those were sympathetic noises," he explained, "the kind I reserve for my un-retired friends. But I take it from what you said over the phone that you want more than commiseration." He handed Doran a glass. "What is it this time, Jerry? Murder, of course."

It had been a number of years since Sheilan had retired from police work and moved into his new home. He seemed quite at ease here in this large cream-colored room, as he hunched a little in his monstrous black armchair.

Sheilan was a very big man – not tall and wiry like Doran – but built on a huge scale. He stood well over six feet, on disproportionately long legs; he was big-boned and slender, with ropy-veined wrists and impressively broad shoulders. He had a ruddy complexion and what might be called ruddy hair – red-tinted where it had not already silvered with age. For all his quietness of manner he cut an imposing figure, and small people with loud voices rarely felt comfortable in his presence. He was quiet now, and the hazel eyes watched his friend's face attentively.

"It's murder," Doran affirmed. "I'm surprised you haven't read about it in the papers. It's been getting front-page coverage ever since it broke this morning."

"I don't read the papers," Sheilan said simply. "What sort of case do you mean?"

"A screwy one. The kind," Doran said with a trace of malice, "that we save for our un-retired friends." Sheilan snorted as Doran went on, "Mr Charles Kimball was killed early this morning in a downtown hotel. During the few seconds that the murder must have taken place, he was alone in an elevator car where no living soul could have come near him. And yet he was murdered."

Sheilan sighed. "You've hooked me, Jerry," he said. "Now I suggest that you begin at the beginning, omit the melodrama, and tell a straight story." Doran looked belligerent. "Suppose you begin with the victim – Mr Kimball."

"All right," said Doran. "Mr Charles Kimball. What do you think Mr Charles Kimball was?"

Sheilan shut his eyes. "A sorcerer," he intoned. "A student of occult mysteries who tampered with forces beyond his control—"

"Bingo!" said Doran. "Got it the first guess. Charles Kimball was a professional magician, a stage illusionist – and a damn good one, from what I hear."

Settling back in his chair, the policeman began to tell the story . . .

Standing in the arctic glare of the blue spotlight, draped like a statue in the black robes of his profession, the magician looked for all the world like the lanky personification of some ancient plague. The skin of his hands was the color of snow, and a madman's shock of white hair, tied with a thin ribbon, crowned his skull; his mouth was like a black sore.

Earlier in the evening the stage had been crowded with gaudy apparatus – coffin-like boxes for sawing a woman in half and cabinets for making her vanish like a puff of smoke. Now the magician stood alone under the spotlight. With a creative gesture of his cupped hands he produced a single white dove which perched for a moment on his arm and then flew away. Then another appeared, and another and another – until it seemed as if there were a hundred of them fluttering around the weirdly lit stage.

The magician was billed as Dr Satanus; he was, of course, none other than Mr Charles Kimball, an entertainer whose checkered career had embraced everything from tightrope acrobatics to cardsharping, from juggling to escape artistry. Somewhere along the line he had married a chorus girl named Margaret Linden and incorporated her into the act as his assistant. Now, after more hard work and disappointment than he cared to remember, Charles

Kimball was at the peak of his career.

Backstage, the Dr Satanus troupe was getting ready to go home – home tonight being three scattered rooms in the Hotel Bowman, a second-rate theatrical establishment just off Broadway. Leo Gurney, a wiry little man with a head of curly black hair and a monkey-ugly face, was leaning against a pile of flats and tinkering with an obscure bit of machinery; in addition to his duties as stage manager, Gurney was Kimball's right-hand man, the mechanical genius who designed and built all the illusions in the show.

There was also Dave Hooker, promotion manager and Jack-of-all-trades – presently off somewhere picking up coffee and sandwiches for a late-night snack. And, of course, there was Margaret Kimball, a still-young woman with a face and figure which could only be described in metaphors of fruit, flowers, and heavenly beings. Still dressed in her Satanic red costume, she stood in the wings and watched the finish of the dove illusion. The curtain came down to a good round of applause, and Charles Kimball swept past, gleamingly spectral in his stage trappings.

It had been a routine performance. However, one thing happened a little later that was out of the ordinary. A few minutes after the curtain dropped, Dave Hooker reappeared, a fair-haired, innocuous young man with an armful of paper bags from some nearby diner, which he quickly distributed. With one bag left over, he went to the door of Kimball's dressing room, rapped once, and stuck in his head.

Charles Kimball started up out of his chair, his hand darting instinctively for something hidden in the dressing-table drawer. Seeing Hooker, he seemed to collect himself; he said something pleasant in reply to a question only half heard, but his hand still hovered over the drawer.

When Hooker had gone, Kimball reached inside and took out a worn-looking .32 automatic. He gripped it tightly, seeming to draw comfort from it. But his hand still shook, and when he looked at his face in the mirror he saw fear as plainly as if the word had been written there in phosphorescent letters . . .

The lobby of a hotel is seldom an inspiring sight. The lobby of the Hotel Bowman at seven o'clock on this particular morning was no exception. It was small, and it was dirty; the fake marble linoleum wasn't fooling anybody.

There were never many people loitering about, especially this early in the morning. Now there were only two: the sandy-haired, shirt-sleeved desk clerk and a fat well-dressed man who looked like a hog. The latter, it appeared, was waiting for someone. He had strolled in and plumped himself down a few minutes before, and now he sat quietly scanning his morning newspaper and eyeing the elevator.

As it happened, the desk clerk was also watching the elevator, which had gone up a few minutes before and was now presumably descending. He watched because he was curious about the hoggish gentleman, and because he had nothing else to do. This was important, because it meant that there were two witnesses to what happened next.

Both men heard the bump of the arriving car, and the hoggish gentleman rose from his seat, depositing the newspaper behind him like an egg. Then the elevator doors rolled open and they both saw that the only occupant of the car was lying down. Startled, the clerk moved around in front of his desk to get a closer look, and suddenly something turned over in his stomach. There was a ragged tear in the man's coat, and something dark staining the fabric.

The next thing he knew, the desk clerk was standing at the elevator doors watching dazedly as the hoggish gentleman lowered himself beside the body. He touched nothing, but he surveyed the scene as if fixing it in his mind. Then he rose with difficulty and turned to the white-faced clerk. His own face might have been stuffed with sawdust, for all the emotion it betrayed.

"My name is Bailey," the hoggish man said, flipping out some sort of identification. "I'm a private detective, I'll stay here while you call the police." The clerk's oyster eyes blinked. "Call the Homicide Squad," the fat man added ominously.

The body on the floor of the elevator was that of Charles Kimball, and – let it be said now – he was dead before the elevator doors opened . . .

"We'll begin," said Doran, "with the elevator." He leaned forward, folding his hands under his chin like a preacher meditating before a sermon.

"First, Mrs Kimball's testimony. She says that her husband was up early this morning, around six-thirty, and that he woke her up at about the same time. He shaved and showered and dressed, talking at some length about a mysterious appointment, but refusing to answer any of her questions. She says he looked worried, that he'd been acting a little odd all week – nervous and scared. Just before he left he said something that frightened her. He said, quote: 'I'm going to see a man who knows secrets.'"

Sheilan said nothing. Doran went on, "Kimball's appointment was for seven o'clock. He was already late when he left – Mrs K. glanced at his watch, when he asked her for it and she handed it to him, and saw that it was just after seven.

"The elevator was directly across from the Kimballs' room, which is on the eleventh floor. Mrs Kimball followed her husband to the elevator door and stood there watching him as he pushed the button for the car, got in, and started down. Since she had her own reasons, which I'll get to in a minute, for being worried about this mysterious appointment, she watched the floor indicator over the door, and she swears that he went straight down to the lobby *without making any stops*.

"Fortunately for Mrs K., we have a second witness, a celebrity-conscious maid who was in the hall at the time and recognized Kimball. We have her corroborative testimony that he was alive when he got into the car, and that he went straight down to the lobby without making any stops."

Doran's voice became grim. "In the lobby," he said, "there was a man named Bailey, a licensed investigator for the Powell Detective Agency. Now, the Powell Agency is one of the finest in the city, and Bailey is one of their best men. He was in the lobby because he was waiting for Kimball; he had an appointment to meet him there at seven and turn over evidence which Kimball had hired him to collect. The evidence was to be used in divorce proceedings against Kimball's wife."

Sheilan smiled, but still said nothing, "There was also a desk clerk," Doran said, "a man named Boyd. Both men were watching when the elevator reached the lobby with Kimball, dead of a knife wound in the back. They both saw it; there cannot be the slightest doubt. The inevitable conclusion—"

"– is that Kimball was killed between the time he got into the elevator on the eleventh floor and the time the car arrived in the lobby," said Sheilan. "I think you've established that. How long would it take the car to make the descent?"

"About forty-five seconds. The timing checks. Mrs Kimball says it was a little after seven when her husband left their room. Bailey noted the time on the clock in the lobby when the car arrived; it was exactly 7:03.

"Now there were two ways for someone to get into that car while it was traveling between floors – through the inner car-doors or through the escape panel in the ceiling. But both ways have been definitely ruled out.

"The inner doors of the car are solid steel. As long as the car is in motion, those doors are automatically held locked in place: the car can move only so long as the inner doors remain closed. Since the car never stopped, no one could have gotten through them; for all practical purposes they were welded shut.

"The second means of entrance is also eliminated. The escape panel is a simple trap door installed at the top of most elevators as an emergency exit. Normally, it would have been possible for someone to drop through there, catch Kimball by surprise, and kill him before he had a chance to resist. But about a year ago one of the hotel's younger guests went climbing up through this hatch and nearly got himself squashed in the elevator mechanism. The management decided on the lesser of two evils and had the trap door padlocked – from the inside.

"So you see where that leaves us. No one could have gotten through the trap door to kill Kimball; and even if he did, he couldn't have gotten out again and left the hatch as it was found, padlocked on the inside. Unless we postulate a kind of Dr Fu Manchu elevator containing a secret passage, there was no way in and no way out. It's an absolutely impossible crime!"

"I suppose," said Sheilan, "that you've ruled out the possibility of suicide?"

"Unquestionably. For one thing, no weapon was found in the car. For another, the nature of the wounds was such that they could not have been self-inflicted. There were actually three wounds – two shallow gashes on the left arm and one deep stab wound under the left shoulder blade, penetrating straight to the heart. The blade that was used was over six inches long and about half an inch wide. Very sharp."

Reaching into his pocket, the policeman pulled out a gun, nickel-plated with a yellowed ivory grip. He said, "We found this gun lying on the floor by the body. It's a Colt .32 automatic, equipped with a hair-trigger and–" he produced a stubby black cylinder and clipped it on the muzzle. "– a Maxim silencer. Not the sort of thing I'd care to come up against in an enclosed space as small as an elevator car." He handed the gun over for Sheilan's inspection.

"I suppose," said Sheilan, "this is Kimball's own gun."

"It's his, all right – his wife identified it positively. She found it last week, hidden under a pile of underwear. He has a permit to own one, but he hasn't carried a gun in years. But from what we've heard from other members of the troupe, Kimball had been acting funny all week – nervous, as if he were afraid of his own shadow. And the gun, as I pointed out, was recently acquired. It all ties in with the theory that Kimball knew he was in danger and carried this to protect himself. And the gun was never fired – he didn't even have time to pull the trigger."

"Hmm," said Sheilan. "Did this notion of impending doom have anything to do with the assignment he gave to the private detective?"

"No. Kimball saw Bailey only once – three weeks ago when the magic show first came to town. He hired Bailey to do some unobtrusive prying into Mrs Kimball's relations with Leo Gurney."

"Aha!" said Sheilan, twirling an imaginary mustache.

"Well, now," said Doran, "Margaret Kimball is no Lady Macbeth, but she's good-looking enough to stir up plenty of homicidal intentions in a close-knit little theatrical family like this one. What's more, Gurney is a first-rate mechanic with a good working knowledge of abracadabra and Hop-o-my-Thumb – modern style. And just to round things out, Gurney's got a record. Before joining up with Kimball he served time for armed robbery. Would he commit murder to get a troublesome husband out of the way? He'd naturally be cautious, with his record, but I still wouldn't put it past him."

"Undeniable possibility," said Sheilan. "I wonder that he isn't locked up in a cell already."

"Two reasons," said Doran. "One: I'm not arresting anyone until I know how that elevator trick was worked. Two: I've been building a case against a straw dummy. Gurney had no more motive to kill Kimball than I do. Private eye Bailey dropped a bombshell – it seems that Kimball was barking up the wrong tree. His wife *was* playing around – but not with Gurney."

"Dave Hooker?"

"Correct. By process of elimination. It's not too surprising when you come to think about it. Hooker is good-looking, in a fuzzy sort of way. But he has a way of making himself – well, sort of invisible; it takes a real effort of concentration to pay attention to him when he talks. So it's really no wonder that Kimball picked the wrong man."

"Did Bailey communicate his discovery to his client?"

"No. Bailey's instructions were to avoid any contact until seven this morning, at which time he planned to present his evidence and watch Kimball's jaw drop. But somebody got to Kimball before he did."

Sheilan raised his eyebrows. "The question being – who? Whom do you favor, Jerry? The so-called Invisible Man, with his shining motive? Leo Gurney, with his sinister past? Or Margaret Kimball, with her ironclad alibi? How did they stand up under questioning?"

"A more nerveless bunch of suspects I never saw," said Doran, "I questioned them individually and collectively for three solid hours without extracting one useful piece of information. Hooker and his lady friend expressed no regrets about their activities; she remained calm the whole time, and he was even helpful. Suggested I look for some way the knife could have been fired like a bullet from a gun—" Doran made vague, harpoon-like gestures "– and reeled back on a string through one of the air vents in the car. I informed him that the air vents were covered with a fine wire mesh which showed no signs of tampering; he shrugged and grinned and looked *oh* so apologetic.

"Gurney grinned the whole time, like a damned orangutan. Volunteered nothing, swore he'd never had a thing to do with Kimball's wife, and didn't bat an eye when I brought up the little matter of his record." Doran grimaced and took a pull at his drink. "Dead end," he said, "to an embarrassing afternoon. Bailey sat in on the whole interrogation, wooden-faced as a cigar-store Indian. I gather that his opinion of the abilities of the force have been confirmed in spades." But then Doran saw that his host wasn't listening.

Sheilan had moved from his chair and was standing in front of one of the big windows. Outside, the twilight had vanished and been replaced by blind darkness.

Doran was silent for a moment. Then he said, "Well, the force is asking for a second opinion. What do you make of it?"

Sheilan turned and looked at him speculatively. "I make a great deal of it," he said, "Before I can be sure, you'll have to answer three questions."

"Three questions," said Doran, settling back, "Fire away."

"One: can you tell me what floor of the hotel each of the three suspects was staying on?"

Silently Doran pulled out his notebook and consulted it. "The Kimballs had a room on the eleventh floor," he said. "Gurney and Hooker had single rooms on the ninth and fifth floors, respectively."

"Excellent," said Sheilan. "Question Number Two: can you tell me something more about the elevator? The outer doors – not what you called the inner doors, but the ones on the various floors – how can they be opened?"

"They open automatically, of course, when the elevator comes to rest at each floor. When the elevator is on some other floor, they can be opened from the outside with a key, and from the inside by exerting pressure on a lock-bar—"

"And Question Number Three," Sheilan interrupted, rubbing his palms together. "Is there a laundry chute?"

Doran blinked. "I'll have to use your phone," he said. And a few minutes later, in a brief conversation with the hotel manager, Doran established that there was no laundry chute in the Hotel Bowman.

Sheilan seemed satisfied. "Just a frill," he explained, "but a possibility that had to be considered. If there had been a laundry chute, it would have spoiled the logical symmetry of my deductions."

"I'm listening," said Doran.

"I should hope you would be," said Sheilan. "Now, to begin with, you will have noticed the imprint of a magician on this murder. A very special kind of legerdemain was required to bring off the elevator trick. Does that suggest anything to you?"

"Not much," said Doran. "Our suspects are really a trio of magicians. Leo Gurney knows every trick of the trade, so does Dave Hooker, and for that matter, so does Margaret Kimball, who was her husband's assistant for a number of years – although as you pointed out she *does* have an ironclad alibi."

"Now that you mention it," said Sheilan, "there's a very close resemblance between the Problem of the Hermetically Sealed Room and the Problem of the Ironclad Alibi. No, I'm not talking about Margaret Kimball – not, for that matter, any of your trio of magician-suspects."

"Do you mean there's someone else? A fourth magician?"

"Precisely. A fourth magician who has played the Invisible Man much better than Dave Hooker and completely eluded your hawklike instincts. Someone who had a better motive for murder than Margaret Kimball, Dave Hooker, and Leo Gurney all rolled into one. Someone who is apparently safe from suspicion—"

"Bailey!" breathed Doran. "The one person—"

"Bailey!" Sheilan let out a snort. "Let's not be fantastic! He and the desk clerk alibi each other. No, the person I am referring to is safe from suspicion for a very convincing reason – he happens to be dead. That's right, the person I'm talking about is Charles Kimball."

"I see," said Doran slowly.

"No, I'm afraid you don't," said Sheilan, "It's a complicated business. Charles Kimball is dead, but he is still the only murderer we have to deal with. Jerry, you've been holding this puzzle upside down.

"Suppose I take it from the beginning and reconstruct. Didn't it strike you as strange that Kimball should carry a gun with a *silencer*? If he were carrying a gun for protection against a person or persons unspecified, surely he'd *want* noise, wouldn't he? He'd have nothing to hide; on the contrary, he'd want people to hear the shots and come running to help him, wherever and whenever he was attacked. No, the silencer indicated a guiltier purpose."

"I see what you mean," said Doran. "You mean *Kimball* was going to commit a murder."

"Exactly," said Sheilan, "and all that abracadabra with the elevator was arranged *by* Kimball – to give himself an alibi. But that alibi backfired and presented you with an impossible situation.

"The person Kimball was planning to murder was obviously the man he suspected of being his wife's lover – Leo Gurney. He had no way of knowing, of course, that Dave Hooker was really the culprit, and that he was planning to kill the wrong man."

"But if that was the case," said Doran, "why didn't he wait for confirmation from Bailey?"

"Two reasons. First, because it would look better for Kimball if the murder took place *before* he received confirmation from Bailey. That was why he instructed Bailey to avoid making contact with him before the time set for the appointment. Who would suspect that a man would hire a detective to investigate his wife's infidelity and then murder the lover even before the investigator made his report? The second reason is more important: Bailey wasn't hired as a detective at all; he was hired as part of the murder plan –

because Kimball needed an unsuspecting, unimpeachable witness for his alibi.

"Kimball knew he would be suspected immediately if Gurney were found murdered, so he set about creating a foolproof alibi. He did it the same way he would create an illusion for his show, making full use of his talents as an acrobat and escape artist.

"The crux of your impossible situation, you see, is that you were looking at it the wrong way. It was a closed circle with no way for a murderer to get *in*, but the circle could be broken if the 'victim' got *out*.

"The plan was probably suggested to him when he saw that the elevator door on the eleventh floor was directly across from his room. His first step was to hire Bailey and arrange for him to be waiting in the lobby on the morning of the murder. Then he acquired a gun and waited. The telltale symptoms of nervousness which were so widely misinterpreted were just that – the nervousness of a man about to engage in the most dangerous of enterprises – committing a murder.

"When he came back to the hotel last night, he did two things. First, he picked the padlock on the trap door and left it open, arranging the lock so that it would appear as usual to any ordinary inspection. Then, before he went to bed, he set his watch ahead about fifteen minutes.

"He got up early this morning and deliberately awakened his wife so that she would testify that she'd been with him from, say, 6:30 to 7:02. He asked her to hand him the watch so that the false time would be fixed in her mind. Kimball actually left the room a good ten minutes *before* seven, not a few minutes after.

"He was certain she would be sufficiently curious about his hints of 'secrets' to follow him to the elevator door and try to get some idea of where he was going. And so she watched the indicator and saw that he went straight down to the lobby.

"Or rather, the *car* traveled straight down. The escape panel was already open; all Kimball had to do was climb through and stay perched on top of the car. The car reached the lobby, but it seemed to arrive empty, and Bailey, the carefully planted witness, noticed nothing.

"In the meantime, Kimball stepped from the roof of the car up to the second floor – a short enough distance – forced the outer door in the manner you indicated was possible, and got out. Then he simply turned around, pushed the button for the elevator again, and rode back up to the ninth floor to complete his plan. On the way up he erased any traces of the deception by setting his watch back and padlocking the trap door again.

"The rest was simple. He picked the lock of Gurney's door, stepped inside, intending to put a bullet through Gurney's head. It was still early in the morning and Kimball, expecting his victim would still be asleep, did not even consider the possibility of encountering resistance. By the time he'd get back to the elevator and ride down to meet Bailey, no more than ten minutes would have elapsed.

"Bailey would be waiting with the evidence which presumably would confirm his suspicions of Gurney. Kimball could then play the outraged husband and ask Bailey to accompany him to Gurney's room and stage a confrontation.

"And what would they find in Gurney's room? Gurney with a bullet in his head. To Bailey's professional eye it would be clear that Gurney had been killed only minutes before. And Kimball would have an indisputable alibi. From 6:30 to 7:02 he had been with his wife in their room. At 7:02 he had left his wife and ridden straight down to meet Bailey, who would then supply him with the rest of his alibi. In short, it would be an illusion – exactly the kind of production by which Kimball made his living and on which he would be perfectly willing to stake his life. If the illusion succeeded, he would have gotten away with murder.

"But, unfortunately for Kimball, the magician paid more attention to the mechanics of the illusion than to the mechanics of the murder itself. What must have happened when Kimball got to Leo Gurney's room seems clear enough. Kimball went there to kill Gurney, but because of stupidity, jitters, or just plain bad luck the attempt backfired and Kimball died instead.

"We can infer that, for some reason or other, Leo Gurney was not asleep when Kimball got to his room; if he had been, he would be dead now, not Kimball. And it certainly seems likely, judging from his record, that Gurney was a man who knew how to protect himself, that he would be able to get the gun away from his attacker before he had a chance to fire. Then again, it would be very much in character for a man like Gurney to carry some sort of weapon – a switchblade knife, say, that could cause a wound like the one which killed Kimball.

"So Kimball is disarmed, but he is still determined. He attacks with his bare hands, overcomes Gurney – a much smaller man –

and begins to choke the life out of him. Gurney manages to pull out his knife, and using his right hand he hacks twice at Kimball's left arm in an attempt to dislodge his grip. Then, in desperation, and as they are struggling, Gurney aims to kill, burying the blade in his opponent's back. Kimball died instantly.

"All speculation, of course, but soundly based on the known facts. The next part, however, is a logical certainty. Gurney has a choice to make: he can plead self-defense or he can try to conceal the crime. Since he has remained silent, we know that he must have panicked and chosen the more dangerous second course. Once he had made his decision, he was faced with one inescapable necessity – to get rid of the body, as soon as possible.

"If the body were found, not just in his room but anywhere on the ninth floor of the hotel, where he alone of the Satanus troupe was staying, it would be extremely dangerous for him. But how was he to get rid of it? Carry it up two flights of stairs to Kimball's floor, or down four flights to Hooker's floor? Any trip up or down the stairway, carrying a bulky corpse, would be much too risky. A laundry chute in the hall would have been safer – but there was no such chute.

"There was only one other possibility, and that was, as luck would have it, the easiest of all: the self-service elevator. Gurney acted quickly. He made sure the coast was clear, lugged the corpse to the elevator, pressed the button for the car, dumped the body in, and sent the car down to the lobby.

"Bear in mind that Gurney knew nothing of Kimball's planned alibi for himself, or of the witness waiting in the lobby; he was simply disposing of the body as quickly and as safely as he could. But the result turned into a perfect illusion. A little over ten minutes had elapsed since Kimball said goodbye to his wife, his first witness, and stepped into the elevator on the eleventh floor. Now it was two or three minutes past seven, and the elevator was on its way to the lobby and its rendezvous with Bailey, the second witness, who would assume the car had just come from the eleventh floor. The closed circle was complete; the incontrovertible alibi was forged. The only discrepancy was that Gurney, the intended victim, was alive, while Kimball, the murderer, was dead."

"Well," Doran exploded, "I'll be a double-dyed prestidigitator!"

Sheilan shrugged modestly. "It's not really so amazing. Once you tumble to the significance of the silencer on the gun, the rest follows inevitably from the logic of the so-called 'impossible situation'."

Doran grinned. "I suppose, in keeping with hoary tradition, the wise old detective will now insist that it was all the work of a celestial Fifth Magician who stood back in the shadows, invisible and omniscient, pulling the strings—"

"Oh, yes," said Sheilan, "I believe in that, most definitely. Fate does work startling tricks at times. In fact," he said, smiling, "that's the only kind of magic I do believe in."

The Stuart Sapphire

Peter Tremayne

Peter Tremayne (b. 1943) is best known for his series of historical mystery novels set in seventh century Europe and featuring Sister Fidelma. The first of them was Absolution by Murder *(1994) and you will find several impossible mysteries amongst the novels and stories. Under his real name, Peter Berresford Ellis is a noted Celtic scholar, author of such books as* The History of the Irish Working Class *(1972),* The Celtic Dawn *(1993) and* The Ancient World of the Celts *(1999). He has also written biographies of the authors H. Rider Haggard, W. E. Johns and Talbot Mundy. The following story features a puzzle involving the last of the Stuart Pretenders to the throne of Great Britain.*

A full-grown man in the grip of uncontrolled panic is not a pleasant sight. Worse still, was the sight of His Majesty, James II, King of England, Scotland and Ireland, Duke of York, Earl of Ulster and Duke of Normandy, wringing his hands, his lips quivering and eyes flitting from side to side in fear, pacing the entrance hall of Dublin Castle.

"Are the horses ready yet?" he paused and demanded of Henry FitzJames, the Lord Grand Prior of England, who stood nervously near the great doors that opened onto the cobbled courtyard. It was not for the first time that he had asked his son the same question in petulant, fearful tone.

"Your Majesty's Life Guards are not yet fully assembled."

"God rot them! What ails them to be so negligent of the safety of their King at such an hour?"

"Sire, it is hard to obtain fresh horses in the city at this time. His Grace, the Duke of Powis, has scoured every stable unsuccessfully for fresh mounts."

"It is already dawn." The King pointed with shaking hand to the early morning light outside. "Have I not been given intelligence that my son-in-law's army," he referred to William, Prince of Orange's relationship to him, with a sneer, "that his piquets have already marched within cannon shot of the outer defences of the city?"

"A report greatly exaggerated, sire. My brother, His Grace of Berwick, has his regiments encamped far to the north and there are no rumours of any alarums."

The King was not listening.

"Men of the like that flock to the banners of the Prince of Orange captured, tried and executed my poor father when I was but sixteen years old. They cut off his head in front of his own palace of Whitehall. I do not intend to suffer the same fate. We must mount immediately and ride for the coast, fresh horses or not. See that it is so!"

The Lord Grand Prior left to obey his father's orders.

Her Grace, Lady Frances, the Duchess of Tyrconnell, had roused herself in the early morning hours to witness the King's departure from the city of Dublin. Now she stood watching him with a look of contempt. With her in the hall was the Lord Mayor of Dublin, Terence McDermott, while at her side stood Father Taafe, her husband's chaplain who had just arrived in the city. Her husband, Richard, was James' Lord Lieutenant of Ireland, and was even now in continued danger at the head of his cavalry regiment somewhere between Dublin and the River Boyne, facing the Prince of Orange's army. Her Grace had tried her best to calm the panic of the King.

"Majesty, our Irish troops will hold the army of the Prince of Orange long before they reach the city. You are safe as yet."

"Hold them?" The King sneered, turning an ugly countenance to her. "Did they hold them at Oldbridge, madam, when the Prince of Orange and his men swarmed across the Boyne River? Cowards, every one. They fled before William like greyhounds in a race. Your countrymen, madam, can run well."

Her Grace of Tyrconnell's lips twitched in anger. She was not

Irish. She had been born near St Albans in Hertfordshire but she felt a desire to defend her husband, the Duke of Tyrconnell, and his countrymen against this insult.

"Not so well as your majesty," she snapped back, "for I see that you have won the race."

Her companions could not disguise the smiles that sprang to their lips, for King James had been in continued panic since he had galloped into the city at midnight, directly from an engagement at the Boyne, shouting that all was lost.

"The horses are ready, Your Majesty," cried the Lord Grand Prior, coming swiftly back into the hall and saving the King from trying to think of a suitable retort.

James turned quickly, without even bidding farewell to the wife of his Lord Lieutenant of Ireland, the Duke of Tyrconnell. The King seemed to have forgotten her presence and those of her companions as he scuttled towards the doors. Then a thought seemed to strike him. He paused and crashed one pale fist into the palm of his hand.

"Pox take me! Have I no one to remind me?"

The Lord Grand Prior looked in bewilderment as his father turned and almost ran towards the room where he had spent the last few hours. It was a small study in which he had previously been engaged in writing his final orders to the Comte de Lauzun, commander of his army. The King hurried to the desk. Ah, thank God he had remembered. A small metal box stood on the desk where he had left it. He picked up the heavy object, unlocked and pushed back the lid. It was filled with jewellery. On top of the diamonds and emeralds and assorted jewels lay a glittering blue stone about one and a half inches in length by an inch wide. The Stuart Sapphire was the pride of his collection. His brother, Charles II, had saved it from falling into Cromwellian hands after his defeat at Worcester. It was worth a king's fortune; it was the fortune of this King, anyway. These were all that were left of the Crown Jewels of the Stuart Dynasty. He snapped the lid shut and turned the key again.

"This casket is to stay with me at all times. It is the guarantee of the survival of the House of Stuart," he grunted at his bewildered son, the Lord Grand Prior. "Now, let us ride for Waterford with all speed."

Without another word, he swept by Lady Tyrconnell, who performed a courtly curtsey; her every movement was filled with irony. Her companions merely inclined their heads.

Lady Tyrconnell waited a few moments until she heard the clattering of horses leaving the castle yard and then her features twisted in disdain.

"I wonder if His Majesty knows what his good subjects of Ireland are already calling him?" She smiled grimly at the troubled faces of the Lord Mayor MacDermott and Father Taafe. "I learnt the Irish from my maid. *Séamus an Chaca* – James the Shit! Methinks my sister, Sarah, the Lady Marlborough, is right when she agreed with her husband that these realms will be better off without such a petty, devious and faint-hearted man as James Stuart on the throne."

Conte Salvatore Volpe of the Ordo Equester Nobile de Nostro Signore, the Papal bodyguard, paused for a moment outside the tall ornate doors with their gilt covered carvings and brass fixtures. He adjusted his sword and raised a hand to ensure his cravat was in place. Then he nodded to the nervous looking *sacredotti* who stood ready. The young trainee priest smote the door twice and then opened it and announced in a whispering tone to the occupant:

"Count Volpe, prefect commander of the Order of the Noble Knights of Our Lord."

Volpe strode into an antechamber and then halted in momentary surprise. He had been expecting to be greeted by the elderly Cardinal York of Frascati but a ruddy-faced man with dark hair and clothes that bespoke more of a man of fashion and elegance greeted him. He was fair of skin and his features seemed to identify him as a foreigner but he greeted Volpe in fluent courtly Italian as one born to the language.

"I have surprised you, count," the man observed. "I am sorry but it is necessary to have a word with you before you are received by my master. I am . . ."

"The Marchese Glenbuchat." Volpe had difficulty pronouncing the Scottish name.

"You are well informed, Conte."

"It is my duty to be so, Marchese, for I am placed in charge of the safety of all the Cardinal princes of Holy Mother Church who are gathering here."

"Then you may also know, who my master is? I want to tell you, before you speak with him, that I have met with great reluctance from him in allowing you privy to a matter, which is of the greatest gravity to him and his cause. He does not want this matter to be voiced abroad. So I must hear from you that you are willing to treat it in utmost secrecy."

"Without knowing the nature of the matter, I cannot take such an oath," replied Volpe. "But if it does not offend the holy office that I hold sacred, I will treat the matter with discretion. Perhaps I can be told the nature of this problem that your master wishes to consult me about?"

Lord Glenbuchat hesitated.

"I will leave that to him."

He crossed to a door and knocked on it discreetly, opened it and announced Volpe's presence.

Count Volpe crossed the marble tiled floor to the chair by an ornate fire carved in the same stone. The slight figure of the elderly man in the robes of a Cardinal was seated to receive him. Volpe came to a halt and bent to kiss the ring of the frail hand that the Cardinal had reached out towards him.

He wondered how he should address someone whom many recognized as the rightful King of England, Scotland and Ireland, but who was Bishop of Frascati and known to his fellow prelates as Cardinal York.

"Eminence," he managed to mutter as he bent over the bishop's ring. He paused a moment and then straightened looking into the pale face and dark haunted eyes of Henry Benedict Maria Clement Stuart, grandson and only surviving legitimate heir of James II who had fled his kingdoms to a life of exile over a century before. Since the death of his elder brother, Prince Charles Edward in 1788, the Cardinal had been hailed as Henry IX of England and I of Scotland. The last of the Stuart claimants to the throne.

"How may I serve your Eminence?" Volpe said, taking the regulatory step backwards from the Cardinal's chair. He was aware that Lord Glenbuchat was standing anxiously behind him.

The old man sighed deeply, raising his tired eyes to gaze on the commander of the Pontifical Guard.

"You are acquainted with my family's sad history?" he asked.

"Eminence." Volpe made the word an affirmation, feeling sorry for this apparently exhausted old man. However, these were times of hardship for everyone. The armies of revolutionary France were scouring the Italian countryside, looting and plundering, and with Pius VI recently dead in Valence, after a mere six months in office, and the godless French agents suspected of complicity in his death, the Cardinals had been unable to find a sanctuary to meet to elect a new Holy Father. They had even been driven from Rome by the French invasion. Volpe was uncomfortably reminded that the old man before him had also had to flee from his villa at Frascati, when it had been attacked and sacked by the French army. Now the Cardinals were gathering on this little island in Venice, in the old Benedictine Monastery of San Giorgio Maggiore, to enter into the conclave in the hope of electing a new Holy Father.

Count Volpe had only recently been appointed to command the old aristocratic bodyguard of the Papal successors. He was a young man and conscious of his office.

Cardinal York spoke in a tired tone.

"A thief has broken into these apartments and made off with jewellery worth a great fortune."

Volpe's eyes widened but he said nothing. After a moment, the Cardinal continued.

"The jewellery was my personal property, family property, bequeathed to me by my brother, Charles."

Volpe knew well of the dissolute and drunken Prince Charles Edward, pretender to the English throne who had died of apoplexy in Rome some ten years before.

"Eminence, what manner of jewellery has gone missing?"

"The wealth of over three centuries of my family's history as Kings of Scotland and then of England and Ireland," replied the old Cardinal. "Among them, the great Stuart Sapphire. I brought them safely from Frascati, as my grandfather had also brought them safely when he was forced to flee into exile. Before that my great-uncle had hidden them safely when his father was executed by his subjects."

Volpe tried to restrain a grim smile.

"Eminence, your family have borne many misfortunes," he remarked with what he hoped was sympathy.

"The Stuart Crown Jewels are beyond mere commercial wealth," intervened Lord Glenbuchat. "They are the symbols of His Majesty's rightful claims to the throne that has been usurped by the family of the Duke of Brunswick-Lüneberg-Celle, the so-called House of Hanover. The jewels must be found and the culprit punished."

"Eminence, I shall do my utmost to bring this matter to a satisfactory and immediate conclusion," Volpe assured the old Cardinal, addressing him rather than turning to Lord Glenbuchat.

The old man sighed and waved his hand to the Marquess.

"I have had my chamberlain, Lord Glenbuchat, make out a list of the items that are missing."

"You say that these apartments were broken into?" Volpe queried. "May I see where the entrance was forced?"

Cardinal York coughed nervously.

"I did not mean to be taken literally," he said as if in bad temper. "There was no sign of anyone actually breaking into these chambers, was there, Glenbuchat?"

The Marchese shook his head.

"No doors nor windows bore signs of forced entry nor even the secret cabinet in which the jewels were kept for safety."

Volpe frowned.

"I presume that the doors to these apartments are locked when there is no one present?"

"Of course, though there is usually myself or my chamberlain here. If we are not, there is my bodyguard, Colonel O'Sullivan, and my manservant, Iain."

"These have access to the chamber where the jewels were kept?"

The Cardinal nodded.

"No one else?"

"None that have free access to these rooms."

"If someone will be so good as to show me where these jewels were kept . . . ?" asked Volpe after a moment's reflection.

Cardinal York glanced to his chamberlain.

Lord Glenbuchat took Volpe by the arm and led him to another door.

"This is His Majesty's bedchamber," he confided. Volpe could not get used to the form of address. He supposed that, to his followers, the Cardinal was totally accepted as the rightful king. Glenbuchat had opened the door and pointed to the key in the lock.

"This key is always in the possession of His Majesty or myself when His Majesty was not in this room. The room was always kept locked because of the presence of the jewels."

"There is only one key?"

"So I am told by the abbot of this monastery."

"And where were the jewels kept?"

Lord Glenbuchat led the way into the chamber, which was covered with frescoes from the time of Palladio who had built the church of San Giorgio Maggiore. Most of them were framed either in the ornate cornices of the ceiling or with raised plasterwork on the walls. There were copies of Tintoretto paintings such as the

"Gathering of Manna" which had been executed by his students. The room was also sumptuously furnished. Volpe saw that there was one window, a small one that he knew only gave access of view to an inner courtyard, some ten metres below.

The Marchese went to the head of the bed, by the right hand side and leaned forward, pressing a panel, which slid aside and reveal a small iron door. He reached for a key on the table and unlocked the door, swinging it open to reveal a tiny metal safe beyond. Apart from some papers, it was empty.

"This is where the jewels were kept," he said, standing aside.

Count Volpe glanced quickly at the safe. It would tell him nothing, except that the lock had not been forced.

"Where was the key kept?" he asked.

"So far as we knew, it was with His Majesty the entire time."

"There being no other key?"

"Again I was assured by the abbot that there was none."

Volpe moved to the window and noticed the latches were secured. He opened it and peered out. It was only a tiny window, no bigger than to allow one's head to be put through. Certainly no one could exit nor gain access through this aperture, even if they had a ladder long enough to reach up from the courtyard.

"Who knew of this secret panel and the safe?"

"Apart from His Majesty and myself as chancellor, only Colonel O'Sullivan and the manservant."

"I presume the previous occupants of this chamber and, of course, the abbot, would know of the safe," Volpe dryly pointed out.

"But they would not have known of the valuables that had been placed there," replied Lord Glenbuchat.

Volpe conceded that it was a point.

"Who knew about these jewels? I do not mean their exact location but of their existence?"

"Of the existence of the Stuart Crown Jewels? I would say, countless people. Now and then emissaries from the usurper Hanoverian court came to make offers to His Late Majesty, when I served him."

"His Late Majesty?" frowned Volpe.

"Charles the Third," replied Glenbuchat irritably. "And, when his brother succeeded, twice they came with offers. The House of Hanover would like possession of the jewels in order to boost the legitimacy of their claims. But the exact whereabouts was only known to we of the household. Indeed, Colonel O'Sullivan deemed it best, when we fled from Frascati, to put it abroad that the French had taken the jewels when they sacked the villa at Frascati."

Volpe was thoughtful.

"Are you saying that no one outside the four of you knew that these jewels were here in the monastery?"

"That I am."

"Then this makes my work either very easy or very hard."

Lord Glenbuchat turned with a quizzical gaze.

"Let us return to His . . . His Eminence," Volpe suggested. "I would like to hear when the jewels were last seen and when and how they were discovered to be missing."

The elderly Cardinal was still sitting before the fire but now there was a young man in attendance to him, serving a pewter goblet whose contents proved to be with mulled wine. Volpe presumed, with accuracy, that this was the Cardinal's servant, Iain, and sought confirmation after he had withdrawn from the room.

"Now, Eminence, would you recall for me the last time you saw the jewels secured in your room?"

Cardinal York pursed his lips.

"I think I ascertained their safety late yesterday."

"It was in the evening, Majesty," added Glenbuchat quickly. "You will recall the evening Angelus was sounding but you had felt a distemper, deciding to retire early for the night."

"Ah, so I did, so I did."

"And why were the jewels inspected?" queried Volpe.

"Some papers had arrived, which I felt that His Majesty should lock away for safekeeping until we were able to deal with them."

"Papers?"

"A report from our chief agent in London which was not for eyes other than myself and His Majesty," replied Glenbuchat.

"And did they also disappear?"

"They did not. Only the jewels."

"So, Eminence, you retired to bed early last night . . . and then what?"

"My servant Iain had brought me some hot brandy and, having partaken of it, I fell asleep and was not roused until this morning."

Volpe unconsciously stroked his chin in thought.

"So you were not disturbed during the night?"

"I slept soundly."

"And, Marchese, you told me it was the custom for His Eminence's bedchamber to be secured?"

Glenbuchat nodded.

"There have been, from time to time, agents of the Hanoverians who might believe assassination was a solution to the claims of His Majesty to the throne of England. This is the first time in years that we have been in a more public place than in the confines of the villa at Frascati. We have to be vigilant. Indeed, you must know that there are some representatives of the clergy attending this conclave who declare their allegiance to the Hanoverian usurpers. Even the Irish bishops have had their allegiance bought by promises of seminaries and an easing of the Penal Laws against the Catholic population in Ireland.

"The Archbishop of Dublin, for example, Troy, is bending over backwards claiming that only those expressing loyalty to the Hanoverian Kings in London should be promoted as Irish bishops. He has condemned the uprising of the Irish last year and is even preaching legislative union of Ireland with England and Scotland. If such is the position of Irish Catholics, then the Stuart cause is lost forever. Such supporters of Archbishop Troy have the effrontery to come here to Venice to support the election of the new Holy Father."

It was clear that Lord Glenbuchat was impassioned with his cause.

"So the bedchamber was secured?"

"We ensure that His Majesty secures his bedchamber door from the inside. And when he retires for the night O'Sullivan or Iain take it in turn to stay outside the door."

"And this was faithfully carried out last night?"

"It was."

"So when were the jewels discovered missing?"

"About mid-morning," replied Glenbuchat.

"In what circumstances?"

It was the Cardinal who answered.

"I arose early and Iain helped me to dress so that I could go to the church to attend the early morning Angelus and mass. As I left my chamber, I locked the door behind me, as was my custom. When I returned I opened the chamber door so that Iain could clean my bedchamber and prepare the bed."

"You were in the chamber when this was being done?"

The Cardinal shook his head.

"I was sitting here with Lord Glenbuchat on matters of business. I dictated some letters, for his lordship acts in the position of my secretary as well as chancellor." The old man smiled wanly. "Thus have the Kings of England and Scotland in exile fallen on hard times."

"It was the secret report from our agent which prompted me to open the safe," added Glenbuchat. "I saw the jewellery box was gone. We questioned the household first. His Majesty was reluctant to send for outside assistance in case the news was spread abroad. But I hope we have your assurance of discretion."

If it was an implied question, Volpe chose to ignore it.

"So, what you are saying is that the theft must have occurred in the hours when His Eminence left the bedchamber and went to attend early morning mass and the time when he returned to this apartment, there being no other opportunity for anyone to enter the chamber and remove the jewels?"

Glenbuchat shrugged helplessly.

"It would seem so. But His Majesty had taken both keys. Iain was here, as was I, awaiting the return of His Majesty. O'Sullivan had accompanied His Majesty to the mass as bodyguard. So we would have surely heard if anyone had forced an entry and remember that there were no signs of a forced entry."

"No, whoever took the jewels had a key," agreed Volpe.

"And we have been assured that there was no other key. Neither key to the safe nor to the bedchamber."

"With your permission, Eminence, I would like a word with your servant, Iain, and also with Colonel O'Sullivan," Volpe said rising.

"They can tell you nothing more than what my lord Glenbuchat and myself have furnished you with," the old Cardinal pointed out.

Volpe smiled softly.

"In such an investigation as this, Eminence, it is always best to confirm things at first hand. A word here, a gesture there, may tell one far more . . . And, with your permission, I would like to see them alone, in their own quarters."

He questioned the manservant Iain, a lad whose great-grandfather had come from Scotland to serve the House of Stuart, but whose connection with that country was solely his name. He was a young, excitable man with a Roman accent and a fast way of speaking, uttering half a dozen words in one breath, pausing and uttering half a dozen more. To Volpe, he seemed rather naïve. At first, Volpe thought he might be somewhat simple but then realized it was due to the youth's unworldly attitude. He confirmed everything that the Cardinal and Glenbuchat had said. During the morning he had not stirred outside the apartments, as his task was to clean and maintain them for the Cardinal's entire household. He was in and out of the main chamber, where the Marquess of Glenbuchat was working on some papers, within sight of the locked bedchamber door, until the return of Cardinal York and Colonel O'Sullivan.

Count Volpe then went to see Colonel O'Sullivan.

O'Sullivan was a tall man with a mane of golden-red hair, flushed fair features and a ready smile. Unlike the others of the Cardinal's household who were descended from exiles, O'Sullivan was an Irishman born but had spent ten years in Dillon's Regiment of the Irish Brigade in French service until the French Revolution had caused the Brigade to be disbanded in 1792. Too many Irish families, in service with the Irish Brigade of France, had risen to be ennobled in the French aristocracy. The new National Assembly of the French Republic did not trust the loyalty of the Irish regiments as many of their commanders had declared themselves as royalists.

Colonel O'Sullivan had made for Rome and offered his service to the Stuart household. He was too bombastic for Volpe's liking. A man quick to temper and equally quick to humour. He was of too ephemeral a nature.

Volpe interviewed him in the colonel's small, rudely furnished bedchamber in which there was room for scarcely anything other than a camp bed, a canvas campaign chair and a travelling chest. Volpe perched himself on the chest and motioned the big man to be seated. O'Sullivan dropped to the bed with a grin.

"Well, it seems as if this is the last throw of the dice for the Stuarts. After this I scarce imagine His so-called Majesty will be able to employ the likes of me."

Volpe's brows drew together. There seemed a certain amount of disrespect in O'Sullivan's tone for one whom, so Volpe presumed, he regarded as his rightful king.

Catching sight of his expression, O'Sullivan slapped his hand on his knee and let out a laugh.

"Lord bless you, but I am a pragmatist. Sure, the Stuarts have provided me with an income after the French disbanded my regiment. But I am not the fool to forget that they never did my poor benighted country any good. Wasn't it the Stuart king who sent the English and Scottish colonists pouring into Ireland and driving the likes of me to their deaths by the thousands? Thousands more of us had to escape to France, Spain or Austria. I serve the money, not the man."

Volpe's eyes widened.

"You are either an honest fellow or a fool," he observed. "You have just provided me with a reason why I should suspect you of this theft."

O'Sullivan grinned.

"You are at liberty to search my room. What you see is all I have. But as for stealing these jewels . . . why, I might have done had I known of their whereabouts. I didn't know until this morning of the cunning hiding hole in the wall. Then that plumped-up jackanapes, Glenbuchat, started his ranting and raving. The old man was a closed mouth. As for Iain, God help him, he knows his station and will not depart from it. If he had found the Crown Jewels in a dark alley he would have come obediently to his master and handed them over without thought of recompense."

"Are you saying that you did not know of their existence?"

"Sure, my Italian is not fluent but I think I made myself clear," chided the other. "I knew of their existence. I knew the Cardinal had them but I did not know where he had hid them until this morning when I was told they had gone."

"So you were told after you returned with His . . . His Eminence from mass this morning?"

"Lord, but you are a sharp one," chuckled the big man.

"And during the preceding night you and Iain, the servant, took turns to stay outside the door of the Cardinal's bedchamber."

"That we did. The Cardinal returned to bed early, so Iain took the early part of the evening. I took my turn on watch when it lacked an hour until midnight. I did a four hour watch and then Iain relieved me and, of course, his watch was relatively short being but two hours before he had to rouse the old . . . the Cardinal to get him up for the Angelus and Mass."

"And you were not disturbed during this time?"

"Not I. No, I had a candle and good reading to occupy me. A countryman had sent me Mister Tone's *Argument on Behalf of the Catholics of Ireland* . . . a fascinating little book the like of which I wish I had come across sooner. It put me in mind of returning home and offering my sword arm to these United Irishmen to strike for the liberty of my own country. I'd be better occupied than with a lost cause like . . ."

He nodded towards the door.

"Nevertheless, you are paid to be a bodyguard to His Eminence," pointed out Volpe.

"And, by the saints, I earn my pay," replied O'Sullivan quickly. "I guard the old man and no one can claim that I have allowed a single assassin to get near him."

"You believe there are such assassins abroad?"

Again, O'Sullivan laughed sharply.

"The enemies that the Stuarts have in London are not beyond paying a fellow a few golden sovereigns to rid them of an irritant if they cannot buy them off. The old man has been growing fearful in recent years. It is not to be wondered at. Why, I'll tell you an irony, an English agent in Madrid in Spain assassinated my own kinsman, The O'Sullivan, chieftain of Beare. The irony being that assassin was sent by a Stuart king who feared poor wee Felim O'Sullivan. The current King of England, Farmer George as he is called, has more to fear from the last of the Stuarts than ever the Stuarts had to fear from my forebear."

Volpe frowned, not really understanding.

"So," he said, trying to make sense of things, "you believe there is justification to fear assassination?"

O'Sullivan leaned forward with a wink and tapped Volpe's arm in a conspiratorial manner.

"Justification, indeed. Didn't I see that wee man, Father Vane, sneaking near these chambers these last two days?"

"Father Vane?" Volpe mentally tried to remember the delegates and their attendants.

"Aye, a weasel of a man. One of the delegates from England. A Catholic? What Englishman is truly a Catholic these days? I'd sooner believe that he has an assassin's dagger in his cassock than a rosary."

Volpe smiled thinly.

"You are prejudiced, my friend."

"If an Irishman can't be prejudiced about the English, then I have no understanding of this world."

"Are you saying that this Father Kane has been seen lurking near these apartments?"

O'Sullivan didn't understand the word *nascondersi* and Volpe had to use a simile to express the action of someone hiding themselves near the apartments.

"Not exactly hiding themselves," confirmed O'Sullivan, "but keeping to the shadows. In fact, before I took over my watch from Iain last night I was sure I saw the little ferret below in the courtyard."

Now it was Volpe's turn to be lost.

"You saw a *furetto* in the courtyard?" he exclaimed.

"Vane, the wee fella," explained the Irishman.

"Ah. How did you observe him?"

O'Sullivan rose and went to the tall windows, the *porta-finestra*, in his room and opened one of them. Outside was a small balcony. O'Sullivan beckoned Volpe to join him.

"Was I not having me a pipe out here when I saw him. The old man does not like the smell of tobacco and, seeing that tobacco is one of the few pleasures I can indulge in, I have my smoke outside."

Volpe saw that the balcony overlooked the courtyard below.

"It must have been dark at the time," he said. "How could you recognize anyone down there as Father Vane?"

"Bless ye, and ye are no fool," chuckled O'Sullivan. "However, at dusk along comes one of your own men and helpfully lights those torches you see on the walls there."

"And you can swear that you saw this Father Vane standing down there . . . show me exactly where."

O'Sullivan pointed to an area further along. It was a spot immediately below the small window of Cardinal York's bed-chamber some ten metres above.

"You say that you suspect Father Vane of evil intentions towards His Eminence and yet you had no fear when you saw him there? You raised no alarm?"

"Love you for a cautious man, but what harm? Have you seen the piddling little window in the old man's bedroom? Even had he been able to climb the wall, he wouldn't have gained entrance by that means. No, if Vane is your thief, he came in through the door. If he came in through the door, he must have had a key. If he had a key, then he must have taken it from somewhere. If not from the hand of the old man, then there must be two keys. And even if there was another key, he must have had the other key to the safe and knew of the secret panel. And if he had all that, then he also had the miraculous ability to have made himself invisible to pass either Iain or myself last night."

"Then there are two possibilities," observed Volpe in a dry tone.

The big Irishman stared at him for a moment.

"Which are?"

"Either Iain or yourself allowed the thief to enter or one or other of you are the thief."

There was a silence. Then O'Sullivan roared with laughter.

"There is no denying that you are a sharp one, Count Volpe. There's yet another explanation. If the jewels were not removed through the door then the only possible method was through the small window, and who can get through it but the wee fairy folk. Have you thought that the *sidhe* might be at work here . . . the wee folk of the hills?"

Volpe left O'Sullivan enjoying his obscure joke and returned to the main chamber.

Cardinal York had retired to his bedchamber for his private devotionals and the Marchese Glenbuchat was pacing the room in front of the fireplace.

"Well?" he demanded roughly, when Volpe re-entered. "Have you come upon a solution?"

Volpe smiled thinly.

"Let us say that I have a few lines of inquiry that need to be pursued. If I may suggest, Marchese, let us be seated for a moment."

Reluctantly, Glenbuchat sat down and Volpe took a chair and pulled it opposite him.

"As I understand it, you are more concerned with His Eminence's political position rather than his ecclesiastical one? You serve him as rightful claimant to the English throne than as Bishop of Frascati, am I correct?"

Glenbuchat frowned.

"As rightful King of England and Scotland," he corrected. "I am a faithful subject and servant of His Majesty, Henry Ninth, by divine right . . ."

"Just so," intervened Volpe. "How long have you served the Stuart Household?"

"All my life. My grandfather was a young man on the staff of His Grace, the Duke of Berwick. He served both His Majesty James the Second and James the Third while they were in exile at St Germain-en-Laye. He went back to Scotland and fought at Glenshiels in Seventeen-Nineteen. My father was born in St Germain-en-Laye and continued that service. He was in Lord Drummond's

Regiment when we defeated that fat German who called himself the Duke of Cumberland at Fontenoy and, a few months later, sailed with Prince Charles Edward back home to Scotland. When Charles Edward came back to exile and then became Charles III, my father returned with him. I was born in Rome and continued in that service. When Charles died, I went to serve the next Stuart monarch, King Henry at Frascati."

Glenbuchat recited all this with a great deal of passion and pride in his voice.

Volpe nodded thoughtfully.

"So you know much of the politics of the conflict between the Hanoverians and Stuarts?"

"Of course."

"His Eminence is considered the last of the Stuarts?"

"The last of the direct line although there are relatives by consanguinity."

"I am told that His Eminence is poor?"

"This last decade has seen his fortune vanish because of this revolutionary fever among the French. The French have taken all the Stuart possessions that remained to them."

"Except the Crown Jewels."

"Except the Stuart Crown Jewels," confirmed Glenbuchat. "The Stuart cause is bereft of wealth. Why do you wish to know this? Your task is to find the thief who took them last night."

Volpe smiled.

"I know my task, Marchese. And that is precisely my intention. I am pursuing it in my own way. Tell me, do you really think that the people of England or Scotland are interested in the return of the Stuarts to the throne?"

Glenbuchat's mouth tightened.

"Whether they are interested or not, the Stuarts are the rightful kings."

Volpe sighed wistfully.

"Kings are not the currency they once were. They can be easily deposed as the French have just shown. The creed of the republicans has swept Europe like a forest fire."

"The French!" sneered Glenbuchat.

"Wasn't it the English who showed the way? They executed one Stuart king and chased another out of the kingdom. For over a hundred years the Stuarts have been in exile. Now we have a frail old man, a Cardinal no less, as the last of the line. Do you think anyone really cares now whether this old man can suddenly be restored to the throne of his grandfather?"

Glenbuchat had turned almost apoplectic with rage.

"How dare you, sir! You insult my King. I have fought duels for less."

Volpe sat back unperturbed.

"I am prefect commander of the guard protecting all the princes of the church meeting at this monastery to elect a new Holy Father. You, Marchese, are here on sufferance only because you are employed by one of the Cardinal delegates. I should be careful with your threats. Now, I make the point, that monarchy is unfashionable, the Irish seem to have turned to republicanism, even your own Scottish nation with its Friends of the People seem to be declaring for a republic. The Stuart cause is no longer justified."

Glenbuchat was still angered.

"I called you here to investigate a theft and bring a criminal to justice. My family and I have devoted our lives, our estates and our good name to the cause of the Stuarts and we are still prepared to defend that cause."

Count Volpe rose abruptly.

"I can see that, Glenbuchat. I think that you may be what the English call the last of the Jacobites. I believe you to be an honest man in that cause."

Glenbuchat regarded him in bewilderment at his conciliatory tone.

"Well, sir, are you to proceed in solving and resolving this theft and naming the culprit?"

"I think I already see a solution to this affair," Volpe replied complacently. "Before the culprit is named, I would like another word with His Eminence."

Glenbuchat looked surprised.

"You have . . . if you have the name of the culprit, give it to me. I am chancellor to . . ."

Volpe raised a hand.

"Please, Marchese. I have little time to indulge in discourse on protocols."

Glenbuchat stood up in annoyance.

"I will see if His Majesty will receive you," he said stiffly. He turned to the Cardinal's bedchamber, knocking softly before entering. A moment later, he reappeared and beckoned to Count Volpe.

The old Cardinal was sitting in a chair by his bed.

When Glenbuchat made no move to withdraw, Volpe said: "Eminence, I would have a few words with you alone."

At once Glenbuchat began to protest but Cardinal York said quietly: "You may wait outside, my lord. I will call you when needed."

With an expression of annoyance, Glenbuchat withdrew, shutting the door behind him. For a few seconds the Cardinal and Count Volpe remained in silence, their searching eyes meeting as if duellists preparing to engage.

"Well, Eminence," Volpe said, after a while, "is it worth my while to order a search of the room and belongings of Father Vane for your jewels?"

A few moments passed and then the Cardinal gave a long, low sigh.

"You are undoubtedly a very clever man, Count Volpe," he said.

Volpe shook his head.

"It required little cleverness, only logic. To make this look like theft it was but poorly done. Little thought was given to arranging opportunities by which a thief might have stolen the jewels, which might have confused me. With few opportunities to dwell on, what was left, however improbable, had to be the solution. You, yourself, removed the jewels and dropped them out of the tiny window to where this Father Vane was waiting below to receive them. Is that not so?"

Cardinal York lowered his head.

"I thought that I would have had a little more time to arrange things, but before I had a chance, Glenbuchat demanded sight of the document which we had put in the safe the night before and, in doing so, realized the jewels were no longer there. I tried to stop him making an official furore but there was little I could do."

"So no theft had been committed?"

"As you have deduced. Count Volpe, I am old and weary. Tired of pretending to something that I know that I cannot have and, frankly, that I do not want to have. My grandfather suffered a mental decline after his exile and took refuge in religion. My father was, all his life, a depressed and gloomy individual, resigned to failure from the years of ill fortune. He became a refugee, dying in Rome with only the Holy Father insisting on addressing him as

King of England. My brother, as you well know, ended his life ended his years as a depressive and a drunk. I have found solace in serving Holy Mother Church. I live frugally and in poverty. Why should I keep these remaining baubles of happier times for my family? I will never be, and never want to be, King of England, Scotland or Ireland."

Volpe waited patiently and then asked: "But the descendants of your family? They might have been entrusted with the jewels?"

"There is no issue after me. My brother had a daughter, illegitimate, who married the Duke of Albany and died the same year as my brother. I am the last of the Stuarts. Let the offspring of the Brunswick-Lúneberg-Celle family keep the throne. After all, they've had it for so long I'll wager no one in England can even remember our family except with bitterness."

"So I presume that this incident was but a surreptitious hand-over of these Crown Jewels to . . . ?"

"Let us say that they have been passed on to the nations over which our family once ruled."

"What will you tell the likes of Glenbuchat? He will be angered at the demise of his cause."

"He has lived in the past too long. I will make my confession in due course and hope the new Holy Father, once we have elected him, will allow me to retire to Frascati to end my days in peace as a due servant of the Church."

On 14 March 1800, after three months in conclave in the monastery of San Giorgio Maggiore in Venice, the Cardinals elected Giorgio Barnaba Chiaramonti as Holy Father. He took the name of Pius VII. One of his first acts was to disband the Order of the Noble Knights of Our Lord and replace them with a new unit called the *Guardia Nobile del Corpo di Nostro Signore*. Count Volpe refused to renew his commission and retired to his estates of Ferarra and Imola, south of Venice. In the same year, George William Frederick, King of Great Britain and Ireland, Duke and Elector of Hanover, agreed to pay to Cardinal York, Bishop of Frascati, a pension of £4,000 for life. The last of the royal Stuarts died at the age of 82 at Frascati on 13 July 1807, and was buried in St Peter's Basilica in the Vatican.

And the mystery of the Stuart Crown Jewels? When the Princess Alexandrina Victoria was crowned Queen of the United Kingdom of Great Britain and Ireland and Empress of India at Westminster

Abbey on 28 June 1838, she wore a newly reworked State Crown. The famous Stuart Sapphire occupied a prominent position on it and today it is one of the two famous sapphires that rest in the collection of the British Crown Jewels.

The Flung-Back Lid

Peter Godfrey

Peter Godfrey (1917–92) was a South African born writer and journalist who settled in England in 1962, because of his opposition to the apartheid regime, and continued his career as a reporter for the Daily Herald, *the* Sun *and* The Times. *He wrote scores of stories for South African and American magazines and newspapers but during his lifetime only a handful were collected between covers in* Death Under the Table *(1954). More recently his son Ronald, also a journalist, compiled a new volume,* The Newtonian Egg *(2002). They all feature the cases of Rolf le Roux, a detective in the Johannesburg police force. All are unusual, but here is possibly the most perplexing.*

All that day, the last day of March, the cableway to the top of Table Mountain had operated normally. Every half hour the car on the summit descended, and the car below ascended, both operating on the same endless cable. The entire journey took seven minutes.

Passengers going up or coming down gawked at the magnificent panorama over the head of the blase conductor in each car. In his upper-station cabin the driver of the week, Clobber, hunched conscientiously over his controls during each run, and was usually able to relax for the rest of the half hour.

In the restaurant on the summit, Mrs Orvin worked and chatted and sold curios and postcards and buttered scones, and showed customers how to post their cards in the little box which would ensure their stamps would be canceled with a special Table Mountain franking.

In the box-office at the lower station, the station master, Brander, sold tickets for the journey, and chatted with the conductor who happened to be down at the time, and drank tea.

Then, at 5.30 p.m., the siren moaned its warning that the last trip of the day was about to commence. Into the upper car came the last straggling sightseers, the engineer on duty, Mrs Orvin, and the conductor, Skager. Alone in the lower car was the other conductor, Heston, who would sleep overnight on the summit.

Then two bells rang, and the cars were on their way. For the space of seven minutes Clobber and the Native labourer, Ben, were the only two on top of the mountain. Then the cars docked, and Heston stepped jauntily on to the landing platform.

He joined Clobber, but neither spoke. Their dislike was mutual and obvious. They ate their evening meal in silence.

Clobber picked up a book. Heston took a short walk, and then went to bed.

Some hours later, he woke up. Somewhere in the blackness of the room he could hear Clobber snoring softly.

Heston bared his teeth. Snore now, he thought, snore now. But tomorrow . . .

The night began to grow less black. The stars faded first, then the lights far below in the city also winked out. The east changed colour. The sun rose.

It was tomorrow.

Brander came into the room which housed the lower landing platform, and peered myopically up along the giant stretch of steel rope.

The old Cape Coloured, Piet, was sweeping out the car which had remained overnight at the lower station – the right-hand car. He said: "*Dag**, Baas Brander."

"*Dag*, Piet," said Brander.

Two thousand feet above, the upper station looked like a doll's house, perched on the edge of the cliff. The outlines of Table Mountain stood deep-etched by the morning sun. On the flat top of the elevation there was no sign of cloud – the tablecloth, as people in Cape Town call it – and there was no stirring of the air.

* *Afrikaans: "Good day."*

Brander thought: Good weather. We will be operating all day.

Piet was sweeping carefully, poking the broom edgeways into the corners of the car. He noticed Brander looking at him, and his old parchment flat-nosed face creased suddenly into a myriad of grins "Baas Dimble is the engineer today," he said. "The car must be very clean."

"That's right, Piet," said Brander. "Make a good job for Baas Dimble. You still have twenty minutes."

In the upper station, Clobber settled himself in his chair in the driver's cabin, and opened the latest issue of *Armchair Scientist*. He had just about enough time, he reckoned, to finish the latest article on the new rocket fuels before the test run at nine-thirty.

Line by line his eyes swallowed words, phrases and sentences. Then, interrupting the even flow of his thoughts, he felt the uneasy consciousness of eyes staring at the back of his neck. He had an annoying mental image of Heston's thin lips contorting in a sardonic smile.

He turned. It was Heston, but this time his face was unusually serious. "Did I interrupt you?" he asked.

"Oh, go to hell," said Clobber. He marked the place in his magazine, and put it down. He asked: "Well?"

"I wanted a few words with you," said Heston.

"If it's chit-chat you're after, find someone else."

Heston looked hurt. "It's . . . well, it's rather a personal problem. Do you mind?"

"All right. Go ahead."

"I'm a bit worried about the trip down."

"Why? You know as well as I do that nothing can go wrong with the cable."

"No, it's not that. It's just . . . Look, Clobber, I don't want you to think I'm pulling your leg, because I'm really very serious. I don't think I'm going to get down alive. You see, yesterday was my birthday – I turned thirty-one and it was 31 March – and I had to spend last night up here. Now, I'm not being superstitious or anything, but I've been warned that the day after my birthday I'd not be alive if my first trip was from the top to the bottom of the mountain. If I hadn't forgotten, I'd have changed shifts with someone, but as it is . . ."

"Look here, Heston, if you're not bluffing, you're the biggest damned fool—"

"I'm not bluffing, Clobber. I mean it. You see, I haven't got a relation in the world. If anything does happen, I'd like to see that each of the men gets something of mine as a sort of keepsake. You can have my watch. Dimble gets my binoculars—"

"Sure, sure. And your million-rand bank account goes to Little Orphan Annie. Don't be a damned fool. Who gave you this idiotic warning, anyway?"

"I had a dream—"

"Get to hell out of here, you little rat! Coming here and—"

"But I mean it, Clobber—"

"Get out! It would be a damned good thing for all of us if you didn't reach the bottom alive!"

Dimble, neat and officious but friendly, arrived at the lower station wagon, and with him were Skager and Mrs Orvin.

Brander shuffled forward to meet them.

"Nice day," said Dimble. "What's your time, Brander? Nine twenty-five? Good, our watches agree. Everything ship-shape here? Fine."

Skager scratched a pimple on his neck.

Mrs Orvin said: "How's your hand, Mr Brander?"

The station-master peered below his glasses at his left hand, which was neatly bound with fresh white bandages. "Getting better slowly, thanks. It's still a little painful. I can't use it much, yet."

"Don't like that Heston," said Dimble. "Nasty trick he played on you, Brander."

"Perhaps it wasn't a trick, Mr Dimble. Perhaps he didn't know the other end of the iron was hot."

"Nonsense," said Mrs Orvin. "He probably heated it up, specially. I can believe anything of him. Impertinent, that's what he is."

"Even if he did do it," said Brander, "I can't bear any hard feelings."

Dimble said: "You're a religious man, eh, Brander? All right in its way, but too impractical. No good turning the other cheek to a chap like Heston. Probably give you another clout for good measure. No, I'm different. If he'd done it to me, I'd have my knife into him."

"He'll get a knife into him one of these days," said Skager, darkly. He hesitated. "He'll be coming down in the first car, won't he?"

"Yes," said Brander.

"And it's just about time," said Dimble. "We'd better get in our car. After you, Mrs Orvin. So long, Brander."

"Goodbye, Mr Dimble – Mrs Orvin – Skager."

Heston came through the door leading to the landing platform at the upper station. In the car, the Native Ben was still sweeping.

"Hurry up, you lazy black swine," said Heston. "What in hell have you been doing with yourself this morning? It's almost time to go, and you're still messing about. Get out of my way."

The Native looked at him with a snarl. "You mustn't talk to me like that. I'm not your dog. I've been twenty years with this company, and in all that time nobody's ever spoken to me like that—"

"Then it's time someone started. Go on – get out!"

Ben muttered: "I'd like to—"

"You'd like to what? Come up behind me when I'm not looking, I suppose? Well, you won't get much chance for that. And don't hang around – *voetsak!*"*

From the driver's cabin they heard the two sharp bells that indicated that the cars were ready to move. Ben stepped aside. As the upper car began to slide down and away Heston went through the door, up the short flight of stairs and into the driver's cabin. Ben looked over Clobber's shoulder at the plate-glass window.

The upper car was then 20 or 30 yards from the station. Both men saw Heston lean over the side of the car, and salute them with an exaggerated sweep of his right arm. Both men muttered under their breath.

As the seconds ticked by, the two cars approached each other in mid-air.

In the ascending car Dimble looked at the one that was descending with a critical eye. Suddenly, he became annoyed. "That fool," he said. "Look how he's leaning out over the door. Dangerous . . ."

His voice tailed off. As the cars passed each other, he saw something protruding from Heston's back – something that gleamed silver for an inch or two, and was surmounted by a handle of bright scarlet. Dimble said: "God!" He reached and jerked the emergency brake. Both cars stopped suddenly, swaying drunkenly over the abyss.

* *Afrikaans: "Scram!"*

Skager moaned: "He's not leaning . . ."

Mrs Orvin gulped audibly. "That's my knife," she said, "the one he said . . ."

The telephone bell in the car rang shrilly. Dimble answered it.

"What's the trouble?" came Clobber's voice.

"It's Heston. He's slumped over the door of the car. There seems to be a knife in his back."

"A knife? Hell! He was alive when he left here. He waved to me . . . What should we do?"

"Hang on a second. Brander, are you on the other end? Have you heard this conversation?"

"Yes, Mr Dimble."

"Okay, Clobber. I'm releasing the brake now. Speed it up a little."

"Sure."

The cars moved again.

At the top, Dimble led the rush up the stairs to the driver's cabin, where Clobber's white face greeted them. They waited.

The telephone rang.

Clobber stretched out a tentative hand, but Dimble was ahead of him.

"I've seen him," said Brander, queerly. "He's dead."

"Are you sure?"

"Yes. He's dead."

"Now look, Brander, we must make sure nothing is touched. Get on the outside phone to the police right away. And let Piet stand guard over the body until they get here, OK?"

"It might be difficult, Mr Dimble. There are people here already for tickets, so I can't leave here, and Piet is scared. He's said so. I've locked the door leading to the landing stage – won't that be enough?"

"No. If anyone there is curious, they can climb round the side of the station to the car, and possibly spoil evidence. Let me speak to Piet."

"Here he is, Mr Dimble."

"Hullo, Piet. Now listen – I want you to stand guard on the landing stage and see nobody touches the car until the police arrive."

"No, Baas. Not me, Baas. Not with a dead body, Baas."

"Oh, dammit. OK, Let me speak to Mr Brander. Brander? Listen – this is the best plan. Don't sell any tickets – we won't be

operating today, anyway. We'll start the cars and stop them half-
way so nobody will be able to get near them. In the meantime you
telephone the police. Do you get that?"

"Yes, I will telephone the police."

"And give me a ring the moment they are here."

"Yes, Mr Dimble."

The police came. Caledon Square had sent its top murder team.
Lieutenant Dirk Joubert was in charge of the party, and with him
was his uncle, Rolf le Roux, the "expert on people" as he jocularly
styled himself, the inevitable *kromsteel*★ protruding through the
forest of his beard. Happy Detective-Sergeant Johnson was there,
Lugubrious Sergeant Botha, Doc McGregor and several uniformed men. They mounted the steps to the lower station building
and found Brander waiting for them.

"Where is the body?" asked Joubert.

Brander pointed out the two tiny cars on their thin threads a
thousand feet above. "Will you please speak on the internal phone
to Mr Dimble, the engineer in charge, who's at the upper station?"
he asked.

"Get him for me," said Joubert.

Brander made the connection, and then handed over the phone.

"Mr Dimble? I am Inspector Joubert of the Cape Town C.I.D.
I want the cable car with the body to be allowed to come down
here. What? No, it'd be better if you people stayed on top of the
mountain while we do our preliminary work here. I'll ring you
when we're ready. Hullo! Just one moment, just bring me up to
date on the discovery of the crime – briefly, please. I see. You were
going up in the right-hand car, and when you passed the other one
at halfway, you saw a knife sticking out of the conductor's back.
His name? Heston . . . yes, I have that. And then? I see. Yes. Yes.
And why did you move the car with the body half-way back up the
mountain? Mm. No, that's all right – it was a good idea. Right,
better get the body back here now."

Almost as soon as he put the receiver down, the cable began to
whine.

From the landing-stage they watched the approaching car. Even
at some distance they could see the slumped figure quite clearly,

---

★ *Curved Boer pipe.*

with the scarlet splash of the knife handle protruding from its back.

"I can tell you one thing right now," said McGregor. "It's not a suicide."

As the car came closer to the landing-stage, Johnson began checking his photographic and fingerprint equipment.

Brander mumbled: "It is the will of the Lord . . ."

He looked almost grateful when Joubert said: "There's nothing we can do here, Brander. Let's go into the ticket office. There are one or two questions . . ."

Rolf went with them.

Joubert said: "I've had the rough details of the story from Mr Dimble. You were here when the body first came down. Did you examine it?"

"No."

"Why not?"

"He was dead. I could see that."

"And did anyone else come near the body? This Coloured, Piet?"

"No, not Piet. He was afraid. He wouldn't go near the car. He stood at the door until the motors-started, though, in case anyone else wanted to go through."

"Anyone else? Who else was here?"

"Well, there was a man and two women – passengers – but they left when I wouldn't sell them tickets."

Joubert tried a new tack. "This Heston, now. Tell me, Brander, what sort of a man was he? Was there anyone working here who hated him?"

Brander hesitated. "I do not like to talk about him. He is dead now. What does it matter what he was like in life?"

Joubert said: "Answer my question. Is there anyone here who hated him?"

"He was not liked," said Brander, "but nobody here hated him enough to kill him."

"No? Someone stuck a knife in his back, all the same. Who could have done it?"

"What does it matter?" said Brander. "He's dead now. Let him rest in peace."

The experts had finished. Two constables carried a long basket clumsily down the steps to a waiting ambulance.

"Well, Doc?" asked Joubert.

"One blow," said McGregor. "A very clean swift blow. No mess. The murderer struck him from behind and above. Either the killer stood on something, or he was a very tall man."

"Or woman?"

"Maybe. I canna say one way or another."

Johnson made his report. "No fingerprints on the knife, Dirk. Couple of blurred smears, that's all. Probably wore gloves."

Joubert said: "All right. Doc, you go back with the body, and do the P.M. If you come up with anything new, telephone me here . . . Now let's talk to this Coloured, Piet."

But Piet knew nothing. He was old and superstition-ridden. He had not even looked at the body. The nearest he had come to it was to stand on guard on the other side of a closed door.

Joubert phoned Dimble. "We're coming up. What is the signal for starting the car? Two bells – right. I'm not interested in rules about conductors on every trip. We're coming up without one, and the car at the top must come down completely empty. All right – so it's irregular. So is murder. I'll take the responsibility . . . We'll want to interview you one at a time. Is there a room there we can use? The restaurant? Right. You'll hear the signal in a couple of minutes."

Joubert, Rolf le Roux and Johnson. Four uniformed policemen. Going up in the car in which death had come down.

"I don't think we'll be long," said Joubert. "The solution's on top, obviously."

Rolf said: "How do you make that out?"

"When the cars reached the middle of the run, Heston already had the knife in his back. He was alone in the cable-car. Therefore he must have been killed before he left the summit. One of the men stationed up there is the chap we're looking for."

Rolf looked worried. He said: "I hope you are right."

"Of course I'm right. It's the only possible explanation."

"So you'll start off by concentrating on the men who were on the mountain when the cars started this morning?"

"No, let them stew in their own juice for a while. This Dimble seems a proper fuss-pot – better get him over first."

Dimble

". . . And so I told Brander to see the body was guarded, and when I found Piet was afraid I told him . . ."

"Right, Dimble. We've got all that. Now, let me get one thing clear. Apart from Heston, there were two men who stayed overnight at the summit – Clobber, and the Native, Ben?"

"Yes."

"Did either of these two have anything against Heston?"

"Probably. Heston wasn't very likable, you know. But I don't think anyone would murder him."

Joubert said again: "Someone did. Now look, Dimble – to your knowledge did either Clobber or Ben have anything against Heston?"

"Not to my knowledge, no. They may have. For that matter, we all disliked him. He was always doing something . . . objectionable. Like practical jokes – only there was malice behind them, and he never acted as though he was joking. Never could be sure. Nasty type."

Rolf asked: "Exactly what sort of objectionable actions do you mean, Mr Dimble?"

"Well, like putting an emetic in my sandwiches when I wasn't looking. Couldn't prove it was him, though. And burning Brander's hand."

Joubert said: "I noticed his left hand was bandaged. What happened?"

"Heston handed him a length of iron to hold, and his end was all but red-hot."

"I see. So it would appear that both you and Brander had cause to hate the man?"

"Cause, yes, and I must admit I didn't like him. But Brander's different. We were talking about it this morning, and he didn't seem to bear any grudge. He's a religious type, you know."

"So I gathered," said Joubert, drily.

Dimble went on: "And that reminds me – Skager had it in for Heston too. When I mentioned that if it had been my hand he burnt, I'd have my knife in for him, Skager said that one day someone would . . . Hey! That's ironic, isn't it?"

"Yes," said Joubert. "All right, Dimble. Let's have Skager."

Skager

A pasty, pimply young man, with a chip on his shoulder.

"I didn't mean anything by it, Inspector. It's just an expression. I didn't like him."

"So you didn't like him, and you just used an expression?

Doesn't it strike you as strange that a few minutes later Heston did have a knife in his back?"

"I didn't think about it."

"Well, think now, Skager. Why did you hate him?"

"Look, Inspector, I had nothing to do with the murder. How could I have killed him?"

"How do you know how he was killed? I tell you, Skager, I am prepared to arrest any man who attempts to hide his motives . . . Now answer my question?"

A slight pause of defiance, then –

"Well, I don't suppose it makes any difference. I've got a girlfriend. Some time ago, someone rang her up and warned her not to go out with me because I had an incurable disease. It took me weeks before I could convince her it was a lie."

"And you thought Heston made the phone call?"

"Yes."

"Why?"

"Maybe because he was always making snide remarks about my pimples. Besides, it's just the kind of sneaky trick he would get up to."

"So you hated him, eh, Skager – hated him enough to kill him?"

"Why do you pick on me, Inspector? I know nothing about any murder. Why don't you speak to Mrs Orvin? At least she recognised the knife . . ."

Mrs Orvin

Mrs Orvin said: "Yes, the knife is mine. My brother-in-law sent it to me from the Congo."

"What did you use it for?"

"Mainly as an ornament. Occasionally for cutting. It was kept on this shelf under the glass of the counter."

"So anyone could have taken it while you were in the kitchen?"

"Yes, that's what must have happened."

"When did you find it was missing?"

"Yesterday afternoon."

"And before that, when did you last notice it?"

"Only a few minutes earlier. I'd been using it to cut some string, and I put it down to attend to something in the kitchen—"

"Was there anyone else in the restaurant at the time?"

"Yes, quite a few people. Four or five tourists and Heston and Clobber."

"Clobber was here?"

"Yes, having his tea. He sat at the far corner table."

"And Heston?"

"At first he was on the balcony, but when I came back from the kitchen he was sitting at this table."

"So when you missed the knife, what did you do?"

"I spoke to Heston . . ."

Heston looked up innocently at her. "Yes, Mrs Orvin?"

"Mr Heston, have you by any chance seen my knife?"

"You mean the big one with the red handle? The voodoo knife? Of course I have. You were using it a minute ago."

"Well, it's gone now. Did you see anyone take it?"

"No, I didn't see anyone take it, Mrs Orvin, but I know what happened to it all the same."

"What?"

"It suddenly rose in the air, and sort of fluttered out through the door. All by itself . . ."

"Mr Heston, you're being stupid and impertinent—"

"But it's true, Mrs Orvin, it's true. Some of the other people here must have seen it, too. Why don't you ask Clobber?"

Joubert said: "And did you ask Clobber, Mrs Orvin?"

"Yes."

"And what did he say?"

"He knew nothing about the knife. He was very angry when I told him about Heston."

"Well, thanks, Mrs Orvin – I think that'll be all for now."

Mrs Orvin left.

Rolf allowed a puff of smoke to billow through his beard. He said to Johnson: "So now we have a flying voodoo dagger."

"Utter nonsense," said Joubert. "This is murder, not fantasy. Someone wearing gloves killed Heston, and the murder was done on top of the mountain. It can only be one of two – the Native or Clobber. I fancy Clobber."

"You're quite sure, eh?" said Rolf. "What will you say if we find Heston was alive when he left the summit?"

"It just couldn't happen. There is no possible way of stabbing a man alone in a cable-car in mid-journey."

Rolf said: "I still have a feeling about this case . . ."

"There are too many feelings altogether. What we need are a few facts. Let's send for Clobber."

Clobber

Clobber was pale. He was still wearing the soiled dustcoat he used while driving. Joubert looked at something protruding from the pocket and glanced significantly at Johnson and Rolf.

"Do you always wear cotton gloves?" he asked.

"Yes. They keep my hands clean."

"They also have another very useful purpose. They don't leave fingerprints."

Clobber's face went even whiter. "What are you getting at? I didn't kill Heston. He was alive when he left the summit."

"And dead when he passed the other car half-way down? Come off it, Clobber. He must have been killed up here. Either you or Ben are guilty."

Clobber said, stubbornly: "Neither of us did it. I tell you he was alive when he left."

"That's what you say. The point is, can you prove it?"

"Yes, I think so. After the car had started, when he was about twenty yards out, he leant over the side of the car and waved to me. Ben had just come into my cabin. He saw him too."

"Where was Ben before that?"

"He was with Heston at the car."

A new gleam came into Joubert's eye. "Look, Clobber," he said, "couldn't Ben have stabbed Heston just as the car pulled away?"

"I suppose he could, but don't forget, Ben was with me when Heston waved."

"Are you sure it was a wave? Couldn't it have been a body wedged upright, and then slumping over the door?"

"No, definitely not. The arm moved up and down two or three times. He was alive. I'm sure of that."

Joubert flung up his hands in a gesture of impatience. "All right, then. Say he was alive. Then how did the knife get in his back half-way down?" Clobber looked harassed. "I don't know. He had an idea . . . but that's nonsense—"

"Idea? What idea?"

"He told me this morning he didn't expect to get to the bottom of the mountain alive."

Rolf echoed: "Didn't expect?"

"Yes. He said he'd been warned. His thirty-first birthday was yesterday – the 31st of the month – and he'd been told that if he spent last night on top of the mountain, he'd never reach the bottom alive. I thought he was pulling my leg."

"Who was supposed to have told him that?

"He said it was a dream."

Joubert said: "Oh, my God!" but Rolf's face was serious.

"Tell me, Mr Clobber," he said, "did Heston ever mention prophetic dreams to you before?"

"Just once. About a month ago."

"And the circumstances?"

"I'd just come off duty, and I was at the lower station with Heston and Brander. Somehow or the other the conversation led to the subject of death . . ."

Clobber said: "When a man dies, he's dead. Finished. A lot of chemical compounds grouped round a skeleton. No reason to hold a body in awe. The rituals of funerals and cremations are a lot of useless hooey. There should be a law compelling the use of bodies for practical purposes – for transplants, medical research, making fertiliser – anything except burning them up or hiding them in holes in the ground under fancy headstones."

Brander was uneasy. "I don't think I can agree with you . . ."

"The trouble with you, Brander, is that you're a religious man, which also means you are a superstitious one. Try looking at hard facts. What we do with our dead is not only irrational, it's also economically wasteful.

"Last night I went to a municipal-election meeting. The speaker made what the crowd thought was a joke, but he was really being sensible. He said the wall round Woltemade cemetery was an example of useless spending – the people outside didn't want to get in, and the people inside couldn't get out . . . What's the matter with you, Brander?"

Heston suddenly interrupted. "You've upset him with all your callous talk. Can't you realise that Brander's a decent religious man who has a proper respect for the dead?"

Brander dabbed his forehead and his lips in an obvious effort to pull himself together. "No . . . no . . . it's not just that. This business about the wall and the people inside reminds me of something that's always horrified me. The idea of the dead coming to life. Even the Bible story of Lazarus . . . you see, ever since I can remember, every now and again I have a terrible nightmare. I'm with a coffin at a funeral, and suddenly from inside the box there's a loud knock . . . I feel my insides twisting in fear . . ."

Clobber said, hastily: "Sorry, Brander. Didn't mean to upset you. But if you think about it for a moment, you'll realise the whole thing's a lot of nonsense – the dead coming to life, and things like that. Absolute rubbish."

"Really?" said Heston. "What about Zombies?"

Brander gasped: "What?"

"Zombies. Dead men brought to life by voodoo in the West Indies to work in the fields. And dreams, too. I know all about prophetic dreams."

Clobber was almost spitting with rage. "What do you mean, you know? What are you getting at?"

"I'll tell you some other time," said Heston. "Here's the station wagon, and I'm in a hurry."

Joubert said: "And the next time he mentioned a dream to you was to tell you he wouldn't reach the lower station alive?"

"Yes."

"And now do you believe in prophetic dreams?"

"It's got so I don't know what to believe."

Joubert rose. "Well, I do. There are no prophesies and nothing here except a cleverly planned murder, and God help you if you did it, Clobber – because I'm going to smash your alibi."

"You can't smash the truth," said Clobber. "In any case, why should I be the one under suspicion?"

"One of the reasons," said Joubert, "is that you wear gloves."

Clobber grinned for the first time. "Then you'll have to widen your suspect list. We all wear them up here. Dimble has a pair. Ben, too. And, yes, Mrs Orvin generally carries kid gloves."

"All right," said Joubert savagely. "That's enough for now. Tell Ben we want to see him."

Ben came, gave his evidence, and went.

"If I could prove that he and Clobber were collaborating," Joubert started, but Rolf stopped him with a shake of his head.

"No, Dirk. There is nothing between them. I could see that. You could see it, too."

"We're stymied," said Johnson. "Apparently nobody could have done it. I examined the cable-car myself, and I'm prepared to swear there's no sign of any sort of apparatus which could explain the stabbing of a man in mid-air. He was alive when he left the top, and dead at the half-way mark. It's just . . . plain impossible."

"Not quite," said Joubert. "We do know some facts. First, this is a carefully premeditated crime. Secondly, it was done before the car left the summit—"

Rolf said: "No, Dirk. The most important facts in this case lie in what Heston told Clobber – his dream of death – his thirty-first birthday—"

"What are you getting at, Oom?"

"I think I know how and why Heston was killed, Dirk. It's only a theory now, and I do not like to talk until I have proof. But you can help me get that proof . . ."

The word went round. A reconstruction of the crime. Everyone must do exactly as he did when Heston was killed.

Whispers.

"Who's going to take Heston's place?"

"The elderly chap with a beard: le Roux I think his name is. The one they call Oom Rolf."

"Do you think they'll find out anything? Do you think – ?"

"We'll know soon enough, anyway."

On the lower station Joubert rang the signal for the reconstruction to start. Dimble, Mrs Orvin and Skager went towards the bottom car. Sergeant Botha went, too.

Rolf le Roux came through the door of the upper landing platform, and looked at Ben sweeping out the empty car.

He said: "Baas Heston spoke to you, and you stopped sweeping?"

"Yes. And then I came out of the car, like this."

"And then?"

"Then we talked."

"Where did Baas Heston stand?"

"He got into the car, and stood near the door. Yes, just about there." He paused. "Do you think you will find out who killed him?"

"It is possible."

"I hope not, Baas. This Heston was a bad man."

"All the same, it is not right that he should be killed. The murderer must be punished."

Two sharp bells rang in the driver's cabin. The car began to move. Ben went through the door up the stairs and stood in the cabin with Clobber and Johnson. They saw Rolf lean over and wave with an exaggerated gesture.

Clobber reached to lift a pair of binoculars, but Johnson gripped his arm. "Wait. Did you pick them up at this stage the first time?"

"No. I only used them after the emergency brake was applied,"

"Then leave them alone now."

They watched the two cars crawling slowly across space towards each other.

In the ascending car Dimble peered approvingly at the one which was descending. "That's right," he said to Botha. "He's leaning over the door exactly as Heston . . . Good God!"

He pulled the emergency brake. Mrs Orvin sobbed and then screamed.

The telephone rang. Botha clapped the instrument to his ear.

"Everything OK?" asked Johnson.

"No!" said Botha, "no! Something's happened to Rolf. There's a knife sticking out of his back. It looks like the same knife . . ."

From the lower station Joubert cut in excitedly. "What are you saying, Botha? It's impossible . . ."

"It's true, Inspector. I can see it quite clearly from here. And he's not moving . . ."

"Get him down here," said Joubert. "Quick!"

The cars moved again.

In the driver's cabin Johnson, through powerful binoculars, watched the car with the sagging figure go down, down, losing sight of it only as it entered the lower station.

Joubert, with Brander, stood on the landing-stage watching the approaching car. He felt suddenly lost and bewildered and angry.

"Oom Rolf," he muttered.

Brander's eyes were sombre with awe. "The Lord has given," he said, "and the Lord has taken away. Blessed be the name of the Lord."

He and Joubert stepped forward as the car bumped to a stop.

The head of the corpse with the knife in its back suddenly twisted, grinned, said gloatingly: "April fool!"

Brander shivered into shocked action. His arms waved in an ecstacy of panic. His bandaged left hand gripped the hilt of the knife held between Rolf's left arm and his body, and raised it high in a convulsive gesture. Rolf twisted away, but his movement was unnecessary. Joubert had acted, too.

Brander struggled, but only for a second. Then he stood meekly peering in myopic surprise at the handcuffs clicking round his wrists.

"And that is how Heston was killed," said Rolf. "He died because he remembered today was April the first – All Fools Day – and because he had that type of mind, he thought of a joke, and he played it to the bitter end. A joke on Clobber, on the people in the ascending car, on Brander.

"But to Brander it was not a joke – it was horror incarnate. A dead man come to life. This was infinitely more terrible than the dream he feared of a knock from a coffin. This was like the very lid being suddenly flung open in his face. And his reaction was the typical response to panic when there is no escape – a wild uncontrollable aggression, striking out in every direction – as he struck out at me when the unthinkable happened again.

"The first time he plunged the knife into Heston. The joke became reality. The dead stopped walking.

"And now you see why there were no fingerprints on the knife. Brander is left-handed – he reached for the hot iron with that hand, remember. So it was burnt and bandaged. Bandages – no fingerprints. The way Heston was crouched, too, explains the angle of the wound."

Joubert said: "So it was not premeditated after all." Then, to Brander: "Why did you not tell the truth?"

Brander said, meekly: "Who would believe the truth?" Then, louder, with undertones of a new hysteria: "The dead are dead. They must rest in peace. Always rest. They are from hell if they walk . . ."

Then he mumbled, and his voice tailed off as he raised his eyes, and his gaze saw far beyond the mountain and the blue of the sky.

The Poisoned Bowl

Forrest Rosaire

*Forrest Rosaire (1902–77), who also wrote under the name J. J.
des Ormeaux, is little remembered today. Originally in the oil
industry, he settled in California from Chicago in the 1930s and
turned to writing. He appeared regularly in both the pulps and
slick magazines producing a number of high quality crime or
suspense stories. He continued writing until the 1950s but did not
make the transition fully to the book market. He published only
three books,* East of Midnight *(1945),* Uneasy Years *(1950)
and* White Night *(1956), the last his only straight suspense
novel in book form. He is another of those writers whose talents
have been forgotten. The following, which betrays some of the
pulp stereotypes of the day, is nevertheless ingeniously plotted
and keeps you guessing to the end.*

I

All kinds of people came into the welfare office, and Sandra
Grey was so well versed in the diverse aspects of human
misery that nothing much surprised her. But this visitor did. Both
physically and by contrast. She had closed up her desk and was
putting on her hat after a long day when his voice from the
doorway made her jump.

"I say, is this where I'm to leave this?"

Sandra turned and saw a big-shouldered, floridly handsome
man in an expensive raglan topcoat. He was holding in his arms a

tiny ragged child – awkwardly, in the way men do who do not know how to handle babies.

Sandra stared at him. For a second she was completely at a loss – his appearance, the child, the request. In his turn the man stared at her. Sandra was enough to take any man aback. He looked jerkily around, as if he could not connect the drab office, with its heaps of cast-off clothing, boxes of canned goods, bushel baskets of shoes, with this radiant, slim, smart girl, whose wide brown eyes were like deep velvet.

He said uncertainly: "This *is* the welfare office, isn't it?"

"Yes," said Sandra. "What's the trouble?"

He nodded his big florid face at the child. "I found this boy down in the building entry with a note on him. I stopped in at the clinic downstairs and they said to bring him up here, or to call the police."

"Oh!" said Sandra.

She stepped quickly across, took the boy from him. He was a little, laughing, curly-headed fellow, no more than three at the most. He reached up a chubby hand, experimentally took hold of the end of Sandra's nose.

"What a darling!" Sandra sat him down on her desk. He had wide gentian-colored eyes, bright with a baby's mischief. He began chuckling to himself, exploring in a tall basket of shoes beside the desk. Sandra's eyes flashed up to the stranger. "A note! You mean—"

"He's abandoned."

"Oh, how terrible!" Sandra had found the note by now, sewed into the ragged collar of his thin blouse. It read simply, in crude printing: "Be good to him."

Sandra felt compassion well up, an ache in her heart. "How could anyone abandon such a darling?"

The man shook his head. He had an abrupt, awkward manner, entirely out of keeping with his air of breeding, his expensively tailored clothes, his big, impressive handsomeness. He said gruffly:

"What will you do with him?"

Sandra shook her head. "Take him to the orphanage, I suppose." She took her slip-over sweater from a chair, began to roll it up. "I'll drop him off on my way home. Thank you for bringing him up, Mr—"

"Gawdy."

"Mr Gawdy." Sandra decided the name aptly described his type of handsomeness. His ruddy face was too high-colored, his eyes too brightly blue, his topcoat too brilliantly golden.

She slipped the sweater over the boy's head. A sudden, curiously sharp feeling of fear caught her. She realized afterward it was an intuition: if she had only caught up the child, sweater and all, rushed away with him, out of the office, away, away, anywhere – she might have avoided the horrible event looming so close at hand. Instead she went on pulling the chubby little hands through the knitted sleeves. The big man cleared his throat.

"I'd kind of like to give something, to give him a help along." He was fishing in a shark-skin billfold.

"Oh, thank you," said Sandra. "That's generous of you. I'll see that it—"

There was a knock on the jamb of the open door.

Sandra turned. A Chinese stood there, young, moon faced, bland, dressed in a loud herringbone suit with a snap-brimmed hat jauntily on the back of his head. He immediately started to back out.

"So sorry. You are busy."

"No, no, come in; don't mind me," said the big man. He sat down, as if interested to observe the workings of a welfare office.

The Chinese came in. He had a squat and powerful body, that rippled with the same smooth blandness, the same easy suavity, as his voice.

"You are Miss Sandra Grey?"

"Yes."

The Chinese creased his almond eyes. "I have come to beg your indulgence, Miss Grey. A very great favor. Having heard of your generosity, which is indeed a byword in the neighborhood" – he creased his eyes still more – "I have come to ask your help in a distressing family matter."

His English was perfect, impeccable, as smooth as oil. He gestured slightly with two squat fingers, between which was an unlighted gold-tipped cigarette.

"I am here in behalf of my uncle, an old man who speaks only Cantonese. The matter concerns his daughter – my cousin – a young lady who has disappeared after a violent family quarrel. I have come to ask if you, Miss Grey, will find her."

Sandra blinked. "You want *me* to find your cousin?"

The Chinese lifted his squat shoulders, dropped them. His bland smile was sad. "You are our last hope."

"Won't you sit down, Mr—"

"Dow."

Mr Dow did not sit down, but lighted the gold-tipped cigarette, which emitted a rank odor of violet. "The old man is heartbroken. If he could only get this message to her, asking her to return, he would be happy." He took from his pocket a bamboo tube, gave it to Sandra. "In this, after the Cantonese fashion, is the individual plea of every member of the family. If you could get it to her, you would make an old man happy, reunite a family."

Sandra turned over the tube. It was about ten inches long and sealed elaborately at one end with red sealing wax, in which a gold cord was embedded to break the wax. She said uncertainly:

"I don't know how I could locate her."

"I believe she has taken a job through an employment agency called the Acme. Unfortunately she has left instructions not to tell her whereabouts to any of her race, so my efforts with the Acme are fruitless. I believe she has a job as housemaid; and for *you*, Miss Grey, I am sure the Acme—"

The big figure of Gawdy showed a sudden interest. "What's that? I have some friends who have a Chinese housemaid."

"Indeed." Dow's round face turned in polite surprise.

"Their name is Delaunay." Gawdy spelled it. "I can give you their address."

"Thank you." Dow's smile was faintly deprecatory. "There are, of course, many Chinese girls in service. But the Acme could verify it for *you*, Miss Grey."

"What is your cousin's name?"

"Helen Ying."

"I'll try to locate her for you, Mr Dow."

"The lady is as generous as she is lovely." Dow's creased eyes inclined over his cigarette. "I will stop in myself, tomorrow, to learn if you have any success. Permit me to depart in the American manner."

He extended his hand, and as Sandra took it, she felt he was palming something in it. She looked down at her hand in surprise, and as she looked up again, the Chinese was gone. Gawdy was staring after him.

"Queer customer," he said. "See here. I'm going by the Delaunays' and—"

"What on earth—" Sandra was staring at what Dow had left in her hand. It was a compact, compressed, folded square of paper. She unfolded it, saw a rice-paper envelope, carefully sealed. On it was typed:

Give this to her employer.

Sandra red lips parted. "Give this to her employer!" Her eyes flashed to Gawdy. "Look. He gave me this. He must mean, give it to his *cousin's* employer!"

Gawdy was staring at it. "He gave that to you?"

"Yes, slipped it in my hand as he was going out!"

"Well, I'll be—" Gawdy got up. "See here. He looked shady to me. Open it, see what it says!"

A piercing scream rent their ears.

They whirled. The little boy had picked up the bamboo tube, hammered it on the desk, knocked the sealing wax loose. Liquid, spurting from it like a geyser, sprayed over his knees and feet, fuming, bubbling, viscous liquid.

"Great God!" cried Sandra. "Acid!"

It was a moment that would remain stamped on her soul as long as she lived. She saw his creamy flesh, his little knees, quivering, contracting, under that searing, slow-crawling flood. She caught his little body in her arms, bucking, wild, convulsive, screaming as only a child can in unendurable pain. Sandra hardly knew what she was doing. She heard Gawdy yell, "Get that Chinaman!" and dash out the door like a bull. She ran headlong at the glass water cooler, plunged the boy's feet and knees into the deluge of water. The choking fumes caught at her, throat-tearing, strangling. She whirled, burst through the door, went like an arrow downstairs toward the clinic one flight below.

She didn't know who was there, whom she plunged through. She saw the white blot of a doctor's apron.

"Acid! Acid! He's burned!"

Strong hands took the boy from her. Other hands guided her, made her sit down. She was blinded, choking and coughing from the fumes. For a time she could only gag, try to catch her breath, listen to that unendurable screaming. A nurse she knew had her by both shoulders.

"Sandra! Are you all right?"

"Yes, yes." The screaming had stopped. She saw the doctor's white form, caught at him. "Will he live? Will he—"

"Yes. You got him in water; best thing you could do." The doctor's eyes were tight. "I've given him morphine. It was sulphuric acid. How did it ever get on the child?"

Sandra heard herself trying to explain. It sounded garbled, impossible. Her mind was still stunned, uncollected. *Acid* was in that tube the bland, suave Dow had given her. Her brain was a maze of horror.

The doctor was aghast. "He was sending sulphuric acid – by you – to a girl?"

"Yes, yes. A Chinese housemaid who—"

For the first time she opened her clenched right hand, saw the rice-paper envelope still clutched in it. It acted on her like an electric shock. "Give this to her employer."

She sprang up, so abruptly she almost pushed the nurse over. Her eyes were not like velvet now, but like tawny flame.

"Ellen, lock up upstairs for me, will you? Call the police; tell them to talk to that man Gawdy!" She was already at the door. "I'll be back, I don't know when!"

The Delaunay house sat stately and brooding among twilight shadows when Sandra rang the bell under its aristocratic portico. The lank, grave face of a butler answered the soft sound of its triple door chime. Sandra burst out:

"Do you have a housemaid here named Helen Ying?"

The butler stared. "Why, yes, miss."

"Let me speak to Mr Delaunay."

The butler blinked. "Who shall I say is—"

A deep voice said from behind: "Who is it, Sanders?"

Sandra pushed in. "You're Mr Delaunay?"

"I'm John Delaunay, yes."

He was an old man, as thin as a grasshopper, leaning on a thick blackthorn cane. His mild and benignant face was filled with wrinkles like transparent wax paper that has been crumpled and then flattened out.

"I'm Sandra Grey. I run the welfare office for St. Luke's charities. Something terrible has happened, and if I could speak to you a moment—"

"Of course. Of course."

He guided her into the paneled entrance of a library. The first thing Sandra saw as she came in the room was a man on a sofa with his arms around a girl trying to kiss her. They both sprang up;

Sandra backed out; the old man gently impelled her in again and snapped on the wall switch.

"Well, bless me," he said mildly, "I didn't know you two were in here Miss Grey, this is my daughter Marceline."

Marceline was a flashily pretty brunette with brilliant black eyes. The brilliant eyes glared at Sandra. She did not say anything. She sat down at the extreme end of the sofa and gave her whole attention to a bowl of goldfish. The man was sitting in an armchair leafing through the pages of a book. He was hawk-faced, olive-cheeked, with a Vandyke beard cupping his chin like a spearhead. It was a ridiculous and awkward second for Sandra. She turned to speak to Mr Delaunay, but the old man was puttering forward to take the Vandyked man by the arm.

"This is Miss Grey. Miss Grey, this is Rupert de Saules, a long-lost distant relative."

De Saules rose, bowed with the greatest aplomb.

"Delighted."

He had cool, sly eyes, that traveled over Sandra with insolent appreciation. Sandra hardly looked at him. She sat down, burst at once into an account of what had happened. The old man sat down, looked at her agape. De Saules' hawklike head came forward sharply. Even Marceline turned from her preoccupation with the goldfish.

The old man gasped: "Acid! To the Chinese maid! How frightful!" He tugged a bell pull. "We'll have her in here." The butler put in his lank head. "Send the Chinese maid in at once."

Sandra was taking the rice-paper envelope from her bag. "The Chinese, Dow, gave me this surreptitiously. It's for you, Mr Delaunay."

"For me!" The astounded old man took it with a blue-veined hand. " 'Give this to her employer' – you're right." He set it in his lap, unsnapped a spectacles case, set his glasses on his nose.

A Chinese girl stood in the door.

"You sent for me, sir?"

"Ah . . . oh . . . yes."

Sandra sprang up.

"You're Helen Ying?" she asked.

The girl turned her oval face to her. She was comely, with jetblack, long-lashed, modest eyes. She curtseyed. "Yes, ma'am."

"Do you know who would try to send acid to you?"

"Acid!" The girl's eyes went wide. "To me! No, ma'am!"

"A Chinese man just came to my office and tried to get me to bring you a bamboo tube filled with sulphuric acid. It was fixed so that if you held it toward you, the natural way to open it, the acid would have spurted all over your face and throat."

The girl clutched at herself, aghast. Her eyes were like saucers.

"He said his name was Dow. He claimed to be your cousin. Do you know him?"

The girl shook her head dumbly. Sandra searched the wide jet-black eyes. They were as candid as her own.

"A young, flashily dressed man, very well educated, smoked gold-tipped cigarettes. Have you any idea who he was?"

"No, ma'am. None . . . none at all."

The Vandyked De Saules asked with a sly smile: "No love affairs, or anything like that?"

"No, sir." The girl did not raise her eyes. "I do not know any men here in the city at all."

"My dear girl, don't lie." De Saules fingered his point of beard. "You must know him, otherwise there'd be no point—"

"Suppose we hear what this says," said old Mr Delaunay, ripping open the rice-paper envelope. He took out a typed sheet of paper, read in a slow, loud voice:

Mr John Delaunay:
    You are about to die.
.   The acid sent to the maid is merely a subordinate matter.
    Do not stay alone by yourself.
    Do not eat or drink anything.
    This is the only way to show that your death is not suicide, but murder.
    No human agency can prevent your death.

"What's this?" For an instant the old man's tongue moved speechlessly in his open mouth. "Me! *My* death! What infernal madness is this?"

His daughter Marceline gasped: "It's a death threat!"

De Saules cried to Sandra: "This Chinaman, this Dow, gave that to you?"

"Yes! Yes!" Sandra was stunned, bewildered. "Dow – Dow, the same one that gave me the acid tube!"

"Who would *dare* do such a thing!" With the quick irascibility of age the old man flew into a rage. His mild eyes flashed, he banged his cane on the floor, he ground his teeth, flung the note down and stamped on it. "Call the police! I'll have that scoundrel if it's the last thing—"

He lurched suddenly sideways. It was not a step; it was as though he had been struck from the side. The blackthorn cane flew from him. He screamed out:

"My tongue! My throat!"

Sandra could only see his face, twisted, demoniac. He was tearing at his mouth in a frenzy. Then he fell backward in a frightful spasm, struck a floor lamp, plunged like a senseless blind hammer to the floor.

II

It was so horrible and swift it left them riveted. Sandra felt only a jar in both shoulder blades, as though she had been driven back in her chair. Then De Saules was plunging at the body.

"Mr Delaunay! Mr Delaunay!"

He had one arm beneath the old man's neck, lifting his head. He froze. It was when the head came into the glare of the overturned lamp. The multitudinously wrinkled face lolled at them, eyeballs bulging, staring, glazed. It was not that which cut the breath in their throats; not the hideous grimace on his face – not even the fact of his death.

The old man's tongue protruded from his lips. It was the color of paper. It had a coarse, pitted texture; it looked like a spongy head of swollen fungus, plugged like a stopper between his lips.

The butler was there. The maid was rocking back and forth like someone on the edge of a precipice. The bell was ringing its triple musical chime. Nobody paid any attention to it.

Marceline reeled against Sandra, clutched her arm with hands that almost tore the muscle out.

"Poisoned!" the girl gasped. "He's poisoned!"

"Poisoned!" De Saules whipped to her. "You're mad! How could he be?"

"The note!" Marceline screamed the words. "The note! It *said* he would die!"

Sandra grabbed the butler by the arm. It was like shaking a wooden image.

"Call the police! The police!"

"They're" – the butler waved one arm wildly; he was trying, to indicate the door – "coming up—"

Sandra flashed by him, darted down the hall. Men were hammering at the door. She saw two detectives, behind them the gold bulk of Gawdy's topcoat, his florid handsome face. She snatched open the door; the hard-eyed man in the lead touched his hat.

"Hullo, Miss Grey. We're following up that acid business—"

Sandra caught him by the arm. "Captain Corrigan! There's a dead man in here! Come on!"

The hard-eyed detective captain went by her in two strides. He turned long enough to snap to his companion: "Get the M. E. He's in the car."

Gawdy got Sandra by the arm. His bright-blue eyes were wide. "What's the matter? What's happened?"

"Mr Delaunay's dead! Murdered! That note Dow gave me – it *said* he would die!"

Gawdy's high-colored features blanched. He said only one word: "Marceline!" He plunged by Sandra into the library.

The library was a scene of confusion. Marceline was screaming; the loud, continuous screams of hysteria. De Saules was ineffectually shouting at her, pleading with her. Captain Corrigan took one look out of his hard eyes, walked up and slapped her across the face.

"Shut up!" he said. "Sit down."

It acted like magic. Marceline fell onto the sofa, stopped screaming. The room jolted into calm as if ice water had been sluiced through it.

Captain Corrigan turned around, looked at the dead man. Sandra saw even the scalp on his blunt bullet head move with surprise as he observed that outthrust paper-white tongue.

"When'd this happen?" His hard eyes swiveled like turret guns at De Saules.

"Just now, not two minutes ago!"

"What had he been drinking?"

"Drinking!" De Saules' point of beard jabbed up and down with the irregular movement of his jaw. "Nothing! He was reading that note – that note that prophesied his death!" He darted across, picked up the crumpled rice paper from the rug. "Here! This!"

Corrigan read it. A little man with a black bag bustled in and kneeled down by the corpse, but Corrigan paid no attention. The mouth in his blunt face opened with a jerk as he looked up at De Saules.

"Where'd this come from?"

"*I* brought it!" Sandra's eyes were like vivid stars. "It's from that Chinese, Dow – the one that gave me the acid tube!"

"What!" The difference in tone as Corrigan spoke to Sandra was noticeable. "That Chinaman who brought you the acid tube! You mean he's mixed up in this?"

"Yes! Yes! Mr Delaunay had just read it. He got very angry. He jumped up and—" She groped for words. "He simply fell over, crying out something about his tongue! That was all! He didn't take anything; he didn't drink anything; we all saw him!"

Corrigan looked from her to De Saules to Marceline. He looked at the note. His hard eyes had an expression as if he were surrounded by a group of lunatics. His voice reflected it. "He's dead of a corrosive poison. He must have swallowed it right in front of you."

"Perfectly correct." The medical examiner's voice was as precise as an icicle. "Absolutely typical reaction – the white tongue, the serrated mucous membrane. The throat shows the same bleaching, all the way to the head of the pharynx. It's oxalic acid, the quickest-acting of the common poisons."

Corrigan's eyes shot to the group. "The quickest-acting! You hear that?" His glance swung back to the doctor. "Could it be used for murder?"

"Impossible." The doctor pursed his lips flatly. "Not unless one of them fed it to him a moment before he fell dead. He's a feeble old man. The reaction was instantaneous."

Marceline burst in. It sounded for a moment as if her hysteria were about to recur. "But we *saw* him! We *saw* him! He didn't take anything! He didn't!"

"Yes!" De Saules' hawklike head jabbed out. "Two, three, four of us saw it! Are you telling us we're all mad?"

Corrigan's eyes looked jarred in their hard depths. This weight of testimony was beginning to tell on him. His glance shot to the doctor.

"Could he have held it in his mouth?"

The doctor gave an incredulous thin snort. "My dear man, this is a corrosive acid. It serrates the mucous membrane. The first touch of it would erode his tongue."

"But this is impossible! Impossible!" Corrigan's eyes battered everyone in savage bewilderment. "Do you realize this is not a poison like arsenic – that's tasteless, that you can take an hour or so before it acts – this is a corrosive, it acts instantly! He couldn't have held it in his mouth! He couldn't! Yet you say he didn't take anything! How did he get it?"

"The only possibility is a capsule," said the doctor's thin, piercing voice. He was primly polishing a pair of half-moon glasses. "Suppose – an absurdity even on the face of it – that in some manner a capsule had been lodged in his mouth. With the swelling of the tongue, the membranes, the capsule would still be there. There is no capsule. I have examined his mouth and throat thoroughly."

There was entire silence. Captain Corrigan sat down on the table, a slow, jarring movement. The manifest impossibility of what was before them locked them all in a kind of mental blankness. A man had been killed, before the eyes of four witnesses, in a perfectly obvious way – he had swallowed a corrosive poison – yet the thing was as impossible as that a railroad tie could be put into the mouth of a milk bottle.

Into the silence a man stumbled, executing an unsteady semicircle through the library door like the reel of a dervish. A dressing gown made a disheveled scarlet circle around him. He came up at sight of the corpse, grabbing hold of a chair and staring down with haggard, puffy eyes.

"Who's this?" snapped Corrigan.

Marceline spoke rapidly. "He's a guest. His name's Lonnie Wyatt. He's been asleep all afternoon."

"A guest!"

Corrigan stared at Wyatt. Mud splattered his patent leather shoes, the black serge bottoms of his Tuxedo trousers. The stale fumes of liquor reeked from him; his weakly boyish face, puffed with dissipation, gave a series of jerks as though he were about to fall headlong over the body. The plain-clothes man accompanying Corrigan grabbed hold of Wyatt, shoved him in a chair. Marceline's voice cut in with the same quick rapidity. There was no hint of hysteria in it now.

"It's a little difficult to explain. We found him lying outside our entry in this condition this morning. I . . . we . . . took him in and took care of him because he's a friend."

The singularity of this explanation, along with the singularity of the man's appearance, caused Captain Corrigan to look, not at the drunken Wyatt, but at Marceline. A slight movement of his head indicated the corpse.

"You're his daughter?"

"Yes. I was legally adopted at seventeen."

Corrigan narrowed his hard eyes slightly. "Oh." He switched his glance to the Vandyked De Saules.

"You're a relative, too?"

"A very distant one." De Saules stopped fingering his beard to make a deprecating gesture. "I met Mr Delaunay for the first time yesterday."

"I see." Corrigan's head shot around. "Where's that Chinese maid?"

The butler bustled out hurriedly into the hall. Sandra sat down quietly in a corner chair, pressed her hands to her temples. It was useless to question the maid. Captain Corrigan was making random gestures like a man who has run into a brick wall. Events still whirled, a mad patchwork, in her own mind. Tags of them flared out at her. Dow's bland yellow face smiling over his cigarette; the feel of the note in her hand; the old man's tongue gaping speechlessly in his mouth as he read it; his frightful plunge headlong into the lamp to the floor. She shuddered. What vicious, horrible enigma, spurting flashes of bizarre color like some enigmatic jewel, was here?

She looked at Gawdy, sitting with his big florid face outthrust, his eyes like robins' eggs. He had seen part of it, the others another part, but only she had seen it all. Gropingly she tried to reconstruct events.

Dow – that incomprehensible Chinese, with his suave, creased eyes, his impeccable English, his violet-perfumed cigarette – had come up to her office, given her the bamboo tube and the note. The tube contained a horrible fate for the Delaunay maid, the note a prophecy of Mr Delaunay's death. She had carried the note to Mr Delaunay; the old man had no more than read it, when, as if by conjunction of cause and effect, he had screamed up to his feet, plunged down dead. Dead by a corrosive poison – oxalic acid – which seared, burned, bleached his mouth, whose action was instantaneous, which no one had administered to him!

It was impossible. It was incredible. Only the evidence of her eyes assured her of something as impossible as witchcraft. Dow – the squat, suave Dow – *knew* this! *Knew* Mr Delaunay was to die! Warned him of it! Why? How did Dow know about it? What was

Dow to that secluded old man? Why, if Dow were behind the attempt, should he warn the very object of the crime? Was the Chinese merely a tool in the hands of—

She stared at the others. Her eyes roamed over Marceline, with her flashy brunet prettiness, heightened now by a kind of feverish acuteness, her eyes as brilliant as black jewels. She looked at De Saules, fingering his spike of beard, the sly eyes in his hawklike olive face retracted, withdrawn. She looked at the drunken Wyatt, sprawled backward, breathing stertorously, his puffy weak young face already sinking into the coma of sleep. What parts did they play in this hideous, incredible puzzle?

And the baby! The boy! That tiny waif of humanity, caught up in the meshes of this horrible thing, his little body an innocent sacrifice to its hideous aim! Every time she closed her eyes, she heard him screaming. She gripped her hands until her nails pierced her palms. In some way she felt responsible for him; she could not get the sight of him off her mind, the load of him off her heart.

She stared at the Chinese maid. Corrigan was jabbing questions at her; the girl's sloe-black eyes were pitiful in terror. Sandra was sure the girl was as innocent, as ignorant of all this, as she herself. Corrigan grabbed up the note. He was reading out the part of it that said: "The acid sent to the maid is merely a subordinate matter." De Saules suddenly shoved out his hawklike head, a sharp hand.

"Look. There's something written on the other side of that!"

"What?" Corrigan whipped the paper over. He stared at a single typed sentence, read in a loud voice: "The murderer will attempt to conceal the means of murder in the garage."

"In the—" Corrigan gaped round.

"The garage! What kind of—"

The butler plunged into the room. His eyes were bulging like duck eggs.

"Sir," he shouted, "the garage is on fire!"

There was a simultaneous rush that way. Sandra went, too, as far as the kitchen entry, when a kind of jolt, an inner hunch, brought her up. It was an intuition of the same sort she had had about the baby in the office. This time she obeyed it. The others had poured out of the house. She turned and darted back to the library.

Immediately she was in the doorway a nameless fear clutched her. The lights were out. That long window had not been open, plunging a bar of moonlight across the floor.

She whirled, drawing in air for a shout, when someone slammed her against the wall, jabbed a gun into her warm throat.

"Be perfectly quiet."

She was staring into the yellow face of Dow!

The scream froze in her throat. She could no more have cried out than a block of stone. His oblique eyes were very close, creased as they had been in the office, but glittering with a lethal quality like the button eyes of an adder. He was breathing very hard. Sweat made a saffron sheen on his round face. But his voice, quicker perhaps, more hissing, had still the oily blandness of the office.

"Sit down. Here."

He forced her into a chair. She was cold, paralyzed. Not three feet from her came the stertorous breathing of the drunken Wyatt; there before her was that yellow face, coolly talking.

"Do not move, Miss Grey. If you do, I shall most certainly kill you. A little diversion – the garage fire – to get everyone out. One moment, and your utter silence, are all I need."

He was gone from her, dragging something on the floor. At first she thought it was the stupefied Wyatt; then she realized it was the corpse. His voice was once more at her elbow.

"I will be right here, very close, so if you move, I can shoot at once." He touched her with the cold barrel. Then he was crouching, busy beside the chair.

Her mind was sick, spinning. Her eyes crawled sideways. She saw, vaguely in the dark, his squat body kneeling on the corpse, saw his shoulders working, saw the dead head move up in answer to his movements. Her soul swooned in the nadir of horror. He was doing something – doing something to the body! Her frozen mind could only picture, snatched from some long-lost childhood book, the sight of ghouls – ghouls hunched so over dead bodies, their talons busy with dead flesh.

He had not stopped talking. His voice flowed on with the same oily suaveness, only a flooding together of the sibilants showing his tremendous haste. There was even a fleering, mocking note in it, as though, in spite of the desperate jeopardy of his position, whatever horrible game he was playing, he was playing it with imperturbable coolness, even bravado.

"One moment. One short moment, Miss Grey. Am I the murderer? No, dear lady. I would not be so insanely rash as to be here if I were." She heard the thud of his knees on the floor.

"The murderer is, shall we say, a friend – a mutual friend, Miss Grey."

There was the tinkle on the floor as of some metallic instrument.

"What am I here for? What is my object?" His voice had a hideous relish. "A simple thing. Profit. I did not want this taken for suicide. That was *his* aim, Miss Grey. Mine is absolutely different. And now it is accomplished."

He was past her, a squat powerful figure, as soft-footed as a cat. He was silhouetted for one second in the moonlit window, gone.

Sandra found that scream then. It was piercing, wild, full-bodied, all her healthy young lungs could do. Feet crashed in the back, Corrigan's yell: "Who is it?"

The house was alive with noise. Corrigan was in the room; the lights went on.

She could only gasp: "Dow . . . Dow! He's gone . . . through that window!"

Corrigan was already plunging through the open casement.

Sandra turned. She was beside the corpse. She could feel it, sense it there beside her left foot. Her hands were over her face. Something stronger than shuddering reaction, an irresistible, horrible attraction drew her like a magnet. She took her hands away.

The glazed eyes in that staring white face looked up at her. Just the same – but not the same. In that gaping mouth the hammer-headed, fungously white plug was missing.

Dow had cut out the corpse's tongue!

III

Sunlight through the Venetian blinds of Captain Corrigtan's office made bars of light and shade over the heap of police photographs on his desk, over Sandra's slim hands, leafing through them. As she dropped each photograph, Gawdy picked it up, scrutinizing it with his big florid face outthrust, his blue eyes sharp. Captain Corrigan paced up and down the office. The floor creaked under his heavy step. His bullet head looked jammed between his shoulders, his hard eyes as if he had not slept all night. De Saules, incessantly fingering his spike of beard, sat a little removed, his cool eyes flitting, not over the photographs of Captain Corrigan, but over Sandra's trim body, her velvety absorbed eyes, the color in her young cheeks.

Sandra tossed aside the last photograph of a Chinese with a criminal record.

"I can't find him, Captain Corrigan. He's just not here."

Captain Corrigan looked at Gawdy as if here were his last hope. Gawdy shook his head. "He's none of these."

Corrigan came up. His voice was like an explosion. "We've *got* to find out! We've ransacked the Chinese quarter, combed the city all night!" His jaws clicked shut, worked. "There was nothing in the old man's mouth to take out! Nothing! What was he after? The tongue was cut – cut by a scalpel – sliced out at the roots! Why? Why?"

His eyes raged at all three. Gawdy's handsome face was blank. De Saules took his hand from his beard, smoothed his brows, shook his head. Sandra bit her lip. She was thinking: "They're stumped. The police. They can't get anywhere. How could they? They know even less than I do."

Corrigan slapped the fingers of one hand on the palm of the other. "That yellow devil put that sentence on the back of the note – about the garage – merely to make us rush out pell-mell when he started the fire. He was hiding, watching the house, slipped in when we swallowed the bait. But what for? Why did he cut out the tongue? Why?"

It was as though the repetition might batter the answer out of thin air. He jabbed both hands downward with a slicing motion. "The M. E.'s made a complete autopsy on the head. There's nothing – nothing out of the ordinary, nothing abnormal. But there was nothing there when he examined the mouth *before* the tongue was cut out!"

He was glaring at De Saules. De Saules' eyes drifted by him as he said:

"The maid's the only link."

Corrigan swore. "The maid's only been here from San Francisco a month. Her record's spotless. We've grilled her for hours. I'm convinced she doesn't know Dow."

Gawdy said in his abrupt, gruff voice: "She *must*."

Corrigan did not deign to reply. He seemed to be hoarsely talking to himself. "There's only one way to figure it. The Chink *helped* – helped in some way. The acid was to get the maid for something she may not even realize she knows. Dow's double-crossing his confederate, playing some game of his own. But what is it? What is it? Why send the acid to the maid – help his confederate on one hand, harm him on the other?"

That was what did it. At first it was only a shock in Sandra's mind, a kind of blankness. Corrigan's voice hammered on:

"Motive! Where's the motive? Dow has no motive. The old man didn't even know him. Hardly knew anybody. A secluded, parsimonious, harmless old man, rich as Midas. Didn't have an enemy in the world."

Sandra was sitting bolt upright, her hands in a tight ball in her lap, looking nowhere.

De Saules' eyes met Corrigan's coolly. "You mean, that puts the motive squarely in the family?"

Corrigan stared at him bluntly. "Since you ask it, yes. But since he died without a will, it puts it squarely at one person – his sole heir, his daughter Marceline."

Sandra had moved to the window. She had the phone book in her hands. With quivering fingers she whipped through it. There was the page – the column – the name. The tiny black type seemed to throb and dance before her eyes.

Slowly she closed the book. She looked out at the street below. The moving traffic seemed blinded out from her sight as by a sunburst.

No! It was impossible! Could it be? Could it be? She felt her heart hammering wildly. There, in that tiny black type, was the address, the name, everything, as plain as a pikestaff, for anyone to read.

Suite 405–406 Mohican Building.

She— No, she couldn't breathe even in her own heart that she had the answer! It was too wild, too crazy. Suite 405–406 Mohican Building! Tell Captain Corrigan? He would laugh! It was preposterous! Ridiculous! And yet—

Already a plan had leaped like a wild javelin into her brain. Her eyes had the same tawny fire as when she sprang bolt upright from the clinic chair. Her lips were parted, hot.

They can't get anywhere. Maybe I can.

Heavy lowering clouds, lighted by the afterglow, dappled and dull, hung over the Mohican Building. It was the end of day, when every building roundabout was pouring its outflow of bus-bound stenographers into the street. Sandra slipped into the little drugstore in the Mohican's lobby, approached the clerk at the back.

"A small bottle of concentrated ammonia, please."

With the bottle she slipped into the phone booth, loaded the only weapon she ever owned. It was an old double compact, with a flat rubber sac in the back, which she filled from the bottle like a fountain pen. She adjusted the rubber neck to fit the hole in the compact, slipped it into her bag.

The foyer of the Mohican was noisy, swarming. The elevators had just disgorged a load of heel-clicking, chattering secretaries, gum-chewing office boys. Drifting salesmen, toothpick in mouth, gave Sandra the eye, coughed, stared after her. Sandra did not take the elevator. She walked up to the third floor, toured it rapidly, got its general layout. Particularly she noted the women's washroom at the far end of the corridor where the stairs angled up.

She could almost feel, like a living, ominous presence upstairs, those two rooms, Suite 405–406.

The women's washroom door was locked. This she hadn't counted on. She wondered, with a quick swallow, if the cold chisel in her bag would force a door.

She saw a beauty shop around the bend of the corridor, walked into it. The woman proprietor was just putting her hat on.

"I'm *so* sorry." Sandra turned on the utmost persuasiveness of her velvety eyes. "Can you give me a manicure? It's something special."

The woman sighed, took off her hat. Sandra was hardly seated at the little table when she reeled irregularly, clutched her head.

"I'm awfully dizzy. I don't – Could I—"

"Here, dearie, here's the key to the washroom."

Sandra went out, unlocked it, shot the bolt in the door. She left it that way, came back looking considerably refreshed, and had her manicure. When it was over, she went directly to the washroom, went in, reversed the bolt so as to lock herself in. Then she waited. She heard the woman fussing around to close up, the jingle of her keys in the door, her echoing steps toward the elevator.

Sandra composed herself for a long wait. Dusk faded into night and the fire escape outlined outside the washroom window blotted into the general blackness. Little by little all sounds in the building diminished, spaced themselves farther and farther apart, died away entirely.

In the darkness the whole hideous affair seemed to throb in pulsing outline in her head. It was so clear! So perfectly clear! That one revealing move – done right in front of her – that one act that gave everything away! How had she missed it at the time? Now it

seemed to stand out like a headlight. Her racing mind thought back
to that sentence of Captain Corrigan's that had jarred realization to
her. Yes, why did Dow help the murderer with one hand, harm
him with the other? Because he *had* to! That had flashed the truth
to her – the truth at least in her own mind, the answer that she had
leaped to arrow-swift, with a woman's cut-the-corners rapidity,
complete disregard of details. The old man had been murdered. By
oxalic acid – by a corrosive poison that he didn't take – by an
inexplicable means! Yet it was so fantastically simple! But what a
chance the murderer had taken! Except that of course it would be
taken for suicide, normally, for the old man would have been found
dead, alone somewhere by himself. When Dow had come up to the
office the preparations had been set, ready, the murder an inevitable, imminent fact – and Dow had coolly thrown a monkey
wrench into them. He was playing a game of his own, playing a
gambit against the murderer; and she – her breath came quick – she
was playing a gambit against them both.

Why? Her brown eyes rolled sideways. It wasn't too late to go
back. It was absolute, mad folly, what she was doing. She could
still slip down out of the building, tell the watchman—

No. She shook her head. What was she doing it for? For a
feverish little waif lying in pain in a clinic, a little laughing-eyed
boy who had no part in anything, who had been thrown under this
murder juggernaut, crushed beneath it.

Upstairs – she sank her teeth hard in her lip – in Suite 405–406,
was the crux of the whole thing. It *must* be. In there, in those two
rooms, *something* must remain, perhaps a bottle of oxalic acid,
perhaps— She didn't know. If she could get in, get out, in five
minutes she might have the evidence in her hand.

Down the corridor she heard a new, ascending, plodding step.
She heard the loud clearing of an old throat, the snap of light
switches. That would be the watchman. Motionless, guarding her
breath, she heard his raspings and hawkings make the tour of the
whole building, return with the creaking yawn of the elevator to
the lobby. She heard him drag a chair along the floor, settle himself
before the door.

Then, and only then, Sandra groped out of the washroom. The
hall was pitch-black. She slipped the catch, let the washroom door
softly close. Quietly, gliding like a wraith, she went up the rear
stairway. She knew where Rooms 405–406 were, by her preliminary tour. They were hardly twenty feet from the stairhead, on a

corner, one room on each side. But as she turned the stairhead, she stopped abruptly. Light was coming through the door of 405.

Someone was there! This cut the ground from under her feet. On the glass oblong she could see the words: "Private – Entrance 406." She stood motionless. Who was there? What was—

She heard the echoing scrape of a chair, the booming sound of the watchman's voice. He was talking to someone below. Their conversation was too distorted by echo to follow.

The elevator began its yawning ascent. Sandra flattened to the wall, immersed in shadow by the stairway as in a well. The door clanged open; she saw a fan of light, the watchman's face, a figure emerging. It stepped very quickly out, but Sandra recognized the brilliant black eyes, the flashy brunet prettiness, of Marceline!

Marceline! Coming up to Suite 405–406! Sandra felt a kind of explosion in her mind. What had she bagged here? Almost before she caught her breath, Marceline was inside, not by the entrance door, but by the very door marked "Private". Sandra was watching. Voices began immediately inside. Loud, excited – one of them. The other – Sandra froze – was the bland, oily tone of Dow!

Dow – with Marceline! Sandra's pulse clipped off for an instant, began going like a trip hammer. The door clanged, the elevator began its yawning descent. It was now or never. Sandra slipped out, darted to the door, listened.

Marceline's voice came very clear. It was passionate, savage.

"What does this mean to me?"

"Much, dear lady." Dow's voice had that mocking silkiness that made leap into the mind his moon-round face, his slit-creased, almond eyes. "Why did you come here? Why did you come, for a telephone call merely naming this place? I see you are well acquainted here. Too well acquainted. Do not blanch so, dear lady. I understand. I understand completely. Come, calm yourself, please sit down, let us talk."

Sandra could not detect the quality of Marceline's voice. It was too low. "What do you want?"

"First let us look calmly at what I hold in my hand. It is very old-fashioned. Perhaps you do not recognize it. But I see you do. It has been among your father's possessions a long time; you have seen it many times over many years. Only, dear lady, I turn it over slightly, and you see it is not quite the same. Not the original. A beautiful copy." His voice fleered. "Why not? I made it myself.

Now you understand, perhaps, a certain reckless action of mine last evening."

Marceline's voice was like a physical shudder.

"You horrible fiend."

"Not at all. Such a pretty thing, to me, for example. What is it, so small, so bright, that I turn thus in my palm and let the light fall upon? Why, it is the whole murder. I turn it so; you look where I point to—"

His voice stopped on a rising note. There was an instant's silence, then his voice flowed on. "Control yourself, dear lady. It is a shock. I see you understand. You clutch your throat, you look around, you see how the preparations were made. It was very simple. There, in that very chair, he sat. Yesterday there was no assistant, or, shall we say, I was the assistant. I held it, so. I passed it across, saying: 'What a beautiful repair!' And it is done, so, in the twinkling of an eye, without noise or fanfare, a simple, innocent—"

A low sound came from Marceline like the cry of an animal. There was a rush, a scuffling, a gasped: "Give it to me!"

"Not quite so fast, dear lady." Dow's oily voice hardly faltered. "It is my whole purpose to give it to you – for a price."

"What price?"

The bland voice was like honey. "Now that you are a rich woman, much money is accessible to you. Ten thousand dollars will not be too much. You will have a certified check for that amount tomorrow at nine thirty. On your discretion I can count. There is so much I know, you see, so much you did not tell the police."

Marceline said in a terribly altered voice: "Is that all?"

"That is all, dear lady, until the morning."

Marceline came out so precipitately she almost smashed the door into Sandra's face. Sandra reeled flat to the wall. Marceline didn't look back. She went down the corridor almost at a run.

The lights went out. Dow was coming out. Sandra started back toward the staircase, froze. She saw, vague in the darkness, a blank bulk standing at the head of the stairs.

Sandra's heart seemed to leap out of her mouth like a jackrabbit. Pure primordial instinct, the kind that freezes animals into replicas of posts, of weed clumps, glued her like an integral part of the darkness to the wall. She might have been a piece of the fire extinguisher whose bulging cylinder touched her forehead. A man, waiting there – for what? For her? Had he seen her?

Her eyes swung wildly. She was caught between two fires. Already Dow was coming out; she heard the pad of his feet, the door closing.

It was an interminable moment, a moment that seemed to scream in the silence with all the voices of pandemonium. Behind her was Dow, his hand on the knob; ahead was that shape, looming silent, waiting.

A voice from the stairhead said: "Dow."

Dow whirled around. Flame roared in a blasting streak across the dark. She saw Dow leap completely across the corridor like a chimpanzee. The dark was a wild havoc of noise. The man was plunging this way. Sandra had only one way to go. She flung down the fire extinguisher, fled like an antelope over its deafening crash. She made the stairhead, flew down the staircase like a streak in blackness. She twisted into the washroom, flung up the window, and darted down the fire escape.

IV

The sunlight gilded De Saules' hawklike head, his back, the black spike of his beard, as he stood in the apartment lobby. His narrow eyes shifted down the line of bells, read the card opposite one: "Miss Sandra Grey." The odor of breakfast drifted down to him through the open lobby door, muted morning noises. De Saules did not ring the bell. He lifted the topcoat on his left arm, glanced once at the bulb-like swelling, the thin tubular nose that extended one pocket. He went rapidly up the carpeted steps to Sandra's apartment.

Sandra herself opened the door. She was ready to go out. The morning light made a halo around her trim little shako hat, touched the freshness of her face, made her eyes vividly brown, her lips as red as cyclamen. De Saules' hat was in his hand.

"Good morning, Miss Grey. You'll pardon such an early call? You're going out, but may I have just a moment?"

"Of course." Sandra's eyes widened as she let him in. De Saules did not sit down. He stood in the center of the living room, immaculate in dove-gray tweed, perfectly poised, his cool eyes mild and disarming.

"This is rather abrupt, Miss Grey, but I am a busy man and have not much time. This will only take a moment. I have been so impressed by your splendid welfare work that I wish to make a donation to it."

Sandra sat down. She stared at the smiling olive face, so freshly barbered, almost purringly soft. De Saules stepped across the rug. He sat very close to Sandra. It was a confidential, gliding movement.

"The size of the donation depends only upon yourself."

Sandra was very still. It was curious, what that simple statement did to the room. One moment the air was calm, relaxed; the next bristling with tension as though electricity crackled through it.

Sandra opened her mouth. "Oh," she said. "I understand."

"There is only one stipulation." De Saules' cool eyes were very close. "That is, that you devote your attention to welfare work from now on."

"From now on?"

The cool eyes inclined forward.

"That means, from this morning on?"

De Saules' eyebrows rose, fell. "We understand each other perfectly, Miss Grey."

Sandra ran her tongue between her lips. She was a fool ever to have closed the apartment door. She felt the blood pound, racing in her ears.

"And if I do not accept this – contribution?"

De Saules studied her. His eyes narrowed very slightly, as though he thought there might be some misunderstanding between them.

"Perhaps you have not seen the morning papers?"

"No."

De Saules unfolded an edition from his pocket. The headline screamed in blackface:

COMPLETE REVERSAL OF TESTIMONY
Three Witnesses Admit Delaunay
Took Poison in their Presence

Sandra's mind went blank. A reversal of testimony! It was impossible! Impossible! Admitted he *took* the poison! What on—

De Saules' voice cut across her stupefaction. "It happened late last night. Captain Corrigan is extremely bewildered, but he will be obliged to accept the fact."

Sandra gasped: "All . . . all of you . . . *you* and Marceline—"

"Precisely."

"The Chinese maid, too?"

De Saules smiled with his eyes. "In her position it is, shall we say, difficult to get another job if discharged under suspicion of murder. She is a very level-headed girl."

Sandra managed to get the words out of her mouth.

"You want me to corroborate this absurd lie?"

"Not at all, Miss Grey." De Saules' tone was unruffled. "The gift – I mean the settlement gift, of course – will enable you to study conditions abroad very comfortably, even luxuriously, provided you take the boat that leaves at noon. There are excellent airplane connections which I have already arranged."

Sandra sprang up. She was already at the telephone before De Saules cried:

"What are you doing?"

"I will call up Captain Corrigan at once."

De Saules was across like the crack of a whip. He snatched the telephone from her.

"No. I do not think so." His voice was low, staccato. "If you do not make it easy for me, you will make it hard. If you will not go as I suggest, you will stay – here – and see no one."

Sandra hurled the words in his face. "Until after the appointment at half past nine, is that it?"

"Perhaps." His eyes were very narrow. "Perhaps much longer."

Sandra laughed in his face. "How will you keep me?"

There was nothing cool or composed about De Saules' face now. Everything had been wiped off it but the elementals – a savage locked bleakness like a bird of prey. "You are dealing with someone much more intelligent than you, Miss Grey. One who has thought of every contingency. I would hardly have come up here without being prepared for your refusal."

Sandra should have screamed then. The next moment she could not. One supple movement and his arm snaked under hers, a grip had her by the neck such as she had never felt before in her life. It was like two points of fire – freezing fire at the base of her brain – two closing, clamping points of a vice that flooded paralysis through her whole muscular system. She knew then. The man was a jujitsu expert. She felt herself crumpling, as weak as a doll. His topcoat was half over her head. From it his free hand had snatched a glass atomizer with a long, thin nose.

His breath was close to her ear. "Cycloprophane is a relatively new anæsthetic. Mixed with oxygen, it induces a very sound sleep. You will rest very quietly, quietly be carried downstairs, out of the house."

He had her over the chair back, crushing her down, the coat tented over her head. Fumes were pouring in her face, sickening, suffocating fumes. She tried to hit, kick, whirl, felt the strength suck out of her with each gasp of that sickening flood. The cold nose of the atomizer was between her teeth. He had to shift his hand for that. His thumb slued down across her mouth, keeping her lips open. With every last ounce of strength she bit his thumb. He gave a cry, dropped the atomizer on the front of her dress. She snatched it, blind, wild, smashed it into his face. She saw the bulb burst, the contents splash starwise over his face.

It was like the long, slow, incredibly endless movements of a nightmare. The room was reeling around her; the space to the door seemed to stretch out to infinity. He was there on the floor, gasping, clawing weakly, no longer able to make coordinated movements. She blundered into the table, sent it crashing. Her bag was there on the floor, spinning like a top before the door. She caught it up, plunged sobbing, gasping, through the door.

The taxi driver stared at Sandra. She was very pale.

"You feel all right, lady?"

"Yes! Yes!" She gasped out the Delaunay address. "Please hurry! Hurry!"

The cab buzzed like a hornet through early morning traffic. Sandra sat in the window corner, gulped in great mouthfuls of fresh air. Her head was steadying; if the nausea would only sub-side— The appointment! Dow and Marceline! Sandra glanced for the twentieth time at her watch, watched the minutes crawl across the dial. 9:39 . . . 9:40 . . . Would she be too late? Too late?

The cab swung into the sweeping lawns, the rippling trees of the Delaunay street. She rapped hard on the glass partition.

"Pull over to the side behind those trees."

She was out the door almost before the cab reached the curb. "Wait here!" She was gone between the massed shrubbery of the Delaunay drive.

Before her the big house stood quiet, dappled with sun and shade. She darted around the side, in the service door. Bulky packages from market were lying, still unretrieved, within – that told her Marceline had dismissed the servants. As Sandra's feet sounded in the kitchen, she heard Marceline's startled voice:

"Who's there?"

Sandra whirled through the kitchen, down the hall, straight into the library.

Marceline was standing bolt upright against the very casement Dow had used for his ghoul's visit. She was alone. In the blaze of yellow light behind her, her face looked extraordinarily white, her black eyes feverishly brilliant. Whatever movements she had had time to make between Sandra's entrance and Sandra's appearance in the library were few and brief. She wore an ornate house coat, whose gorgeous flowers of scarlet and gold emphasized her frightful pallor, the brilliance of her eyes. She let her hands drop from behind her back as she exclaimed:

"You!"

Then Sandra knew what she had been doing with her hands. She had been closing the casement. That told her the story; that and the faint but unmistakable reek of violet in the air. Dow had just gone; Sandra had caught her almost in the act of receiving what Dow had brought; she had not had time to dispose of it. The crisis of the whole affair swung like a pendulum in the quiet room. Sandra felt strangely cool, knife-hard. It was woman against woman, and it was going to be fought out with women's weapons.

Her velvety eyes were as soft as Irish honey. "Why, darling, how upset you look! Did I frighten you by running in?"

Marceline sat down on the sofa. It was a quick, crouching movement. Sandra could see the pulse beat in her throat. Her voice was unkeyed.

"What are you doing here?"

"I've the most wonderful thing to tell you!" Sandra's voice rippled with excitement. *That* wasn't hard. Under that locked coolness she had never been so excited in her life. She crossed to the sofa, sat quickly by Marceline. "Mr de Saules has just made me the most wonderful gift for my welfare work!"

Marceline stared at her. It could be seen from her wild, uncollected eyes just how unready this sidelong shot caught her. Their brilliant depths had almost a stupid blankness. She was in the position of one who cannot estimate her antagonist, has no idea what she knows, and is so caught by the jeopardy of her own position that she cannot collect herself to fence. Sandra didn't give her time to marshal herself. She burst out:

"I'm so excited, darling! I just *had* to rush over! May I have one of your cigarettes?"

With quick, hard hands she patted the pockets of Marceline's house coat. It had only two pockets; its zippered length was otherwise unrelieved. The two pockets were empty.

"Oh, you've got them here, of course." Sandra picked up Marceline's bag, unsnapped it, raked inside. A compact, lipstick, gold pencil, rolled away beneath her fingers. Nothing else. Her eyes darted around the room. That damning bit of evidence was here somewhere. Where had she put it? Where? The room was singularly bare of places of quick concealment. The books lining three walls were packed solid, behind glass. There was only a cloisonné jar on the mantel, a tabouret with a red drawer, and the massive bulk of a combination radio and victrola.

Marceline said harshly: "What are you doing here, if you took the gift?"

Sandra crossed to the mantel. "I *had* to thank you." She took the cover off the cloisonné jar. It was empty. That left only the tabouret drawer and the radio combination. Once she lifted the lid of the radio, the game was up.

"Thank me? What do you mean?"

"I *knew* it came from you." Sandra snapped open the tabouret drawer, looked at blank red wood. Her voice rippled, flute-soft. "You *do* keep your cigarettes in the most outlandish places." She crossed to the radio, lifted the lid, saw nothing inside whatever.

Marceline sprang up. The buttons were off the foils now. She cried:

"What are you doing?"

Then Sandra saw it. The sight gave her such a rush of relief she felt for an instant free and giddy as if swept into mountain air. She crossed, almost in a run, to the far end of the sofa. She knelt on the cushions. She leaned over the arm. She said, in the same dulcet, flute-soft voice:

"Why, darling, the fish are all dead."

The goldfish in the bowl were floating bellies up. Around the little ornamental castle that had been their home the water was colorless, the green fernlike fronds of bladder-wort undisturbed. Only in the sand before the castle something half immersed was gleaming that might have been the polished side of a small shell.

Sandra murmured: "*What* could have killed them? Poison, do you suppose? Poison, on something that's been dropped in?"

She lifted her hand to dip into the bowl. Marceline took two wild, darting movements toward a wing chair and came up with a gun from beneath the cushion.

"Put your hand in that bowl and I swear I'll kill you."

Her brilliant eyes were like a leopard's. Sandra took one look at them and knew that she meant exactly what she said. Slowly she let her hand drop by her side, slowly sat down on the sofa.

"Marceline, the game's up. You don't think I took that bribe from De Saules, do you?" Sandra talked very rapidly. She held Marceline's eyes, not letting that dilated gaze escape for a second. She didn't dare. "I left him lying in my apartment. I called the police before I left the apartment lobby. You see, I was in the Mohican Building last night."

It was hard to tell, from the wildness of those eyes, whether she heard or not. Sandra drove the words in hard.

"Do you love him very much?"

A quiver went over that face. The brilliant eyes seemed stricken to their depths. Sandra slipped her compact from her pocket. Now her voice was low, soothing, as one speaks to a child.

"Did your father have great hopes for you, Marceline? Would he have disinherited you if he knew what you had done? Is that why you kept the marriage a secret?"

Marceline began to shake. She could not control it. It was all over her body, from her lips to the elbow of the arm holding the gun. The words seemed to jerk out without her volition.

"Marriage? How did you know?"

"It had to be, Marceline. He *had* to be your husband to have a motive. I know how you feel. You love him. You want to protect him at all costs. He's going to kill you, Marceline. He has to, now. Because you know. Marceline, he's standing right behind you in the door."

Marceline whirled. Sandra was across like a flash, smashed at the gun with her hand. It exploded point-blank into the floor; the recoil knocked it from Marceline's hand.

Sandra snatched it up, flung it to the far end of the room. She whirled toward the fishbowl. She was too centered, going too headlong, to see the casement swing open. Even the fan of sunlight, leaping like a spear across her path, didn't warm her. She was two steps from the bowl. She never reached it. Something crashed down on her head. That fan of sunlight seemed to leap up, swallow the whole room in a bursting yellow star.

It didn't knock her out. She could thank her shako hat, her thick hair, for that. She felt herself hit the sofa, go headlong into its cushions. Strong hands twisted her on her back. Whipsaws of sound were whanging and snapping in her brain. She was staring as through the wrong end of a telescope at the yellow face of Dow.

"Very lucky, dear lady, I remained to overhear." His voice poured like thin oil from far away. "It would do for the proper party to have it, but never for you. In that case I will take it back."

She saw Marceline spring at him, a screaming, clawing form. She saw the yellow man tear her from him like a kitten, fling her across the room. He hardly stopped talking to Sandra.

"I see you are not the naïve, child-like little lady I took you for. It was you, then, who were in the Mohican Building last night. I made a mistake not to kill you the last time. This time I most certainly shall."

Sandra tried to roll off the sofa. She could not. The fishbowl was above her. Dow was holding it, staring into it. She would always see his face, distorted through the curved glass like the flat, prodigiously wide face of a sting ray.

Then he dipped in his yellow hand, took out the bright object.

"So," he said, "the little item returns to me. The little item that places the murder so exactly. This time it will not leave me."

The shot seemed to come from nowhere. Dow was still holding the fishbowl. He jammed it into his own face with a convulsive jerk, smashing a great half-moon out of it. He whirled on his heels with a surprised look, cast the bowl like a shot-put at the floor. He kept revolving, his face a horrible gray and stretched with surprise, plunged headlong over Sandra on the sofa.

Sandra did not know if she was screaming or not. Her mind was like a black blind space riven by two forked bolts. One of them was: the murderer! The murderer was in the room! The other was: under the form quivering convulsively above her, the bright object was there on the cushions beside her!

It was a moment of such hideous chaos nothing seemed coherent – not the yellow head, batting blindly at the sofa back, not her own hand jammed into her face, not her frantic animal convulsions to throw off that shuddering body.

Then Marceline's scream cut through everything.

"Oh, no! Not me! You're not going to kill *me*!"

The gun crashed again. She heard Marceline's scream. Sandra seemed sucked out of reality, her soul yawing and heeling over in blackness. She was free of that twitching form. She was half off the sofa. A new bedlam was awake – a bedlam that was not in her mind. Voices. Pounding feet. Batterings. Yells.

Captain Corrigan! The police!

She was on her knees. A hand got hold of her. It got her under the jaw from behind, a hand like a steel vice. It yanked her completely from the ground, a swooping arc that almost made her swoon. She saw the bright blaze of sunlight rushing toward her, felt her fierce propulsion across the rug. Then she knew – he was going to use her for a shield!

She was at the casement. He was behind her. She could feel the rigid strength of his body, the sharp pressure of his hip. His breath panted hoarsely in her hair. His left arm was clamped like a bar across her neck, both her wrists pinioned beneath it.

Outside were faces. They were picked out vivid against the green lawn, the brilliant sunshine. Captain Corrigan, his bullet head forward, his eyes like two slits of a knife, his hard jaw working. The policemen, the sun flashing from their shields, their guns half extended. The hawklike face of De Saules, his black spear point of beard jabbing up and down with irregular motions. All were staring at the face behind her, their faces etched alike with stunned, stark blankness.

They were looking into the face of the murderer – the face she could not see!

Then his coat sleeve brushed by her body as he raised his arm to fire. She couldn't do anything. She couldn't move her wrists. All she could do was turn over the compact in her hand. She couldn't aim it. But her hand was jammed almost against his jaw. She got the hole in the metal cover around just as his arm swung down to shoot.

She squeezed the compact for all she was worth. The jet of ammonia shot like a cascade into his face. The contraction of his body threw her headfirst against the wall. But before she spun into blackness, before the rush through the window reached that floundering, gagging form, she caught one glimpse of his face – the too florid, too blue-eyed, too handsome face of Gawdy!

Captain Corrigan was beside her. She was sitting on the sofa. The rush, tumult and furor had all gone out, now, out of the room and out of the house, taking the gold-coated bulk of Gawdy with it. Out of her mind, too – she was once more clear and collected, her shako hat straight on her head, her face freshened, and except for the ache in her head, could even look back on things with a certain perspective.

Captain Corrigan's head was lowered. He was leafing through a telephone book. He jabbed his thumb at a name.

"You're right! There it is! A dentist! Dr Gawdy! Now why the devil didn't I look the guy up? Is that all you did to find it?"

"That's all." Sandra put her slim forefinger beside his thumb. "There it was in the book – George Gawdy, D.D.S., Suite 405–406, Mohican Building. He was Mr Delaunay's dentist – for how long I don't know, but probably after he married Marceline."

Corrigan had dropped the book and was staring at a bright object on the sofa flanked by two circular gold prongs. "An old-fashioned denture – a one-tooth removable bridge!" He turned it over. "And there, there's the hole in it where it was filled with the pulverized crystals of oxalic acid!"

"Yes, and through the same hole the acid got out." Sandra could not look at it without repulsion. "It's a duplicate, made by the dental laboratory man Dow, to be slipped into Mr Delaunay's mouth in place of the one he had. Under the guise of having it repaired, Gawdy got hold of it and had the hollow duplicate made."

Corrigan began a curse, checked himself. "All Gawdy did was fill it with the pulverized crystals, and plug it with a little soluble cement, so the poison would come out when the cement did!"

"Of course. And that moment happened to be when Mr Delaunay got so angry over reading Dow's warning note. He ground his teeth and dislodged the plug – and the acid poured into his mouth."

Corrigan stared at her. His eyes went over her trim head, her vivid young cheeks, her wide brown eyes, in a kind of mystified stupefaction.

"How the devil did you ever happen to pick out Gawdy?"

"*You* helped me, Captain Corrigan." Sandra's brown eyes flashed a smile. "It was yesterday morning, in your office, when you said of Dow: 'Why help his confederate on one hand, harm him on the other?' Only because he *had* to. Women's minds make strange quirks, Captain Corrigan, and that made mine flash back to when Dow, in the welfare office, had given me the note. It made me see what I had entirely overlooked – that Dow *palmed* the note he gave me. He *hid* it in his hand. Why? Why not hand me the note openly? It could only have been because of the presence of someone he didn't want to see it – and the only other person there was Gawdy. That made it" – she gestured – "oh, so plain, it was just like a bombshell! So then I went and looked Gawdy up in the phone book, and there he was – a dentist. That almost proved it, at least to me. Of course the poison had to be something to do with his teeth! It was the only way it *could* get into his mouth! So you see, at the bottom of the crazy way a woman's mind works, *you* really supplied the answer."

Corrigan took his hat off. He almost blushed.

"There's precious little credit in this for me. Go on. I'm listening. My hat's off to you. I've got my mouth open."

Sandra said with a gesture of both hands: "There *wasn't* anything else. I had a wild idea there might be a dental chart of Mr Delaunay's in Gawdy's office. I went up to the Mohican Building – and found Dow selling the bridge to Marceline. Of course I didn't know it was a bridge, but I knew it was something that looked like a tooth."

A shadow crossed her face. "Maybe what kept me from thinking of Gawdy so long was the fact that he brought the baby up to my office. That was pure coincidence. He was coming up to see that Dow delivered the bamboo tube to me without any hitch, and finding the baby gave him a good excuse to come in." She shook her head. "I can see what Dow's whole aim was all through, to make the affair plainly a murder, so he could blackmail Gawdy's secret bride. But I still don't know *why*, Captain Corrigan, they sent the acid to the Chinese maid."

Corrigan grunted. "You were still unconscious when Dow gasped that part out to us with what must have been his last gallon of breath. The maid was the one that overheard Gawdy talking to the old man, examining his bridge, and suggesting that he come up to the office and have it repaired."

"So that's it!" Sandra gave a breath of relief. "I'm so glad she's cleared; I had a feeling she was honest all through."

Corrigan gave his knee a vicious cut with his hat. "No wonder the M. E. or the autopsy didn't find anything wrong with the old man's mouth! When the M. E. first looked into it, the duplicate bridge was there; when the autopsy was conducted, his honest old original bridge was there!"

"Of course. And all Dow cut the tongue out for was to get at the poisoned bridge, remove it, and replace the original harmless one; and of course *then* there was not the slightest thing wrong with the old man's mouth."

Corrigan's hard eyes flicked over the broken remnants of the goldfish bowl. "The young lady Marceline can consider herself damned lucky she only got a flesh wound. Gawdy was in here to clean up. He was going to get her and Dow and everyone he figured knew a solitary thing about it."

Sandra's eyes blazed. "And after what Marceline went through for him, did for him, out of pure, unadulterated love for him! She begged De Saules to reverse his testimony – probably at the cost of saying she herself was implicated – and De Saules, out of family loyalty and because he really was gone on her, agreed." She broke off suddenly. She didn't tell how De Saules had come up, tried to stop her with cycloprophane. Let bygones be bygones. She had a feeling the whole answer to Marceline's shattered life lay in De Saules.

"By George! I wish I was ten years younger!" Captain Corrigan was staring at her with his widest-open look. He got up and stood with his blunt hands on his hips. "Think of it, a girl like you, smart as they make 'em, pretty as a little dream, running around loose!" His thundering voice broke off with a grin. "How come no man has appropriated you?"

"One has." The smile in Sandra's eyes was like the deepest velvet in the world. She picked up her bag. "I'm on the way to see him now, Captain Corrigan. He's not very big, but he's gone through a lot on my account. He's waiting for me over at the clinic."

Proof of Guilt

Bill Pronzini

Bill Pronzini (b. 1943) is both an aficionado of the pulp and mystery magazines and a highly respected writer of crime and mystery fiction. He is best known for his long-running series featuring the unnamed private eye and former cop known simply as Nameless. His first novel appearance was with The Snatch *(1971) and his adventures include the double locked-room puzzler* Hoodwink *(1981). Pronzini has won many awards including the Private Eye Writers of America Lifetime Achievement. He is married to author Marcia Muller. The following does not include any of his series characters and is probably the most audacious of the stories in this volume.*

I've been a city cop for 32 years now, and during that time I've heard of and been involved in some of the weirdest, most audacious crimes imaginable – on and off public record. But as far as I'm concerned, the murder of an attorney named Adam Chillingham is *the* damnedest case in my experience, if not in the entire annals of crime.

You think I'm exaggerating? Well, listen to the way it was.

My partner Jack Sherrard and I were in the Detective Squad-room one morning last summer when this call came in from a man named Charles Hearn. He said he was Adam Chillingham's law clerk, and that his employer had just been shot to death; he also said he had the killer trapped in the lawyer's private office.

It seemed like a fairly routine case at that point. Sherrard and I drove out to the Dawes Building, a skyscraper in a new business development on the city's south side, and rode the elevator up to Chillingham's suite of offices on the sixteenth floor. Hearn, and a woman named Clarisse Tower, who told us she had been the dead man's secretary, were waiting in the anteroom with two uniformed patrolmen who had arrived minutes earlier.

According to Hearn, a man named George Dillon had made a 10:30 appointment with Chillingham, had kept it punctually, and had been escorted by the attorney into the private office at that exact time. At 10:40 Hearn thought he heard a muffled explosion from inside the office, but he couldn't be sure because the walls were partially soundproofed.

Hearn got up from his desk in the anteroom and knocked on the door and there was no response; then he tried the knob and found that the door was locked from the inside. Miss Tower confirmed all this, although she said she hadn't heard any sound; her desk was farther away from the office door than was Hearn's.

A couple of minutes later the door had opened and George Dillon had looked out and calmly said that Chillingham had been murdered. He had not tried to leave the office after the announcement; instead, he'd seated himself in a chair near the desk and lighted a cigarette. Hearn satisfied himself that his employer was dead, made a hasty exit, but had the presence of mind to lock the door from the outside by the simple expediency of transferring the key from the inside to the outside – thus sealing Dillon in the office with the body. After which Hearn put in his call to Headquarters.

So Sherrard and I drew our guns, unlocked the door, and burst into the private office. This George Dillon was sitting in the chair across the desk, very casual, both his hands up in plain sight. He gave us a relieved look and said he was glad the police had arrived so quickly.

I went over and looked at the body, which was sprawled on the floor behind the desk; a pair of French windows were open in the wall just beyond, letting in a warm summer breeze. Chillingham had been shot once in the right side of the neck, with what appeared by the size of the wound to have been a small-caliber bullet; there was no exit wound, and there were no powder burns.

I straightened up, glanced around the office, and saw that the only door was the one which we had just come through. There was no balcony or ledge outside the open windows – just a sheer drop of 16 stories to a parklike, well-landscaped lawn which stretched away for several hundred yards. The nearest building was a hundred yards distant, angled well to the right. Its roof was about on a level with Chillingham's office, it being a lower structure than the Dawes Building; not much of the roof was visible unless you peered out and around.

Sherrard and I then questioned George Dillon – and he claimed he hadn't killed Chillingham. He said the attorney had been standing at the open windows, leaning out a little, and that all of a sudden he had cried out and fallen down with the bullet in his neck. Dillon said he'd taken a look out the windows, hadn't seen anything, checked that Chillingham was dead, then unlocked the door and summoned Hearn and Miss Tower.

When the coroner and the lab crew finally got there, and the doc had made his preliminary examination, I asked him about the wound. He confirmed my earlier guess – a small-caliber bullet, probably a .22 or .25. He couldn't be absolutely sure, of course, until he took out the slug at the post-mortem.

I talked things over with Sherrard and we both agreed that it was pretty much improbable for somebody with a .22 or .25 caliber weapon to have shot Chillingham from the roof of the nearest building; a small caliber like that just doesn't have a range of a hundred yards and the angle was almost too sharp. There was nowhere else the shot could have come from – except from inside the office. And that left us with George Dillon, whose story was obviously false and who just as obviously had killed the attorney while the two of them were locked inside this office.

You'd think it was pretty cut and dried then, wouldn't you? You'd think all we had to do was arrest Dillon and charge him with homicide, and our job was finished. Right?

Wrong.

Because we couldn't find the gun.

Remember, now, Dillon had been locked in that office – except for the minute or two it took Hearn to examine the body and slip out and relock the door – from the time Chillingham died until the time we came in. And both Hearn and Miss Tower swore that Dillon hadn't stepped outside the office during that minute or two. We'd already searched Dillon and he had nothing on him. We searched the office – I mean, we *searched* that office – and there was no gun there.

We sent officers over to the roof of the nearest building and down onto the landscaped lawn; they went over every square inch of ground and rooftop, and they didn't find anything. Dillon hadn't thrown the gun out the open windows then, and there was no place on the face of the sheer wall of the building where a gun could have been hidden.

So where was the murder weapon? What had Dillon done with it? Unless we found that out, we had no evidence against him that would stand up in a court of law; his word that he *hadn't* killed Chillingham, despite the circumstantial evidence of the locked room, was as good as money in the bank. It was up to us to prove him guilty, not up to him to prove himself innocent. You see the problem?

We took him into a large book-filled room that was part of the Chillingham suite – what Hearn called the "archives" – and sat him down in a chair and began to question him extensively. He was a big husky guy with blondish hair and these perfectly guileless eyes; he just sat there and looked at us and answered in a polite voice, maintaining right along that he hadn't killed the lawyer.

We made him tell his story of what had happened in the office a dozen times, and he explained it the same way each time – no variations. Chillingham had locked the door after they entered, and then they sat down and talked over some business. Pretty soon Chillingham complained that it was stuffy in the room, got up, and opened the French windows; the next thing Dillon knew, he said, the attorney collapsed with the bullet in him. He hadn't heard any shot, he said; Hearn must be mistaken about a muffled explosion.

I said finally, "All right, Dillon, suppose you tell us why you came to see Chillingham. What was this business you discussed?"

"He was my father's lawyer," Dillon said, "and the executor of my father's estate. He was also a thief. He stole three hundred and fifty thousand dollars of my father's money."

Sherrard and I stared at him. Jack said, "That gives you one hell of a motive for murder, if it's true."

"It's true," Dillon said flatly. "And yes, I suppose it does give me a strong motive for killing him. I admit I hated the man, I hated him passionately."

"You admit that, do you?"

"Why not? I have nothing to hide."

"What did you expect to gain by coming here to see Chillingham?" I asked. "Assuming you didn't come here to kill him."

"I wanted to tell him I knew what he'd done, and that I was going to expose him for the thief he was."

"You tell him that?"

"I was leading up to it when he was shot."

"Suppose you go into a little more detail about this alleged theft from your father's estate."

"All right." Dillon lit a cigarette. "My father was a hard-nosed businessman, a selfmade type who acquired a considerable fortune in textiles; as far as he was concerned, all of life revolved around money. But I've never seen it that way; I've always been something of a free spirit and to hell with negotiable assets. Inevitably, my father and I had a falling-out about fifteen years ago, when I was twenty-three, and I left home with the idea of seeing some of the big wide world – which is exactly what I did.

"I traveled from one end of this country to the other, working at different jobs, and then I went to South America for a while. Some of the wanderlust finally began to wear off, and I decided to come back to this city and settle down – maybe even patch things up with my father. I arrived several days ago and learned then that he had been dead for more than two years."

"You had no contact with your father during the fifteen years you were drifting around?"

"None whatsoever. I told you, we had a falling-out. And we'd never been close to begin with."

Sherrard asked, "So what made you suspect Chillingham had stolen money from your father's estate?"

"I am the only surviving member of the Dillon family; there are no other relatives, not even a distant cousin. I knew my father wouldn't have left me a cent, not after all these years, and I didn't particularly care; but I *was* curious to find out to whom he had willed his estate."

"And what did you find out?"

"Well, I happen to know that my father had three favorite charities," Dillon said. "Before I left, he used to tell me that if I didn't 'shape-up,' as he put it, he would leave every cent of his money to those three institutions."

"He didn't, is that it?"

"Not exactly. According to the will, he left two hundred thousand dollars to each of two of them – the Cancer Society and the Children's Hospital. He also, according to the will, left three hundred and fifty thousand dollars to the Association for Medical Research."

"All right," Sherrard said, "so what does that have to do with Chillingham?"

"Everything," Dillon told him. "My father died of a heart attack – he'd had a heart condition for many years. Not severe, but he fully expected to die as a result of it one day. And so he did. And because of this heart condition his third favorite charity – the one he felt the most strongly about – was the Heart Fund."

"Go on," I said, frowning.

Dillon put out his cigarette and gave me a humorless smile. "I looked into the Association for Medical Research and I did quite a thorough bit of checking. It doesn't exist; there *isn't* any Association for Medical Research. And the only person who could have invented it is or was my father's lawyer and executor, Adam Chillingham."

Sherrard and I thought that over and came to the same conclusion. I said, "So even though you never got along with your father, and you don't care about money for yourself, you decided to expose Chillingham."

"That's right. My father worked hard all his life to build his fortune, and admirably enough he decided to give it to charity at his death. I believe in worthwhile causes, I believe in the work being done by the Heart Fund, and it sent me into a rage to realize they had been cheated out of a substantial fortune which could have gone toward valuable research."

"A murderous rage?" Sherrard asked softly.

Dillon showed us his humorless smile again. "I didn't kill Adam Chillingham," he said. "But you'll have to admit, he deserved killing – and that the world is better off without the likes of him."

I might have admitted that to myself, if Dillon's accusations were valid, but I didn't admit it to Dillon. I'm a cop, and my job is to uphold the law; murder is murder, whatever the reasons for it, and it can't be gotten away with.

Sherrard and I hammered at Dillon a while longer, but we couldn't shake him at all. I left Jack to continue the field questioning and took a couple of men and re-searched Chillingham's private office. No gun. I went up onto the roof of the nearest building and searched that personally. No gun. I took my men down into the lawn area and supervised another minute search. No gun.

I went back to Chillingham's suite and talked to Charles Hearn and Miss Tower again, and they had nothing to add to what they'd already told us; Hearn was "almost positive" he had heard a muffled explosion inside the office, but from the legal point of view that was the same as not having heard anything at all.

We took Dillon down to Headquarters finally, because we knew damned well he had killed Adam Chillingham, and advised him of his rights and printed him and booked him on suspicion. He asked for counsel, and we called a public defender for him, and then we grilled him again in earnest. It got us nowhere.

The F.B.I. and state check we ran on his fingerprints got us nowhere either; he wasn't wanted, he had never been arrested, he had never even been printed before. Unless something turned up soon in the way of evidence – specifically, the missing murder weapon – we knew we couldn't hold him very long.

The next day I received the lab report and the coroner's report and the ballistics report on the bullet taken from Chillingham's neck – 22 caliber, all right. The lab's and coroner's findings combined to tell me something I'd already guessed: the wound and the calculated angle of trajectory of the bullet did not entirely rule out the remote possibility that Chillingham had been shot from the roof of the nearest building. The ballistics report, however, told me something I hadn't guessed – something which surprised me a little.

The bullet had no rifling marks.

Sherrard blinked at this when I related the information to him. "No rifling marks?" he said. "Hell, that means the slug wasn't fired from a gun at all, at least not a lawfully manufactured one. A homemade weapon, you think, Walt?"

"That's how it figures," I agreed. "A kind of zip gun probably. Anybody can make one; all you need is a length of tubing or the like and a bullet and a grip of some sort and a detonating cap."

"But there was no zip gun, either, in or around Chillingham's office. We'd have found it if there was."

I worried my lower lip meditatively. "Well, you can make one of those zips from a dozen or more small component parts, you know; even the tubing could be soft aluminum, the kind you can break apart with your hands. When you're done using it, you can knock it down again into its components. Dillon had enough time to have done that, before opening the locked door."

"Sure," Sherrard said. "But then what? We *still* didn't find anything – not a single thing – that could have been used as part of a homemade zip."

I suggested we go back and make another search, and so we drove once more to the Dawes Building. We re-combed Chillingham's private office – we'd had a police seal on it to make sure nothing could be disturbed – and we re-combed the surrounding area. We didn't find so much as an iron filing. Then we went to the city jail and had another talk with George Dillon.

When I told him our zipgun theory, I thought I saw a light flicker in his eyes; but it was the briefest of reactions, and I couldn't be sure. We told him it was highly unlikely a zipgun using a .22 caliber bullet could kill anybody from a distance of a hundred yards, and he said he couldn't help that, *he* didn't know anything about such a weapon. Further questioning got us nowhere.

And the following day we were forced to release him, with a warning not to leave the city.

But Sherrard and I continued to work doggedly on the case; it was one of those cases that preys on your mind constantly, keeps you from sleeping well at night, because you know there has to be an answer and you just can't figure out what it is. We ran checks into Chillingham's records and found that he had made some large private investments a year ago, right after the Dillon will had been probated. And as George Dillon had claimed, there was no Association for Medical Research; it was a dummy charity, apparently set up by Chillingham for the explicit purpose of stealing old man Dillon's $350,000. But there was no definite proof of this, not enough to have convinced Chillingham of theft in a court of law; he'd covered himself pretty neatly.

As an intelligent man, George Dillon had no doubt realized that a public exposure of Chillingham would have resulted in nothing more than adverse publicity and the slim possibility of disbarment – hardly sufficient punishment in Dillon's eyes. So he had decided on what to him was a morally justifiable homicide. From the law's point of view, however, it was nonetheless Murder One.

But the law still had no idea what he'd done with the weapon, and therefore, as in the case of Chillingham's theft, the law had no proof of guilt.

As I said, though, we had our teeth into this one and we weren't about to let go. So we paid another call on Dillon, this time at the hotel where he was staying, and asked him some questions about his background. There was nothing more immediate we could investigate, and we thought that maybe there was an angle in his past which would give us a clue toward solving the riddle.

He told us, readily enough, some of what he'd done during the 15 years since he'd left home, and it was a typical drifter's life:

lobster packer in Maine, ranch hand in Montana, oil worker in Texas, road construction in South America. But there was a gap of about four years which he sort of skimmed over without saying anything specific. I jumped on that and asked him some direct questions, but he wouldn't talk about it.

His reluctance made Sherrard and me more than a little curious; we both had that cop's feeling it was important, that maybe it was the key we needed to unlock the mystery. Unobtrusively we had the department photographer take some pictures of Dillon; then we sent them out, along with a request for information as to his whereabouts during the four blank years, to various law enforcement agencies in Florida – where he'd admitted to being just prior to the gap, working as a deckhand on a Key West charter-fishing boat.

Time dragged on, and nothing turned up, and we were reluctantly forced by sheer volume of other work to abandon the Chillingham case; officially, it was now buried in the Unsolved File. Then, three months later, we had a wire from the Chief of Police of a town not far from Fort Lauderdale. It said they had tentatively identified George Dillon from the pictures we'd sent and were forwarding by airmail special delivery something which might conceivably prove the nature of Dillon's activities during at least part of the specified period.

Sherrard and I fidgeted around waiting for the special delivery to arrive, and when it finally came I happened to be the only one of us in the Squadroom. I tore the envelope open and what was inside was a multicolored and well-aged poster, with a picture of a man who was undeniably George Dillon depicted on it. I looked at the picture and read what was written on the poster at least a dozen times.

It told me a lot of things all right, that poster did. It told me exactly what Dillon had done with the homemade zipgun he had used to kill Adam Chillingham – an answer that was at once fantastic and yet so simple you'd never even consider it. And it told me there wasn't a damned thing we could do about it now, that we couldn't touch him, that George Dillon actually had committed a perfect murder.

I was brooding over this when Jack Sherrard returned to the Squadroom. He said, "Why so glum, Walt?"

"The special delivery from Florida finally showed up," I said, and watched instant excitement animate his face. Then I saw some of it fade while I told him what I'd been brooding about, finishing with, "We simply can't arrest him now, Jack. There's no evidence, it doesn't exist any more; we can't prove a thing. And maybe it's just as well in one respect, since I kind of liked Dillon and would have hated to see him convicted for killing a crook like Chillingham. Anyway, we'll be able to sleep nights now."

"Damn it, Walt, will you tell me what you're talking about!"

"All right. Remember when we got the ballistics report and we talked over how easy it would be for Dillon to have made a zipgun? And how he could make the whole thing out of a dozen or so small component parts, so that afterward he could break it down again into those small parts?"

"Sure, sure. But I still don't care if Dillon used a hundred components, we didn't find a single one of them. Not one. So what, if that's part of the answer, did he do with them? There's not even a connecting bathroom where he could have flushed them down. What did he do with the damned zipgun?"

I sighed and slid the poster – the old carnival sideshow poster – around on my desk so he could see Dillon's picture and read the words printed below it: STEAK AND POTATOES AND APPLE PIE IS OUR DISH; NUTS, BOLTS, PIECES OF WOOD, BITS OF METAL IS HIS! YOU HAVE TO SEE IT TO BELIEVE IT: THE AMAZING MR GEORGE, THE MAN WITH THE CAST-IRON STOMACH.

Sherrard's head jerked up and he stared at me open-mouthed.

"That's right," I said wearily. "He *ate* it."

Slaughterhouse

Barry Longyear

Barry Longyear (b. 1942) is best known for his science fiction, and his early work, which included the now classic short story "Enemy Mine" (1979), filmed in 1985, won him a clutch of awards. Other books include Manifest Destiny *(1980),* Circus World *(1981),* Sea of Glass *(1987) and* Naked Came the Robot *(1988). It may come as a surprise to many to find that he also wrote this one mystery story early in his career, which is not only an impossible mystery but almost a perfect one.*

K illing Martha Griever was the only thing Nathan Griever had ever really done well, and he had done that very well indeed. The sole heir, Nathan had netted nearly twenty-three million dollars after taxes. Of course, his inheritance made him the number-one suspect, especially after it was learned that Nathan had only known his wife a scant few months before her unfortunate passing.

A clever fellow, Nathan had seen no way to divert suspicion from himself. Therefore, he did the next best thing – he made sure no one could prove he did it. The game had dragged on for a while, but the final score was L.A.P.D. nothing, Nathan Griever multi-millionaire.

The money had bought Nathan his place in the world. Even the suspicion of guilt now worked to his advantage. He was not only wealthy, he had an air of mystery about him that interested the ladies and encouraged people to invite him to dinners and parties. Before, his conversation had been banal and witless; now, though it hadn't changed in the least, he was considered urbane and clever by his new circle of friends. Nathan Griever belonged.

Smiling, he tipped his bowler over one eye and aimed the other in the direction of his new friend, Sir James Owens Cockeral. That's me, folks, Nathan thought as he looked his distinguished friend over – that's Nathan Griever walking down a London street with Sir James Owens Cockeral. Nathan thumbed his Bond Street threads and restrained himself from bursting out with a very ungentlemanly whistle and whoop.

"You seem chipper, Nate. What is it? The spring air?"

"No, Sir James—"

"Call me Jim."

"Why, certainly, Jim, old boy. As I was about to say, I'm looking forward to joining the club."

Sir James furrowed his brow and shook his head. "I do wish you'd take this more seriously, Nate. You know I'm going out on a limb by sponsoring you?"

"Not to worry, Jim. I think I can make a real contribution."

"You know, if any of those fellows guess how you've done it, I'm afraid there's nothing to do but try again at a later date."

"I understand, and, as I said, not to worry." Nathan frowned, then looked at Sir James. "I have to admit I'm a little reluctant to spill the story in front of a bunch of strangers."

Sir James nodded. "As well you should be. However, we are very careful about selecting candidates for membership. And there is also the guarantee, Nate. Once you are accepted, each of us will recount his own story. That way, if any one of us talks, we all suffer. So no one ever talks.

"Did you bring the application fee?" Sir James continued.

Nathan patted his breast pocket. "It's right here – and in cash, as specified. Why the uneven amount? Instead of $13,107.17, why not just make it thirteen or fourteen thousand?"

"I suppose our customs seem strange to an American."

"No, no – not at all. I just wondered."

Sir James aimed his walking stick at the ornate entrance of an ancient greystone structure. "Here we are."

They turned in the entrance and Sir James pulled a hand-wrought chain extending from the mouth of a brass lion's head set in the stone to the right of the iron-strapped double-oak doors. The left door opened and a liveried doorman, complete with powdered wig, stood in the entrance.

"Sir James," he said.

"Yes, Collins. This is my guest, Mr Nathan Griever. Would you announce us?"

"Certainly. If you gentlemen would follow me."

Nathan followed Sir James through the door and they handed their hats to a second bewigged servant. Dark gilded frames surrounded even darker portraits of distinguished persons in uniforms or high-collared formal wear. The servant opened another set of doors, and inside the room five distinguished gentlemen rose as he announced the pair.

One of the gentlemen, with monocle, three-piece tweed suit, and handlebar moustache, approached Nathan and held out his hand. "Ah, Mr Griever, I am happy to make your acquaintance. Welcome to Slaughterhouse."

Nathan grasped the outstretched hand and was pleased at the firmness of the fellow's grip. "Thank you."

"I am Major Evan Sims-Danton, late of Her Majesty's Irish Guard." As Nathan thrilled at the hyphenated name, Sims-Danton turned and held out a hand toward his four companions. "Mr Griever, may I introduce the other members of Slaughterhouse – Wallace Baines, Edward Stepany, Charles Humpheries, and our treasurer, Malcolm Jordon."

Nathan nodded at each in turn, shaking hands and smiling. After shaking Malcolm Jordon's hand, Nathan looked at his new friends, bounced a bit on his toes, and grinned. "I'm very pleased to make your acquaintance."

Sims-Danton cleared his throat and leaned his head in Nathan's direction. "I believe you have something for Mr Jordon?"

"Oh, yes." Nathan reached into his pocket, withdrew a heavy letter-size envelope, and handed it to the treasurer.

Jordon nodded as he took it. "Thank you. I'm certain it's all here, Mr Griever, but club policy requires that I count it. I hope you understand."

"Certainly."

Jordon opened the envelope, quickly thumbed through the bills, dumped the change into his hand, glanced at it, then nodded at Sims-Danton. "$13,107.17."

Sims-Danton nodded, took Nathan by the elbow, and held his other hand out toward an imposing marble staircase. "Then shall we be off to the problem room?"

They turned and led the procession up the staircase, followed by

Baines, Stepany, Humpheries, Jordon, and, at the very end, Sir James Owens Cockeral. Nathan turned toward Sims-Danton. "If I pass, will I be accepted today?"

"Yes. Of course, you understand that each of us in turn will have a crack at guessing how you did it. If any of us is successful, then I'm afraid you don't qualify for membership."

"I see."

Sims-Danton slapped Nathan on the back as they reached the top of the stairs. "Have faith, my boy. If Sir James sponsors you, I'm certain you'll give us a run for our money."

Nathan smiled. "You mean a run for *my* money, don't you?"

Sims-Danton frowned, then barked out a sharp laugh. "Yes, a run for *your* money! Good. Very good, by Jove." He held out a hand toward a flat white-painted door that stood ajar. The doorjamb was splintered, indicating the doorway had been forced. "Here we are, Mr Griever."

The procession came to a halt. "Now, according to the police report, this is exactly the way the room was found. As you can see, the door has been forced. The report states that Angela, the maid, heard a single shot as she was sitting in the kitchen downstairs having a cup of coffee. She rushed out of the kitchen, through the dining room, down the main hall, then up the staircase to Mrs Griever's bedroom."

Sims-Danton pointed toward a doorway at the other end of the upstairs hall. "As she came to the door, Angela noticed you, Mr Griever, in your robe and slippers, leaving your room. Is that correct?"

Nathan nodded. "This is amazing. The hallway looks just like the one in my house. How did you get copies of the police report?"

Sims-Danton waved his hand. "We try to be thorough here at Slaughterhouse, Mr Griever." He studied the paper in his hand and rubbed his chin. "Now, Angela stated that you rushed to her side. With both of you standing in front of Mrs Griever's door, you asked, 'What was it? Did you hear something?' Angela replied in the affirmative. Then both of you tried to rouse Mrs Griever by pounding on the door and shouting."

The Major rapped on the door, producing a clanging sound. "The door to Mrs Griever's bedroom was made of steel, and the doorjamb was made of wood-filled steel. For these reasons, neither you nor you and Angela together were able to break down the door. Hence, the gardener, Oshiro, was called. Oshiro subsequently broke down the door by bending and splintering the doorjamb. Correct?"

Nathan nodded. "So far, very accurate."

The Major nodded. "The door was pushed open and Mrs Griever was found in her bed, shot through the right temple, a .32-caliber pistol in her right hand. You, Mr Griever, went to her side, determined she was dead, then ordered Oshiro and Angela from the room. You accompanied them, leaving the door as we find it now. Correct thus far, sir?"

Nathan nodded. "You are thorough, aren't you?"

The Major nodded. "We try to be." He pushed against the door. "Gentlemen, you will notice that the door is spring-loaded in the closed position. The only reason it stood ajar is because of the solenoid-controlled deadbolt, in an extended position, leaning against the splintered doorjamb." He held out a hand toward the open door. "Gentlemen?"

The members, led by Nathan, entered the room. Baines immediately began studying the solenoid lock, while Jordon began tracing the wire from the lock around the room to the push button located on the night stand next to the bed. Nathan walked to the edge of the bed and looked down at the representation of his former wife, gun in hand, staring with sightless eyes at the canopy. In the mannequin's right temple was a dark hole pocked with powder burns above a slight trickle of reddish-brown blood. Nathan bit his lower lip and felt the cold sweat on his forehead.

"Quite realistic, isn't it?"

Nathan turned to see Sims-Danton standing by his side. He nodded. "Yes, very."

Sims-Danton clapped his hands. "Very well, gentlemen. Baines, Jordon – you're jumping the gun." The two errant members gathered with the others around the Major as he introduced the problem.

"First, gentlemen, we have Martha Griever, the former Mrs Stanton Atwood. When Mr Atwood passed away, he left her a fortune of some eighteen million dollars, which she subsequently doubled. Then—" the Major bowed toward Nathan "– Mr Griever entered the picture."

Nathan turned away from the still figure on the bed. The Major drew a small notebook from his left breast pocket and continued. "After a brief period of courtship, Nathan Griever was wed to the former Mrs Atwood, who promptly became an alcoholic as well as a raving paranoiac." He plucked the monocle from his eye and raised an eyebrow in Nathan's direction. "Forgive me if my description is harsh, Mr Griever."

Nathan shrugged. "It was more than generous, Major." He pointed toward the door. "You can see how she rigged up her bedroom. No one could enter or leave unless she pressed the button on her night stand and, even so, you had to stand outside her door and shout for twenty minutes to convince her to press the button. She probably would have had a closed-circuit TV camera put in if she could have allowed a stranger in to do the installation."

Stepany raised a hand and cleared his throat. "If you please, Mr Griever – how was she able to leave the room herself?"

Nathan shook his head. "Except for two visits to the hospital, she never did. Both of those times, she had me prop the door open with a wooden chock."

Baines nodded, then rubbed his chin. "That, I think, would give Mr Griever ample opportunity to examine the room undisturbed." He turned to Nathan. "Correct?"

"Yes."

Sims-Danton held up a hand. "One moment, gentlemen – I am almost finished." He flipped a page of his notebook. "After the discovery of the body, the police found the room as you now see it. The pistol in Mrs Griever's hand was registered to her, and only her own fingerprints were on the weapon. However, the bullet's entry path aroused suspicion, since for Mrs Griever to have done herself in, she would have had to hold the pistol in a possible, but very awkward, position." Sims-Danton formed a representation of a gun with his right forefinger and thumb, held the "barrel" next to his right temple, then rotated his wrist until the "gun" was in front of his face. The path at such an angle would enter the right temple and exit behind the left ear.

Humpheries frowned and shook his head. "Sloppy. Very sloppy, Mr Griever."

The Major held up a hand. "One moment, Charles. The test is whether or not Mr Griever got away with it. As you can see by his presence here, he obviously did. In fact, though his motive was undeniable and Mrs Griever's death a highly probable murder, our candidate for membership was not even brought to trial. He was held on suspicion for a few days, but they had to release him because they couldn't figure out how he did it."

He turned to Nathan. "Mr Griever, before the members begin

trying to crack this nut, I would like you to examine the room very closely to make sure everything is as it was when the police entered the room."

Nathan went to the door and examined the lock, checked the pictures on the walls, noted the absence of windows and air vents, and went to the night stand and checked the objects there. He raised his eyebrows as he checked the labels on the numerous prescription pills, drops, sprays, and powders his wife had always kept handy. Everything was accurate, down to and including the printed name of the pharmacy. The half-filled, open bottle of whiskey – her brand – stood behind the pills next to a pitcher of ice water and a half-filled glass of the whiskey-water mixture she loved so well. The push button that controlled the door lock was in its proper place on the edge of the night stand near the bed, and Nathan would have sworn that even the scratches in the brass cover surrounding the button were identical to the original. He reached out his hand, pushed the button, and heard the lock buzz and click open. He released the button, the buzzing stopped, and the lock's heavy spring shot the bolt into its extended position.

Nathan nodded and looked at the wiring that led from the back of the night stand, in which the battery was contained. It was stapled around the baseboard behind the bed and around the room, until it came to the door, where it was attached to the solenoid's contacts. He examined the wire to make certain it hadn't been disturbed. The wires in the original bedroom had been painted down the last time the room had been decorated. Nathan raised his brows and nodded in admiration. The paint was the identical color.

He faced the members. "As far as I can see, everything is exactly the way it was when the police entered the room."

Sims-Danton smiled. "Before we begin, gentlemen, I should add that from the time the maid Angela met Mr Griever at the door, he was under constant observation. In addition, the police conducted a thorough search of his room and the rest of the house. Nothing that could have been used in the murder was found – at least, in the opinion of the police. Shall we begin?"

Jordon rubbed his chin and held one hand toward the lock and the other toward the push button. "There seems little doubt that the problem is to keep the lock open long enough for the murderer to escape, but then to allow the lock to close, fastening the door shut." He turned to Sims-Danton. "I say, Evan, do we have a replica of the door in good condition – before the doorjamb was splintered?"

"Of course." The Major went to the door, pulled it open, and waved his hand. The doorman and another liveried servant carried in a pre-hung steel door fitted with a stand. They set it upright in the center of the room, bowed, and left.

Baines examined the door, pressed the push button, and nodded as the lock buzzed and clicked open. He pulled the door open and released the push button. "Jolly good." He pointed at the lock. "Now, gentlemen, I prefer the simple to the complex. Let us say that the murderer gains entrance to the room, uses the wooden block to chock it open—" he smiled "– kills Mrs Griever, then leaves. He holds the door open, removes the chock, takes a credit card thusly—" Baines removed a plastic card from his pocket "– pushes in the lock's bolt, closes the door, and pulls the card out through the space between the doorjamb and the door."

Major Sims-Danton nodded. "Is that your choice, Wallace?"

"Yes."

The Major turned to the others. "Very well, gentlemen – have at it."

Stepany stepped to the door replica, placed a finger against the lock's dead bolt, and pushed. "Wallace, old man, I'm afraid this ends your theory."

Baines stooped over and looked at the lock. "Eh?"

"The bolt doesn't move. Obviously, the solenoid operates a key of some kind that falls in place when the solenoid is not energized."

Baines shrugged and the Major nodded at Stepany. "Eddie, are you ready to have a go?"

Stepany nodded. "I agree with Wallace as to the nature of the problem, and even the method – however, the bolt must be held back before the key can fall in place. This means that a clamp must be placed over the lock before Mrs Griever releases the button to let in the murderer. Then the deed is done, the clamp is removed – the bolt still being held in – and then the door is closed, using a credit card in the manner Baines has suggested."

Jordon examined the door, the lock, and the doorjamb. "I think I see a problem, old fellow. The lip on the doorjamb is at least three quarters of an inch thick, and fitted with a rubber molding. If the door fits snugly, I don't see how one could pull the card free. Since the lip extends around the entire door, including the bottom, that would appear to exclude using a string on the card and pulling it through in some other place."

Stepany pushed the button, held the bolt in with his thumb, then released the button. The bolt immediately slammed back into an extended position. "Dear me!" Stepany waved his hand. "The spring driving that bolt is certainly a strong one. I couldn't hold it." He smiled. "I suppose that shoots me down, even if the card could be pulled through the doorjamb. If that bolt is to be held open, it would have to be done electrically."

Jordon nodded. "I agree. And, where something as thick as a credit card might not have made it, a pair of strong thin wires probably could. If the murderer placed a battery on the hall floor, gained entrance to the room, chocked open the door, then did the deed, he could run his wires through the hinged side of the opening, connect into the circuit where the wire jumps the gap between the baseboard and the door, and thus hold the lock open. Then he closes the door and pulls the wires after him, breaking the circuit and thereby closing the bolt."

Humpheries shook his head, went to the door of the room, and stooped to examine the wire where it jumped the hinge between the baseboard and door. "See here, Malcolm. The insulation on the wire hasn't been disturbed." He stood and examined the contacts to the solenoid. "Hmmm. He could have connected here, then pulled the wires out."

Sims-Danton held out a hand. "Gentlemen, the scheme now being pondered requires just the sort of equipment the police were looking for when they searched the rest of the house."

Humpheries stood. "Yes, Evan, but a battery and two lengths of wire can be made to appear very innocent. For example, the battery could easily be put into a radio or some other appliance. The wires could be tucked into a television set or just hidden in some small niche."

He smirked. "As we all know, gentlemen, the usual run of police inspector is not terribly bright. Could we send Collins for wires and a battery?"

After a few moments, equipment in hand, Humpheries nodded his thanks and Collins left the room. He removed the insulation from the tips of two lengths of steel bell wire, screwed the ends of the pair to a large dry-cell battery, then carried it to the "outside" of the unbroken door. "Very well – if one of you will play Mrs Griever and push the button, I will show you how it was done."

Jordon reached out a hand and pushed the button set in the doorjamb. The lock buzzed and clicked open, then Humpheries pushed the door open and turned to Baines. "Wallace, old man, would you play the door chock and hold it open?"

"Yes, of course." Baines held the door open while Humpheries stepped through, carrying the wired battery.

"Now, gentlemen, I move to the bed, kill the victim, rush back, and attach these leads." He frowned at Jordon. "Release the button."

Jordon removed his finger from the button. "Sorry."

With the bolt extended, Humpheries bent one of the leads around one of the solenoid contacts. "And now, the other." As soon as he touched the second lead to the second solenoid contact, the lock buzzed, retracting the bolt. He bent the lead around the second contact and, still holding the battery, stepped through the door. "Now I remove the chock and close the door." The door closed on the wires and the lock controlled by the doorknob caught, while the solenoid lock remained retracted. "Now all I do is pull the wires through—" Humpheries grunted as he tugged at the wires. "Drat! That door does have a snug fit, doesn't it?" One last grunt and the solenoid de-energized, slamming the bolt home.

Jordon laughed. "Good show! Well done, Humpheries."

Sims-Danton pointed at the solenoid contacts. The wires were still attached. Humpheries walked around the door, sheepishly holding out the battery.

"I'm afraid I broke the wires."

Sims-Danton rubbed his chin. "Charles, try it again, but don't let the door latch. Leave it open just enough to pull the wires through."

The experiment was repeated, with the door held open a bit. As the wires were pulled from the solenoid, the bolt shot home, forcing the door to shut on the wires. "It's no use. I pulled them as fast as I could, but it's just not fast enough."

Sims-Danton pulled the door open. "Hook it up and try it again – but this time open the door a little further."

The experiment was repeated but, instead of forcing the door shut, the bolt forced the door open. "Hmmm. That would never do." Sims-Danton again pressed the button and opened the door. "The taper on the bolt seems to do it. When the door is in an approximate position, the bolt shoots for the bolt hole and either finds its way in, forcing the door closed, or hits the sharp edge of this lip, forcing the door open." He closed the door, released the button, and shrugged. "I'm afraid that exhausts my theory as well." He faced Nathan. "In which case, Mr Griever, it looks as though Slaughterhouse has another member."

Nathan beamed but, feeling reckless, shook his head. "Sir James hasn't had a crack at it yet."

Cockeral cleared his throat. "Nate, you must understand that I am your sponsor. It wouldn't be proper for me to make an attempt against my own candidate."

Nathan shrugged and held out his hands. "Please – I insist."

The membership looked at Sir James, who smiled and turned toward Nathan. "Very well, then. I'll take a crack at it. Most of the solutions thus far appear to take up too much time. How long does it take to run from the kitchen, through the dining room and hall, then up the stairs to the bedroom door?"

Sims-Danton pulled out his notebook. "According to the police investigation, at the most Mr Griever would have fourteen to sixteen seconds from the time of the shooting to place the gun in the victim's hand, leave the room, and make it into his own bedroom. One of the officers making the run did it in eleven seconds, but he was, I gather, an exceptional athlete."

Sir James nodded. "That would appear to preclude anything complicated and time-consuming. If he used any extra equipment, I can't imagine where he could have put it. He would only have time enough to get to his room before he had to turn around and come out to meet Angela, thereby making it appear that he too had been drawn by the sound of the shot." He turned to Nathan. "Tell me, Nate – what physical shape was Angela in – old, young, slender, obese?"

"She was twenty-nine, but quite plump."

Sir James nodded. "Then, for the sake of argument, let's say the sixteen-second run was what she made." He went to the side of the bed. "Therefore, within sixteen seconds he had to place the gun in the victim's hand – say four seconds. Then he had to traverse the distance from the bed to the door." Sir James turned to Jordon. "Give it a try, will you, old man? I'll keep your time."

"Of course." Jordon moved to the side of the bed.

Sir James examined his watch. "Go!"

Jordon ran to the door and opened it, stepped through, and let the door close behind him. He opened the door and looked through. "How did I do?"

Sir James nodded. "Three seconds." He turned to Sims-Danton. "Do we have the hallway outside the bedroom plotted? I would like to time a run from Mrs Griever's door to Mr Griever's door."

Sims-Danton turned again to his notebook. "We don't have it plotted, but tests by the police on the scene made the run at about four seconds, which includes opening his bedroom door, entering, and closing the door." The Major closed the notebook and smiled at Sir James.

"Very well." Sir James nodded and turned back to the bed. "Very well. On the sixteen-second run, that leaves only five seconds for Mr Griever to do whatever it was that he did to effect his exit. That would leave no time either to use or dispose of batteries, wires, and the like." Sir James opened the front of the night stand, stooped, and looked inside. He then stood, looked at the back of the night stand, and carefully traced the wire to the solenoid lock. When he was satisfied, he turned and faced the room. "The insulation along the entire length is undisturbed, and I saw no discreet little holes in the wall, which would appear to preclude any sort of timing mechanism prepared in advance." He rubbed his chin. "Hence, to my mind, it seems that whatever was used should still be in the room."

Wallace Baines cleared his throat. "Sir James, it really is bad form to work against your own candidate. If you should guess the method, Mr Griever would be disqualified for admission. I would think that would cause bad feeling between you."

The other members nodded and Sims-Danton stepped forward. "I agree."

Nathan Griever held out his hands and grinned. "Please, gentlemen. I insist that Jim have his go at it. I'm not worried." He turned to Sir James. "Go ahead, old boy. Give it your best shot."

Sir James shrugged and walked to the side of the bed, then turned to the night stand and placed his finger on the push button. He tried it several times and listened as the solenoid energized and clicked back the bolt. Removing his finger from the button, he looked at the articles on the night stand, then lifted up the glass half filled with whiskey and water. He sniffed at it, replaced it, then opened several of the plastic containers of pills, uncapped the three plastic nasal-spray bottles, and unscrewed the tops on a bottle of nose drops and a bottle of eye drops. Then, replacing all the caps, he again lifted the glass of whiskey and water. He turned to Sims-Danton. "Tell me, did the police laboratory find anything unusual in any of these containers?"

Sims-Danton frowned. "Surely, Sir James, you don't suspect that the victim was poisoned."

Sir James looked back at the glass. "Oh." He nodded and replaced the glass. "Of course not. How silly of me." He turned to Nathan. "Well, Nate, it looks as though you're a member of Slaughterhouse. We all seem to be baffled. Please accept my congratulations."

Nathan shook the hands that were extended toward him, his face wreathed in smiles. "Thank you. Should I demonstrate now?"

Sims-Danton patted his forehead with a handkerchief and nodded. "Please do."

Nathan walked to the side of the bed. "I suppose that all I have to do is to account for those five seconds?"

Sims-Danton replaced his handkerchief. "That is correct."

Nathan nodded. "Jim, old boy, if you would time what I do, I'd like someone else to time how long the lock on the door is open."

Sims-Danton pushed back his sleeve, uncovering the watch on his left wrist. "Any time, Mr Griever."

Nathan smiled, rubbed his hands together, and nodded. "Go!" Nathan turned from the bed, uncapped the bottle of nose drops, put the end of the dropper into the water and whiskey, and sucked up barely enough to fill it past the tapered tip. Then he held the dropper over the push button, squeezed out four drops, and replaced the cap on the bottle as the liquid seeped into the space between the button and case, and shorted out the circuit. Nathan replaced the bottle as the solenoid buzzed and clicked open. "Of course the timing might be a bit off since I am using a different push button," he said.

A moment later the buzzing stopped and the bolt shot back out. Sims-Danton looked up from his watch. "Seven seconds. That would enable him to get through the door with time to spare."

Sir James nodded. "I have five seconds on the nose, Nate. Bravo! That accounts for the missing time, lets you absent the premises, baffles the police – and gets you into Slaughterhouse."

Nathan beamed. "You see, when my wife was in the hospital, I was able to try out a variety of liquids and numbers of drops. As chance would have it, four drops of her favorite drink did the trick.

All I had to do was wait for the maid to be settled down in the kitchen. My wife always had a drink on the night stand."

Jordon nodded. "Excellent."

"Four drops is just enough to short out the push button. Between the short, evaporation opens the circuit in just a little—"

Malcolm Jordon slapped Nathan on the back, took his elbow, and steered him toward the door. "Come, we must celebrate!"

Stepany, Humpheries, and Baines followed the pair through the door and down the stairs.

Sir James turned to his companion. "I almost muffed it, didn't I, Lieutenant Danton?"

Danton nodded as he removed his handlebar moustache. "You had me worried, Inspector Cockeral, no doubt about that."

Cockeral nodded. "Of course your laboratory found nose drops in the glass and whiskey in the nose drops."

"Yes. As soon as we got the results, we knew how he had done it. The problem was getting him to admit it. The District Attorney was certain he'd never be able to convince a jury that Nathan Griever could be that imaginative. The defense could easily produce a thousand bits of evidence that his client is about as sharp as a pound of wet silage."

"Still, it is rather imaginative."

Danton nodded. "Twenty-three million dollars can mother a lot of invention."

Cockeral nodded his head toward the door. "What happens to him now?"

"First, a party welcoming him to the club. Then, an epic pub crawl will begin that will end with his delivery back at the Los Angeles airport, where he will be arrested."

Cockeral shook his head. "Pity. The fellow did so want to belong."

"Oh, he'll belong – and wait till he gets a load of his new clubhouse." Danton turned and walked toward the door. Cockeral followed.

"You must have been awfully certain he would fall for your charade."

Danton smiled. "I studied Nathan Griever very carefully. He's nothing but a small-time grifter who only made one clever score in his entire life. Can you imagine how frustrated he must have felt not being able to tell his story? All we did was provide an audience worthy of his confidence."

"Danton, what about the strange amount for the initiation fee?
The $13,107.17?"

Danton shrugged. "Proposition Thirteen."

"Eh?"

"Proposition Thirteen. Money is very, very tight, and the only
way I could get my superiors to go along with this was if it didn't
cost us anything. $13,107.17 was the exact cost of the charade. We
could have gotten more from him, of course, but it wouldn't have
been sporting to make profit, don't you agree?"

The Birdman of Tonypandy

Bernard Knight

Bernard Knight (b. 1931) was for many years a Home Office Pathologist and is Emeritus Professor of Forensic Pathology at the University of Wales College of Medicine. He has written such key texts as Forensic Medicine *(1985),* Lawyer's Guide to Forensic Medicine *(1982) and the definitive* Knight's Forensic Pathology, *now in its third edition (2004). Knight has also turned his talents to fiction and is the author of the historical mystery series featuring the twelfth-century coroner Sir John de Wolfe, which began with* The Sanctuary Seeker *(1998). Knight had previously written fiction under the alias Bernard Picton, starting with* The Lately Deceased *(1963). He also contributed several story lines to the TV series,* The Expert, *which ran from 1968 to 1974, and adapted a novel based on the series in 1976. But perhaps his main claim to fame will be that Knight oversaw the recovery of all twelve bodies of the victims from the garden of Fred and Rosemary West in Gloucester in 1994.*

If anyone could concoct the undetectable perfect crime, Bernard Knight is surely our man. Maybe I ought to preface the following with "don't try this at home".

He laid his binoculars on the window ledge and decided that it was time that he murdered his wife.

Pondering for a few minutes, Lewis Lloyd reviewed the various methods that had been going through his mind for the past few weeks. He had more or less decided on one, the prime considera-

tion being that he should never be convicted of the crime. There
was no doubt that he would be strongly suspected – and if his luck
was out, he might even be brought to trial, given their past record
of domestic discord.

But found guilty – never!

Having made the decision, Lloyd gave a sigh of relief and turned
his attention back to the window. Picking up his glasses again, he
trained them at the line of scraggy rowan trees and stunted oaks
that rimmed the top of the mountain, high above his hut. He
watched a group of magpies strutting about under the trees, until
his attention was diverted by a pair of buzzards soaring high over
the old coal tip, beyond the ruined lime-kiln.

Lewis Lloyd loved birds and this ramshackle hut was his only
refuge from the nagging and abuse that he suffered down in the
valley bottom. He often came up early in the morning, or when the
pub was shut in the afternoon. Sometimes he even stayed overnight, in winter huddled over the little pot-bellied stove, blissful in
his solitude.

Lewis smiled complacently behind his binoculars, thinking that
when the deed was done, he could come up even more often, with
no Rita to screech objections at him.

Yes, it was high time to put Plan A into action.

"Bloody nonsense!" growled Mordecai Evans, tossing the letter on
to his cluttered desk. "We've got enough aggravation already
without daft women writing us letters."

"Mind you, boss, that family's got a bit of previous," murmured
his sergeant, peeved that Mordecai had dismissed his offering in
such a cavalier fashion. The detective-inspector, a squat bruiser
who could have doubled for John Prescott, scowled up at Willy
Williams.

"What previous? A bit of form for couple of domestics?"

"Lloyd broke her arm once – and another time she got a couple
of busted ribs," said Willy defensively. "The beak gave him six
months, suspended on account of provocation."

"Big deal!" sneered the DI. "So we're supposed to take her
seriously, are we?"

He hauled himself to his feet and grabbed the crumpled letter
from the desk, going to the window for better light. Though he was
reluctant to admit it, he couldn't see so well these days and a visit to
Specsavers was on the cards soon. Peering at the cheap notepaper

in the grey light that managed to percolate through the dark clouds looming over Pontypridd, he glowered at the unwelcome message.

"How did you come by this, Willy?"

"Eddie Morgan, the desk sergeant at the nick up in Ton Pentre gave it me yesterday, when I was up there about the break-in at the Co-op."

"And where did he get it?" grumbled Mordecai, slumping back into his chair.

"Rita Lloyd brought it in a few days ago. Apparently, she bent his ear something terrible, saying her old man was threatening to kill her, so she was making an official complaint." The detective-sergeant delivered this with some relish. "Eddie said he forgot all about it, knowing what a nutter Rita was – but as I was there, he said he thought he'd better pass it on to us."

"Oh, Gawd!" sighed Mordecai. "Was she battered and bruised this time?"

"No sign of it, he said. But half-pissed, as usual."

Wearily, the DI pulled a stack of case folders across the desk towards him. "Well, I haven't got bloody time to waste on that now. If she comes in with two black eyes, we'll have a word with her, otherwise it goes in my 'pending' file." He opened the top folder and peered myopically at the first page of endless police bumf, so his sergeant took the hint and sloped off to the canteen for his refreshments.

Ten minutes later, his lanky ginger-haired figure slid back through the door and he came to stand in front of the desk, his knuckles resting on the edge.

"I think you'd better have another read of that letter, boss," he said in sepulchral tones. "I just had a cup of tea with the coroner's officer. He happened to mention that Rita Lloyd was found dead yesterday morning!"

"Nothing! What d'you mean, nothing?" demanded Mordecai Evans. "There must be something, for God's sake!"

On hearing his sergeant's news, the DI had gone storming downstairs to the little room where the coroner's officer presided, Willy trailing in his wake. He stood over Jimmy Armstrong, a large, placid man who had been a police officer before he returned after retirement to the same job as a civilian.

Jimmy shook his head sadly. "Sorry, guv, we got nothing. There was a post-mortem this morning and the doc found nothing that could have killed her. He's kept some samples for analysis, just in case."

Mordecai brandished Rita's letter under Armstrong's nose. "She wrote to us, saying her husband was threatening to kill her, man! Now she's dead!"

The coroner's officer shrugged. "Don't blame me, I'm just the dogsbody round here. Perhaps you'd better have a word with the coroner."

"Damn right I will," muttered the detective. "And a few words with the flaming husband as well." His irritation subsided as the possible consequences of this affair began to sink in. He sat on one of the hard chairs provided for grieving relatives when being interviewed by Armstrong and stared pensively at the coroner's officer.

"You live in Tonypandy, Jimmy. What's the gossip on these Lloyds these days?"

Armstrong, whose tweed suit and tidy grey hair made him look like everyone's favourite uncle, clasped his hands as if in prayer.

"Queer pair, a disaster waiting to happen, I reckon."

"He still runs the pub? I thought he'd have had the sack, after his run-in with the law," growled the DI.

"It's a Free House, he's not just a manager," cut in the sergeant. "The Elliot Arms is a bit of a dump, but we don't get much trouble there. It's too old-fashioned to attract the yobs, no strippers or live music, just a quiz-night once a week."

"Why were he and his missus at each other's throats then?" demanded Mordecai.

Armstrong shrugged his big shoulders. "Incompatible, they are! He's a quiet sort of bloke, until he gets his rag out, then he's got a terrible temper. She's an old slag – booze, bingo and blokes. Rita'll go for anything in trousers – at least, when she's sober enough to stand up."

The DI grunted and hauled himself to his feet. He tapped the letter. "So there might be something in this, eh?"

The coroner's officer held up his hands defensively. "Don't ask me, that's your job. But I'd have a word with my boss first."

The coroner was a local solicitor who conducted his business from his offices above a shoe shop in Pontypridd's Taff Street, a few hundred yards from the Divisional Police Headquarters. Mordecai Evans and his sergeant took a walk there, pushing impatiently through the ambling throng in the narrow road, which was the town's main shopping street.

They turned in at a door on which a worn brass plate declared "*Thomas, Evans and Rees – Solicitors*" though these gentlemen were long dead and the present senior partner was Mr David Mostyn, Her Majesty's Coroner for East Glamorgan.

In a seedy reception area at the top of a narrow flight of stairs, a girl with a bad head-cold showed them into his office. Mostyn was a rotund man with a shiny bald head and a round, pink face that always seemed to have a smile on it, even when he was discussing death in all its often horrible forms. He ushered the two detectives to hard chairs and sat down again behind his paper-infested desk.

"My officer has told me about the situation over the phone," he began, picking up a form from a pile in front of him. "We already had a bit of a problem in that Doctor Carlton hasn't yet been able to give me a cause of death." He gave them a cheery grin, as if he had just won the Lottery.

"Surely that's unusual in itself, sir?" muttered Mordecai, picking at a pimple on his neck.

The coroner shook his head happily. "Not that unusual, Inspector. Especially if tablets or alcohol are involved, nothing may be found at the post-mortem, but the answer may come later from laboratory tests."

The DI delved into his inside pocket and pulled out Rita Lloyd's letter, now encased in a clear plastic envelope. He handed it across the desk.

"You see our problem, sir. I get this this morning, then I'm told she's already dead!"

David Mostyn scanned through the single page of writing, then handed it back and rubbed his bald head as an aid to thought.

"It certainly requires us to proceed with caution, officer. What do you know about this pair?"

Mordecai motioned with his head towards his sergeant. "Williams here knows them best, he comes from that part of the valley."

Willy cleared his throat and began to speak as if he was in the witness box, though he managed to avoid phrases like, "I was proceeding in a northerly direction."

"Sir, Lewis and Rita Lloyd have been known to me for a long while. In fact, I arrested him some time ago for assaulting his wife. He is the owner and licensee of the Elliot Arms in Tonypandy, a free house where he lives with the now deceased."

The coroner nodded, his benign smile still firmly in place. "Have you spoken to him about this yet?"

Mordecai shook his head. "We've only known about this for an hour, sir. It was only by chance that Lewis Armstrong mentioned to my sergeant that she was dead."

The coroner stared down at the paper he held in his hand.

"All I've got is Lewis's daily notification to me. It just says that the family doctor was called to the house – Dr Battachirya, that would be – who then phoned in to say he was reporting a death, as he couldn't give a certificate. The woman was found dead in bed by the husband at seven-thirty yesterday morning."

Mordecai Evans's pugnacious face stared at David Mostyn.

"That's all you have, sir?" he demanded, as if he suspected that the coroner was holding out on him.

"At this stage, yes. If the p.m. had shown a natural cause of death, like a coronary or a stroke, I would have issued a disposal certificate and that would be an end of it. As it is, I have to wait for the pathologist, Dr Carlton, to come back to me eventually with an update based on the results of the tests he sent away."

"How long will that take, sir?" ventured Willy Williams.

Mostyn beamed back at him. "Varies a lot, sergeant. Some things, like alcohol and carbon monoxide, he can have done in his own hospital the same day. More complicated tests for drugs have to be sent away and can take weeks."

The inspector glowered at the coroner as if it was his fault. "We may not be able to wait that long, sir. I've spoken to my Superintendent and he's told me to see the husband and if I feel there's any doubt, to proceed as if it's a criminal investigation."

David Mostyn's smile faded a little. "And what would that entail in this case?"

Mordecai shrugged his bull-like shoulders. "We may have to call in the Scenes-of-Crime team to the pub, sir. And possibly ask the Home Office pathologist to carry out a second autopsy – with your consent, of course."

He could almost see the figures ringing up like a cash register in the coroner's eyes, as Mostyn calculated the extra cost to the budget he received from the local authority. However, he rallied and with his grin at maximum rictus, he agreed with good grace.

"Well, have a talk with this Lloyd chap, Inspector – and keep me informed as to what's happening."

* * *

The Elliot Arms was an ugly red-brick building on the main road through the Rhondda Valley, a twisting, congested route lined with terraced houses, betting shops and Chinese take-aways. Built in 1900 to wash the coal-dust from the throats of thousands of miners, the public house had fallen on hard times, now that not a single pit remained in the valley. Lewis Lloyd had managed to survive by accepting a frugal life-style, most of his custom coming from the old colliers whom came to the Elliot mainly out of habit. There was also a hard core of pigeon fanciers, whose Club met once a week in the barren room above the Public Bar. Lewis was himself a pigeon man, with a large loft out in the backyard where he kept a dozen cherished Fantails. He also had a moderate lunch-time trade in ham-rolls and pasties bought mainly by the workers from a small plastics factory further up Mafeking Terrace, the side street on the corner of which his pub was situated.

Just past the factory, the road angled up at almost forty-five degrees, climbing out of the valley bottom to the green heights five hundred feet above, where his bird-watching retreat lay beyond the last houses and then the allotments.

This Wednesday, the day after his wife had been carried out feet first by Caradoc Builders and Undertakers, Lewis Lloyd drew back the bolts on the doors to the Public Bar on the dot of twelve. He did this every day, closing up at three and opening again from six until eleven.

Yesterday was an exception, not because of overwhelming grief, but because he had had to go down to the coroner's office and the undertaker's to sign forms, which threw his usual routine out of kilter. The loss of his wife made little difference to his staffing problems, as Rita rarely appeared in the bar, except when she wanted a fresh bottle of gin or when the fancy took her for a flirtatious gossip with some of the less geriatric patrons.

At lunch times, Sharon, a fat adenoidal girl from Mafeking Street, helped behind the bar, mainly employed in inserting a lettuce leaf and a slice of reconstituted ham into bread rolls. She also removed the cellophane from cloned Cornish pasties and popped them into the microwave, to satiate the appetites of the workers from Panda Plastics. On alternate evenings, the gloomy mahogany bar was manned by either Wayne or Alvis. The first of these two young men was a deserter from the Army, the other on bail awaiting trial for burglary.

With the doors opened, the landlord walked across the cavernous room, its half-panelled walls and ceiling yellowed with decades of cigarette smoke. He sat on a stool at the end of the bar, next to the hinged panel that gave access to the serving area and his sitting room and kitchen beyond. Picking up the *Western Mail*, he began reading the sports pages, ignoring the sympathetic looks from Sharon, who having been nurtured on television soap-operas from the age of three, was convinced that his nonchalant manner concealed abject grief. In fact, Lewis's mind was not on the current aberrations of the Welsh Rugby Union, but was busy reviewing the likely consequences of his recent homicidal behaviour.

Jim Armstrong, the coroner's officer, had offered nothing more than gruff sympathy and efficient form-filling, when he had gone down to the police station to give him details about his lately deceased wife. Then he had phoned Lloyd about an hour ago, to tell him that there had been a hitch in the proceedings and that he should not make any arrangements for the funeral until he heard again from the coroner's office. For form's sake, the publican tried to sound concerned and asked what the problem was, but the officer was evasive.

From previous less serious brushes with the law and from some research in the Public Library at Porth, he was aware of what would be the likely sequence of events. The post-mortem would show nothing and there would most probably be an adjournment of an inquest until further futile tests were done. With luck, the coroner would then throw in the towel, hold a resumed inquest with an "open" verdict and let burial go ahead. If he was less fortunate, the rozzers would come sniffing round, given that he had had some domestic trouble with Rita in the past. As long as he stonewalled them, there was nothing to fear, as they had absolutely nothing to go on, even though there was a large insurance policy riding on the death.

Though Lewis Lloyd was relatively uneducated, having left school at sixteen, he was intelligent and cunning and had worked out all the possible permutations of what may happen after he had done the deed. He had no remorse, as the drunken, unfaithful, vituperative Rita had it coming and all that now remained was to weather any stormy passages that might be in store.

There was only one aspect that Lloyd had been unable to factor into his equations – and that was because he had known nothing about the letter that his wife had sent the police.

*   *   *

Willy Williams parked the CID car in Mafeking Terrace an hour later and as they walked back to the drab building on the corner, Mordecai asked him what sort of chap this Lewis Lloyd was.

"Bloke about forty-five, ordinary enough, I suppose. Used to be on the railway, but got run over by an engine, still limps a bit. Had a nice bit of 'compo', so he bought the pub with it, they say. Mad keen on birds, he is – the feathered sort."

"What's all this with his missus, then?"

"Rita? Frizzy blonde, quite a looker in her time, but she got too fond of the bottle. Used to be a hairdresser, but I reckon she was too lazy to make anything of it."

"So why would she marry a bird-watching wimp like Lloyd?"

"Probably the compensation he had – keep her in gin for life, that would! Though I hear the pub's not doing too well these days, so Lloyd's probably a bit skint."

They reached the corner and Willy's proffered *curriculum vitae* was curtailed as they pushed open the door of the pub. Inside the bar, an old man slumped in one corner, reading a racing paper. Half a dozen younger men and women were crowded round a couple of tables in the centre, chattering, drinking lager and eating Sharon's offerings off paper plates.

A dark-haired man was sitting at the bar reading a newspaper, but when he saw Willy, he folded it up and came towards them.

"Mr Lloyd?" said Mordecai Evans, managing to make the simple words sound menacing.

Lewis nodded a greeting to Willy, who he had good cause to recognise and then nodded at the DI to agree that he was indeed Mr Lloyd.

"Detective Inspector Evans from Ponty," grated Mordecai. "Can we go somewhere more private?"

In the gloomy back room, which had a worn three-piece suite, a dining table and a small television set, Lloyd motioned the police officers to sit and perched himself on the edge of a dining chair.

"This is just where we come when we're serving in the bar," he said apologetically. "Our proper living quarters are upstairs."

Mordecai ran a finger round his thick neck, jammed into a tight collar. It was hot in here and he suddenly fancied one of his suspect's pints.

"Your wife died yesterday, Mr Lloyd. I'm sorry to disturb you at a time like this, but we need to ask a few questions." He didn't sound in the least sorry, thought Willy.

"I found her dead in bed, officer. I can't understand it, it was a terrible shock. She hadn't been ill – at least, no more than usual."

"What do you mean by that?" grunted the DI, suspiciously.

Lloyd's rather swarthy face looked down at his fingernails. "Well, it's no great secret round here that she was too fond of the sauce, if you get my meaning, especially living on licensed premises. Dr Battachirya warned her about it many times. He sent some tests away last year, but we didn't hear any more."

"But the doctor said he couldn't give a certificate, so it couldn't be that," chipped in Willy.

"I don't know, then," replied Lloyd, shrugging his shoulders. "I expect the hospital will find something."

"You had a conviction for assaulting her not long ago? What do you say to that?" demanded Mordecai, accusingly.

The publican's dark eyebrows rose in surprise. "I don't see why you bring that up! She wasn't beaten to death, was she?"

"I'll ask the questions, if you don't mind," snapped the detective. "Have you caused any further physical harm since then?"

Lloyd bridled at this. His indignation was genuine, as he knew perfectly well that Rita would not have so much as a scratch on her at the post-mortem.

"Of course not! And I resent you even suggesting such a thing."

Unperturbed, Mordecai dipped into his pocket and brought out the plastic-covered letter, which he held out to Lloyd.

"Your wife handed this in to the police only a few days ago. What do you say to that?"

The publican had never played poker, but he might have been a great success at the game, for as he read the letter, his face betrayed none of the concern that flooded through him. Stupid bitch, he thought, what did she want to go and do this for, just before he saw her off! But confidence in his plan soon overcame the shock of her accusing him to the police. Whatever they thought, nothing could ever be proved.

He handed the letter back to Mordecai. "She was hardly *compos mentis* much of the time, inspector. Tipsy most of the day. Emotional and dramatic, I think she imagined she lived in Coronation Street or Emmerdale!"

"What d'you mean by that?" snapped the inspector, suspiciously.

Lewis Lloyd shrugged and turned up his hands, continental-fashion.

"Out of touch with reality, I think they call it. She spent all her time accusing me of something, very often ranting and raving, usually about money. No wonder she drove me to giving her a slap now and then."

Willy Williams decided to join the debate.

"Well, she tells the police she's in fear of her life from you – and then turns up dead within a day or two. What about that?"

Lloyd turned a dead-pan face towards the sergeant. "What about it, then? You tell me what she died of? What makes you think I could have killed her?"

There was no answer to that and the two officers turned in some frustration to routine questions about where and when.

"She was found dead in bed, so where were you?" grated Mordecai.

"In the back bedroom, we hadn't slept together for a couple of years," said Lewis. "I might have caught something, she went with so many other blokes," he added bitterly.

After a number of further questions and getting unrewarding answers, DI Evans got up and hovered menacingly over Lewis.

"I'm not satisfied, Mr Lloyd, so while we're waiting for more information from the hospital, I'd like to search your premises. Do you consent or shall I have to get a warrant?"

"No, you carry on, lad!" said Lewis affably. "I've got nothing to hide, so help yourself!"

Willy tried to look menacing, but he didn't have the face for it like Mordecai. "You've got a hut up the mountain, too, haven't you?" he said.

The landlord nodded. "Just an old shanty, it used to be for the fitters at the top end of the slag hoist when the colliery was working. I rent it from a farmer now, somewhere to watch the birds from and get a bit of peace from Rita."

"Well, we'll want to search that too, so I'll be sending some officers up here later today."

With that feeble threat, the detectives marched out, leaving Lloyd to once again carefully review all his actions, to check that they had been foolproof.

The rest of the day saw a lot of action, with little result. After reporting back to his Detective-Superintendent at Headquarters in Bridgend, Mordecai Evans got his blessing to crank up the investigation and by mid-afternoon, a white Scenes-of-Crime van pulled up in Mafeking Street, followed by a Ford Focus carrying a civilian photographer. Three SOCOs delighted the gawping inhabitants of the street by ostentatiously standing at the back of their van to pull on their white paper suits and then trooping into the pub, carrying an assortment of metal cases.

Meanwhile, after a number of phone calls to the coroner and to the Forensic Pathology department in Cardiff, Mordecai and Willy made their way up to the new Abercynon General Hospital, a few miles away.

This was a large concrete edifice, looking like a grain-silo with windows. It had been built on the site of a former colliery and on the bulldozed slag at the back, the mortuary occupied the exact spot where the winding-house had once stood. The detectives found the consultant pathologist, Dr Archie Carlton, waiting for them in the little office, looking somewhat disgruntled. He was a thin, gangling man, with a lock of mousey hair flopping over his forehead and was a born pessimist.

"Don't see why you want that Home Office chap coming up here," he said peevishly. "I had a word with him on the phone, when he rang to say he was coming. If I say there's nothing to be found, then no one else is going to be able to say anything different."

After the usual ritual of cups of dark-brown tea being supplied by the mortuary attendant, Mordecai attempted to be diplomatic.

"It's the coroner and my chief, doc. They insisted, as there's some dodgy background to this death." He explained the circumstances and managed to placate the hospital pathologist's wounded pride before a screech of rubber on gravel outside heralded the arrival of Professor Peter Porteous from Cardiff.

The forensic pathologist was rather like a rubber ball on legs, a bouncy little man of fifty, with receding hair and a toothbrush moustache. He affected a yellow waistcoat and a drooping bow tie and was always in a hurry, inevitably having to be somewhere else before he even arrived.

Grabbing a mug of tea, he went straight into a discussion with Archie Carlton.

"Didn't find a thing, eh?" he gabbled. "All the stuff gone off for histology and toxicology?"

The hospital doctor nodded mournfully. "Asked for everything, even insulin. Blood, urine, bile, stomach contents, CSF, vitreous fluid, the lot."

"She was forty, I gather. No problem in her coronaries?"

"Clean as a whistle, could drive a bus down them. Normal sized heart, no pulmonary embolism, damn all."

"She was bit cyanosed, you said on the phone?"

Carlton shrugged. "Just a bit blue round the lips by the time she got here. Nothing specific about that, no petechiae in the eyes or any other signs of asphyxia."

Porteous nodded briskly. "Don't believe in the signs of asphyxia myself. Lot of bullshit, used as an excuse by people who should know better."

Mordecai decided to add his pennyworth. "She was a heavy drinker, professor. Rarely sober!"

Porteous took a mouthful of tea. "Liver look all right?" he asked Carlton.

"Touch of fat, nothing out of the way," grunted the other pathologist.

"I've seen a few boozers throw a double-six with not much to show for it at post-mortem," commented the forensic man. "But it's a diagnosis of despair to suggest that." He put his mug down and looked at his watch.

"Right, let's get to it. I should have been in Swansea ten minutes ago."

Five days after the second autopsy, Lewis Lloyd was sitting in his hut on the mountain, wondering what was happening to the investigation.

Both Willy Williams and Mordecai Evans had been back twice, first with another SOCO team to turn the pub over once again – and then to grill him once more. As there was nothing significant to be found or said, they went away with their tails between their legs, Mordecai again muttering empty threats.

Lewis sat in an old armchair, thinking over recent events. He blessed the foresight with which, soon after they were married, he had insured Rita for forty thousand pounds, being flush with his compensation money at the time. She had done her best to go through his windfall with her extravagance on clothes, drink and dubious "shopping trips" to Bristol and London, a thin cover for her numerous brief affairs. Now the money from the Prudential would come in very nicely to clear his debts and let him build a brand-new pigeon loft in the back-yard.

The thought of birds made him get up and scan the mountain-top for feathered friends, but the light was already failing. The autumn was well advanced and even at five in the afternoon, it was getting dusk. It was a poor time of year for bird-watchers and he decided to have a day off next Monday and drive up to Llangorse Lake to see what water-fowl were about. It was cold in the old hut and he contemplated lighting the stove for the first time since last Spring, but as he had to be back for opening time, it seemed hardly worth it, so he subsided into his chair again.

As he sat there wondering when they would release Rita's body for the funeral, another conference was going on in the CID office in Pontypridd.

The coroner, his officer, and an inspector in charge of the SOCOs were crowded into Mordecai's cluttered office, along with the DI and his sergeant.

"So what are we going to do about it, Mr Evans?" asked the coroner, with a cheery smile.

"We're stumped, that's what we are, sir," growled Mordecai. "Can't get a thing out of Lloyd, though my gut tells me the bugger did it!"

"All the investigations have turned out negative," put in Willy. "At least, unless you've got anything new?" He looked enquiringly at the SOCO.

Albert Whistler, a tall, grizzled man nearing retirement, shook his head.

"Sweet Fanny Adams, I'm afraid. We went over that pub with a fine-tooth-comb, as well as that hut up on the mountain."

"Nothing at all?" queried David Mostyn, with a leer.

"She had no injuries, sir, so there would be no blood. We checked everywhere for poison containers or pills, but nothing but cough medicine and aspirin."

Jimmy Armstrong, the coroner's officer, waved a thin file of papers.

"We've had both post-mortem reports now, the one from Doctor Carlton and another from the Prof in Cardiff. No help at all."

The coroner nodded. "I read them before I came across here, they both agree that there was no anatomical cause of death whatsoever. Heart, brain, lungs – everything all normal."

"What about something like suffocation?" asked Mordecai, still grasping at straws.

"I spoke to Professor Porteous on the phone this morning," said

Mostyn. "He was very helpful, but of no help, if you know what I mean. He said there are some forms of suffocation which can leave no signs at all, but that's just a negative finding, of no legal use whatsoever."

"What about that thing with a syringe-full of air that Dorothy L. Sayers got wrong in one of her books?" asked Willy, an avid reader of thrillers.

"The Professor mentioned that as well, actually," said the coroner cheerfully. "He said it would be impossible, there were no needle marks on the body and Dr Carlton had found no bubbles anywhere in the circulation."

The Detective-Inspector now glared at the Scenes-of-Crime Officer. 'Isn't there something that bloody forensic lab can do to help? What about all those samples that were sent up to them? It's already cost us a fortune to fast-track the tests."

Whistler hefted his own file of reports. "They've done all they can, Mordecai. All negative results, apart from a fair whack of alcohol. But not enough to kill her, especially as she was used to the juice."

"How high was it?" asked Willy Williams.

"A hundred and sixty-five milligrams per hundred mill," answered Whistler. "Over twice the legal limit for driving, but nothing like dangerous to life, according to the lab. Put her to sleep, most likely, but with a hardened drinker like Rita Lloyd, perhaps not even that."

There was a thoughtful silence. "And nothing else?" demanded Mordecai, eventually.

The SOCO shook his head again. "No drugs, no aspirin, no insulin, nothing."

"I asked Professor Porteous if he had any further suggestions," offered the coroner. "He mentioned a few things, but the lab had already excluded them. Another possibility was potassium chloride poisoning, but that can't be analysed after death, apparently, as it's a natural constituent of the body. And it has to be injected directly into a vein."

Mordecai Evans glowered. "Can't see Lewis Lloyd knowing about that stuff. And where the hell would he get it from, anyway."

"And the body showed no injection marks at all," reminded Lewis Armstrong. "The second post-mortem was very thorough. The Prof looked particularly for any needle marks, even in the feet."

There was another bitter silence.

"So where are we?" asked the coroner, with a bland smile. "If you're not going to charge Lloyd, then I've got to get on with my inquest and draw a line under this matter."

Mordecai ground his teeth. "I hate to see the bastard getting away with it! I even had a word with the Crown Prosecutor, but he laughed down the phone at me. He said the CPS wouldn't touch it with a barge-pole, unless we came up with something definite."

The coroner rose to his feet and motioned with his head at his officer.

"Well, there's nothing more to be gained by sitting here, Inspector. Unless you can get a confession out of this man by tomorrow – or come up with some solid evidence, I'm going to have to complete the inquest. We can't keep the poor woman above ground for much longer."

When all the others had left his office, Mordecai Evans glowered at his sergeant.

"Confession be damned! That crafty bugger Lloyd wouldn't confess to giving short weight in a packet of his crisps!"

A week later, Lewis Lloyd attended the coroner's inquest, held in a vacant room in the Magistrate's Court. He wore a dark suit and a black tie as he sat avoiding the poisonous looks thrown across the court at him by Mordecai Evans. Apart from the police and a couple of bored young reporters from the local papers, the only other people present were three nosey old men, whiling away their retirement in the warmth of the court, as the weather had turned frosty outside.

As prophesied, the proceedings were short and unproductive. Doctor Carlton appeared in person to give his post-mortem findings, but the coroner had accepted the written report of the Home Office man, which contributed nothing more useful. With the Detective-Inspector glowering at every word, David Mostyn rattled through the evidence and rapidly summed up the negative findings. There was no jury and he wisely made no comments about any suspicious circumstances, as this was outside a coroner's jurisdiction. After asking Lloyd if he wanted to ask any questions, which Lewis mutely declined, Mostyn brought in a "open verdict", leaving the cause of death unascertained. Even the fact that he had refused a cremation certificate was not mentioned in open court, leaving the option open for an exhumation at a later date if any further evidence came to light, unlikely though that seemed.

As Lewis Lloyd walked out into the cold street, Mordecai "accidentally" stumbled against him, making the publican stagger.

"Think you're such a clever bastard, don't you, Lloyd! But I'll have you one of these days!" he snarled.

Ignoring the empty threat, Lewis drove back to Tonypandy just in time for lunchtime opening and a plea from Sharon.

"The lager's off, Mr Lloyd. Can you put another one on, please?"

He opened the trap in the floor behind the bar and went down the steps to the cellar, switching on the lights as he went. For a few minutes, he trundled aluminium kegs about and connected pipes with the ease born of long familiarity.

"All right, girl, try it now!" he called up the steps. When all was working again, he prepared to climb up to the bar, but took a moment with his hand on the light switch to look around the large cellar. Apart from the row of metal casks and cylinders with their complex piping connected to the bar above, there were racks and cases of bottles, boxes of crisps and peanuts and a collection of oddments which made part of the chamber look like a jumble sale.

As his eyes roved over the old wooden barrels, off-cuts of carpet, plastic bags, broken table lamps, discarded chairs, a dilapidated wardrobe and two bicycles, he grinned to himself. Those silly buggers of policemen had searched this place several times and had seen and even handled the instruments of Rita's death without the faintest notion of recognizing them as such.

Satisfied that he was now safe for ever, he clicked the switch and went up to check that the lager was flowing properly.

Early that evening, he decided to celebrate by staying the night in his cabin high above the valley. Leaving Wayne to look after the bar, he climbed up Mafeking Street to reach the hut that used to shelter the men maintaining the cable hoist that once brought the black waste up from the colliery. It was almost dark when he unlocked the door. Inside, the cabin felt cold and damp and he shivered for the first time that autumn. Looking though the window to see if there were any birds about, there was just enough light to see as far as the old lime kiln, which had given him the idea in the first place.

As he crumpled up some newspaper and pushed it into his stove with a handful of firewood, he recalled reading about those kilns, which burned endlessly in the old days, turning lumps of limestone into quick-lime for farmers and builders. On winter nights, tramps used to sleep huddled near them for warmth – and quite a few never woke up. The heavy carbon dioxide gas produced by the kilns used to settle over them and, though not poisonous in itself, displaced all the oxygen and peacefully extinguished their dismal lives.

Intrigued, Lewis had pursued his researches in the Reference Library and discovered that such deaths left no physical signs whatsoever, the explanation being derived only from the circumstances. He also read that not only lime-kilns, but wells dug deeply into chalk and even grain silos on farms could produce this fatal heavy vapour that killed so silently.

He put more wood and coal on the fire and lit a butane camping-lamp to give him enough light to read his latest bird-watching magazine, for there was no electricity in the hut. Sitting in the tattered but comfortable arm-chair, he leafed through the pages, with a can of Boddington's Bitter and a Cornish pasty for sustenance. As the room warmed up, Lewis became comfortably drowsy but, before falling asleep, he went over yet again in his mind, the details of the plot which had defeated the best brains of the police and the forensic experts.

That memorable night, Rita had been out for the evening, allegedly at a hen-party, but Lewis was well aware that she had gone out to a club in Merthyr with her latest chap, a used-car dealer from Aberdare. She had returned at one in the morning, reeling drunk and this had decided him that tonight was the night – or, rather, morning. After giving him some semi-coherent abuse, Rita tottered off to her bed and within minutes was flat on her back, snoring like a hog.

Lewis Lloyd had swung into action, going down to the cellar for his equipment. From the old wardrobe, he took four wire coat-hangers saved from the dry-cleaners and bent them at right-angles. He took them upstairs with a few black plastic rubbish bags and carefully constructed a kind of open-topped well around his wife's head. By sliding one end of each hanger under the pillow and the duvet, he erected four supports around which he arranged the plastic bags, securing them with sellotape.

At this stage, he checked that she was undisturbed, but as expected, Rita was out cold and, even if she had woken up, would have been too confused to know what was going on. Satisfied, he went downstairs again and humped up one of the gas cylinders that was used to pressurize the metal beer kegs. Propping it against the bedside cabinet, he used a length of spare tubing to fill his improvised gas chamber with carbon dioxide. He left the end of the tube inside, keeping a slow but steady flow to displace all the air from inside his little tent. Lewis was well aware that it would overflow, but the heavy gas would sink to the floor and was no danger to himself. He checked at intervals with a cigarette lighter to make sure that the chamber was full, the flame going out from lack of oxygen as soon as he dipped it below the top edge of the plastic bags.

"Worked like a dream!" he murmured, as he slumped in his arm-chair, then giggled as he wondered if Rita had had any last dreams that night. Her breathing changed after a few minutes from noisy snoring to a rasping hiss, and quickened in rate. Then it began to diminish, both in volume and speed, and after another five or six minutes appeared to cease altogether. By the light of his little flame, he could see that her face and lips had become faintly violet and he suspected that she was already dead. To be on the safe side, he left the gas running and went outside for half an hour, to avoid any possible effects upon himself. When he came back, he knew she had gone, but checked the absence of a pulse in her neck just to make sure.

Turning off the gas, he opened the window to dissipate any remaining vapour. Then he dismantled his apparatus and returned the cylinder to the cellar, where he reconnected it to the barrel of lager, ready for business when they opened. He straightened out the hangers and hung them back in the wardrobe, then filled the plastic bags with old papers and other rubbish and dumped them out in the yard, ready for the bin-men. His work done, he made one last check to make sure that Rita had not managed some kind of resurrection, then he went to bed himself and slept soundly with no twinge of guilt or conscience until it was time to "discover" her body.

Now with a sigh of satisfaction, Lewis sleepily finished his beer and putting aside his birdy magazine, slid further down in his chair for a doze and to think about a trip he had planned to Mid-Wales next month to look for red kites.

"Now we'll never bloody know what happened to his missus!" grumbled Mordecai Evans, as they left the coroner's court a week later.

"It certainly wasn't carbon monoxide poisoning, that's for sure!" said Willy Williams. "Did you see the colour of his skin in the mortuary? Now I know what they mean by 'being in the pink'!"

The Detective-Inspector ignored his sergeant's feeble attempt at witticism. "The SOCOs say the flue-pipe of that stove must have been blocked since last Spring. Bloody ironic, really!"

Willy nodded sagely. "Lewis Lloyd would have appreciated that, if he'd known. A jackdaw's nest, of all things!"

"Serve the bugger right," grunted Mordecai.

Other titles available from Robinson

The Mammoth Book of Roaring Twenties Whodunnits £7.99 [ ]
Ed. Mike Ashley
The Roaring Twenties, the Jazz Age, the Age of Wonderful Nonsense – this
was the decade when everyone went a little bit crazy but beneath the dazzle
and glitter lay a darker side. A simply fabulous collection including stories by
Max Allan Collins, Cornell Woolrich, Gillian Linscott and H.R.F. Keating.

The Mammoth Book of Roman Whodunnits £7.99 [ ]
Ed. Mike Ashley
With dramatic settings ranging from the Eternal City of Rome to the most
remote outposts of her Empire, here are new tales from masters of the
detective story plus a special introduction and a Gordianus the Finder novella
from Steven Saylor.

The Mammoth Book of Vintage Whodunnits £7.99 [ ]
Ed. Maxim Jakubowski
1850 to 1905 was the original era of marvellously creative mystery fiction. This
compelling anthology includes a surprising number of authors not commonly
associated with crime fiction today – names like Alexandre Dumas, Alexander
Pushkin, Charles Dickens, Mark Twain and Rudyard Kipling.

*Robinson books are available from all good bookshops or direct from the
publisher. Just tick the titles you want and fill in the form below.*

FREEPOST RLUL-SJGC-SGKJ, Cash Sales/Direct Mail Dept., The Book
Service, Colchester Road, Frating Green, Colchester, Essex CO7 7DW
Tel: +44 (0) 1206 255800
Fax: +44 (0) 1206 255930
Email: sales@tbs-ltd.co.uk

Customers should allow £2.50 per order for p&p.

Please send me the titles ticked above.

NAME (Block letters) . . . .

ADDRESS. . . . .

. . . .

POSTCODE. . . . .

I enclose a cheque/PO (payable to TBS Direct) for . . . .

I wish to pay by Switch/Credit card

Number . . . .

Card Expiry Date . . . .

Switch Issue Number . . . .